A RAW YOUTH

A NOVEL IN THREE PARTS BY
FYODOR DOSTOEVSKY

FROM THE RUSSIAN BY
CONSTANCE GARNETT

University Press of the Pacific
Honolulu, Hawaii

A Raw Youth
a Novel in Three Parts

by
Fyodor Dostoevsky

From the Russian by Constance Garnett

ISBN 0-89875-317-1

Copyright © 2001 by University Press of the Pacific

Reprinted from the 1916 edition

University Press of the Pacific
Honolulu, Hawaii
http://www.universitypressofthepacific.com

PART I

CHAPTER I

1

I CANNOT resist sitting down to write the history of the first steps in my career, though I might very well abstain from doing so. . . . I know one thing for certain : I shall never again sit down to write my autobiography even if I live to be a hundred. One must be too disgustingly in love with self to be able without shame to write about oneself. I can only excuse myself on the ground that I am not writing with the same object with which other people write, that is, to win the praise of my readers. It has suddenly occurred to me to write out word for word all that has happened to me during this last year, simply from an inward impulse, because I am so impressed by all that has happened. I shall simply record the incidents, doing my utmost to exclude everything extraneous, especially all literary graces. The professional writer writes for thirty years, and is quite unable to say at the end why he has been writing for all that time. I am not a professional writer and don't want to be, and to drag forth into the literary market-place the inmost secrets of my soul and an artistic description of my feelings I should regard as indecent and contemptible. I foresee, however, with vexation, that it will be impossible to avoid describing feelings altogether and making reflections (even, perhaps, cheap ones), so corrupting is every sort of literary pursuit in its effect, even if it be undertaken only for one's own satisfaction. The reflections may indeed be very cheap, because what is of value for oneself may very well have no value for others. But all this is beside the mark. It will do for a preface, however. There will be nothing more of the sort. Let us get to work, though there is nothing more difficult than to begin upon some sorts of work—perhaps any sort of work.

2

I am beginning—or rather, I should like to begin—these notes from the 19th of September of last year, that is, from the very day I first met . . .

But to explain so prematurely who it was I met before anything else is known would be cheap ; in fact, I believe my tone is cheap. I vowed I would eschew all literary graces, and here at the first sentence I am being seduced by them. It seems as if writing sensibly can't be done simply by wanting to. I may remark, also, that I fancy writing is more difficult in Russian than in any other European language. I am now reading over what I have just written, and I see that I am much cleverer than what I have written. How is it thât what is expressed by a clever man is much more stupid than what is left in him ? I have more than once during this momentous year noticed this with myself in my relations with people, and have been very much worried by it.

Although I am beginning from the 19th of September, I must put in a word or two about who I am and where I had been till then, and what was consequently my state of mind on the morning of that day, to make things clearer to the reader, and perhaps to myself also.

3

I have passed the leaving examination at the grammar school, and now I am in my twenty-first year. My surname is Dolgoruky, and my legal father is Makar Ivanov Dolgoruky, formerly a serf in the household of the Versilovs. In this way I am a legitimate son, although I am, as a matter of fact, conspicuously illegitimate, and there is not the faintest doubt about my origin.

The facts are as follows. Twenty-two years ago Versilov (that is my father), being twenty-five years old, visited his estate in the province of Tula. I imagine that at that time his character was still quite unformed. It is curious that this man who, even in my childhood, made such an impression upon me, who had such a crucial influence on the whole bent of my mind, and who perhaps has even cast his shadow over the whole of my future, still remains, even now, a complete enigma to me in many respects. Of this, more particulars later. There is no describing him straight off. My whole manuscript will be full of this man, anyway.

He had just been left a widower at that time, that is, when he was twenty-five. He had married one of the Fanariotovs— a girl of high rank but without much money—and by her he had a son and a daughter. The facts that I have gathered about this wife whom he lost so early are somewhat scanty, and are lost among my materials, and, indeed, many of the circumstances of Versilov's private life have eluded me, for he has always been so proud, disdainful, reserved and casual with me, in spite of a sort of meekness towards me which was striking at times. I will mention, however, to make things clear beforehand, that he ran through three fortunes in his lifetime, and very big ones too, of over fourteen hundred souls, and maybe more. Now, of course, he has not a farthing.

He went to the village on that occasion, " God knows why," so at least he said to me afterwards. His young children were, as usual, not with him but with relations. This was always his method with his children, legitimate and illegitimate alike. The house-serfs on this estate were rather numerous, and among them was a gardener called Makar Ivanov Dolgoruky. Here I will note in parenthesis, to relieve my mind once and for all, I doubt whether anyone can ever have raged against his surname as I have all my life ; this is stupid, of course, but so it has been. Every time I entered a school or met persons whom I had to treat with respect as my elders, every wretched little teacher, tutor, priest—anyone you like—on asking my name and hearing it was Dolgoruky, for some reason invariably thought fitting to add, " Prince Dolgoruky ? " And every single time I was forced to explain to these futile people, " No, simply Dolgoruky."

That simply began to drive me mad at last. Here I note as a curious phenomenon that I don't remember a single exception ; every one asked the question. For some it was apparently quite superfluous, and indeed I don't know how the devil it could have been necessary for anyone. But all, every one of them asked it. On hearing that I was simply Dolgoruky, the questioner usually looked me up and down with a blank and stupidly apathetic stare that betrayed that he did not know why he had asked the question. Then he would walk away. My comrades and schoolfellows were the most insulting of all. How do schoolboys question a new-comer ? The new boy, abashed and confused on the first day of entering a school (whatever school it may be), is the victim of all ; they order him about, they tease him, and treat him like a lackey. A stout, chubby urchin suddenly stands still before his victim and watches him persistently for some moments with a stern and haughty stare. The new boy stands facing him in silence, looks at him out of the corner of his eyes, and, if he is not a coward, waits to see what is going to happen.

" What's your name ? "

" Dolgoruky."

" Prince Dolgoruky ? "

" No, simply Dolgoruky."

" Ah, simply ! Fool."

And he was right ; nothing could be more foolish than to be called Dolgoruky without being a prince. I have to bear the burden of that foolishness through no fault of my own. Later on, when I began to get very cross about it, I always answered the question " Are you a prince ? " by saying, " No, I'm the son of a servant, formerly a serf."

At last, when I was roused to the utmost pitch of fury, I resolutely answered :

" No, simply Dolgoruky, the illegitimate son of my former owner."

I thought of this when I was in the sixth form of the grammar school, and though I was very soon after thoroughly convinced that I was stupid, I did not at once give up being so. I remember that one of the teachers opined—he was alone in his opinion, however—that I was " filled with ideas of vengeance and civic rights." As a rule this reply was received with a sort of meditative pensiveness, anything but flattering to me.

At last one of my schoolfellows, a very sarcastic boy, to whom I hardly talked once in a year, said to me with a serious countenance, looking a little away :

" Such sentiments do you credit, of course, and no doubt you have something to be proud of ; but if I were in your place I should not be too festive over being illegitimate . . . you seem to expect congratulations ! "

From that time forth I dropped *boasting* of being illegitimate.

I repeat, it is very difficult to write in Russian : here I have covered three pages with describing how furious I have been all my life with my surname, and after all the reader will, no doubt, probably have deduced that I was really furious at not being a prince but simply Dolgoruky. To explain again and defend myself would be humiliating.

4

And so among the servants, of whom there were a great number besides Makar Ivanitch, there was a maid, and she was eighteen when Makar Dolgoruky, who was fifty, suddenly announced his intention of marrying her. In the days of serfdom marriages of house-serfs, as every one knows, only took place with the sanction of their masters, and were sometimes simply arranged by the latter. At that time "auntie" was living on the estate ; not that she was my aunt, though : she had, in fact, an estate of her own ; but, I don't know why, every one knew her all her life as "auntie"—not mine in particular but an aunt in general, even in the family of Versilov, to whom she can hardly have been related. Her name was Tatyana Pavlovna Prutkov. In those days she still had, in the same province and district, a property of thirty-five serfs of her own. She didn't exactly administer Versilov's estate (of five hundred serfs), but, being so near a neighbour, she kept a vigilant eye on it, and her superintendence, so I have heard, was as efficient as that of any trained steward. However, her efficiency is nothing to do with me. But, to dispose of all suspicion of cringing or flattery on my part, I should like to add that this Tatyana Pavlovna was a generous and even original person.

Well, far from checking the gloomy Makar Dolgoruky's matrimonial inclinations (I am told he was gloomy in those days), she gave them the warmest encouragement.

Sofia Andreyevna, the serf-girl of eighteen (that is, my mother), had been for some years fatherless and motherless. Her father, also a serf, who had a great respect for Makar Dolgoruky and was under some obligation to him, had six years before, on his death-bed, beckoned to the old gardener and, pointing significantly to his daughter, had, in the presence of the priest and all the servants, bequeathed her to him, saying, " When she's grown up, marry her." This was, so they say, a quarter of an hour before he expired, so that it might, if need be, have been put down to delirium ; besides which, he had no right to dispose of property, being a serf. Every one heard his words. As for Makar Ivanovitch, I don't know in what spirit he afterwards entered upon the marriage, whether with great eagerness or simply as the fulfilment of a duty. Probably he preserved an appearance of complete indifference. He was a man who even at that time knew how to " keep up his dignity." It was not that he was a particularly well-educated or reading man (though he knew the whole of the church service and some lives of the saints, but this was only from hearing them). It was not that he was a sort of backstairs philosopher; it was simply that he was a man of obstinate, and even at times rash character, was conceited in his talk, autocratic in his judgment, and " respectful in his life," to use his own surprising expression; that is what he was like at that time. Of course, he was universally respected, but, I am told, disliked by every one. It was a different matter when he ceased to be a house-serf; then he was spoken about as a saint and a man who had suffered much. That I know for a fact.

As for my mother, Tatyana Pavlovna had kept her till the age of eighteen in her house, although the steward had urged that the girl should be sent to Moscow to be trained. She had given the orphan some education, that is, taught her sewing and cutting out clothes, ladylike deportment, and even a little reading. My mother was never able to write decently. She looked upon this marriage with Makar Ivanovitch as something settled long ago, and everything that happened to her in those days she considered very good and all for the best. She went to her wedding looking as unmoved as anyone could on such an occasion, so much so that even Tatyana Pavlovna called her a fish. All this about my mother's character at that time I heard from Tatyana Pavlovna herself. Versilov arrived just six months after this wedding.

5

I only want to say that I have never been able to find out or to guess to my own satisfaction what led up to everything between him and my mother. I am quite ready to believe, as he himself assured me last year with a flushed face, though he talked of all this with the most unconstrained and flippant air, that there was no romance about it at all, that it had just happened. I believe that it did just happen, and that little phrase *just happened* is delightful, yet I always wanted to know how it could have come about. I have always hated that sort of nastiness all my life and always shall. It's not simply a disgraceful curiosity on my part, of course. I may remark that I knew absolutely nothing of my mother till a year ago. For the sake of Versilov's comfort I was sent away to strangers, but of that later, and so I can never picture what she looked like at that time. If she had not been at all pretty, what could a man such as Versilov was then have found attractive in her ? This question is of importance to me because it throws a light on an extremely interesting side of that man's character. It is for that reason I ask it and not from depravity. Gloomy and reserved as he always was, he told me himself on one occasion, with that charming candour which he used to produce (from the devil knows where—it seemed to come out of his pocket when he saw it was indispensable) that at that time he was a " very silly young puppy " ; not that he was exactly sentimental, but just that he had lately read " Poor Anton " and " Polinka Sachs," two literary works which exerted an immense, humanizing influence on the younger generation of that day. He added that it was perhaps through " Poor Anton " that he went to the country, and he added it with the utmost gravity. How did that " silly puppy " begin at first with my mother ? I have suddenly realized that if I had a single reader he would certainly be laughing at me as a most ridiculous raw youth, still stupidly innocent, putting himself forward to discuss and criticize what he knows nothing about. It is true that I know nothing about it, though I recognize that not at all with pride, for I know how stupid such inexperience is in a great dolt of twenty ; only I would tell such a gentleman that he knows nothing about it himself, and I will prove it to him. It is true that I know nothing about women, and I don't want to either, for I shall always despise that sort of thing, and I have sworn I will all my life.

But I know for certain, though, that some women fascinate by their beauty, or by anything you like, all in a minute, while you may ruminate over another for six months before you understand what is in her ; and that to see through and love such a woman it is not enough to look at her, it is not enough to be simply ready for anything, one must have a special gift besides. Of that I am convinced, although I do know nothing about it : and if it were not true it would mean degrading all women to the level of domestic animals, and only keeping them about one as such ; possibly this is what very many people would like.

I know from several sources that my mother was by no means a beauty, though I have never seen the portrait of her at that age which is in existence. So it was impossible to have fallen in love with her at first sight. Simply to " amuse himself " Versilov might have pitched on some one else, and there was some one else in the house, an unmarried girl too, Anfisa Konstantinovna Sapozhkov, a housemaid. To a man who had brought " Poor Anton " with him to the country it must have seemed shameful to take advantage of his seignorial rights to violate the sanctity of a marriage, even that of his serf, for I repeat, he spoke with extreme seriousness of this " Poor Anton " only a few months ago, that is, twenty years after the event. Why, " Poor Anton " only had his horse taken from him, but this was a wife ! So there must have been something peculiar in this case, and Mlle. Sapozhkov was the loser by it (or rather, I should say, the gainer). I attacked him with all these questions once or twice last year when it was possible to talk to him (for it wasn't always possible to talk to him). And, in spite of all his society polish and the lapse of twenty years, I noticed that he winced. But I persisted. On one occasion, anyway, although he maintained the air of worldly superciliousness which he invariably thought fit to assume with me, he muttered strangely that my mother was one of those " defenceless " people whom one does not fall in love with—quite the contrary, in fact— but whom one suddenly pities for their gentleness, perhaps, though one cannot tell what for. That no one ever knows, but one goes on pitying them, one pities them and grows fond of them. " In fact, my dear boy, there are cases when one can't shake it off." That was what he told me. And if that was how it really happened I could not look upon him as the " silly puppy " he had proclaimed himself. That is just what I wanted.

He went on to assure me, however, that my mother loved him " through servility." He positively pretended it was because he was her master ! He lied, thinking this was chic ! He lied against his conscience, against all honour and generosity.

I have said all this, of course, as it were to the credit of my mother. But I have explained already that I knew nothing whatever of her as she was then. What is more, I know the rigidity of her environment, and the pitiful ideas in which she had become set from her childhood and to which she remained enslaved for the rest of her life. The misfortune happened, nevertheless. I must correct myself, by the way. Letting my fancy run away with me, I have forgotten the fact which I ought to have stated first of all, that is, that the misfortune happened at the very outset (I hope that the reader will not be too squeamish to understand at once what I mean). In fact, it began with his exercising his seignorial rights, although Mlle. Sapozhkov was passed over. But here, in self-defence, I must declare at once that I am not contradicting myself. For—good Lord!—what could a man like Versilov have talked about at that date with a person like my mother even if he had felt the most overwhelming love for her? I have heard from depraved people that men and women very often come together without a word being uttered, which is, of course, the last extreme of monstrous loathsomeness. Nevertheless, I do not see how Versilov could have begun differently with my mother if he had wanted to. Could he have begun by expounding "Polinka Sachs" to her? And besides, they had no thoughts to spare for Russian literature; on the contrary, from what he said (he let himself go once), they used to hide in corners, wait for each other on the stairs, fly apart like bouncing balls, with flushed cheeks if anyone passed by, and the "tyrant slave-owner" trembled before the lowest scrubbing-maid, in spite of his seignorial rights. And although it was at first an affair of master and servant, it was that and yet not that, and after all, there is no really explaining it. In fact, the more you go into it the more obscure it seems. The very depth and duration of their love makes it more mysterious, for it is a leading characteristic of such men as Versilov to abandon as soon as their object is attained. That did not happen, though. To transgress with an attractive, giddy flirt who was his serf (and my mother was not a flirt) was not only possible but inevitable for a depraved young puppy (and they were all depraved, every one of them, the progressives as well as the reactionaries), especially considering his romantic position as a young widower and his having nothing to do. But to love her all his life is too much. I cannot guarantee that he did love her, but he has dragged her about with him all his life—that's certain.

I put a great many questions to my mother, but there is one, most important, which, I may remark, I did not venture to ask her directly, though I got on such familiar terms with her last year; and, what is more, like a coarse, ungrateful puppy, considering she had wronged me, I did not spare her feelings at all. This was the question: how she after six months of marriage, crushed by her ideas of the sanctity of wedlock, crushed like some helpless fly, respecting her Makar Ivanovitch as though he had been a god—how she could have brought herself in about a fortnight to such a sin ? Was my mother a depraved woman, perhaps ? On the contrary, I may say now at once that it is difficult to imagine anyone more pure-hearted than she was then and has been all her life. The explanation may be, perhaps, that she scarcely knew what she was doing (I don't mean in the sense in which lawyers nowadays urge this in defence of their thieves and murderers), but was carried away by a violent emotion, which sometimes gains a fatal and tragic ascendancy when the victim is of a certain degree of simplicity. There is no telling : perhaps she fell madly in love with . . . the cut of his clothes, the Parisian style in which he parted his hair, his French accent—yes, French, though she didn't understand a word of it—the song he sang at the piano ; she fell in love with something she had never seen or heard of (and he was very handsome), and fell in love with him straight away, once for all, hopelessly, fell in love with him altogether—manners, song, and all. I have heard that this did sometimes happen to peasant girls in the days of serfdom, and to the most virtuous, too. I understand this, and the man is a scoundrel who puts it down to nothing but servility. And so perhaps this young man may have had enough direct power of fascination to attract a creature who had till then been so pure and who was of a different species, of an utterly different world, and to lead her on to such evident ruin. That it was to her ruin my mother, I hope, realized all her life ; only probably when she went to it she did not think of ruin at all; but that is how it always is with these " defenceless " creatures, they know it is ruin and they rush upon it.

Having sinned, they promptly repented. He told me flippantly that he sobbed on the shoulder of Makar Ivanovitch, whom he sent for to his study expressly for the purpose, and she—she meanwhile was lying unconscious in some little back room in the servants' quarters. . . .

6

But enough of questions and scandalous details. After paying Makar Ivanovitch a sum of money for my mother, Versilov went away shortly afterwards, and ever since, as I have mentioned already, he dragged her about with him, almost everywhere he went, except at certain times when he absented himself for a considerable period. Then, as a rule, he left her in the care of "auntie," that is, of Tatyana Pavlovna Prutkov, who always turned up on such occasions. They lived in Moscow, and also in other towns and villages, even abroad, and finally in Petersburg. Of all that later, though perhaps it is not worth recording. I will only mention that a year after my mother left Makar Ivanovitch, I made my appearance, and a year later my sister, and ten or eleven years afterwards a sickly child, my younger brother, who died a few months later. My mother's terrible confinement with this baby was the end of her good looks, so at least I was told : she began rapidly to grow older and feebler.

But a correspondence with Makar Ivanovitch was always kept up. Wherever the Versilovs were, whether they lived for some years in the same place, or were moving about, Makar Ivanovitch never failed to send news of himself to the "family." Strange relations grew up, somewhat ceremonious and almost solemn. Among the gentry there is always an element of something comic in such relations, I know. But there was nothing of the sort in this case. Letters were exchanged twice a year, never more nor less frequently, and they were extraordinarily alike. I have seen them. There was scarcely anything personal in them. On the contrary, they were practically nothing but ceremonious statements of the most public incidents, and the most public sentiments, if one may use such an expression of sentiments ; first came news of his own health, and inquiries about their health, then ceremonious hopes, greetings and blessings—that was all.

I believe that this publicity and impersonality is looked upon as the essence of propriety and good breeding among the peasants. "To our much esteemed and respected spouse, Sofia Andreyevna, we send our humblest greetings. . . ." "We send to our beloved children, our fatherly blessing, ever unalterable." The children were mentioned by name, including me. I may remark here that Makar Ivanovitch had so much wit as never to describe "His high-born most respected master, Andrey Petrovitch" as his "benefactor"; though he did invariably, in each letter, send him his most humble greetings, beg for the continuance of his favour, and call down upon him the blessing of God. The answers to Makar Ivanovitch were sent shortly after by my mother, and were always written in exactly the same style. Versilov, of course, took no part in the correspondence. Makar Ivanovitch wrote from all parts of Russia, from the towns and monasteries in which he sometimes stayed for a considerable time. He had become a pilgrim, as it is called. He never asked for anything ; but he invariably turned up at home once in three years on a holiday, and stayed with my mother, who always, as it happened, had her own lodgings apart from Versilov's. Of this I shall have to say more later, here I will only mention that Makar Ivanovitch did not loll on the sofa in the drawing-room, but always sat discreetly somewhere in the background. He never stayed for long : five days or a week.

I have omitted to say that he had the greatest affection and respect for his surname, "Dolgoruky." Of course this was ludicrous stupidity. And what was most stupid was that he prized his name just because there were princes of the name. A strange, topsy-turvy idea.

I have said that the family were always together, but I mean except for me, of course. I was like an outcast, and, almost from my birth, had been with strangers. But this was done with no special design, but simply because it had happened so. When I was born my mother was still young and good-looking, and therefore necessary to Versilov ; and a screaming child, of course, was always a nuisance, especially when they were travelling. That was how it happened that until I was nineteen I had scarcely seen my mother except on two or three brief occasions. It was not due to my mother's wishes, but to Versilov's lofty disregard for people.

7

Now for something quite different. A month earlier, that is a month before the 19th of September, I had made up my mind in Moscow to renounce them all, and to retire into my own idea, finally. I record that expression "retire into my own idea " because that expression may explain my leading motive, my object in life. What that " idea " of mine is, of that there will be only too much said later. In the solitary years of my dreamy life in Moscow it sprang up in my mind before I had left the sixth form of the grammar school, and from that time perhaps never left me for an instant. It absorbed my whole existence. Till then I had lived in dreams ; from my childhood upwards I have lived in the world of dreams, always of a certain colour. But after this great and all-absorbing idea turned up, my dreams gained in force, took a definite shape ; and became rational instead of foolish. School did not hinder my dreams, and it did not hinder the idea either. I must add, however, that I came out badly in the leaving exam, though I had always been one of the first in all the forms up to the seventh, and this was a result of that same idea, a result of a false deduction from it perhaps. So it was not school work that hindered the idea, but the idea that hindered school work, and it hindered university work too. When I left school I intended at once not only to cut myself off from my family completely, but from all the world if necessary, though I was only nineteen at the time. I wrote through a suitable person to tell them to leave me entirely alone, not to send me any more money for my maintenance, and, if possible, to forget me altogether (that is if they ever did remember me), and finally "nothing would induce" me to enter the university. An alternative presented itself from which there was no escaping : to refuse to enter the university and go on with my education, or to defer putting my idea into practice for another four years. I went for the idea without faltering, for I was absolutely resolved about it. In answer to my letter, which had not been addressed to him, Versilov, my father, whom I had only seen once for a moment when I was a boy of ten (though even in that moment he made a great impression upon me), summoned me to Petersburg in a letter written in his own hand, promising me a private situation. This cold, proud man, careless and disdainful of me, after bringing me into the world and packing me off to strangers, knew nothing of me at all and had never even regretted his conduct ; who knows, perhaps he had only a vague and confused idea of my existence, for it appeared afterwards that the money for my maintenance in Moscow had not been furnished by him but by other people. Yet the summons of this man who so suddenly remembered me and deigned to write to me with his own hand, by flattering me, decided my fate. Strange to say, what pleased me in his note (one tiny sheet of paper) was that he said not a word about the university, did not ask me to change my mind, did not blame me for not wanting to continue my studies, did not, in fact, trot out any parental flourishes of the kind usual in such cases, and yet this was wrong of him since it betrayed more than anything his lack of interest in me. I resolved to go, the more readily because it would not hinder my great idea. "I'll see what will come of it," I argued, "in any case I shall associate with them only for a time ; possibly a very short time. But as soon as I see that this step, tentative and trifling as it is, is keeping me from the *great object*, I shall break off with them, throw up everything and retreat into my shell." Yes, into my shell ! " I shall hide in it like a tortoise." This comparison pleased me very much. " I shall not be alone," I went on musing, as I walked about Moscow those last days like one possessed. " I shall never be alone as I have been for so many awful years till now ; I shall have my idea to which I will never be false, even if I like them all there, and they make me happy, and I live with them for ten years ! " It was, I may remark beforehand, just that impression, that is, just the twofold nature of the plans and objects definitely formed before leaving Moscow, and never out of my mind for one instant in Petersburg (for I hardly think there was a day in Petersburg which I had not fixed on beforehand as the final date for breaking off with them and going away), it was this, I say, that was, I believe, one of the chief causes of many of the indiscretions I have been guilty of during this year, many nasty things, many even low things, and stupid ones of course. To be sure, a father, something I had never had before, had appeared upon the scene. This thought intoxicated me as I made my preparations in Moscow and sat in the railway carriage. That he was my father would be nothing. I was not fond of sentimentality, but this man had humiliated me and had not cared to know me, while all those years I had been chewing away at my dreams of him, if one may use such an expression. From my childhood upward, my dreams were all coloured by him ; all hovered about him as the final goal. I don't know whether I hated him or loved him ; but his figure dominated the future and all my schemes of life. And this happened of itself. It grew up with me.

Another thing which influenced me in leaving Moscow was a tremendous circumstance, a temptation which even then, three months before my departure (before Petersburg had been mentioned), set my heart leaping and throbbing. I was drawn to this unknown ocean by the thought that I could enter it as the lord and master of other people's destinies, and what people, too ! But the feelings that were surging in my heart were generous and not despotic—I hasten to declare it that my words may not be mistaken. Moreover, Versilov might think (if he ever deigned to think of me) that a small boy who had just left

school, a raw youth, was coming who would be agape with wonder
at everything. And meanwhile I knew all his private life, and
had about me a document of the utmost importance, for which
(I know that now for a fact) he would have given some years of
his life, if I had told him the secret at the time. But I notice
that I am talking in riddles. One cannot describe feelings without
facts. Besides which, there will be enough about all this in its
proper place ; it is with that object I have taken up my pen.
Writing like this is like a cloud of words or the ravings of
delirium.

8

Finally, to pass once for all to the 19th of September, I
will observe briefly and, so to say, cursorily, that I found them
all, that is Versilov, my mother and my sister (the latter I saw
for the first time in my life) in difficult circumstances, almost
destitute, or at least, on the verge of destitution. I knew of
this before leaving Moscow, but yet I was not prepared for
what I saw. I had been accustomed from childhood to imagine
this man, this " future father of mine " in brilliant surroundings,
and could not picture him except as the leading figure everywhere. Versilov had never shared the same lodgings with my
mother, but had always taken rooms for her apart. He did this,
of course, out of regard for their very contemptible " proprieties."
But here they were all living together in a little wooden lodge
in a back street in the Semyonovsky Polk. All their things
were in pawn, so that, without Versilov's knowledge, I gave my
mother my secret sixty roubles. *Secret*, because I had saved
them up in the course of two years out of my pocket money,
which was five roubles a month. I had begun saving from the
very day I had conceived my " idea," and so Versilov must
know nothing about the money. I trembled at the thought of
that.

My help was like a drop in the ocean. My mother worked
hard and my sister too took in sewing. Versilov lived in
idleness, indulged his whims and kept up a number of his former
rather expensive habits. He grumbled terribly, especially at
dinner, and he was absolutely despotic in all his ways. But my
mother, my sister, Tatyana Pavlovna and the whole family of
the late Andronikov (the head of some department who used also
to manage Versilov's affairs and had died three months before),
consisting of innumerable women, grovelled before him as

though he were a fetish. I had not imagined this. I may remark that nine years before he had been infinitely more elegant. I have said already that I had kept the image of him in my dreams surrounded by a sort of brilliance, and so I could not conceive how it was possible after only nine years for him to look so much older and to be so worn out ; I felt at once sad, sorry, ashamed. The sight of him was one of the most painful of my first impressions on my arrival. Yet he was by no means an old man, he was only forty-five. Looking at him more closely I found in his handsome face something even more striking than what I had kept in my memory. There was less of the brilliance of those days, less external beauty, less elegance even ; but life had, as it were, stamped on that face something far more interesting than before.

Meanwhile poverty was not the tenth or twentieth fraction of his misfortunes, and I knew that. There was something infinitely more serious than poverty, apart from the fact that there was still a hope that Versilov might win the lawsuit he had been contesting for the last year with the Princes Sokolsky and might in the immediate future come into an estate to the value of seventy thousand or more. I have said above that Versilov had run through three fortunes in his life, and here another fortune was coming to his rescue again ! The case was to be settled very shortly. It was just then that I arrived. It is true that no one would lend him money on his expectations, there was nowhere he could borrow, and meanwhile they had to suffer.

Versilov visited no one, though he sometimes was out for the whole day. It was more than a year since he had been *banished* from society. In spite of all my efforts, this scandal remained for the most part a mystery though I had been a whole month in Petersburg. Was Versilov guilty or not guilty—that was what mattered to me, that is what I had come to Petersburg for ! Every one had turned against him—among others all the influential and distinguished people with whom he had been particularly clever in maintaining relations all his life—in consequence of rumours of an extremely low and—what was much worse in the eyes of the " world "—scandalous action which he was said to have committed more than a year ago in Germany. It was even reported that he had received a slap in the face from Prince Sokolsky (one of those with whom he was now in litigation) and had not followed it by a challenge. Even his children (the legitimate ones), his son and daughter, had turned against him and were holding aloof. It is true that through the influence of the Fanariotovs and old Prince Sokolsky (who had been a friend of Versilov) the son and daughter moved in the very highest circles. Yet, watching him all that month, I saw a haughty man who had rather cast off " society " than been cast off by it, so independent was his air. But had he the right to look like that—that was the question that agitated me. I absolutely had to find out the whole truth at the earliest possible date, for I had come—to judge this man. I still kept my power hidden from him, but I had either to accept him or to reject him altogether. But that would have been too painful to me and I was in torment. I will confess it frankly at last : the man was dear to me !

And meanwhile I was living in the same flat with him, working, and scarcely refraining from being rude. In fact I did not refrain. After spending a month with him I became more convinced every day that I could not possibly appeal to him for a full explanation. This man in his pride remained an enigma to me, while he wounded me deeply. He was positively charming to me, and jested with me, but I should have liked quarrels better than such jests. There was a certain note of ambiguity about all my conversations with him, or more simply, a strange irony on his part. From our first meeting, on my arrival from Moscow, he did not treat me seriously. I never could make out why he took up this line. It is true that by this means he succeeded in remaining impenetrable, but I would not have humbled myself so far as to ask him to treat me seriously. Besides, he had certain wonderful and irresistible ways which I did not know how to deal with. In short he behaved to me as though I were the greenest of raw youths, which I was hardly able to endure, though I knew it would be so. I, too, gave up talking seriously in consequence, and waited ; in fact, I almost gave up talking altogether. I waited for a person on whose arrival in Petersburg I might finally learn the truth ; that was my last hope. In any case I prepared myself for a final rupture, and had already taken all necessary measures. I was sorry for my mother but—" either him or me," that was the choice I meant to offer her and my sister. I had even fixed on the day ; and meanwhile I went to my work.

CHAPTER II

1

On that 19th of September I was also to receive my first salary
for the first month of my work in Petersburg in my " private "
situation.   They did not ask me about this job but simply
handed me over to it, I believe, on the very first day of my arrival.
This was very unmannerly, and it was almost my duty to protest.
The job turned out to be a situation in the household of old
Prince Sokolsky.   But to protest then would have meant breaking off relations on the spot, and though I was not in the least
afraid of that, it would have hindered the attainment of my
primary objects ;   and so in silence I accepted the job for the
time, maintaining my dignity by silence.   I must explain from
the very first that this Prince Sokolsky, a wealthy man and a
privy councillor, was no relation at all of the Moscow princes
of that name (who had been poor and insignificant for several
generations past) with whom Versilov was contesting his lawsuit.
It was only that they had the same name.   Yet the old prince
took a great interest in them, and was particularly fond of one
of them who was, so to speak, the head of the family—a young
officer.   Versilov had till recently had an immense influence
in this old man's affairs and had been his friend, a strange sort
of friend, for the poor old prince, as I detected, was awfully
afraid of him, not only at the time when I arrived on the scene,
but had apparently been always afraid of him all through their
friendship.   They had not seen each other for a long time,
however.   The dishonourable conduct of which Versilov was
accused concerned the old prince's family.   But Tatyana Pavlovna had intervened and it was through her that I was placed
in attendance on the old prince, who wanted a " young man "
in his study.   At the same time it appeared that he was very
anxious to do something to please Versilov, to make, so to speak,
the first advance to him, and Versilov *allowed* it.   The old man
had made the arrangement in the absence of his daughter, the
widow of a general, who would certainly not have permitted him
to take this step.   Of this later, but I may remark that the
strangeness of his relations with Versilov impressed me in the
latter's favour.   It occurred to the imagination that if the head
of the injured family still cherished a respect for Versilov, the

rumours of Versilov's scoundrelly behaviour must be absurd, or
at least exaggerated, and might have more than one explanation.
It was partly this circumstance which kept me from protesting against the situation ; in accepting it I hoped to verify all
this.

Tatyana Pavlovna was playing a strange part at the time when
I found her in Petersburg. I had almost forgotten her, and had
not at all expected to find her possessed of such influence. She
had met me three or four times during my life in Moscow, and
had always turned up, goodness knows where from, sent by
some one or other whenever I needed fitting out—to go into
Touchard's boarding school, or two and a half years later, when
I was being transferred to the grammar school and sent to
board with Nikolay Semyonovitch, a friend I shall never forget.
She used to spend the whole day with me and inspect my linen and
my clothes. She drove about the town with me, took me to
Kuznetsky Street, bought me what was necessary, provided me
with a complete outfit, in fact, down to the smallest box and pen-
knife. All the while she nagged at me, scolded me, reproached
me, cross-examined me, quoting as examples to me various phantom boys among her relations and acquaintances who were all said
to be better than I was. She even pinched me and actually gave
me several vicious pokes. After fitting me out and installing
me, she would disappear completely for several years. On this
occasion, too, she turned up at once on my arrival to instal me
again. She was a spare little figure with a sharp nose like a beak,
and sharp little eyes like a bird's. She waited on Versilov like a
slave, and grovelled before him as though he were the Pope,
but she did it through conviction. But I soon noticed with
surprise that she was respected by all and, what was more,
known to every one everywhere. Old Prince Sokolsky treated
her with extraordinary deference ; it was the same thing with
his family ; the same with Versilov's haughty children ; the same
with the Fanariotovs ; and yet she lived by taking in sewing, and
washing lace, and fetched work from the shops. She and I fell
out at the first word, for she thought fit to begin nagging at me
just as she had done six years before. And from that time forward we quarrelled every day, but that did not prevent us from
sometimes talking, and I must confess that by the end of the
month I began to like her : for her independent character, I
believe. But I did not tell her so.

I realized at once that I had only been given this post at the old invalid prince's in order to " amuse " him, and that that was my whole duty. Naturally this was humiliating, and I should at once have taken steps, but the queer old fellow soon made an unexpected impression upon me. I felt something like compassion for him, and by the end of the month I had become strangely attached to him ; anyway I gave up my intention of being rude. He was not more than sixty, however, but there had been a great to-do with him a year and a half before, when he suddenly had a fit. He was travelling somewhere and went mad on the way, so there was something of a scandal of which people talked in Petersburg. As is usual in such cases, he was instantly taken abroad, but five months later he suddenly reappeared perfectly well, though he gave up the service. Versilov asserted seriously (and with noticeable heat) that he had not been insane at all, but had only had some sort of nervous fit. I promptly made a note of Versilov's warmth about it. I may observe, however, that I was disposed to share his opinion. The old man only showed perhaps an excessive frivolity at times, not quite appropriate to his years, of which, so they say, there was no sign in him before. It was said that in the past he had been a councillor of some sort, and on one occasion had quite distinguished himself in some commission with which he had been charged. After knowing him for a whole month, I should never have supposed he could have any special capacity as a councillor. People observed (though I saw nothing of it) that after his fit he developed a marked disposition to rush into matrimony, and it was said that he had more than once reverted to this idea during the last eighteen months, that it was known in society and a subject of interest. But as this weakness by no means fell in with the interests of certain persons of the prince's circle, the old man was guarded on all sides. He had not a large family of his own ; he had been a widower for twenty years, and had only one daughter, the general's widow, who was now daily expected from Moscow. She was a young person whose strength of will was evidently a source of apprehension to the old man. But he had masses of distant relatives, principally through his wife, who were all almost beggars, besides a multitude of protégés of all sorts, male and female, all of whom expected to be mentioned in his will, and so they all supported the general's widow in keeping watch over the old man. He had, moreover, had one strange propensity from his youth up (I don't know whether it was ridiculous or not) for making matches for poor girls. He had been finding husbands for the last twenty-five years—for distant relations, for the step-daughters of his wife's cousins, for his god-daughters; he even found a husband for the daughter of his house porter. He used to take his protégées into his house when they were little girls, provide them with governesses and French mademoiselles, then have them educated in the best boarding schools, and finally marry them off with a dowry. The calls upon him were continually increasing. When his protégées were married they naturally produced more little girls ; and all these little girls became his protégées. He was always having to stand as god-father. The whole lot turned up to congratulate him on his birthdays, and it was all very agreeable to him.

I noticed at once that the old man had lurking in his mind a painful conviction (it was impossible to avoid noticing it, indeed) that every one had begun to look at him strangely, that every one had begun to behave to him not as before, not as to a healthy man. This impression never left him even at the liveliest social functions. The old man had become suspicious, had begun to detect something in every one's eyes. He was evidently tormented by the idea that every one suspected him of being mad. He sometimes looked mistrustfully even at me. And if he had found out that some one was spreading or upholding such rumours, the benevolent old man would have become his implacable foe. I beg that this circumstance may be noted. I may add that it was what decided me from the first day not to be rude to him ; in fact, I was glad if I were able sometimes to amuse or entertain him ; I don't think that this confession can cast any slur on my dignity.

The greater part of his money was invested. He had since his illness become a partner in a large joint stock enterprise, a very safe one, however. And though the management was in other hands he took a great interest in it, too, attended the shareholders' meetings, was appointed a director, presided at the board-meetings, opposed motions, was noisy and obviously enjoyed himself. He was very fond of making speeches : every one could judge of his brain anyway. And in general he developed a great fancy for introducing profound reflections and *bon mots* in his conversation, even in the intimacy of private life. I quite understand it.

On the ground floor of his house there was something like a private office where a single clerk kept the books and accounts and also managed the house. This clerk was quite equal to the work alone, though he had some government job as well, but by the prince's own wish I was engaged to assist him ; but I was immediately transferred to the prince's study, and often had no work before me, not even books or papers to keep up appearances. I am writing now sobered by time ; and about many things feel now almost like an outsider ; but how can I describe the depression (I recall it vividly at this moment) that weighed down my heart in those days, and still more, the excitement which reached such a pitch of confused feverishness that I did not sleep at night—all due to my impatience, to the riddles I had set myself to solve.

2

To ask for money, even a salary, is a most disgusting business, especially if one feels in the recesses of one's conscience that one has not quite earned it. Yet the evening before, my mother had been whispering to my sister apart from Versilov (" so as not to worry Andrey Petrovitch ") that she intended to take the ikon which for some reason was particularly precious to her to the pawnbroker's. I was to be paid fifty roubles a month, but I had no idea how I should receive the money ; nothing had been said to me about it.

Meeting the clerk downstairs three days before, I inquired of him whom one was to ask for one's salary. He looked at me with a smile as though of astonishment (he did not like me).

" Oh, you get a salary ? "

I thought that on my answering he would add :

" What for ? "

But he merely answered drily, that he " knew nothing about it," and buried himself in the ruled exercise book into which he was copying accounts from some bills.

He was not unaware, however, that I did something. A fortnight before I had spent four days over work he had given me, making a fair copy, and as it turned out, almost a fresh draft of something. It was a perfect avalanche of " ideas " of the prince's which he was preparing to present to the board of directors. These had to be put together into a whole and clothed in suitable language. I spent a whole day with the prince over it afterwards, and he argued very warmly with me, but was well satisfied in the end. But I don't know whether he read the paper or not. I say nothing of the two or three letters, also about business, which I wrote at his request.

It was annoying to me to have to ask for my salary because I had already decided to give up my situation, foreseeing that I should be obliged through unavoidable circumstances to go away. When I waked up and dressed that morning in my garret upstairs, I felt that my heart was beating, and though I pooh-poohed it, yet I was conscious of the same excitement as I walked towards the prince's house. That morning there was expected a woman, whose presence I was reckoning upon for the explanation of all that was tormenting me! This was the prince's daughter, the young widow of General Ahmakov, of whom I have spoken already and who was bitterly hostile to Versilov. At last I have written that name! I had never seen her, of course, and could not imagine how I should speak to her or whether I should speak, but I imagined (perhaps on sufficient grounds) that with her arrival there would be some light thrown on the darkness surrounding Versilov in my eyes. I could not remain unmoved. It was frightfully annoying that at the very outset I should be so cowardly and awkward; it was awfully interesting, and, still more, sickening—three impressions at once. I remember every detail of that day!

My old prince knew nothing of his daughter's probable arrival, and was not expecting her to return from Moscow for a week. I had learnt this the evening before quite by chance: Tatyana Pavlovna, who had received a letter from Mme. Ahmakov, let it out to my mother. Though they were whispering and spoke in veiled allusions, I guessed what was meant. Of course I was not eavesdropping, I simply could not avoid listening when I saw how agitated my mother was at the news of this woman's arrival. Versilov was not in the house.

I did not want to tell the old prince because I could not help noticing all that time how he was dreading her arrival. He had even let drop three days before, though only by a timid and remote hint, that he was afraid of her coming on my account; that is that he would have trouble about me. I must add, however, that in his own family he preserved his independence and was still master in his own house, especially in money matters. My first judgment of him was that he was a regular old woman, but I was afterwards obliged to revise my opinion, and to recognize that, if he were an old woman, there was still a fund of obstinacy, if not of real manliness, in him. There were moments when one could hardly do anything with him in spite of his apprehensive and yielding character. Versilov explained this to me more fully later. I recall now with interest that the old prince and I scarcely ever spoke of his daughter, we seemed to avoid it : I in particular avoided it, while he, on his side, avoided mentioning Versilov, and I guessed that he would not answer if I were to ask him one of the delicate questions which interested me so much.

If anyone cares to know what we did talk about all that month I must answer that we really talked of everything in the world, but always of the queerest things. I was delighted with the extraordinary simplicity with which he treated me. Sometimes I looked with extreme astonishment at the old man and wondered how he could ever have presided at meetings. If he had been put into our school and in the fourth class too, what a nice school-fellow he would have made. More than once, too, I was surprised by his face ; it was very serious-looking, almost handsome and thin ; he had thick curly grey hair, wide-open eyes ; and he was besides slim and well built ; but there was an unpleasant, almost unseemly, peculiarity about his face, it would suddenly change from excessive gravity to an expression of exaggerated playfulness, which was a complete surprise to a person who saw him for the first time. I spoke of this to Versilov, who listened with curiosity ; I fancy that he had not expected me to be capable of making such observations ; he observed casually that this had come upon the prince since his illness and probably only of late.

We used to talk principally of two abstract subjects—of God and of His existence, that is, whether there was a God or not—and of women. The prince was very religious and sentimental. He had in his study a huge stand of ikons with a lamp burning before them. But something seemed to come over him—and he would begin expressing doubts of the existence of God and would say astounding things, obviously challenging me to answer. I was not much interested in the question, speaking generally, but we both got very hot about it and quite genuinely. I recall all those conversations even now with pleasure. But what he liked best was gossiping about women, and he was sometimes positively disappointed at my disliking this subject of conversation, and making such a poor response to it.

He began talking in that style as soon as I went in that morning. I found him in a jocose mood, though I had left him the night before extremely melancholy. Meanwhile it was absolutely necessary for me to settle the matter of the salary—before the arrival of certain persons. I reckoned that that morning we should certainly be interrupted (it was not for nothing my heart was beating) and then perhaps I should not be able to bring my-self to speak of money. But I did not know how to begin about money and I was naturally angry at my stupidity. And, as I remember now in my vexation at some too jocular question of his, I blurted out my views on women point-blank and with great vigour.

And this led him to be more expansive with me than ever.

3

" I don't like women because they've no manners, because they are awkward, because they are not self-reliant, and because they wear unseemly clothes ! " I wound up my long tirade incoherently.

" My dear boy, spare us ! " he cried, immensely delighted, which enraged me more than ever.

I am ready to give way and be trivial only about trifles. I never give way in things that are really important. In trifles, in little matters of etiquette, you can do anything you like with me, and I curse this peculiarity in myself. From a sort of putrid good nature I've sometimes been ready to knuckle under to some fashionable snob, simply flattered by his affability, or I've let myself be drawn into argument with a fool, which is more unpardonable than anything. All this is due to lack of self-control, and to my having grown up in seclusion, but next day it would be the same thing again : that's why I was some-times taken for a boy of sixteen. But instead of gaining self-control I prefer even now to bottle myself up more tightly than ever in my shell—" I may be clumsy—but good-bye ! "—however misanthropic that may seem. I say that seriously and for good. But I don't write this with reference to the prince or even with reference to that conversation.

" I'm not speaking for your entertainment," I almost shouted at him. " I am speaking from conviction."

" But how do you mean that women have no manners and are unseemly in their dress ? That's something new."

" They have no manners. Go to the theatre, go for a walk. Every man knows the right side of the road, when they meet they step aside, he keeps to the right, I keep to the right. A woman, that is a lady—it's ladies I'm talking about—dashes straight at you as though she doesn't see you, as though you were absolutely bound to skip aside and make way for her. I'm prepared to make way for her as a weaker creature, but why has she the right, why is she so sure it's my duty—that's what's offensive. I always curse when I meet them. And after that they cry out that they're oppressed and demand equality ; a fine sort of equality when she tramples me under foot and fills my mouth with sand."

" With sand ? "

" Yes, because they're not decently dressed—it's only depraved people don't notice it. In the law-courts they close the doors when they're trying cases of indecency. Why do they allow it in the streets, where there are more people ? They openly hang bustles on behind to look as though they had fine figures ; openly ! I can't help noticing ; the young lad notices it too ; and the child that's growing into a boy notices it too ; it's abominable. Let old rakes admire them and run after them with their tongues hanging out, but there is such a thing as the purity of youth which must be protected. One can only despise them. They walk along the parade with trains half a yard long behind them, sweeping up the dust. It's a pleasant thing to walk behind them : you must run to get in front of them, or jump on one side, or they'll sweep pounds of dust into your mouth and nose. And what's more it's silk, and they'll drag it over the stones for a couple of miles simply because it's the fashion, when their husbands get five hundred roubles a year in the Senate : that's where bribes come in ! I've always despised them. I've cursed them aloud and abused them."

Though I describe this conversation somewhat humorously in the style that was characteristic of me at that time, my ideas are still the same.

" And how do you come off ? " the prince queried.

" I curse them and turn away. They feel it, of course, but they don't show it, they prance along majestically without turning their heads. But I only came to actual abuse on one occasion with two females, both wearing tails on the parade ; of course I didn't use bad language, but I said aloud that long tails were offensive."

" Did you use that expression ? "

" Of course I did. To begin with, they trample upon the rules of social life, and secondly, they raise the dust, and the parade is meant for all. I walk there, other men walk, Fyodor, Ivan, it's the same for all. So that's what I said. And I dislike the way women walk altogether, when you look at their back view ; I told them that too, but only hinted at it."

" But, my dear boy, you might get into serious trouble ; they might have hauled you off to the police station."

" They couldn't do anything. They had nothing to complain of : a man walks beside them talking to himself. Every one has the right to express his convictions to the air. I spoke in the abstract without addressing them. They began wrangling with me of themselves ; they began to abuse me, they used much worse language than I did ; they called me milksop, said I ought to go without my dinner, called me a nihilist, and threatened to hand me over to the police ; said that I'd attacked them because they were alone and weak women, but if there'd been a man with them I should soon sing another tune. I very coolly told them to leave off annoying me, and I would cross to the other side of the street. And to show them that I was not in the least afraid of their men, and was ready to accept their challenge, I would follow them to their house, walking twenty paces behind them, then I would stand before the house and wait for their men. And so I did."

" You don't say so ? "

" Of course it was stupid, but I was roused. They dragged me over two miles in the heat, as far as the 'institutions,' they went into a wooden house of one storey—a very respectable-looking one I must admit—one could see in at the windows a great many flowers, two canaries, three pug-dogs and engravings in frames. I stood for half an hour in the street facing the house. They peeped out two or three times, then pulled down all the blinds. Finally an elderly government clerk came out of the little gate ; judging from his appearance he had been asleep and had been waked up on purpose ; he was not actually in a dressing-gown, but he was in a very domestic-looking attire. He stood at the gate, folded his hands behind him, and proceeded to stare at me—I at him. Then he looked away, then gazed at me again, and suddenly began smiling at me. I turned and walked away."

" My dear boy, how Schilleresque ! I've always wondered at you ; with your rosy cheeks, your face blooming with health, and such an aversion, one may say, for women ! How is it possible that woman does not make a certain impression on you at your age ? Why, when I was a boy of eleven, *mon cher*, my tutor used to notice that I looked too attentively at the statues in the Summer Gardens."

" You would like me to take up with some Josephine here,

and come and tell you all about it! Rather not; I saw a woman completely naked when I was thirteen; I've had a feeling of disgust ever since."

"Do you mean it? But, *cher enfant*, about a fresh, beautiful woman there's a scent of apples; there's nothing disgusting."

"In the little boarding school I was at before I went to the grammar school, there was a boy called Lambert. He was always thrashing me, for he was three years older than I was, and I used to wait on him, and take off his boots. When he was going to be confirmed an abbé, called Rigaud, came to congratulate him on his first communion, and they dissolved in tears on each other's necks, and the abbé hugged him tightly to his bosom. I shed tears, too, and felt very envious. He left school when his father died, and for two years I saw nothing of him. Then I met him in the street. He said he would come and see me. By that time I was at the grammar school and living at Nikolay Semyonovitch's. He came in the morning, showed me five hundred roubles, and told me to go with him. Though he had thrashed me two years before, he had always wanted my company, not simply to take off his boots, but because he liked to tell me things. He told me that he had taken the money that day out of his mother's desk, to which he had made a false key, for legally all his father's money was his, and so much the worse for her if she wouldn't give it to him. He said that the Abbé Rigaud had been to lecture him the day before, that he'd come in, stood over him, begun whimpering, and described all sorts of horrors, lifting up his hands to heaven. "And I pulled out a knife and told him I'd cut his throat" (he pronounced it 'thr-r-roat'). We went to Kuznetsky Street. On the way he informed me that his mother was the abbé's mistress, and that he'd found it out, and he didn't care a hang for anything, and that all they said about the sacrament was rubbish. He said a great deal more, and I felt frightened. In Kuznetsky Street he bought a double-barrelled gun, a game bag, cartridges, a riding-whip, and afterwards a pound of sweets. We were going out into the country to shoot, and on the way we met a bird-catcher with cages of birds. Lambert bought a canary from him. In a wood he let the canary go, as it couldn't fly far after being in the cage, and began shooting at it, but did not hit it. It was the first time in his life he had fired off a gun, but he had wanted to buy a gun years before; at Touchard's even we were dreaming of one.

He was almost choking with excitement. His hair was black, awfully black, his face was white and red, like a mask, he had a long aquiline nose, such as are common with Frenchmen, white teeth and black eyes. He tied the canary by a thread to a branch, and an inch away fired off both barrels, and the bird was blown into a hundred feathers. Then we returned, drove to an hotel, took a room, and began eating, and drinking champagne ; a lady came in. . . . I remember being awfully impressed by her being so splendidly dressed ; she wore a green silk dress. It was then I saw . . . all that I told you about. . . . Afterwards, when we had begun drinking, he began taunting and abusing her ; she was sitting with nothing on, he took away her clothes and when she began scolding and asking for her clothes to dress again, he began with all his might beating her with the riding-whip on her bare shoulders. I got up, seized him by the hair, and so neatly that I threw him on the ground at once. He snatched up a fork and stuck it in my leg. Hearing the outcry, people ran in, and I had time to run away. Ever since then it's disgusted me to think of nakedness ; and, believe me, she was a beauty."

As I talked, the prince's face changed from a playful expression to one of great sadness.

" *Mon pauvre enfant!* I have felt convinced all along that there have been very many unhappy days in your childhood."

" Please don't distress yourself ! "

" But you were alone, you told me so yourself, but for that Lambert ; you have described it so well, that canary, the confirmation and shedding tears on the abbé's breast, and only a year or so later saying that of his mother and the abbé ! . . . Oh, *mon cher*, the question of childhood in our day is truly awful ; for a time those golden heads, curly and innocent, flutter before one and look at one with their clear eyes like angels of God, or little birds, and afterwards . . . and afterwards it turns out that it would have been better if they had not grown up at all ! "

" How soft you are, prince ! It's as though you had little children of your own. Why, you haven't any and never will have."

" *Tiens !* " His whole face was instantly transformed, " that's just what Alexandra Petrovna said—the day before yesterday, he-he !—Alexandra Petrovna Sinitsky—you must have met her here three weeks ago—only fancy, the day before yesterday, in reply to my jocular remark that if I do get married now I could set my mind at rest, there'd be no children, she suddenly said, and with such spite, ' On the contrary, there certainly would be ; people like you always have them, they'll arrive the very first year, you'll see.' He-he ! And they've all taken it into their heads, for some reason, that I'm going to get married ; but though it was spiteful I admit it was—witty ! ''

" Witty—but insulting ! "

" Oh, *cher enfant*, one can't take offence at some people. There's nothing I prize so much in people as wit, which is evidently disappearing among us ; though what Alexandra Petrovna said—can hardly be considered wit."

" What ? What did you say ? " I said, catching at his words—" one can't take offence at some people. That's just it ! Some people are not worth noticing—an excellent principle ! Just the one I need. I shall make a note of it. You sometimes say the most delightful things, prince."

He beamed all over.

" *N'est ce pas ? Cher enfant*, true wit is vanishing ; the longer one lives the more one sees it. *Eh, mais . . . c'est moi qui connait les femmes !* Believe me, the life of every woman, whatever she may profess, is nothing but a perpetual search for some one to submit to . . . so to speak a thirst for submission. And mark my words, there's not a single exception."

" Perfectly true ! Magnificent ! " I cried rapturously. Another time we should have launched into philosophical disquisitions on this theme, lasting for an hour, but suddenly I felt as though something had bitten me, and I flushed all over. I suddenly imagined that in admiring his *bon mots* I was flattering him as a prelude to asking for money, and that he would certainly think so as soon as I began to ask for it. I purposely mention this now.

" Prince, I humbly beg you to pay me at once the fifty roubles you owe me for the month," I fired off like a shot, in a tone of irritability that was positively rude.

I remember (for I remember every detail of that morning) that there followed between us then a scene most disgusting in its realistic truth. For the first minute he did not understand me, stared at me for some time without understanding what money I was talking about. It was natural that he should not realize I was receiving a salary—and indeed, why should I ? It is true that he proceeded to assure me afterwards that he had forgotten, and when he grasped the meaning of my words, he instantly began taking out fifty roubles, but he was flustered and turned crimson. Seeing how things stood, I got up and abruptly announced that I could not take the money now, that in what I had been told about a salary they had made a mistake, or deceived me to induce me to accept the situation, and that I saw only too well now, that I did nothing to earn one, for I had no duties to perform. The prince was alarmed and began assuring me that I was of the greatest use to him, that I should be still more useful to him in the future, and that fifty roubles was so little that he should certainly add to it, for he was bound to do so, and that he had made the arrangement himself with Tatyana Pavlovna, but had "unpardonably forgotten it." I flushed crimson and declared resolutely that it was degrading for me to receive a salary for telling scandalous stories of how I had followed two draggle-tails to the 'institutions,' that I had not been engaged to amuse him but to do work, and that if there was no work I must stop it, and so on, and so on. I could never have imagined that anyone could have been so scared as he was by my words. Of course it ended in my ceasing to protest, and his somehow pressing the fifty roubles into my hand : to this day I recall with a blush that I took it. Everything in the world always ends in meanness, and what was worst of all, he somehow succeeded in almost proving to me that I had unmistakably earned the money, and I was so stupid as to believe it, and so it was absolutely impossible to avoid taking it.

"*Cher, cher enfant!*" he cried, kissing and embracing me (I must admit I was on the point of tears myself, goodness knows why, though I instantly restrained myself, and even now I blush as I write it). "My dear boy, you're like one of the family to me now ; in the course of this month you've won a warm place in my heart ! In 'society' you get 'society' and nothing else. Katerina Nikolaevna (that was his daughter's name) is a magnificent woman and I'm proud of her, but she often, my dear boy, very often, wounds me. And as for these girls (*elles sont charmantes*) and their mothers who come on my birthday, they merely bring their embroidery and never know how to tell one anything. I've accumulated over sixty cushions embroidered by them, all dogs and stags. I like them very much, but with you I feel as if you were my own—not son, but brother, and I particularly like it when you argue against me ; you're literary, you have read, you can be enthusiastic. . . ."

" I have read nothing, and I'm not literary at all.   I used to
read what I came across, but I've read nothing for two years
and I'm not going to read."

" Why aren't you going to ? "

" I have other objects."

" Cher . . . it's a pity if at the end of your life you say, like
me, ' Je sais tout, mais je ne sais rien de bon.'   I don't know in
the least what I have lived in this world for !   But . . . I'm
so much indebted to you . . . and I should like, in fact . . ."

He suddenly broke off, and with an air of fatigue sank into
brooding.   After any agitation (and he might be overcome by
agitation at any minute, goodness knows why) he generally
seemed for some time to lose his faculties and his power of self-
control, but he soon recovered, so that it really did not matter.
We sat still for a few minutes.   His very full lower lip hung
down . . . what surprised me most of all was that he had
suddenly spoken of his daughter, and with such openness too.
I put it down, of course, to his being upset.

" Cher enfant, you don't mind my addressing you so familiarly,
do you ? " broke from him suddenly.

" Not in the least.   I must confess that at the very first I
was rather offended by it and felt inclined to address you in the
same way, but I saw it was stupid because you didn't speak
like that to humiliate me."

But he had forgotten his question and was no longer listening.

" Well, how's your father ? " he said, suddenly raising his
eyes and looking dreamily at me.

I winced.   In the first place he called Versilov my father,
which he had never permitted himself to do before, and secondly,
he began of himself to speak of Versilov, which he had never
done before.

" He sits at home without a penny and is very gloomy," I
answered briefly, though I was burning with curiosity.

" Yes, about money.   His lawsuit is being decided to-day,
and I'm expecting Prince Sergay as soon as he arrives.   He
promised to come straight from the court to me.   Their whole
future turns on it.   It's a question of sixty or seventy thousand.
Of course, I've always wished well to Andrey Petrovitch "
(Versilov's name), " and I believe he'll win the suit, and Prince
Sergay has no case.   It's a point of law."

" The case will be decided to-day ? " I cried, amazed.   The
thought that Versilov had not deigned to tell me even that

was a great shock to me. "Then he hasn't told my mother, perhaps not anyone," it suddenly struck me. "What strength of will!"

"Then is Prince Sokolsky in Petersburg?" was another idea that occurred to me immediately.

"He arrived yesterday. He has come straight from Berlin expressly for this day."

That too was an extremely important piece of news for me. And he would be here to-day, that man who had given *him* a slap in the face!

"Well, what then?" The old prince's face suddenly changed again. "He'll preach religion as before and . . . and . . . maybe run after little girls, unfledged girls, again. He-he! There's a very funny little story about that going about even now. . . . He-he!"

"Who will preach? Who will run after little girls?"

"Andrey Petrovitch! Would you believe it, he used to pester us all in those days. 'Where are we going?' he would say. 'What are we thinking about?' That was about it, anyway. He frightened and chastened us. 'If you're religious,' he'd say, 'why don't you become a monk?' That was about what he expected. *Mais quelle idée!* If it's right, isn't it too severe? He was particularly fond of frightening me with the Day of Judgment—me of all people!"

"I've noticed nothing of all this, and I've been living with him a month," I answered, listening with impatience. I felt fearfully vexed that he hadn't pulled himself together and was rambling on so incoherently.

"It's only that he doesn't talk about that now, but, believe me, it was so. He's a clever man, and undoubtedly very learned; but is his intellect quite sound? All this happened to him after his three years abroad. And I must own he shocked me very much and shocked every one. *Cher enfant, j'aime le bon Dieu.* . . . I believe, I believe as much as I can, but I really was angry at the time. Supposing I did put on a frivolous manner, I did it on purpose because I was annoyed—and besides, the basis of my objection was as serious as it has been from the beginning of the world. 'If there is a higher Being,' I said, ' and He has a *personal* existence, and isn't some sort of diffused spirit for creation, some sort of fluid (for that's even more difficult to understand), where does He live?' *C'était bête,* no doubt, my dear boy, but, you know, all the arguments come to that.

C

Un domicile is an important thing. He was awfully angry. He had become a Catholic out there."

" I've heard that too. But it was probably nonsense."

" I assure you by everything that's sacred. You've only to look at him. . . . But you say he's changed. But in those days how he used to worry us all ! Would you believe it, he used to behave as though he were a saint and his relics were being displayed. He called us to account for our behaviour, I declare he did ! Relics ! *En voilà un autre !* It's all very well for a monk or a hermit, but here was a man going about in a dress-coat and all the rest of it, and then he sets up as a saint ! A strange inclination in a man in good society, and a curious taste, I admit. I say nothing about that ; no doubt all that's sacred, and anything may happen. . . . Besides, this is all *l'inconnu*, but it's positively unseemly for a man in good society. If anything happened to me and the offer were made me I swear I should refuse it. I go and dine to-day at the club and then suddenly make a miraculous appearance as a saint ! Why, I should be ridiculous. I put all that to him at the time. . . . He used to wear chains."

I turned red with anger.

" Did you see the chains yourself ? "

" I didn't see them myself but . . ."

" Then let me tell you that all that is false, a tissue of loathsome fabrications, the calumny of enemies, that is, of one chief and inhuman enemy—for he has only one enemy—your daughter ! "

The old prince flared up in his turn.

" *Mon cher*, I beg and insist that from this time forth you never couple with that revolting story the name of my daughter."

I stood up. He was beside himself. His chin was quivering.

" *Cette histoire infame !* . . . I did not believe it, I never would believe it, but . . . they tell me, believe it, believe it, I . . ."

At that instant a footman came in and announced visitors. I dropped into my chair again.

4

Two ladies came in. They were both young and unmarried. One was a stepdaughter of a cousin of the old prince's deceased wife or something of the sort, a protégée of his for whom he had already set aside a dowry, and who (I mention it with a view to later events) had money herself : the other was Anna Andreyevna Versilov, the daughter of Versilov, three years older than I. She lived with her brother in the family of Mme. Fanariotov. I had only seen her once before in my life, for a minute in the street, though I had had an encounter, also very brief, with her brother in Moscow. (I may very possibly refer to this encounter later—if I have space, that is, for it is hardly worth recording.) Anna Andreyevna had been from childhood a special favourite of the old prince (Versilov's acquaintance with the prince dated from very long ago). I was so overcome by what had just happened that I did not even stand up on their entrance, though the old prince rose to greet them. Afterwards I thought it would be humiliating to get up, and I remained where I was. What overwhelmed me most was the prince's having shouted at me like that three minutes before, and I did not know whether to go away or not. But the old man, as usual, had already forgotten everything, and was all pleasure and animation at sight of the young ladies. At the very moment of their entrance he hurriedly whispered to me, with a rapid change of expression and a mysterious wink :

" Look at Olympiada, watch her, watch her ; I'll tell you why after. . . ."

I did look at her rather carefully, but I saw nothing special about her. She was a plump, not very tall young lady, with exceedingly red cheeks. Her face was rather pleasing, of the sort that materialists like. She had an expression of kindness, perhaps, but with a touch of something different. She could not have been very brilliant intellectually—that is, not in the higher sense—for one could see cunning in her eyes. She was not more than nineteen. In fact, there was nothing remarkable about her. In our school we should have called her a cushion. (I only give this minute description of her because it will be useful later on.)

Indeed, all I have written hitherto with, apparently, such unnecessary detail is all leading up to what is coming and is necessary for it. It will all come in in its proper place ; I cannot avoid it ; and if it is dull, pray don't read it.

Versilov's daughter was a very different person. She was tall and somewhat slim, with a long and strikingly pale face and splendid black hair. She had large dark eyes with an earnest expression, a small mouth, and most crimson lips. She was the first woman who did not disgust me by her horrid way of walking. She was thin and slender, however. Her expression was not altogether good-natured, but was dignified. She was twenty-two. There was hardly a trace of resemblance to Versilov in her features, and yet, by some miracle, there was an extraordinary similarity of expression. I do not know whether she was pretty ; that is a matter of taste. They were both very simple in their dress, so that it is not worth while to describe it. I expected to be at once insulted by some glance or gesture of Mlle. Versilov, and I was prepared for it. Her brother had insulted me in Moscow the first time we ever met. She could hardly know me by sight, but no doubt she had heard I was in attendance on the prince. Whatever the prince did or proposed to do at once aroused interest and was looked upon as an event in the whole gang of his relations and expectant beneficiaries, and this was especially so with his sudden partiality for me. I knew for a fact that the old prince was particularly solicitous for Anna Andreyevna's welfare and was on the look-out for a husband for her. But it was more difficult to find a suitor for Mlle. Versilov than for the ladies who embroidered on canvas.

And, lo and behold ! contrary to all my expectations, after shaking hands with the prince and exchanging a few light, conventional phrases with him, she looked at me with marked curiosity, and, seeing that I too was looking at her, bowed to me with a smile. It is true that she had only just come into the room, and so might naturally bow to anyone in it, but her smile was so friendly that it was evidently premeditated ; and, I remember, it gave me a particularly pleasant feeling.

" And this . . . this is my dear young friend Arkady Andreyevitch Dol . . ." The prince faltered, noticing that she bowed to me while I remained sitting—and he suddenly broke off ; perhaps he was confused at introducing me to her (that is, in reality, introducing a brother to a sister). The " cushion " bowed to me too ; but I suddenly leapt up with a clumsy scrape of my chair : it was a rush of simulated pride, utterly senseless, all due to vanity.

" Excuse me, prince, I am not Arkady Andreyevitch but Arkady Makarovitch ! " I rapped out abruptly, utterly forgetting that I ought to have bowed to the ladies. Damnation take that unseemly moment !

" *Mais tiens !* " cried the prince, tapping his forehead with his finger.

" Where have you studied ? " I heard the stupid question drawled by the " cushion," who came straight up to me.

" In Moscow, at the grammar school."

" Ah ! so I have heard. Is the teaching good there ? "

" Very good."

I remained standing and answered like a soldier reporting himself.

The young lady's questions were certainly not appropriate, but she did succeed in smoothing over my stupid outbreak and relieving the embarrassment of the prince, who was meanwhile listening with an amused smile to something funny Mlle. Versilov was whispering in his ear, evidently not about me. But I wondered why this girl, who was a complete stranger to me, should put herself out to smooth over my stupid behaviour and all the rest of it. At the same time, it was impossible to imagine that she had addressed me quite casually ; it was obviously premeditated. She looked at me with too marked an interest ; it was as though she wanted me, too, to notice her as much as possible. I pondered over all this later, and I was not mistaken.

" What, surely not to-day ? " the prince cried suddenly, jumping up from his seat.

" Why, didn't you know ? " Mlle. Versilov asked in surprise. " Olympie ! the prince didn't know that Katerina Nikolaevna would be here to-day. Why, it's to see her we've come. We thought she'd have arrived by the morning train and have been here long ago. She has just driven up to the steps ; she's come straight from the station, and she told us to come up and she would be here in a minute. . . . And here she is ! "

The side-door opened and—*that woman walked in !*

I knew her face already from the wonderful portrait of her that hung in the prince's study. I had been scrutinizing the portrait all that month. I spent three minutes in the study in her presence, and I did not take my eyes off her face for a second. But if I had not known her portrait and had been asked, after those three minutes, what she was like, I could not have answered, for all was confusion within me.

I only remember from those three minutes the image of a really beautiful woman, whom the prince was kissing and signing with the cross, and who looked quickly at once—the very minute she came in—at me. I distinctly heard the prince muttering something, with a little simper, about his new secretary and mentioning my name, evidently pointing at me. Her face seemed to contract; she threw a vicious glance at me, and smiled so insolently that I took a sudden step forward, went up to the prince, and muttered, trembling all over and unable to finish my words (I believe my teeth were chattering) :

"From this time I . . . I've business of my own. . . . I'm going."

And I turned and went out. No one said a word to me, not even the prince; they all simply stared. The old prince told me afterwards that I turned so white that he "was simply frightened."

But there was no need.

CHAPTER III

1

Indeed there was no need: a higher consideration swallowed up all petty feelings, and one powerful emotion made up to me for everything. I went out in a sort of ecstasy. As I stepped into the street I was ready to sing aloud. To match my mood it was an exquisite morning, sunshine, people out walking, noise, movement, joyousness, and crowds. Why, had not that woman insulted me ? From whom would I have endured that look and that insolent smile without instant protest however stupid it might be. I did not mind about that. Note that she had come expressly to insult me as soon as she could, although she had never seen me. In her eyes I was an " envoy from Versilov," and she was convinced at that time, and for long afterwards, that Versilov held her fate in his hands and could ruin her at once if he wanted to, by means of a certain document; she suspected that, anyway. It was a duel to the death. And yet —I was not offended ! It was an insult, but I did not feel it. How should I ? I was positively glad of it; though I had come here to hate her I felt I was beginning to love her.

I don't know whether the spider perhaps does not hate the fly he has marked and is snaring. Dear little fly ! It seems to me that the victim is loved, or at least may be loved. Here I love my enemy; I am delighted, for instance, that she is so beautiful. I am delighted, madam, that you are so haughty and majestic. If you were meeker it would not be so delightful. You have spat on me—and I am triumphant. If you were literally to spit in my face I should really not be angry because you—are my victim ; *mine* and not *his*. How fascinating was that idea ! Yes, the secret consciousness of power is more insupportably delightful than open domination. If I were a millionaire I believe I should take pleasure in going about in the oldest clothes and being taken for a destitute man, almost a beggar, being jostled and despised. The consciousness of the truth would be enough for me.

That is how I should interpret my thoughts and happiness, and much of what I was feeling that day. I will only add that in what I have just written there is too much levity ; in reality my feeling was deeper and more modest. Perhaps even now I am more modest in myself than in my words and deeds—God grant it may be so !

Perhaps I have done amiss in sitting down to write at all. Infinitely more remains hidden within than comes out in words. Your thought, even if it is an evil one, is always deeper while it is in your mind ; it becomes more absurd and dishonourable when it is put into words. Versilov once said to me that the opposite was true only with horrid people, they simply tell lies, it is easy for them ; but I am trying to write the whole truth, and that's fearfully difficult !

2

On that 19th of September I took one other " step."

For the first time since I arrived I had money in my pocket, for the sixty roubles I had saved up in two years I had given to my mother, as I mentioned before. But, a few days before, I had determined that on the day I received my salary I would make an " experiment " of which I had long been dreaming. The day before I had cut out of the paper an address ; it was an advertisement that on the 19th of September at twelve o'clock in the morning, in such-and-such a street, at number so-and-so, there would be a sale by the local police authority of the effects of Mme. Lebrecht, and that the catalogue, valuation, and property for sale could be inspected on the day of the auction, and so on.

It was just past one. I hurried to the address on foot. I had not taken a cab for more than two years—I had taken a vow not to (or I should never have saved up my sixty roubles). I had never been to an auction, I had never *allowed* myself this indulgence. And though my present step was only an *experiment*, yet I had made up my mind not to take even that step till I had left the grammar school, when I should break off with everything, hide myself in my shell, and become perfectly free. It is true that I was far from being in my shell and far from being free yet, but then I was only taking this step by way of an experiment—simply to look into it, as it were to indulge a fancy, and after that not to recur to it perhaps for a long while, till the time of beginning seriously. For every one else this was only a stupid little auction, but for me it was the first plank in the ship in which a Columbus would set out to discover his America. That was my feeling then.

When I arrived I went into the furthest corner of the yard of the house mentioned in the advertisement, and entered Mme. Lebrecht's flat, which consisted of an entry and four small low-pitched rooms. In the first room there was a crowd of about thirty persons, half of them people who had come to bargain, while the rest, judging from their appearance, were either inquisitive outsiders, or connoisseurs, or representatives of Mme. Lebrecht. There were merchants and Jews gloating over the objects made of gold, and a few people of the well-dressed class. The very faces of some of these gentlemen remain stamped in my memory. In the doorway leading to the room on the right there was placed a table so that it was impossible to pass ; on it lay the things catalogued for sale. There was another room on the left, but the door into it was closed, though it was continually being opened a little way, and some one could be seen peeping through the crack, no doubt some one of the numerous family of Mme. Lebrecht, who must have been feeling very much ashamed at the time. At the table between the doors, facing the public, sat the warrant officer, to judge by his badge, presiding over the sale. I found the auction half over ; I squeezed my way up to the table as soon as I went in. Some bronze candlesticks were being sold. I began looking at the things.

I looked at the things and wondered what I could buy, and what I could do with bronze candlesticks, and whether my object would be attained, and how the thing would be done, and whether my project would be successful, and whether my project were not childish. All this I wondered as I waited. It was like the sensation one has at the gambling table at the moment before one has put down a card, though one has come to do so, feeling, " if I like I'll put it down, if I don't I'll go away—I'm free to choose ! " One's heart does not begin to throb at that point, but there is a faint thrill and flutter in it—a sensation not without charm. But indecision soon begins to weigh painfully upon one : one's eyes grow dizzy, one stretches out one's hand, picks up a card, but mechanically, almost against one's will, as though some one else were directing one's hand. At last one has decided and thrown down the card—then the feeling is quite different—immense. I am not writing about the auction ; I am writing about myself ; who else would feel his heart throbbing at an auction ?

Some were excited, some were waiting in silence, some had bought things and were regretting it. I felt no sympathy with a gentleman who, misunderstanding what was said, bought an electro-plated milk-jug in mistake for a silver one for five roubles instead of two ; in fact it amused me very much. The warrant officer passed rapidly from one class of objects to another : after the candlesticks, displayed earrings, after earrings an embroidered leather cushion, then a money-box—probably for the sake of variety, or to meet the wishes of the purchasers. I could not remain passive even for ten minutes. I went up to the cushion, and afterwards to the cash-box, but at the critical moment my tongue failed me : these objects seemed to me quite out of the question. At last I saw an album in the warrant officer's hand.

" A family album in real morocco, second-hand, with sketches in water-colour and crayon, in a carved ivory case with silver clasps—priced two roubles ! "

I went up : it looked an elegant article, but the carving was damaged in one place. I was the only person who went up to look at it, all were silent ; there was no bidding for it. I might have undone the clasps and taken the album out of the case to look at it, but I did not make use of my privilege, and only waved a trembling hand as though to say " never mind."

" Two roubles, five kopecks," I said. I believe my teeth were chattering again.

The album was knocked down to me. I at once took out the money, paid for it, snatched up the album, and went into a corner of the room. There I took it out of its case, and began looking through it with feverish haste—it was the most trumpery thing possible—a little album of the size of a piece of notepaper, with rubbed gilt edges, exactly like the albums girls used to keep in former days when they left school. There were crayon and colour sketches of temples on mountain-sides, Cupids, a lake with floating swans ; there were verses :

> *On a far journey I am starting,*
> *From Moscow I am departing,*
> *From my dear ones I am parting.*
> *And with post-horses flying South.*

They are enshrined in my memory !

I made up my mind that I had made a mess of it ; if there ever was anything no one could possibly want it was this.

"Never mind," I decided, " one's bound to lose the first card ; it's a good omen, in fact."

I felt thoroughly light-hearted.

"Ach, I'm too late ; is it yours ? You have bought it ? " I suddenly heard beside me the voice of a well-dressed, presentable-looking gentleman in a blue coat. He had come in late.

"I am too late. Ach, what a pity ! How much was it ? "

"Two roubles, five kopecks."

"Ach, what a pity ! Would you give it up ? "

"Come outside," I whispered to him, in a tremor.

We went out on the staircase.

"I'll let you have it for ten roubles," I said, feeling a shiver run down my back.

"Ten roubles ! Upon my word ! "

"As you like."

He stared at me open-eyed. I was well dressed, not in the least like a Jew or a second-hand dealer.

"Mercy on us—why it's a wretched old album, what use is it to anyone ? The case isn't worth anything certainly. You certainly won't sell it to anyone."

"I see you will buy it."

"But that's for a special reason. I only found out yesterday. I'm the only one who would. Upon my word, what are you thinking about ! "

"I ought to have asked twenty-five roubles, but as there was, after all, a risk you might draw back, I only asked for ten to make sure of it. I won't take a farthing less."

I turned and walked away.

"Well, take four roubles," he said, overtaking me in the yard, " come, five ! "

I strode on without speaking.

" Well, take it then ! "

He took out ten roubles. I gave him the album.

" But you must own it's not honest ! Two roubles—and then ten, eh ? "

" Why not honest ? It's a question of market."

" What do you mean by market ? " He grew angry.

" When there's a demand one has a market—if you hadn't asked for it I shouldn't have sold it for forty kopecks."

Though I was serious and didn't burst out laughing I was laughing inwardly—not from delight—I don't know why myself, I was almost breathless.

" Listen," I muttered, utterly unable to restrain myself, but speaking in a friendly way and feeling quite fond of him. " Listen, when as a young man the late James Rothschild, the Parisian one, who left seventeen hundred million francs (he nodded), heard of the murder of the Duc de Berri some hours before anybody else he sent the news to the proper quarter, and by that one stroke in an instant made several millions—that's how people get on ! "

" So you're a Rothschild, are you ? " he cried as though indignant with me for being such a fool.

I walked quickly out of the house. One step, and I had made seven roubles ninety-five kopecks. It was a senseless step, a piece of child's play I admit, but it chimed in with my theories, and I could not help being deeply stirred by it. But it is no good describing one's feelings. My ten roubles were in my waistcoat pocket, I thrust in two fingers to feel it—and walked along without taking my hand out. After walking a hundred yards along the street I took the note out to look at it, I looked at it and felt like kissing it. A carriage rumbled up to the steps of a house. The house porter opened the door and a lady came out to get into the carriage. She was young, handsome and wealthy-looking, gorgeously dressed in silk and velvet, with a train more than two yards long. Suddenly a pretty little portfolio dropped out of her hand and fell on the ground ; she got into the carriage. The footman stooped down to pick the thing up, but I flew up quickly, picked it up and handed it to the lady, taking off my hat. (The hat was a silk one, I was suitably dressed for a young man.) With a very pleasant smile, though with an air of reserve, the lady said to me : " *Merci, M'sieu !* " The carriage rolled away. I kissed the ten-rouble note.

3

That same day I was to go and see Efim Zvyerev, one of my old schoolfellows at the grammar school, who had gone to a special college in Petersburg. He is not worth describing, and I was not on particularly friendly terms with him ; but I looked him up in Petersburg. He might (through various circumstances which again are not worth relating) be able to give me the address of a man called Kraft, whom it was very important for me to see as soon as he returned from Vilna. Efim was expecting him that day or the next, as he had let me know two days before. I had to go to the Petersburg Side, but I did not feel tired.

I found Efim (who was also nineteen) in the yard of his aunt's house, where he was staying for the time. He had just had dinner and was walking about the yard on stilts. He told me at once that Kraft had arrived the day before, and was staying at his old lodgings close by, and that he was anxious to see me as soon as possible, as he had something important to tell me.

" He's going off somewhere again," added Efim.

As in the present circumstances it was of great importance to see Kraft I asked Efim to take me round at once to his lodging, which it appeared was in a back street only a few steps away. But Efim told me that he had met him an hour ago and that he was on his way to Dergatchev's.

" But come along to Dergatchev's. Why do you always cry off ? Are you afraid ? "

Kraft might as a fact stay on at Dergatchev's, and in that case where could I wait for him ? I was not afraid of going to Dergatchev's, but I did not want to go to his house, though Efim had tried to get me there three times already. And on each occasion had asked " Are you afraid ? " with a very nasty smile at my expense. It was not a case of fear I must state at once ; if I was afraid it was of something quite different. This time I made up my mind to go. Dergatchev's, too, was only a few steps away. On the way I asked Efim if he still meant to run away to America.

" Maybe I shall wait a bit," he answered with a faint smile.

I was not particularly fond of him ; in fact I did not like him at all. He had fair hair, and a full face of an excessive fairness, an almost unseemly childish fairness, yet he was taller than I was, but he would never have been taken for more than seventeen. I had nothing to talk to him about.

"What's going on there? Is there always a crowd?" I asked.

"But why are you always so frightened?" he laughed again.

"Go to hell!" I said, getting angry.

"There won't be a crowd at all. Only friends come, and they're all his own set. Don't worry yourself."

"But what the devil is it to me whether they're his set or not! I'm not one of his set. How can they be sure of me?"

"I am bringing you and that's enough. They've heard of you already. Kraft can answer for you, too."

"I say, will Vassin be there?"

"I don't know."

"If he is, give me a poke and point him out as soon as we go in. As soon as we go in. Do you hear?"

I had heard a good deal about Vassin already, and had long been interested in him.

Dergatchev lived in a little lodge in the courtyard of a wooden house belonging to a merchant's wife, but he occupied the whole of it. There were only three living rooms. All the four windows had the blinds drawn down. He was a mechanical engineer, and did work in Petersburg. I had heard casually that he had got a good private berth in the provinces, and that he was just going away to it.

As soon as we stepped into the tiny entry we heard voices. There seemed to be a heated argument and some one shouted:

"Quae medicamenta non sanant, ferrum sanat, quae ferrum non sanat—ignis sanat!"

I certainly was in some uneasiness. I was, of course, not accustomed to society of any kind. At school I had been on familiar terms with my schoolfellows, but I was scarcely friends with anyone; I made a little corner for myself and lived in it. But this was not what disturbed me. In any case I vowed not to let myself be drawn into argument and to say nothing beyond what was necessary, so that no one could draw any conclusions about me; above all—to avoid argument.

In the room, which was really too small, there were seven men; counting the ladies, ten persons. Dergatchev was five-and-twenty, and was married. His wife had a sister and another female relation, who lived with them. The room was furnished after a fashion, sufficiently though, and was even tidy. There was a lithographed portrait on the wall, but a very cheap one ; in the corner there was an ikon without a setting, but with a lamp burning before it.

Dergatchev came up to me, shook hands and asked me to sit down.

"Sit down ; they're all our own set here."

"You're very welcome," a rather nice-looking, modestly dressed young woman added immediately, and making me a slight bow she at once went out of the room. This was his wife, and she, too, seemed to have been taking part in the discussion, and went away to nurse the baby. But there were two other ladies left in the room ; one very short girl of about twenty, wearing a black dress, also rather nice-looking, and the other a thin, keen-eyed lady of thirty. They sat listening eagerly, but not taking part in the conversation. All the men were standing except Kraft, Vassin and me. Efim pointed them out to me at once, for I had never seen Kraft before, either. I got up and went up to make their acquaintance. Kraft's face I shall never forget. There was no particular beauty about it, but a positive excess of mildness and delicacy, though personal dignity was conspicuous in everything about him. He was twenty-six, rather thin, above medium height, fair haired, with an earnest but soft face ; there was a peculiar gentleness about his whole personality. And yet if I were asked I would not have changed my own, possibly very commonplace, countenance for his, which struck me as so attractive. There was something in his face I should not have cared to have in mine, too marked a calm (in a moral sense) and something like a secret, unconscious pride. But I probably could not have actually formed this judgment at the time. It seems so to me now, in the light of later events.

"I'm very glad you've come," said Kraft. "I have a letter which concerns you. We'll stay here a little and then go home."

Dergatchev was a strong, broad-shouldered, dark-complexioned man of medium height, with a big beard. His eyes showed acuteness, habitual reserve, and a certain incessant watchfulness ; though he was for the most part silent, he evidently controlled the conversation. Vassin's face did not impress me much, though I had heard of him as extraordinarily intelligent : he had fair hair, large light grey eyes, and a very open face. But at the same time there was something, as it were, too hard in it ; one had a presentiment that he would not be communicative ;

but he looked undeniably clever, cleverer than Dergatchev, of a more profound intellect—cleverer than anyone in the room. But perhaps I am exaggerating. Of the other young men I only recall two ; one a tall, dark man of twenty-seven, with black whiskers, who talked a great deal, a teacher or something of the sort ; the other was a fellow of my own age, with good lines in his face, wearing a Russian tunic without sleeves. He was silent, and listened attentively. He turned out afterwards to be a peasant.

"No, that's not the way to put it," the black-whiskered teacher began, obviously continuing the previous discussion. He talked more than anyone in the room.

"I'm not talking of mathematical proofs, but that idea which I am prepared to believe without mathematical proof . . ."

"Wait a bit, Tihomirov," Dergatchev interrupted loudly, "the new-comers don't understand. You see," he suddenly addressed himself to me alone (and I confess if he intended to put me as a novice through an examination or to make me speak, it was adroitly done on his part ; I felt it and prepared myself) "it's all our friend Kraft, who is well known to us all for his character and the solidity of his convictions. From a very ordinary fact he has deduced a very extraordinary conviction that has surprised us all. He has deduced that the Russians are a second-rate people . . ."

"Third-rate," shouted some one.

"A second-rate people destined to serve as the raw material for a nobler race, and not to play an independent part in the history of humanity. In view of this theory of his, which is perhaps correct, Kraft has come to the conclusion that the activity of every Russian must in the future be paralysed by this idea, that all, so to speak, will fold their hands and . . ."

"Excuse me, Dergatchev, that's not the way to put it," Tihomirov interrupted impatiently again (Dergatchev at once gave way), "considering that Kraft has made a serious study of the subject, has made on a physiological basis deductions which he regards as mathematically proved, and has spent perhaps two years on his idea (which I should be prepared a priori to accept with equanimity), considering all this, that is considering Kraft's excitement and earnestness, the case must be considered as a phenomenon. All this leads up to a question which Kraft cannot understand, and that's what we must attend to—I mean, Kraft's not understanding it, for that's the phenomenon. We

must decide whether this phenomenon belongs to the domain
of pathology as a solitary instance, or whether it is an occurrence
which may be normally repeated in others ; that's what is of
interest for the common cause. I believe Kraft about Russia,
and I will even say that I am glad of it, perhaps ; if this idea
were assimilated by all it would free many from patriotic preju-
dice and untie their hands . . ."

"I am not influenced by patriotism," said Kraft, speaking with
a certain stiffness. All this debate seemed distasteful to him.

" Whether patriotism or not we need not consider," observed
Vassin, who had been very silent.

" But how, tell me, please, could Kraft's deduction weaken the
impulse to the cause of humanity," shouted the teacher. (He
was the only one shouting. All the others spoke in a low voice.)
" Let Russia be condemned to second-rateness, but we can still
work and not for Russia alone. And, what's more, how can
Kraft be a patriot if he has ceased to believe in Russia ? "

" Besides being a German," a voice interrupted again.

" I am a Russian," said Kraft.

" That's a question that has no direct bearing on the subject,"
observed Dergatchev to the speaker who had interrupted.

"Take a wider view of your idea," cried Tihomirov, heeding
nothing. " If Russia is only the material for nobler races why
shouldn't she serve as such material ? It's a sufficiently attractive part for her to play. Why not accept the idea calmly, considering how it enlarges the task ? Humanity is on the eve of
its regeneration, which is already beginning. None but the
blind deny the task before us. Let Russia alone, if you've lost
faith in her, and work for the future, for the future unknown
people that will be formed of all humanity without distinction
of race. Russia would perish some time, anyway; even the most
gifted peoples exist for fifteen hundred or at the most two thousand years. Isn't it all the same whether it's two thousand or
two hundred ? The Romans did not last fifteen hundred years
as a vital force, they too have turned into material. They ceased
to exist long ago, but they've left an idea, and it has become
an element in the future of mankind. How can one tell a man
there's nothing to be done ? I can't conceive of a position in
which there ever could be nothing to do ! Work for humanity
and don't trouble about the rest. There's so much to do that
life isn't long enough if you look into it more closely."

" One must live in harmony with the laws of nature and

truth," Mme. Dergatchev observed from the doorway. The door was slightly ajar and one could see that she was standing there, listening eagerly, with the baby at her breast which was covered.

Kraft listened with a faint smile and brought out at last with a somewhat harassed face, but with earnest sincerity :

" I don't understand how, if one is under the influence of some over-mastering idea which completely dominates one's mind and one's heart, one can live for something else which is outside that idea."

" But if it is logically, mathematically proved to you that your deduction is erroneous—that your whole idea is erroneous, that you have not the slightest right to exclude yourself from working for the welfare of humanity simply because Russia is predestined to a second-rate part, if it is pointed out to you, that in place of your narrow horizon infinity lies open before you, that instead of your narrow idea of patriotism . . ."

" Ah ! " Kraft waved his hand gently, " I've told you there is no question of patriotism."

" There is evidently a misunderstanding," Vassin interposed suddenly, " the mistake arises from the fact that Kraft's conclusion is not a mere logical theory but, so to say, a theory that has been transmuted into a feeling. All natures are not alike ; in some men a logical deduction is sometimes transmuted into a very powerful emotion which takes possession of the whole being, and is sometimes very difficult to dislodge or alter. To cure such a man the feeling itself must be changed, which is only possible by replacing it by another, equally powerful one. That's always difficult, and in many cases impossible."

" That's a mistake," roared the argumentative teacher, " a logical proof of itself will dissipate prejudices. A rational conviction will give rise to feeling, too. Thought arises from feeling, and dominating a man in its turn formulates new feeling."

" People are very different. Some change their feelings readily, while for others it's hard to do so," responded Vassin, as though disinclined to continue the argument ; but I was delighted by his idea.

" That's perfectly true what you say," I said, turning to him, all at once breaking the ice and suddenly beginning to speak ; " that to change a feeling one must replace it by another. Four years ago a general in Moscow . . . I didn't know him, you see, but . . . Perhaps he couldn't have inspired respect of himself.

D

. . . And the fact itself may seem irrational but . . . But he had lost a child, that's to say two little girls who had died one after another of scarlatina. And he was utterly crushed, and did nothing but grieve, so that one couldn't bear to go and look at him, and he ended by dying scarcely six months later. It's a fact that he died of it ! What could have saved him ? The answer is—a feeling of equal strength. One would have had to dig those two little girls out of the grave and give them back to him—that would have been the only thing, I mean in that way. And he died. Yet one might have presented him with excellent reflections : that life is transitory, that all are mortal ; one might have produced statistics to show how many children do die of scarlatina . . . he was on the retired list. . . ."

I stopped, out of breath, and looked round.

" That's nothing to do with it," said some one.

" The instance you have quoted, though it's not quite in the same category, is very similar and illustrates the subject," said Vassin, turning to me.

4

Here I must confess why I was so delighted with what Vassin had said about the " idea transmuted into feeling," and at the same time I must confess to a fiendish disgrace. Yes, I was afraid to go to Dergatchev's, though not for the reason Efim imagined. I dreaded going because I had been afraid of them even before I left Moscow. I knew that they (or some of their sort, it's all the same) were great in argument and would perhaps shatter " my idea." I was firmly resolved in myself that I wouldn't give away my idea or say a word to them about it ; but they (or again some of their sort) might easily say something to me which would destroy my faith in my " idea," even though I might not utter a syllable about it. There were questions connected with my " idea " which I had not settled, but I did not want anyone to settle them but myself. For the last two years I had even given up reading for fear of meeting with some passage opposed to my " idea " which might shake me. And all at once Vassin had solved the difficulty and reassured me on the most essential point. After all, what was I afraid of and what could they do to me, whatever skill in argument they might have ? I perhaps was the only one who understood what Vassin meant by " an idea transformed into an emotion." It's not enough to refute a fine idea, one must replace it by something fine of equal strength ; or else, refusing absolutely to part with my feeling, in my heart I should refute the refutation, however strong the argument might be, whatever they might say. And what could they give me in place of it ? And therefore I might be braver, I was bound to be more manly. While I was delighted with Vassin, I felt ashamed, and felt myself an insignificant child.

Then there followed fresh ignominy. It was not a contemptible desire to show off my intelligence that made me break the ice and speak, it was an impulse to " throw myself on his neck." The impulse to throw myself on people's necks that they might think well of me and take me to their hearts or something of the sort (pure beastliness, in fact) I look upon as the most abject of my weaknesses, and I suspected it in myself long ago ; in fact, when I was in the corner in which I entrenched myself for so many years, though I don't regret doing so, I knew I ought to behave in company with more austerity. What comforted me after every such ignominious scene was that my " idea " was as great a secret as ever, and that I hadn't given it away. With a sinking at my heart I sometimes imagined that when I did let out my idea to some one I should suddenly have nothing left, that I should become like every one else, and perhaps I should give up the idea ; and so I was on my guard and preserved it, and trembled at the thought of chattering. And now at Dergatchev's, almost at the first contact with anyone, I broke down. I hadn't betrayed anything, of course, but I had chattered unpardonably ; it was ignominious. It is a horrid thing to remember ! No, I must not associate with people. I think so even now. Forty years hence I will speak. My idea demands a corner.

5

As soon as Vassin expressed approval I felt irresistibly impelled to talk.

" I consider that every one has a right to have his own feelings . . . if they are from conviction . . . and that no one should reproach him with them," I went on, addressing Vassin. Though I spoke boldly, it was as though I was not speaking, not my own tongue moving in my mouth.

" Re-all-ly ? " the same voice which had interrupted Dergatchev and shouted at Kraft that he was a German interposed with an ironical drawl. Regarding the speaker as a complete

nonentity, I addressed the teacher as though he had called out
to me.

"It's my conviction that I should not dare to judge anyone,"
I said, quivering, and conscious that I was going to make a fool
of myself.

"Why so mysterious ?" cried the voice of the nonentity again.

"Every man has his own idea," I went on, gazing persistently
at the teacher, who for his part held his tongue and looked at me
with a smile.

"Yours is ?" cried the nonentity.

"Too long to describe. . . . But part of my idea is that I
should be left alone. As long as I've two roubles I want to be
independent of every one (don't excite yourself, I know the
objection that will be made) and to do nothing—not even to work
for that grand future of humanity which Mr. Kraft is invited to
work for. Personal freedom, that is, my own, is the first thing,
and I don't care about anything else."

My mistake was that I lost my temper.

"In other words you advocate the tranquillity of the well-fed
cow ?"

"So be it. Cows don't hurt anyone. I owe no one anything.
I pay society in the form of taxes that I may not be robbed,
killed or assaulted, and no one dare demand anything more.
I personally, perhaps, may have other ideas, and if I want to serve
humanity I shall, and perhaps ten times as much as those who
preach about it ; only I want no one to dare to demand it of me,
to force me to it like Mr. Kraft. I must be perfectly free not to
lift a finger if I like. But to rush and 'fall on everybody's neck'
from love to humanity, and dissolve in tears of emotion—is only a
fashion. And why should I be bound to love my neighbour, or
your future humanity which I shall never see, which will never
know anything about me, and which will in its turn disappear
and leave no trace (time counts for nothing in this) when the
earth in its turn will be changed into an iceberg, and will fly off
into the void with an infinite multitude of other similar icebergs ;
it's the most senseless thing one could possibly imagine. That's
your teaching. Tell me why I am bound to be so noble,
especially if it all lasts only for a moment ?"

"P-pooh !" cried a voice.

I had fired off all this with nervous exasperation, throwing
off all restraint. I knew that I was making a fool of myself,
but I hurried on, afraid of being interrupted. I felt that my

words were pouring out like water through a sieve, incoherently, nineteen to the dozen, but I hurried on to convince them and get the better of them. It was a matter of such importance to me. I had been preparing for it for three years. But it was remarkable that they were all suddenly silent, they said absolutely nothing, every one was listening. I went on addressing my remarks to the teacher.

"That's just it. A very clever man has said that nothing is more difficult than to answer the question ' Why we must be honourable.' You know there are three sorts of scoundrels in the world ; naïve scoundrels, that is, convinced that their villany is the highest virtue ; scoundrels who are ashamed, that is, ashamed of their own villany, though they fully intend to persevere with it; and lastly simple scoundrels, pure-bred scoundrels. For example I had a schoolfellow called Lambert who told me at sixteen that when he came into his fortune it would be his greatest satisfaction to feed on meat and bread while the children of the poor were dying of hunger ; and when they had no fuel for their fires he would buy up a whole woodstack, build it up in a field and set fire to it there, and not give any of it to the poor. Those were his feelings ! Tell me, what am I to say to a pure-blooded scoundrel like that if he asks me why he should be honourable ? Especially now in these times which you have so transformed, for things have never been worse than they are now. Nothing is clear in our society. You deny God, you see, deny heroism. What blind, deaf, dull-witted stagnation of mind can force me to act in one way, if it's more to my advantage to do the opposite ? You say ' a rational attitude to humanity is to your own advantage, too ' ; but what if I think all these rational considerations irrational, and dislike all these socialist barracks and phalanxes ? What the devil do I care for them or for the future when I shall only live once on earth ! Allow me to judge of my advantage for myself ; it's more amusing. What does it matter to me what will happen in a thousand years to your humanity if, on your principles, I'm to get for it neither love, nor future life, nor recognition of my heroism ? No, if that's how it is I'd rather live in the most ignorant way for myself and let them all go to perdition ! "

" An excellent sentiment ! "

" Though I'm always ready to go with them."

" That's one better ! "—the same voice again.

The others still remained silent, they all scrutinized me,

staring; but little by little in different parts of the room there rose a titter, subdued indeed, but they were all laughing at me to my face. Vassin and Kraft were the only ones not laughing, the gentleman with the black whiskers was sniggering too ; he sneered at me persistently and listened.

"I'm not going to tell you my idea," I cried, quivering all over, "nothing would induce me, but I ask you on the other hand, from your point of view—don't imagine I'm speaking for myself, for I dare say I love humanity a thousand times more than all of you put together ! Tell me, and you must, you are bound now to answer because you are laughing, tell me, what inducement do you hold out to me to follow you ? Tell me, how do you prove to me that you'll make things better ? How will you deal with my individual protest in your barracks ? I have wanted to meet you, gentlemen, for ever so long. You will have barracks, communistic homes, *stricte necessaire*, atheism, and communistic wives without children—that's your ideal, I know all about it. And for all this, for this little part of mediocre advantage which your rational system guarantees me, for a bit of bread and a warm corner you take away all my personal liberty ! For instance ; if my wife's carried off, are you going to take away my personal liberty so that I mayn't bash my rival's brains in ? You'll tell me I shall be more sensible then myself, but what will the wife say to a husband so sensible, if she has the slightest self-respect ? Why it's unnatural ; you ought to be ashamed ! "

"You're a specialist on the woman question then ? " the voice of the nonentity pronounced malignantly.

For one instant I had an impulse to fly at him and pommel him with my fists. He was a short fellow with red hair and freckles . . . though what the devil does his appearance matter ?

"Don't excite yourself. I've never once had relations with a woman," I rapped out, for the first time addressing him directly.

"A priceless avowal which might have been made more politely in the presence of ladies."

But there was a general movement among them ; they were all looking for their hats and taking leave—not on my account, of course, but simply because it was time to break up. But I was crushed with shame at the way they all ignored me. I jumped up, too.

"Allow me to ask your name. You kept looking at me." said the teacher, coming up to me with a very nasty smile.

"Dolgoruky."

" Prince Dolgoruky ? "

" No, simply Dolgoruky, legally the son of a former serf, Makar Dolgoruky, but the illegitimate son of my former master, Monsieur Versilov. Don't make a mistake, gentlemen, I don't tell you this to make you all fall upon my neck and begin howling like calves from sentimentality."

There was a loud and unceremonious roar of laughter, so much so that the baby, who was asleep in the next room, waked up and began squealing. I trembled with fury. Every one shook hands with Dergatchev and went out without taking the slightest notice of me.

" Come along," said Kraft, touching me.

I went up to Dergatchev, pressed his hand and shook it vigorously several times.

" You must excuse Kudryumov's being so rude to you " (Kudryumov was the red-haired man), said Dergatchev.

I followed Kraft out. I was not in the least ashamed.

6

There is of course an immense difference between what I am now and what I was then.

Still " not in the least ashamed " I overtook Vassin on the stairs, leaving Kraft behind as of secondary importance, and with the most natural air as though nothing had happened I asked :

" I believe you know my father, I mean Versilov.

" He's not exactly an acquaintance of mine," Vassin answered at once (and without a trace of that insulting refinement of politeness which delicate people adopt when they speak to people who have just disgraced themselves), " but I do know him a little ; I have met him and I've heard him talk."

" If you've heard him no doubt you do know him, for you are you ! What do you think of him ? Forgive the abrupt question but I need to know. It's what *you* would think, just your opinion that I need."

" You are asking a great deal of me. I believe that man is capable of setting himself tremendous tasks and possibly carrying them through—but without rendering an account of his doings to anyone."

" That's true, that's very true—he's a very proud man ! Is he a sincere man ? Tell me, what do you think about his being a Catholic ? But I forgot, perhaps you don't know ? "

If I had not been so excited I should not, of course, have fired off such questions so irrelevantly at a man of whom I had heard but whom I had never seen before. I was surprised that Vassin did not seem to notice how rude I was.

" I heard something about it, but I don't know how far it may be true," he answered in the same calm and even tone as before.

" Not a bit ! It's false ! Do you suppose he can believe in God ? "

" He—is a very proud man, as you said just now, and many very proud people like to believe in God, especially those who despise other people. Many strong natures seem to have a sort of natural craving to find some one or something to which they can do homage. Strong natures often find it very difficult to bear the burden of their strength."

" Do you know that must be awfully true," I cried again. " Only I should like to understand . . ."

" The reason is obvious. They turn to God to avoid doing homage to men, of course without recognizing how it comes about in them ; to do homage to God is not so humiliating. They become the most fervent of believers—or to be more accurate the most fervently desirous of believing ; but they take this desire for belief itself. These are the people who most frequently become disillusioned in the end. As for Monsieur Versilov, I imagine that he has some extremely sincere characteristics. And altogether he interested me."

" Vassin ! " I cried, " you rejoice my heart ! It's not your intelligence I wonder at ; I am astonished that you, a man of such a lofty nature and so far above me, can walk with me and talk to me as simply and courteously as though nothing had happened ! "

Vassin smiled.

" You are too flattering, and all that has happened is that you have shown a weakness for abstract conversation. You have probably been through a long period of silence."

" For three years I have been silent ; for three years I have been preparing to speak. . . . You couldn't of course have thought me a fool, you're so extraordinarily clever, though no one could have behaved more stupidly ; but you must have thought me a scoundrel."

" A scoundrel ! "

" Yes, certainly ! Tell me, don't you secretly despise me for saying I was Versilov's illegitimate son. . . . Boasting I was the son of a serf ? "

" You worry yourself too much. If you think you did wrong in saying so you've only to avoid saying it again. You have fifty years before you."

" Oh, I know that I ought to be very silent with other people. This throwing oneself on people's necks is the lowest of all vices ; I told them so just now, and here I am doing it to you ! But there is a difference, isn't there ? If you realize that difference, if you are capable of realizing it, then I bless this moment ! "

Vassin smiled again.

" Come and see me if you care to," he said. " I have work now and am busy, but I shall be pleased to see you."

" I thought from your face just now that you were too hard and uncommunicative."

" That may very well be true. I saw something of your sister Lizaveta Makarovna at Luga, last year. . . . Kraft has stopped and I believe is waiting for you. He has to turn here."

I pressed Vassin's hand warmly, and ran up to Kraft, who had walked on ahead all the while I talked to Vassin. We walked in silence to his lodgings. I could not speak to him and did not want to. One of the strongest traits in Kraft's character was delicacy.

CHAPTER IV

1

Kraft had been somewhere in the service, and at the same time had been a paid assistant of Andronikov's in the management of the private business which the deceased gentleman had always carried on in addition to his official duties. What mattered to me was, that from his close association with Andronikov, Kraft might well know a great deal of what interested me. But Marie Ivanovna, the wife of Nikolay Semyonovitch, with whom I had boarded so many years while I was at the grammar school in Moscow, was a favourite niece of Andronikov and was brought up by him, and from her I learnt that Kraft had actually been " commissioned " to give me something. I had been expecting him for a whole month.

He lived in a little flat of two rooms quite apart from the rest of the house, and at the moment, having only just returned, he had no servant. His trunk stood open, not yet unpacked. His belongings lay about on the chairs, and were spread out on the table in front of the sofa : his travelling bag, his cashbox, his revolver and so on. As we went in, Kraft seemed lost in thought, as though he had altogether forgotten me. He had perhaps not noticed that I had not spoken to him on the way. He began looking for something at once, but happening to catch a glimpse of himself in the looking-glass he stood still for a full minute gazing at his own face. Though I noticed this peculiar action, and recalled it all afterwards, I was depressed and disturbed. I was not feeling equal to concentrating my mind. For a moment I had a sudden impulse to go straight away and to give it all up for ever. And after all what did all these things amount to in reality ? Was it not simply an unnecessary worry I had taken upon myself ? I sank into despair at the thought that I was wasting so much energy perhaps on worthless trifles from mere sentimentality, while I had facing me a task that called for all my powers. And meanwhile my incapacity for any real work was clearly obvious from what had happened at Dergatchev's.

" Kraft, shall you go to them again ? " I asked him suddenly.

He turned slowly to me as though hardly understanding me. I sat down on a chair.

" Forgive them," said Kraft suddenly.

I fancied, of course, that this was a sneer, but looking attentively at him, I saw such a strange and even wonderful ingenuousness in his face that I positively wondered at his asking me so earnestly to " forgive " them. He brought up a chair and sat down beside me.

" I know that I am perhaps a medley of all sorts of vanities and nothing more," I began, " but I'm not apologizing."

" And you've no need to apologize to anyone," he said, quietly and earnestly. He talked all the time quietly and very slowly.

" I may be guilty in my own eyes. . . . I like being guilty in my own eyes. . . . Kraft, forgive me for talking nonsense. Tell me, surely you don't belong to that circle ? That's what I wanted to ask."

" They are no sillier than other people and no wiser ; they are mad like every one else. . . ."

" Why, is every one mad ? " I asked, turning towards him with involuntary curiosity.

" All the best people are mad nowadays ; it's the carnival of mediocrity and ineptitude and nothing else. . . . But it's not worth talking about."

As he talked he looked away into the air and began sentences and broke off without finishing them. I was particularly struck by a note of despondency in his voice.

" Surely Vassin is not one of them, Vassin has a mind, Vassin has a moral idea ! " I cried.

" There are no moral ideas now. It suddenly appears that there is not one left and, what's worse, that there never have been any."

" Never have been any in the past ? "

" Let us leave that ! " he brought out with unmistakable weariness.

I was touched by his sorrowful earnestness. Ashamed of my own egoism I began to drop into his tone.

" The present day," he began after a pause lasting two minutes, looking away into space, " the present day is the golden age of mediocrity and callousness, of a passion for ignorance, idleness, inefficiency, a craving for everything ready-made. No one thinks ; it's rare for anyone to work out an idea for himself."

He broke off again and paused for a while ; I listened. " Now-adays they are stripping Russia of her forests, and exhausting her natural wealth, turning the country into a waste and making it only fit for the Kalmucks. If a man looks forward and plants a tree every one laughs at him, and tells him he won't live to enjoy it. On the other hand those with aspirations discuss nothing but what will be in a thousand years. The idea that sustained men has utterly gone. It's as though they were all at an hotel and were leaving Russia to-morrow. They are alive if they could only . . ."

" Excuse me, Kraft, you said they worried their heads about what would happen in a thousand years. But you despair about the future of Russia . . . isn't that an anxiety of the same sort ? "

" It—it's the most essential question in the world ! " he said irritably, and jumped up quickly from his seat.

" Ah, yes ! I forgot," he said suddenly in quite a different voice, looking at me in perplexity. " I asked you to come for something special and meanwhile . . . for heaven's sake excuse me."

He seemed suddenly to wake up from a sort of dream, and was almost disconcerted ; he took a letter out of a portfolio on the table and gave it to me.

" This is what I have to give you. It's a document of some importance," he began, speaking collectedly and with a businesslike air. Long afterwards, when I recalled it, I was struck by this faculty in him (at an hour such as this was—for him !) of turning such wholehearted attention on another person's affairs and going into them with such firmness and composure.

" It is a letter of Stolbeyev's, that is of the man whose will gave rise to Versilov's lawsuit with the Princes Sokolsky. The case is just being decided in the court, and will certainly be decided in Versilov's favour ; the law is on his side. Meanwhile, in this letter, a private letter written two years ago, the deceased sets forth his real dispositions, or more accurately his desires, and expresses them rather in favour of the Sokolskys than of Versilov. At any rate the points on which the Sokolskys rest their case in contesting the will are materially strengthened by this letter. Versilov's opponents would give a great deal for this letter, though it really has no positive legal value. Alexey Nikanoritch (Andronikov), who managed Versilov's affairs, kept this letter and not long before his death gave it to me, telling me to ' take care of it ' ; perhaps he had a presentiment that he was dying and was anxious about his papers. I was unwilling to judge of Alexey Nikanoritch's intentions in the case, and I must confess that at his death I found myself in disagreeable uncertainty what to do with this document, especially as the case was so soon to be concluded. But Marie Ivanovna, in whom Alexey Nikanoritch seems to have put great confidence in his lifetime, helped me out of the difficulty, She wrote to me three weeks ago telling me that I was to give the letter to you, as this would, she *believed* (her own expression) be in accordance with the wishes of the deceased, and I am very glad that I can at last give it to you."

" Tell me," I said, dumbfounded at this new and unexpected information, " what am I to do with this letter now ? How am I to act ? "

" That's for you to decide."

" Impossible ; my hands are tied, you must admit that! Versilov is so reckoning on this fortune . . . and, you know, he'll be utterly lost without it ; and it suddenly appears that a document like this exists ! "

" It only exists here in this room."

" Is that really so ? " I looked at him attentively.

" If you can't decide how to act in this case, what can I advise you ? "

" But I can't give it to the Sokolskys either. I should ruin all Versilov's hopes, and be a traitor to him besides. . . . On the other hand if I give it to Versilov I plunge the innocent into poverty, and I should put Versilov in a hopeless dilemma too ; he would either have to give up the fortune or become a thief."

" You exaggerate the importance of the matter."

" Tell me one thing : is this letter decisive, conclusive ? "

" No, it isn't. I'm not much of a lawyer. A lawyer on the other side would, no doubt, know how to make use of such a document and to turn it to account ; but Alexey Nikanoritch considered positively that if this letter were put forward it would have no great legal value, so that Versilov's case might be won all the same. This letter is more a matter of conscience, so to say. . . ."

" But that's what matters most of all," I interrupted, " just because it would put Versilov in a hopeless dilemma."

" He may on the contrary destroy the document, and so escape all danger."

" Have you any grounds for supposing such a thing of him, Kraft ? That's what I want to know ; that's why I'm here."

" I believe every one would do the same in his place."

" Would you behave so, yourself ? "

" I'm not going to receive a fortune, so I can't tell about myself."

" Very well," I said, putting the letter in my pocket. " The matter's settled for the present. Listen, Kraft. Marie Ivanovna, who has, I assure you, told me a great deal, said to me that you and only you could tell me the truth of what happened at Ems a year and a half ago between Versilov and Mme. Ahmakov. I've been looking forward to seeing you as a sun that would throw light on everything. You don't know my position, Kraft. I beseech you to tell me the whole truth. What I want to know is what kind of man *he* is, and now—now I need to know it more than ever."

" I wonder Marie Ivanovna did not tell you all about it herself ; she might have heard it all from Andronikov, and of course she has heard it and very likely knows more than I do."

" Andronikov was not clear about it himself, so Marie Ivanovna told me. It seems a maze to which no one has the clue. The devil himself would be lost in it. I know that you were at Ems yourself at the time."

" I never knew the whole of it, but what I do know I will willingly tell you if you like, though I doubt whether I shall satisfy you."

2

I won't reproduce his story word for word, but will only give a brief summary of it.

A year and a half before, Versilov (through the old prince) became a constant visitor at the Ahmakovs' (they were all abroad then, at Ems) and made a great impression on the general himself, a man who had during three years of marriage squandered all his wife's large dowry over cards, and as a result of his irregular life had already had a paralytic stroke, though he was not an old man. He had recovered from it before going abroad, and was staying at Ems for the sake of his daughter by his first wife. She was a girl of seventeen, in delicate health—consumptive—and said to be extremely beautiful, but at the same time very fantastical. She had no dowry ; but they rested their hopes, as usual, on the old prince. Mme. Ahmakov was said to be a good stepmother, but the girl, for some reason, became particularly attached to Versilov. He was preaching at that time " something impassioned," as Kraft expressed it, some sort of new life ; " was in a state of religious fervour of the most exalted kind," in the strange and perhaps ironical phrase of Andronikov, which was repeated to me. But it was noticeable that they all soon began to dislike him. The general was positively afraid of him. Kraft did not altogether deny the rumour that Versilov succeeded in instilling into the invalid husband's mind the suspicion that his wife, Katerina Niko-laevna, was not indifferent to the young Prince Sokolsky (who had left Ems and was at that time in Paris). He did this not directly, but " after his usual fashion "—by hints, inferences, and all sorts of roundabout ways, " at which he is a great master," said Kraft. I may say that Kraft considered him, and preferred to consider him, altogether rather as an impostor and an invete-rate intriguer than as a man genuinely possessed by some exalted, or at least original. idea. I knew, apart from Kraft, that Versilov, who had at first had an extraordinary influence on Katerina Nikolaevna, had by degrees come to an open rupture with her. What lay behind all this I could not find out from Kraft, but every one confirmed the story of the mutual hatred that had sprung up between them after their friendship. Then

came a strange circumstance : Katerina Nikolaevna's invalid
stepdaughter apparently fell in love with Versilov, or was struck
by something in him, or was inflamed by his eloquence or I
don't know what ; but it is known that at one time Versilov
spent almost every day at her side. It ended by the young
lady's suddenly announcing to her father that she wanted to
marry Versilov. That this actually had happened was confirmed by every one—by Kraft, by Andronikov, and by Marie
Ivanovna, and even Tatyana Pavlovna once spoke about it
before me. They asserted also that Versilov not only desired
it himself but positively insisted on a marriage with this girl,
and that these two creatures of such different species, one old
and the other young, were in complete agreement about it. But
the father was alarmed at the idea. As he became more estranged
from Katerina Nikolaevna, whom he had been very fond of,
he now began almost to idolize his daughter, especially after his
stroke. But the bitterest opposition to the idea of such a
marriage came from Katerina Nikolaevna. There followed a
great number of secret and extremely unpleasant family wrangles,
disputes, mortifying and in fact revolting scenes. At last the
father began to give way before the persistence of the love-sick
girl who was, as Kraft expressed it, " fanaticized " by Versilov.
But Katerina Nikolaevna still resisted it with implacable hatred.
And it is at this stage that the muddle begins which no one can
understand. But this was Kraft's conjecture based on the
facts—only a conjecture, however.

He thought Versilov had succeeded, *in his characteristic way*,
in subtly suggesting to the young person that the reason Katerina
Nikolaevna would not agree was that she was in love with him
herself, and had been for a long time past worrying him with
her jealousy, pursuing him and intriguing ; that she had declared
her feeling to him and was now ready to horsewhip him for
loving some one else : something of that sort, anyway. Worst
of all, that he had " hinted " this to the girl's father, the husband
of the " unfaithful " wife, explaining that the prince had only
been a passing amusement. The house, of course, began to be
a perfect hell. In some versions of the story Katerina Nikolaevna was devoted to her stepdaughter and now was in despair
at being calumniated to her, to say nothing of her relations
with her invalid husband. And, what is more, there existed
another version, which, to my grief, I found Kraft fully believed,
and therefore I believed myself (of all this I had heard already).

It was maintained (Andronikov, it was said, had heard it from Katerina Nikolaevna herself) that, on the contrary, Versilov had in the past, before his feeling for the girl, made love to Katerina Nikolaevna ; that though she had been his friend and had been for a time carried away by his religious exaltation, yet she had constantly opposed and mistrusted him, and that she had met Versilov's declaration with deep resentment and had ridiculed him vindictively ; that she had formally dismissed him for having openly suggested that she should become his wife as her husband was expected to have a second attack very shortly. On this theory Katerina Nikolaevna must have felt a peculiar hatred for Versilov when she saw him afterwards so openly trying to win her stepdaughter's hand. Marie Ivanovna, who told me all this in Moscow, believed in both versions—both together, that is ; she maintained that there was nothing inconsistent in all this, that it was something in the style of *la haine dans l'amour*, of the wounded pride of love on both sides, etc. etc.—something, in fact, like a very subtle, intricate romance, quite out of keeping with any serious and common-sense man and, moreover, with an element of nastiness in it. But Marie Ivanovna, in spite of her estimable character, had been from childhood upwards saturated with sentiment, from the novels which she read day and night. The sequel exhibited Versilov's evident baseness, his lying and intriguing, something dark and loathsome in him, the more so as the affair had a tragic ending. The poor infatuated girl poisoned herself, they say, by means of phosphorus matches, though even now I don't know whether to believe that last detail. They did their utmost to hush it up, anyway. The young lady was ill for a fortnight and then died. So the matches remained an open question, but Kraft firmly believed in them. Shortly afterwards the young lady's father died too—it was said from his grief, which brought on a second stroke, though this did not occur till three months later. But after the young lady's funeral the young Prince Sokolsky, who had returned to Ems from Paris, gave Versilov a slap in the face in a public garden, and the latter had not replied with a challenge but had, on the contrary, showed himself next day on the promenade as though nothing had happened. Then every one turned against him, in Petersburg as well. Though Versilov kept up with some acquaintances, they were quite in a different circle. All his aristocratic friends blamed him, though, as a fact, scarcely anyone knew the details ;

they only knew something of the young lady's romantic death and the slap in the face. Only two or three persons knew the story fully, so far as that was possible. The one who had known most of all was the deceased, Andronikov, who had for many years had business relations with the Ahmakovs, and had had to do with Katerina Nikolaevna particularly in one case. But he kept all these secrets even from his own family and had only told part of the story to Kraft and Marie Ivanovna, and that from necessity.

"The chief point is that there is a document in existence," concluded Kraft, "which Mme. Ahmakov is very much afraid of."

And this was what he told me about that. When the old prince, Katerina Nikolaevna's father, was abroad, beginning to recover from his attack, she was so indiscreet as to write to Andronikov in dead secret (Katerina Nikolaevna put implicit faith in him) an extremely compromising letter. During his convalescence the old prince actually did, it was said, display a propensity to waste his money—almost to fling it away, in fact; he began buying, when he was abroad, quite useless but expensive objects, pictures, vases, making donations and subscriptions of large sums to various institutions out there, and goodness knows what. He almost bought, on the sly, for an immense sum, a ruined and encumbered estate from a fashionable Russian spendthrift; and, finally, began even dreaming of matrimony. And in view of all this, Katerina Nikolaevna, who had never left her father's side during his illness, wrote to Andronikov, as a "lawyer" and "an old friend," inquiring whether "it would be legally possible to put the old prince under guardianship or to declare him incompetent to manage his own affairs, and, if so, how it could best be done without scandal, that no one might blame her and that her father's feelings might be spared, etc. etc." It was said that Andronikov advised her against this and dissuaded her; and later on, when the old prince had completely recovered, it was impossible to return to the idea: but the letter remained in Andronikov's hands. And now he had died, and Katerina Nikolaevna had at once remembered the letter: if it turned up among the deceased's papers and fell into the old prince's hands, he would, no doubt, have cast her off for ever, cut her out of his will and not have given her another farthing during his lifetime. The thought that his own daughter did not believe in his sanity,

E

and even wanted to have him certified as a lunatic would change the lamb into a wild beast. Her husband's gambling habits had left her at his death without a farthing, and she had only her father to look to. She fully hoped to receive from him a second dowry as ample as the first.

Kraft did not quite know what had become of the letter, but observed that Andronikov never tore up papers of consequence, and he was, besides, a man of " broad principles " as well as " broad intelligence." (I was positively surprised at the independence of Kraft's criticism of Andronikov, whom he had loved and respected so much.) But Kraft felt convinced that Versilov had obtained possession of the compromising document through his close relations with Andronikov's widow and daughters ; it was known, indeed, that they had at once, of necessity, handed over all the deceased's papers to Versilov. He knew, too, that Katerina Nikolaevna was already aware that the letter was in Versilov's possession and that she was frightened on account of it, imagining that Versilov would take the letter straight to her old father ; that on her return from abroad she had searched for the document in Petersburg, had been at the Andronikovs', and was still hunting for it now, so that she must still have some hope that the letter was not in Versilov's hands ; and, finally, that she had gone to Moscow simply with the same object, and had entreated Marie Ivanovna to look for it among the papers that had remained with her. She had only recently, since her return to Petersburg, heard of the existence of Marie Ivanovna, and of the footing on which the latter had stood with Andronikov.

" You don't think she found it at Marie Ivanovna's ? " I asked. " I have my own ideas."

" If Marie Ivanovna has not told even you about it, probably she hasn't got it."

" Then you suppose the document is in Versilov's hands ? "

" Most likely it is. I don't know, though. Anything is possible," he answered with evident weariness.

I gave up questioning him, and indeed there was no object in doing so. All that mattered most had been made clear to me, in spite of all this sordid tangle ; all that I feared most was confirmed.

" It's all like a delirious nightmare," I said, deeply dejected. as I took up my hat.

" Is the man so dear to you ? " asked Kraft. I read his deep sympathy on his face at that minute.

"I felt I shouldn't learn the whole story from you," said I. "Mme. Ahmakov is the only hope left me. I was resting my hopes on her. Perhaps I shall go to her and perhaps not."

Kraft looked at me with some surprise.

"Good-bye, Kraft," I said. "Why force oneself on people who don't want to see one? Isn't it better to break with everything, eh?"

"And what then?" he asked almost sullenly, keeping his eyes on the ground.

"Retreat within oneself! Break with everything and withdraw within oneself!"

"To America?"

"To America! Within oneself, simply within oneself! That's my whole idea, Kraft!" I said enthusiastically.

He looked at me with some curiosity.

"Have you such a place 'within yourself'?"

"Yes. Good-bye, Kraft; thank you. I am sorry to have troubled you. If I were in your place and had that sort of Russia in my head I'd send them all to hell; I'd say: 'Get out with you; keep your fretting and intriguing to yourselves— it's nothing to do with me.'"

"Stay a little longer," he said suddenly when he was already with me at the front door.

I was a little surprised. I went back and sat down again. Kraft sat opposite. We looked at each other with a sort of smile. I can see it all now. I remember that I felt a sort of wonder at him.

"What I like in you is that you're so—courteous," I said suddenly.

"Yes?"

"I feel that, because I don't often succeed in being courteous myself, though I should like to. And yet perhaps it's better for people to be rude to one; at least they save one from the misfortune of liking them."

"What hour of the day do you like best?" he asked, evidently not listening to me.

"What hour? I don't know. I don't like sunset."

"No?" he brought out with a peculiar curiosity.

"Are you going away again?"

"Yes. I'm going away."

"Soon?"

"Yes."

" Surely you don't want a revolver to get to Vilna ? " I asked, without the faintest hidden meaning in my words—and indeed there was no meaning at all ! I asked the question simply because I happened to glance at the revolver and I was at a loss for something to say.

He turned and looked intently at the revolver.

" No, I take it simply from habit."

" If I had a revolver I should keep it hidden somewhere, locked up. It really is a temptation, you know. I may not believe in an epidemic of suicide, but if it's always catching my eye, there really are moments, you know, when it might tempt one."

" Don't talk about it," he said, and suddenly got up from his chair.

" I wasn't thinking of myself," I said, standing up too. " I'm not going to use it. If you were to give me three lives it wouldn't be enough for me."

" Long life to you," broke from him.

He gave me an absent-minded smile and, strange to say, walked straight into the passage as though to show me out, probably not noticing what he was doing.

" I wish you every sort of success, Kraft," I said, as I went out on to the stairs.

" That's as it may be," he answered firmly.

" Till we meet again."

" That's as it may be, too."

I remember his last glance at me.

3

And this was the man for whom my heart had been beating all those years ! And what had I expected from Kraft, what new information ?

As I came away from Kraft's I felt very hungry. It was evening and I had had no dinner. I went to a little restaurant in Great Prospect that I might not have to spend more than twenty, or at most twenty-five, kopecks—I would not have allowed myself to spend more at that time. I took some soup for myself, and as I ate it I sat looking out of window. There were a great many people in the room, and there was a smell of burnt meat, restaurant napkins, and tobacco. It was nasty. Over my head a dumb nightingale, gloomy and pensive, was pecking at the bottom of its cage. There was a noise in the adjoining billiard-room, but I sat there and sank into deep thought. The setting sun (why was Kraft surprised at my not liking the sunset ?) aroused in me a new and unexpected sensation quite out of keeping with my surroundings. I was haunted by the soft look in my mother's eyes, her dear eyes which had been watching me so timidly the whole month. Of late I had been very rude at home, to her especially. I had a desire to be rude to Versilov, but not daring, in my contemptible way tormented her instead. I had thoroughly frightened her, in fact ; often she looked at me with such imploring eyes when Andrey Petrovitch came in, afraid of some outburst on my part. It was a very strange thing that, sitting here in the restaurant, I realized for the first time that, while Versilov spoke to me familiarly, she always addressed me deferentially. I had wondered at it before and had not been impressed in her favour by it, but now I realized it particularly, and strange ideas passed one after another through my brain. I sat there a long time, till it got quite dark. I thought about my sister too.

It was a fateful moment for me. At all costs I must decide. Could I be incapable of decision ? What is the difficulty of breaking with them if they don't want me either ? My mother and sister ? But I should not leave them, anyway, however things turned out.

It is true that the entrance of that man into my life, though only for an instant in my early childhood, was the turning-point from which my conscious development began. Had he not met me then, my mind, my way of thinking, my fate, would certainly have been different, even in spite of the character ordained me by destiny, which I could not anyway have escaped.

But it turned out that this man was only a dream, the dream of my childhood. I had invented him myself, and in reality he was a different man who fell far below my imagination. I had come to find a genuine man, not a man like this. And why had I fallen in love with him once and for ever in that brief moment when I saw him as a child ? That " for ever " must vanish. Some time, if I have space for it, I will describe that meeting, the most futile incident leading up to nothing. But I had built it up into a pyramid. I had begun building that pyramid as I lay in my little bed, when, falling asleep, I could dream and weep—what for I cannot tell. Because I had been abandoned ? Because I was tormented ? But I was only tormented a little, and only for two years at Touchard's, the school into which he thrust me before leaving me for ever. Afterwards no one tormented me ; quite the contrary ; I looked scornfully at my schoolfellows. And I can't endure the self-pity of the forlorn. There is no rôle more revolting than that of the orphan, the illegitimate, the outcast and all such wretched creatures, for whom I never feel any pity when they solemnly parade before the public and begin piteously but insistently whining of how they have been treated. I could beat them all ! Will none of the filthy, conventional herd understand that it would be ten times as creditable to hold their tongues, not to whine and not to *deign* to complain ! And if he does deign he deserves his fate, the bastard. That's my view !

But what is absurd is not that I used to dream of him in my little bed but that, almost forgetting my chief object, I have come here for the sake of him, of that " imagined " man. I have come to help him to stamp out a calumny, to crush his enemies. The document of which Kraft had spoken, that woman's letter to Andronikov about which she was so afraid, which might ruin her and reduce her to poverty, which she supposed to be in Versilov's hands, was not in his possession but in mine, sewn up in my coat pocket ! I had sewn it there myself, and no one in the whole world knew of it. The fact that the romantic Marie Ivanovna, in whose keeping the letter was left " to be preserved," thought fit to give it to me and to no one else was only her own idea and a matter for her to decide, which I am not called upon to explain, though I may discuss it later if it seems appropriate. But, armed with this unexpected weapon, I could not help yielding to the temptation to come to Petersburg. Of course, I proposed to assist this man secretly without display or excitement, without expecting his praise or his embraces. And never, never would I condescend to reproach him for anything. And indeed, was it his fault that I had fallen in love with him and had created a fantastic ideal of him ? Though, indeed, I did not perhaps love him at all ! His original mind, his interesting character, his intrigues and adventures, and what my mother had been to him—all that, it seemed could not keep me. It was enough that my fantastic doll was shattered, and that I could not, perhaps, love him any more. And so what was keeping me ? why was I sticking there ?— that was the question. The upshot of it all was that only I was a fool. no one else.

But, expecting honesty from others, I will be honest myself. I must confess that the letter sewn up in my pocket did not only arouse in me the passionate desire to rush to Versilov's aid. Now it is quite clear to me, and even then I thought of it with a blush. I had visions of a woman—a proud, aristocratic creature—whom I should meet face to face. She would laugh at me, despise me, as though I were a mouse ; she would not even suspect that her future was in my power. This idea intoxicated me even in Moscow, and still more in the train on the way ; I have confessed this already. Yes, I hated that woman, but already I loved her as my victim ; and all this was true, all this was real. But this was childishness which I should not have expected even from anyone like me. I am describing my feelings then, that is, what passed through my mind as I sat in the restaurant under the nightingale and made up my mind to break with them for ever. The memory of my recent meeting with that woman sent a rush of colour to my face. An ignominious meeting ! An ignominious and stupid impression, and—what mattered most—it showed my incapacity for action. It proved—I thought then—that I was not strong enough to withstand the stupidest lure, though I told Kraft myself just now that I had my place " within myself," and work of my own, and that if I had three lives they wouldn't be enough for me. I said that proudly. My having abandoned my idea and mixed myself up with Versilov's affairs was to some extent excusable, but that I should run from side to side like a frightened hare and be drawn into every trifle—that, of course, was simply my own folly. What induced me to go to Dergatchev's and to burst out with my imbecilities, though I knew long ago that I am incapable of saying anything cleverly or sensibly, that it is always better for me to be silent ? And some Vassin or other reassures me with the reflection that I've fifty years of life ahead of me and so I've no need to worry. It was a good reply, I admit, and did credit to his unmistakable intelligence ; it was good because it was the simplest, and what is simplest is never understood till the last, when everything that is cleverer or stupider has been tried already. But I knew that answer before Vassin ; I'd had an inkling of that thought more than three years ago ; what's more, my " idea " was to some extent included in it. Such were my reflections in the restaurant.

I felt disgusted as I made my way towards Semyonovsky Polk at eight o'clock in the evening, worn out with walking and with thinking. It was quite dark by then and the weather had changed ; it was dry, but a horrid Petersburg wind had sprung up, blowing keenly and malignantly on my back and whirling up the dust and sand. How many sullen faces of poor people hurrying home to their corners from work and trade ! Every one had his own sullen anxiety in his face, and there was perhaps not one common uniting thought in the crowd ! Kraft was right ; every one was different. I met a little boy, so little that it was strange he could be out alone in the street at that hour ; he seemed to have lost his way. A peasant-woman stopped for a minute to listen to him, but, not understanding what he said, waved her hand and went on, leaving him alone in the darkness. I was going towards him, but he suddenly took fright and ran away.

As I approached the house I made up my mind that I should never go and see Vassin. I had an intense longing as I went up the stairs to find them at home alone, without Versilov, that I might have time before he came in to say something nice to my mother or to my dear sister, to whom I had scarcely said anything particular all that month. It so happened that he was not at home.

4

By the way, as I am bringing on to the scene this "new character " (I am speaking of Versilov), I will introduce briefly a formal account of him, though it is of no significance. I do this to make things more comprehensible for the reader, and because I can't foresee where this account could fit in in the later part of my story.

He studied at the university but went into a cavalry regiment of the guards. He married Mlle. Fanariotov and retired from the army. He went abroad, and on his return lived a life of worldly gaiety in Moscow. On his wife's death he spent some time in the country ; then came the episode with my mother. Then he lived for a long time somewhere in the south. During the war with Europe he served in the army but did not reach the Crimea and was never in action. At the conclusion of the war he left the service and went abroad. He took my mother with him, though he left her at Königsberg. The poor woman used sometimes, shaking her head, to tell with a sort of horror, how she had spent six months there with her little girl, not knowing the language, absolutely friendless, and in the end penniless, as though she were lost in a forest. Then Tatyana Pavlovna came to fetch her and took her back to some place in the Novgorod Province. Then, on the emancipation of the serfs, Versilov became one of the first "mediators," and is said to have performed his duties admirably; but he soon gave this up, and in Petersburg was occupied with the conduct of various private lawsuits. Andronikov always had a high opinion of his capacity; he had a great respect for him, and only said he did not understand his character. Then Versilov gave that up too, and went abroad again—this time for a long period, several years. Then came his close intimacy with old Prince Sokolsky. During this period his financial position underwent two or three radical changes. At one time he fell into complete poverty, then grew wealthy and rose again.

Having brought my story to this point, I am determined to describe my "idea" too. For the first time since its conception I will translate it into words. I am determined to reveal it, so to speak, to the reader, partly for the sake of greater clearness in what I have to explain further. And it is not only confusing for the reader; even I, the author, am beginning to get muddled by the difficulty of explaining each step without explaining what led up to it and induced me to take it. By keeping up this "attitude of silence" I have clumsily descended to one of those "literary graces" which I have ridiculed above. Before entering upon my Petersburg romance with all my ignominious adventures in it, I find this preface is necessary. But I was not tempted to silence for the sake of literary "grace" but was forced to it by the nature of the case, that is, the difficulty of the case; even now, when it is all over, I find it very difficult to put this idea into words. Besides, I must describe it in its aspect at that time, that is, the form it took and the way I looked at it, not now, but then, and that is a fresh difficulty. To describe some things is almost impossible. The ideas that are the simplest and the clearest are the most difficult to understand. If before the discovery of America Columbus had begun telling his idea to other people, I am convinced that for a very long time people would not have understood him. And indeed they did not understand him. I don't mean to compare myself with Columbus, and if anyone imagines that I do he ought to be ashamed of himself, that's all.

CHAPTER V

1

My " idea " is—to become a Rothschild. I invite the reader to keep calm and not to excite himself.

I repeat it. My " idea " is to become a Rothschild, to become as rich as Rothschild, not simply rich, but as rich as Rothschild. What objects I have in view, what for, and why—all that shall come later. First I will simply show that the attainment of my object is a mathematical certainty.

It is a very simple matter ; the whole secret lies in two words : *obstinacy* and *perseverance*.

" We have heard that ; it's nothing new," people will tell me. Every " *vater*," in Germany repeats this to his children, and meanwhile your Rothschild (James Rothschild the Parisian, is the one I mean) is unique while there are millions of such " *vaters*."

I should answer :

" You assert that you've heard it, but you've heard nothing. It's true that you're right about one thing. When I said that this was ' very simple,' I forgot to add that it is most difficult. All the religions and the moralities of the world amount to one thing : ' Love virtue and avoid vice.' One would think nothing could be simpler. But just try doing something virtuous and giving up any one of your vices ; just try it. It's the same with this.

" That's why your innumerable German ' *vaters* ' may, for ages past reckoning, have repeated those two wonderful words which contain the whole secret, and, meanwhile, Rothschild remains unique. It shows it's the same but not the same, and these ' *vaters* ' don't repeat the same idea.

" No doubt they too have heard of obstinacy and perseverance, but to attain my object what I need is not these German ' *vaters*' ' obstinacy or these ' *vaters*' ' perseverance."

" The mere fact that he is a ' *vater* '—I don't mean only the Germans—that he has a family, that he is living like other people, has expenses like other people, has obligations like other people, means that he can't become a Rothschild, but must remain an average man. I understand quite clearly that in becoming a Rothschild, or merely desiring to become one, not in the German ' *vaters*' ' way but seriously, I must at the same time cut myself off from society."

Some years ago I read in the newspaper that on one of the steamers on the Volga there died a beggar who went about begging in rags and was known to every one. On his death they found sewn up in his shirt three thousand roubles in notes. The other day I read of another beggar of the " respectable " sort, who used to go about the restaurants holding out his hand. He was arrested and there was found on him five thousand roubles. Two conclusions follow directly from this. The first, that *obstinacy* in saving even the smallest coin will produce enormous results in the long run (time is of no account in this), and secondly that the most unskilful form of accumulation if only *persevering* is mathematically certain of success.

Meanwhile there are perhaps a good number of respectable, clever, obstinate people who cannot save either three or five thousand, however much they struggle, though they would be awfully glad to have such a sum. Why is that ? The answer is clear : it is because not one of them, in spite of all their wishing it, *desires* it to such a degree that, for instance, if he is not able to save by other means, he is ready to become a beggar, and so persistent that after becoming a beggar, he will not waste the first farthing he is given on an extra crust of bread for himself or his family. With this system of saving, that is in beggary, one must live on bread and salt and nothing more, to save up such sums ; at least, so I imagine. That is no doubt what the two beggars I have mentioned above did do ; they must have eaten nothing but bread and have lived almost in the open air. There is no doubt that they had no intention of becoming Rothschilds ; they were simply Harpagons or Ilyushkins in their purest form, nothing more ; but, when there is intelligent accumulation in quite a different form with the object of becoming a Rothschild, no less strength of will is needed than in the case of those two beggars. The German " *vater* " does not show such strength of will. There are many kinds of strength in the world, especially of strength of will and of desire. There is the temperature of boiling water and there is the temperature of molten iron.

One wants here the same thing as in a monastery, the same heroic asceticism. Feeling is wanted, not only idea. What for ? Why ? Is it moral and not monstrous to wear sackcloth and eat black bread all one's life to heap up filthy lucre ? These questions I will consider later. Now I am discussing only the possibility of attaining the object. When I thought of my " idea " and it was forged in white heat, I began asking myself— am I capable of asceticism ? With this object, for the whole of the first month I took bread and water, not more than two and a half pounds of black bread a day. To do this I was obliged to deceive Nikolay Semyonovitch who was clever, and Marie Ivanovna who was anxious for my welfare. Though I wounded her and somewhat surprised Nikolay Semyonovitch who was a man of great delicacy, I insisted on having my dinner brought to my room. There I simply got rid of it. I poured the soup out of window on to the nettles or elsewhere, the meat I either flung out of window to a dog, or wrapping it up in paper put it in my pocket and threw it away after, and so on. As the bread given me for dinner was much less than two and a half pounds I bought bread on the sly. I stood this for a month perhaps, only upsetting my stomach a little, but the next month I added soup to the bread and drank a glass of tea morning and evening, and I assure you I passed a year like that in perfect health and content, as well as in a moral ecstasy and perpetual secret delight. Far from regretting the dainties I missed, I was overjoyed. At the end of the year, having convinced myself I was capable of standing any fast, however severe, I began eating as they did, and went back to dine with them. Not satisfied with this experiment I made a second ; apart from the sum paid to Nikolay Semyonovitch for my board I was allowed five roubles a month for pocket money. I resolved to spend only half. This was a very great trial, but after at most two years I had in my pocket by the time I went to Petersburg seventy roubles saved entirely in this way, besides other money. The result of these two experiments was of vast importance to me : I had learnt positively that I could so will a thing as to attain my objects, and that I repeat is the essence of " my idea " —the rest is all nonsense.

2

Let us, however, look into the nonsense too.

I have described my two experiments. In Petersburg, as the reader knows, I made a third. I went to the auction and at one stroke made a profit of seven roubles ninety-five kopecks. This of course was not a real experiment, it was only by way of sport and diversion. I simply wanted to filch a moment from the future, and to test how I should go and behave. I had decided even at the very first, in Moscow, to put off really beginning till I was perfectly free. I fully realized that I must, for instance, finish my work at school. (The university, as the reader knows already, I sacrificed.) There is no disputing that I went to Petersburg with concealed anger in my heart. No sooner had I left the grammar school and become free for the first time, than I suddenly saw that Versilov's affairs would distract me from beginning my enterprise for an indefinite period. But though I was angry I went to Petersburg feeling perfectly serene about my object.

It is true I knew nothing of practical life ; but I had been thinking about it for three years and could have no doubt about it. I had pictured a thousand times over how I should begin. I should suddenly find myself, as though dropped from the clouds, in one of our two capitals (I pitched on Petersburg or Moscow for my beginning, and by choice Petersburg, to which I gave the preference through certain considerations), perfectly free, not dependent on anyone, in good health, and with a hundred roubles hidden in my pocket, as the capital for my first investment. Without a hundred roubles it would be impossible to begin, as, without it, even the earliest period of success would be too remote. Apart from my hundred roubles I should have, as the reader knows already, courage, obstinacy, perseverance, absolute isolation and secrecy. Isolation was the principal thing. I greatly disliked the idea of any connection or association with others until the last moment. Speaking generally I proposed beginning my enterprise alone, that was a *sine qua non*. People weigh upon me, and with them I should have been uneasy, and uneasiness would have hindered my success. Generally speaking, all my life up to now, in all my dreams of how I would behave with people, I always imagined myself being very clever ; it was very different in reality—I was always very stupid ; and I confess sincerely, with indignation, I always gave myself away and was flustered, and so I resolved to cut people off altogether. I should gain by it independence, tranquillity of mind and clearness of motive.

In spite of the terrible prices in Petersburg I determined once for all that I should never spend more than fifteen kopecks on food, and I knew I should keep my word. This question of food I had thought over minutely for a long time past. I resolved, for instance, sometimes to eat nothing but bread and salt for two days together, and to spend on the third day what I had saved on those two days. I fancied that this would be better for my health than a perpetual uniform fast on a minimum of fifteen kopecks. Then I needed a corner, literally a " corner," solely to sleep the night in and to have a refuge in very bad weather. I proposed living in the street, and, if necessary, I was ready to sleep in one of the night refuges where they give you a piece of bread and a glass of tea as well as a night's lodging. Oh, I should be quite capable of hiding my money so that it should not be stolen in the " corner," or in the refuge, and should not even be suspected, I'll answer for that !

"Steal from me ? Why, I'm afraid of stealing myself ! " I once heard a passer-by in the street say gaily. Of course I only apply to myself the caution and smartness of it, I don't intend to steal. What is more, while I was in Moscow, perhaps from the very first day of my " idea," I resolved that I would not be a pawnbroker or usurer either ; there are Jews for that job, and such Russians as have neither intelligence nor character. Pawnbroking and usury are for the commonplace.

As for clothes, I resolved to have two suits, one for every day and one for best. When once I had got them I felt sure I should wear them a long time. I purposely trained myself to wear a suit for two and a half years, and in fact I discovered a secret : for clothes always to look new and not to get shabby they should be brushed as often as possible, five or six times a day. Brushing does not hurt the cloth. I speak from knowledge. What does hurt it is dust and dirt. Dust is the same thing as stones if you look at it through the microscope, and, however hard a brush is, it is almost the same as fur. I trained myself to wear my boots evenly. The secret lies in putting down the whole sole at once, and avoiding treading on the side. One can train oneself to this in a fortnight, after that the habit is unconscious. In this way boots last on an average a third as long again. That is the experience of two years.

Then followed my activity itself.

I started with the hypothesis that I had a hundred roubles. In Petersburg there are so many auction sales, petty hucksters' booths and people who want things, that it would be impossible not to sell anything one bought for a little more. Over the album I had made seven roubles ninety-five kopecks profit on two roubles five kopecks of capital invested. This immense profit was made without any risk : I could see from his eyes that the purchaser would not back out. Of course I know quite well that this was only a chance ; but it is just such chances I am on the look-out for, that is why I have made up my mind to live in the street. Well, granted that such a chance is unusual, no matter ; my first principle will be to risk nothing, and the second to make every day more than the minimum spent on my subsistence, that the process of accumulation may not be interrupted for a single day.

I shall be told that "all this is a dream, you don't know the streets, and you'll be taken in at the first step." But I have will and character, and the science of the streets is a science like any other : persistence, attention and capacity can conquer it. In the grammar school right up to the seventh form I was one of the first ; I was very good at mathematics. Why, can one possibly exaggerate the value of experience and knowledge of the streets to such a fantastic pitch as to predict my failure for certain ? That is only what people say who have never made an experiment in anything, have never begun any sort of life, but have grown stiff in second-hand stagnation. "One man breaks his nose, so another must break his." No, I won't break mine. I have character and if I pay attention I can learn anything. But is it possible to imagine that with constant persistence, with incessant vigilance, and continual calculation and reflection, with perpetual activity and alertness one could fail to find out how to make twenty kopecks to spare every day ? Above all I resolved not to struggle for the maximum profit, but always to keep calm. As time went on after heaping up one or two thousand I should, of course, naturally rise above second-hand dealing and street trading. I know, of course, far too little as yet about the stock exchange, about shares, banking and all that sort of thing. But to make up for that I know, as I know I have five fingers on my hand, that I should learn all the stock exchange and banking business as well as anyone else, and that the subject would turn out to be perfectly simple, because one is brought to it by practice. What need is there of the wisdom of Solomon so long as one has character ; efficiency, skill and knowledge come of themselves. If only one does not leave off " willing."

The great thing is to avoid risks, and that can only be done if one has character. Not long ago in Petersburg I had before me a subscription list of shares in some railway investments ; those who succeeded in getting shares made a lot of money.

For some time the shares went up and up. Well, if one day some one who had not succeeded in getting a share, or was greedy for more, had offered to buy mine at a premium of so much per cent., I should certainly have sold it. People would have laughed at me, of course, and have said that if I had waited I should have made ten times as much. Quite so, but my premium is safer, for it's a bird in the hand while yours is on the bush. I shall be told that one can't make much like that; excuse me, that's your mistake, the mistake of all our Kokorevs, Polyakovs, and Gubonins. Let me tell you the truth; perseverance and persistence in money making and still more in saving is much more effective than these cent. per cent. profits.

Not long before the French Revolution there was a man called Law in Paris who invented of himself a scheme what was theoretically magnificent but which came utterly to grief in practice afterwards. All Paris was in excitement. Law's shares were bought up at once before allotment. Money from all parts of Paris poured as from a sack into the house where the shares were subscribed. But the house was not enough at last, the public thronged the street, people of all callings, all classes, all ages : bourgeois, noblemen, their children, countesses, marquises, prostitutes, were all struggling in one infuriated, half-crazy, rabid mob. Rank, the prejudices of birth and pride, even honour and good name were all trampled in the same mire; all, even women, were ready to sacrifice anyone to gain a few shares. The list at last was passed down into the streets, but there was nothing to write on. Then it was suggested to a hunchback that he should lend his back for the time as a table on which people could sign their names for shares. The hunchback agreed—one can fancy at what a price. Some time (a very short time) after, they were all bankrupt, the whole thing went smash, the whole idea was exploded and the shares were worth nothing. Who got the best of it ? Why, the hunchback, because he did not take shares but louis-d'or in cash. Well, I am that hunchback ! I had strength of will enough not to eat, and to save seventy-two roubles out of my kopecks; I shall have strength enough to restrain myself and prefer a safe profit to a large one, even when every one around me is carried away by a fever of excitement. I am trivial only about trifles, not in what is important. I have often lacked fortitude for enduring little things ever since the inception of my idea, but for enduring big things I shall always have enough. When in the morning my mother gave me cold coffee before I set out to work, I was angry and rude to her, and yet I was the same person who had lived a whole month on bread and water.

In short not to make money, not to learn how to make money, would be unnatural. It would be unnatural, too, in spite of incessant and regular saving, unflagging care and mental sobriety, self-control, economy, and growing energy—it would be unnatural, I repeat, to fail to become a millionaire. How did the beggar make his money if not by fanatical determination and perseverance ? Am I inferior to a beggar ? "And after all, supposing I don't arrive at anything, suppose my calculation is incorrect, suppose I fail and come to grief; no matter, I shall go on, I shall go on, because I want to." That is what I said in Moscow.

I shall be told that there is no " idea " in this, absolutely nothing new. But I say, and for the last time, that there are an immense number of ideas in it, and a vast amount that is new.

Oh, I foresaw how trivial all objections would be, and that I should be as trivial myself in expounding my " idea " : why, what have I said after all ? I haven't told a hundredth part of it. I feel that it is trivial, superficial, crude, and, somehow, too young for my age.

3

I've still to answer the questions, " What for ? " and " Why ? " " Whether it's moral," and all the rest of it. I've undertaken to answer them.

I am sad at disappointing the reader straight off, sad and glad too. Let him know that in my idea there is absolutely no feeling of " revenge," nothing " Byronic "—no curses, no lamentations over my orphaned state, no tears over my illegitimacy, nothing, nothing of the sort. In fact, if a romantic lady should chance to come across my autobiography she would certainly turn up her nose. The whole object of my " idea " is—isolation. But one can arrive at isolation without straining to become a Rothschild. What has Rothschild got to do with it ?

Why, this. That besides isolation I want power.

Let me tell the reader, he will perhaps be horrified at the candour of my confession, and in the simplicity of his heart will wonder how the author could help blushing : but my answer is that I'm not writing for publication, and I may not have a reader for ten years, and by that time everything will be so thoroughly past, settled and defined that there will be no need to blush. And so, if I sometimes in my autobiography appeal to my reader it is simply a form of expression. My reader is an imaginary figure.

No, it was not being illegitimate, with which I was so taunted at Touchard's, not my sorrowful childhood, it was not revenge, nor the desire to protest, that was at the bottom of my idea; my character alone was responsible for everything. At twelve years old, I believe, that is almost at the dawn of real consciousness, I began to dislike my fellow-creatures. It was not that I disliked them exactly, but that their presence weighed upon me. I was sometimes in my moments of purest sincerity quite sad that I never could express everything even to my nearest and dearest, that is, I could but will not ; for some reason I restrain myself, so that I'm mistrustful, sullen and reserved. Again, I have noticed one characteristic in myself almost from childhood, that I am too ready to find fault, and given to blaming others. But this impulse was often followed at once by another which was very irksome to me : I would ask myself whether it were not my fault rather than theirs. And how often I blamed myself for nothing ! To avoid such doubts I naturally sought solitude. Besides, I found nothing in the company of others, however much I tried, and I did try. All the boys of my own age anyway, all my schoolfellows, all, every one of them, turned out to be inferior to me in their ideas. I don't recall one single exception.

Yes, I am a gloomy person ; I'm always shutting myself up. I often love to walk out of a room full of people. I may perhaps do people a kindness, but often I cannot see the slightest reason for doing them a kindness. People are not such splendid creatures that they are worth taking much trouble about. Why can't they approach me openly and directly, why must I always be forced to make the first overtures ?

That is the question I asked myself. I am a grateful creature, and have shown it by a hundred imbecilities. If some one were frank with me, I should instantly respond with frankness and begin to love them at once. And so I have done, but they have all deceived me promptly, and have withdrawn from me with a sneer. The most candid of them all was Lambert, who beat me so much as a child, but he was only an open brute and scoundrel. And even his openness was only stupidity. Such was my state of mind when I came to Petersburg.

When I came out from Dergatchev's (and goodness only

knows what made me go to him) I had gone up to Vassin, and in a rush of enthusiasm I had begun singing his praises. And that very evening I felt that I liked him much less. Why ? Just because by my praise of him I had demeaned myself before him. Yet one might have thought it would have been the other way : a man just and generous enough to give another his due, even to his own detriment, ought to stand higher in personal dignity than anyone. And though I quite understood this, I did like Vassin less, much less in fact. I purposely choose an example with which the reader is familiar. I even thought of Kraft with a bitter, sickly feeling, because he had led me into the passage, and this feeling lasted till the day when Kraft's state of mind at the time was revealed, and it was impossible to be angry with him. From the time when I was in the lowest class in the grammar-school, as soon as any of my comrades excelled me in school work, or witty answers or physical strength, I immediately gave up talking or having anything to do with them. Not that I disliked them or wished them not to succeed ; I simply turned away from them because such was my character.

Yes, I thirsted for power, I've thirsted for it all my life, power and solitude. I dreamed of it at an age when every one would have laughed at me to my face if they could have guessed what was in my head. That was why I so liked secrecy. And indeed all my energy went into dreams, so much so that I had no time to talk. This led to my being unsociable, and my absent-mindedness led people to more unpleasant conclusions about me, but my rosy cheeks belied their suspicions.

I was particularly happy when, covering myself up in bed at night, I began in complete solitude, with no stir or sound of other people round me, to re-create life on a different plan. I was most desperately dreamy up to the time of the " idea," when all my dreams became rational instead of foolish, and passed from the fantastic realms of romance to the reasonable world of reality.

Everything was concentrated into one object. Not that they were so very stupid before, although there were masses and masses of them. But I had favourites . . . there is no need to bring them in here, however.

Power ! I am convinced that very many people would think it very funny if they knew that such a " pitiful " creature was struggling for power. But I shall surprise them even more : perhaps from my very first dreams that is, almost from my earliest childhood, I could never imagine myself except in the foremost place, always and in every situation in life. I will add a strange confession : it is the same perhaps to this day. At the same time, let me observe that I am not apologizing for it.

That is the point of my idea, that is the force of it, that money is the one means by which the humblest nonentity may rise to the *foremost place*. I may not be a nonentity, but I know from the looking-glass that my exterior does not do me justice, for my face is commonplace. But if I were as rich as Rothschild, who would find fault with my face ? And wouldn't thousands of women be ready to fly to me with all their charms if I whistled to them ? I am sure that they would honestly consider me good-looking. Suppose I am clever. But were I as wise as Solomon some one would be found wiser still, and I should be done for. But if I were a Rothschild what would that wise man be beside me ? Why, they would not let him say a word beside me ! I may be witty, but with Talleyrand or Piron I'm thrown into the shade ; but if I were Rothschild, where would Piron be, and where Talleyrand even, perhaps ? Money is, of course, despotic power, and at the same time it is the greatest leveller, and that is its chief power. Money levels all inequality. I settled all that in Moscow.

You will see, of course, in this idea nothing but insolence, violence, the triumph of the nonentity over the talented. I admit that it is an impudent idea (and for that reason a sweet one). But let it pass : you imagine that I desire power to be able to crush, to avenge myself. That is just the point, that that is how the commonplace would behave. What is more, I'm convinced that thousands of the wise and talented who are so exalted, if the Rothschilds' millions suddenly fell to their lot could not resist behaving like the most vulgar and commonplace, and would be more oppressive than any. My idea is quite different. I'm not afraid of money. It won't crush me and it won't make me crush others.

What I want isn't money, or rather money is not necessary to me, nor power either. I only want what is obtained by power, and cannot be obtained without it ; that is, the calm and solitary consciousness of strength ! That is the fullest definition of liberty for which the whole world is struggling ! Liberty ! At last I have written that grand word. . . . Yes, the solitary consciousness of strength is splendid and alluring.

I have strength and I am serene. With the thunderbolts in his hands Jove is serene ; are his thunders often heard ? The fool fancies that he is asleep. But put a literary man or a peasant-woman in Jove's place, and the thunder would never cease !

If I only have power, I argued, I should have no need to use it. I assure you that of my own free will I should take the lowest seat everywhere. If I were a Rothschild, I would go about in an old overcoat with an umbrella. What should I care if I were jostled in the crowd, if I had to skip through the mud to avoid being run over ? The consciousness that I was myself, a Rothschild, would even amuse me at the moment. I should know I could have a dinner better than anyone, that I could have the best cook in the world, it would be enough for me to know it. I would eat a piece of bread and ham and be satisfied with the consciousness of it. I think so even now.

I shouldn't run after the aristocracy, but they would run after me. I shouldn't pursue women, but they would fly to me like the wind, offering me all that women can offer. "The vulgar" run after money, but the intelligent are attracted by curiosity to the strange, proud and reserved being, indifferent to everything. I would be kind, and would give them money perhaps, but I would take nothing from them. Curiosity arouses passion, perhaps I may inspire passion. They will take nothing away with them I assure you, except perhaps presents that will make me twice as interesting to them.

> . . . *to me enough*
> *The consciousness of this.*

It is strange, but true, that I have been fascinated by this picture since I was seventeen.

I don't want to oppress or torment anyone and I won't, but I know that if I did want to ruin some man, some enemy of mine, no one could prevent me, and every one would serve me, and that would be enough again. I would not revenge myself on anyone. I could never understand how James Rothschild could consent to become a Baron ! Why, for what reason, when he was already more exalted than anyone in the world. " Oh, let that insolent general insult me at the station where we are both waiting for our horses ! If he knew who I was he would run himself to harness the horses and would hasten to assist me into my modest vehicle ! They say that some foreign count or baron at a Vienna railway station put an Austrian banker's slippers on for him in public ; and the latter was so vulgar as to allow him to do it. Oh, may that terrible beauty (yes, terrible, there are such !), that daughter of that luxurious and aristocratic lady meeting me by chance on a steamer or somewhere, glance askance at me and turn up her nose, wondering contemptuously how that humble, unpresentable man with a book or paper in his hand could dare to be in a front seat beside her ! If only she knew who was sitting beside her ! And she will find out, she will, and will come to sit beside me of her own accord, humble, timid, ingratiating, seeking my glance, radiant at my smile." . . . I purposely introduce these early day-dreams to express what was in my mind. But the picture is pale, and perhaps trivial. Only reality will justify everything.

I shall be told that such a life would be stupid : why not have a mansion, keep open house, gather society round you, why not have influence, why not marry ? But what would Rothschild be then ? He would become like every one else. All the charm of the " idea " would disappear, all its moral force. When I was quite a child I learnt Pushkin's monologue of the " Miserly Knight." Pushkin has written nothing finer in conception than that ! I have the same ideas now.

" But yours is too low an ideal," I shall be told with contempt. " Money, wealth. Very different from the common weal, from self-sacrifice for humanity."

But how can anyone tell how I should use my wealth ? In what way is it immoral, in what way is it degrading, that these millions should pass out of dirty, evil, Jewish hands into the hands of a sober and resolute ascetic with a keen outlook upon life ? All these dreams of the future, all these conjectures, seem like a romance now, and perhaps I am wasting time in recording them. I might have kept them to myself. I know, too, that these lines will very likely be read by no one, but if anyone were to read them, would he believe that I should be unable to stand the test of the Rothschild millions ? Not because they would crush me, quite the contrary. More than once in my dreams I have anticipated that moment in the future, when my consciousness will be satiated, and power will not seem enough for me. Then, not from ennui, not from aimless weariness, but because I have a boundless desire for what is great, I shall give all my millions away, let society distribute all my wealth, and I—I will mix with nothingness again ! Maybe I will turn into a beggar like the one who died on the steamer, with the only difference that they wouldn't find money sewn up in my shirt. The mere consciousness that I had had millions in my hands and had flung them away into the dirt like trash would sustain me in my solitude. I am ready to think the same even now. Yes, my " idea " is a fortress in which I can always, at every turn, take refuge from every one, even if I were a beggar dying on a steamer. It is my poem ! And let me tell you I must have the *whole* of my vicious will, simply to prove *to myself* that I can renounce it.

No doubt I shall be told that this is all romance, and that if I got my millions I should not give them up and become a beggar. Perhaps I should not. I have simply sketched the ideal in my mind.

But I will add seriously that if I did succeed in piling up as much money as Rothschild, that it really might end in my giving it all up to the public (though it would be difficult to do so before I reached that amount). And I shouldn't give away half because that would be simply vulgar : I should be only half as rich, that would be all. I should give away all, all to the last farthing, for on becoming a beggar I should become twice as rich as Rothschild ! If other people don't understand this it's not my fault ; I'm not going to explain it.

" The fanaticism, the romanticism of insignificance and impotence ! " people will pronounce, " the triumph of common-placeness and mediocrity ! " Yes, I admit that it is in a way the triumph of commonplaceness and mediocrity, but surely not of impotence. I used to be awfully fond of imagining just such a creature, commonplace and mediocre, facing the world and saying to it with a smile, " You are Galileos, and Copernicuses, Charlemagnes and Napoleons, you are Pushkins and Shake-speares, you are field-marshals and generals, and I am incom-petence and illegitimacy, and yet I am higher than all of you, because you bow down to it yourself." I admit that I have pushed this fancy to such extremes that I have struck out even my education. It seemed to me more picturesque if the man were sordidly ignorant. This exaggerated dream had a positive influence at the time on my success in the seventh form of the grammar-school. I gave up working simply from fanaticism, feeling that lack of education would add a charm to my ideal. Now I've changed my views on that point ; education does not detract from it.

Gentlemen, can it be that even the smallest independence of

mind is so distasteful to you ? Blessed he who has an ideal of beauty, even though it be a mistaken one ! But I believe in mine. It is only that I've explained it clumsily, crudely. In ten years, of course, I should explain it better, and I treasure that in my memory.

4

I've finished with my idea. If my account of it has been commonplace and superficial it is I that am to blame and not the idea. I have already pointed out that the simplest ideas are always the most difficult to understand.

Now I will add that they are also the most difficult to explain ; moreover, I have described my " idea " in its earliest phase. The converse is the rule with ideas : commonplace and shallow ideas are extraordinarily quickly understood, and are invariably understood by the crowd, by the whole street. What is more, they are regarded as very great, and as the ideas of genius, but only for the day of their appearance. The cheap never wears. For a thing to be quickly understood is only a sign of its commonplaceness. Bismarck's idea was received as a stroke of genius instantly, and Bismarck himself was looked on as a genius, but the very rapidity of its reception was suspicious. Wait for ten years, and then we shall see what remains of the idea and of Bismarck himself. I introduce this extremely irrelevant observation, of course, not for the sake of comparison, but also for the sake of remembering it. (An explanation for the too unmannerly reader.)

And now I will tell two anecdotes to wind up my account of the " idea," that it may not hinder my story again.

In July, two months before I came to Petersburg, when my time was all my own, Marie Ivanovna asked me to go to see an old maiden lady who was staying in the Troitsky suburb to take her a message of no interest for my story. Returning the same day, I noticed in the railway carriage an unattractive-looking young man, not very poorly though grubbily dressed, with a pimply face and a muddy dark complexion. He distinguished himself by getting out at every station, big and little, to have a drink. Towards the end of the journey he was surrounded by a merry throng of very low companions. One merchant, also a little drunk, was particularly delighted at the young man's power of drinking incessantly without becoming drunk. Another person, who was awfully pleased with him, was a very stupid young fellow who talked a great deal. He was wearing European dress and smelt most unsavoury—he was a footman as I found out afterwards ; this fellow got quite friendly with the young man who was drinking, and, every time the train stopped, roused him with the invitation : " It's time for a drop of vodka," and they got out with their arms round each other. The young man who drank scarcely said a word, but yet more and more companions joined him. He only listened to their chatter, grinning incessantly with a drivelling snigger, and only from time to time, always unexpectedly, brought out a sound something like " Ture-lure-loo ! " while he put his finger up to his nose in a very comical way. This diverted the merchant, and the footman and all of them, and they burst into very loud and free and easy laughter. It is sometimes impossible to understand why people laugh. I joined them too, and, I don't know why, the young man attracted me too, perhaps by his very open disregard for the generally accepted conventions and proprieties. I didn't see, in fact, that he was simply a fool. Anyway, I got on to friendly terms with him at once, and, as I got out of the train, I learnt from him that he would be in the Tverskoy Boulevard between eight and nine. It appeared that he had been a student. I went to the Boulevard, and this was the diversion he taught me : we walked together up and down the boulevards, and a little later, as soon as we noticed a respectable woman walking along the street, if there were no one else near, we fastened upon her. Without uttering a word we walked one on each side of her, and with an air of perfect composure as though we didn't see her, began to carry on a most unseemly conversation. We called things by their names, preserving unruffled countenances as though it were the natural thing to do ; we entered into such subtleties in our description of all sorts of filth and obscenity as the nastiest mind of the lewdest debauchee could hardly have conceived. (I had, of course, acquired all this knowledge at the boarding school before I went to the grammar school, though I knew only words, nothing of the reality.) The woman was dreadfully frightened, and made haste to try and get away, but we quickened our pace too—and went on in the same way. Our victim, of course, could do nothing ; it was no use to cry out, there were no spectators ; besides, it would be a strange thing to complain of. I repeated this diversion for eight days. I can't think how I

can have liked doing it ; though, indeed, I didn't like doing it—
I simply did it. At first I thought it original, as something
outside everyday conventions and conditions, besides I couldn't
endure women. I once told the student that in his "Confessions" Jean Jacques Rousseau describes how, as a youth, he
used to behave indecently in the presence of women. The
student responded with his "ture-lure-loo!" I noticed that
he was extraordinarily ignorant, and that his interests were
astonishingly limited. There was no trace in him of any latent
idea such as I had hoped to find in him. Instead of originality I
found nothing in him but a wearisome monotony. I disliked
him more and more. The end came quite unexpectedly. One
night when it was quite dark, we persecuted a girl who was
quickly and timidly walking along the boulevard. She was very
young, perhaps sixteen or even less, very tidily and modestly
dressed ; possibly a working girl hurrying home from work to
an old widowed mother with other children ; there is no need to
be sentimental though. The girl listened for some time, and
hurried as fast as she could with her head bowed and her veil
drawn over her face, frightened and trembling. But suddenly
she stood still, threw back her veil, showing, as far as I remember,
a thin but pretty face, and cried with flashing eyes :

" Oh, what scoundrels you are ! "

She may have been on the verge of tears, but something
different happened. Lifting her thin little arm, she gave the
student a slap in the face which could not have been more
dexterously delivered. It did come with a smack ! He would
have rushed at her, swearing, but I held him back, and the girl
had time to run away. We began quarrelling at once. I told
him all I had been saving up against him in those days. I told
him he was the paltriest commonplace fool without the trace of
an idea. He swore at me. . . . (I had once explained to him
that I was illegitimate), then we spat at each other, and I've
never seen him since. I felt frightfully vexed with myself that
evening, but not so much the next day, and by the day after I
had quite forgotten it. And though I sometimes thought of
that girl again, it was only casually, for a moment. It was only
after I had been a fortnight in Petersburg, I suddenly recalled
the whole scene. I remembered it, and I was suddenly so
ashamed that tears of shame literally ran down my cheeks.
I was wretched the whole evening, and all that night, and I am
rather miserable about it now. I could not understand at first

how I could have sunk to such a depth of degradation, and still less how I could have forgotten it without feeling shame or remorse. It is only now that I understand what was at the root of it; it was all due to my " idea." Briefly, I conclude that, having something fixed, permanent and overpowering in one's mind in which one is terribly absorbed, one is, as it were, removed by it from the whole world, and everything that happens, except the one great thing, slips by one. Even one's impressions are hardly formed correctly. And what matters most—one always has an excuse. However much I worried my mother at that time, however disgracefully I neglected my sister," Oh, I've my ' idea,' nothing else matters," was what I said to myself, as it were. If I were slighted and hurt, I withdrew in my mortification and at once said to myself, " Ah, I'm humiliated, but still I have my idea, and they know nothing about that." The " idea " comforted me in disgrace and insignificance. But all the nasty things I did took refuge, as it were, under the " idea." It, so to speak, smoothed over everything, but it also put a mist before my eyes ; and such a misty understanding of things and events may, of course, be a great hindrance to the " idea " itself, to say nothing of other things.

Now for another anecdote.

On the 1st of April last year, Marie Ivanovna was keeping her name-day; some visitors, though only a few, came for the evening. Suddenly Agrafena rushed in, out of breath, announcing that a baby was crying in the passage before the kitchen, and that she didn't know what to do. We were all excited at the news. We went out and saw a bark basket, and in the basket a three or four weeks old child, crying. I picked up the basket and took it into the kitchen. Then I immediately found a folded note : " Gracious benefactors, show kind charity to the girl christened Arina, and we will join with her to send our tears to the Heavenly throne for you for ever, and congratulate you on your name-day,

Persons unknown to you."

Then Nikolay Semyonovitch, for whom I have such a respect, greatly disappointed me. He drew a very long face and decided to send the child at once to the Foundling Home. I felt very sad. They lived very frugally but had no children, and Nikolay Semyonovitch was always glad of it. I carefully took little Arina out of the basket and held her up under the arms. The basket had that sour, pungent odour characteristic of a small child which has not been washed for a long time. I opposed Nikolay Semyonovitch, and suddenly announced that I would keep the child at my expense. In spite of his gentleness he protested with some severity, and, though he ended by joking, he adhered to his intention in regard to the foundling. I got my way, however. In the same block of buildings, but in a different wing, there lived a very poor carpenter, an elderly man, given to drink, but his wife, a very healthy and still youngish peasant woman, had only just lost a baby, and, what is more, the only child she had had in eight years of marriage, also a girl, and by a strange piece of luck also called Arina. I call it good luck, because while we were arguing in the kitchen, the woman, hearing of what had happened, ran in to look at the child, and when she learned that it was called Arina, she was greatly touched. She still had milk, and unfastening her dress she put the baby to her breast. I began persuading her to take the child home with her, saying I would pay for it every month. She was afraid her husband would not allow it, but she took it for the night. Next morning, her husband consented to her keeping it for eight roubles a month, and I immediately paid him for the first month in advance. He at once spent the money on drink. Nikolay Semyonovitch, still with a strange smile, agreed to guarantee that the money should be paid regularly every month. I would have given my sixty roubles into Nikolay Semyonovitch's keeping as security, but he would not take it. He knew, however, that I had the money, and trusted me. Our momentary quarrel was smoothed over by this delicacy on his part. Marie Ivanovna said nothing, but wondered at my undertaking such a responsibility. I particularly appreciated their delicacy in refraining from the slightest jest at my expense, but, on the contrary, taking the matter with proper seriousness. I used to run over to the carpenter's wife three times a day, and at the end of a week I slipped an extra three roubles into her hand without her husband's knowledge. For another three I bought a little quilt and swaddling clothes. But ten days later little Arina fell ill. I called in a doctor at once, he wrote a prescription, and we were up all night, tormenting the mite with horrid medicine. Next day he declared that he had been sent for too late, and answered my entreaties—which I fancy were more like reproaches—by saying with majestic evasiveness : " I am not God." The baby's little tongue and lips and whole mouth were covered with a minute white rash, and towards evening she died, gazing at me with her big black eyes, as though she understood already. I don't know why I never thought to take a photograph of the dead baby. But will it be believed, that I cried that evening, and, in fact, I howled as I had never let myself do before, and Marie Ivanovna had to try to comfort me, again without the least mockery either on her part or on Nikolay Semyonovitch's. The carpenter made a little coffin, and Marie Ivanovna finished it with a frill and a pretty little pillow, while I bought flowers and strewed them on the baby. So they carried away my poor little blossom, whom it will hardly be believed I can't forget even now. A little afterwards, however, this sudden adventure made me reflect seriously. Little Arina had not cost me much, of course ; the coffin, the burial, the doctor, the flowers, and the payment to the carpenter's wife came altogether to thirty roubles. As I was going to Petersburg I made up this sum from the forty roubles sent me by Versilov for the journey, and from the sale of various articles before my departure, so that my capital remained intact. But I thought : " If I am going to be turned aside like this I shan't get far." The affair with the student showed that the " idea " might absorb me till it blurred my impressions and drew me away from the realities of life. The incident with little Arina proved, on the contrary, that no " idea " was strong enough to absorb me, at least so completely that I should not stop short in the face of an overwhelming fact and sacrifice to it at once all that I had done for the " idea " by years of labour. Both conclusions were nevertheless true.

CHAPTER VI

1

My hopes were not fully realized. I did not find them alone though Versilov was not at home, Tatyana Pavlovna was sitting with my mother, and she was, after all, not one of the family. Fully half of my magnanimous feelings disappeared instantly. It is wonderful how hasty and changeable I am in such cases ; a straw, a grain of sand is enough to dissipate my good mood and replace it by a bad one. My bad impressions, I regret to say, are not so quickly dispelled, though I am not resentful. . . . When I went in, I had a feeling that my mother immediately

and hastily broke off what she was saying to Tatyana Pavlovna;
I fancied they were talking very eagerly. My sister turned from
her work only for a moment to look at me and did not come out
of her little alcove again. The flat consisted of three rooms.
The room in which we usually sat, the middle room or drawing-
room, was fairly large and almost presentable. In it were soft,
red armchairs and a sofa, very much the worse for wear, however
(Versilov could not endure covers on furniture); there were rugs
of a sort and several tables, including some useless little ones. On
the right was Versilov's room, cramped and narrow with one
window; it was furnished with a wretched-looking writing-table
covered with unused books and crumpled papers, and an equally
wretched-looking easy chair with a broken spring that stuck up
in one corner and often made Versilov groan and swear. On an
equally threadbare sofa in this room he used to sleep. He
hated this study of his, and I believe he never did anything in it;
he preferred sitting idle for hours together in the drawing-room.
On the left of the drawing-room there was another room of the
same sort in which my mother and sister slept. The drawing-
room was entered from the passage at the end of which was the
kitchen, where the cook, Lukerya, lived, and when she cooked,
she ruthlessly filled the whole flat with the smell of burnt fat.
There were moments when Versilov cursed his life and fate aloud
on account of the smell from the kitchen, and in that one matter
I sympathized with him fully; I hated that smell, too, though it
did not penetrate to my room : I lived upstairs in an attic under
the roof, to which I climbed by a very steep and shaky ladder.
The only things worth mentioning in it were a semicircular
window, a low-pitched ceiling, a sofa covered with American
leather on which at night Lukerya spread sheets and put a pillow
for me. The rest of the furniture consisted of two articles,
a perfectly plain deal table and a wooden rush-bottomed chair.
We still preserved, however, some relics of former comfort. In
the drawing-room, for instance, we had a fairly decent china
lamp, and on the wall hung a large and splendid engraving of
the Sistine Madonna; facing it on the other wall was an immense
and expensive photograph of the cast-bronze gates of the cathedral
of Florence. In the corner of the same room was a shrine of
old-fashioned family ikons, one of which had a gilt-silver setting
—the one they had meant to pawn, while another (the image of
Our Lady) had a velvet setting embroidered in pearls. Under
the ikons hung a little lamp which was lighted on every holiday.

Versilov evidently had no feeling for the ikons in their inner meaning and religious significance, but he restrained himself. He merely screwed up his eyes, sometimes complaining that the lamplight reflected in the gilt setting hurt them, but he did not hinder my mother from lighting the lamp.

I usually entered in gloomy silence, looking away into some corner, and sometimes without even greeting anyone. As a rule I returned earlier than to-day, and they used to send my dinner to me upstairs. Going into the room I said, " Good evening, mother," a thing I had never done before. Though even this time I was unable from a sort of bashfulness to make myself look at her, and I sat down in the opposite corner of the room. I was awfully tired, but I did not think of that.

"That lout of yours still walks in as rudely as ever," Tatyana Pavlovna hissed at me. She had been in the habit in old days of using abusive epithets to me and it had become an established tradition between us.

My mother faltered " Good evening " to me, using the formal mode of address, and evidently embarrassed at my greeting her. " Your dinner has been ready a long while," she added, almost overcome by confusion : " I hope the soup is not cold, I will order the cutlets at once. . . ." She was hastily jumping up to go to the kitchen and, for the first time perhaps during that whole month, I felt ashamed that she should run about to wait on me so humbly, though till that moment I had expected it of her.

"Thank you very much, mother, I have had dinner already. May I stay and rest here if I am not in the way ? "

" Oh . . . of course. . . . how can you ask, pray sit down . . . ."

" Don't worry yourself, mother, I won't be rude to Andrey Petrovitch again," I rapped out all at once.

" Good heavens ! how noble of him," cried Tatyana Pavlovna. " Sonia darling, you don't mean to say you still stand on ceremony with him ? Who is he to be treated with such deference, and by his own mother, too ! Look at you, why you behave as though you were afraid of him, it is disgraceful."

"I should like it very much, mother, if you would call me Arkasha."

" Oh . . . yes . . . certainly, yes I will," my mother said hurriedly. " I . . . don't always . . . henceforward I will."

She blushed all over. Certainly her face had at times a great charm. . . . It had a look of simplicity, but by no means of stupidity. It was rather pale and anæmic, her cheeks were very thin, even hollow; her forehead was already lined by many wrinkles, but there were none round her eyes, and her eyes were rather large and wide open, and shone with a gentle and serene light which had drawn me to her from the very first day. I liked her face, too, because it did not look particularly depressed or drawn; on the contrary, her expression would have been positively cheerful, if she had not been so often agitated, sometimes almost panic-stricken over trifles, starting up from her seat for nothing at all. or listening in alarm to anything new that was said, till she was sure that all was well and as before. What mattered to her was just that all should be as before; that there should be no change, that nothing new should happen, not even new happiness. . . . It might have been thought that she had been frightened as a child. Besides her eyes, I liked the oval of her rather long face, and I believe if it had been a shade less broad across the cheekbones she might have been called beautiful, not only in her youth but even now. She was not more than thirty-nine, but grey hairs were already visible in her chestnut hair.

Tatyana Pavlovna glanced at her in genuine indignation.

"A booby like him! And you tremble before him, you are ridiculous, Sofia, you make me angry, I tell you!"

"Ah, Tatyana Pavlovna, why should you attack him now? But you are joking perhaps, eh?" my mother added, detecting something like a smile on Tatyana Pavlovna's face. Her scoldings could not indeed be always taken seriously. But she smiled (if she did smile) only at my mother, of course, because she loved her devotedly, and no doubt noticed how happy she was at that moment at my meekness.

"Of course, I can't help feeling hurt, if you will attack people unprovoked, Tatyana Pavlovna, and just when I've come in saying 'Good evening, mother,' a thing I've never done before," I thought it necessary to observe at last.

"Only fancy," she boiled over at once: "He considers it as something to be proud of. Am I to go down on my knees to you, pray, because for once in your life you've been polite? and as though it were politeness! Why do you stare into the corner when you come in? I know how you tear and fling about before her! You might have said 'Good evening' to me, too, I wrapped you in your swaddling clothes, I am your godmother."

I need not say I did not deign to answer. At that moment my sister came in and I made haste to turn to her.

"Liza, I saw Vassin to-day and he inquired after you. You have met him ? "

"Yes, last year in Luga," she answered quite simply, sitting down beside me and looking at me affectionately. I don't know why, but I had fancied she would flush when I spoke of Vassin. My sister was a blonde ; very fair with flaxen hair, quite unlike both her parents. But her eyes and the oval of her face were like our mother's. Her nose was very straight, small, and regular ; there were tiny freckles in her face, however, of which there was no sign in my mother's. There was very little resemblance to Versilov, nothing but the slenderness of figure, perhaps, her tallness and something charming in her carriage. There was not the slightest likeness between us—we were the opposite poles.

"I knew his honour for three months," Liza added.

"Is it Vassin you call ' his honour,' Liza ? You should call him by his name. Excuse my correcting you, sister, but it grieves me that they seem to have neglected your education."

"But it's shameful of you to remark upon it before your mother," cried Tatyana Pavlovna, firing up ; "and you are talking nonsense, it has not been neglected at all."

"I am not saying anything about my mother," I said sharply, defending myself. "Do you know, mother, that when I look at Liza it's as though it were you over again ; you have given her the same charm of goodness, which you must have had yourself, and you have it to this day and always will have it. . . . I was only talking of the surface polish, of the silly rules of etiquette, which are necessary, however. I am only indignant at the thought that when Versilov has heard you call Vassin ' his honour ' he has not troubled to correct you at all—his disdain and his indifference to us are so complete. That's what makes me furious."

"He is a perfect bear himself, and he is giving us lessons in good manners ! Don't you dare talk of Versilov before your mother, sir, or before me either, I won't stand it ! " Tatyana Pavlovna flashed out.

"I got my salary to-day, mother, fifty roubles ; take it, please ; here ! "

I went up to her and gave her the money ; she was in a tremor of anxiety at once.

G

" Oh, I don't know about taking it," she brought out, as though afraid to touch the money. I did not understand.

" For goodness' sake, mother, if you both think of me as one of the family, as a son and a brother. . . ."

" Oh, I've been to blame, Arkady : I ought to have confessed something to you, but I am afraid of you. . . ."

She said this with a timid and deprecating smile ; again I did not understand and interrupted.

" By the way, did you know, mother, that Andrey Petrovitch's case against the Sokolskys is being decided to-day ? "

" Ah ! I knew," she cried, clasping her hands before her (her favourite gesture) in alarm.

" To-day ? " cried Tatyana Pavlovna startled, " but it's impossible, he would have told us. Did he tell you ? " she turned to my mother.

" Oh ! no . . . that it was to-day . . . he didn't. But I have been fearing it all the week. I would have prayed for him to lose it even, only to have it over and off one's mind, and to have things as they used to be again."

" What ! hasn't he even told you, mother ? " I exclaimed. " What a man ! There's an example of the indifference and contempt I spoke of just now."

" It's being decided, how is it being decided ? And who told you ? " cried Tatyana Pavlovna, pouncing upon me. " Speak, do."

" Why, here he is himself ! Perhaps he will tell you," I announced, catching the sound of his step in the passage and hastily sitting down again beside Liza.

" Brother, for God's sake, spare mother, and be patient with Andrey Petrovitch . . ." she whispered to me.

" I will, I will," with that I turned to her and pressed her hand.

Liza looked at me very mistrustfully, and she was right.

2

He came in very much pleased with himself, so pleased that he did not feel it necessary to conceal his state of mind. And, indeed, he had become accustomed of late to displaying himself before us without the slightest ceremony, not only in his bad points but even where he was ridiculous, a thing which most people are afraid to do ; at the same time, he fully recognized that we should understand to the smallest detail. In the course of the last year, so Tatyana Pavlovna observed, he had become slovenly in his dress : his clothes though old were always well cut and free from foppishness. It is true that he was prepared to put on clean linen only on every alternate day, instead of every day, which was a real distress to my mother ; it was regarded by them as a sacrifice, and the whole group of devoted women looked upon it as an act of heroism. He always wore soft wide-brimmed black hats. When he took off his hat his very thick but silvery locks stood up in a shock on his head ; I liked looking at his hair when he took off his hat.

" Good evening; still disputing; and is he actually one of the party ? I heard his voice from outside in the passage ; he has been attacking me I suppose ? "

It was one of the signs of his being in a good humour for him to be witty at my expense ; I did not answer, of course. Lukerya came in with a regular sackful of parcels and put them on the table.

" Victory ! Tatyana Pavlovna ! the case is won, and the Sokolskys certainly won't venture to appeal. I've won the day ! I was able to borrow a thousand roubles at once. Sonia, put down your work, don't try your eyes. Back from work, Liza ? "

" Yes, father," answered Liza, looking at him affectionately ; she used to call him father ; nothing would have induced me to submit to doing the same.

" Tired ? "

" Yes."

" Give up your work, don't go to-morrow, and drop it altogether."

" Father, that will be worse for me."

" I beg you will . . . I greatly dislike to see women working, Tatyana Pavlovna."

" How can they get on without work ? a woman's not to work ? "

" I know, I know ; that's excellent and very true, and I agree with it beforehand, but—I mean needlework particularly. Only imagine, I believe that's one of the morbid anomalous impressions of my childhood. In my dim memories of the time when I was five or six years old I remember more often than anything—with loathing, of course—a solemn council of wise women, stern and forbidding, sitting at a round table with scissors, material, patterns, and a fashion-plate. They thought they knew all about it, and shook their heads slowly and majestically, measuring, calculating, and preparing to cut out. All those kind people who were so fond of me had suddenly become unapproachable, and if I began to play I was carried out of the room at once. Even my poor nurse, who held me by the hand and took no notice of my shouting and pulling at her, was listening and gazing enraptured, as though at a kind of paradise. The sternness of those sensible faces and the solemnity with which they faced the task of cutting out is for some reason distressing for me to picture even now. Tatyana Pavlovna, you are awfully fond of cutting out. Although it may be aristocratic, yet I do prefer a woman who does not work at all. Don't take that as meant for you, Sonia. . . . How could you, indeed! Woman is an immense power without working. You know that, though, Sonia. What's your opinion, Arkady Makarovitch? No doubt you disagree?"

"No, not at all," I answered—"that's a particularly good saying that woman is an immense power, though I don't understand why you say that about work. And she can't help working if she has no money—as you know yourself."

"Well, that's enough," and he turned to my mother, who positively beamed all over (when he addressed me she was all of a tremor); "at least, to begin with, I beg you not to let me see you doing needlework for me. No doubt, Arkady, as a young man of the period you are something of a socialist; well, would you believe it, my dear fellow, none are so fond of idleness as the toiling masses."

"Rest perhaps, not idleness."

"No, idleness, doing nothing; that's their ideal! I knew a man who was for ever at work, though he was not one of the common people, he was rather intellectual and capable of generalizing. Every day of his life, perhaps, he brooded with blissful emotion on visions of utter idleness, raising the ideal to infinity, so to speak, to unlimited independence, to everlasting freedom, dreaming, and idle contemplation. So it went on till he broke down altogether from overwork. There was no mending him, he died in a hospital. I am sometimes seriously disposed to believe that the delights of labour have been invented by the idle, from virtuous motives, of course. It is one of the 'Geneva ideas' of the end of last century. Tatyana Pavlovna, I cut an advertisement out of the newspaper the day before yesterday, here it is"; he took a scrap of paper out of his waist-

coat pocket. " It is one of those everlasting students, proficient
in classics and mathematics and prepared to travel, to sleep
in a garret or anywhere. Here, listen : ' A teacher (lady)
prepares for all the scholastic establishments (do you hear, for
all) and gives lessons in arithmetic ! ' Prepares for all the
scholastic establishments—in arithmetic, therefore, may we
assume ? No, arithmetic is something apart for her. It is a
case of simple hunger, the last extremity of want. It is just
the ineptitude of it that's so touching : it's evident that the lady
has never prepared anyone for any school, and it is doubtful
whether she is fit to teach anything. Yet at her last gasp she
wastes her one remaining rouble and prints in the paper that
she prepares for all the scholastic establishments, and what's
more, gives lessons in arithmetic. *Per tutto mundo e in altri
siti.*"

" Oh, Andrey Petrovitch, she ought to be helped ! Where
does she live ? " cried Tatyana Pavlovna.

" Oh, there are lots of them ! " He put the advertisement
in his pocket. " That bag's full of treats for you, Liza, and
you, Tatyana Pavlovna ; Sonia and I don't care for sweet things.
And perhaps for you, young man. I bought the things myself
at Eliseyev's and at Ballé's. Too long we've gone hungry, as
Lukerya said. (N.B.—None of us had ever gone hungry.) Here
are grapes, sweets, *duchesses* and strawberry tarts ; I've even
brought some excellent liqueur ; nuts, too. It's curious that to this
day I'm fond of nuts as I have been from a child, Tatyana
Pavlovna, and of the commonest nuts, do you know. Liza
takes after me ; she is fond of cracking nuts like a squirrel. But
there's nothing more charming, Tatyana Pavlovna, than sometimes when recalling one's childhood to imagine oneself in a
wood, in a copse, gathering nuts. . . . The days are almost
autumnal, but bright ; at times it's so fresh, one hides in the
bushes, one wanders in the wood, there's a scent of leaves. . . .
I seem to see something sympathetic in your face, Arkady
Makarovitch ? "

" The early years of my childhood, too, were spent in the
country."

" But I thought you were brought up in Moscow, if I am not
mistaken."

" He was living in Moscow at the Andronikovs' when you
went there ; but till then he used to live in the country with
your aunt, Varvara Stepanovna," Tatyana Pavlovna put in.

" Sonia, here's some money, put it away. I promise you, in a few days, five thousand."

" So there's no hope then for the Sokolskys ? " asked Tatyana Pavlovna.

" Absolutely none, Tatyana Pavlovna."

" I have always sympathized with you and all of yours, Andrey Petrovitch, and I have always been a friend of the family, but though the Sokolskys are strangers, yet, upon my word, I am sorry for them. Don't be angry, Andrey Petrovitch."

" I have no intention of going shares with them, Tatyana Pavlovna ! "

" You know my idea, of course, Andrey Petrovitch ; they would have settled the case out of court, if at the very beginning you had offered to go halves with them ; now, of course, it is too late. Not that I venture to criticize. . . . I say so because I don't think the deceased would have left them out of his will altogether."

" Not only he wouldn't have left them out, he'd have certainly left them everything, and would have left none out but me, if he'd known how to do things and to write a will properly ; but as it is, the law's on my side, and it's settled. I can't go shares, and I don't want to, Tatyana Pavlovna, and that is the end of the matter."

He spoke with real exasperation, a thing he rarely allowed himself to do. Tatyana Pavlovna subsided. My mother looked down mournfully. Versilov knew that she shared Tatyana Pavlovna's views.

" He has not forgotten that slap in the face at Ems," I thought to myself. The document given me by Kraft and at that moment in my pocket would have a poor chance if it had fallen into his hands. I suddenly felt that the whole responsibility was still weighing upon me, and this idea, together with all the rest, had, of course, an irritating effect upon me.

" Arkady, I should like you to be better dressed, my dear fellow ; your suit is all right, but for future contingencies I might recommend you to an excellent Frenchman, most conscientious and possessed of taste."

" I beg you never to make such suggestions again," I burst out suddenly.

" What's that ? "

" It is not that I consider it humiliating, of course, but we are not agreed about anything ; on the contrary, our views are entirely

opposed, for in a day or two—to-morrow—I shall give up going
to the prince's, as I find there is absolutely no work for me to
do there."

"But you are going and sitting there with him—that is the
work."

"Such ideas are degrading."

"I don't understand ; but if you are so squeamish, don't take
money from him, but simply go. You will distress him horribly,
he has already become attached to you, I assure you. . . . However, as you please. . . ." He was evidently put out.

"You say, don't ask for money, but thanks to you I did a
mean thing to-day : you did not warn me, and I demanded my
month's salary from him to-day."

"So you have seen to that already ; I confess I did not
expect you to ask for it ; but how sharp you all are nowadays !
There are no young people in these days, Tatyana Pavlovna."
He was very spiteful : I was awfully angry too.

"I ought to have had things out with you . . . you made me
do it, I don't know now how it's to be."

"By the way, Sonia, give Arkady back his sixty roubles at
once ; and you, my dear fellow, don't be angry at our repaying
it so quickly. I can guess from your face that you have some
enterprise in your mind and that you need it. . . . So invest it
. . . or something of the sort."

"I don't know what my face expresses, but I did not expect
mother would have told you of that money when I so particularly
asked her. . . ." I looked at my mother with flashing eyes, I
cannot express how wounded I felt.

"Arkasha, darling, for God's sake forgive me, I couldn't
possibly help speaking of it. . . ."

"My dear fellow, don't make a grievance of her telling me your
secrets : besides, she did it with the best intentions—it was
simply a mother's longing to boast of her son's feeling for her.
But I assure you I should have guessed without that you were
a capitalist. All your secrets are written on your honest
countenance. He has 'his idea,' Tatyana Pavlovna, as I told
you."

"Let's drop my honest countenance," I burst out again.
"I know that you often see right through things, but in some
cases you see no further than your own nose, and I have marvelled
at your powers of penetration. Well then, I have 'my idea.'
That you should use that expression, of course, was an accident,

but I am not afraid to admit it ; I have ' an idea ' of my own,
I am not afraid and I am not ashamed of it."

" Don't be ashamed, that's the chief thing."

" And all the same I shall never tell it you."

" That's to say you won't condescend to ; no need to, my dear
fellow, I know the nature of your idea as it is ; in any case it
implies :

Into the wilderness I flee.

Tatyana Pavlovna, my notion is that he wants . . . to become a
Rothschild, or something of the kind, and shut himself up in his
grandeur. . . . No doubt he'll magnanimously allow us a pension,
though perhaps he won't allow me one—but in any case he will
vanish from our sight. Like the new moon he has risen, only
to set again."

I shuddered in my inmost being; of course, it was all chance;
he knew nothing of my idea and was not speaking about it, though
he did mention Rothschild ; but how could he define my feelings
so precisely, my impulse to break with them and go away ? He
divined everything and wanted to defile beforehand with his
cynicism the tragedy of fact. That he was horribly angry, of
that there could be no doubt.

" Mother, forgive my hastiness, for I see that there's no hiding
things from Andrey Petrovitch in any case," I said, affecting to
laugh and trying if only for a moment to turn it into a joke.

" That's the very best thing you can do, my dear fellow, to
laugh. It is difficult to realize how much every one gains by
laughing even in appearance ; I am speaking most seriously.
He always has an air, Tatyana Pavlovna, of having something
so important on his mind, that he is quite abashed at the circumstance himself."

" I must ask you in earnest, Andrey Petrovitch, to be more
careful what you say."

" You are right, my dear boy ; but one must speak out once
for all, so as never to touch upon the matter again. You have
come to us from Moscow, to begin making trouble at once.
That's all we know as yet of your object in coming. I say
nothing, of course, of your having come to surprise us in some
way. And all this month you have been snorting and sneering
at us. Yet you are obviously an intelligent person, and as such
you might leave such snorting and sneering to those who have
no other means of avenging themselves on others for their own

insignificance. You are always shutting yourself up, though your honest countenance and your rosy cheeks bear witness that you might look every one straight in the face with perfect innocence. He's a neurotic; I can't make out, Tatyana Pavlovna, why they are all neurotic nowadays. . . ? "

" If you did not even know where I was brought up, you are not likely to know why a man's neurotic."

" Oh, so that's the key to it ! You are offended at my being capable of forgetting where you were brought up ! "

" Not in the least. Don't attribute such silly ideas to me. Mother ! Andrey Petrovitch praised me just now for laughing ; let us laugh—why sit like this ! Shall I tell you a little anecdote about myself ? Especially as Andrey Petrovitch knows nothing of my adventures."

I was boiling. I knew this was the last time we should be sitting together like this, that when I left that house I should never enter it again, and so on the eve of it all I could not restrain myself. He had challenged me to such a parting scene himself.

" That will be delightful, of course, if it is really amusing," he observed, looking at me searchingly. " Your manners were rather neglected where you were brought up, my dear fellow, though they are pretty passable. He is charming to-day, Tatyana Pavlovna, and it's a good thing you have undone that bag at last."

But Tatyana Pavlovna frowned ; she did not even turn round at his words, but went on untying the parcels and laying out the good things on some plates which had been brought in. My mother, too, was sitting in complete bewilderment, though she had misgivings, of course, and realized that there would be trouble between us. My sister touched my elbow again.

3

" I simply want to tell you all," I began, with a very free-and-easy air, " how a father met for the first time a dearly loved son : it happened ' wherever you were brought up ' . . ."

" My dear fellow, won't it be . . . a dull story ? You know, *tous les genres*. . . ."

" Don't frown, Andrey Petrovitch, I am not speaking at all with the object you imagine. All I want is to make every one laugh."

" Well, God hears you, my dear boy. I know that you love us

all . . . and don't want to spoil our evening," he mumbled with a sort of affected carelessness.

"Of course, you have gusesed by my face that I love you ? "

"Yes, partly by your face, too."

"Just as I guessed from her face that Tatyana Pavlovna's in love with me. Don't look at me so ferociously, Tatyana Pavlovna, it is better to laugh ! it is better to laugh ! "

She turned quickly to me, and gave me a searching look which lasted half a minute.

"Mind now," she said, holding up her finger at me, but so earnestly that her words could not have referred to my stupid joke, but must have been meant as a warning in case I might be up to some mischief.

"Andrey Petrovitch, is it possible you don't remember how we met for the first time in our lives ? "

"Upon my word I've forgotten, my dear fellow, and I am really very sorry. All that I remember is that it was a long time ago . . . and took place somewhere. . . ."

"Mother, and don't you remember how you were in the country, where I was brought up, till I was six or seven I believe, or rather were you really there once, or is it simply a dream that I saw you there for the first time ? I have been wanting to ask you about it for a long time, but I've kept putting it off ; now the time has come."

"To be sure, Arkasha, to be sure I stayed with Varvara Stepanovna three times ; my first visit was when you were only a year old, I came a second time when you were nearly four, and afterwards again when you were six."

"Ah, you did then ; I have been wanting to ask you about it all this month."

My mother seemed overwhelmed by a rush of memories, and she asked me with feeling :

"Do you really mean, Arkasha, that you remembered me there ? "

"I don't know or remember anything, only something of your face remained in my heart for the rest of my life, and the fact, too, that you were my mother. I recall everything there as though it were a dream, I've even forgotten my nurse. I have a faint recollection of Varvara Stepanovna, simply that her face was tied up for toothache. I remember huge trees near the house —lime-trees I think they were—then sometimes the brilliant sunshine at the open windows, the little flower garden, the little path, and you, mother, I remember clearly only at one moment when I was taken to the church there, and you held me up to receive the sacrament and to kiss the chalice ; it was in the summer, and a dove flew through the cupola, in at one window and out at another. . . ."

" Mercy on us, that's just how it was," cried my mother, throwing up her hands, " and the dear dove I remember, too, now. With the chalice just before you, you started, and cried out, ' a dove, a dove.' "

" Your face or something of the expression remained in my memory so distinctly that I recognized you five years after in Moscow, though nobody there told me you were my mother. But when I met Andrey Petrovitch for the first time, I was brought from the Andronikovs' ; I had been vegetating quietly and happily with them for five years on end. I remember their flat down to the smallest detail, and all those ladies who have all grown so much older here ; and the whole household, and how Andronikov himself used to bring the provisions, poultry, fish, and sucking-pigs from the town in a fish-basket. And how at dinner instead of his wife, who always gave herself such airs, he used to help the soup, and how we all laughed at his doing it, he most of all. The young ladies there used to teach me French. But what I liked best of all was Krylov's Fables. I learned a number of them by heart and every day I used to recite one to Andronikov. . . .going straight into his tiny study to do so without considering whether he were busy or not. Well, it was through a fable of Krylov's that I got to know you, Andrey Petrovitch. I see you are beginning to remember."

" I do recall something, my dear fellow, that you repeated something to me . . . a fable or a passage from ' Woe from Wit,' I fancy. What a memory you have, though ! "

" A memory ! I should think so ! it's the one thing I've remembered all my life."

" That's all right, that's all right, my dear fellow, you are quite waking me up."

He actually smiled ; as soon as he smiled, my mother and sister smiled after him, confidence was restored ; but Tatyana Pavlovna,who had finished laying out the good things on the table and settled herself in a corner, still bent upon me a keen and disapproving eye. " This is how it happened," I went on : " one fine morning there suddenly appeared the friend of my childhood, Tatyana Pavlovna, who always made her entrance on the stage of my existence with dramatic suddenness. She took me away in a carriage to a grand house, to sumptuous apartments. You were staying at Madame Fanariotov's, Andrey Petrovitch, in her empty house, which she had bought from you ; she was abroad at that time. I always used to wear short jackets ; now all of a sudden I was put into a pretty little blue greatcoat, and a very fine shirt. Tatyana Pavlovna was busy with me all day and bought me lots of things ; I kept walking through all the empty rooms, looking at myself in all the looking-glasses. And wandering about in the same way the next morning, at ten o'clock, I walked quite by chance into your study. I had seen you already the evening before, as soon as I was brought into the house, but only for an instant on the stairs. You were coming downstairs to get into your carriage and drive off somewhere ; you were staying alone in Moscow then, for a short time after a very long absence, so that you had engagements in all directions and were scarcely ever at home. When you met Tatyana Pavlovna and me you only drawled ' Ah ! ' and did not even stop."

"He describes it with a special love," observed Versilov, addressing Tatyana Pavlovna ; she turned away and did not answer.

"I can see you now as you were then, handsome and flourishing. It is wonderful how much older and less good-looking you have grown in these years ; please forgive this candour, you were thirty-seven even then, though. I gazed at you with admiration ; what wonderful hair you had, almost jet black, with a brilliant lustre without a trace of grey ; moustaches and whiskers, like the setting of a jewel : I can find no other expression for it ; your face of an even pallor ; not like its sickly pallor to-day, but like your daughter, Anna Andreyevna, whom I had the honour of seeing this morning ; dark, glowing eyes, and gleaming teeth, especially when you laughed. And you did laugh, when you looked round as I came in ; I was not very discriminating at that time, and your smile rejoiced my heart. That morning you were wearing a dark blue velvet jacket, a sulphur coloured necktie, and a magnificent shirt with Alençon lace on it ; you were standing before the looking-glass with a manuscript in your hand, and were busy declaiming Tchatsky's monologue, and especially his last exclamation : ' A coach, I want a coach.' "

"Good heavens ! " cried Versilov. "Why, he's right !

Though I was only in Moscow for so short a time, I undertook to
play Tchatsky in an amateur performance at Alexandra Petrovna
Vitovtov's in place of Zhileyko, who was ill ! ''

" Do you mean to say you had forgotten it ? " laughed
Tatyana Pavlovna.

" He has brought it back to my mind ! And I own that those
few days in Moscow were perhaps the happiest in my life ! We
were still so young then . . . and all so fervently expecting
something. . . . It was then in Moscow I unexpectedly met so
much. . . . But go on, my dear fellow : this time you've done
well to remember it all so exactly. . . .''

" I stood still to look at you and suddenly cried out, ' Ah, how
good, the real Tchatsky ' You turned round at once and
asked : ' Why, do you know Tchatsky already ? ' and you sat
down on a sofa, and began drinking your coffee in the most
charming humour—I could have kissed you. Then I informed
you that at the Andronikovs' every one read a great deal, and
that the young ladies knew a great deal of poetry by heart,
and used to act scenes out of ' Woe from Wit ' among themselves,
and that all last week we had been reading aloud in the evening
' A Sportsman's Sketches,' but what I liked best of all was
Krylov's Fables, and that I knew them by heart. You told
me to repeat one, and I repeated ' The Girl who was Hard to
Please.' ''

A maid her suitor shrewdly scanned.

" Yes ! Yes ! I remember it all now," cried Versilov again ;
" but, my dear fellow, I remember you, too, clearly now ; you
were such a charming boy then, a thoughtful boy even, and, I
assure you, you, too, have changed for the worse in the course of
these nine years."

At this point all of them, even Tatyana Pavlovna, laughed.
It was evident that Andrey Petrovitch had deigned to jest, and
had paid me out in the same coin for my biting remark about his
having grown old. Every one was amused, and indeed, it was
well said.

" As I recited, you smiled, but before I was half-way through
the fable you rang the bell and told the footman who answered
it to ask Tatyana Pavlovna to come, and she ran in with such
a delighted face, that though I had seen her the evening before
I scarcely knew her. For Tatyana Pavlovna, I began the fable
again, I finished it brilliantly, even Tatyana Pavlovna smiled,

and you, Andrey Petrovitch cried 'Bravo!' and observed with warmth that if it had been 'The Ant and the Grasshopper' it would not be wonderful that a sensible boy of my age should recite it sensibly, but this fable

> *A maid her suitor shrewdly scanned.*
> *Indeed, that's not a crime.*

was different. "Listen how he brings out 'Indeed, that's not a crime,'" you said; in fact, you were enthusiastic. Then you said something in French to Tatyana Pavlovna, and she instantly frowned and began to protest, and grew very hot, in fact; but as it was impossible to oppose Andrey Petrovitch if he once took an idea into his head, she hurriedly carried me off to her room, there my hands and face were washed again, my shirt was changed, my hair was pomaded and even curled.

"Then towards evening Tatyana Pavlovna dressed herself up rather grandly as I had never expected to see her, and she took me with her in the carriage. It was the first time in my life I had been to a play; it was at a private performance at Mme. Vitovtov's. The lights, the chandeliers, the ladies, the officers, the generals, the young ladies, the curtain, the rows of chairs, were utterly unlike anything I had seen before. Tatyana Pavlovna took a very modest seat in one of the back rows, and made me sit down beside her. There were, of course, other children like me in the room, but I had no eyes for anything, I simply waited with a sinking of my heart for the performance. When you came on, Andrey Petrovitch, I was ecstatic to the point of tears. What for and why, I don't understand. Why those tears of rapture? It has been a strange recollection for me ever since, for these last nine years! I followed the drama with a throbbing heart; all I understood of it, of course, was that *she* was deceiving *him*, and that he was ridiculed by stupid people who were not worth his little finger. When he was reciting at the ball I understood that he was humiliated and insulted, that he was reproaching all these miserable people, but that he was— great, great! No doubt my training at the Andronikovs' helped me to understand, and your acting, Andrey Petrovitch! It was the first time I had seen a play! When you went off shouting 'A coach, a coach!' (and you did that shout wonderfully) I jumped up from my seat, and while the whole audience burst into applause, I, too, clapped my hands and cried 'bravo' at the top of my voice. I vividly recall how at that instant I felt as though I had been pierced by a pin in my back 'a little below the waist'; Tatyana Pavlovna had given me a ferocious pinch; but I took no notice of it. As soon as 'Woe from Wit' was over, Tatyana Pavlovna took me home, of course. 'You can't stay for the dancing, and it's only on your account I am not staying!' you hissed at me all the way home in the carriage, Tatyana Pavlovna. All night I was delirious, and by ten o'clock the next morning I was standing at the study door, but it was shut; there were people with you and you were engaged in some business with them; then you drove off and were away the whole day till late at night—so I did not see you again! What I meant to say to you, I have forgotten, of course, and indeed I did not know then, but I longed passionately to see you as soon as possible. And at eight o'clock next morning you were graciously pleased to set off for Serpuhov; at that time you had just sold your Tula estate to settle with your creditors, but there was still left in your hands a tempting stake; that was why you had come at that time to Moscow, where you had not been able to show yourself till then for fear of your creditors, and this Serpuhov ruffian was the only one of them who had not agreed to take half of what you owed him instead of the whole. When I questioned Tatyana Pavlovna, she did not even answer me. 'It's no business of yours, but the day after to-morrow I shall take you to your boarding school: get your exercise-books ready, take your lesson books, put them all in order, and you must learn to pack your little box yourself, you can't expect to be waited on, sir.' You were drumming this and that into my ears all those three days, Tatyana Pavlovna. It ended in my being taken in my innocence to school at Touchard's, adoring you, Andrey Petrovitch; our whole meeting was a trivial incident, perhaps, but would you believe it, six months afterwards I longed to run away from Touchard's to you!"

"You describe it capitally, you have brought it all back so vividly," Versilov pronounced incisively; "but what strikes me most in your story is the wealth of certain strange details, concerning my debts, for instance. Apart from the fact that these details are hardly a suitable subject for you to discuss, I can't imagine how you managed to get hold of them."

"Details? how I got hold of them? Why I repeat, for the last nine years I have been doing nothing but getting hold of facts about you."

"A strange confession, and a strange way of spending your time."
He turned half-reclining in his easy chair, and even yawned
slightly, whether intentionally or not I could not say.

"Well, shall I go on telling you how I wanted to run to you
from Touchard's?"

"Forbid him, Andrey Petrovitch; suppress him and send him
away," Tatyana Pavlovna burst out.

"That won't do, Tatyana Pavlovna," Versilov answered her
impressively. "Arkasha has evidently something on his mind,
and so he must be allowed to finish. Well, let him speak!
When he's said what he's got to say, it will be off his mind, and
what matters most to him is that he should get it off his mind.
Begin your new story, my dear fellow; I call it new, but you may
rest assured that I know how it ends."

4

"I ran away, that is, I tried to run away to you, very simply.
Tatyana Pavlovna, do you remember after I had been there a
fortnight Touchard wrote you a letter—didn't he? Marie
Ivanovna showed me the letter afterwards; that turned up
among Andronikov's papers, too. Touchard suddenly discovered
that the fees he had asked were too small, and with ' dignity '
announced in his lettr to you ' that little princes and senator's
children were educated in his establishment, and that it was
lowering its tone to keep a pupil of such humble origin as me
unless the remuneration were increased."

"*Mon cher*, you really might. . . ."

"Oh that's nothing, that's nothing," I interrupted, "I am
only going to say a little about Touchard. You wrote from the
provinces a fortnight later, Tatyana Pavlovna, and answered
with a flat refusal. I remember how he walked into our classroom, flushing crimson. He was a very short thick-set little
Frenchman of five-and-forty, a Parisian cobbler by origin,
though he had from time immemorial held a position in Moscow
as an instructor in the French language, and even had an
official rank, of which he was extremely proud; he was a man of
crass ignorance. There were only six of us pupils; among them
there actually was a nephew of a Moscow senator; and we all
lived like one family under the supervision of his wife, a very
affected lady, who was the daughter of a Russian government
clerk. During that fortnight I had given myself great airs

before my school-fellows. I boasted of my blue overcoat, and my papa, Andrey Petrovitch, and their questions : why I was called Dolgoruky and not Versilov did not embarrass me in the least, since I did not know why."

"Andrey Petrovitch !" cried Tatyana Pavlovna, in a voice almost menacing. My mother, on the contrary, was watching me intently, and evidently wished me to go on.

"*Ce Touchard* . . . I actually recall him now . . . he was a fussy little man," Versilov admitted ; "but he was recommended to me by the very best people. . . ."

"*Ce Touchard* walked in with the letter in his hand, went up to the big oak table, at which all six of us were seated learning something by heart; he seized me firmly by the shoulder, picked me up from the chair, and ordered me to collect my exercise-books. 'Your place is not here but there,' he said, pointing to a tiny room on the left of the passage, where there was nothing but a plain deal table, a rush-bottom chair, and an American leather sofa—exactly like what I have upstairs in the attic. I went into it in amazement, very much downcast ; I had never been roughly treated before. Half an hour later when Touchard had gone out of the schoolroom, I began to exchange glances and smiles with my schoolfellows ; they, of course, were laughing at me ; but I had no suspicion of it and thought we were laughing because we were merry. At that moment Touchard darted in, seized me by the forelock, and dragged me about.

"'Don't you dare sit with gentlemanly boys, you are a child of low origin and no better than a lackey.'

"And he gave me a stinging blow on my chubby, rosy cheek. He must have enjoyed doing so and he struck me a second time, and a third. I cried violently and was terribly astonished. For a whole hour I sat with my face hidden in my hands crying and crying. Something had happened which was utterly beyond my comprehension. I don't understand how a man, not of spiteful character, a foreigner like Touchard, who rejoiced at the emancipation of the Russian peasants, could have beaten a foolish child like me. I was only amazed, not resentful, how-ever. I had not yet learnt to resent an insult. It seemed to me that I had somehow been naughty, that when I was good again I should be forgiven, and that we should all be merry again at once, that we should go out to play in the yard and live happy ever after."

"My dear fellow, if I had only known. . . ." Versilov drawled

H

with the careless smile of a rather weary man. " What a scoundrel
that Touchard was, though ! I have not given up all hope,
however, that you may make an effort and forgive us for all that
at last, and that we may all live happy ever after."

He yawned decisively.

" But I am not blaming you at all, and believe me, I am
not complaining of Touchard," I cried, a little disconcerted.
" Though, indeed, he beat me for ten months or so. I remember I was always trying to appease him in some way ; I used
to rush to kiss his hands, I was always kissing them, and I was
always crying and crying. My schoolfellows laughed at me and
despised me, because Touchard began to treat me sometimes like a
servant, he used to order me to bring him his clothes when he was
dressing. My menial instincts were of use to me there ; I did my
very utmost to please him, and was not in the least offended, because I did not at that time understand it at all, and I am surprised to this day that I could have been so stupid as not to realize
that I was not on an equal footing with the rest. It's true my
schoolfellows made many things clear to me even then ; it was a
good school. Touchard came in the end to prefer giving me a
kick to slapping me in the face, and six months later he even
began to be affectionate ; only he never failed to beat me once
a month or so to remind me not to forget myself. He soon let
me sit with the other boys, too, and allowed me to play with
them,but not once during those two and a half years did Touchard
forget the difference in our social positions, and from time to
time, though not very frequently, he employed me in menial
tasks, I verily believe, to remind me of it.

" I was running away ; that's to say, I was on the point of
running away for five months after those first two months. I
have always been slow in taking action. When I got into bed
and pulled the quilt over me, I began thinking of you at once,
Andrey Petrovitch, only of you, of no one else ; I don't in the
least know why it was so. I dreamed about you too. I used
always to be passionately imagining that you would walk in,
and I would rush up to you and you would take me out of that
place, and bring me home with you to the same study, and that
we would go to the theatre again, and so on. Above all, that we
should not part again—that was the chief thing ! As soon as I
had to wake up in the morning the jeers and contempt of the
boys began again ; one of them actually began beating me and
making me put on his boots for him ; he called me the vilest

names, particularly aiming at making my origin clear to me, to the diversion of all who heard him. When at last Touchard himself became comprehensible, something unbearable began in my soul. I felt that I should never be forgiven here. Oh, I was beginning by degrees to understand what it was they would not forgive me and of what I was guilty! And so at last I resolved to run away. For two whole months I dreamed of it incessantly; at last—it was September—I made up my mind. I waited for Saturday, when my schoolfellows used to go home for the week-end, and meanwhile I secretly and carefully got together a bundle of the most necessary things; all the money I had was two roubles. I meant to wait till dusk; 'then I will go downstairs,' I thought, 'and I'll go out and walk away!' Where? I knew that Andronikov had moved to Petersburg, and I resolved that I would look for Mme. Fanariotov's house in Arbaty; 'I'll spend the night walking or sitting somewhere, and in the morning I'll ask some one in the courtyard of the house, where Andrey Petrovitch is now, and if not in Moscow, in what town or country. They will be sure to tell me. I'll walk away, and then ask some one, somewhere else, by which gate to go out to reach such a town; and then I'll go and walk and walk, I shall keep on walking; I shall sleep somewhere under the bushes; I shall eat nothing but bread, and for two roubles I can get bread enough for a long time.'

"I could not manage to run away on Saturday, however; I had to wait till next day, Sunday, and as luck would have it, Touchard and his wife were going away somewhere for the Sunday; there was no one left in the house but Agafya and me. I awaited the night in terrible agitation, I remember. I sat at the window in the schoolroom, looking out at the dusty street, the little wooden houses, and the few passers-by. Touchard lived in an out-of-the-way street; from the windows I could see one of the city gates; 'Isn't it the one?' I kept wondering. The sun set in a red glow, the sky was so cold-looking, and a piercing wind was stirring up the dust, just as it is to-day. It was quite dark at last; I stood before the ikon and began to pray, only very, very quickly, I was in haste; I caught up my bundle, and went on tip-toe down the creaking stairs, horribly afraid that Agafya would hear me from the kitchen. The door was locked, I turned the key, and at once a dark, dark night loomed black before me like a boundless perilous unknown land, and the wind snatched off my cap. I was just going out on the same side of the pavement; I heard a hoarse volley of oaths from a drunken man in the street. I stood, looked, and slowly turned, slowly went upstairs, slowly took off my things, put down my little bundle and lay down flat, without tears, and without thoughts, and it was from that moment, Andrey Petrovitch, that I began to think. It was from that moment that I realized that besides being a lackey, I was a coward, too, and my real development began ! "

" Well, I see through you once and for all from this minute," cried Tatyana Pavlovna, jumping up from her seat, and so suddenly, that I was utterly unprepared for it ; " yes, you were not only a lackey then, you are a lackey now ; you've the soul of a lackey ! Why should not Andrey Petrovitch have apprenticed you to a shoemaker ? it would have been an act of charity to have taught you a trade ! Who would have expected more than that of him ? Your father, Makar Ivanovitch, asked—in fact, he insisted—that you, his children, should not be brought up to be above your station. Why, you think nothing of his having educated you for the university, and that through him you have received class rights. The little rascals teased him, to be sure, so he has sworn to avenge himself on humanity. . . . You scoundrel ! "

I must confess I was struck dumb by this outburst, I got up and stood for some time staring and not knowing what to say.

" Well, certainly Tatyana Pavlovna has told me something new," I said at last, turning resolutely to Versilov ; " yes, certainly I am such a lackey that I can't be satisfied with Versilov's not having apprenticed me to a shoemaker ; even ' rights ' did not touch me. I wanted the whole of Versilov, I wanted a father . . . that's what I asked for—like a regular lackey. Mother, I've had it on my conscience for eight years—when you came to Moscow alone to see me at Touchard's, the way I received you then, but I have no time to speak of it now. Tatyana Pavlovna won't let me tell my story, Good-bye till to-morrow, mother; we may see each other again. Tatyana Pavlovna ! what if I am so utterly a lackey that I am quite unable to admit the possibility of a man's marrying again when his wife is alive ? Yet you know that all but happened to Andrey Petrovitch at Ems ! Mother, if you don't want to stay with a husband who may take another wife to-morrow, remember you have a son who promises to be a dutiful son to you for ever; remember, and let us go away, only on condition that it is ' either he, or I ' will you ? I don't ask you for an answer at once, of course : I know that such questions can't be answered straight off."

But I could not go on, partly because I was excited and confused. My mother turned pale and her voice seemed to fail her : she could not utter a word. Tatyana Pavlovna said something in a very loud voice and at great length which I could not make out, and twice she pushed me on the shoulder with her fist. I only remember that she shouted that " my words were a sham, the broodings of a petty soul, counted over and turned inside out." Versilov sat motionless and very serious, he was not smiling. I went upstairs to my room. The last thing I saw as I went out was the reproach in my sister's eyes ; she shook her head at me sternly.

CHAPTER VII

1

I DESCRIBE all these scenes without sparing myself, in order to recall it clearly and revive the impression. As I went up to my attic, I did not know in the least whether I ought to be ashamed or triumphant as though I had done my duty. Had I been ever so little more experienced, I should have had a misgiving that the least doubt in such cases must be taken as a bad sign. but another fact threw me out in my reckoning : I don't know what I was pleased about, but I felt awfully pleased, in spite of my being uncertain, and of my realizing distinctly that I had not come off with flying colours downstairs. Even Tatyana Pavlovna's spiteful abuse of me struck me as funny and amusing and did not anger me at all. Probably all this was because I had anyway broken my chains and for the first time felt myself free.

I felt, too, that I had weakened my position : how I was to act in regard to the letter about the inheritance was more obscure than ever. Now it would be certainly taken for granted that I was revenging myself on Versilov. But while all this discussion was going on downstairs I had made up my mind to submit the question of the letter to an impartial outsider and to appeal to Vassin for his decision, or, failing Vassin, to take it to some one else. I had already made up my mind to whom. I would go to see Vassin once, for that occasion only, I thought to myself, and then —then I would vanish for a long while, for some months, from the sight of all, especially of Vassin. Only my mother and sister I might see occasionally. It was all inconsistent and confused; I felt that I had done something, though not in the right way, and I was satisfied : I repeat, I was awfully pleased anyway.

I meant to go to bed rather early, foreseeing I should have a lot to do next day. Besides finding a lodging and moving, I had another project which in one way or another I meant to carry out. But the evening was not destined to end without surprises, and Versilov succeeded in astonishing me extremely. He had certainly never been into my attic, and lo and behold, before I had been an hour in my room I heard his footsteps on the ladder : he called to me to show a light. I took a candle, and stretching out my hand, which he caught hold of, I helped him up.

"*Merci,* my dear fellow; I've never climbed up here before, not even when I took the lodgings. I imagined what sort of place it was, but I never supposed it was quite such a hole as this." He stood in the middle of my attic, looking around with curiosity. "Why, this is a coffin, a regular coffin."

It really had a resemblance to the inside of a coffin, and I positively admired the way he had described it in one word. It was a long narrow box of a room, the ceiling sloped away from the wall at the height of my shoulder, and the top of it was within easy reach of my hand. Versilov unconsciously stood stooping, afraid of hitting his head against the ceiling ; he did not knock it, however, and, finally more or less reassured, he seated himself on the sofa, where my bed had already been made up. But I did not sit down, I looked at him in the greatest amazement.

"Your mother says she does not know whether to take the money you gave her this evening for your board for the month. But for a coffin like this, instead of taking your money, we ought rather to offer you compensation ! I have never been up and . . . . I can't conceive how you can exist here ! "

"I am used to it. But what I can't get used to is seeing you in my room after what has just happened downstairs."

"O, yes, you were distinctly rude downstairs, but . . . I, too, have a special object which I will explain to you, though indeed there is nothing extraordinary in my coming ; even the scene downstairs is in the regular order of things ; but for mercy's sake do explain this : what you told us downstairs after preparing us and approaching the subject so solemnly was surely not all you meant to disclose or communicate ? Was there really nothing else ? "

"That was all, or we'll assume it was all."

" It's not much, my dear fellow : I must own that from your beginning and the way you urged us to laugh, in fact from your eagerness to talk, I expected more."

" But that does not matter to you, surely ? "

" But I speak simply from a sense of proportion; it was not worth making such a fuss about, it was quite disproportionate; you've been sitting mute a whole month, preparing to speak, and when it comes—it's nothing."

" I meant to say more, but I am ashamed of having said even that. Not everything can be put into words, there are things it's better never to say at all ; I said a good deal, but you did not understand."

"Why, so you, too, are sometimes distressed at the impossibility of putting thought into words ! That's a noble sorrow, my dear fellow, and it's only vouchsafed to the elect : the fool is always satisfied with what he has said, and always, too, says more than he need ; they love to have something to spare."

" As I see I did, for instance ; I said more than I need : I asked for the ' whole of Versilov,' that was a great deal too much ; I don't need Versilov at all."

" My dear fellow, I see you want to retrieve your failure downstairs. It is very evident you repent it, and as repentance among us always involves immediately attacking some one, you are very anxious to hit hard this time. I have come too soon, and you have not yet cooled down, and besides you are not very good at standing criticism. But sit down, for mercy's sake ; I have come to tell you something ; thank you, that's right. From what you said to your mother, as you went out, it's quite clear that it is better for us to separate. I have come to persuade you to do so as gently and with as little fuss as possible, to avoid grieving and alarming your mother any further. My coming up here even has cheered her. She believes in a way that we may still be reconciled and that everything will go on as before. I imagine that if we were to laugh heartily once or twice we should fill their timid hearts with delight. They may be simple souls, but they are sincere and true-hearted in their love. Why not humour them on occasion ? Well, that's one thing. Another thing : why should we necessarily part thirsting for revenge, gnashing our teeth, vowing vengeance, etc. Of course there is no manner of need to fall on each other's necks, but we might part, so to say, with mutual respect, mightn't we ? "

" That's all nonsense ! I promise to go away without a fuss—

and that's enough. And is it for my mother's sake you are anxious ? But it strikes me that my mother's peace of mind has absolutely nothing to do with it, and you are simply saying that."

" You don't believe it ? "

" You talk to me just as though I were a baby."

" I am ready to beg your pardon a thousand times over for that, in fact for everything you bring up against me, for those years of your childhood and the rest of it, but, *cher enfant,* what will be the use of it ? You are too clever to want to be put into such a stupid position. To say nothing of my not understanding, so far, the exact nature of your accusations. What is it you blame me for in reality ? For your not having been born a Versilov ? Bah ! You laugh contemptuously and wave your hands, so that's not it ? "

" No, I assure you. I assure you I don't think it an honour to be called Versilov."

" Let's leave honour out of the question ; and, besides, your answer was bound to be democratic ; but if so, what are you blaming me for ? "

" Tatyana Pavlovna told me just now all I needed to know, and had always failed to grasp, till she spoke. That is, that you did not apprentice me to a shoemaker, and that consequently I had to be grateful, too. I can't understand why it is I am not grateful, even now, even after I have been taught my lesson. Isn't it the pride of your race showing itself in me, Andrey Petrovitch ? "

" Probably not, and apart from that, you must admit that by your sallies downstairs you've only bullied and tormented your mother instead of crushing me, as you intended. Yet I should have thought it was not for you to judge her. Besides, what wrong has she done you ? Explain to me, too, by the way, my dear fellow : for what reason and with what object did you spread abroad that you were illegitimate, at your boarding school and at the grammar school, and everywhere you have been, to every casual stranger, as I hear you have ? I hear that you did this with a peculiar relish. And yet that's all nonsense, and a revolting calumny : you are legitimate, a Dolgoruky, the son of Makar Ivanovitch Dolgoruky, a respectable man, remarkable for his intelligence and character. That you have received a superior education is entirely owing to your former master, Versilov, and what's the upshot of it ? By proclaiming your illegitimacy, which is a calumny in itself, you first and foremost gave away your mother's secret, and from a false pride exposed your mother to the criticism of every dirty stranger. My dear fellow, that was very discreditable, especially as your mother is in no way to blame : she has a nature of the greatest purity, and that her name is not Versilov is simply because her husband is still living."

" Enough, I entirely agree with you, and I have enough faith in your intelligence to hope that you won't go on rating at me too long for it. You are so fond of moderation ; and yet there's a moderation in all things, even in your sudden love for my mother. I'll tell you what would be better : since you have gone so far as to come up and see me and mean to spend a quarter of an hour or half an hour with me (I still don't know what for, we'll assume for my mother's peace of mind), and what's more, in spite of the scene downstairs, seem so eager to talk to me, you had better tell me about my father—tell me about Makar Ivanovitch the pilgrim. I want to hear from you about him : I have been intending to ask you for some time past. Now that we are parting perhaps for a long time, I should very much like to get from you an answer to another question : has it really been impossible for you during these twenty years to affect my mother's traditional ideas—and now my sister's, too—so as to dissipate by your civilizing influence the primitive darkness of her environment ? Oh, I am not speaking of the purity of her nature. She's infinitely nobler than you, morally anyway, excuse my saying so . . . but she's only an infinitely noble corpse. Versilov is the only one living, everything else about him and everything connected with him exists only on the express condition of having the honour to nourish him with its force, its living sap. But I suppose she, too, was once alive, wasn't she ? I suppose you loved something in her, didn't you ? I suppose she was once a woman ? "

" My dear fellow, she never was, if you will have it," he assured me, at once dropping into his habitual manner with me, with which I was so familiar, and by which I was so enraged, that is he was apparently all sincerity and open-heartedness, but if one looked more closely there was nothing in him but the deepest irony : "she never was. The Russian woman never is a woman."

" Is the Polish woman, the French woman ? Or the Italian, the passionate Italian, that's the sort to fascinate the civilized upper-class Russian of the type of Versilov ? "

" Well, I certainly did not expect to meet a Slavophil," laughed Versilov.

I remember his story, word for word : he began talking with great readiness indeed, and with evident pleasure. It was quite clear to me, that he had come up not to have a gossip with me, and not to pacify my mother either, but with some other object.

2

" Your mother and I have spent these twenty years together in silence," he began, prattling on (it was utterly affected and unnatural), " and all that passed between us took place in silence. The chief characteristic of our twenty years' connection has been its—dumbness. I believe we have never once quarrelled. It is true I have often gone away and left her alone, but it has always ended in my coming back. *Nous revenons toujours ;* indeed, it's a fundamental characteristic of men ; it's due to their magnanimity. If marriage depended on women alone, not a single marriage would last. Meekness, submissiveness, self-abasement, and at the same time firmness, strength, real strength, that's your mother's character. Take note, that she's the best of all the women I've met in my life. And that she has strength I can bear witness : I have seen how that strength has supported her. When it's a matter, I won't say of convictions—convictions are out of the question—but what they look upon as convictions, and so, to their thinking, sacred, she is ready to face torture. Well, I leave you to judge, whether I am much like a torturer. That's why I have preferred to remain silent about almost everything, and not simply because it was more convenient, and I confess I don't regret it. In this way our life has gone on of itself on broad and humane lines, so that indeed I take no credit to myself for it. I must say by the way in parenthesis, that for some reason she never believed in my humanity, and so was always in a tremor ; but, though she has trembled, she has never given in to any advanced ideas. They are so good at that, while we never understand that sort of thing, and in fact they are much better at managing things for themselves than we are. They are able to go on living their own lives in positions most unnatural to them, and in positions most strange to them they remain always the same. But we can't do that."

" Who are ' they ' ? I don't quite understand you."

" The people, my dear fellow, I'm speaking of the common people. They have shown their great living force, and their historical breadth both morally and politically. But, to come back to ourselves, I may remark about your mother, that she is not always dumb; your mother sometimes speaks, but she speaks in such a way that you see at once that you simply waste time in talking to her, even though you might have been preparing her for five years beforehand. Moreover, she makes the most unexpected objections. Note again, that I am far from calling her a fool; on the contrary, she has intelligence of a sort, and even remarkable intelligence; though perhaps you will not believe in her intelligence . . ."

"Why not? What I don't believe is that you really believe in her intelligence yourself, and are not pretending."

"Yes? You look upon me as such a chameleon? My dear fellow, I am allowing you a little too much licence . . . like a spoilt son . . . So be it for the time."

"Tell me if you can the truth about my father."

"About Makar Ivanovitch? Makar Ivanovitch was, as you are aware, a house-serf, who, so to speak, had a yearning for glory of a sort . . ."

"I bet that at this minute you feel envious of him!"

"On the contrary, my dear fellow, on the contrary, and if you like I am very glad to see you in such a flippant mood; I swear that I am in a penitent frame of mind, and just now, at this moment, I regret a thousand times over all that happened twenty years ago. And besides, God knows, it all happened quite accidentally . . . well, and, so far as in me lay, humanely too; —as I conceived of an act of humanity in those days anyway. Oh, in those days we were all boiling over with zeal for doing good, for serving the public weal, for a higher ideal; we disapproved of class distinctions, of the privileges of our rank, of our property and even of usury, at least some of us did. . . . I declare we did. There were not many of us, but we said good things, and sometimes, I assure you, did good things, too."

"That was when you sobbed on his shoulder."

"I am ready to agree with you on every point beforehand. By the way, you heard of that shoulder from me, and so, at this moment, you are making spiteful use of my frankness and confidence in you; but you must admit that there was not so much harm in that episode as might seem at the first glance, especially for that period. To be sure we were only making a beginning then. Of course it was a pose, but I did not know at the time that it was a pose. Have you, for instance, never posed in practical affairs?"

" I was rather sentimental downstairs, just now, and as I came up here I felt horribly ashamed at the thought that you might imagine I had been posing. It is true in some cases, though one's feelings are sincere, one makes a display of one's feelings. I swear that everything I said downstairs was absolutely genuine."

" That's exactly it ; you have very successfully defined it in a phrase, ' though one's feelings are sincere one makes a display of one's self ' ; but do you know it was just the same with me. Though I was making a display of them, my sobs were perfectly genuine. I don't deny that Makar Ivanovitch might, if he had been wittily disposed, have looked upon my sobs as the climax of mockery, but in those days he was too honest to be so clear-sighted. I don't know whether he felt sorry for me or not. I remember that I had a great desire that he should."

" Do you know," I interrupted him," you're jeering now when you say that ? And in fact, all this last month whenever you have talked to me, you have been jeering. Why have you done so, whenever you have talked with me ? "

" You think so ? " he answered mildly ; " you are very suspicious ; however, if I do laugh it's not at you, or, at least not only at you, don't be uneasy. But I am not laughing now, and then— in short I did everything I could then, and, believe me, not for my personal advantage. We, that is, superior people, unlike the common people, do not know how to act for our personal advantage : on the contrary, we made a mess of it as far as we possibly could, and I suspect that that was considered among us in those days ' our higher advantage,' in an exalted sense of course. The present generation of advanced people are much keener on the main chance than we were. Even before our ' sin ' I explained the whole position to Makar Ivanovitch with extraordinary directness. I am ready to admit now, that a great deal need not have been explained at all, especially with such directness ; to say nothing of humanity it would have been far more polite, but . . . but there's no pulling up when you once begin dancing, and want to cut a fine caper. And perhaps our cravings for the fine and exalted only amount to that in reality. All my life I have never been able to make up my mind about it. However, that is too deep a subject for our superficial conversation, but I assure you I am sometimes ready to die with shame, when I recall it. I offered him at the time three thousand roubles, and I remember he did not say a word and I did all the talking. Only fancy, I imagined that he was afraid of me, that

is of my rights of ownership over him, and I remember I did my
utmost to reassure him ; I kept trying to persuade him to have
no apprehension, but to tell me his wishes frankly and without
sparing me. By way of guarantee I promised him, that if he did
not accept my terms, that is three thousand with freedom (for
himself and his wife, of course)—and a journey wherever he
pleased (without his wife, of course)—then let him say so straight
out, and I would at once give him his freedom, let his wife go,
and compensate them both with the same three thousand, I believe, and they should not go away from me, but I would go away
myself in solitude for three years to Italy. *Mon ami*, I should
not have taken Mlle. Sapozhkov with me to Italy, you may be sure
of that. I was extremely pure at that epoch. And, do you know,
Makar Ivanovitch knew perfectly well that I should do as I
promised ; but he still remained silent, and only when I was about
to throw myself on his neck, for the third time, he drew back,
waved his hand, and went out of the room with a certain lack
of ceremony,indeed, which I assure you surprised me at the time.
I caught a glimpse of myself in the looking-glass and I can't
forget it.

" As a rule when they don't speak it's worst of all, and he was a
gloomy character, and I must confess that far from feeling sure
of him I was awfully afraid of him, when I summoned him to my
study. In that class there are types, and many of them, who
are, so to speak, the very incarnation of all that's ill-bred, and
one's more afraid of that than a beating. Sic. And what a risk
I was running, what a risk ! Why, what if he had begun shouting
for all the servants to hear, had howled, this village Uriah, what
would have become of me, such a juvenile David, and what
should I have done then ? That's why I trotted out the three
thousand first of all, that was instinctive ; but luckily I was mistaken : this Makar Ivanovitch was something quite different."

" Tell me, had you ' sinned ' then ? You said just now that
you summoned the husband beforehand."

"Well, do you see . . . that is . . . as one understands
it . . ."

" Oh, you had then. You said just now you were mistaken in
him, that he was something different ; how different ? "

"Well, how exactly I don't know to this day, but somehow
different, and, do you know, positively very decent. I think so
because in the end I felt more than ever ashamed to face him. Next
day he agreed to the journey, without any words, but without,

of course, forgetting one of the inducements I had offered him."

"He took the money ? "

"I should think so ! And you know, my dear fellow, in that point he surprised me too. I had not, of course, three thousand at the time in my pocket, but I procured seven hundred and handed it over to him as the first instalment ; and what do you think ? He demanded the remaining two thousand three hundred from me in the form of a credit note made payable to a certain merchant for security. And two years later, by means of that credit note, he got the money out of me before a court, and with interest too, so that he surprised me again, especially as he had literally gone collecting funds for building a church, and has been a pilgrim ever since, that is, for the last twenty years. I don't understand what a pilgrim should want money of his own for. . . . money which is such a worldly thing. . . . I offered the money at the minute of course with perfect sincerity, and, so to speak, in the first flush of feeling, but afterwards, after the lapse of so many minutes, I might naturally have thought better of it . . . and might have reckoned that he would spare me . . . or, so to say, spare *us*, me and her, and would have waited for a time at least. But he lost no time however . . ."

Here I must make a necessary note. If my mother were to outlive M. Versilov, she would have been left literally without a farthing in her old age, had it not been for Makar Ivanovitch's three thousand, which had been doubled long ago by the accumulation of interest, and which he had the previous year left her intact in his will. He had seen through Versilov even in those days.

"You told me once that Makar Ivanovitch had come several times on a visit to you, and always stayed at mother's lodgings ? "

"Yes, my dear boy : and I must confess at first I was awfully frightened of these visits. He has come six or seven times altogether during this period, that is, the last twenty years, and on the first occasions I used to hide myself if I were in the house when he arrived. At first I could not make out what it meant, and why he had turned up. But afterwards I thought that from certain points of view it was by no means so stupid on his part. Afterwards it somehow occurred to me to feel curious about him ; I came out to have a look at him, and formed, I assure you, a very original impression of him. This was on his third or fourth visit, at the time when I had just been appointed a mediator, and when, of course, I was getting all my energies to work to study Russia. I heard from him a very great deal that was new to me. I found in him, besides, what I had never expected to find: a sort of benign serenity, an evenness of temper, and what was more surprising than anything, something almost like gaiety. Not the faintest allusion to *that* (*tu comprends*) and a very great capacity for talking sense, and talking extremely well, that is, with none of that silly servantish profundity, which I confess to you I can't endure, democratic as I am, and with none of those far-fetched Russian expressions which 'the genuine Russian peasant' makes use of in novels and on the stage. At the same time very little about religion, unless one begins upon the subject, and most charming descriptions of the monastery and monastic life, if one asks questions about it. And above all—respectfulness, that modest courtesy, just that courtesy which is essential for the truest equality, and without which, indeed, in my opinion, one cannot be really superior. The truest good-breeding is in such cases attained through the complete absence of conceit, and the man shows himself secure in his self-respect in his own station of life whatever that may be, and whatever fate may befall him. This power of respecting one's self in one's own position is extremely rare, as rare, anyway, as real personal dignity. . . . You will see that for yourself if you live long enough. But what struck me most of all, especially later on, and not at the beginning," added Versilov, " was the fact that this Makar had an extraordinary stateliness, and was, I assure you, very handsome. It is true he was old, but—

Dark visaged, tall, erect,

simple and dignified ; I actually wondered how my poor Sonia could have preferred me *then ;* at that time he was fifty, but he was still a fine fellow, and compared with him I was such a featherhead. I remember, however, that he was unpardonably grey even then ; so he must have been just as grey-headed when he married her. . . . Perhaps that had an influence."

Versilov had a very nasty aristocratic trick: after saying (when he could not help it) some particularly clever and fine things, he would all at once intentionally cap them with some stupid saying such as this remark about Makar Ivanovitch's grey hair, and the influence it had on my mother. He did this on purpose probably without knowing why he did it, from a silly snobbish habit. To hear him, one would suppose he was speaking quite seriously, and all the while he was posing to himself, or laughing.

3

I don't know why but I was suddenly overcome by an intense exasperation, In fact, I recall with extreme dissatisfaction some of my behaviour during those minutes ; I suddenly got up from my seat.

" I tell you what," I said : " you say you came up chiefly that my mother might imagine we were reconciled. Time enough has passed for her to imagine it ; will you be so good as to leave me alone ? "

He flushed slightly and got up from his place.

" My dear boy, you are extremely unceremonious with me. However, good-bye ; there is no winning love by force. I will only venture upon one question : do you really want to leave the prince ? "

" Aha ! I knew you had some object in your mind. . . . ."

" That is, you suspect I came up to induce you to stay with the prince, for some purpose of my own. But do you suppose, my dear fellow, that I sent for you from Moscow for some purpose of my own ? Oh ! how suspicious you are. On the contrary, I was anxious for your good in every way. And even now, since my position has so improved, I should have liked you to let me and your mother help you sometimes."

" I don't like you, Versilov."

" And ' Versilov ' too ! By the way, I greatly regret that I can't transmit you the name, seeing that in reality constitutes my whole offence, if offence there is, doesn't it ? but again I couldn't marry a married woman, could I ? "

" That was why, I suppose, you wanted to marry an unmarried one ? "

A slight spasm passed over his face.

" You are thinking of Ems. Listen, Arkady, you went so far as to allude to that downstairs, pouring contempt upon me before your mother. You must know that that's where you make your greatest mistake. You know nothing whatever of what happened with Lidya Ahmakov. You don't know how much your mother had to do with it all, although she was not with me at the time, and if I have ever seen a good woman it was when

I looked at your mother then. But that's enough; all that is a secret still, and you—you talk of what you don't know, and have heard about from outsiders."

" Only to-day the prince told me that you have a special fancy for unfledged girls."

"The prince said that ?"

" Yes, listen, would you like me to tell you exactly what you have come up to me for ? I have been sitting here all this time wondering what was the secret object of this visit, and now I believe I've guessed it."

He was just going out, but he stopped and turned to me in expectation.

" I blurted out just now that Touchard's letter to Tatyana Pavlovna was among Andronikov's papers, and at his death came into the hands of Marie Ivanovna. I saw how your face suddenly twitched, and I only guessed why just now, when your face twitched again in the same way. The idea suddenly occurred to you that if one letter in Andronikov's keeping had come into Marie Ivanovna's hands, why shouldn't another ? And Andronikov might have left very important letters, mightn't he ? "

" So I came up here hoping to make you talk about it ? "

" You know that yourself."

He turned very pale.

" You did not imagine that of yourself ; there's a woman's influence in it ; and what hatred there is in your words—in your coarse supposition ! "

" A woman ? I have seen that woman for the first time to-day ! Perhaps it's just to spy on her you want me to stay on with the old prince."

" I see, though, that you will do well in your new line. Isn't that perhaps ' your idea ' ? Go on, my dear fellow, you have an unmistakable gift for detective work. Given talent, one must perfect it."

He paused to take breath.

" Take care, Versilov, don't make me your enemy ! "

" My dear fellow, in such cases no one gives utterance to his last thoughts, but keeps them to himself. And with that, show me a light, if you please ; though you are my enemy you are not so much so as to want me to break my neck, I suppose. *Tiens, mon ami*, only fancy," he went on, as he descended the ladder, " all this month I have been taking you for a good-natured

I

fellow.   You so want to live and are so thirsting for life that I do believe three lives would not be enough for you : one can see that in your face, and people like that are generally good-natured. And how mistaken I've been ! " '

4

I can't express how my heart ached when I was left alone ; it was as though I had cut off a piece of my own living flesh ! Why I had so suddenly lost my temper, and why I had so insulted him—so persistently and intentionally—I couldn't say now ; nor could I at the time, of course.   And how pale he had turned !   And who knows, perhaps that paleness was the expression of the truest and purest .feeling and the deepest sorrow, and not of anger or of offence.   I always fancied that there had been a moment when he really loved me.   Why, why could I not believe that now, especially when so much had been made clear ?

I had flown into a sudden fury and actually driven him away, partly perhaps by my sudden guess that he had come to find out whether there were not another letter left by Andronikov in Marie Ivanovna's possession.   That he must have been on the lookout for those letters, and that he was on the look-out for them I knew.   But who knows, perhaps at that minute I had made a horrible blunder !   And who knows, perhaps, by that blunder I had led him to think of Marie Ivanovna and the possibility of her having letters.

And finally, there was something else that was strange : again he had repeated word for word my own thought (about three lives), which I had expressed to Kraft that evening, and, what is more, in my very words.   The coincidence was of course a chance again, but how he knew the inmost core of my nature ; what insight, what penetration !   But if he so well understood one thing, why was it he utterly failed to understand something else ?   Was it possible he was not pretending, could he really be incapable of divining that it was not the noble rank of a Versilov I wanted, that it was not my birth I could not forgive him, but that all my life I had wanted Versilov himself, the whole man, the father, and that this idea had become part of myself.   Was it possible that so subtle a man could be so crude and so stupid ?   And if not, why did he drive me to fury, why did he pretend ?

CHAPTER VIII

1

I TRIED to get up as early as possible in the morning. As a rule we, that is my mother, my sister and I, used to get up about eight o'clock. Versilov used to lie comfortably in bed till half-past nine. Punctually at half-past eight my mother used to bring me up my coffee. But this time I slipped out of the house at eight o'clock without waiting for it. I had the day before mapped out roughly my plan of action for the whole of this day. In spite of my passionate resolve to carry out this plan I felt that there was a very great deal of it that was uncertain and indefinite in its most essential points. That was why I lay all night in a sort of half-waking state; I had an immense number of dreams, as though I were light-headed, and I hardly fell asleep properly all night. In spite of that I got up feeling fresher and more confident than usual. I was particularly anxious not to meet my mother. I could not have avoided speaking to her on a certain subject, and I was afraid of being distracted from the objects I was pursuing by some new and unexpected impression.

It was a cold morning and a damp, milky mist hovered over everything. I don't know why, but I always like the early workaday morning in Petersburg in spite of its squalid air; and the self-centred people, always absorbed in thought, and hurrying on their affairs, have a special attraction for me at eight o'clock in the morning. As I hasten on my road I particularly like either asking some one a practical question, or being asked one by some passer-by : both question and answer are always brief, clear, and to the point ; they are spoken without stopping and almost always in a friendly manner, and there is a greater readiness to answer than at any other hour. In the middle of the day, or in the evening, the Petersburger is far more apt to be abusive or jeering. It is quite different early in the morning, before work has begun, at the soberest and most serious hour of the day. I have noticed that.

I set off again for the Petersburg Side. As I had to be back in Fontanka by twelve o'clock to see Vassin (who was always more likely to be at home at midday), I hurried on without stopping, though I had a great longing to have a cup of coffee. It was absolutely necessary to find Efim Zvyerev at home too ;

I went to him and almost missed him ; he had finished his coffee and was just ready to go out.

"What brings you here so often ? " was how he greeted me without getting up from his seat.

" I will explain that directly."

The early morning everywhere, including Petersburg, has a sobering effect on a man's nature. Some of the passionate dreams of night evaporate completely with the light and chill of morning, and it has happened to me myself sometimes to recall in the morning my dreams and even my actions of the previous night, with shame and self-reproach. But I will remark, however, in passing, I consider a Petersburg morning—which might be thought the most prosaic on the terrestrial globe—almost the most fantastic in the world. That is my personal view, or rather impression, but I am prepared to defend it. On such a Petersburg morning, foul, damp and foggy, the wild dream of some Herman out of Pushkin's " Queen of Spades " (a colossal figure, an extraordinary and regular Petersburg type —the type of the Petersburg period !) would, I believe, be more like solid reality. A hundred times over, in such a fog, I have been haunted by a strange but persistent fancy : " What if this fog should part and float away, would not all this rotten and slimy town go with it, rise up with the fog, and vanish like smoke, and the old Finnish marsh be left as before, and in the midst of it, perhaps, to complete the picture, a bronze horseman on a panting, overdriven steed." In fact I cannot find words for my sensations, for all this is fantastic after all—poetic, and therefore nonsensical ; nevertheless I have often been and often am haunted by an utterly senseless question : " Here they are all flitting to and fro, but how can one tell, perhaps all this is some one's dream, and there is not one real person here, nor one real action. Some one who is dreaming all this will suddenly wake up—and everything will suddenly disappear." But I am digressing.

I must say by way of preface that there are projects and dreams in every one's experience so eccentric that they might well be taken at first sight for madness. It was with such a phantasy in my mind that I arrived that morning at Efim's,— I went to Efim because I had no one else in Petersburg to whom I could apply on this occasion. Yet Efim was the last person to whom I should have gone with such a proposition if I had had any choice. When I was sitting opposite him, I was actually struck myself with the thought that I was the incarnation of fever and delirium, sitting opposite the incarnation of prose and the golden mean. Yet on my side there was an idea and true feeling, while on his there was nothing but the practical conviction, that things were not done like that. In short I explained to him briefly and clearly that I had absolutely no one else in Petersburg whom I could send by way of a second in a matter vitally affecting my honour ; that he, Efim, was an old comrade, and therefore had no right to refuse, and that I wanted to challenge a lieutenant in the Guards, Prince Sokolsky, because more than a year ago he had given my father a slap in the face at Ems. I may mention by the way that Efim knew all the details of my family circumstances, my relations with Versilov, and almost all that I knew myself of Versilov's career ; I had on various occasions talked to him of my private affairs, except, of course, of certain secrets. He sat and listened as his habit was, all ruffling up his feathers like a sparrow in a cage, silent and serious, with his puffy face and his untidy, flaxen-white hair. A set smile of mockery never left his lips. This smile was all the nastier for being quite unintentional and unconscious ; it was evident that he genuinely and sincerely considered himself at that moment vastly superior to me in intellect and character. I suspected, too, that he despised me for the scene the evening before at Dergatchev's ; that was bound to be so. Efim was the crowd, Efim was the man in the street, and the man in the street has no reverence for anything but success.

" And Versilov knows nothing of this ? " he asked.

" Of course not."

" Then what right have you to meddle in his affairs ? That's the first question. And the second one is, what do you want to show by it ? "

I was prepared for the objection, and at once explained to him that it was not so stupid as he supposed. To begin with, the insolent prince would be shown that there are people, even in our class, who know what is meant by honour ; and secondly, Versilov would be put to shame and learn a lesson. And in the third place, what mattered most of all, even if Versilov had been right in refusing to challenge him in accordance with his convictions at the time, he would see that there was some one who was capable of feeling the insult to him so keenly that he accepted it as an insult to himself, and was prepared to lay down his life for his, Versilov's, interests ... although he was leaving him for ever....

" Wait a minute, don't shout, my aunt does not like it. Tell me, is it this same Prince Sokolsky that Versilov is at law with about a will ? If so, this will be quite a new and original way of winning a lawsuit—to kill your opponent in a duel."

I explained to him *en toutes lettres*, that he was simply silly and impertinent, and that if his sarcastic grin was growing broader and broader, it only showed his conceit and common-placeness, and that he was incapable of imagining that I had had the lawsuit in my mind from the very beginning, and that reflection on that subject was not confined to his sagacity. Then I informed him that the case was already decided, and, moreover, it had not been brought by Prince Sokolsky but by the Princes Sokolsky, so that if a Prince Sokolsky were killed the others would be left, but that no doubt it would be necessary to put off the challenge till the end of the time within which an appeal was possible, not that the Solkoskys would as a fact appeal, but simply as a matter of good form. When the latest possible date for an appeal had passed, the challenge would follow ; that I had come about it now, not that the duel would take place immediately, but that I must be prepared at any rate in time to find a second, if he, Efim, refused, as I knew no one. That was why, I said, I had come.

" Well, come and talk about it then, or else you'll be leading us a wild-goose chase."

He stood up and took his cap.

" So you'll go then ? "

" No, of course I won't."

" Why not ? "

" Well, for one reason if I agreed now that I would go then, you would begin hanging about here every evening till the time for the appeal was over. And besides, it's simply nonsense, and that's all about it. And am I going to mess up my career for you ? Why, Prince Sokolsky will ask me at once : ' Who sent you ? '—' Dolgoruky '—' And what's Dolgoruky got to do with Versilov ? ' And am I to explain your pedigree to him, pray ? Why, he'd burst out laughing ! "

" Then you give him a punch in the face ! "

" But it's all gibberish."

" You're afraid ! You so tall and the strongest at the grammar school ! "

" I'm afraid, of course, I am afraid. Besides, the prince won't fight, for they only fight their equals."

" I am a gentleman, too, by education. I have rights, I am his equal . . . on the contrary, he is not my equal."

" You are a small boy."

" How a small boy ? "

" Just a small boy ; we are both boys but he is grown up."

" You fool ! But I might have been married a year ago by the law."

" Well, get married then, but anyway you are a ——! you will grow up one day ! "

I saw, of course, that he thought fit to jeer at me. I might not indeed have told all this foolish episode, and it would have been better in fact for it to have perished in obscurity ; besides, it's revolting in its pettiness and gratuitousness, though it had rather serious consequences.

But to punish myself still further I will describe it fully. Realizing that Efim was jeering at me, I permitted myself to push him on the shoulder with my right hand, or rather my right fist. Then he took me by the shoulder, turned me upside down and—proved to me conclusively that he was the strongest of us at the grammar school.

2

The reader will doubtless imagine that I was in a terrible state of mind when I came out from Efim's ; he will be mistaken, however. I quite realized that what had happened was only schoolboyishness, but the gravity of my purpose remained unchanged. I got some coffee at Vassilyevsky Island, purposely avoiding the restaurant I had been at the evening before on the Petersburg Side ; the restaurant and its nightingale were doubly hateful to me. It is a strange characteristic of mine that I am capable of hating places and things as though they were people. On the other hand I have happy places in Petersburg, that is places where I have at some time or other been happy. And I am careful of those places, and purposely avoid visiting them as far as possible, that later on when I am alone and unhappy I may go back to them to brood over my griefs and my memories. Over my coffee I did full justice to Efim and his common sense. Yes, he was more practical than I was, but I doubt whether he was in closer touch with reality. A realism that refuses to look beyond the end of its nose is more dangerous than the maddest romanticism, because it is blind. But while I did justice to Efim (who probably at that moment imagined that I was wandering about the streets swearing)—I did not give up one point in my convictions, and I have not to this day. I have seen people who at the first bucket of cold water have abandoned their course of action, and even their idea, and begun laughing themselves at what an hour before they looked upon as sacred. Oh, how easily that is done ! Even if Efim were more right than I in the main, and I were foolish beyond all foolishness and giving myself airs, yet at the very bottom of it all there was a point of view upon which I was right : there was something to be said on my side also, and what is more, too, it was something they could never understand.

I reached Vassin's in Fontanka, near the Semyonovsky bridge, at twelve o'clock punctually, but I did not find him at home. His work was in Vassilyevsky Island, and he was only at home at certain fixed hours, almost always at midday. And as it was a holiday I made sure of finding him ; not finding him I decided to wait, although it was my first visit.

I reasoned that the matter of the letter was a question of conscience, and in choosing Vassin to decide it I was showing him the deepest respect, which no doubt must be flattering to him. Of course, I was really worried by this letter and was genuinely persuaded of the necessity of an outside opinion ; but I suspect that I could have got out of my difficulty without any outside help. And what is more I was aware of that myself ; I had only to give the letter to Versilov, to put it into his hands and then let him do what he liked with it—that would have settled it. To set myself up as judge, as arbitrator in a matter of this sort was indeed utterly irregular. By confining myself to handing over the letter, especially in silence, I should have scored at once, putting myself into a position of superiority over Versilov. For renouncing all the advantages of the inheritance as far as I was concerned (for some part of it would have been sure, sooner or later, to have fallen to me as Versilov's son), I should have secured for ever a superior moral attitude in regard to Versilov's future action. Nobody, on the other hand, could reproach me for ruining the Sokolskys, since the document had no decisive legal value. All this I thought over and made perfectly clear to myself, sitting in Vassin's empty room, and it even occurred to me suddenly that I had come to Vassin's, so thirsting for his advice how to act, simply to show him what a generous and irreproachable person I was, and so to avenge myself for my humiliation before him the previous evening.

As I recognized all this, I felt great vexation ; nevertheless I did not go away, but sat on, though I knew for certain that my vexation would only grow greater every five minutes.

First of all, I began to feel an intense dislike for Vassin's room. " Show me your room and I will tell you your character," one really may say that. Vassin had a furnished room in a flat belonging to people evidently poor, who let lodgings for their living and had other lodgers besides Vassin. I was familiar with poky apartments of this sort, scarcely furnished, yet with pretensions to comfort : there is invariably a soft sofa from the second-hand market, which is dangerous to move ; a washing-stand and an iron bed shut off by a screen. Vassin was evidently the best and the most to be depended on of the lodgers. Lodging-house keepers always have one such best lodger, and particularly try to please him. They sweep and tidy his room more carefully, and hang lithographs over his sofa ; under the table they lay an emaciated-looking rug. People who are fond of stuffy tidiness and, still more, of obsequious deference in their landladies are to be suspected. I felt convinced that Vassin himself was flattered by his position as best lodger. I don't know why, but the sight of those two tables piled up with books gradually enraged me. The books, the papers, the inkstand, all were arrayed with a revolting tidiness, the ideal of which would have coincided with the loftiest conceptions of a German landlady and her maidservant. There were a good many books, not merely magazines and reviews, but real books, and he evidently read them, and he probably sat down to read or to write with an extremely important and precise expression. I don't know why, but I prefer to see books lying about in disorder. Then, at any rate, work is not made into a sacred rite. No doubt Vassin was extremely polite to his visitors, but probably every gesture he made told them plainly, " I will spend an hour and a half with you, and afterwards, when you go away, I'll set to work." No doubt one might have a very interesting conversation with him and hear something new from him, but he would be thinking, " Here we are talking now, and I am interesting you very much, but when you go away, I shall proceed to something more interesting. . . ." Yet I did not go away, but went on sitting there. That I had absolutely no need of his advice I was by now thoroughly convinced.

I stayed for over an hour sitting on one of the two rush-bottom chairs which had been placed by the window. It enraged me, too, that time was passing and that before evening I had to find a lodging. I was so bored that I felt inclined to take up a book, but I did not. At the very thought of distracting my mind I felt more disgusted than ever. For more than an hour there had been an extraordinary silence, when I began gradually and unconsciously to distinguish the sound of whispering, which kept growing louder, and came from somewhere close by, the other side of a door that was blocked up by the sofa. There were two voices, evidently women's, so much I could hear, but I could not distinguish the words. And yet I was so bored that I began to listen. It was obvious that they were talking earnestly and passionately, and that they were not talking about patterns. They were discussing or disputing about something, or one voice was persuading, or entreating, while the other was refusing or protesting. They must have been other lodgers. I soon got tired, and my ear became accustomed to the sound, so that though I went on listening, it was only mechanically, and sometimes quite without remembering that I was listening, when suddenly something extraordinary happened, as though some one had jumped down off a chair on to both feet, or had suddenly leapt up and stamped ; then I heard a moan, then suddenly a shriek, or rather not a shriek but an infuriated animal squeal, reckless whether it could be overheard or not.

I rushed to the door and opened it ; another door at the end of the corridor was opened simultaneously, the door of the landlady's room as I learned later, and from it two inquisitive faces peeped out. The shriek, however, ceased at once, and suddenly the door next to mine opened, and a young woman— so at least she seemed to me—dashed out, and rushed downstairs. The other woman, who was elderly, tried to stop her, but did not succeed, and could only moan after her :

" Olya, Olya, where are you going ? Och ! " But noticing our two open doors, she promptly closed hers, leaving a crack through which she listened till Olya's footsteps had died away completely on the stairs. I turned to my window. All was silence. It was a trivial and perhaps ridiculous incident, and I left off thinking of it.

About a quarter of an hour later I heard in the corridor at Vassin's door a loud and free-and-easy masculine voice. Some one took hold of the door-handle, and opened the door far enough for me to see in the passage a tall man who had already obviously seen and indeed had carefully scrutinized me, although he had not yet entered the room, but still holding the door-handle went on talking to the landlady at the other end of the passage. The landlady called back to him in a thin, piping little voice which betrayed that he was an old acquaintance, respected and valued by her as a visitor of consequence, and a gentleman of a merry disposition. The merry gentleman shouted witticisms, but his theme was only the impossibility of finding Vassin at home. He declared that this was his destiny from his birth up, that he would wait again as before. And all this, no doubt, seemed the height of wit to the landlady. Finally the visitor flung the door wide open and came in.

He was a well-dressed gentleman, evidently turned out by a good tailor, as they say, "like a real gentleman," though there was nothing of "the real gentleman" about him, in spite, I fancy, of his desire to appear one. He was not exactly free and easy, but somehow naturally insolent, which is anyway less offensive than an insolence practised before the looking-glass. His brown, slightly grizzled hair, his black eyebrows, big beard and large eyes instead of helping to define his character, actually gave him something universal, like every one else. This sort of man laughs and is ready to laugh, but for some reason one is never cheerful in his company. He quickly passes from a jocular to a dignified air, from dignity to playfulness or winking, but all this seems somehow put on and causeless. . . . However, there is no need to describe him further. I came later on to know this gentleman more intimately, and therefore I have a more definite impression of him now than when he opened the door and came into the room. However, even now I should find it difficult to say anything exact or definite about him, because the chief characteristic of such people is just their incompleteness, their artificiality and their indefiniteness.

He had scarcely sat down when it dawned upon me that he must be Vassin's stepfather, one M. Stebelkov, of whom I had already heard something, but so casually that I couldn't tell what it was : I could only remember that it was not to his advantage. I knew that Vassin had long ago been left an orphan under this gentleman's control, but that for some years past he had not been under his influence, that their aims and interests were different, and that they lived entirely separated in all respects. It came back to my mind, too, that this Stebelkov had some money, that he was, indeed, something of a speculator and spendthrift; in fact I had probably heard something more definite about him, but I have forgotten. He looked me up and down, without bowing to me, however, put his top hat down on a table in front of the sofa, kicked away the table with an air of authority, and instead of quietly sitting down, flung himself full length on the sofa (on which I had not ventured to sit) so that it positively creaked, and dangling his legs held his right foot up in the air and began admiring the tip of his patent-leather boot. Of course he turned at once to me and stared at me with his big and rather fixed-looking eyes.

" I don't find him in," he gave me a slight nod.

I did not speak.

" Not punctual ! He has his own ideas. From the Petersburg Side ? "

" You mean you've come from the Petersburg Side ? " I asked him in my turn.

" No, I asked whether you had."

" I . . . yes, I have . . . but how did you know ? "

" How did I know ? H'm ! " He winked, but did not deign to explain.

" I don't live on the Petersburg Side, but I've just been there and have come from there."

He remained silent, still with the same significant smile, which I disliked extremely. There was something stupid in his winking.

" From M. Dergatchev's ? " he said at last.

" From Dergatchev's ? " I opened my eyes. He gazed at me triumphantly. " I don't know him."

" H'm ! "

" Well, as you please," I answered. I began to loathe him.

" H'm. . . . To be sure. No, excuse me : you buy a thing at a shop, at another shop next door another man buys something else, and what, do you suppose ? Money from a tradesman who is called a money-lender . . . for money too is an article of sale, and a money-lender is a tradesman too. . . . You follow me ? "

" Certainly I follow."

" A third purchaser comes along, and pointing to one shop, he says, ' This is sound.' Then he points to the other shop and says, ' This is unsound.' What am I to conclude about this purchaser ? "

"How can I tell."

"No, excuse me. I'll take an example, man lives by good example. I walk along the Nevsky Prospect, and observe on the other side of the street a gentleman whose character I should like to investigate more closely. We walk, one each side of the street as far as the gate leading to Morskaya, and there, just where the English shop is, we observe a third gentleman, who has just been run over. Now mark : a fourth gentleman walks up, and wishes to investigate the character of all three of us, including the man who has been run over, from the point of view of practicability and soundness. . . . Do you follow ? "

"Excuse me, with great difficulty."

"Quite so ; just what I thought. I'll change the subject. I was at the springs in Germany, the mineral springs, as I had frequently been before, no matter which springs. I go to drink the waters and see an Englishman. It is difficult as you know to make acquaintance with an Englishman ; two months later, having finished my cure, we were walking, a whole party of us, with alpenstocks on the mountain, no matter what mountain. At a pass there is an étape, the one where the monks make Chartreuse, note that. I meet a native standing in solitude looking about him in silence. I wish to form my conclusions in regard to his soundness : what do you think, can I apply for conclusions to the crowd of Englishmen with whom I am travelling solely because I was unable to talk to them at the springs ? "

"How can I tell ? Excuse me, it's very difficult to follow you."

"Difficult, is it ? "

"Yes, you weary me."

"H'm." He winked and made a gesture, probably intended to suggest victory and triumph ; then with stolid composure he took out of his pocket a newspaper which he had evidently only just bought, unfolded it and began reading the last page, apparently intending to leave me undisturbed. For five minutes he did not look at me.

"Brestograevskies haven't gone smash, eh ! Once they've started, they go on ! I know a lot that have gone smash."

He looked at me with intense earnestness.

"I don't know much about the Stock Exchange so far," I answered.

" You disapprove of it."

" What ? "

" Money."

" I don't disapprove of money but . . . but I think ideas come first and money second."

" That is, allow me to say. . . . Here you have a man, so to say, with his own capital. . . ."

" A lofty idea comes before money, and a society with money but without a lofty idea comes to grief."

I don't know why, but I began to grow hot. He looked at me rather blankly, as though he were perplexed, but suddenly his whole face relaxed in a gleeful and cunning smile.

" Versilov, hey ? He's fairly scored, he has ! Judgment given yesterday, eh ? "

I suddenly perceived to my surprise that he knew who I was, and perhaps knew a great deal more. But I don't understand why I flushed and stared in a most idiotic way without taking my eyes off him. He was evidently triumphant. He looked at me in high glee, as though he had found me out and caught me in the cleverest way.

" No," he said, raising both his eyebrows ; " you ask me about M. Versilov. What did I say to you just now about soundness ? A year and a half ago over that baby he might have made a very perfect little job, but he came to grief."

" Over what baby ? "

" The baby who is being brought up now out of the way, but he won't gain anything by it . . . because . . ."

" What baby ? What do you mean ? "

" His baby, of course, his own by Mlle. Lidya Ahmakov. . . . 'A charming girl very fond of me. . . .' phosphorus matches—eh ? "

" What nonsense, what a wild story ! He never had a baby by Mlle. Ahmakov ! "

" Go on ! I've been here and there, I've been a doctor and I've been an accoucheur. My name's Stebelkov, haven't you heard of me ? It's true I haven't practised for a long time, but practical advice on a practical matter I could give."

" You're an accoucheur . . . did you attend Mlle. Ahmakov ? "

" No, I did not attend her. In a suburb there was a doctor Granz, burdened with a family ; he was paid half a thaler, such is the position of doctors out there, and no one knew him either, so he was there instead of me. . . . I recommended him, indeed, because he was so obscure and unknown. You follow? I only gave practical advice when Versilov, Andrey Petrovitch, asked for it ; but he asked me in dead secret, *tête-à-tête*. But Andrey Petrovitch wanted to catch two hares at once."

I listened in profound astonishment.

" ' Chase two hares, catch neither,' according to the popular, or rather peasant, proverb. What I say is : exceptions continually repeated become a general rule. He went after another hare, or, to speak plain Russian, after another lady, and with no results. Hold tight what you've got. When he ought to be hastening a thing on, he potters about : Versilov, that ' petticoat prophet,' as young Prince Sokolsky well described him before me at the time. Yes, you had better come to me ! If there is anything you want to know about Versilov, you had better come to me ! "

He was evidently delighted at my open-mouthed astonishment. I had never heard anything before about a baby. And at that moment the door of the next room slammed as some one walked rapidly in.

" Versilov lives in Mozhaisky Street, at Litvinov's house, No. 17 ; I have been to the address bureau myself ! " a woman's voice cried aloud in an irritable tone ; we could hear every word. Stebelkov raised his eyebrows and held up his finger. " We talk of him here, and there already he's. . . . Here you have exceptions continually occurring ! *Quand on parle d'une corde. . . .*"

He jumped up quickly and sitting down on the sofa, began listening at the door in front of which the sofa stood. I too was tremendously struck. I reflected that the speaker was probably the same young girl who had run down the stairs in such excitement. But how did Versilov come to be mixed up in this too ? Suddenly there came again the same shriek, the furious shriek of some one savage with anger, who has been prevented from getting or doing something. The only difference was that the cries and shrieks were more prolonged than before. There were sounds of a struggle, a torrent of words, " I won't, I won't," " Give it up, give it up at once ! " or something of the sort, I don't remember exactly. Then, just as before, some one rushed to the door and opened it. Both the people in the room rushed out into the passage, one just as before, trying to restrain the other. Stebelkov, who had leapt up from the sofa, and been

listening with relish, fairly flew to the door, and with extreme
lack of ceremony dashed into the passage straight upon the two.
I too, of course, ran to the door.   But his appearance in the
passage acted like a pail of cold water.   The two women
vanished instantly, and shut the door with a slam.

Stebelkov was on the point of dashing after them, but he
stopped short, held up his finger with a smile, and stood considering.   This time I detected in his smile something nasty,
evil and malignant.   Seeing the landlady, who was again standing in her doorway, he ran quickly across the passage to her on
tiptoe; after whispering to her for a minute or two, and no
doubt receiving information, he came back to the room, re-
suming his air of ponderous dignity, picked up his top-hat from
the table, looked at himself in the looking-glass as he passed,
ruffled up his hair, and with self-complacent dignity went
to the next door without even a glance in my direction.   For
an instant he held his ear to the door, listening, then winked
triumphantly across the passage to the landlady, who shook
her finger and wagged her head at him, as though to say, " Och,
naughty man, naughty man ! "   Finally with an air of resolute,
even of shrinking delicacy, he knocked with his knuckles at the
door.   A voice asked :

" Who's there ? "

" Will you allow me to enter on urgent business ? "   Stebelkov
pronounced in a loud and dignified voice.

There was a brief delay, yet they did open the door, first only
a little way ; but Stebelkov at once clutched the door-handle
and would not let them close it again.   A conversation followed,
Stebelkov began talking loudly, still pushing his way into the
room.   I don't remember the words, but he was speaking about
Versilov, saying that he could tell them, could explain everything—" Yes, I can tell you," " Yes, you come to me "—or
something to that effect.   They quickly let him in, I went back
to the sofa and began to listen, but I could not catch it all,
I could only hear that Versilov's name was frequently mentioned.
From the intonations of his voice I guessed that Stebelkov by
now had control of the conversation, that he no longer spoke
insinuatingly but authoritatively, in the same style as he had
talked to me—" you follow ? " " kindly note that," and so on.
With women, though, he must have been extraordinarily affable.
Already I had twice heard his loud laugh, probably most inappropriate, because accompanying his voice, and sometimes

rising above it, could be heard the voices of the women, and they sounded anything but cheerful, and especially that of the young woman, the one who had shrieked : she talked a great deal, rapidly and nervously, making apparently some accusation or complaint, and seeking judgment or redress. But Stebelkov did not give way, he raised his voice higher and higher, and laughed more and more often ; such men are unable to listen to other people. I soon jumped up from the sofa, for it seemed to me shameful to be eavesdropping, and went back again to the rush-bottom chair by the window. I felt convinced that Vassin did not think much of this gentleman, but that, if anyone else had expressed the same opinion, he would have at once defended him with grave dignity, and have observed that, " he was a practical man, and one of those modern business people who were not to be judged from our theoretical and abstract stand-points." At that instant, however, I felt somehow morally shattered, my heart was throbbing and I was unmistakably expecting something.

About ten minutes passed ; suddenly in the midst of a resound-ing peal of laughter some one leapt up from a chair with just the same noise as before, then I heard shrieks from both the women. I heard Stebelkov jump up too and say something in quite a different tone of voice, as though he were justifying himself and begging them to listen. . . . But they did not listen to him ; I heard cries of anger : " Go away ! You're a scoundrel, you're a shameless villain ! " In fact it was clear that he was being turned out of the room. I opened the door at the very minute when he skipped into the passage, as it seemed literally thrust out by their hands. Seeing me he cried out at once, pointing at me : " This is Versilov's son ! If you don't believe me, here is his son, his own son ! I assure you ! " And he seized me by the arm as though I belonged to him. " This is his son, his own son ! " he repeated, though he added nothing by way of explanation, as he led me to the ladies.

The young woman was standing in the passage, the elderly one a step behind her, in the doorway. I only remember that this poor girl was about twenty, and pretty, though thin and sickly looking ; she had red hair, and was somehow a little like my sister ; this likeness flashed upon me at the time, and re-mained in my memory ; but Liza never had been, and never could have been in the wrathful frenzy by which the girl stand-ing before me was possessed : her lips were white, her light grey

K

eyes were flashing, she was trembling all over with indignation. I remember, too, that I was in an exceedingly foolish and undignified position, for, thanks to this insolent scoundrel, I was at a complete loss what to say.

"What do you mean, his son! If he's with you he's a scoundrel too. If you are Versilov's son," she turned suddenly to me, "tell your father from me that he is a scoundrel, that he's a mean, shameless wretch, that I don't want his money. . . . There, there, there, give him this money at once!"

She hurriedly took out of her pocket several notes, but the elder lady (her mother, as it appeared later) clutched her hand:

"Olya, but you know . . . perhaps it's not true . . . perhaps it's not his son!"

Olya looked at her quickly, reflected, looked at me contemptuously and went back into the room; but before she slammed the door she stood still in the doorway and shouted to Stebelkov once more:

"Go away!"

And she even stamped her foot at him. Then the door was slammed and locked. Stebelkov, still holding me by the shoulder, with his finger raised and his mouth relaxed in a slow doubtful grin, bent a look of inquiry on me.

"I consider the way you've behaved with me ridiculous and disgraceful," I muttered indignantly. But he did not hear what I said, though he was still staring at me.

"This ought to be looked into," he pronounced, pondering.

"But how dare you drag me in? Who is this? What is this woman? You took me by the shoulder, and brought me in—what does it mean?"

"Yes, by Jove! A young person who has lost her fair fame . . . a frequently recurring exception—you follow?" And he poked me in the chest with his finger.

"Ech, damnation!" I pushed away his finger. But he suddenly and quite unexpectedly went off into a low, noiseless, prolonged chuckle of merriment. Finally he put on his hat and, with a rapid change to an expression of gloom, he observed, frowning:

"The landlady must be informed . . . they must be turned out of the lodgings, to be sure, and without loss of time too, or they'll be . . . you will see! Mark my words, you will see! Yes, by Jove!" he was gleeful again all at once. "You'll wait for Grisha, I suppose?"

" No, I shan't wait," I answered resolutely.

" Well, it's all one to me. . . ."

And without adding another syllable he turned, went out, and walked downstairs, without vouchsafing a glance in the landlady's direction, though she was evidently expecting news and explanations. I, too, took up my hat, and asking the landlady to tell Vassin that I, Dolgoruky, had called, I ran downstairs.

3

I had merely wasted my time. On coming out I set to work at once to look for lodgings; but I was preoccupied. I wandered about the streets for several hours, and, though I went into five or six flats with rooms to let, I am sure I passed by twenty without noticing them. To increase my vexation I found it far more difficult to get a lodging than I had imagined. Everywhere there were rooms like Vassin's, or a great deal worse, while the rent was enormous, that is, not what I had reckoned upon. I asked for nothing more than a " corner " where I could turn round, and I was informed contemptuously that if that was what I wanted, I must go where rooms were let " in corners." Moreover, I found everywhere numbers of strange lodgers, in whose proximity I could not have lived; in fact, I would have paid anything not to have to live in their proximity. There were queer gentlemen in their waistcoats without their coats, who had dishevelled beards, and were inquisitive and free-and-easy in their manners. In one tiny room there were about a dozen such sitting over cards and beer, and I was offered the next room. In another place I answered the landlady's inquiries so absurdly that they looked at me in surprise, and in one flat I actually began quarrelling with the people. However, I won't describe these dismal details; I only felt that I was awfully tired. I had something to eat in a cookshop when it was almost dark. I finally decided that I would go and give Versilov the letter concerning the will, with no one else present (making no explanation), that I would go upstairs, pack my things in my trunk and bag, and go for the night, if need be, to an hotel. At the end of the Obuhovsky Prospect, at the Gate of Triumph, I knew there was an inn where one could get a room to oneself for thirty kopecks; I resolved for one night to sacrifice that sum, rather than sleep at Versilov's. And as I was passing the Institute of Technology, the notion suddenly struck me to call on Tatyana Pavlovna, who lived just opposite the institute. My pretext for going in was this same letter about the will, but my overwhelming impulse to go in was due to some other cause, which I cannot to this day explain. My mind was in a turmoil, brooding over "the baby," the "exceptions that pass into rules." I had a longing to tell some one, or to make a scene, or to fight, or even to have a cry—I can't tell which, but I went up to Tatyana Pavlovna's. I had only been there once before, with some message from my mother, soon after I came from Moscow, and I remember I went in, gave my message, and went out a minute later, without sitting down, and indeed she did not ask me to.

I rang the bell, and the cook at once opened the door to me, and showed me into the room without speaking. All these details are necessary that the reader may understand how the mad adventure, which had so vast an influence on all that followed, was rendered possible. And to begin with, as regards the cook. She was an ill-tempered, snub-nosed Finnish woman, and I believe hated her mistress Tatyana Pavlovna, while the latter, on the contrary, could not bring herself to part with her from a peculiar sort of infatuation, such as old maids sometimes show for damp-nosed pug dogs, or somnolent cats. The Finnish woman was either spiteful and rude or, after a quarrel, would be silent for weeks together to punish her mistress. I must have chanced upon one of these dumb days, for even when I asked her, as I remember doing, whether her mistress were at home, she made no answer, but walked off to the kitchen in silence. Feeling sure after this that Tatyana Pavlovna was at home, I walked into the room, and finding no one there, waited expecting that she would come out of her bedroom before long ; otherwise, why should the cook have shown me in ? Without sitting down, I waited two minutes, three ; it was dusk and Tatyana Pavlovna's dark flat seemed even less hospitable from the endless yards of cretonne hanging about. A couple of words about that horrid little flat, to explain the surroundings of what followed. With her obstinate and peremptory character, and the tastes she had formed from living in the country in the past, Tatyana Pavlovna could not put up with furnished lodgings, and had taken this parody of a flat simply in order to live apart and be her own mistress. The two rooms were exactly like two bird-cages, set side by side, one

smaller than the other ; the flat was on the third storey, and
the windows looked into the courtyard. Coming into the flat,
one stepped straight into a tiny passage, a yard and a half wide ;
on the left, the two afore-mentioned bird-cages, and at the end
of the passage the tiny kitchen. The five hundred cubic feet
of air required to last a human being twelve hours were perhaps
provided in this room, but hardly more. The rooms were
hideously low-pitched, and, what was stupider than anything,
the windows, the doors, the furniture, all were hung or draped
with cretonne, good French cretonne, and decorated with
festoons ; but this made the room twice as dark and more
than ever like the inside of a travelling-coach. In the room
where I was waiting it was possible to turn round, though it
was cumbered up with furniture, and the furniture, by the way,
was not at all bad : there were all sorts of little inlaid tables,
with bronze fittings, boxes, an elegant and even sumptuous
toilet table. But the next room, from which I expected her to
come in, the bedroom, screened off by a thick curtain, consisted
literally of a bedstead, as appeared afterwards. All these
details are necessary to explain the foolishness of which I was
guilty.

So I had no doubts and was waiting, when there came a ring
at the bell. I heard the cook cross the little passage with lagging
footsteps, and admit the visitors, still in silence, just as she had
me. They were two ladies and both were talking loudly, but
what was my amazement when from their voices I recognized
one as Tatyana Pavlovna, and the other as the woman I was
least prepared to meet now, above all in such circumstances !
I could not be mistaken : I had heard that powerful, mellow,
ringing voice the day before, only for three minutes it is true,
but it still resounded in my heart. Yes, it was " yesterday's
woman." What was I to do ? I am not asking the reader
this question, I am only picturing that moment to myself, and
I am utterly unable to imagine even now how it came to pass
that I suddenly rushed behind the curtain, and found myself
in Tatyana Pavlovna's bedroom. In short, I hid myself, and
had scarcely time to do so when they walked in. Why I hid
and did not come forward to meet them, I don't know. It all
happened accidentally and absolutely without premeditation.

After rushing into the bedroom and knocking against the
bed, I noticed at once that there was a door leading from the
bedroom into the kitchen, and so there was a way out of my

horrible position, and I could make my escape but—oh, horror ! the door was locked, and there was no key in it. I sank on the bed in despair ; I realized that I should overhear their talk, and from the first sentence, from the first sound of their conversation, I guessed that they were discussing delicate and private matters. Oh, of course, a straightforward and honourable man should even then have got up, come out, said aloud, " I'm here, stop ! " and, in spite of his ridiculous position, walked past them ; but I did not get up, and did not come out ; I didn't dare, I was in a most despicable funk.

" My darling Katerina Nikolaevna, you distress me very much," Tatyana Pavlovna was saying in an imploring voice. " Set your mind at rest once for all, it's not like you. You bring joy with you wherever you go, and now suddenly . . . I suppose you do still believe in me ? Why, you know how devoted I am to you. As much so as to Andrey Petrovitch, and I make no secret of my undying devotion to him. . . . But do believe me, I swear on my honour he has no such document in his possession, and perhaps no one else has either ; and he is not capable of anything so underhand, it's wicked of you to suspect him. This hostility between you two is simply the work of your own imaginations. . . ."

" There is such a document, and he is capable of anything. And there, as soon as I go in yesterday, the first person I meet is *ce petit espion*, whom he has foisted on my father."

" Ach, *ce petit espion !* To begin with he is not an *espion* at all, for it was I, I insisted on his going to the prince, or else he would have gone mad, or died of hunger in Moscow—that was the account they sent us of him ; and what's more, that unmannerly urchin is a perfect little fool, how could he be a spy ? "

" Yes, he is a fool, but that does not prevent his being a scoundrel. If I hadn't been so angry, I should have died of laughing yesterday : he turned pale, he ran about, made bows and talked French. And Marie Ivanovna talked of him in Moscow as a genius. That that unlucky letter is still in existence and is in dangerous hands somewhere, I gathered chiefly from Marie Ivanovna's face."

" My beauty ! why you say yourself she has nothing ! "

" That's just it, that she has ; she does nothing but tell lies, and she is a good hand at it, I can tell you ! Before I went to Moscow, I still had hopes that no papers of any sort were left, but then. then. . . ."

" Oh, it's quite the contrary, my dear, I am told she is a good-natured and sensible creature ; Andronikov thought more of her than of any of his other nieces. It's true I don't know her well—but you should have won her over, my beauty ! It's no trouble to you to win hearts—why, I'm an old woman, but here I'm quite in love with you already, and can't resist kissing you. . . . But it would have been nothing to you to win her heart."

" I did, Tatyana Pavlovna, I tried ; she was enchanted with me, but she's very sly too. . . . Yes, she's a regular type, and a peculiar Moscow type. . . . And would you believe it, she advised me to apply to a man here called Kraft, who had been Andronikov's assistant. ' Maybe he knows something,' she said. I had some idea of what Kraft was like, and in fact, I had a faint recollection of him ; but as she talked about Kraft, I suddenly felt certain that it was not that she simply knew nothing but that she knew all about it and was lying."

" But why, why ? Well, perhaps you might find out from him ! That German, Kraft, isn't a chatterbox, and I remember him as very honest—you really ought to question him ! Only I fancy he is not in Petersburg now. . . ."

" Oh, he came back yesterday evening, I have just been to see him. . . . I have come to you in such a state, I'm shaking all over. I wanted to ask you, Tatyana Pavlovna, my angel, for you know every one, wouldn't it be possible to find out from his papers, for he must have left papers, to whom they will come now ? They may come into dangerous hands again ! I wanted to ask your advice."

" But what papers are you talking about ? " said Tatyana Pavlovna, not understanding. " Why, you say you have just been at Kraft's ? "

" Yes, I have been, I have, I have just been there, but he's shot himself ! Yesterday evening."

I jumped up from the bed. I was able to sit through being called a spy and an idiot, and the longer the conversation went on the more impossible it seemed to show myself. It was impossible to contemplate ! I inwardly determined with a sinking heart to stay where I was till Tatyana Pavlovna went to the door with her visitor (if, that is, I were lucky, and she did not before then come to fetch something from the bedroom), and afterwards, when Mme. Ahmakov had gone out, then, if need be, I'd fight it out with Tatyana Pavlovna. . . . But now, when, suddenly hearing about Kraft, I jumped up from the bed, I shuddered all over. Without thinking, without reflecting, or realizing what I was doing, I took a step, lifted the curtain, and appeared before the two of them. It was still light enough for them to see me, pale and trembling. . . . They both cried out, and indeed they well might.

"Kraft ? " I muttered, turning to Mme. Ahmakov—" he has shot himself ? Yesterday ? At sunset ? "

"Where were you ? Where have you come from ? " screamed Tatyana Pavlovna, and she literally clawed my shoulder. " You've been spying ? You have been eavesdropping ? "

"What did I tell you just now ? " said Katerina Nikolaevna, getting up from the sofa and pointing at me.

I was beside myself.

"It's a lie, it's nonsense ! " I broke in furiously. " You called me a spy just now, my God ! You are not worth spying on, life's not worth living in the same world with such people as you, in fact ! A great-hearted man has killed himself, Kraft has shot himself—for the sake of an idea, for the sake of Hecuba. . . . But how should you know about Hecuba ? . . . And here—one's to live among your intrigues, to linger in the midst of your lying, your deceptions and underhand plots. . . . Enough ! "

"Slap him in the face ! Slap him in the face ! " cried Tatyana Pavlovna, and as Katerina Nikolaevna did not move, though she stared fixedly at me (I remember it all minutely), Tatyana Pavlovna would certainly have done so herself without loss of time, so that I instinctively raised my hand to protect my face ; and this gesture led her to imagine that I meant to strike her.

"Well, strike me, strike me, show me that you are a low cur from your birth up : you are stronger than women, why stand on ceremony with them ! "

"That's enough of your slander ! " I cried. " I have never raised my hand against a woman ! You are shameless, Tatyana Pavlovna, you've always treated me with contempt. Oh, servants must be treated without respect ! You laugh, Katerina Nikolaevna, at my appearance I suppose ; yes, God has not blessed me with the elegance of your young officers. And, yet I don't feel humbled before you, on the contrary I feel exalted. . . . I don't care how I express myself, only I'm not to blame ! I got here by accident, Tatyana Pavlovna, it's all the fault of your cook, or rather of your devotion to her : why did she bring me in here without answering my question ? And afterwards to dash out of a woman's bedroom seemed so monstrous, that I made up my mind not to show myself, but to sit and put up with your insults. . . . You are laughing again, Katerina Nikolaevna ! "

"Leave the room, leave the room, go away ! " screamed Tatyana Pavlovna, almost pushing me out. "Don't think anything of his abuse, Katerina Nikolaevna : I've told you that they sent us word that he was mad ! "

"Mad ? They sent word ? Who sent you word ? No matter, enough of this, Katerina Nikolaevna ! I swear to you by all that's sacred, this conversation and all that I've heard shall remain hidden. . . . Am I to blame for having learned your secrets ? Especially as I am leaving your father's service to-morrow, so as regards the letter you are looking for, you need not worry yourself ! "

"What's that. . . . What letter are you talking about ? " asked Katerina Nikolaevna in such confusion that she turned pale, or perhaps I fancied it. I realized that I had said too much.

I walked quickly out; they watched me go without a word, with looks of intense amazement. I had in fact set them a riddle.

CHAPTER IX

1

I HURRIED home and—marvellous to relate—I was very well satisfied with myself. That's not the way one talks to women, of course, and to such women too—it would be truer to say such a woman, for I was not considering Tatyana Pavlovna. Perhaps it's out of the question to say to a woman of that class that one spits on her intrigues, but I had said that, and it was just that that I was pleased with. Apart from anything else, I was convinced that by taking this tone I had effaced all that was ridiculous in my position. But I had not time to think much about that : my mind was full of Kraft. Not that the thought of him distressed me very greatly, but yet I was shaken to my inmost depths, and so much so that the ordinary human feeling of pleasure at another man's misfortune—at his breaking his leg or covering himself with disgrace, at his losing some one dear to him, and so on—even this ordinary feeling of mean satisfaction was completely eclipsed by another absolutely single-hearted feeling, a feeling of sorrow, of compassion for Kraft—at least I don't know whether it was compassion, but it was a strong and warm-hearted feeling. And I was glad of this too. It's marvellous how many irrelevant ideas can flash through the mind at the very time when one is shattered by some tremendous piece of news, which one would have thought must overpower all other feelings and banish all extraneous thoughts, especially petty ones ; yet petty ones, on the contrary, obtrude themselves. I remember, too, that I was gradually overcome by a quite perceptible nervous shudder, which lasted several minutes, in fact all the time I was at home and talking to Versilov.

This interview followed under strange and exceptional circumstances. I had mentioned already that we lived in a separate lodge in the courtyard ; this lodging was marked " No. 13." Before I had entered the gate I heard a woman's voice asking loudly, with impatience and irritation, " Where is No. 13 ? " The question was asked by a lady who was standing close to the gate and had opened the door of the little shop ; but apparently she got no answer there, or was even repulsed, for she came down the steps, resentful and angry.

" But where is the porter ? " she cried, stamping her foot. I had already recognized the voice.

" I am going to No. 13," I said, approaching her. " Whom do you want ? "

" I have been looking for the porter for the last hour. I keep asking every one ; I have been up all the staircases."

" It's in the yard. Don't you recognize me ? "

But by now she had recognized me.

" You want Versilov ; you want to see him about something, and so do I," I went on. " I have come to take leave of him for ever. Come along."

" You are his son ? "

" That means nothing. Granted, though, that I am his son, yet my name's Dolgoruky ; I am illegitimate. This gentleman has an endless supply of illegitimate children. When conscience and honour require it a son will leave his father's house. That's in the Bible. He has come into a fortune too, and I don't wish to share it, and I go to live by the work of my hands. A noble-hearted man will sacrifice life itself, if need be ; Kraft has shot himself, Kraft for the sake of an idea, imagine, a young man, yet he overcame hope. . . . This way, this way! We live in a lodge apart. But that's in the Bible; children leave their parents and make homes for themselves. . . . If the idea draws one on . . . if there is an idea! The idea is what matters, the idea is everything. . . ."

I babbled on like this while we were making our way to the lodge. The reader will, no doubt, observe that I don't spare myself much, though I give myself a good character on occasion; I want to train myself to tell the truth. Versilov was at home. I went in without taking off my overcoat; she did the same. Her clothes were dreadfully thin: over a wretched gown of some dark colour was hung a rag that did duty for a cloak or mantle; on her head she wore an old and frayed sailor-hat, which was very unbecoming. When we went into the room my mother was sitting at her usual place at work, and my sister came out of her room to see who it was, and was standing in the doorway. Versilov, as usual, was doing nothing, and he got up to meet us. He looked at me intently with a stern and inquiring gaze.

"It's nothing to do with me," I hastened to explain, and I stood on one side. "I only met this person at the gate; she was trying to find you and no one could direct her. I have come about my own business, which I shall be delighted to explain afterwards. . . ."

Versilov nevertheless still scrutinized me curiously.

"Excuse me," the girl began impatiently. Versilov turned towards her.

"I have been wondering a long while what induced you to leave money for me yesterday. . . . I . . . in short . . . here's your money!" she almost shrieked, as she had before, and flung a bundle of notes on the table. "I've had to hunt for you through the address bureau, or I should have brought it before. Listen, you!" She suddenly addressed my mother, who had turned quite pale. "I don't want to insult you; you look honest, and perhaps this is actually your daughter. I don't know whether you are his wife, but let me tell you that this gentleman gets hold of the advertisements on which teachers and governesses have spent their last farthing and visits these luckless wretches with dishonourable motives, trying to lure them to ruin by money. I don't understand how I could have taken his money yesterday: he looked so honest. . . . Get away, don't say a word! You are a villain, sir! Even if you had honourable intentions I don't want your charity. Not a word, not a word! Oh, how glad I am that I have unmasked you now before your women! Curse you!"

She ran to the door, but turned for one instant in the doorway to shout.

"You've come into a fortune, I'm told."

With that she vanished like a shadow. I repeat again, it was frenzy. Versilov was greatly astonished; he stood as though pondering and reflecting on something. At last he turned suddenly to me:

"You don't know her at all?"

"I happened to see her this morning when she was raging in the passage at Vassin's; she was screaming and cursing you. But I did not speak to her and I know nothing about it, and just now I met her at the gate. No doubt she is that teacher you spoke of yesterday, who also gives lessons in arithmetic."

"Yes, she is. For once in my life I did a good deed and . . . But what's the matter with you?"

"Here is this letter," I answered. "I don't think explanation necessary: it comes from Kraft, and he got it from Andronikov. You will understand what's in it. I will add that no one but me in the whole world knows about that letter, for Kraft, who gave me that letter yesterday just as I was leaving him, has shot himself."

While I was speaking with breathless haste he took the letter and, holding it lightly poised in his left hand, watched me attentively. When I told him of Kraft's suicide I looked at him with particular attention to see the effect. And what did I see? The news did not make the slightest impression on him. If he had even raised an eyebrow! On the contrary, seeing that I had paused, he drew out his eyeglasses, which he always had about him hanging on a black ribbon, carried the letter to the candle and, glancing at the signature, began carefully examining it. I can't express how mortified I was at this supercilious callousness. He must have known Kraft very well: it was, in any case, such an extraordinary piece of news! Besides, I naturally desired it to produce an effect. Knowing that the letter was long, I turned, after waiting, and went out. My trunk had been packed long ago, I had only to stuff a few things into my bag. I thought of my mother and that I had not gone up to speak to her. Ten minutes later, when I had finished my preparations and was meaning to go for a cab, my sister walked into my attic.

"Here are your sixty roubles; mother sends it and begs you again to forgive her for having mentioned it to Andrey Petrovitch. And here's twenty roubles besides. You gave her fifty yesterday for your board; mother says she can't take more than thirty from you because you haven't cost fifty, and she sends you twenty roubles back."

"Well, thanks, if she is telling the truth. Good-bye, sister, I'm going."

"Where are you going now?"

"For the time being to an hotel, to escape spending the night in this house. Tell mother that I love her."

"She knows that. She knows that you love Andrey Petrovitch too. I wonder you are not ashamed of having brought that wretched girl here!"

"I swear I did not; I met her at the gate."

"No, it was your doing."

"I assure you . . ."

"Think a little, ask yourself, and you will see that you were the cause."

"I was only very pleased that Versilov should be put to shame. Imagine, he had a baby by Lidya Ahmakov . . . but what am I telling you!"

"He? A baby? But it is not his child! From whom have you heard such a falsehood?"

"Why, you can know nothing about it."

"Me know nothing about it? But I used to nurse the baby in Luga. Listen, brother: I've seen for a long time past that you know nothing about anything, and meanwhile you wound Andrey Petrovitch—and . . . mother too."

"If he is right, then I shall be to blame. That's all, and I love you no less for it. What makes you flush like that, sister? And more still now! Well, never mind, anyway, I shall challenge that little prince for the slap he gave Versilov at Ems. If Versilov was in the right as regards Mlle. Ahmakov, so much the better."

"Brother, what are you thinking of?"

"Luckily, the lawsuit's over now. . . . Well, now she has turned white!"

"But the prince won't fight you," said Liza, looking at me with a wan smile in spite of her alarm.

" Then I will put him to shame in public. What's the matter with you, Liza ? "

She had turned so pale that she could not stand, and sank on to my sofa.

" Liza," my mother's voice called from below.

She recovered herself and stood up ; she smiled at me affectionately.

" Brother, drop this foolishness, or put it off for a time till you know about ever so many things : it's awful how little you understand."

" I shall remember, Liza, that you turned pale when you heard I was going to fight a duel."

" Yes, yes, remember that too ! " she said, smiling once more at parting, and she went downstairs.

I called a cab, and with the help of the man I hauled my things out of the lodge. No one in the house stopped me or opposed my going. I did not go in to say good-bye to my mother as I did not want to meet Versilov again. When I was sitting in the cab a thought flashed upon me :

" To Fontanka by Semyonovsky Bridge," I told the man, and went back to Vassin's.

2

It suddenly struck me that Vassin would know already about Kraft, and perhaps know a hundred times more than I did ; and so it proved to be. Vassin immediately informed me of all the facts with great precision but with no great warmth ; I concluded that he was very tired, and so indeed he was. He had been at Kraft's himself in the morning. Kraft had shot himself with a revolver (that same revolver) after dark, as was shown by his diary. The last entry in the diary was made just before the fatal shot, and in it he mentioned that he was writing almost in the dark and hardly able to distinguish the letters, that he did not want to light a candle for fear that it should set fire to something when he was dead. " And I don't want to light it and then, before shooting, put it out like my life," he added strangely, almost the last words. This diary he had begun three days before his death, immediately on his return to Petersburg, before his visit to Dergatchev's. After I had gone away he had written something in it every quarter of an hour : the last three or four entries were made at intervals of five minutes. I expressed aloud my surprise that though Vassin had had this diary so long in his hands (it had been given him to read), he had not made a copy of it, especially as it was not more than a sheet or so and all the entries were short. " You might at least have copied the last page ! " Vassin observed with a smile that he remembered it as it was ; moreover, that the entries were quite disconnected, about anything that came into his mind. I was about to protest that this was just what was precious in this case, but without going into that I began instead to insist on his recalling some of it, and he did recall a few sentences—for instance, an hour before he shot himself, " That he was chilly," " That he thought of drinking a glass of wine to warm himself, but had been deterred by the idea that it might cause an increase in the flow of blood." " It was almost all that sort of thing," Vassin remarked in conclusion.

" And you call that nonsense ! " I cried.

" And when did I call it nonsense ? I simply did not copy it. But though it's not nonsense, the diary certainly is somewhat ordinary, or rather, natural—that is, it's just what it's bound to be in such circumstances. . . ."

" But the last thoughts, the last thoughts ! "

" The last thoughts sometimes are extremely insignificant. One such suicide complained, in fact, in a similar diary that not one lofty idea visited him at that important hour, nothing but futile and petty thoughts."

" And that he was chilly, was that too a futile thought ? "

" Do you mean his being chilly, or the thought about the blood ? Besides, it's a well-known fact that very many people who are capable of contemplating their approaching death, whether it's by their own hand or not, frequently show a tendency to worry themselves about leaving their body in a presentable condition. It was from that point of view that Kraft was anxious about the blood."

" I don't know whether that is a well-known fact . . . or whether that is so," I muttered ; " but I am surprised that you consider all that natural, and yet it's not long since Kraft was speaking, feeling, sitting among us. Surely you must feel sorry for him ? "

" Oh, of course, I'm sorry, and that's quite a different thing ; but, in any case, Kraft himself conceived of his death as a logical deduction. It turns out that all that was said about him yesterday at Dergatchev's was true. He left behind him a manuscript book full of abtruse theories, proving by phrenology, by cranio-logy, and even by mathematics, that the Russians are a second-rate race, and that therefore, since he was a Russian, life was not worth living for him. What is more striking about it, if you like, is that it shows one can make any logical deduction one pleases ; but to shoot oneself in consequence of a deduction does not always follow."

" At least one must do credit to his strength of will."

" Possibly not that only," Vassin observed evasively ; it was clear that he assumed stupidity or weakness of intellect. All this irritated me.

" You talked of feeling yourself yesterday, Vassin."

" I don't gainsay it now ; but what has happened betrays something in him so crudely mistaken that, if one looks at it critically, it checks one's compassion in spite of oneself."

" Do you know that I guessed yesterday from your eyes that you would disapprove of Kraft, and I resolved not to ask your opinion, that I might not hear evil of him ; but you have given it of yourself, and I am forced to agree with you in spite of myself ; and yet I am annoyed with you ! I am sorry for Kraft."

" Do you know we are going rather far . . ."

" Yes, yes," I interrupted, " but it's a comfort, anyway, that in such cases those who are left alive, the critics of the dead, can say of themselves : ' Though a man has shot himself who was worthy of all compassion and indulgence, we are left, at any rate, and so there's no great need to grieve.' "

" Yes, of course, from that point of view. . . . Oh, but I believe you are joking, and very cleverly ! I always drink tea at this time, and am just going to ask for it : you will join me, perhaps."

And he went out, with a glance at my trunk and bag.

I had wanted to say something rather spiteful, to retaliate for his judgment of Kraft, and I had succeeded in saying it, but it was curious that he had taken my consoling reflection that "such as we are left" as meant seriously. But, be that as it may, he was, anyway, more right than I was in everything, even in his feelings. I recognized this without the slightest dissatis-faction, but I felt distinctly that I did not like him.

When they had brought in the tea I announced that I was going to ask for his hospitality for one night only, and if this were impossible I hoped he would say so, and I would go to an hotel. Then I briefly explained my reasons, simply and frankly stating that I had finally quarrelled with Versilov, without, however, going into details. Vassin listened attentively but without the slightest excitement. As a rule he only spoke in reply to questions, though he always answered with ready courtesy and sufficient detail. I said nothing at all about the letter concerning which I had come to ask his advice in the morning, and I explained that I had looked in then simply to call on him. Having given Versilov my word that no one else should know of the letter, I considered I had no right to speak of it to anyone. I felt it for some reason peculiarly repugnant to speak of certain things to Vassin—of some things and not of others; I succeeded, for instance, in interesting him in my description of the scenes that had taken place that morning in the passage, in the next room, and finally at Versilov's. He listened with extreme attention, especially to what I told him of Stebelkov. When I told him how Stebelkov asked about Dergatchev he made me repeat the question again, and seemed to ponder gravely over it, though he did laugh in the end. It suddenly occurred to me at that moment that nothing could ever have disconcerted Vassin; I remember, however, that this idea presented itself at first in a form most complimentary to him.

"In fact, I could not gather much from what M. Stebelkov said," I added finally; "he talks in a sort of muddle . . . and there is something, as it were, feather-headed about him. . . ."

Vassin at once assumed a serious air.

"He certainly has no gift for language, but he sometimes manages to make very acute observations at first sight, and in fact he belongs to the class of business men, men of practical affairs, rather than of theoretical ideas; one must judge them from that point of view. . . ."

It was exactly what I had imagined him saying that morning.

"He made an awful row next door, though, and goodness knows how it might have ended."

Of the inmates of the next room, Vassin told me that they had been living there about three weeks and had come from somewhere in the provinces; that their room was very small, and that to all appearance they were very poor; that they stayed in and seemed to be expecting something. He did not know the young woman had advertised for lessons, but he had heard that Versilov had been to see them; it had happened in

L

his absence, but the landlady had told him of it. The two ladies had held themselves aloof from every one, even from the landlady. During the last few days he had indeed become aware that something was wrong with them, but there had been no other scenes like the one that morning. I recall all that was said about the people next door because of what followed. All this time there was a dead silence in the next room. Vassin listened with marked interest when I told him that Stebelkov had said he must talk to the landlady about our neighbours and that he had twice repeated, " Ah ! you will see ! you will see ! "

" And you will see," added Vassin, " that that notion of his stands for something ; he has an extraordinarily keen eye for such things."

" Why, do you think the landlady ought to be advised to turn them out ? "

" No, I did not mean that they should be turned out . . . simply that there might be a scandal . . . but all such cases end one way or another. . . . Let's drop the subject."

As for Versilov's visit next door, he asolutely refused to give any opinion.

" Anything is possible : a man feels that he has money in his pocket . . . but he may very likely have given the money from charity ; that would perhaps be in accordance with his traditions and his inclinations."

I told him that Stebelkov had chattered that morning about " a baby."

" Stebelkov is absolutely mistaken about that," Vassin brought out with peculiar emphasis and gravity (I remembered this particularly). " Stebelkov sometimes puts too much faith in his practical common sense, and so is in too great a hurry to draw conclusions to fit in with his logic, which is often very penetrating ; and all the while the actual fact may be far more fantastic and surprising when one considers the character of the persons concerned in it. So it has been in this case ; having a partial knowledge of the affair, he concluded the child belonged to Versilov ; and yet the child is not Versilov's."

I pressed him, and, to my great amazement, learned from him that the infant in question was the child of Prince Sergay Sokolsky. Lidya Ahmakov, either owing to her illness or to some fantastic streak in her character, used at times to behave like a lunatic. She had been fascinated by the prince before

she met Versilov, " and he had not scrupled to accept her love,"
to use Vassin's expression. The liaison had lasted but for a
moment ; they had quarrelled, as we know already, and Lidya
had dismissed the prince, " at which the latter seems to have
been relieved." " She was a very strange girl," added Vassin ;
" it is quite possible that she was not always in her right mind.
But when he went away to Paris, Prince Sokolsky had no idea
of the condition in which he had left his victim, he did not
know until the end, until his return. Versilov, who had become
a friend of the young lady's, offered her his hand, in view of her
situation (of which it appears her parents had no suspicion up
to the end). The lovesick damsel was overjoyed, and saw in
Versilov's offer " something more than self-sacrifice," though
that too she appreciated. " Of course, though, he knew how
to carry it through," Vassin added. " The baby (a girl) was
born a month or six weeks before the proper time ; it was placed
out somewhere in Germany but afterwards taken back by Versilov
and is now somewhere in Russia—perhaps in Petersburg."

" And the phosphorus matches ? "

" I know nothing about that," Vassin said in conclusion.
" Lidya Ahmakov died a fortnight after her confinement : what
had happened I don't know. Prince Sokolsky, who had only
just returned from Paris, learned there was a child, and seems
not to have believed at first that it was his child. . . . The
whole affair has, in fact, been kept secret by all parties up till
now."

" But what a wretch this prince must be," I cried indignantly.
" What a way to treat an invalid girl ! "

" She was not so much of an invalid then. . . . Besides, she
sent him away herself. . . . It is true, perhaps, that he was in
too great a hurry to take advantage of his dismissal."

" You justify a villain like that ! "

" No, only I don't call him a villain. There is a great deal in
it besides simple villainy. In fact, it's quite an ordinary thing."

" Tell me, Vassin, did you know him intimately ? I should
particularly value your opinion, owing to a circumstance that
touches me very nearly."

But to this Vassin replied with excessive reserve. He knew
the prince, but he was, with obvious intention, reticent in regard
to the circumstances under which he had made his acquaintance.
He added further that one had to make allowances for Prince
Sokolsky's character. " He is impressionable and full of honour-

able impulses, but has neither good sense nor strength of will enough to control his desires. He is not a well-educated man ; many ideas and situations are beyond his power to deal with, and yet he rushes upon them. He will, for example, persist in declaring, ' I am a prince and descended from Rurik ; but there's no reason why I shouldn't be a shoemaker if I have to earn my living ; I am not fit for any other calling. Above the shop there shall be, " Prince So-and-so, Bootmaker "—it would really be a credit.' He would say that and act upon it, too, that's what matters," added Vassin ; " and yet it's not the result of strong conviction, but only the most shallow impression-ability. Afterwards repentance invariably follows, and then he is always ready to rush to an opposite extreme ; his whole life is passed like that. Many people come to grief in that way nowadays," Vassin ended, " just because they are born in this age."

I could not help pondering on his words.

" Is it true that he was turned out of his regiment ? " I asked.

" I don't know whether he was turned out, but he certainly did leave the regiment through some unpleasant scandal. I suppose you know that he spent two or three months last autumn at Luga."

" I . . . I know that you were staying at Luga at that time."

" Yes, I was there too for a time. Prince Sokolsky knew Lizaveta Makarovna too."

" Oh ! I didn't know. I must confess I've had so little talk with my sister. . . . But surely he was not received in my mother's house ? " I cried.

" Oh, no ; he was only slightly acquainted with them through other friends."

" Ah, to be sure, what did my sister tell me about that child ? Was the baby at Luga ? "

" For a while."

" And where is it now."

" No doubt in Petersburg."

" I never will believe," I cried in great emotion, " that my mother took any part whatever in this scandal with this Lidya ! "

" Apart from these intrigues, of which I can't undertake to give the details, there was nothing particularly reprehensible in Versilov's part of the affair," observed Vassin, with a condescend-ing smile. I fancy he began to feel it difficult to talk to me, but he tried not to betray it.

"I will never, never believe," I cried again, "that a woman could give up her husband to another woman ; that I won't believe ! . . . I swear my mother had no hand in it ! "

"It seems, though, she did not oppose it."

"In her place, from pride I should not have opposed it."

"For my part, I absolutely refuse to judge in such a matter," was Vassin's final comment.

Perhaps, for all his intelligence, Vassin really knew nothing about women, so that a whole cycle of ideas and phenomena remained unknown to him. I sank into silence. Vassin had a temporary berth in some company's office, and I knew that he used to bring work home with him. When I pressed him, he admitted that he had work to do now, accounts to make up, and I begged him warmly not to stand on ceremony with me. I believe this pleased him ; but before bringing out his papers he made up a bed for me on the sofa. At first he offered me his bed, but when I refused it I think that too gratified him. He got pillows and a quilt from the landlady. Vassin was extremely polite and amiable, but it made me feel uncomfortable, seeing him take so much trouble on my account. I had liked it better when, three weeks before, I had spent a night at Efim's. I remember how he concocted a bed for me, also on a sofa, and without the knowledge of his aunt, who would, he thought, for some reason, have been vexed if she had known he had a school-fellow staying the night with him. We laughed a great deal. A shirt did duty for a sheet and an overcoat for a pillow. I remember how Efim, when he had completed the work, patted the sofa tenderly and said to me :

"*Vous dormirez comme un petit roi.*"

And his foolish mirth and the French phrase, as incongruous in his mouth as a saddle on a cow, made me enjoy sleeping at that jocose youth's. As for Vassin, I felt greatly relieved when he sat down to work with his back to me. I stretched myself on the sofa and, looking at his back, pondered deeply on many things.

3

And indeed I had plenty to think about. Everything seemed split up and in confusion in my soul, but certain sensations stood out very definitely, though from their very abundance I was not dominated by any one of them. They all came, as it were, in disconnected flashes, one after another, and I had no inclination, I remember, to dwell on any one of my impressions or to establish any sequence among them. Even the idea of Kraft had imperceptibly passed into the background. What troubled me most of all was my own position, that here I had " broken off," and that my trunk was with me, and I was not at home, and was beginning everything new. It was as though all my previous intentions and preparations had been in play, " and only now—and above all so *suddenly*—everything was beginning in reality." This idea gave me courage and cheered me up, in spite of the confusion within me over many things.

But . . . but I had other sensations ; one of them was trying to dominate the others and to take possession of my soul, and, strange to say, this sensation too gave me courage and seemed to hold out prospects of something very gay. Yet this feeling had begun with fear : I had been afraid for a long time, from the very hour that in my heat I had, unawares, said too much to Mme. Ahmakov about the " document." " Yes, I said too much," I thought, "and maybe they will guess something . . . it's a pity ! No doubt they will give me no peace if they begin to suspect, but . . . let them ! Very likely they won't find me, I'll hide ! And what if they really do run after me . . . ? " And then I began recalling minutely in every point, and with growing satisfaction, how I had stood up before Katerina Nikolaevna and how her insolent but extremely astonished eyes had gazed at me obstinately. Going away, I had left her in the same amazement, I remembered ; " her eyes are not quite black, though . . . it's only her eyelashes that are so black, and that's what makes her eyes look so dark. . . ."

And suddenly, I remember, I felt horribly disgusted at the recollection . . . and sick and angry both at them and at myself. I reproached myself and tried to think of something else. " Why did I not feel the slightest indignation with Versilov for the incident with the girl in the next room ? " it suddenly occurred to me to wonder. For my part, I was firmly convinced that he had had amorous designs and had come to amuse himself, but I was not particularly indignant at this. It seemed to me, indeed, that one could not have conceived of his behaving differently, and although I really was glad he had been put to shame, yet I did not blame him. It was not that which seemed important to me ; what was important was the exasperation with which he had looked at me when I came in with the girl, the way he had looked at me as he had never done before.

" At last he has looked at me *seriously*," I thought, with a flutter at my heart. Ah, if I had not loved him I should not have been so overjoyed at his hatred !

At last I began to doze and fell asleep. I can just remember being aware of Vassin's finishing his work, tidying away his things, looking carefully towards my sofa, undressing and putting out the light.

It was one o'clock at night.

4

Almost exactly two hours later I woke up with a start and, jumping up as though I were frantic, sat on my sofa. From the next room there arose fearful lamentations, screams, and sounds of weeping. Our door was wide open, and people were shouting and running to and fro in the lighted passage. I was on the point of calling to Vassin, but I realized that he was no longer in his bed. I did not know where to find the matches ; I fumbled for my clothes and began hurriedly dressing in the dark. Evidently the landlady, and perhaps the lodgers, had run into the next room. Only one voice was wailing, however, that of the older woman : the youthful voice I had heard the day before, and so well remembered, was quite silent ; I remember that this was the first thought that came into my mind. Before I had finished dressing Vassin came in hurriedly. He laid his hand on the matches instantly and lighted up the room. He was in his dressing-gown and slippers, and he immediately proceeded to dress.

" What's happened ? " I cried.

" A most unpleasant and bothersome business," he answered almost angrily ; " that young girl you were telling me about has hanged herself in the next room."

I could not help crying out. I cannot describe the pang at my heart ! We ran out into the passage. I must own I did not dare go into the room, and only saw the unhappy girl afterwards, when she had been taken down, and even then, indeed, at some distance and covered with a sheet, beyond which the two narrow soles of her shoes stood out. So I did not for some reason look into her face. The mother was in a fearful condition ; our landlady was with her—not, however, greatly alarmed.

All the lodgers in the flat had gathered round. There were only three of them : an elderly naval man, always very peevish and exacting, though on this occasion he was quite quiet, and an elderly couple, respectable people of the small functionary class who came from the province of Tver. I won't attempt to describe the rest of that night, the general commotion and afterwards the visit of the police. Literally till daylight I kept shuddering and felt it my duty to sit up, though I did absolutely nothing. And indeed every one had an extraordinarily cheery air, as though they had been particularly cheered by something. Vassin went off somewhere. The landlady turned out to be rather a decent woman, much better than I had imagined her. I persuaded her (and I put it down to my credit) that the mother must not be left alone with the daughter's corpse, and that she must, at least until to-morrow, take her into her room. The landlady at once agreed, and though the mother struggled and shed tears, refusing to leave her daughter, she did at last move into the landlady's room, and the latter immediately ordered the samovar to be brought. After that the lodgers went back to their rooms and shut the doors, but nothing would have induced me to go to bed, and I remained a long time with the landlady, who was positively relieved at the presence of a third person, and especially one who was able to give some information bearing on the case.

The samovar was most welcome, and in fact the samovar is the most essential thing in Russia, especially at times of particularly awful, sudden, and eccentric catastrophes and misfortunes ; even the mother was induced to drink two cups—though, of course, only with much urging and almost compulsion. And yet I can honestly say that I have never seen a bitterer and more genuine sorrow that that poor mother's.

After the first paroxysms of sobbing and hysterics she was actually eager to talk, and I listened greedily to her story. There are unhappy people, especially women, who must be allowed to talk as freely as possible when they are in trouble. Moreover, there are characters too, blurred so to speak by sorrow, who all their life long have suffered, have suffered terribly much both of great sorrow and of continual worry about trifles, and who can never be surprised by anything, by any sort of sudden calamity, and who, above all, never, even beside the coffin of their dearest, can forget the rules of behaviour for propitiating people, which they have learnt by bitter experience.

And I don't criticize it: there is neither the vulgarity of egoism nor the insolence of culture in this; there is perhaps more genuine goodness to be found in these simple hearts than in heroines of the loftiest demeanour, but the long habit of humiliation, the instinct of self-preservation, the years of timid anxiety and oppression, leave their mark at last. The poor girl who had died by her own hand was not like her mother in this. They were alike in face, however, though the dead girl was decidedly good-looking. The mother was not a very old woman, fifty at the most; she, too, was fair, but her eyes were sunken, her cheeks were hollow, and she had large yellow, uneven teeth. And indeed everything had a tinge of yellowness: the skin on her hands and face was like parchment; her dark dress had grown yellow with age, and the nail on the forefinger of her right hand * had been, I don't know why, carefully and tidily plastered up with yellow wax.

The poor woman's story was in parts quite disconnected. I will tell it as I understood it and as I remember it.

5

They had come from Moscow. She had long been a widow—"the widow of an official, however." Her husband had been in the government service, but had left them practically nothing "except a pension of two hundred roubles." But what are two hundred roubles? Olya grew up, however, and went to the high school—"and how well she did, how good she was at her lessons; she won the silver medal when she left" (at this point, of course, prolonged weeping). The deceased husband had lost a fortune of nearly four thousand roubles, invested with a merchant here in Petersburg. This merchant had suddenly grown rich again. "I had papers, I asked advice; I was told, 'Try, and you will certainly get it. . . .' I wrote, the merchant agreed: 'Go yourself,' I was told. Olya and I set off, and arrived a month ago. Our means were small: we took this room because it was the smallest of all and, as we could see ourselves, in a respectable house, and that's what mattered most to us. We were inexperienced women; every one takes advantage of us. Well, we paid you for one month. With

* This must be an error on Dostoevsky's part. Russian women some‐ times plaster with wax the forefinger of the left hand to protect it from eing pricked in sewing.—Translator's Note.

one thing and another, Petersburg is ruinous. Our merchant gives us a flat refusal—' I don't know you or anything about you '; and the paper I had was not regular, I knew that. Then I was advised to go to a celebrated lawyer; he was a professor, not simply a lawyer but an expert, so he'd be sure to tell me what to do. I took him my last fifteen roubles. The lawyer came out to me, and he did not listen to me for three minutes : ' I see,' says he, ' I know,' says he. ' If the merchant wants to,' says he, ' he'll pay the money; if he doesn't want to, he won't, and if you take proceedings you may have to pay yourself, perhaps; you had far better come to terms.' He made a joke, then, out of the Gospel : ' Make peace,' said he, ' while your enemy is in the way with you, lest you pay to the uttermost farthing.' He laughed as he saw me out. My fifteen roubles were wasted ! I came back to Olya; we sat facing one another. I began crying. Olya did not cry; she sat there, proud and indignant. She has always been like that with me; all her life, even when she was tiny, she was never one to moan, she was never one to cry, but she would sit and look fierce; it used to make me creep to look at her. And—would you believe it ?— I was afraid of her, I was really quite afraid of her; I've been so for a long time past. I often wanted to grieve, but I did not dare before her. I went to the merchant for the last time. I cried before him freely : he said it was all right, and would not even listen. Meanwhile I must confess that, not having reckoned on being here for so long, we had been for some time without a penny. I began taking our clothes one by one to the pawn-broker's; we have been living on what we have pawned. I stripped myself of everything; she gave me the last of her linen, and I cried bitterly at taking it. She stamped, then she jumped up and ran off to the merchant herself. He was a widower; he talked to her. ' Come at five o'clock the day after to-morrow,' says he, ' perhaps I shall have something to say to you.' She came home quite gay : ' He says he may have something to say to me.' Well, I was pleased too, but yet I somehow felt a sort of chill at my heart. ' Something will come of it,' I thought, but I did not dare to question her. Two days later she came back from the merchant's, pale and trembling all over, and threw herself on her bed. I saw what it meant, and did not dare to question her. And—would you believe it ?— the villain had offered her fifteen roubles. ' If I find you pure and virtuous I'll hand you over another forty.' He said that to her face—he wasn't ashamed to. At that she flew at him, so she told me ; he thrust her out, and even locked himself in the next room. And meanwhile I must confess, to tell the truth, we had nothing to eat. We brought out a jacket lined with hare-fur ; we sold it. She went to a newspaper and put in an advertisement at once : she offered lessons in all subjects and in arithmetic. 'If they'll only pay thirty kopecks,' she said. And in the end I began to be really alarmed at her : she would sit for hours at the window without saying a word, staring at the roof of the house opposite, and then she would suddenly cry out, 'If I could only wash or dig !' She would say one sentence like that and stamp her foot. And there was no one we knew here, no one we could go to : I wondered what would become of us. And all the while I was afraid to talk to her. One day she fell asleep in the daytime. She waked up, opened her eyes, and looked at me ; I was sitting on the box, and I was looking at her too. She got up, came to me without saying a word, and threw her arms round me. And we could not help crying, both of us ; we sat crying and clinging to each other. It was the first time in her life I had seen her like that. And just as we were sitting like that, your Nastasya came in and said, 'There's a lady inquiring for you.' This was only four days ago. The lady came in ; we saw she was very well dressed, though she spoke Russian, it seemed to me, with a German accent. 'You advertised that you give lessons,' she said. We were so delighted then, we made her sit down. She laughed in such a friendly way : 'It's not for me,' she said, ' but my niece has small children ; and if it suits you, come to us, and we will make arrangements.' She gave an address, a flat in Voznessensky Street. She went away. Dear Olya set off the same day ; she flew there. She came back two hours later ; she was in hysterics, in convulsions. She told me after-wards : 'I asked the porter where flat No. so-and-so was.' The porter looked at her and said, 'And what do you want to go to that flat for ?' He said that so strangely that it might have made one suspicious, but she was so self-willed, poor darling, so impatient, she could not bear impertinent questions. 'Go along, then,' he said, and he pointed up the stairs to her and went back himself to his little room. And what do you think ! She went in, asked for the lady, and on all sides women ran up to her at once—horrid creatures, rouged ; they rushed at her, laughing. 'Please come in, please come in,' they cried ;

they dragged her in. Some one was playing the piano. ' I tried to get away from them,' she said, ' but they would not let me go.' She was frightened, her legs gave way under her. They simply would not let her go ; they talked to her coaxingly, they persuaded her, they uncorked a bottle of porter, they pressed it on her. She jumped up trembling, screamed at the top of her voice ' Let me go, let me go ! ' She rushed to the door ; they held the door, she shrieked. Then the one who had been to see us the day before ran up and slapped my Olya twice in the face and pushed her out of the door : ' You don't deserve to be in a respectable house, you skinny slut ! ' And another shouted after her on the stairs : ' You came of yourself to beg of us because you have nothing to eat, but we won't look at such an ugly fright ! ' All that night she lay in a fever and delirious and in the morning her eyes glittered ; she got up and walked about. ' Justice,' she cried, ' she must be brought to justice ! ' I said nothing, but I thought, ' If you brought her up how could we prove it ? ' She walked about with set lips, wringing her hands and tears streaming down her face. And her whole face seemed darkened from that time up to the very end. On the third day she seemed better ; she was quiet and seemed calmer. And then at four o'clock in the afternoon M. Versilov came to us. And I must say I can't understand, even now, how Olya, who was always so mistrustful, was ready to listen to him almost at the first word. What attracted us both more than anything was that he had such a grave, almost stern air ; he spoke gently, impressively, and so politely—more than politely, respectfully even—and yet at the same time he showed no sign of trying to make up to us : it was plain to see he had come with a pure heart. ' I read your advertisement in the paper,' said he. ' You did not word it suitably, madam, and you may damage your prospects by that.' And he began explaining—I must own I did not understand—something about arithmetic, but I saw that Olya flushed and seemed to brighten up altogether. She listened and talked readily (and, to be sure, he must be a clever man !) ; I heard her even thank him. He questioned her so minutely about everything, and it seemed that he had lived a long time in Moscow, and it turned out that he knew the head mistress of the high school. ' I will be sure to find you lessons,' said he, ' for I know a great many people here, and I can, in fact, apply to many influential people, so that if you would prefer a permanent situation we might look out for that. . . . Meanwhile,' said he, ' forgive me one direct question : can I be of some use to you at once ? It will be your doing me a favour, not my doing you one,' said he, ' if you will allow me to be of use to you in any way. Let it be a loan,' said he, ' and as soon as you have a situation, in a very short time, you will be able to repay me. Believe me, on my honour,' said he, ' if ever I were to come to poverty and you had plenty of everything I would come straight to you for some little help. I would send my wife and daughter ' . . . at least, I don't remember all his words, only I was moved to tears, for I saw that Olya's lips were trembling with gratitude too. ' If I take it,' she answered him, ' it is because I trust an honourable and humane man, who might have been my father. . . .' That was very well said by her, briefly and with dignity. ' A humane man,' said she. He stood up at once : ' I will get you lessons and a situation without fail. I will set to work this very day, for you have quite a satisfactory diploma too. . . .' I forgot to say that he looked through all her school certificates when he first came in ; she showed them to him, and he examined her in several subjects. . . . ' You see, he examined me, mamma,' Olya said to me afterwards, ' and what a clever man he is,' she said ; ' it is not often one speaks to such a well-educated, cultured man. . . .' And she was quite radiant. The money—sixty roubles, lay on the table : ' Take it, mamma,' said she ; ' when I get a situation we will pay it back as soon as possible. We will show that we are honest and that we have delicacy : he has seen that already, though.' Then she paused. I saw her draw a deep breath. ' Do you know, mamma,' she said to me suddenly, ' if we had been coarse we should perhaps have refused to take it through pride, but by taking it now we only show our delicacy of feeling and that we trust him completely, out of respect for his grey hair, don't we ? ' At first I did not quite understand : ' But why, Olya, not accept the benevolence of a wealthy and honourable man if he has a good heart too ? ' She scowled at me. ' No, mamma,' she said, ' that's not it ; I don't want benevolence, but his humanity is precious. And it would have been better really not to have taken the money at all, since he has promised to get me a situation ; that's enough . . . though we are in need.' ' Well, Olya,' said I, ' our need is so great that we could not have refused it.' I actually laughed. Well, I was pleased, but an hour later she turned to me : ' Don't spend that money yet, mamma,' said she resolutely. ' What ? '

said I. ' I mean it,' she said, and she broke off and said no
more. She was silent all the evening, only at two o'clock in
the night I waked up and heard Olya tossing in her bed : ' Are
you awake, mamma ? ' ' Yes, I am awake.' ' Do you know,
he meant to insult me.' ' What nonsense, what nonsense,' I
said. ' There is no doubt of it,' she said ; ' he is a vile man ;
don't dare to spend a farthing of his money.' I tried to talk
to her. I burst out crying, in bed as I was. She turned away to
the wall. ' Be quiet,' she said, ' let me go to sleep ! ' In the
morning I looked at her ; she was not like herself. And you
may believe it or not, before God I swear she was not in her
right mind then ! From the time that she was insulted in that
infamous place there was darkness and perplexity in her heart
. . . and in her brain. Looking at her that morning, I had
misgivings about her ; I was alarmed. I made up my mind I
would not say a word to contradict her. ' He did not even
leave his address, mamma,' she said. ' For shame, Olya,' I
said ; ' you listened to him last night ; you praised him and
were ready to shed tears of gratitude.' That was all I said,
but she screamed and stamped. ' You are a woman of low
feelings,' she said, ' brought up in the old slavish ideas. . . .'
And then, without a word, she snatched up her hat, ran out.
I called after her. I wondered what was the matter with her,
where she had run. She had run to the address bureau to find
out where Versilov lived. ' I'll take him back the money to-
day and fling it in his face ; he meant to insult me,' she said, ' like
Safronov (that is the merchant), but Safronov insulted me like
a coarse peasant, but he like a cunning Jesuit.' And just then,
unhappily, that gentleman knocked at the door : ' I hear the
name of Versilov,' he said ; ' I can tell you about him.' When
she heard Versilov's name she pounced on him. She was in a
perfect frenzy ; she kept talking away. I gazed at her in
amazement. She was always a silent girl and had never talked
to anyone like that, and with a perfect stranger too. Her cheeks
were burning, her eyes glittered. . . . And he said at once :
' You are perfectly right, madam. Versilov,' said he, ' is just
like the generals here, described in the newspapers ; they dress
themselves up with all their decorations and go after all the
governesses who advertise in the papers. Sometimes they
find what they want, or, if they don't, they sit and talk a
little, make bushels of promises and go away, having got diversion out of it, anyway.' Olya actually laughed, but so bitterly,

and I saw the gentleman take her hand and press it to his heart. 'I am a man of independent means, madam,' said he, 'and might well make a proposal to a fair maiden, but I'd better,' said he, 'kiss your little hand to begin with. . . .' And he was trying to kiss her hand. How she started! But I came to the rescue, and together we turned him out of the room. Then, towards evening, Olya snatched the money from me and ran out. When she came back she said, 'I have revenged myself on that dishonourable man, mamma.' 'Oh, Olya, Olya,' I said, 'perhaps we have thrown away our happiness. You have insulted a generous, benevolent man!' I cried—I was so vexed with her I could not help it. She shouted at me. 'I won't have it, I won't have it!' she cried; 'if he were ever so honest, I don't want his charity! I don't want anyone to pity me!' I went to bed with no thought of anything. How many times I had looked on that nail in your wall where once there had been a looking-glass—it never entered my head, never; I never thought of it yesterday and I'd never thought of it before; I had no inkling of it, and I did not expect it of Olya at all. I usually sleep heavily and snore; it's the blood going to my head, and sometimes it goes to my heart. I call out in my sleep so that Olya wakes me up at night. 'What is the matter with you, mamma?' she would say; 'you sleep so heavily there's no waking you.' 'Oh, Olya,' I said, 'I do, I do.' That's how I must have slept this night, so that, after waiting a bit, she got up without fear of waking me. The strap, a long one from our trunk, had been lying about all that month where we could see it; only yesterday morning I had been thinking of tidying it away. And the chair she must have kicked away afterwards, and she had put her petticoat down beside it to prevent its banging on the floor. And it must have been a long time afterwards, a whole hour or more afterwards, that I waked up and called 'Olya, Olya'; all at once I felt something amiss, and called her name. Either because I did not hear her breathing in her bed, or perhaps I made out in the dark that the bed was empty—anyway, I got up suddenly and felt with my hand; there was no one in the bed and the pillow was cold. My heart sank; I stood still as though I were stunned; my mind was a blank. 'She's gone out,' I thought. I took a step, and by the bed I seemed to see her standing in the corner by the door. I stood still and gazed at her without speaking, and through the darkness she seemed to look at me without stirring.

. . . ' But why has she got on a chair,' I wondered. ' Olya,' I whispered. I was frightened. ' Olya, do you hear ? ' But suddenly, as it were, it all dawned upon me. I went forward, held out both arms and put them round her, and she swayed in my arms ; I swayed and she swayed with me. I understood and would not understand. . . . I wanted to cry out, but no cry came. . . . Ach ! I fell on the floor and shrieked. . . ."

.   .   .   .   .   .

"Vassin," I said at six o'clock in the morning, "if it had not been for your Stebelkov this might not have happened."

"Who knows ?—most likely it would have happened. One can't draw such a conclusion ; everything was leading up to it, apart from that. . . . It is true that Stebelkov sometimes . . ."

He broke off and frowned disagreeably. At seven o'clock he went out again ; he still had a great deal to do. I was left at last entirely alone. It was by now daylight. I felt rather giddy. I was haunted by the figure of Versilov : this lady's story had brought him out in quite a different light. To think this over better, I lay down on Vassin's bed just as I was, in my clothes and my boots, just for a minute, with no intention of going to sleep—and suddenly I fell asleep ; I don't remember how it happened, indeed. I slept almost four hours ; nobody waked me.

CHAPTER X

1

I WOKE about half-past ten, and for a long time I could not believe my eyes : on the sofa on which I had slept the previous night was sitting my mother, and beside her—the unhappy mother of the dead girl. They were holding each other's hands, they were talking in whispers, I suppose, that they might not wake me, and both were crying. I got up from the bed, and flew straight to kiss my mother. She positively beamed all over, kissed me and make the sign of the cross over me three times with the right hand. Before we had time to say a word the door opened, and Versilov and Vassin came in. My mother at once got up and led the bereaved woman away. Vassin gave me his hand, while Versilov sank into an armchair without saying a word to me. Mother and he had evidently been here for some time. His face looked overcast and careworn.

" What I regret most of all," he began saying slowly to Vassin, evidently in continuation of what they had been discussing outside, " is that I had no time to set it all right yesterday evening ; then probably this terrible thing would not have happened ! And indeed there was time, it was hardly eight o'clock. As soon as she ran away from us last night, I inwardly resolved to follow her and to reassure her, but this unforeseen and urgent business, though of course I might quite well have put it off till to-day . . . or even for a week—this vexatious turn of affairs has hindered and ruined everything. That's just how things do happen ! "

" Perhaps you would not have succeeded in reassuring her ; things had gone too far already, apart from you," Vassin put in.

" No, I should have succeeded, I certainly should have succeeded. And the idea did occur to me to send Sofia Andreyevna in my place. It flashed across my mind, but nothing more. Sofia Andreyevna alone would have convinced her, and the unhappy girl would have been alive. No, never again will I meddle . . . in ' good works ' . . . and it is the only time in my life I have done it ! And I imagined that I had kept up with the times and understood the younger generation. But we elders grow old almost before we grow ripe. And, by the way, there are a terrible number of modern people who go on considering themselves the younger generation from habit, because only yesterday they were such, and meantime they don't notice that they are no longer under the ban of the orthodox."

" There has been a misunderstanding, and the misunderstanding is quite evident," Vassin observed reasonably. " Her mother maintains that after the cruel way she was insulted in that infamous house, she seemed to lose her reason. Add to that her circumstances, the insult in the first place from the merchant . . . all this might have happened in the past, and, to my mind, is in no way particularly characteristic of the younger generation of to-day."

" It's impatient, the present generation, and has little understanding of reality ; and, although that's true of all young people in all ages, it's particularly so in this . . . tell me, what part had Mr. Stebelkov in the trouble ? "

" Mr. Stebelkov," I put in suddenly, " was the cause of it all. If it hadn't been for him nothing would have happened, he poured oil on the flames."

Versilov listened, but he did not glance at me. Vassin frowned.

M

"I blame myself for one ridiculous circumstance," Versilov went on deliberately, dwelling on each syllable as before, "I believe that in my usual stupid way I allowed myself to be lively after a fashion—this frivolous little laugh—in fact, I was not sufficiently abrupt, dry and gloomy, three characteristics which seem to be greatly prized by the young generation. In fact, I gave her grounds for suspecting me of being a gay deceiver."

"Quite the opposite," I put in abruptly again, "the mother lays particular stress on your having made the best possible impression through your gravity, severity even, and sincerity—those were her very words. The dead girl herself praised you on the same grounds directly after you'd gone."

"Y-yes?" Versilov mumbled with a cursory glance in my direction at last. "Take this scrap of paper, it's essential to the business"—he held out a tiny sheet to Vassin. Vassin took it, and seeing I was looking at him with curiosity, gave it to me to read. It was a note of two straggling lines scrawled in pencil, and perhaps in the dark:

"Mother darling, forgive me for cutting short my début into life. Your Olya who is causing you such grief."

"That was only found this morning," Vassin explained.

"What a strange letter!" I cried in astonishment.

"Why strange?" asked Vassin.

"How can anyone use humorous expressions at such a minute?"

Vassin looked at me inquiringly.

"And the humour is strange too," I went on. "It's the conventional school jargon that schoolfellows use with one another. Who could write 'cut short my début into life' at such a moment, in such a letter to her unhappy mother—and she seems to have loved her mother too."

"Why not write it?" said Vassin, still not understanding.

"There's absolutely no humour about it," observed Versilov at last, "the expression, of course, is inappropriate, and quite incongruous, and may, as you say, have been picked up from some high-school slang or from some journalistic stuff; but the dead girl used it in that awful letter quite simply and earnestly."

"That's impossible; she had completed her studies and won the silver medal."

"A silver medal has nothing to do with it. Lots of them complete their studies as brilliantly nowadays."

" The younger generation again," said Vassin, smiling.

" Not at all," said Versilov, getting up and taking his hat. " If the present generation is deficient on the literary side there's no doubt that it possesses other qualifications," he added with unusual gravity. " At the same time ' many ' does not mean ' all ' : you, for instance, I don't accuse of being badly educated on the literary side, and you're a young man too."

" Vassin saw nothing wrong in the use of ' début ' either," I could not resist saying.

Versilov held out his hand to Vassin without speaking. The latter took up his cap to go with him, calling out to me : " Good-bye for now." Versilov went out without noticing me. I too had no time to lose. Come what might, I had to run and find a lodging—now more necessary than ever. My mother was not with the landlady. She had gone out, taking the bereaved woman with her. I went out into the street, feeling particularly cheerful and confident. A new and mighty feeling had sprung up in my soul. As luck would have it, everything helped to maintain this mood. I was exceptionally fortunate and quickly found a lodging in every way suitable. Of this lodging later, but for the moment I will continue with what is more important.

It was past one when I went back to Vassin's to fetch my trunk, and again found him at home. When he saw me he cried with a sincere and good-humoured air :

" How glad I am you've caught me ! I was just going out. I can tell you a piece of news that I think will interest you particularly."

" I'm sure of that," I cried.

" I say, you do look cheerful ! Tell me, did you know anything about a letter that was preserved by Kraft, and came into Versilov's hands yesterday, something concerning the lawsuit he has just won ? In this letter, the testator declares intentions contrary to the decision in the lawcourts yesterday. The letter was written long ago. I know nothing definite about it in fact, but don't you know something ? "

" To be sure I do. The day before yesterday Kraft took me home with him from those people on purpose to give me the letter, and I gave it to Versilov yesterday."

" Yes ? That's just what I thought. Only fancy, that's just the business Versilov was speaking of just now, that prevented him from coming yesterday evening to see that girl—it was owing to that letter. Versilov went straight yesterday evening to Prince Sokolsky's lawyer, handed in the letter, and refused to take the fortune he had won. By now this refusal has been put into legal form. Versilov is not making Prince Sokolsky a present of the money, but declares that he acknowledges his claim to it."

I was dumbfoundered, but ecstatic. I had in reality been convinced that Versilov would destroy the letter, and, what is more, though I had told Kraft that this would be dishonourable, and although I had repeated this to myself in the restaurant, and had told myself that " it was to find a true man, not a man like this that I had come "—yet deeper down, that is, in my inmost soul, I felt that there was nothing to be done but to destroy the letter, that is to say, I looked upon this as quite a natural thing to do. If I blamed Versilov for it afterwards I simply blamed him on purpose, to keep up appearances, and to maintain my moral superiority. But hearing now of Versilov's noble action I was moved to genuine and whole-hearted enthusiasm, blaming myself with shame and remorse for my cynicism and indifference to principle, and instantly exalting Versilov to heights far above me. I almost embraced Vassin.

"What a man ! What a man ! " I exclaimed, rapturously. " Who else would have done it ? "

"I quite agree with you that very many people would not have done it . . . and that it was undoubtedly an extremely disinterested action. . . ."

"But . . . ? Finish, Vassin. You have a ' but ' ? "

"Yes, of course there is a ' but ' ; Versilov's action, to my mind, is a little too hasty, and not quite ingenuous," said Vassin with a smile.

"Not ingenuous ? "

"Yes. There's too much of the ' hero on the pedestal ' about it. For in any case he might have done the same thing without injuring himself. Some part of the inheritance, if not half of it, might well have remained with him, even from the most scrupulous standpoint, especially as the letter has no legal significance, and he has already won the case. The lawyer on the other side shares my opinion. I've just been talking to him. His conduct would have been no less handsome ; but simply through a whim due to pride, things have turned out differently. What's more, Mr. Versilov let himself be carried away by his feelings, and acted too precipitately. He said himself yesterday that he might have put it off for a whole week. . . .''

"Do you know, Vassin, I can't help agreeing with you, but . . . I like it better so, it pleases me more ! "

"However, it's a matter of taste ! You asked for my opinion or I should have held my tongue."

"Even if there is something of the ' pedestal ' about it, so much the better," I said. "A pedestal may be a pedestal but in itself it's a very precious thing. This ' pedestal ' is, anyway, an ' ideal ' of a sort, and it's by no means an improvement that some modern souls are without it : it's better to have it even in a slightly distorted form ! And I'm sure you think so yourself, Vassin darling, Vassin, my dear Vassin ! I am raving but of course you understand me. That's what you're for, Vassin. In any case I embrace and kiss you, Vassin ! "

"So pleased ? "

"Yes, awfully pleased. For the man ' was dead and liveth, he was lost and is found ' ! Vassin, I'm a miserable wretch of a boy, I'm not as good as you. I recognize it just because at some moments I'm different, deeper and loftier. I say this because the day before yesterday I flattered you to your face (and I did that because I had been humiliated and crushed)—I hated you for it for two whole days. I swore the same night that I would never come and see you, and I came to you yesterday morning simply from spite, do you understand, *from spite*. I sat here alone criticizing your room and you, and every one of your books and your landlady. I tried to humble you and laugh at you."

"You shouldn't say that . . . ."

"Yesterday evening, when I concluded from some phrase of yours that you did not understand women, I felt glad that I was able to detect you in it. This morning, when I scored off you over the ' début,' I was awfully pleased again, and all because I had praised you up so before."

"I should think so indeed ! " Vassin cried at last (he still went on smiling, not in the least surprised at me). "Why, that happens with almost every one, only no one admits it, and one ought not to confess it at all, because in any case it passes, and leads to nothing."

"Is it really the same with every one ? Is every one the same ? And you say that quite calmly ? Why, one can't go on living with such views ! "

" You think then that :

> *To me more dear the lie ennobling*
> *Than Truth's dark infamy revealed !* "

" But that's true, you know," I cried. " There's a sacred axiom in those two lines ! "

" I don't know. I can't undertake to decide whether those lines are true or not. Perhaps, as always, the truth lies in the mean : that is, that in one case truth is sacred and in another falsehood. The only thing I know for certain is that that idea will long remain one of the questions most disputed among men. In any case I observe that at the moment you're longing to dance. Well, dance away then, exercise is wholesome ; but I have a mass of work to get through this morning . . . and I've lingered on with you till I'm late ! "

" I'm going ! I'm going ! I'm just off ! One word only," I cried, after seizing my trunk, " my ' throwing myself on your neck' again; it's simply because when I came in you told me this news with such genuine pleasure and were ' so glad ' I had found you, and after the ' début ' incident this morning ; that real gladness of yours turned my ' youthful ardent soul ' to you again. Well, good-bye, good-bye, I'll do my best not to come in the future, and I know that that will please you very much, as I see from your eyes, and it will be an advantage to both of us."

Chattering like this, and almost spluttering in my joyful babble, I hauled up my trunk and set off with it to my lodging. What delighted me most of all was that Versilov had been so unmistakably angry with me, and had been unwilling to speak to me or look at me. As soon as I had deposited my trunk, I at once flew off to my old prince. I must confess that I had rather felt not seeing him those two days. Besides, he would no doubt have heard already about Versilov.

2

I knew he would be delighted to see me, and I protest that I should have gone, apart from Versilov altogether. What had alarmed me yesterday and that morning was the thought that I might meet Katerina Nikolaevna ; but now I was afraid of nothing.

He embraced me joyfully.

" About Versilov ! Have you heard ? " I began forthwith on the great news.

" *Cher enfant*, my dear boy, it's so magnanimous, so noble— in fact it made an overwhelming impression even on Kilyan " (this was the clerk downstairs). " It's injudicious on his part, but it's magnificent, it's heroic ! One must cherish the ideal ! "

" Yes, one must, mustn't one ? We were always agreed about that."

" My dear boy, we always have agreed. Where have you been ? I wanted very much to come and see you but I didn't know where to find you . . for I couldn't go to Versilov's anyway. . . . Though now, after all this . . . you know, my boy, I believe it's by this he has always conquered the women's hearts, by these qualities, no doubt of it. . . ."

" By the way, for fear I forget it, I've been saving this up for you. A very low fellow, a ridiculous fool, abusing Versilov to my face yesterday, used the expression that he was a ' petticoat prophet ' ; what an expression—was it his own expression ? I have been treasuring it up for you. . . ."

" A ' petticoat prophet ' ? *Mais . . . c'est charmant !* Ha-ha ! But that fits him so well, or rather it doesn't—foo ! . . . But it's so apt . . . at least it's not apt at all but . . ."

" Never mind, never mind, don't worry yourself, look upon it simply as a *bon mot !* "

" It's a capital *bon mot*, and do you know, it has a deep signi-ficance. . . . There's a perfectly true idea in it. That is, would you believe it . . . In fact, I'll tell you a tiny little secret. Have you noticed that girl Olympiada ? Would you believe it, she's got a little heartache for Andrey Petrovitch ; in fact it goes so far as cherishing a . . ."

" Cherishing ! What doesn't she deserve ? " I cried with a gesture of contempt.

" *Mon cher*, don't shout, it's all nonsense, it may be you're right from your point of view. By the way, what was the matter with you last time you were here and Katerina Niko-laevna arrived ? . . . You staggered ; I thought you were going to fall down, and was on the point of rushing to support you."

" Never mind that now. The fact is I was simply confused for a special reason. . . ."

" You're blushing now."

" And you must rub it in of course. You know that she's on bad terms with Versilov . . . and then all this ; so it upset me. Ech, leave that ; later ! "

" Yes, let's leave it ! I'm delighted to. . . . In fact, I've been very much to blame in regard to her and I remember I grumbled about her to you. . . . Forget it, my dear ; she will change her opinion of you, too. I quite foresee that. . . . Ah, here's Prince Sergay ! "

A handsome young officer walked in. I looked at him eagerly, I had never seen him before. I call him handsome for every one called him so, but there was something not altogether attractive in that handsome young face. I note this as the impression made the first instant, my first view of him, which remained with me always.

He was thin and finely built, with brown hair, a fresh but somewhat sallow skin and an expression of determination. There was a rather hard look in his beautiful dark eyes even when he was perfectly calm. But his resolute expression repelled one just because one felt that its resoluteness cost him little. But I cannot put it into words. . . . It is true that his face was able to change suddenly from hardness to a wonderfully friendly, gentle and tender expression, and, what is more, with unmistakable frankness. It was just that frankness which was attractive. I will note another characteristic : in spite of its friendliness and frankness his face never looked gay ; even when he laughed with whole-hearted mirth there was always a feeling that there was no trace in his heart of genuine, serene, light-hearted gaiety. . . . But it is extremely difficult to describe a face like this. I'm utterly incapable of it. In his usual stupid way the old prince hastened to introduce us.

" This is my young friend Arkady Andreyevitch Dolgoruky " (again " Andreyevitch ! ").

The young man turned to me with redoubled courtesy, but it was evident that my name was quite unknown to him.

" He's . . . a relation of Andrey Petrovitch's," murmured my vexatious old prince. (How tiresome these old men sometimes are with their little ways !) The young man at once realized who I was.

" Ach ! I heard of you long ago. . . ." he said quickly. " I had the very great pleasure of making the acquaintance of your sister Lizaveta Makarovna last year at Luga. . . . She talked to me about you too."

I was surprised ; there was a glow of real pleasure in his face.

"Excuse me, prince," I answered, drawing back both my hands, " I ought to tell you frankly, and I'm glad to be speaking in the presence of our dear prince, that I was actually desirous of meeting you, and quite recently, only yesterday, desired it with very different motives. I tell you this directly although it may surprise you. In short, I wanted to challenge you for the insult you offered to Versilov a year and a half ago in Ems. And though perhaps you would not have accepted my challenge, as I'm only a school-boy, and not of age, yet I should have sent you the challenge, however you might have taken it or whatever you might have done, and I confess I have the same intention still."

The old prince told me afterwards that I succeeded in pronouncing these words with great dignity.

There was a look of genuine distress on the young man's face.

" You didn't let me finish," he answered earnestly. " The real cordiality with which I greeted you is due to my present feeling for Andrey Petrovitch. I'm sorry I cannot at once tell you all the circumstances. But I assure you on my honour that I have long regarded my unfortunate conduct at Ems with the greatest regret. I resolved on my return to Petersburg to make every reparation within my power, that is, literally to make him an apology in any form he might select. The highest and weightiest considerations have caused this change in my views. The fact that we were at law with one another would not have affected my determination in the least. His action in regard to me yesterday has, so to speak, moved me to the depths of my soul, and even now, would you believe it, I can't get over it. And now, I must tell you, I've come to the prince to inform him of an astounding circumstance. Three hours ago, that is, just at the time when he was drawing up the deed with the lawyer, a friend of Andrey Petrovitch's came to me bringing a challenge from him to a duel . . . a formal challenge for the affair at Ems. . . ."

" He challenged you ? " I cried, and I felt that my eyes glowed and the blood rushed into my face.

" Yes, challenged me. I at once accepted the challenge, but resolved before our meeting to send him a letter in which I explain my view of my conduct, and my deep regret for my horrible blunder . . . for it was only a blunder, an unlucky, fatal blunder ! I may observe that my position in the regiment forced me to run the risk of this duel, and that by sending such a letter before our meeting I have exposed myself to public censure . . . do you understand ? But in spite of that, I made up my mind to send it, and I've only not done so because an hour after the challenge I received another letter from him in which he apologizes for having troubled me, asks me to forget the challenge, and adds that he regrets his ' momentary outburst of cowardice and egoism '—his own words. So that he relieves me from all obligation to send the letter. I had not yet dispatched it, but I have come to say something about this to the prince. . . . And I assure you I have suffered far more from the reproaches of my conscience than anyone. . . . Is this sufficient explanation for you, Arkady Makarovitch, for the time at any rate ? Will you do me the honour to believe in my complete sincerity ? "

I was completely conquered. I found a perfect frankness, which was the last thing I had expected. Indeed, I had expected nothing of this kind. I muttered something in reply and forthwith held out both hands. He shook both of them in his delightedly. Then he drew the old prince away and talked to him for five minutes in the latter's bedroom.

" If you want to do me particular pleasure," he said frankly in a loud voice, addressing me as he came out of the prince's room, " come back straight with me and I will show you the letter I am just sending to Andrey Petrovitch and with it his letter to me."

I consented with the utmost readiness. My old prince made a great bustle at seeing us off and called me, too, apart into his room for a minute.

" *Mon ami*, how glad I am, how glad I am. . . . We'll talk of it all later. By the way, I've two letters here in my portfolio. One has to be delivered with a personal explanation and the other must go to the bank—and there too . . ."

And he at once gave me two commissions which he pretended were urgent and required exceptional effort and attention. I should have to go, deliver them myself, give a receipt and so on.

" Ha, you are cunning ! " I cried as I took the letters, " I swear all this is nonsense and you've no work for me to do at all. You've invented these two jobs on purpose to make me believe that I am of use and not taking money for nothing."

" *Mon enfant,* I protest that you are mistaken. They are both urgent matters. *Cher enfant !* " he cried, suddenly overcome by a rush of emotion, " my dear young friend " (he put both hands on my head), " I bless you and your destiny. Let us always be as true-hearted as to-day . . . as kind-hearted and good as possible, let us love all that is fair and good . . . in all its varied forms. . . . Well, *enfin . . . enfin rendons grâce . . . et je te benis !* "

He could not go on, but whimpered over my head. I must confess I was almost in tears too ; anyway I embraced my queer old friend with sincere and delighted feeling. We kissed each other warmly.

3

Prince Sergay as I shall call him (that is Prince Sergay Petrovitch Sokolsky) drove me in a smart victoria to his flat, and my first impression was one of surprise at its magnificence. Not that it was really magnificent, but it was a flat such as " well-to-do people " live in, light, large, lofty rooms (I saw two of them) and the furniture well padded, comfortable, abundant and of the best—though I've no idea whether it was in the Versailles or Renaissance style. There were rugs, carvings, and statuettes, though everybody said that the Sokolskys were beggars, and had absolutely nothing. I had heard, however, that Prince Sergay had cut a dash wherever he could, here, in Moscow, in his old regiment and in Paris, that he was a gambler and that he had debts. My coat was crumpled and covered with fluff, too, because I had slept in it without undressing, and this was the fourth day I had worn my shirt. My coat was not really shabby but when I went into Prince Sergay's, I recalled Versilov's suggestion that I should have a new suit.

"Only fancy, owing to a case of suicide, I slept all night without undressing," I observed with a casual air, and as he immediately looked attentive I briefly told the story. But what interested him most was evidently his letter. What seemed strangest to me was that he had not smiled nor betrayed the slightest symptom of amusement when I had told him I meant to challenge him to a duel. Though I should have been able to prevent his laughing, his gravity was strange in a man of his class. We sat opposite one another in the middle of the room, at his immense writing table, and he handed me for my inspection the fair copy of his letter to Versilov. The letter was very much like all that he had just told me at the old prince's ; it was written with warmth, indeed. I really did not know at first what to make of his evident frankness and his apparent leaning towards what was good and right, but I was already beginning to be conquered by it, for after all what reason had I for disbelieving it ? Whatever he was like, and whatever stories were told of him, he yet might have good impulses. I looked, too, at Versilov's second note, which consisted of seven lines—his withdrawal of his challenge. Though he did, it is true, speak of his own cowardice and egoism, yet on the whole the note was suggestive of a sort of disdain . . . or rather there was apparent in the whole episode a superlative nonchalance. I did not, however, utter this thought aloud.

" What do you think of this withdrawal, though ? " I asked, " you don't suppose he acted from cowardice, do you ? "

" Of course not," said Prince Sergay with a smile, though a very grave one, and in fact he was becoming more and more preoccupied. " I know quite well how manly he is. It's a special point of view . . . his peculiar turn of ideas."

" No doubt," I broke in warmly. " A fellow called Vassin says that there's too much of the ' pedestal ' about the line he has taken with this letter and his refusing to take the fortune. . . . But to my mind things like that aren't done for effect but correspond with something fundamental within."

" I know Mr. Vassin very well," observed Prince Sergay.

" Oh, yes, you must have seen him in Luga."

We suddenly glanced at one another, and, I remember, I flushed a little. Anyway he changed the subject. I had a great longing to talk, however. The thought of one person I had met the day before tempted me to ask him certain questions, but I did not know how to approach the subject. And altogether I felt ill at ease. I was impressed, too, by his perfect breeding, his courtesy, his manner, his absence of constraint, in fact by the polish which these aristocrats acquire almost from the cradle. I saw two glaring mistakes in grammar in his letter. And as a rule, when I meet such people I'm not at all overawed and only become more abrupt, which is sometimes, perhaps, a mistake. But on this occasion the thought that I was covered with fluff contributed to my discomfiture so that, in fact, I floundered a little and dropped into being overfamilar. I caught Prince Sergay eyeing me very intently at times.

"Tell me, prince," I blurted out suddenly, "don't you secretly think it absurd that a youngster like me should think of challenging you, especially for an affront to some one else ? "

"An affront to a father may well be resented. No, I don't think it's absurd."

"It seems to me that it's dreadfully absurd . . . from one point of view, not of course from my own. Especially as my name is Dolgoruky and not Versilov. And if you're telling me a falsehood, or are trying to smoothe things over simply from worldly politeness, it stands to reason that you are deceiving me in everything else."

"No, I don't think it's absurd," he repeated with great seriousness. "How could you help feeling like a son to your father ? It's true, you're young . . . because . . . I don't know . . . I believe that a youth not of age can't fight a duel . . . and a challenge can't be accepted from him . . . by the rules. . . . But there is, if you like, one serious objection to be made : if you send a challenge without the knowledge of the offended party on whose behalf you are acting, you seem to be guilty of a certain lack of respect to him, don't you ? . . ."

Our conversation was interrupted by a footman who came in to make some announcement. Prince Sergay, who seemed to have been expecting him, went at once to meet him without finishing what he was saying. So the announcement was made in an undertone and I did not hear it.

"Excuse me," said Prince Sergay, turning to me, "I'll be back in a moment."

And he went out. I was left alone ; I walked up and down the room, thinking. Strange to say, he attracted me and at the same time repelled me intensely. There was something in him for which I could not find a name, though it was very repellent. "If he isn't laughing at me he certainly must be very guileless, but if he has been laughing at me then . . . perhaps I should think him cleverer. . . ." I thought rather oddly. I went up to the table, and read the letter to Versilov once more. In my abstraction I didn't notice the time, but when I roused myself I found that the prince's minute had lasted at least a quarter of an hour. This disturbed me a little ; I walked up and down once more, at last I took my hat and decided, I remember, to go out to try and find some one to send to Prince Sergay, and when he came, to say good-bye to him at once, declaring that I had work to do and could stay no longer. I fancied that that would be the most suitable thing to do, for I was rather tormented by the idea that he was treating me very casually in leaving me so long.

There were two doors in the room, both shut, and on the same side, one at each end of it. Forgetting which door I had come in by, or rather lost in thought, I opened one of them, and suddenly, in a long narrow room, I saw, sitting on the sofa, my sister Liza. There was no one else in the room and she was certainly waiting for some one. But before I had time even to feel surprised, I heard the voice of Prince Sergay speaking loudly to some one, and returning to the study. I hurriedly closed the door and Prince Sergay, coming in at the other, noticed nothing. I remember he began to apologize and said something about " Anna Fyodorovna." But I was so amazed and confused that I hardly took in what he said, and could only mutter that I simply must go home, and stubbornly persisting in this, I beat a hasty retreat. The well-bred prince must have looked with curiosity at my manners. He came with me right into the hall, still talking, and I neither answered nor looked at him.

4

I turned to the left when I got into the street and walked away at random. There was nothing coherent in my mind. I walked along slowly and I believe I had walked a good way, some five hundred paces, when I felt a light tap on my shoulder. I turned and saw Liza ; she had overtaken me and tapped me on the shoulder with her umbrella. There was a wonderful gaiety and a touch of roguishness in her beaming eyes.

" How glad I am you came this way, or I shouldn't have met you to-day ! " She was a little out of breath from walking fast.

" How breathless you are."

" I've been running so as to catch you up."

" Liza, was it you I saw just now ? "

" Where ? "

" At the prince's. . . . At Prince Sokolsky's."

" No, it wasn't me. You didn't see me. . . ."

I made no answer and we walked on for ten paces.   Liza burst into a fit of laughter.

" It was me, of course it was !   Why, you saw me yourself, you looked into my eyes, and I looked into yours, so how can you ask whether you saw me ?   What a character !   And do you know I dreadfully wanted to laugh when you looked at me then.   You looked so awfully funny."

She laughed violently.   I felt all the anguish in my heart fade away at once.

" But tell me how did you come to be there ? "

" To see Anna Fyodorovna."

" What Anna Fyodorovna ? "

" Mme. Stolbyeev.   When we were staying in Luga I used to spend whole days with her.   She used to receive mother, too, and used even to come and see us, though she visited scarcely anyone else there.   She is a distant relation of Andrey Petrovitch's, and a relation of Prince Sokolsky's too : she's a sort of old aunt of his."

" Then she lives at Prince Sokolsky's ? "

" No, he lives with her."

" Then whose flat is it ? "

" It's her flat.   The whole flat has been hers for the last year.   Prince Sokolsky has only just arrived and is staying with her.   Yes, and she's only been in Petersburg four days herself."

" I say, Liza, bother her flat and her too ! "

" No, she's splendid."

" Well, let her be, that's her affair.   We're splendid too ! See what a day it is, see how jolly !   How pretty you are to-day, Liza.   But you're an awful baby though."

" Arkady, tell me, that girl, the one who came yesterday. . . ."

" Oh, the pity of it, Liza !   The pity of it ! "

" Ach, what a pity !   What a fate !   Do you know it's a sin for us to be walking here so happily while her soul is hovering somewhere in darkness, in some unfathomable darkness, after her sin and the wrong done her. . . . Arkady, who was responsible for her suicide ?   Oh, how terrible it is !   Do you ever think of that outer darkness ?   Ach, how I fear death, and how sinful it is.   I don't like the dark, what a glorious thing the sun is !   Mother says it's a sin to be afraid. . . . Arkady, do you know mother well ? "

" Very little, Liza.   Very little so far."

" Ah, what a wonderful person she is ; and you ought to get to know her ! She needs understanding. . . ."

" Yes, but you see, I didn't know you either; but I know you now, thoroughly. I've found you out altogether in one minute. Though you are afraid of death, Liza, you must be proud, bold, plucky. Better than I am, ever so much better ! I like you awfully, Liza. Ach, Liza ! let death come when it must, but meantime let us live—let us live ! Oh, let us pity that poor girl, but let us bless life all the same ! Don't you think so ? I have an 'idea,' Liza. Liza, you know, of course, that Versilov has refused to take the fortune ? You don't know my soul, Liza, you don't know what that man has meant to me. . . ."

" Not know indeed ! I know all that."

" You know all about it ? But, of course, you would ! You're clever, cleverer than Vassin. Mother and you have eyes that are penetrating and humane, I mean a point of view that is. I'm talking nonsense. . . . Liza, I'm not good for much, in lots of ways."

" You want taking in hand, that's all."

" Take me in hand, Liza. How nice it is to look at you to-day. Do you know that you are very pretty ? I have never seen your eyes before. . . . I've only seen them for the first time to-day . . . where did you get them to-day, Liza ? Where have you bought them ? What price have you paid for them ? Liza, I've never had a friend, and I've thought the idea of friendship nonsense ; but it's not nonsense with you. . . . Shall we be friends ! You understand what I mean ? "

" I quite understand."

" And you know—we'll simply be friends, no conditions, no contract."

" Yes, simply, simply, with only one condition : that if we ever blame one another, if we're displeased about anything, if we become nasty and horrid, even if we forget all this,—we will never forget this day, and this hour ! Let's vow that to ourselves. Let us vow that we will always remember this day and how we walked arm in arm together, and how we laughed and were gay. . . . Yes ? Shall we ? "

" Yes, Liza, yes, I swear. But, Liza, I feel as though I'm hearing you talk for the first time. . . . Liza, have you read much ? "

"He has never asked till now! Only yesterday for the first time, when I said something, you deigned to notice me, honoured sir, Mr. Wiseacre."

"But why didn't you begin to talk to me if I've been such a fool?"

"I kept expecting you'd grow wiser. I've been watching you from the very first, Arkady Makarovitch, and as I watched you I said to myself ' he'll come to me, it's bound to end in his coming'—and I made up my mind I'd better leave you the honour of taking the first step. 'No,' I said to myself, 'you can run after me.'"

"Ah, you coquette! Come, Liza, tell me honestly, have you been laughing at me for the last month?"

"Oh, you are funny, you're awfully funny, Arkady! And do you know, what I've been loving you for most all this month is your being so queer. But in some ways you're a horrid boy too—I say that for fear you should grow conceited. And do you know who else has been laughing at you? Mother's been laughing at you, mother and I together. 'Oh my,' we whispered, 'what a queer boy! My goodness, what a queer boy!' And you sat all the while imagining that we were trembling before you."

"Liza, what do you think about Versilov?"

"I think a great deal about him; but we won't talk about him just now, you know. There's no need to talk of him to-day, is there?"

"Quite so! Yes, you're awfully clever, Liza! You are certainly cleverer than I am. You wait a bit, Liza, I'll make an end of all this, and then I shall have something to tell you. . . ."

"What are you frowning at?"

"I'm not frowning, Liza, it's nothing. . . . You see, Liza, it's best to be open: it's a peculiarity of mine that I don't like some tender spots on my soul being touched upon . . . or rather, it's shameful to be often displaying certain feelings for the admiration of all, isn't it? So that I sometimes prefer to frown and hold my tongue. You're clever, you must understand."

"Yes, and what's more, I'm the same myself; I understand you in everything. Do you know that mother's the same too?

"Ah, Liza! Oh, to live a long while on this earth! Ah? What did you say?"

N

" I said nothing."

" You're looking ? "

" Yes, and so are you.   I look at you and love you."

I went with her almost all the way home and gave her my address.   As we parted, for the first time in my life I kissed her. . . .

5

And all this would have been very nice but there was one thing that was not nice : one painful thought had been throbbing in my mind all night and I could not shake it off.   This was, that when I had met that unhappy girl at the gate I told her I was leaving the house myself, leaving home, that one left bad people and made a home for oneself, and that Versilov had a lot of illegitimate children.   Such words from a son about his father must, of course, have confirmed all her suspicions of Versilov's character and of his having insulted her.   I had blamed Stebelkov, but perhaps I had been the chief one to pour oil on the flames.   That thought was awful, it is awful even now. . . . But then, that morning, though I'd begun to be uneasy, I told myself it was all nonsense.   " Oh, ' things had gone too far already ' apart from me," I repeated from time to time, " it's nothing ; it will pass !   I shall get over it.   I shall make up for this somehow, I've fifty years before me ! "

But yet the idea haunted me.

PART II

CHAPTER I

1

I PASS over an interval of almost two months. The reader need not be uneasy, everything will be clear from the latter part of my story. I start again from the 15th of November, a day I remember only too well for many reasons. To begin with, no one who had known me two months before would have recognized me, externally anyway, that is to say, anyone would have known me but would not have been able to make me out. To begin with I was dressed like a dandy. The conscientious and tasteful Frenchman, whom Versilov had once tried to recommend me, had not only made me a whole suit, but had already been rejected as not good enough. I already had suits made by other, superior, tailors, of a better class, and I even ran up bills with them. I had an account, too, at a celebrated restaurant, but I was still a little nervous there and paid on the spot whenever I had money, though I knew it was *mauvais ton*, and that I was compromising myself by doing so. A French barber on the Nevsky Prospect was on familiar terms with me, and told me anecdotes as he dressed my hair. And I must confess I practised my French on him. Though I know French, and fairly well indeed, yet I'm afraid of beginning to speak it in grand society; and I dare say my accent is far from Parisian. I have a smart coachman, Matvey, with a smart turn-out, and he is always at my service when I send for him; he has a pale sorrel horse, a fast trotter (I don't like greys). Everything is not perfect, however: it's the 15th of November and has been wintry weather for the last three days, and my fur coat is an old one, lined with raccoon, that once was Versilov's. It wouldn't fetch more than twenty-five roubles. I must get a new one, and my pocket is empty, and I must, besides, have money in reserve for this evening whatever happens—without that I shall be ruined and miserable : that was how I put it to myself at the time. Oh, degradation ! Where had these thousands come from, these fast trotters, these expensive restaurants ? How could I all at once change like this and forget everything ? Shame ! Reader, I am beginning now the story of my shame and disgrace, and nothing in life can be more shameful to me than these recollections.

I speak as a judge and I know that I was guilty. Even in the whirl in which I was caught up, and though I was alone without a guide or counsellor, I was, I swear, conscious of my downfall, and so there's no excuse for me. And yet, for those two months I was almost happy—why almost ? I was quite happy ! And so happy—would it be believed—that the consciousness of my degradation, of which I had glimpses at moments (frequent moments !) and which made me shudder in my inmost soul, only intoxicated me the more. " What do I care if I'm fallen ! And I won't fall, I'll get out of it ! I have a lucky star ! " I was crossing a precipice on a thin plank without a rail, and I was pleased at my position, and even peeped into the abyss. It was risky and it was delightful. And " my idea ? " My " idea " later, the idea would wait. Everything that happened was simply " a temporary deviation." " Why not enjoy oneself ? " That's what was amiss with my idea, I repeat, it admitted of all sorts of deviations ; if it had not been so firm and fundamental I might have been afraid of deviating.

And meanwhile I kept on the same humble lodging ; I kept it on but I didn't live in it ; there I kept my trunk, my bag, and my various properties. But I really lived with Prince Sergay. I spent my days there and I slept there at night. And this went on for weeks. . . . How this came to pass I'll tell in a minute, but meanwhile I will describe my little lodging. It was already dear to me. Versilov had come to see me there of himself, first of all after our quarrel, and often subsequently. I repeat, this was a period of shame but of great happiness. . . . Yes, and everything at that time was so successful and so smiling. " And what was all that depression in the past about ? " I wondered in some ecstatic moments, " why those old painful self-lacerations, my solitary and gloomy childhood, my foolish dreams under my quilt, my vows, my calculations, even my ' idea ' ? I imagined and invented all that, and it turns out that the world's not like that at all ; see how happy and gay I am : I have a father—

Versilov ; I have a friend—Prince Sergay ; I have besides . . . but that ' besides ' we'll leave."

Alas, it was all done in the name of love, magnanimity, honour, and afterwards it turned out hideous, shameless and ignominious.

Enough.

2

He came to see me for the first time three days after our rupture. I was not at home, and he waited for me. Though I had been expecting him every day, when I went into my tiny cupboard of a room there was a mist before my eyes, and my heart beat so violently that I stopped short in the doorway. Fortunately my landlord was with him, having thought it necessary to introduce himself at once, that the visitor might not be bored with waiting. He was eagerly describing something to Versilov. He was a titular counsellor, a man about forty, much disfigured by small-pox, very poor, and burdened with a consumptive wife and an invalid child. He was of a very communicative and unassuming character, but not without tact. I was relieved at his presence, which was a positive deliverance for me, for what could I have said to Versilov ? I had known, known in earnest that Versilov would come of his own prompting—exactly as I wanted him to, for nothing in the world would have induced me to go to him first, and not from obstinacy, but just from love of him ; a sort of jealous love—I can't express it. Indeed, the reader won't find me eloquent at any time. But though I had been expecting him for those three days, and had been continually picturing how he would come in, yet though I tried my utmost, I could not imagine what we should say to one another at first, after all that had happened.

" Ah, here you are ! " he said to me affectionately, holding out his hand and not getting up. " Sit down with us ; Pyotr Ippolitovitch is telling me something very interesting about that stone near the Pavlovsky barracks . . . or somewhere in that direction."

" Yes, I know the stone," I made haste to answer, dropping into a chair beside him. They were sitting at the table. The whole room was just fourteen feet square. I drew a deep breath.

There was a gleam of pleasure in Versilov's eyes. I believe

he was uncertain, and afraid I should be demonstrative. He was reassured.

"You must begin again, Pyotr Ippolitovitch." They were already calling each other by their names.

"It happened in the reign of the late Tsar," Pyotr Ippolitovitch said, addressing me nervously and with some uneasiness, anxious as to the effect of his story. "You know that stone—a stupid stone in the street, and what use is it, it's only in the way, you'd say, wouldn't you? The Tsar rode by several times, and every time there was the stone. At last the Tsar was displeased, and with good reason; a rock, a regular rock standing in the street, spoiling it. 'Remove the stone!' Well, he said remove it—you understand what that means—'remove the stone!' The late Tsar—do you remember him? What was to be done with the stone? They all lost their heads, there was the town council, and a most important person, I can't remember his name, one of the greatest personages of the time, who was put in charge of the matter. Well, this great personage listened; they told him it would cost fifteen thousand roubles, no less, and in silver too (for it was not till the time of the late Tsar that paper money could be changed into silver). 'Fifteen thousand, what a sum!' At first the English wanted to bring rails, and remove it by steam; but think what that would have cost! There were no railways then, there was only one running to Tsarskoe-Selo."

"Why, they might have smashed it up!" I cried, frowning. I felt horribly vexed and ashamed in Versilov's presence. But he was listening with evident pleasure. I understood that he was glad to have the landlord there, as he too was abashed with me. I saw that. I remember I felt it somehow touching in him.

"Smash it up! Yes, that was the very idea they arrived at. And Montferant, too,—he was building St. Isaak's Cathedral at the time.—Smash it up, he said, and then take it away. But what would that cost?"

"It would cost nothing. Simply break it up and carry it away."

"No, excuse me, a machine would be wanted to do it, a steam-engine, and besides, where could it be taken? And such a mountain, too! 'Ten thousand,' they said, 'not less than ten or twelve thousand.'"

"I say, Pyotr Ippolitovitch, that's nonsense, you know. It couldn't have been so. . . ."

But at that instant Versilov winked at me unseen, and in that wink I saw such delicate compassion for the landlord, even distress on his account, that I was delighted with it, and I laughed.

"Well, well then," cried the landlord, delighted; he had noticed nothing, and was awfully afraid, as such story-tellers always are, that he would be pestered with questions; "but then a Russian workman walks up, a young fellow, you know the typical Russian, with a beard like a wedge, in a long-skirted coat, and perhaps a little drunk too . . . but no, he wasn't drunk. He just stands by while those Englishmen and Montferant are talking away, and that great personage drives up just then in his carriage, and listens, and gets angry at the way they keep discussing it and can't decide on anything. And suddenly he notices the workman at a distance standing there and smiling deceitfully, that is, not deceitfully though, I'm wrong there, what is it . . . ? "

"Derisively," Versilov prompted him discreetly.

"Derisively, yes, a little derisively, that kind, good Russian smile, you know; the great personage was in a bad humour, you understand : ' What are you waiting here for, big beard ? ' said he. ' Who are you ? '

" ' Why, I'm looking at this stone here, your Highness,' says he. Yes, I believe he said Highness, and I fancy it was Prince Suvorov, the Italian one, the ancestor of the general. . . . But no, it was not Suvorov, and I'm so sorry I've forgotten who it was exactly, but though he was a Highness he was a genuine thorough-bred Russian, a Russian type, a patriot, a cultured Russian heart ; well, he saw what was up.

" ' What is it,' says he. ' Do you want to take away the stone ? What are you sniggering about ? '

" ' At the Englishmen, chiefly, your Highness. They ask a prodigious price because the Russian purse is fat, and they've nothing to eat at home. Let me have a hundred roubles, your Highness,' says he ; ' by to-morrow evening we'll move the stone.'

"Can you imagine such a proposition ? The English, of course, are ready to devour him ; Montferant laughs. But that Highness with the pure Russian heart says : ' Give him a hundred roubles ! But surely you won't remove it ? ' says he.

" ' To-morrow evening, your Highness, we'll have it on the move,' says he.

" ' But how will you do it ? '

" ' If you'll excuse me, your Highness, that's our secret,' he says, and in that Russian way, you know. It pleased him : ' Hey, give him anything he wants.' And so they left it. What would you suppose he did ? "

The landlord paused, and looked from one to the other with a face full of sentiment.

" I don't know," said Versilov, smiling ; I scowled.

" Well, I'll tell you what he did," said the landlord, with as much triumph as though it were his own achievement, " he hired some peasants with spades, simple Russians, and began digging a deep hole just at the edge of it. They were digging all night ; they dug an immense hole as big as the stone and just about an inch and a half deeper, and when they dug it out he told them to dig out the earth from under the stone, cautiously, little by little. Well, naturally, as they'd dug the earth away the stone had nothing to stand upon, it began to overbalance ; and as soon as it began to shake they pushed with their hands upon the stone, shouting hurrah, in true Russian style, and the stone fell with a crash into the hole ! Then they shovelled earth on it, rammed it down with a mallet, paved it over with little stones—the road was smooth, the stone had disappeared ! "

" Only fancy ! " cried Versilov.

" The people rushed up to be sure, in multitudes innumerable ; the Englishmen had seen how it would be long before ; they were furious. Montferant came up : ' That's the peasant style,' says he, ' it's too simple,' says he. ' That's just it, that it's so simple, but you never thought of it, you fools ! ' And so I tell you that commander, that great personage, simply embraced him and kissed him. ' And where do you come from ? ' says he. ' From the province of Yaroslav, your Excellency, we're tailors by trade, and we come to Petersburg in the summer to sell fruit.' Well, it came to the ears of the authorities ; the authorities ordered a medal to be given him, so he went about with a medal on his neck ; but he drank himself to death afterwards, they say ; you know the typical Russian, he has no self-restraint ! That's why the foreigners have got the better of us so far, yes, there it is ! "

" Yes, of course, the Russian mind. . . ." Versilov was beginning.

But at this point, luckily, the landlord was called away by

his invalid wife, and hastened off, or I should have been unable to restrain myself. Versilov laughed.

"He's been entertaining me for a whole hour, my dear. That stone . . . is the very model of patriotic unseemliness among such stories, but how could I interrupt him ? As you saw, he was melting with delight. And what's more, I believe the stone's there still, if I'm not mistaken, and hasn't been buried in the hole at all."

"Good heavens, yes ! " I cried, "that's true ! How could he dare ! . . ."

"What's the matter ? Why, I believe you're really indignant ; he certainly has muddled things up. I heard a story of the sort about a stone when I was a child, only of course it was a little different, and not about the same stone. That ' it came to the ears of the authorities ! ' Why, there was a pæan of glory in his heart when he uttered that phrase ' it came to the ears of the authorities.' In the pitiful narrowness of their lives they can't get on without such stories. They have numbers of them, chiefly owing to their incontinence. They've learnt nothing, they know nothing exactly, and they have a longing to talk about something besides cards and their wares, something of universal interest, something poetic. . . . What sort of man is this Pyotr Ippolitovitch ? "

"A very poor creature, and unfortunate too."

"Well, there, you see, perhaps he doesn't even play cards. I repeat, in telling that foolish story he was satisfying his love for his neighbour : you see, he wanted to make us happy. His sentiment of patriotism was gratified too ; they've got another story, for instance, that the English gave Zavyalov a million on condition that he shouldn't put his stamp on his handiwork."

"Oh, goodness, I've heard that story too."

"Who hasn't heard it, and the teller of it knows, too, that you have heard it, but still he tells it, *intentionally* supposing that you haven't. The vision of the Swedish king, I believe, is a little out of date with them now, but in my youth it used to be repeated unctuously, in a mysterious whisper. And so was the story of some one's having knelt in the Senate before the Senators at the beginning of last century. There were lots of anecdotes about Commander Bashutsky, too, how he carried away a monument. They simply love anecdotes of the court ; for instance, tales of Tchernyshev, a minister in the last reign, how when he was an old man of seventy he got himself up to look like a man of thirty, so much so that the late Tsar was amazed at the levées. . . ."

" I've heard that too."

" Who hasn't heard it ? All these anecdotes are the height of indecency ; but, let me tell you, this kind of indecency is far more deeply rooted and widely spread than we imagine. The desire to lie with the object of giving pleasure to your neighbour one meets even in Russian society of the highest breeding, for we all suffer from this incontinence of our hearts. Only anecdotes of a different type are current among us : the number of stories they tell about America is simply amazing, and they're told by men even of ministerial rank ! I must confess I belong to that indecent class myself, and I've suffered from it all my life."

" I've told anecdotes about Tchernyshev several times myself."

" You've told them yourself ? "

" There's another lodger here besides me, marked with small-pox too, an old clerk, but he's awfully prosaic, and as soon as Pyotr Ippolitovitch begins to speak he tries to refute him and contradict. He's reduced Pyotr Ippolitovitch to such a point that he waits on the old fellow like a slave, and does everything to please him, simply to make him listen."

" That's another type of the indecent, one even perhaps more revolting than the first. The first sort is all ecstasy ! ' You only let me lie,' he seems to say, ' you'll see how nice it will be.' The second sort is all spleen and prose. ' I won't let you lie,' he says, ' where, when, in what year ? '—in fact a man with no heart. My dear boy, we must always let a man lie a little. It's quite innocent. Indeed we may let him lie a great deal. In the first place it will show our delicacy, and secondly, people will let us lie in return—two immense advantages at once. *Que diable !* one must love one's neighbour. But it's time for me to be off. You've arranged the place charmingly," he added, getting up from his chair. " I'll tell Sofia Andreyevna and your sister that I've been here and found you quite well. Good-bye, my dear."

Could this be all ? This was not at all what I wanted. I was expecting something different, something important, though I quite understood that this was how it must be. I got up with a candle to light him down the stairs. The landlord would have come forward, but without Versilov's seeing it I seized him by the arm and thrust him back savagely. He stared with astonishment, but immediately vanished.

"These staircases . . ." Versilov mumbled, dwelling on the syllables evidently in order to say something, and evidently afraid I might say something, "I'm no longer used to such stairs, and you're on the third storey, but now I can find the way. . . . Don't trouble, my dear, you'll catch cold, too."

But I did not leave him. We were going down the second flight. . . .

"I've been expecting you for the last three days," broke from me suddenly, as it were of itself ; I was breathless.

"Thank you, my dear."

"I knew you'd be sure to come."

"And I knew that you knew I should be sure to come. Thank you, my dear."

He was silent. We had reached the outer door, and I still followed him. He opened the door ; the wind rushing in blew out my candle. Then I clutched his hand. It was pitch dark. He started but said nothing. I stooped over his hand and kissed it greedily several times, many times.

"My darling boy, why do you love me so much ? " he said, but in quite a different voice. His voice quivered, there was a ring of something quite new in it as though it were not he who spoke.

I tried to answer something, but couldn't, and ran upstairs. He stood waiting where he was, and it was only when I was back in the flat that I heard the front door open and shut with a slam. I slipped by the landlord, who turned up again, and went into my room, fastened the latch, and without lighting the candle threw myself on my bed, buried my face in the pillow and cried and cried. It was the first time I had cried since I was at Touchard's. My sobs were so violent, and I was so happy . . . but why describe it ?

I write this now without being ashamed of it, for perhaps it was all good, in spite of its absurdity.

3

But didn't I make him suffer for it ! I became frightfully overbearing. There was no reference to this scene between us afterwards. On the contrary, we met three days later as though nothing had happened—what's more, I was almost rude that evening, and he too seemed rather dry. This happened in my room again ; for some reason I had not been to see him in spite of my longing to see my mother.

We talked all this time, that is throughout these two months, only of the most abstract subjects. And I can't help wondering at it ; we did nothing but talk of abstract subjects—of the greatest interest and of vast significance for humanity, of course, but with no bearing whatever on the practical position. Yet many, many aspects of the practical position needed, and urgently needed, defining and clearing up, but of that we did not speak. I did not even say anything about my mother or Liza or . . . or indeed about myself and my whole history. Whether this was due to shame or to youthful stupidity I don't know. I expect it was stupidity, for shame I could have overcome. But I domineered over him frightfully, and absolutely went so far as insolence more than once, even against my own feelings. This all seemed to happen of itself, inevitably ; I couldn't restrain myself. His tone was as before, one of light mockery, though always extremely affectionate in spite of everything. I was struck, too, by the fact that he preferred coming to me, so that at last I very rarely went to see my mother, not more than once a week, especially towards the latter part of the time, as I became more and more absorbed in frivolity. He used always to come in the evenings, to sit and chat with me, he was very fond of talking to the landlord too, which enraged me in a man like him.

The idea struck me that he might have nowhere to go except to see me. But I knew for a fact that he had acquaintances, and that he had, indeed, of late renewed many of his old ties in society, which he had dropped the year before. But he did not seem to be particularly fascinated by them, and seemed to have renewed many of them simply in a formal way ; he preferred coming to see me.

I was sometimes awfully touched by the timid way in which he almost always opened my door, and for the first minute looked with strange anxiety into my eyes. " Am I in the way ? " he seemed to ask, " tell me, and I'll go." He even said as much sometimes. Once, for instance, towards the end he came in when I had just put on a suit, brand new from the tailor's, and was just setting off to Prince Sergay's, to go off somewhere with him (where, I will explain later). He sat down without noticing that I was on the point of going out ; he showed at moments a

remarkable absence of mind. As luck would have it, he began
to talk of the landlord. I fired up.

" Oh, damn the landlord ! "

" Ah, my dear," he said, getting up, " I believe you're going
out and I'm hindering you. . . . Forgive me, please."

And he meekly hastened to depart. Such meekness towards
me from a man like him, a man so aristocratic and independent,
who had so much individuality, at once stirred in my heart all
my tenderness for him, and trust in him. But if he loved me so
much, why did he not check me at the time of my degradation ?
If he had said one word I should perhaps have pulled up. Though
perhaps I should not. But he did see my foppery, my flaunting
swagger, my smart Matvey (I wanted once to drive him back
in my sledge but he would not consent, and indeed it happened
several times that he refused to be driven in it), he could see I
was squandering money—and he said not a word, not a word,
he showed no curiosity even ! I'm surprised at that to this day ;
even now. And yet I didn't stand on ceremony with him, and
spoke openly about everything, though I never gave him a word
of explanation. He didn't ask and I didn't speak.

Yet on two or three occasions we did speak on the money
question. I asked him on one occasion, soon after he renounced
the fortune he had won, how he was going to live now.

" Somehow, my dear," he answered with extraordinary
composure.

I know now that more than half of Tatyana Pavlovna's little
capital of five thousand roubles has been spent on Versilov
during the last two years.

Another time it somehow happened that we talked of my
mother.

" My dear boy," he said mournfully, " I used often to say to
Sofia Andreyevna at the beginning of our life together, though
indeed I've said it in the middle and at the end too : ' My dear,
I worry you and torment you, and I don't regret it as long as
you're before me, but if you were to die I know I should kill
myself to atone for it.' "

I remember, however, that he was particularly open that evening.

" If only I were a weak-willed nonentity and suffered from
the consciousness of it ! But you see that's not so, I know I'm
exceedingly strong, and in what way do you suppose ? Why
just in that spontaneous power of accommodating myself to
anything whatever, so characteristic of all intelligent Russians

of our generation. There's no crushing me, no destroying me, no surprising me. I've as many lives as a cat. I can with perfect convenience experience two opposite feelings at one and the same time, and not, of course, through my own will. I know, nevertheless, that it's dishonourable just because it's so sensible. I've lived almost to fifty, and to this day I don't know whether it's a good thing I've gone on living or not. I like life, but that follows as a matter of course. But for a man like me to love life is contemptible. Of late there has been a new movement, and the Krafts won't accommodate themselves to things, and shoot themselves. But it's evident that the Krafts are stupid, we, to be sure, are clever—so that one can draw no parallel, and the question remains open anyway. And can it be that the earth is only for such as we? In all probability it is; but the idea is a comfortless one. However . . . however, the question remains open, anyway."

He spoke mournfully and yet I didn't know whether he was sincere or not. He always had a manner which nothing would have made him drop.

4

Then I besieged him with questions, I fell upon him like a starving man on bread. He always answered me readily and straightforwardly, but in the end always went off into the widest generalizations, so that in reality one could draw no conclusions from it. And yet these questions had worried me all my life, and I frankly confess that even in Moscow I had put off settling them till I should meet him in Petersburg. I told him this plainly, and he did not laugh at me—on the contrary, I remember he pressed my hand.

On general politics and social questions I could get nothing out of him, and yet in connection with my " idea " those subjects troubled me more than anything. Of men like Dergatchev I once drew from him the remark that " they were below all criticism," but at the same time he added strangely that " he reserved the right of attaching no significance to his opinions." For a very long time he would say nothing on the question how the modern state would end, and how the social community would be built up anew, but in the end I literally wrenched a few words out of him.

" I imagine that all that will come about in a very commonplace way," he said once. " Simply *un beau matin,* in spite of all the balance-sheets on budget days, and the absence of deficits, all the states without exception will be unable to pay, so that they'll all be landed in general bankruptcy. At the same time all the conservative elements of the whole world will rise up in opposition to everything, because they will be the bondholders and creditors, and they won't want to allow the bankruptcy. Then, of course, there will follow a general liquidation, so to speak ; the Jews will come to the fore and the reign of the Jews will begin : and then all those who have never had shares in anything, and in fact have never had anything at all, that is all the beggars, will naturally be unwilling to take part in the liquidation. . . . A struggle will begin, and after seventy-seven battles the beggars will destroy the shareholders and carry off their shares and take their places as shareholders, of course. Perhaps they'll say something new too, and perhaps they won't. Most likely they'll go bankrupt too. Further than that, my dear boy, I can't undertake to predict the destinies by which the face of this world will be changed. Look in the Apocalypse though . . ."

" But can it all be so materialistic ? Can the modern world come to an end simply through finance ? "

" Oh, of course, I've only chosen one aspect of the picture, but that aspect is bound up with the whole by indissoluble bonds, so to speak."

" What's to be done ? "

" Oh dear, don't be in a hurry ; it's not all coming so soon. In any case, to do nothing is always best, one's conscience is at rest anyway, knowing that one's had no share in anything."

" Aië, do stop that, talk sense. I want to know what I'm to do and how I'm to live."

"What you are to do, my dear ? Be honest, never lie, don't covet your neighbour's house ; in fact, read the Ten Commandments—it's written there once for all."

" Don't talk like that, all that's so old, and besides . . . it's all words ; I want something real."

" Well, if you're fearfully devoured by ennui, try to love some one or something, or at any rate to attach yourself to something."

" You're only laughing ! Besides, what can I do alone with your Ten Commandments ? "

"Well, keep them in spite of all your doubts and questions, and you'll be a great man."

"Whom no one will know of."

"'There is nothing hidden that shall not be made manifest.'"

"You're certainly laughing."

"Well, if you take it so to heart you'd better try as soon as possible to specialize, take up architecture or the law, and then when you're busy with serious work you'll be more settled in your mind and forget trifles."

I was silent. What could I gather from this? And yet, after every such conversation I was more troubled than before. Moreover I saw clearly that there always remained in him, as it were, something secret, and that drew me to him more and more.

"Listen," I said, interrupting him one day, "I always suspect that you say all this only out of bitterness and suffering, but that secretly you are a fanatic over some idea, and are only concealing it, or ashamed to admit it."

"Thank you, my dear."

"Listen, nothing's better than being useful. Tell me how, at the present moment, I can be most of use. I know it's not for you to decide that, but I'm only asking for your opinion. You tell me, and what you say I swear I'll do! Well, what is the great thought?"

"Well, to turn stones into bread. That's a great thought."

"The greatest? Yes, really, you have suggested quite a new path. Tell me, is it the greatest?"

"It's very great, my dear boy, very great, but it's not the greatest. It's great but secondary, and only great at the present time. Man will be satisfied and forget; he will say: 'I've eaten it and what am I to do now?' The question will remain open for all time."

"You spoke once of the 'Geneva ideas.' I didn't understand what was meant by the 'Geneva ideas.'"

"The 'Geneva idea' is the idea of virtue without Christ, my boy, the modern idea, or, more correctly, the ideas of all modern civilization. In fact, it's one of those long stories which it's very dull to begin, and it will be a great deal better if we talk of other things, and better still if we're silent about other things."

"You always want to be silent!"

"My dear, remember that to be silent is good, safe, and picturesque."

·" Picturesque ? "

" Of course. Silence is always picturesque, and the man who is silent always looks nicer than the man who is speaking."

" Why, talking as we do is no better than being silent. Damn such picturesqueness, and still more damn such profitableness."

" My dear," he said suddenly, rather changing his tone, speaking with real feeling and even with a certain insistence, " I don't want to seduce you from your ideals to any sort of bourgeois virtue, I'm not assuring you that ' happiness is better than heroism ' ; on the contrary ' heroism is finer than any happiness,' and the very capacity for it alone constitutes happiness. That's a settled thing between us. I respect you just for being able in these mawkish days to set up some sort of an ' idea ' in your soul (don't be uneasy, I remember perfectly well). But yet one must think of proportion, for now you want to live a resounding life, to set fire to something, to smash something, to rise above everything in Russia, to call up storm-clouds, to throw every one into terror and ecstasy, while you vanish yourself in North America. I've no doubt you've something of that sort in your heart, and so I feel it necessary to warn you, for I really love you, my dear."

What could I gather from that either ? There was nothing in it but anxiety for me, for my material prosperity ; it betrayed the father with the father's kindly but prosaic feelings. Was this what I wanted by way of an idea for the sake of which any honest father would send his son to face death, as the ancient Roman Horatius sent his sons for the idea of Rome ?

I often pressed him on the subject of religion, but there the fog was thicker than ever. When I asked him what to do about that, he answered in the stupidest way, as though to a child :

" You must have faith in God, my dear."

" But what if I don't believe in all that ? " I cried irritably once.

" A very good thing, my dear."

" How a good thing ? "

" It's a most excellent symptom, dear boy ; a most hopeful one, for our atheists in Russia, if only they are really atheists and have some little trace of intelligence, are the best fellows in the whole world, and always disposed to be kind to God, for they're invariably good-humoured, and they're good-humoured because they're immensely pleased at being atheists. Our

o

atheists are respectable people and extremely conscientious, pillars of the fatherland, in fact. . . ."

This was something, of course, but it was not what I wanted. On one occasion, however, he spoke out, but so strangely that he surprised me more than ever, especially after the stories of Catholicism and penitential chains that I had heard about him.

"Dear boy," he said one day, not in my room, but in the street, when I was seeing him home after a long conversation, "to love people as they are is impossible. And yet we must. And therefore do them good, overcoming your feelings, holding your nose and shutting your eyes (the latter's essential). Endure evil from them as far as may be without anger, 'mindful that you too are a man.' Of course you'll be disposed to be severe with them if it has been vouchsafed to you to be ever so little more intelligent than the average. Men are naturally base and like to love from fear. Don't give in to such love, and never cease to despise it. Somewhere in the Koran Allah bids the prophet look upon the 'froward' as upon mice, do them good, and pass them by—a little haughty, but right. Know how to despise them even when they are good, for most often it is in that they are base. Oh, my dear, it's judging by myself I say that. Anyone who's not quite stupid can't live without despising himself, whether he's honest or dishonest—it makes no difference. To love one's neighbour and not despise him—is impossible. I believe that man has been created physically incapable of loving his neighbour. There has been some mistake in language here from the very first, and 'love for humanity' must be understood as love for that humanity which you have yourself created in your soul (in other words, you have created yourself and your love is for yourself)—and which, therefore, never will be in reality."

"Never will be ? "

"My dear boy, I agree that if this were true, it would be stupid, but that's not my fault, and I was not consulted at the creation. I reserve the right to have my own opinion about it."

"How is it they call you a Christian, then ? " I cried. "A monk in chains, a preacher ? I don't understand it ! "

"Why, who calls me that ? "

I told him ; he listened very attentively, but cut short the conversation.

I can't remember what led to this memorable conversation ; but he was positively irritated, which scarcely ever happened to him. He spoke passionately and without irony, as though he were not speaking to me. But again I didn't believe him. He could not speak on such subjects seriously to anyone like me.

CHAPTER II

1

On that morning, the 15th of November, I found him at Prince Sergay's. I had brought the prince and him together, but they had ties apart from me (I mean the affair abroad, and all that). Moreover, the prince had promised to divide the disputed fortune with him, giving him a third, which would mean twenty thousand at least. I remember at the time I thought it awfully strange that he was giving him only a third and not the full half ; but I said nothing. Prince Sergay gave this promise of his own accord ; Versilov had not said a syllable to suggest it, had not dropped a hint. Prince Sergay came forward himself and Versilov only let it pass in silence, never once alluded to it, and showed no sign that he had the least recollection of a promise. I may mention, by the way, that Prince Sergay was absolutely enchanted with him at first and still more with the things he said. He fell into positive raptures about him, and several times expressed his feelings to me. Sometimes when he was alone with me he exclaimed about himself, almost with despair, that he was " so ill-educated, that he was on the wrong track ! . . ." Oh, we were still so friendly then ! . . . I kept trying to impress Versilov with Prince Sergay's good points only, and excused his defects though I saw them myself ; but Versilov listened in silence, or smiled.

" If he has faults he has at least as many virtues as defects ! " I once exclaimed to Versilov when I was alone with him.

" Goodness, how you flatter him ! " he said laughing.

" How do I flatter him ? " I said, not understanding.

" As many virtues ! Why he must be a saint if he has as many virtues as defects ! "

But, of course, that was not his opinion. In general he avoided speaking of Prince Sergay at that time, as he did indeed of everything real, but of the prince particularly. I suspected, even then, that he went to see Prince Sergay without me, and that they were on rather peculiar terms, but I did not go into that. I was not jealous either at his talking to him more seriously than to me, more positively, so to speak, with less mockery ; I was so happy at the time that I was actually pleased at it. I explained it too by Prince Sergay's being of rather limited intelligence, and so being fond of verbal exactitude ; some jests he absolutely failed to see.

But of late he had, as it were, begun to emancipate himself. His feelings for Versilov seemed beginning to change. Versilov with his delicate perception noticed it. I may mention at this point that Prince Sergay's attitude to me, too, became different at the same time, rather too obviously, in fact. Only the lifeless forms of our warm earlier relations were maintained. Yet I went on going to see him ; I could not indeed help it, having once been drawn into it. Oh, how clumsy and inexperienced I was then ; it is almost beyond belief that mere foolishness of heart can have brought anyone to such humiliation and lack of perception. I took money from him and thought that it didn't matter, that it was quite right. Yet that is not true : even then I knew that it was not right, but it was simply that I thought very little about it. I did not go to the prince to get money, though I needed the money so much. I knew I did not go for the sake of the money, but I realized that I went every day to borrow money. But I was in a whirl then, and besides all that I had something very different in my soul—it was singing with joy !

When I went in at eleven o'clock in the morning I found Versilov just finishing a long tirade. Prince Sergay was walking about the room listening, and Versilov was sitting down. Prince Sergay seemed in some excitement. Versilov was almost always able to work him into a state of excitement. He was exceedingly impressionable, to a degree of simplicity, indeed, which had often made me look down on him. But, I repeat, of late I had detected in him something like a resentful sneer. He stopped short, seeing me, and a quiver seemed to pass over his face. I knew in my heart to what to attribute the shadow over him that morning, but I had not expected that his face would be so distorted by it. I knew that he had an accumulation of anxieties, but it was revolting that I didn't know more than a tenth part of them—the rest had been kept so far a dead secret from me. What made it stupid and revolting was that I often obtruded my sympathy on him, gave advice and often laughed condescendingly at his weakness at being so upset " about such trifles." He used to be silent; but he must have detested me at those moments; I was in an utterly false position and had no suspicion of it. Oh, I call God to witness that of the chief trouble I had no suspicion!

He courteously held out his hand to me, however; Versilov nodded, without interrupting himself. I stretched myself on the sofa—my tone and manners were horrible at that time! My swagger went even further: I used to treat his acquaintances as though they were my own. Oh, if it could only be done all over again, I should know how to behave very differently!

Two words, that I may not forget. Prince Sergay was still living in the same flat, but now occupied almost the whole of it. Mme. Stolbyeev, whose flat it was, after staying only a month, had gone away again.

2

They were talking of the aristocracy. I may mention that Prince Sergay grew sometimes much excited over this subject in spite of his progressive notions. I suspect indeed that many of his misdoings had their source and origin in this idea. Attaching great significance to his princely rank, he threw money away in all directions although he was a beggar, and became involved in debt. Versilov had more than once hinted that this extravagance was not the essence of princeliness, and tried to instil into him a higher conception of it; but Prince Sergay had begun to show signs of resentment at being instructed. Evidently there had been something of the same sort that morning, but I hadn't arrived in time for the beginning of it. Versilov's words struck me at first as reactionary, but he made up for that later on.

"The word honour means duty," he said (I only give the sense as far as I remember it); "when the upper class rules in a state the country is strong. The upper class always has its sense of honour, and its code of honour, which may be imperfect but almost always serves as a bond and strengthens the country; an advantage morally and still more politically. But the slaves, that is all those not belonging to the ruling class, suffer. They are given equal rights to prevent their suffering. That's what has been done with us, and it's an excellent thing. But in all experience so far (in Europe that is to say) a weakening of the sense of honour and duty has followed the establishment of equal rights. Egoism has replaced the old consolidating principle and the whole system has been shattered on the rock of personal freedom. The emancipated masses, left with no sustaining principle, have ended by losing all sense of cohesion, till they have given up defending the liberties they have gained. But the Russian type of aristocrat has never been like the European nobility. Our nobility, even now that it has lost its privileges, might remain the leading class as the upholders of honour, enlightenment, science, and higher culture, and, what is of the greatest importance, without cutting themselves off into a separate caste, which would be the death of the idea. On the contrary, the entrance to this class has been thrown open long ago among us, and now the time has come to open it completely. Let every honourable and valiant action, every great achievement in science enable a man to gain the ranks of the highest class. In that way the class is automatically transformed into an assembly of the best people in a true and literal sense, not in the sense in which it was said of the privileged caste in the past. In this new, or rather renewed form, the class might be retained."

The prince smiled sarcastically.

" What sort of an aristocracy would that be ? It's some sort of masonic lodge you're sketching ; not an aristocracy."

Prince Sergay had been, I repeat, extremely ill-educated. I turned over with vexation on the sofa, though I was far from agreeing with Versilov. Versilov quite understood that the prince was sneering.

" I don't know in what sense you talk of a masonic lodge," he answered. " Well, if even a Russian prince recoils from such an idea, no doubt the time for it has not arrived. The idea of honour and enlightenment as the sacred keys that unlock for any man the portals of a class thus continually renewed is, of course, a Utopia. But why is it an impossible one ? If the thought is living though only in a few brains it is not yet lost, but shines like a tiny flame in the depths of darkness."

" You are fond of using such words as ' higher culture,' 'great idea,' ' sustaining principle ' and such ; I should like to know what you mean exactly by a ' great idea ' ? "

" I really don't know how to answer that question, dear prince," Versilov responded with a subtle smile. " If I confess to you that I myself am not able to answer, it would be more accurate. A great idea is most often a feeling which sometimes remains too long undefined. I only know that it's that which has been the source of living life, gay joyous life, I mean, not theoretical and artificial; so that the great idea, from which it flows, is absolutely indispensable, to the general vexation, of course."

" Why vexation ? "

" Because, to live with ideas is dreary, and it's always gay without them."

The prince swallowed the rebuke.

" And what do you mean by this living life as you call it ? " (He was evidently cross.)

" I don't know that either, prince ; I only know that it must be something very simple, the most everyday thing, staring us in the face, a thing of every day, every minute, and so simple that we can never believe it to be so simple, and we've naturally been passing it by for thousands of years without noticing it or recognizing it."

" I only meant to say that your idea of the aristocracy is equivalent to denying the aristocracy," observed Prince Sergay.

" Well, if you will have it so, perhaps there never has been an aristocracy in Russia."

" All this is very obscure and vague. If one says something, one ought, to my mind, to explain it. . . ."

Prince Sergay contracted his brows and stole a glance at the clock on the wall. Versilov got up and took his hat.

" Explain ? " he said, " no, it's better not to, besides, I've a passion for talking without explanations. That's really it. And there's another strange thing : if it happens that I try to explain an idea I believe in, it almost always happens that I cease to believe what I have explained. I'm afraid of that fate now. Good-bye, dear prince ; I always chatter unpardonably with you."

He went out ; the prince escorted him politely, but I felt offended.

" What are you ruffling up your feathers about ? " he fired off suddenly, walking past me to his bureau without looking at me.

" I'm ruffling up my feathers," I began with a tremor in my voice, " because, finding in you such a queer change of tone to me and even to Versilov I . . . Versilov may, of course, have begun in rather a reactionary way, but afterwards he made up for it and . . . there was perhaps a profound meaning in what he said, but you simply didn't understand, and . . ."

" I simply don't care to have people putting themselves forward to teach me and treating me as though I were a schoolboy," he snapped out, almost wrathfully.

" Prince, such expressions . . ."

" Please spare me theatrical flourishes—if you will be so kind. I know that what I am doing is—contemptible, that I'm—a spendthrift, a gambler, perhaps a thief. . . . Yes, a thief, for I gamble away the money belonging to my family, but I don't want anybody's judgment. I don't want it and I won't have it. I'm—the judge of my own actions. And why this ambiguity ? If he wants to say anything to me let him say it straight out, and not go in for this mysterious prophetic twaddle. To tell me all this he ought to have the right to, he ought to be an honourable man himself. . . ."

" In the first place I didn't come in at the beginning and I don't know what you were talking about, and, secondly, what has Versilov done dishonourable, allow me to ask ? "

" Please, that's enough, that's enough. You asked me for three hundred roubles yesterday. Here it is. . . ."

He laid the money on the table before me, sat down in the armchair, leaned nervously against the back of it, and crossed one leg over the other. I was thrown into confusion.

" I don't know . . ." I muttered, " though I did ask you for it . . . and though I do need the money now, since you take such a tone . . ."

" Don't talk about tone. If I spoke sharply you must excuse me. I assure you that I've no thoughts to spare for it. Listen to this : I've had a letter from Moscow. My brother Sasha, who was only a child, as you know, died four days ago. My father, as you know too, has been paralysed for the last two years, and now, they write to me, he's worse, he can't utter a word and knows nobody. They were relieved to get the inheritance, and want to take him abroad, but the doctor writes that he's not likely to live a fortnight. So I'm left with my mother and sister . . . that is, almost alone. . . . In fact, I'm —alone. This fortune . . . this fortune—oh, it would have been better perhaps if it had not come to me at all ! But this is what I wanted to tell you : I promised Andrey Petrovitch a minimum of twenty thousand. . . . And, meanwhile, only imagine, owing to legal formalities I've been able to do nothing. I haven't even . . . we, that is . . . my father that is, has not yet been informed of the inheritance. And meanwhile I've lost so much money during the last three weeks, and that scoundrel Stebelkov charges such a rate of interest. . . . I've given you almost the last. . . ."

"Oh, prince, if that's how it is . . ."

"I didn't mean that. I didn't mean that. Stebelkov will bring some to-day, no doubt, and there'll be enough to go on with, but what the devil's one to think of Stebelkov? I entreated him to get me ten thousand, so that I might at least give Andrey Petrovitch that much. It worries me, it plagues me to think of my promise to give him a third. I gave my word and I must keep it. And I swear I'll do my utmost to free myself from obligations in that direction anyhow. They weigh upon me, they weigh upon me, they're insufferable! This burdensome tie. . . . I can't bear to see Andrey Petrovitch, for I can't look him in the face. . . . Why does he take advantage of it?"

"What does he take advantage of, prince?" I stood before him in amazement. "Has he ever so much as hinted at it?"

"Oh, no, and I appreciate it, it's I who reproach myself. And in fact I'm getting more and more involved. . . . This Stebelkov. . . ."

"Listen, prince, do calm yourself, please. I see you get more excited the more you talk, and yet it may be all imagination. Oh, I've got myself into difficulties too, unpardonably, contemptibly. But I know it's only temporary . . . and as soon as I win back a certain sum, then . . . I say, with this three hundred, I owe you two thousand five hundred, don't I?"

"I'm not asking it from you, I believe," the prince said suddenly with a sneer.

"You say ten thousand for Versilov. If I borrow from you now the money will be taken off Versilov's twenty thousand; otherwise I won't consent. But . . . but I shall certainly pay it back myself. . . . But can you possibly imagine that Versilov comes to you to get the money?"

"It would be easier for me if he did come for the money," Prince Sergay observed enigmatically.

"You talk of some 'burdensome tie.' . . . If you mean with Versilov and me, upon my soul it's an insult. And you say why isn't he what he preaches—that's your logic! And, in the first place it's not logic, allow me to tell you, for even if he's not, he can't help saying what's true. . . . And besides, why do you talk about 'preaching'? You call him a 'prophet.'

Tell me, was it you who called him a ' petticoat prophet ' in Germany ? "

" No, it was not I."

" Stebelkov told me it was you."

" He told a lie. I'm—no hand at giving derisive nicknames. But if a man preaches honour he ought to be honourable himself —that's my logic, and if it's incorrect I don't care. I prefer it to be so. And I won't have anyone dare to come and judge me in my own house and treat me like a baby! That's enough ! " he shouted, waving his hand to stop me. . . . " Ah, at last ! "

The door opened and Stebelkov walked in.

3

He was exactly the same, just as jauntily dressed ; and squared his chest and stared into one's face as stupidly as ever, imagining that he was being very sly, and exceedingly well satisfied with himself. On this occasion he looked about him in a strange way on entering ; there was a look of peculiar caution and penetration in his face, as though he wanted to guess something from our countenances. He instantly subsided, however, and his face beamed with a self-satisfied smile, that " pardonably-insolent " smile, which was yet unspeakably repulsive to me.

I had known for a long time that he was a great torment to Prince Sergay. He had come once or twice when I was present. I . . . I too had had a transaction with him during that month, but on this occasion I was rather surprised at the way he came in.

" In a minute," Prince Sergay said, without greeting him, and, turning his back on us both, he began looking in his desk for the necessary papers and accounts. As for me, I was mortally offended by his last words. The suggestion that Versilov was dishonourable was so clear (and so astonishing !) that it could not be allowed to pass without a full explanation. But that was impossible before Stebelkov. I reclined on the sofa again and turned over a book that was lying before me.

" Byelinsky, part two ! That's something new ! Are you trying to cultivate your mind ? " I exclaimed, I fancy, very unnaturally.

He was busily engaged and in great haste, but at my words he turned.

" I beg you to leave that book alone," he brought out sharply.

This was beyond all endurance, especially before Stebelkov ! To make it worse Stebelkov gave a sly and loathsome smirk, and made a stealthy sign to me in Prince Sergay's direction. I turned away from the fool.

" Don't be angry, prince ; I'll leave you to your most important visitor, and meanwhile I'll disappear. . . ."

I made up my mind to be casual in my manner.

" Is that me—the most important visitor ? " Stebelkov put in, jocosely pointing at himself with his finger.

" Yes, you ; you're the most important person and you know it too ! "

" No, excuse me. Everywhere in the world there's a second person. I am a second person. There is a first person and a second person. The first acts and the second takes. So the first person turns into the second person, and the second person turns into the first person. Is that so or not ? "

" It may be so. But as usual I don't understand you."

" Excuse me. In France there was a revolution and every one was executed. Napoleon came along and took everything. The revolution is the first person, and Napoleon the second person. But it turned out that the revolution became the second person and Napoleon became the first person. Is that right ? "

I may observe, by the way, that in his speaking to me of the French Revolution I saw an instance of his own cunning which amused me very much. He still persisted in regarding me as some sort of revolutionist, and whenever he met me thought it necessary to begin on some topic of the sort.

" Come along," said Prince Sergay, and they went together into the other room. As soon as I was alone I made up my mind to give him back the three hundred as soon as Stebelkov had gone. I needed the money terribly, still I resolved to do so.

They remained in the other room, and for ten minutes I heard nothing, then suddenly they began talking loudly. They were both talking, but Prince Sergay suddenly shouted as though in violent irritation, approaching frenzy. He was sometimes very hasty, so that I was not surprised. But at that moment a footman came in to announce a visitor ; I motioned him to the other room and instantly there was silence there. Prince Sergay came out with an anxious face, though he smiled ; the footman hastened away, and half a minute later a visitor came in.

It was a visitor of great consequence, with shoulder-knots and a family crest. He was a gentleman not over thirty, of high rank, and of a severe appearance. I may remark that Prince Sergay did not yet really belong to the highest circles in Petersburg, in spite of his passionate desire to do so (I was aware of this desire), and so he must have been glad to see a visitor like this. The acquaintance had, as I knew, only been formed through great efforts on the part of Prince Sergay. The guest was returning Prince Sergay's visit, and unhappily came upon him at the wrong moment. I saw Prince Sergay look at Stebelkov with an agonized and hopeless expression ; but Stebelkov encountered his eyes as though nothing whatever were the matter, and without the faintest idea of effacing himself, sat down on the sofa with a free-and-easy air and began passing his hand through his hair, probably to display his independence. He even assumed an important countenance, in fact he was utterly impossible. As for me, I knew, of course, how to behave decently even then, and should never have disgraced anyone ; but what was my amazement when I caught on Prince Sergay's face the same hopeless, miserable and vindictive look directed at me : he was ashamed of us both then, and put me on a level with Stebelkov. That idea drove me to fury. I lolled even more at my ease, and began turning over the leaves of the book, as though the position were no concern of mine. Stebelkov, on the contrary, bent forward open-eyed to listen to their conversation, probably supposing that this was a polite and affable thing to do. The visitor glanced once or twice at Stebelkov, and at me too, indeed.

They talked of family news ; this gentleman had at some time known Prince Sergay's mother, who was one of a distinguished family. From what I could gather, in spite of his politeness and the apparent good-nature of his tone, the visitor was very formal and evidently valued his own dignity so highly as to consider a visit from him an honour to anyone whatever. Had Prince Sergay been alone, that is had we not been present, he would certainly have been more dignified and more resourceful. As it was, something tremulous in his smile, possibly an excess of politeness, and a strange absent-mindedness, betrayed him.

They had hardly been sitting there five minutes when another visitor was announced, also of the compromising kind. I knew this one very well and had heard a great deal about him, though he did not know me at all. He was still quite a young man, though twenty-three, who was handsome and elegantly dressed and had a fine house, but moved in distinctly doubtful circles. A year before he had been serving in one of the smartest cavalry regiments, but had been forced to give up his commission, and every one knew for what reason. His relations had even advertised in the papers that they would not be responsible for his debts, but he still continued his profligate manner of life, borrowing money at ten per cent. a month, playing desperately in gambling circles, and squandering his money on a notorious Frenchwoman. A week before, he had succeeded one evening in winning twelve thousand roubles and was triumphant. He was on friendly terms with Prince Sergay: they often played together *tête-à-tête*; but Prince Sergay positively shuddered seeing him now. I noticed this from where I lay. This youth made himself at home everywhere, talked with noisy gaiety, saying anything that came into his head without restraint. And of course it could never have occurred to him that our host was in such a panic over the impression his associates would make upon his important visitor.

He interrupted their conversation by his entrance, and began at once describing his play on the previous day, before he had even sat down.

" I believe you were there too," he said, breaking off at the third sentence to address the important gentleman, mistaking him for one of his own set ; but looking at him more closely he cried at once :

" Oh, I beg your pardon, I mistook you for one of the party yesterday ! "

" Alexey Vladimirovitch Darzan—Ippolit Alexandrovitch Nastchokin," Prince Sergay made haste to introduce them. This youth could still be introduced. He belonged to a good family and it was a distinguished name ; but us he did not introduce, and we went on sitting in our corners. I absolutely refused to turn my head in their direction, but Stebelkov began smirking gleefully at the sight of the young man, and was unmistakably threatening to begin talking. This began to amuse me.

" I met you several times last year at Countess Verigin's," said Darzan.

" I remember you, but I believe you were in military uniform then," Nastchokin observed genially.

" Yes, I was, but thanks to. . . . But Stebelkov here ? How does he come here ? It's just thanks to these pretty gentlemen here that I'm not in the army now ! " he pointed to Stebelkov, and burst out laughing. Stebelkov laughed gleefully too, probably taking it as a compliment. Prince Sergay blushed and made haste to address a question to Nastchokin, and Darzan, going up to Stebelkov, began talking of something very warmly, though in a whisper.

" I believe you saw a great deal of Katerina Nikolaevna Ahmakov abroad ? " the visitor asked Prince Sergay.

" Oh yes, I knew her. . . ."

" I believe we shall soon be hearing a piece of news about her. They say she's engaged to Baron Büring."

" That's true ! " cried Darzan.

" Do you know it for a fact ? " Prince Sergay asked Nastchokin with evident agitation, bringing out his question with peculiar emphasis.

" I've been told so, and people are talking about it ; but I don't know it for a fact."

" Oh, it is a fact ! " said Darzan, going up to him. " Dubasov told me so yesterday, he's always the first to know news like that. Yes, and the prince ought to know. . . ."

Nastchokin waited till Darzan had finished, and turned to Prince Sergay again.

" She's not very often seen now."

" Her father has been ill for the last month," Prince Sergay observed drily.

" She's a lady of many adventures ! " Darzan blurted out suddenly.

I raised my head and sat up.

" I have the pleasure of knowing Katerina Nikolaevna personally, and I take upon myself the duty of declaring that all scandalous stories about her are mere lies and infamy . . . and invented by those who have sought her favour without success."

After this stupid outburst I relapsed into silence, still sitting upright and gazing at them all with a flushed face. Every one turned to me, but Stebelkov suddenly guffawed ; Darzan, too, simpered and seemed surprised.

" Arkady Makarovitch Dolgoruky," said Prince Sergay, indicating me to Darzan.

" Oh, believe me, *prince*," said Darzan, frankly and good-naturedly addressing me, " I am only repeating what

I've heard ; if there are rumours they have not been of my spreading."

" I did not mean it for you ! " I answered quickly, but Stebelkov had burst into an outrageous roar of laughter, caused as he explained afterwards by Darzan's having addressed me as prince. My diabolical surname had got me into a mess again. Even now I blush at the thought that I had not the courage— through shame, of course—to set right this blunder and to protest aloud that I was " simply Dolgoruky." It was the first time in my life I had let it pass. Darzan looked in perplexity at me and at Stebelkov's laughter.

" Ah yes ! Who was the pretty girl I met on the stairs just now, a slim, fair little thing ? " he suddenly asked Prince Sergay.

" I really don't know," the latter answered quickly, reddening.

" How should you ? " laughed Darzan.

" Though . . . it . . . it might have been. . . ." Prince Sergay faltered oddly.

" It was . . . this gentleman's sister, Lizaveta Makarovna ! " said Stebelkov suddenly pointing to me, " for I met her just now too. . . ."

" Ah indeed ! " Prince Sergay put in quickly, speaking this time, however, with an extremely grave and dignified expression, " it must have been Lizaveta Makarovna, who is a great friend of Anna Fyodorovna Stolbyeev, in whose flat I am staying ; she must have come to-day to see Darya Onisimovna, another of Anna Fyodorovna's great friends, whom she left in charge of the house when she went away. . . ."

This was all true. Darya Onisimovna was the mother of poor Olya, whose story I have told already. Tatyana Pavlovna had found a refuge for the poor woman at last with Mme. Stolbyeev. I know very well that Liza had been sometimes at Mme. Stolbyeev's, and had lately visited there Darya Onisimovna, of whom every one at home was very fond ; but after this statement by Prince Sergay—sensible as it was, however— and still more Stebelkov's stupid outburst, and perhaps because I had been called prince, I suddenly flushed all over. Luckily at that very instant Nastchokin stood up to take leave ; he offered his hand to Darzan also. At the moment Stebelkov and I were left alone ; he nodded his head to me in the direction of Darzan, who was standing in the doorway with his back to us ; I shook my fist at Stebelkov.

A minute later Darzan, too, got up to go, after arranging with

Prince Sergay to meet him next day at some place, a gambling house, I believe. As he went out he shouted something to Stebelkov, and made me a slight bow. Hardly had he gone out when Stebelkov jumped up and stood in the middle of the room, pointing to the ceiling with his finger :

"I'll tell you the trick that fine young gentleman played last week. He gave an IOU to Averyanov and signed a false name to it. That IOU is still in existence, but it's not been honoured ! It's criminal ! Eight thousand ! "

"And no doubt that IOU is in your hands ? " I cried, glaring at him savagely.

"I have a bank, I have a *mont-de-piété*, I am not a broker. Have you heard that there is a *mont-de-piété* in Paris ? Bread and benevolence for the poor ; I have a *mont-de-piété*. . . ."

Prince Sergay rudely and angrily cut him short.

"What are you doing here ? What are you staying for ? "

"But," Stebelkov blinked rapidly, "what about that ? Won't it do ? "

"No, no, no," Prince Sergay shouted, stamping ; "I've said so."

"Well, if so . . . that's so. . . . But that's a mistake. . . ." He turned abruptly and with bowed head and bent spine went quickly out of the room. Prince Sergay called after him when he was in the doorway :

"You may as well know, sir, that I am not in the least afraid of you."

He was very much irritated, he was about to sit down, but glancing at me, remained standing. His eyes seemed to say to me also, " Why are you hanging about here too ? "

"Prince, I . . ." I was beginning.

"I've really no time to listen, Arkady Makarovitch, I'm just going out."

"One minute, prince, it's very important ; and, to begin with, take back your three hundred."

"What's this now ? "

He was walking up and down, but he stopped short.

"This now is that after all that has passed . . . and what you've said about Versilov . . . that he was dishonourable, and in fact your tone all the time. . . . In short, I can't possibly take it."

"You've been *taking* it for the last month, though."

He suddenly sat down on the chair. I was standing at the

table, and with one hand I patted the volume of Byelinsky, while I held my hat in the other.

"I had different feelings, prince . . . and, in fact, I would never have brought it to such a sum . . . it was the gambling . . . in short, I can't !"

"You have not distinguished yourself to-day, and so you are in a rage ; I'll ask you to leave that book alone."

"What does that mean : 'not distinguished myself' ? And, in fact, before your visitors you almost put me on a level with Stebelkov."

"So that's the key to the riddle !" he said with a biting smile. "You were abashed by Darzan's calling you prince, too."

He laughed spitefully. I flared up.

"I simply don't understand ; I wouldn't take your title as a gift."

"I know your character. How absurdly you cried out in defence of Mme. Ahmakov . . . let that book alone !"

"What's the meaning of it ?" I cried.

"L-l-let the book alone !" he yelled suddenly, drawing himself up in the low chair, with a ferocious movement, as though about to spring at me.

"This is beyond all limits," I said, and I walked quickly out of the room, but before I had reached the end of the drawing-room, he shouted to me from the study :

"Arkady Makarovitch, come back ! Co-ome ba-ack ! Co-ome ba-ack !"

I went on without heeding. He hastily overtook me, seized me by the arm, and dragged me back into the study. I did not resist.

"Take it," he said, pale with excitement, handing me the three hundred roubles I had thrown on the table. "You must take it . . . or else we . . . you must !"

"Prince, how can I take it ?"

"Oh, I'll beg your pardon . . . if you like . . . all right, forgive me ! . . ."

"I have always liked you, prince, and if you feel the same . . ."

"I do ; take it. . . ."

I took the money. His lips were trembling.

"I can understand, prince, that you are exasperated by that scoundrel . . . but I won't take it, prince, unless we kiss each other, as we have done when we've quarrelled before."

I was trembling, too, as I said this.

P

" Now for sentimentality," muttered Prince Sergay, with an embarrassed smile, but he bent down and kissed me. I shuddered ; at the instant he kissed me I caught on his face an unmistakable look of aversion.

" Did he bring you the money, anyway ? . . ."

" Aie, never mind."

" I was asking on your account. . . ."

" Yes he did, he did."

" Prince, we have been friends . . . and in fact, Versilov. . . ."

" Yes, yes. That's all right ! "

" And in fact . . . I really don't know . . . about this three hundred. . . ."

I was holding the money in my hand.

" Take it, ta-ake it ! " he smiled again, but there was something very vicious in his smile.

I took the money.

CHAPTER III

1

I took the money because I loved him. If anyone disbelieves this I must inform him that at the moment when I took the money I was firmly convinced that I could have obtained it from another source. And so I really took it, not because I was in desperate straits, but from delicacy, not to hurt his feelings. Alas, that was how I reasoned at the time ! But yet my heart was very heavy as I went out from him. I had seen that morning an extraordinary change in his attitude to me ; he had never taken such a tone before, and, as regards Versilov, it was a case of positive mutiny. Stebelkov had no doubt annoyed him very much that morning, but he had begun to be the same before seeing Stebelkov. I repeat once more : the change from his original manner might indeed have been noticed for some days past, but not in the same way, not in the same degree, that was the point.

The stupid gossip about that major, Baron Büring, might have some effect on him. . . . I too had been disturbed by it, but . . . the fact is, I had something else in my heart at that time that shone so resplendent that I heedlessly let many things pass unnoticed, made haste to let them pass, to get rid of them, and to go back to that resplendence. . . .

It was not yet one o'clock. From Prince Sergay's I drove with my Matvey straight off to—it will hardly be believed to whom— to Stebelkov ! The fact is that he had surprised me that morning, not so much by turning up at Prince Sergay's (for he had promised to be there) as by the way he had winked at me ; he had a stupid habit of doing so, but that morning it had been apropos of a different subject from what I had expected. The evening before, a note had come from him by post, which had rather puzzled me. In it he begged me to go to him between two and three to-day, and that " he might inform me of facts that would be a surprise to me."

And in reference to that letter he had that morning, at Prince Sergay's, made no sign whatever. What sort of secrets could there be between Stebelkov and me ? Such an idea was positively ridiculous ; but, after all that had happened, I felt a slight excitement as I drove off to him. I had, of course, a fortnight before applied to him for money, and he was ready to lend it, but for some reason we did not come to terms, and I did not take the money : on that occasion, too, he had muttered something vague, as his habit was, and I had fancied he wanted to make me some offer, to suggest some special conditions ; and as I had treated him disdainfully every time I had met him at Prince Sergay's, I proudly cut short any idea of special terms, though he pursued me to the door. I borrowed the money afterwards from Prince Sergay.

Stebelkov lived in a very comfortable style. He had his own establishment, a flat of four rooms, with handsome furniture, men and women servants, and a housekeeper, who was, however, by no means young. I went in angrily.

" Listen, my good man," I began from the door ; " to begin with, what's the meaning of that letter ? I don't care for letters to be passing between us. And why did you not make any statement you wanted to make at Prince Sergay's this morning ? I was at your service."

" And why did you hold your tongue, too, this morning, instead of questioning me ? " he said with a broad grin of intense self-satisfaction.

" Because it's not I want something of you, but you want something of me," I cried, suddenly growing hot.

" Why have you come to see me, if that's so ? " he cried, almost jumping out of his chair with glee. I turned instantld, and would have gone out, but he seized me by the shoulder.

" No, no, I was joking, it's a matter of importance, as you'll see for yourself."

I sat down, I must admit I was inquisitive. We were seated facing one another at the end of a big writing table. He smiled slyly, and was just holding up his finger.

" None of your slyness, please, and no fingers either, and above all, none of your allegories ! Come straight to the point, or I'll go away at once," I cried angrily again.

" You . . . are proud ! " he pronounced in a tone of stupid reproach, rocking in his easy-chair and turning his wrinkled forehead towards the ceiling.

" One has to be with you ! "

" You . . . took money from Prince Sergay to-day, three hundred roubles ; I have money too, my money is better than his."

" How do you know I took it ? " I asked, greatly astonished. " Can he have told you that himself ? "

" He told me ; don't worry yourself, in the course of conversation it happened to come up, it just happened to come up, it was not on purpose. He told me. And you need not have taken it. Is that so, or not ? "

" But I hear that you squeeze out an exorbitant interest."

" I have a *mont-de-pieté*, but I don't squeeze. I only lend to friends, and not to other people, the *mont-de-piété* is for them. . . ."

This *mont-de-piété* was an ordinary pawnbroker's shop, which flourished under another name, in a different quarter of the town.

" But I lend large sums to friends."

" Why, is Prince Sergay such a friend of yours ? "

" A fri-iend ; but . . . he plays the fool, and he'd better not dare to play the fool."

" Why is he so much in your power ? Does he owe you a great deal ? "

" He . . . does owe a great deal."

" He'll pay you ; he has come into a fortune . . ."

" That is not his fortune ; he owes money, and owes something else, too. The fortune's not enough. I'll lend to you without interest."

" As though I were a ' friend ' too ? How have I earned that ? " I laughed.

" You will earn it." Again he rocked his whole person forward on a level with me, and was again holding up his fingers.

" Stebelkov ! Speak without flourishing your fingers or I go."

" I say, he may marry Anna Andreyevna ! " and he screwed up his left eye fiendishly.

" Listen, Stebelkov, your conversation is taking such a scandalous turn. . . . How dare you utter the name of Anna Andreyevna ! "

" Don't lose your temper."

" I am listening, though it's against the grain, for I see clearly you have something up your sleeve, and I want to find out what it is . . . but you may try my patience too far, Stebelkov ! "

" Don't be angry, don't be proud. Humble your pride a little and listen ; and then you'll be proud again. You know, of course, about Anna Andreyevna. The prince may make a match . . . you know, of course . . ."

" I have heard of the idea, of course, I know all about it, but I have never spoken to Prince Sergay about it, I only know that the idea originated with old Prince Sokolsky, who is ill now ; but I have never talked to him about it and I have had nothing to do with it. I tell you this, simply to make things clear. I will ask you in the first place : what is your object in mentioning it to me ? And secondly, can Prince Sergay possibly discuss such subjects with *you* ? "

" He does not discuss them with me ; he does not want to discuss them with me, but I mention them to him, and he does not want to listen. He shouted at me this morning."

" I should think so ! I commend him."

" Old Prince Sokolsky will give Anna Andreyevna a good dowry ; she's a favourite. Then when the prince marries her, he'll repay me all the money he owes. And he will pay other debts as well. He'll certainly pay them ! But now he has nothing to pay with."

" What do you want of me ? "

" To answer the great question : you are known everywhere, you go everywhere, you can find out anything."

" Oh, damnation . . . find out what ? "

" Whether Prince Sergay wishes it, whether Anna Andreyevna wishes it, whether the old prince wishes it."

" And you dare to propose that I should be your spy, and— for money ! " I burst out indignantly.

" Don't be too proud, don't be too proud, humble your pride only a little, only for five minutes." He made me sit down again.

He was evidently not intimidated by my words or gestures ; but I made up my mind to hear him out.

"I must find out quickly, find out quickly, because . . . because it will soon be too late. You saw how he swallowed the pill this morning, when the officer mentioned the baron for Mme. Ahmakov."

I certainly demeaned myself by listening further, but my curiosity was irresistibly aroused.

"Listen, you worthless fellow ! " I said resolutely. " Though I'm sitting here listening, and allow you to speak of such persons . . . and even answer you, it's not in the least that I admit your right to do so. I simply see in it some piece of rascality. . . . And in the first place, what hopes can Prince Sergay have in reference to Katerina Nikolaevna ? "

"None whatever, yet he is furious."

"That's untrue ! "

"Yes, he is. Mme. Ahmakov is no go, then, now. He has lost that stake. Now he has only Anna Andreyevna to fall back on. I will give you two thousand . . . without interest and without an IOU."

Having delivered himself of this, he sat back in his chair, with a determined and important expression, and stared goggle-eyed at me. I too stared.

"You've a suit from Bolshaya Milliona ; you need money, you want money ; my money's better than his. I will give you more than two thousand . . ."

"But what for ? what for ? damn it all ! " I stamped my foot. He bent towards me and brought out impressively :

"For you not to hinder."

"But I'm not interfering as it is," I shouted.

"I know that you are holding your tongue, that's excellent."

"I don't want your approbation. For my part I am very anxious for it myself, but I consider it's not my business, and in fact that it would be unseemly for me to meddle."

"There, you see, you see, unseemly ! " he held up his finger.

"What do you see ? "

"Unseemly . . . Ha ! " and he suddenly laughed. "I understand, I understand, that it would be unseemly of you, but . . . you won't interfere ? " he winked ; but in that wink there was something so insolent, so low and even jeering : evidently he was assuming some meanness on my part and was reckoning upon it ; that was clear. but I hadn't a notion what was meant.

"Anna Andreyevna is your sister, too," he pronounced insinuatingly.

"Don't you dare to speak of that. And in fact don't dare to speak of Anna Andreyevna at all."

"Don't be too proud, only one more minute! Listen! he will get the money and provide for every one," Stebelkov said impressively, "every one, *every one*, you follow ?"

"So you think I'll take money from him ?"

"You are taking it now."

"I am taking my own."

"How is it your own ?"

"It's Versilov's money, he owes Versilov twenty thousand."

"Versilov then, not you."

"Versilov is my father."

"No, you are a Dolgoruky, not a Versilov."

"It's all the same." Yes, indeed, I was able to argue like that then ! I knew it was not the same, I was not so stupid as all that, but again it was from " delicacy " that I reasoned so.

"Enough !" I cried. "I can't make out what you are talking about, and how dare you ask me to come for such nonsense."

"Can you really not understand ? Is it on purpose or not ?" Stebelkov brought out slowly, looking at me with a penetrating and incredulous smile.

"I swear I don't understand."

"I tell you he'll be able to provide for every one, *every one ;* you've only not to interfere, and don't try to persuade him."

"You must have gone out of your mind. Why do you keep trotting out that 'every one.' Do you mean he'll provide for Versilov ?"

"You're not the only one, nor Versilov either . . . there is some one else, too, and Anna Andreyevna is just as much your sister *as Lizaveta Makarovna !*"

I gazed at him open-eyed. There was a sudden glimpse of something like compassion for me in his loathsome eyes :

"You don't understand, so much the better ! That's good, very good, that you don't understand. It's very laudable . . . if you really don't understand."

I was absolutely furious.

"Go to hell with your silly nonsense, you madman !" I shouted, taking up my hat.

"It's not silly nonsense ! So you are going, but you'll come again, you know."

"No," I rapped out in the doorway.

"You'll come, and then we shall have another talk. That will be the real talk. Two thousand, remember!"

2

He made such a filthy and confused impression on me, that when I got out I tried not to think of it at all, but dismissed it with a curse. The idea that Prince Sergay was capable of talking to him of me and of that money stabbed me like a pin. "I'll win and pay him back to-day," I thought resolutely. Stupid and inarticulate as Stebelkov was, I had seen the full-blown scoundrel in all his glory. And what mattered most to me, it was impossible to avoid intrigue in this business. Only I had not the time just then to go into any sort of intrigues, and that may have been the chief reason why I was as blind as a hen! I looked anxiously at my watch, but it was not yet two o'clock; so it was still possible to pay a call; otherwise I should have been worn out with excitement before three o'clock. I went to Anna Andreyevna Versilov, my sister. I had got to know her some time before at my old prince's, during his illness. He thought that I had not seen him for three or four days fretted my conscience, but I was reckoning on Anna Andreyevna: the old prince had become extremely attached to her of late, and even spoke of her to me as his guardian angel. And by the way, the idea of marrying her to Prince Sergay really had occurred to the old prince, and he had even expressed it more than once to me, in secret of course. I had mentioned this suggestion to Versilov, for I had noticed that though he was so indifferent to all the practical affairs of life, he seemed particularly interested whenever I told him of my meeting Anna Andreyevna. When I mentioned the old prince's idea, Versilov muttered that Anna Andreyevna had plenty of sense, and was quite capable of getting out of a delicate position without the advice of outsiders. Stebelkov was right, of course, in saying that the old man meant to give her a dowry, but how could he dare to reckon on getting anything out of it! Prince Sergay had shouted after him that morning that he was not in the least afraid of him: surely Stebelkov had not actually spoken to him of Anna Andreyevna in the study? I could fancy how furious I should have been in Prince Sergay's place.

I had been to see Anna Andreyevna pretty often of late. But there was one queer thing about my visits : it always happened that she arranged for me to come, and certainly expected me, but when I went in she always made a pretence of my having come unexpectedly and by chance ; I noticed this peculiarity in her, but I became much attached to her nevertheless. She lived with Mme. Fanariotov, her grandmother, as an adopted child, of course (Versilov had never contributed anything for her keep), but she was very far from being in the position in which the protégées of illustrious ladies are usually described as being ; for instance, the one in the house of the old countess, in Pushkin's " Queen of Spades."

Anna Andreyevna was more in the position of the countess herself. She lived quite independently in the house, that is to say, though on the same storey and in the same flat as the Fanariotovs she had two rooms completely apart, so that I, for instance, never once met any of the family as I went in or came out. She was free to receive any visitors she liked, and to employ her time as she chose. It is true that she was in her twenty-third year. She had almost given up going out into society of late, though Mme. Fanariotov spared no expense for her granddaughter, of whom I was told she was very fond. Yet what I particularly liked about Anna Andreyevna was that I always found her so quietly dressed and always occupied with something, a book or needlework. There was something of the convent, even of the nun about her, and I liked it very much. She was not very talkative, but she always spoke with judgment and knew how to listen, which I never did. When I told her that she reminded me of Versilov, though they had not a feature in common, she always flushed a little. She often blushed and always quickly, invariably with a faint flush, and I particularly liked this peculiarity in her face. In her presence I never spoke of Versilov by his surname, but always called him Andrey Petrovitch, and this had somehow come to pass of itself. I gathered indeed that the Fanariotovs must have been ashamed of Versilov, though indeed I only drew this conclusion from Anna Andreyevna, and again I'm not sure that the word " ashamed " is appropriate in this connection ; but there was some feeling of that sort. I talked to her too about Prince Sergay, and she listened eagerly, and was, I fancy, interested in what I told her of him ; but it somehow happened that I always spoke of him of my own accord, and she never questioned me about him. Of the possibility of a marriage between them I had never dared to speak, though I often felt inclined to, for the idea was not without attraction for me. But there were very many things of which, in her room, I could not have ventured to speak, yet on the other hand I felt very much at home there. Another thing I liked was that she was so well educated, and had read so much—real books too ; she had read far more than I had.

She had invited me the first time of her own accord. I realized even at the time that she might be reckoning on getting some information out of me at one time or another. Oh, lots of people were able to get information of all sorts out of me in those days ! " But what of it," I thought, " it's not only for that that she's asking me." In fact I was positively glad to think I might be of use to her . . . and when I sat with her I always felt that I had a sister sitting beside me, though we never once spoke of our relationship by so much as a word or a hint, but behaved as though it did not exist at all. When I was with her it was absolutely unthinkable to speak of it, and indeed looking at her I was struck with the absurd notion that she might perhaps know nothing of our relationship—so completely did she ignore it in her manner to me.

3

When I went in I found Liza with her. This almost astonished me. I knew very well that they had seen each other before ; they had met over the " baby." I will perhaps later on, if I have space, tell how Anna Andreyevna, always so proud and so delicate, was possessed by the fantastic desire to see that baby, and how she had there met Liza. But yet I had not expected that Anna Andreyevna would ever have invited Liza to come to see her. It was a pleasant surprise to me. Giving no sign of this, of course, I greeted Anna Andreyevna, and warmly pressing Liza's hand sat down beside her. Both were busily occupied : spread out on the table and on their knees was an evening dress of Anna Andreyevna's, expensive but " old," that is, worn three times ; and Anna Andreyevna wanted to alter it. Liza was " a master-hand " at such work, and had real taste, and so a " solemn council of wise women " was being held. I recalled Versilov's words and laughed ; and indeed I was in a radiantly happy state of mind.

" You are in very good spirits to-day and that's very pleasant," observed Anna Andreyevna, uttering her words gravely and distinctly. Her voice was a rich mellow contralto, and she always spoke quietly and gently, with a droop of her long eyelashes, and a faint smile on her pale face.

"Liza knows how disagreeable I am when I am not in good spirits," I answered gaily.

"Perhaps Anna Andreyevna knows that too," mischievous Liza gibed at me. My darling! If I had known what was on her mind at that time!

"What are you doing now?" asked Anna Andreyevna. (I may remark that she had asked me to come and see her that day.)

"I am sitting here wondering why I always prefer to find you reading rather than with needlework. Yes, really needlework doesn't suit you, somehow. I agree with Andrey Petrovitch about that."

"You have still not made up your mind to enter the university, then?"

"I am very grateful to you for not having forgotten our conversation: it shows you think of me sometimes, but . . . about the university my ideas are not quite definite . . . besides, I have plans of my own."

"That means he has a secret," observed Liza.

"Leave off joking, Liza. Some clever person said the other day that by our progressive movement of the last twenty years, we had proved above everything that we are filthily uneducated. That was meant for our university men, too."

"No doubt father said that," remarked Liza, "you very often repeat his ideas."

"Liza, you seem to think I've no mind of my own."

"In these days it's a good thing to listen to intelligent men, and repeat their words," said Anna Andreyevna, taking my part a little.

"Just so, Anna Andreyevna," I assented warmly. "The man who doesn't think of the position of Russia to-day is no patriot! I look at Russia perhaps from a strange point of view: we lived through the Tatar invasion, and afterwards two centuries of slavery, no doubt because they both suited our tastes. Now freedom has been given us, and we have to put up with freedom: shall we know how to? Will freedom, too, turn out to suit our taste? That's the question."

Liza glanced quickly at Anna Andreyevna, and the latter immediately cast down her eyes and began looking about for something; I saw that Liza was doing her utmost to control

herself but all at once our eyes chanced to meet, and she burst
into a fit of laughter ; I flared up.

"Liza, you are insupportable ! "

"Forgive me ! " she said suddenly, leaving off laughing and
speaking almost sadly. "Goodness knows what I can be thinking about . . ."

And there was a tremor almost as of tears in her voice. I felt
horribly ashamed ; I took her hand and kissed it warmly.

"You are very good," Anna Andreyevna said. softly, seeing
me kiss Liza's hand.

"I am awfully glad that I have found you laughing this time,
Liza," I said. "Would you believe it, Anna Andreyevna, every
time I have met her lately she has greeted me with a strange
look, and that look seemed to ask, ' has he found out something ?
is everything all right ? ' Really, there has been something like
that about her."

Anna Andreyevna looked keenly and deliberately at her.
Liza dropped her eyes. I could see very clearly, however, that
they were on much closer and more intimate terms than I could
have possibly imagined ; the thought was pleasant.

"You told me just now that I am good ; you would not
believe, Anna Andreyevna, how much I change for the better
when I'm with you, and how much I like being with you," I said
with warmth.

"I am awfully glad that you say that just now," she answered
with peculiar significance. I must mention that she never spoke
to me of the reckless way I was living, and the depths to which
I was sinking, although (I knew it) she was not only aware of all
this, but even made inquiries about it indirectly.

So that this now was something like the first hint on the
subject, and my heart turned to her more warmly than ever.

"How is our patient ? " I asked.

"Oh, he is much better ; he is up, and he went for a drive
yesterday and again to-day. You don't mean to say you
have not been to see him to-day ? He is eagerly expecting
you."

"I have behaved very badly to him, but now you're looking
after him, and have quite taken my place ; he is a gay deceiver,
and has thrown me over for you."

A serious look came into her face, very possibly because my
tone was rather too flippant.

"I have just been at Prince Sergay's," I muttered, "and I

. . . by the way, Liza, you went to see Darya Onisimovna this morning, didn't you ? "

" Yes," she answered briefly, without raising her head. " But you do go to see the invalid every day, I believe, don't you ? " she asked suddenly, probably in order to say something.

" Yes, I go to see him, but I don't get there," I said laughing. " I go in and turn to the left."

" Even the prince has noticed that you go to see Katerina Nikolaevna very often. He was speaking of it yesterday and laughing," said Anna Andreyevna.

" What, what did he laugh at ? "

" He was joking, you know his way. He said that, on the contrary, the only impression that a young and beautiful woman makes on a young man of your age is one of anger and indignation," Anne Andreyevna broke into sudden laughter.

" Listen . . . that was a very shrewd saying of his," I cried. " Most likely it was not he said it, but you said it to him."

" Why so ? No, it was he said it."

" Well, but suppose the beautiful lady takes notice of him, in spite of his being so insignificant, of his standing in the corner and fuming at the thought that he is ' only a boy '; suppose she suddenly prefers him to the whole crowd of admirers surrounding her, what then ? " I asked with a bold and defiant air. My head was throbbing.

" Then you are completely done for," laughed Liza.

" Done for," I cried. " No, I'm not done for. I believe that's false. If a woman stands across my path she must follow me. I am not going to be turned aside from my path with impunity. . . ."

I remember Liza once happened to mention long afterwards that I pronounced this phrase very strangely, earnestly, and as though reflecting deeply : and at the same time it was " so absurd, it was impossible to keep from laughing " ; Anna Andreyevna did, in fact, laugh again.

" Laugh at me, laugh away," I cried in exultation, for I was delighted with the whole conversation and the tone of it ; " from you it's a pleasure to me. I love your laugh, Anne Andreyevna ! It's a peculiarity of yours to keep perfectly quiet, and then suddenly laugh, all in one minute, so that an instant before one could not guess what was coming from your face. I used to know a lady in Moscow, I used to sit in a corner and watch her from a distance. She was almost as handsome as you are, but she did not know how to laugh like you ; her face was as attractive as yours, but it lost all its attractiveness when she laughed ; what's so particularly attractive in you . . . is just that faculty. . . . I have been meaning to tell you so for a long time."

When I said of this Moscow lady that " she was as handsome as you " I was not quite ingenuous. I pretended that the phrase had dropped from me unawares, without my noticing it : I knew very well that such " unconscious " praise is more highly valued by a woman than the most polished compliment. And though Anna Andreyevna might flush, I knew that it pleased her. And indeed I invented the lady : I had known no such lady in Moscow ; I had said so simply to compliment Anna Andreyevna, and give her pleasure.

" One really might imagine," she said with a charming laugh, " that you had come under the influence of some fair lady during the last few days."

I felt I was being carried away . . . I longed indeed to tell them something . . . but I refrained.

" By the way, only lately you spoke of Katerina Nikolaevna with very hostile feelings."

" If I did speak ill of her in any way," I cried with flashing eyes, " what's to blame for it is the monstrous slander—that she is an enemy of Andrey Petrovitch's ; there's a libellous story about him, too, that he was in love with her, made her an offer and other absurdities of the sort. The notion is as grotesque as the other scandalous story, that during her husband's lifetime she promised Prince Sergay to marry him as soon as she should be a widow, and afterwards would not keep her word. But I have it first hand that it was not so at all, and that it was all only a joke. I know it first hand. She did, in fact, when she was abroad, say to him in a playful moment : ' Perhaps in the future ' ; but what did that amount to beyond an idle word ? I know very well that the prince on his side can attach no sort of consequence to such a promise ; and indeed he has no intention of doing so," I added on second thoughts. " I fancy he has very different ideas in his head," I put in slily. " Nastchokin said this morning at Prince Sergay's that Katerina Nikolaevna was to be married to Baron Büring. I assure you he received the news with the greatest equanimity, you can take my word for it."

" Has Nastchokin been at Prince Sergay's ? " Anna Andreyevna asked with grave emphasis, apparently surprised.

" Oh yes ; he seems to be one of those highly respectable people . . ."

" And did Nastchokin speak to him of this match with Büring ? " asked Anna Andreyevna, showing sudden interest.

" Not of the match, but of the possibility of one—he spoke of it as a rumour ; he said there was such a rumour going the round of the drawing-rooms : for my part I am certain it's nonsense."

Anna Andreyevna pondered a moment and bent over her sewing.

" I love Prince Sergay," I added suddenly with warmth. " He has his failings, no doubt ; I have told you so already, especially a certain tendency to be obsessed by one idea . . . and, indeed, his faults are a proof of the generosity of his heart, aren't they ? But we almost had a quarrel with him to-day about an idea ; it's his conviction that one must be honourable if one talks of what's honourable, if not, all that you say is a lie. Now, is that logical ? Yet it shows the high standard of honesty, duty, and truth in his soul, doesn't it ? . . . Oh, good heavens, what time is it," I cried, suddenly happening to glance at the clock on the wall.

" Ten minutes to three," she responded tranquilly, looking at the clock. All the time I had talked of Prince Sergay she listened to me with her eyes cast down, with a rather sly but charming smile : she knew why I was praising him. Liza listened with her head bent over her work. For some time past she had taken no part in the conversation.

I jumped up as though I were scalded.

" Are you late for some appointment ? "

" Yes . . . No . . . I am late though, but I am just off. One word only, Anna Andreyevna," I began with feeling ; " I can't help telling you to-day ! I want to confess that I have often blessed your kindness, and the delicacy with which you have invited me to see you. . . . My acquaintance with you has made the strongest impression on me. . . . In your room I am, as it were, spiritually purified, and I leave you better than when I came. That's true. When I sit beside you I am not only unable to speak of anything evil, I am incapable even of evil thoughts ; they vanish away in your presence and, if I recall anything evil after seeing you, I feel ashamed of it at once, I am cast down and blush inwardly. And do you know, it pleased me particularly to find my sister with you to-day. . . . It's a proof of your generosity . . . of such a fine attitude. . . . In one word, you have shown something so *sisterly*, if I may be allowed to break the ice. to . . ."

As I spoke she got up from her seat, and turned more and more crimson ; but suddenly she seemed in alarm at something, at the overstepping of some line which should not have been crossed, and she quickly interrupted me.

" I assure you I appreciate your feelings with all my heart. . . . I have understood them without words for a long time past. . . ."

She paused in confusion, pressing my hand. Liza, unseen by her, suddenly pulled at my sleeve. I said good-bye and went out, but Liza overtook me in the next room.

4

" Liza, why did you tug at my sleeve ? " I asked her.

" She is horrid, she is cunning, she is not worth it. . . . She keeps hold of you to get something out of you," she murmured in a rapid, angry whisper. I had never before seen such a look on her face.

" For goodness' sake, Liza ! she is such a delightful girl ! "

" Well, then, I'm horrid."

" What's the matter with you ? "

" I am very nasty. She may be the most delightful girl, and I am nasty. That's enough, let me alone. Listen : mother implores you about something ' of which she does not dare to speak,' so she said, Arkady darling ! Give up gambling, dear one, I entreat you . . . and so does mother. . . ."

" Liza, I know, but . . . I know that it's pitiful cowardice, but . . . but it's all of no consequence, really ! You see I've got into debt like a fool, and I want to win simply to pay it off. I can win, for till now I've been playing at random, for the fun of the thing, like a fool, but now I shall tremble over every rouble. . . . It won't be me if I don't win ! I have not got a passion for it ; it's not important, it's simply a passing thing ; I assure you I am too strong to be unable to stop when I like. I'll pay back the money and then I shall be altogether yours, and tell mother that I shall stay with you always. . . ."

" That three hundred roubles cost you something this morning ! "

" How do you know ? " I asked, startled.

" Darya Onisimovna heard it all this morning . . ."

But at that moment Liza pushed me behind the curtain, and

we found ourselves in the so-called "lantern," that is a little circular room with windows all round it. Before I knew where we were I caught the sound of a voice I knew, and the clang of spurs, and recognized a familiar footstep.

"Prince Sergay," I whispered.

"Yes," she whispered.

"Why are you so frightened ? "

"It's nothing ; I don't want him to meet me."

"*Tiens*, you don't mean to say he's trying to flirt with you ? " I said smiling. "I'd give it to him if he did. Where are you going ? "

"Let us go, I will come with you."

"Have you said good-bye ? "

"Yes, my coat's in the hall."

We went out ; on the stairs I was struck by an idea.

"Do you know, Liza, he may have come to make her an offer ! "

"N–n–no . . . he won't make her an offer . . ." she said firmly and deliberately, in a low voice.

"You don't know, Liza, though I quarrelled with him this morning—since you've been told of it already—yet on my honour I really love him and wish him success. We made it up this morning. When we are happy we are so good-natured. . . . One sees in him many fine tendencies . . . and he has humane feelings too. . . . The rudiments anyway . . . and in the hands of such a strong and clever girl as Anna Andreyevna, he would rise to her level and be happy. I am sorry I've no time to spare . . . but let us go a little way together, I should like to tell you something. . . . "

"No, you go on, I'm not going that way. Are you coming to dinner ? "

"I am coming, I am coming as I promised. Listen, Liza, a low brute, a loathsome creature in fact, called Stebelkov, has a strange influence over his doings . . . an IOU. . . . In short he has him in his power, and he has pressed him so hard, and Prince Sergay has humiliated himself so far that neither of them see any way out of it except an offer to Anna Andreyevna. And really she ought to be warned, though that's nonsense ; she will set it all to rights later. But what do you think, will she refuse him ? "

"Good-bye, I am late," Liza muttered, and in the momentary look on her face I saw such hatred that I cried out in horror :

Q

" Liza, darling, what is it ? "

" I am not angry with you ; only don't gamble. . . ."

" Oh, you are talking of that ; I'm not going to."

" You said just now : ' when we are happy.'   Are you very happy then ? "

" Awfully, Liza, awfully !   Good heavens, why it's past three o'clock ! . . . Good-bye, Liza.   Lizotchka darling, tell me : can one keep a woman waiting ?   Isn't it inexcusable ? "

" Waiting to meet you, do you mean ? " said Liza faintly smiling, with a sort of lifeless, trembling smile.

" Give me your hand for luck."

" For luck ? my hand ?   I won't, not for anything."

She walked away quickly.   And she had exclaimed it so earnestly !   I jumped into my sledge.

Yes, yes, this was " happiness," and it was the chief reason why I was as blind as a mole, and had no eyes or understanding, except for myself.

CHAPTER IV

1

Now I am really afraid to tell my story.   It all happened long ago ; and it is all like a mirage to me now.   How could such a woman possibly have arranged a rendezvous with such a contemptible urchin as I was then ?   Yet so it seemed at first sight ! When, leaving Liza, I raced along with my heart throbbing, I really thought that I had gone out of my mind : the idea that she had granted me this interview suddenly appeared to me such an obvious absurdity, that it was impossible for me to believe in it.   And yet I had not the faintest doubt of it ; the more obviously absurd it seemed, the more implicitly I believed in it.

The fact that it had already struck three troubled me : " If an interview has been granted me, how can I possibly be late for it," I thought.   Foolish questions crossed my mind, too, such as : " Which was my better course now, boldness or timidity ? "   But all this only flashed through my mind because I had something of real value in my heart, which I could not have defined.   What had been said the evening before was this : " To-morrow at three o'clock I shall be at Tatyana Pavlovna's," that was all.   But in the first place, she always received me alone in her own room, and she could have said anything she liked to me there, without going to Tatyana Pavlovna's for the purpose ; so why have appointed another place of meeting ? And another question was : would Tatyana Pavlovna be at home or not ? If it were a tryst then Tatyana Pavlovna would not be at home. And how could this have been arranged without telling Tatyana Pavlovna beforehand ? Then was Tatyana Pavlovna in the secret ? This idea seemed to me wild, and in a way indelicate, almost coarse.

And, in fact, she might simply have been going to see Tatyana Pavlovna, and have mentioned the fact to me the previous evening with no object in view, but I had misunderstood her. And, indeed, it had been said so casually, so quickly, and after a very tedious visit. I was for some reason overcome with stupidity the whole evening : I sat and mumbled, and did not know what to say, raged inwardly, and was horribly shy, and she was going out somewhere, as I learnt later, and was evidently relieved when I got up to go. All these reflections surged into my mind. I made up my mind at last that when I arrived I would ring the bell. "The cook will open the door," I thought, "and I shall ask whether Tatyana Pavlovna is at home. If she is not then it's a tryst." But I had no doubt of it, no doubt of it !

I ran up the stairs and when I was at the door all my fears vanished. "Come what may," I thought, "if only it's quickly ! " The cook opened the door and with revolting apathy snuffled out that Tatyana Pavlovna was not at home. "But isn't there some one else ? Isn't there some one waiting for her ? " I wanted to ask, but I did not ask, "I'd better see for myself," and muttering to the cook that I would wait, I took off my fur coat and opened the door. . . .

Katerina Nikolaevna was sitting at the window "waiting for Tatyana Pavlovna."

"Isn't she at home ? " she suddenly asked me, in a tone of anxiety and annoyance as soon as she saw me. And her face and her voice were so utterly incongruous with what I had expected that I came to a full stop in the doorway.

"Who's not at home ? " I muttered.

"Tatyana Pavlovna ! Why, I asked you yesterday to tell her that I would be with her at three o'clock."

"I . . . I have not seen her at all."

"Did you forget ? "

I sat completely overwhelmed. So this was all it meant! And the worst of it was it was all as clear as twice two makes four, and I—I had all this while persisted in believing it.

"I don't remember your asking me to tell her. And in fact you didn't ask me : you simply said you would be here at three o'clock," I burst out impatiently, I did not look at her.

"Oh!" she cried suddenly ; "but if you forgot to tell her, though you knew I should be here, what has brought you here?"

I raised my head ; there was no trace of mockery or anger in her face, there was only her bright, gay smile, and a look more mischievous than usual. Though, indeed, her face always had an expression of almost childish mischief.

"There, you see I've caught you ; well, what are you going to say now?" her whole face seemed to be saying.

I did not want to answer and looked down again. The silence lasted half a minute.

"Have you just come from papa?" she asked.

"I have come from Anna Andreyevna's, I haven't been to see Prince Nikolay Ivanitch at all . . . and you know that," I added suddenly.

"Did anything happen to you at Anna Andreyevna's?"

"You mean that I look as though I were crazy? But I looked crazy before I went to Anna Andreyevna."

"And you didn't recover your wits there?"

"No, I didn't. And what's more I heard that you were going to marry Baron Büring."

"Did she tell you that?" she asked with sudden interest.

"No, it was I told her ; I heard Nastchokin tell Prince Sergay so this morning."

I still kept my eyes cast down and did not look at her ; to look at her meant to be flooded with radiance, joy, and happiness, and I did not want to be happy. Indignation had stung me to the heart, and in one instant I had taken a tremendous resolution. Then I began to speak, I hardly knew what about. I was breathless, and spoke indistinctly, but I looked at her boldly. My heart was throbbing. I began talking of something quite irrelevant, though perhaps not incoherently. At first she listened with a serene, patient smile, which never left her face, but little by little signs of surprise and then of alarm passed over her countenance. The smile still persisted, but from time to time it seemed tremulous. "What's the matter?" I asked her, noticing that she shuddered all over.

" I am afraid of you," she answered, almost in trepidation.

"Why don't you go away ?" I said. "As Tatyana Pavlovna is not at home, and you know she won't be, you ought to get up and go."

" I meant to wait for her, but now . . . really. . . ."

She made a movement to get up.

" No, no, sit down," I said, stopping her ; " there, you shuddered again, but you smile even when you're frightened. . . . You always have a smile. There, now you are smiling all over. . . ."

" You are raving."

" Yes, I am."

" I am frightened . . ." she whispered again.

" Frightened of what ? "

" That you'll begin knocking down the walls . . ." she smiled again, though she really was scared.

" I can't endure your smile . . . ! "

And I talked away again. I plunged headlong. It was as though something had given me a shove. I had never, never talked to her like that, I had always been shy. I was fearfully shy now, but I talked ; I remember I talked about her face.

" I can't endure your smile any longer ! " I cried suddenly. "Why did I even in Moscow picture you as menacing, magnificent, using venomous drawing-room phrases ? Yes, even before I left Moscow, I used to talk with Marie Ivanovna about you, and imagined what you must be like. . . . Do you remember Marie Ivanovna ? You've been in her house. When I was coming here I dreamed of you all night in the train. For a whole month before you came I gazed at your portrait, in your father's study, and could make nothing of it. The expression of your face is childish mischief and boundless good-nature—there! I have been marvelling at it all the time I've been coming to see you. Oh, and you know how to look haughty and to crush one with a glance. I remember how you looked at me at your father's that day when you had arrived from Moscow . . . I saw you then, but if you were to ask me how I went out of the room or what you were like, I could not tell you—I could not even have told whether you were tall or short. As soon as I saw you I was blinded. Your portrait is not in the least like you : your eyes are not dark, but light, it's only the long eyelashes that make them look dark. You are plump, you are neither tall nor short, you have a buxom fullness, the light full figure of a healthy peasant girl. And your face is quite countrified, too, it's the face of a village beauty—don't be offended. Why, it's fine, it's better so—a round, rosy, clear, bold, laughing, and . . . bashful face! Really, bashful. Bashful! of Katerina Nikolaevna Ahmakov! Bashful and chaste, I swear! More than chaste—childlike!—that's your face! I have been astounded by it all this time, and have been asking myself, is the woman so, too ? I know now that you are very clever, but do you know, at first I thought you were a simpleton ? You have a bright and lively mind, but without embellishments of any sort. . . . Another thing I like is that your smile never deserts you ; that's my paradise ! I love your calmness, too, your quietness, and your uttering your words so smoothly, so calmly and almost lazily, it's just that laziness I like. I believe if a bridge were to break down under you, you would say something in a smooth and even voice. . . . I imagined you as the acme of pride and passion, and for the last two months you've been talking to me as one student talks to another. I never imagined that you had such a brow ; it's rather low, like the foreheads of statues, but soft and as white as marble, under your glorious hair. Your bosom is high, your movements are light. You are extraordinarily beautiful, but there's no pride about you. It's only now I've come to believe it, I've disbelieved in it all this time ! "

She listened to this wild tirade with large wide-open eyes, she saw that I was trembling. Several times she lifted her gloved hand with a charming apprehensive gesture to stop me, but every time she drew it back in dismay and perplexity. Sometimes she even stepped back a little. Two or three times the smile lighted up her face again ; at one time she flushed very red, but in the end was really frightened and turned pale. As soon as I stopped she held out her hand, and in a voice that was still even, though it had a note of entreaty, said :

" You must not say that . . . you can't talk like that. . . ."

And suddenly she got up from her place, deliberately gathering up her scarf and sable muff.

" Are you going ? " I cried.

" I'm really afraid of you . . . you are abusing . . ." she articulated slowly and as it were with compassion and reproach.

" Listen, on my honour I won't knock down the walls."

" But you've begun already," she could not refrain from smiling. " I don't even know if you will allow me to pass." And she seemed to be actually afraid I would not let her go.

" I will open the door myself, but let me tell you I've taken a tremendous resolution ; and if you care to give light to my soul, come back, sit down, and listen to just two words. But if you won't, then go away, and I will open the door to you myself ! "

She looked at me and sat down again.

" Some women would have gone out with a show of indignation, but you sit down ! " I cried in exaltation.

" You have never allowed yourself to talk like this before."

" I was always afraid before, I came in now not knowing what I should say. You imagine I'm not afraid now : I am. But I've just taken a tremendous resolution, and I feel I shall carry it out. And as soon as I took that resolution I went out of my mind and began saying all this. . . . Listen, this is what I have to say, am I your spy or not ? Answer me that question ! "

The colour rushed into her face.

" Don't answer yet, Katerina Nikolaevna, but listen to everything and then tell the whole truth."

I had broken down all barriers at once and plunged headlong into space.

2

" Two months ago I was standing here behind the curtain. . . . you know . . . and you talked to Tatyana Pavlovna about the letter. I rushed out, and beside myself, I blurted out the truth. You saw at once that I knew something . . . you could not help seeing it . . . you were trying to find an important document, and were uneasy about it. . . . Wait a bit, Katerina Nikolaevna, don't speak yet. I must tell you that your suspicion was well founded : that document does exist . . . that is to say it did. . . . I have seen it—your letter to Andronikov, that's it, isn't it ? "

" You've seen that letter ? " she asked quickly, in embarrassment and agitation. " When did you see it ? "

" I saw it . . . I saw it at Kraft's . . . you know, the man that shot himself. . . ."

" Really ? You saw it yourself ? What became of it ? "

" Kraft tore it up."

" In your presence, did you see him ? "

" Yes, he tore it up, probably because he was going to die. . . . I did not know then, of course, that he was going to shoot himself. . . ."

" So it has been destroyed, thank God ! " she commented slowly with a deep sigh, and she crossed herself.

I was not lying to her, that is to say I was lying because the letter in question was in my hands and had never been in Kraft's, but that was a mere detail ; in what really mattered I did not lie, because at the instant I told the lie I nerved myself to burn the letter that very evening. I swear that if it had been in my pocket that moment I would have taken it out and given it her ; but I hadn't it with me, it was at my lodging. Perhaps though I should not have given it her because I should have felt horribly ashamed to confess to her then that I had it, and had been keeping it and waiting so long before I gave it back. It made no difference, I should have burnt it at home in any case, and I was not lying ! I swear that at that moment my heart was pure.

"And since that's how it is," I went on, almost beside myself, "tell me, have you been attracting me, have you been welcoming me in your drawing-room because you suspected that I knew of the letter ? Stay, Katerina Nikolaevna, one minute more, don't speak, but let me finish : all the time I've been coming to see you, all this time I've been suspecting that it was only because of that that you made much of me, to get that letter out of me, to lead me on to telling you about it. . . . Wait one more minute : I suspected it, but I suffered. Your duplicity was more than I could bear, for I found you a noble creature ! I tell you plainly ; I was your enemy, but I found you a noble creature ! I was utterly vanquished. But your duplicity, that is the suspicion of your duplicity, was anguish. . . . Now everything must be settled, everything must be explained, the time has come for it ; but wait yet a little longer, don't speak, let me tell you how I look at it myself, just now at this moment ; I tell you plainly, if it has been so I don't resent it . . . that is, I mean, I'm not offended, for it's so natural ; I understand, you see. What is there unnatural or wrong about it ? You were worried about a letter, you suspected that So-and-so knew all about it; well, you might very naturally desire So-and-so to speak out. . . . There's no harm in that, none at all. I am speaking sincerely. Yet now you must tell me something . . . you must confess (forgive the word), I must have the truth. I want it for a reason ! And so tell me, why did you make much of me ? Was it to get that letter out of me . . . Katerina Nikolaevna ? "

I spoke as though I were falling from a height, and my forehead was burning. She was listening to me now without apprehension; on the contrary, her face was full of feeling ; but she looked somehow abashed, as though she were ashamed.

"It was for that," she said slowly and in a low voice. "Forgive me, I did wrong," she added suddenly, with a faint movement of her hands towards me. I had never expected this. had expected anything rather that those two words—even from her whom I knew already.

"And you tell me you did wrong! so simply : 'I did wrong,'" I cried.

"Oh, for a long time I've been feeling that I was not treating you fairly . . . and, indeed, I'm glad to be able to speak of it. . . ."

"For a long time you've been feeling that ? Why did you not speak of it before ? "

"Oh, I did not know how to say it," she smiled ; "that is, I should have known how," she smiled again, "but I always felt ashamed . . . because at first it really was only on that account that I 'attracted' you, as you expressed it; but very soon afterwards I felt disgusted and sick of all this deception, I assure you ! " she added with bitter feeling ; "and of all this troublesome business ! "

"And why—why couldn't you have asked me then straightforwardly ? You should have said : ' you know about the letter, why do you pretend ? ' And I should have told you at once, I should have confessed at once ! "

"Oh, I was . . . a little afraid of you. I must admit I did not trust you either. And after all, if I dissembled, you did the same," she added with a laugh.

"Yes, yes, I have been contemptible ! " I cried, overwhelmed. "Oh, you don't know yet the abyss into which I have fallen."

"An abyss already ! I recognize your style," she smiled softly. "That letter," she added mournfully, "was the saddest and most indiscreet thing I ever did. The consciousness of it was a continual reproach. Moved by circumstances and apprehension, I had doubts of my dear generous-hearted father. Knowing that that letter might fall . . . into the hands of malicious people . . . and I had good reasons for fearing this " (she added hotly), "I trembled that they might use it, might show my father . . . and it might make a tremendous impression on him . . . in his condition . . . on his health . . . and he might be estranged from me. . . . Yes," she added, looking me candidly in the face, and probably catching some shade in my expression ; "yes, and I was afraid for my future too ; I was afraid that he . . . under the influence of his illness . . .

might deprive me of his favour. . . . That feeling came in too ; no doubt I did him an injustice ; he is so kind and generous, that no doubt he would have forgiven me. That's all. But I ought not to have treated you as I did," she concluded, again seeming suddenly abashed. " You have made me feel ashamed."

" No, you have nothing to be ashamed of," I cried.

" I certainly did reckon . . . on your impulsiveness . . . and I recognize it," she brought out, looking down.

" Katerina Nikolaevna ! Who forces you to make such confessions to me, tell me that ? " I cried, as though I were drunk. " Wouldn't it have been easy for you to get up, and in the most exquisite phrases to prove to me subtly and as clearly as twice two make four that though it was so, yet it was nothing of the sort—you understand, as people of your world know how to deal with the truth ? I am crude and foolish, you know, I should have believed you at once, I should have believed anything from you, whatever you said ! It would have cost you nothing to behave like that, of course ! You are not really afraid of me, you know ! How could you be so willing to humiliate yourself like this before an impudent puppy, a wretched raw youth ? "

" In this anyway I've not humiliated myself before you," she enunciated with immense dignity, apparently not understanding my exclamation.

" No, indeed, quite the contrary, that's just what I am saying. . . ."

" Oh, it was so wrong, so thoughtless of me ! " she exclaimed, putting her hand to her face, as though to hide it. "I felt ashamed yesterday, that's why I was not myself when I was with you. . . . The fact is," she added, " that circumstances have made it absolutely essential for me at last to find out the truth about that unlucky letter, or else I should have begun to forget about it . . . for I have not let you come to see me simply on account of that," she added suddenly.

There was a tremor at my heart.

" Of course not," she went on with a subtle smile, " of course not ! I . . . You very aptly remarked, Arkady Makarovitch, that we have often talked together as one student to another. I assure you I am sometimes very much bored in company ; I have felt so particularly since my time abroad and all these family troubles . . . I very rarely go anywhere, in fact, and not simply from laziness. I often long to go into the country. There I could read over again my favourite books, which I have laid aside for so long, and have never been able to bring myself to read again. I have spoken to you of that already. Do you remember, you laughed at my reading the Russian newspapers at the rate of two a day."

"I didn't laugh. . . ."

" Of course not, for you, too, were excited over them, and I confessed, too, long ago, that I am Russian, and love Russia. You remember we always read ' facts ' as you called them " (she smiled). " Though you are at times somewhat . . . strange, yet sometimes you grew so eager and would say such good things, and you were interested just in what I was interested in. When you are a ' student ' you are charming and original. Nothing else suits you so well," she added, with a sly and charming smile. " Do you remember we sometimes talked for hours about nothing but figures, reckoned and compared, and took trouble to find out how many schools there are in Russia, and in what direction progress is being made ? We reckoned up the murders and serious crimes and set them off against the cheering items. . . . We wanted to find out in what direction we were moving, and what would happen to us in the end. In you I found sincerity. In our world men never talk like that to us, to women. Last week I was talking to Prince X. about Bismarck, for I was very much interested, and could not make up my mind about him, and only fancy, he sat down beside me and began telling me about him very fully, indeed, but always with a sort of irony, and that patronizing condescension which I always find so insufferable, and which is so common in ' great men ' when they talk to us women if we meddle with ' subjects beyond our sphere.' . . . Do you remember that we almost had a quarrel, you and I, over Bismarck ? You showed me that you had ideas of your own ' far more definite ' than Bismarck's," she laughed suddenly. " I have only met two people in my whole life who talked to me quite seriously ; my husband, a very, very intelligent and hon-our-able man," she pronounced the words impressively, " and you know whom. . . ."

" Versilov ! " I cried ; I hung breathless on every word she uttered.

" Yes, I was very fond of listening to him, I became at last absolutely open . . . perhaps too open with him, but even then he did not believe in me ! "

" Did not believe in you ? "

" No, no one has ever believed in me."

" But Versilov, Versilov ! "

" He did not simply disbelieve in me," she pronounced, dropping her eyes, and smiling strangely, " but considered that I had all the vices. "

" Of which you have not one ! "

" No, even I have some."

" Versilov did not love you, so he did not understand you," I cried with flashing eyes.

Her face twitched.

" Say no more of that and never speak to me of . . . of that man," she added hotly, with vehement emphasis. " But that's enough : I must be going "—she got up to go. " Well, do you forgive me or not ? " she added, looking at me brightly.

" Me . . . forgive you. . . . Listen, Katerina Nikolaevna, and don't be angry ; is it true that you are going to be married ? "

" That's not settled," she said in confusion, seeming frightened of something.

" Is he a good man ? Forgive me, forgive me that question ! "

" Yes, very."

" Don't answer further, don't vouchsafe me an answer ! I know that such questions from me are impossible ! I only wanted to know whether he is worthy of you or not, but I will find out for myself."

" Ah, listen ! " she said in dismay.

" No, I won't, I won't. I'll step aside. . . . Only this one thing I want to say : God grant you every happiness according to your choice . . . for having given me so much happiness in this one hour ! Your image is imprinted on my heart for ever now. I have gained a treasure : the thought of your perfection. I expected duplicity and coarse coquetry and was wretched . . . because I could not connect that idea with you. I've been thinking day and night lately, and suddenly everything has become clear as daylight ! As I was coming here I thought I should bear away an image of jesuitical cunning, of deception, of an inquisitorial serpent, and I found honour, magnificence, a student. You laugh. Laugh away ! You are holy, you know, you cannot laugh at what is sacred. . . ."

" Oh no, I'm only laughing because you use such wonderful expressions. . . . But what is an ' inquisitorial serpent ' ? " she laughed.

" You let slip to-day a priceless sentence," I went on ecstatically. " How could you to my face utter the words : ' I reckoned on your impulsiveness ' ? Well, granted you are a saint, and confess even that, because you imagined yourself guilty in some way and want to punish yourself . . . though there was no fault of any sort, for, if there had been, from you everything is holy ! But yet you need not have uttered just that word, that expression ! . . . Such unnatural candour only shows your lofty purity, your respect for me, your faith in me ! " I cried incoherently. " Oh, do not blush, do not blush ! . . . And how, how could anyone slander you, and say that you are a woman of violent passions ? ` Oh, forgive me : I see a look of anguish on your face ; forgive a frenzied boy his clumsy words ! Besides, do words matter now ? Are you not above all words ? . . . Versilov said once that Othello did not kill Desdemona and afterwards himself because he was jealous, but because he had been robbed of his ideal. . . . I understand that, because to-day my ideal has been restored to me ! "

" You praise me too much : I don't deserve this," she pronounced with feeling. " Do you remember what I told you about your eyes ? " she added playfully.

" That I have microscopes for eyes, and that I exaggerate every fly into a camel ! No, this time it's not a camel. . . . What, you are going ? "

She was standing in the middle of the room with her muff and her shawl in her hands.

" No, I shall wait till you're gone, and then I shall go afterwards. I must write a couple of words to Tatyana Pavlovna."

" I'm going directly, directly, but once more : may you be happy alone, or with the man of your choice, and God bless you ! All that I need is my ideal ! "

" Dear, good Arkady Makarovitch, believe me I . . . My father always says of you ' the dear, good boy ! ' Believe me I shall always remember what you have told me of your lonely childhood, abandoned amongst strangers, and your solitary dreams. . . . I understand only too well how your mind has been formed . . . but now though we are students," she added, with a deprecating and shamefaced smile, pressing my hand, " we can't go on seeing each other as before and, and . . . no doubt you will understand that ? "

" We cannot ? "

" No, we cannot, for a long time, we cannot . . . it's my fault. . . . I see now that it's quite out of the question. . . . We shall meet sometimes at my father's."

" You are afraid of my ' impulsiveness,' my feelings, you don't believe in me ! " I would have exclaimed, but she was so overcome with shame that my words refused to be uttered.

" Tell me," she said, stopping me all at once in the doorway, " did you see yourself that . . . that letter was torn up ? You are sure you remember it ? How did you know at the time that it was the letter to Andronikov ? "

" Kraft told me what was in it, and even showed it to me. . . . Good-bye ! When I am with you in your study I am shy of you, but when you go away I am ready to fall down and kiss the spot where your foot has touched the floor. . . ." I brought out all at once, unconsciously, not knowing how or why I said it. And without looking at her I went quickly out of the room.

I set off for home ; there was rapture in my soul. My brain was in a whirl, my heart was full. As I drew near my mother's house I recalled Liza's ingratitude to Anna Andreyevna, her cruel and monstrous saying that morning, and my heart suddenly ached for them all !

" How hard their hearts are ! And Liza too, what's the matter with her ? " I thought as I stood on the steps.

I dismissed Matvey and told him to come to my lodging for me at nine o'clock.

CHAPTER V

1

I was late for dinner, but they had not yet sat down to table, they had waited for me. Perhaps because I did not often dine with them, some special additions to the menu had been made on my account : with the savouries there were sardines and so on. But to my surprise and regret, I found them all rather worried and out of humour. Liza scarcely smiled when she saw me, and mother was obviously uneasy ; Versilov gave me a smile, but it was a forced one. " Have they been quarrelling ? " I wondered. Everything went well at first, however ; Versilov only frowned over the soup with dumplings in it, and made wry faces when he was handed the beef olives.

"I have only to mention that a particular dish does not suit me, for it to reappear next day," he pronounced in vexation.

"But how's one to invent things, Andrey Petrovitch? There's no inventing a new dish of any sort," my mother answered timidly.

"Your mother is the exact opposite of some of our newspapers, to whom whatever is new is good," Versilov tried to make a joke in a more playful and amiable voice; but it somehow fell flat, and only added to the discomfiture of my mother, who of course could make nothing of the comparison of herself with the newspapers, and looked about her in perplexity. At that moment Tatyana Pavlovna came in, and announcing that she had already dined, sat down near mother, on the sofa.

I had not yet succeeded in gaining the good graces of that lady, quite the contrary in fact; she used to fall foul of me more than ever, for everything, and about everything. Her displeasure had of late become more accentuated than ever; she could not endure the sight of my foppish clothes, and Liza told me that she almost had a fit when she heard that I kept a coachman and a smart turn-out. I ended by avoiding meeting her as far as possible. Two months before, when the disputed inheritance was given up to Prince Sergay, I had run to Tatyana Pavlovna, meaning to talk over Versilov's conduct with her, but I met with no trace of sympathy; on the contrary she was dreadfully angry: she was particularly vexed that the whole had been given back, instead of half the fortune; she observed sharply:

"I'll bet you are persuaded that he has given up the money and challenged the prince to a duel, solely to regain the good opinion of Arkady Makarovitch."

And indeed she was almost right. I was in reality feeling something of the sort at the time.

As soon as she came in I saw at once that she would infallibly attack me. I was even inclined to believe that she had come in expressly with that object, and so I immediately became exceptionally free-and-easy in my manner; this was no effort to me, for what had just happened had left me still radiant and joyful. I may mention once and for all that a free-and-easy manner never has been right for me, that is to say, it never suits me, but always covers me with disgrace. So it happened now. I instantly said the wrong thing, with no evil intent, but simply from thoughtlessness; noticing that Liza was horribly depressed, I suddenly blurted out, without thinking of what I was saying :

" I haven't dined here for such ages, and now I have come, see how bored you are, Liza ! "

" My head aches," answered Liza.

" Good gracious ! " said Tatyana Pavlovna, instantly catching at it. " What if you are ill ? Arkady Makarovitch has deigned to come to dinner, you must dance and be merry."

" You really are the worry of my life, Tatyana Pavlovna. I will never come again when you are here ! " and I brought my hand down on the table with genuine vexation; mother started, and Versilov looked at me strangely. I laughed at once and begged their pardon.

" Tatyana Pavlovna, I take back the word ' worry,' " I said, turning to her, with the same free-and-easy tone.

" No, no," she snapped out, " it's much more flattering to be a worry to you than to be the opposite, you may be sure of that."

" My dear boy, one must learn to put up with the small worries of life," Versilov murmured with a smile, " life is not worth living without them."

" Do you know, you are sometimes a fearful reactionary," I cried, laughing nervously.

" My dear boy, it doesn't matter."

" Yes, it does ! Why not tell the blunt truth to an ass, if he is an ass ? "

" Surely you are not speaking of yourself ? To begin with, I can't judge anyone, and I don't want to."

" Why don't you want to, why can't you ? "

" Laziness and distaste. A clever woman told me once that I had no right to judge others because ' I don't know how to suffer,' that before judging others, one must gain the right to judge, from suffering. Rather exalted, but, as applied to me, perhaps it's true, so that I very readily accepted the criticism."

" Wasn't it Tatyana Pavlovna who told you that ? " I cried.

" Why, how do you know ? " said Versilov, glancing at me with some surprise.

" I knew it from Tatyana Pavlovna's face : she gave a sudden start."

I guessed by chance. The phrase, as it appeared later, actually had been uttered by Tatyana Pavlovna, the evening before, in a heated discussion. And indeed, I repeat, I had, brimming over with joy and expansiveness, swooped down upon them at an unfortunate moment; all of them had their separate troubles, and they were heavy ones.

" I don't understand it," I went on, " because it's all so abstract; it's dreadful how fond you are of abstract discussion, Andrey Petrovitch; it's a sign of egoism; only egoists are fond of generalization."

" That's not a bad saying, but don't persecute me."

" But let me ask," I insisted expansively, " what's the meaning of ' gaining the right to judge ? ' Anyone who is honest may be a judge, that's my idea."

" You won't find many judges in that case."

" I know one anyway."

" Who's that ? "

" He is sitting and talking to me now."

Versilov laughed strangely, he stooped down to my ear, and taking me by the shoulder whispered, " He is always lying to you."

I don't know to this day what was in his mind, but evidently he was in some agitation at the time (in consequence of something he had learned, as I found out later). But those words, " he is always lying to you," were so unexpected and uttered so earnestly, and with such a strange and far from playful expression, that it gave me a nervous shudder. I was almost alarmed and looked at him wildly; but Versilov made haste to laugh.

" Well, thank God ! " murmured my mother, who was uneasy at seeing him whisper to me, " I was almost thinking. . . . Don't be angry with us, Arkasha; you'll have clever friends apart from us, but who is going to love you, if we don't love one another ? "

" The love of one's relations is immoral, mother, just because it's undeserved; love ought to be earned."

" You'll earn it later on, but here you are loved without."

Every one suddenly laughed.

" Well, mother, you may not have meant to shoot, but you hit your bird ! " I cried, laughing, too.

" And you actually imagined that there's something to love you for," cried Tatyana Pavlovna, falling upon me again: " You are not simply loved for nothing, you are loved in spite of loathing."

"Oh not a bit of it," I cried gaily; "do you know, perhaps, some one told me to-day I was loved."

"Said it laughing at you!" Tatyana Pavlovna said suddenly with a sort of unnatural malignity, as though she had just been waiting for me to say that, "yes, a person of delicacy, especially a woman, would be moved to disgust by the uncleanness of your soul. Your hair is done with a smart parting, you have fine linen, and a suit made by a French tailor, but it's all uncleanness really! Who's paid your tailor's bill, who keeps you, and gives you money to play roulette with? Think who it is you've been so shameless as to sponge on!"

My mother flushed painfully, and I had never seen a look of such shame on her face before. Everything seemed to be giving way within me.

"If I am spending money it's my own, and I am not bound to give an account of it to anyone," I blurted out, turning crimson.

"Whose own? What money's your own?"

"If it's not mine, it's Andrey Petrovitch's. He won't refuse it me. . . . I borrowed from what Prince Sergay owes Andrey Petrovitch. . . ."

"My dear boy," Versilov said firmly, all of a sudden, "not a farthing of that money is mine."

The phrase was horribly significant. I was dumbfounded. Oh, of course, considering my paradoxical and careless attitude at that time, I might quite well have turned it off with some outburst of "generous" feeling, or high-sounding phrase, or something, but I suddenly caught on Liza's face a resentful accusing expression, an expression I had not deserved, almost a sneer, and a devil seemed to prompt me.

"You seem," I said, turning to her suddenly, "to visit Darya Onisimovna very often at Prince Sergay's flat, miss, so will you be pleased to give her this three hundred roubles, which you've given me such a nagging about already to-day?"

I took out the money and held it out to her. But will it be believed that those mean words were uttered entirely without motive, that is, without the faintest allusion to anything. And indeed there could have been no such allusion, for at that moment I knew absolutely nothing. Perhaps I had just a desire to vex her by something comparatively most innocent, by way of a gibe, "Since you are such an interfering young lady, wouldn't you like to return the money yourself to the prince, a charming young man and a Petersburg officer, as you are so anxious to meddle in young men's business." But what was my amazement when my mother got up, and, with a menacing gesture, cried :

"How dare you ! How dare you !"

I could never have conceived of anything like it from her, and I too jumped up from my seat, not exactly in alarm, but with a sort of anguish, a poignant wound in my heart, suddenly realizing that something dreadful had happened. But unable to control herself, mother hid her face in her hands and ran out of the room. Liza followed her out without so much as a glance at me. Tatyana Pavlovna gazed at me for half a minute in silence.

"Can you really have meant to jeer ? " she exclaimed enigmatically, looking at me in profound astonishment, but without waiting for me to answer, she, too, ran out to join them. With an unsympathetic, almost angry expression, Versilov got up from the table, and took his hat from the corner.

"I imagine that you are not so much a fool as an innocent," he mumbled to me ironically. "If they come back, tell them to have their pudding without waiting for me. I am going out for a little."

I remained alone ; at first I felt bewildered, then I felt resentful, but afterwards I saw clearly that I was to blame. However, I did not know exactly how I was to blame, I simply had a feeling of it. I sat in the window and waited. After waiting ten minutes, I, too, took my hat, and went upstairs to the attic, which had been mine. I knew that they, that is my mother and Liza, were there, and that Tatyana Pavlovna had gone away. And so I found them on my sofa, whispering together about something. They left off whispering at once, when I appeared ; to my amazement they were not angry with me ; mother anyway smiled at me.

"I am sorry, mother," I began.

"Never mind !" mother cut me short, "only love each other and never quarrel and God will send you happiness."

"He is never nasty to me, mother, I assure you," Liza said with conviction and feeling.

"If it hadn't been for that Tatyana Pavlovna nothing would have happened," I cried ; "she's horrid !"

"You see, mother ? You hear ? " said Liza with a motion towards me.

"What I want to tell you both is this," I declared : "if

there is anything nasty in the world, it's I that am nasty, and all the rest is delightful ! "

" Arkasha, don't be angry, darling, but if you really would give up . . ."

" Gambling, you mean, gambling ? I will give it up, mother. I am going there for the last time to-day—especially since Andrey Petrovitch himself has declared that not a farthing of that money is his, you can't imagine how I blush. . . . I must go into it with him, though . . . Mother darling, last time I was here I said something clumsy . . . it was nonsense, darling ; I truly want to believe, it was only swagger, I love Christ. . . ."

On my last visit there had been a conversation about religion. Mother had been much grieved and upset. When she heard my words now, she smiled at me as though I were a little child.

" Christ forgives everything, Arkasha ; he forgives your wrong-doing and worse than yours. Christ is our Father, Christ never fails us, and will give light in the blackest night. . . ."

I said good-bye to them, and went away, thinking over the chances of seeing Versilov that day ; I had a great deal to talk over with him, and it had been impossible that afternoon. I had a strong suspicion that he would be waiting for me at my lodging. I walked there on foot ; it had turned colder and begun to freeze and walking was very pleasant.

2

I lived near the Voznesenky Bridge, in a huge block of flats overlooking the courtyard. Almost as I went into the gate I ran into Versilov coming out.

" As usual when I go for a walk, I only get as far as your lodging, and I've been to Pyotr Ippolitovitch's, but I got tired of waiting for you ; your people there are for ever quarrelling, and to-day his wife is even a little tearful ; I looked in and came away."

For some reason I felt annoyed.

" I suppose you never go to see anyone except me and Pyotr Ippolitovitch ; you have no one else in all Petersburg to go to."

" My dear fellow . . . but it doesn't matter."

" Where are you going now ? "

" I am not coming back to you. If you like we'll go for a walk, it's a glorious evening."

" If instead of abstract discussions, you had talked to me like a human being, and had for instance given me the merest hint about that confounded gambling, I should perhaps not have let myself be drawn into it like a fool," I said suddenly.

" You regret it ? That's a good thing," he answered, bringing out his words reluctantly ; " I always suspected that play was not a matter of great consequence with you, but only a temporary aberration. . . . You are right, my dear boy, gambling is beastly, and what's more one may lose."

" And lose other people's money, too."

" Have you lost other people's money ? "

" I have lost yours. I borrowed of Prince Sergay, from what was owing you. Of course it was fearfully stupid and absurd of me . . . to consider your money mine, but I always meant to win it back."

" I must warn you once more, my dear boy, that I have no money in Prince Sergay's hands. I know that young man is in straits himself, and I am not reckoning on him for anything, in spite of his promises."

" That makes my position twice as bad. . . . I am in a ludicrous position ! And what grounds has he for lending me money, and me for borrowing in that case ? "

" That's your affair. . . . But there's not the slightest reason for you to borrow money from him, is there ? "

" Except that we are comrades. . . ."

" No other reason ? Is there anything which has made you feel it possible to borrow from him ? Any consideration whatever ? "

" What sort of consideration do you mean ? I don't understand."

" So much the better if you don't, and I will own, my boy, that I was sure of it. *Brisons-là, mon cher*, and do try to avoid playing somehow."

" If only you had told me before ! You seem half-hearted about it even now."

" If I had spoken to you about it before, we should only have quarrelled, and you wouldn't have let me come and see you in the evenings so readily. And let me tell you, my dear, that all such saving counsels and warnings are simply an intrusion into another person's conscience, at another person's expense. I have done enough meddling with the consciences of others, and in the long run I get nothing but taunts and rebuffs for it.

Taunts and rebuffs, of course, don't matter; the point is that one never obtains one's object in that way : no one listens to you, however much you meddle . . . and every one gets to dislike you."

"I am glad that you have begun to talk to me of something besides abstractions. I want to ask you one thing, I have wanted to for a long time, but it's always been impossible when I've been with you. It is a good thing we are in the street. Do you remember that evening, the last evening I spent in your house, two months ago, how we sat upstairs in my ' coffin,' and I questioned you about mother and Makar Ivanovitch ; do you remember how free and easy I was with you then ? How could you allow a young puppy to speak in those terms of his mother ? And yet you made not the faintest sign of protest ; on the contrary, 'you let yourself go,' and so made me worse than ever."

"My dear boy, I'm very glad to hear . . . such sentiments, from you. . . . Yes, I remember very well; I was actually waiting to see the blush on your cheek, and if I fell in with your tone, it was just to bring you to the limit. . . ."

"And you only deceived me then, and troubled more than ever the springs of purity in my soul! Yes, I'm a wretched raw youth, and I don't know from minute to minute what is good and what is evil. Had you given me the tiniest hint of the right road, I should have realized things and should have been eager to take the right path. But you only drove me to fury."

" *Cher enfant,* I always foresaw that, one way or another, we should understand one another ; that ' blush ' has made its appearance of itself, without my aid, and that I swear is better for you. . . . I notice, my dear boy, that you have gained a great deal of late . . . can it be the companionship of that princeling ? "

"Don't praise me, I don't like it. Don't leave me with a painful suspicion that you are flattering me without regard for truth, so as to go on pleasing me. Well, lately . . . you see . . . I've been visiting ladies. I am very well received, you know, by Anna Andreyevna, for instance."

" I know that from her, my dear boy. Yes, she is very charming and intelligent. *Mais brisons-là, mon cher.* It's odd how sick I feel of everything to-day, spleen I suppose. I put it down to hæmorrhoids. How are things at home ? All right ? You made it up, of course, and embraces followed ? *Celà va sans dire.* It's melancholy sometimes to go back to them, even after the nastiest walk. In fact, I sometimes go a longer way round in the rain, simply to delay the moment of returning to the bosom of my family. . . . And how bored I am there, good God, how bored ! "

" Mother . . ."

" Your mother is a most perfect and delightful creature, *mais.* . . . In short I am probably unworthy of them. By the way, what's the matter with them to-day ? For the last few days they've all been out of sorts somehow. . . . I always try to ignore such things you know, but there is something fresh brewing to-day. . . . Have you noticed nothing ? "

" I know nothing positive, and in fact I should not have noticed it at all it if hadn't been for that confounded Tatyana Pavlovna, who can never resist trying to get her knife in. You are right ; there is something wrong. I found Liza at Anna Andreyevna's this morning, and she was so . . . she surprised me in fact. You know, of course, that she visits Anna Andreyevna ? "

" I know, my dear. And you . . . when were you at Anna Andreyevna's, to-day ? At what time ? I want to know for a reason."

" From two till three. And only fancy as I was going out Prince Sergay arrived. . . ."

Then I described my whole visit very circumstantially. He listened without speaking ; he made no comment whatever on the possibility of a match between Prince Sergay and Anna Andreyevna ; in response to my enthusiastic praise of Anna Andreyevna he murmured again that " she was very charming."

" I gave her a great surprise this morning, with the latest bit of drawing-room gossip that Mme. Ahmakov is to be married to Baron Büring," I said all of a sudden, as though something were torn out of me.

" Yes ? Would you believe it, she told me that ' news ' earlier in the day, much earlier than you can have surprised her with it."

" What do you mean ? " I was simply struck dumb. "From whom could she have heard it ? Though after all, there's no need to ask ; of course she might have heard it before I did ; but only imagine, she listened to me when I told her as though it were absolutely news to her ! But . . . but what of it ? Hurrah for ' breadth ! ' One must take a broad view of people's characters, mustn't one ? I, for instance, should have poured it all out at once, and she shuts it up in a snuff-box . . . and so be it, so be it, she is none the less a most delightful person, and a very fine character ! "

" Oh, no doubt of it, every one must go his own way. And something more original—these fine characters can sometimes baffle one completely—just imagine, Anna Andreyevna took my breath away this morning by asking : ' Whether I were in love with Katerina Nikolaevna Ahmakov or not ? ' "

" What a wild and incredible question ! " I cried, dumbfounded again. There was actually a mist before my eyes. I had never yet broached this subject with him, and here he had begun on it himself. . . .

" In what way did she put it ? "

" No way, my dear boy, absolutely no way ; the snuff-box shut again at once, more closely than ever, and what's more, observe, I've never admitted the conceivability of such questions being addressed to me, nor has she . . . however, you say yourself that you know her and therefore you can imagine how far such a question is characteristic. . . . Do you know any-thing about it by chance ? "

" I am just as puzzled as you are. Curiosity, perhaps, or a joke."

" Oh, quite the contrary, it was a most serious question, hardly a question in fact, more a cross-examination, and evidently there were very important and positive reasons for it. Won't you be going to see her ? Couldn't you find out something ? I would ask you as a favour, do you see . . ."

" But the strangest thing is that she could imagine you to be in love with Katerina Nikolaevna ! Forgive me, I can't get over my amazement. I should never, never have ventured to speak to you on this subject, or anything like it."

" And that's very sensible of you, my dear boy."

" Your intrigues and your relations in the past—well, of course, the subject's out of the question between us, and indeed it would be stupid of me, but of late, the last few days, I have several times exclaimed to myself that if you had ever loved that woman, if only for a moment—oh, you could never have made such a terrible mistake in your opinion of her as you did ! I know what happened, I know of your enmity, of your aversion, so to say, for each other, I've heard of it, I've heard too much of it ; even before I left Moscow I heard of it, but the fact that stands out so clearly is intense aversion, intense hostility, the very *opposite* of love, and Anna Andreyevna suddenly asks point-blank, ' Do you love her ? ' Can she have heard so little about it ? It's wild ! She was laughing, I assure you she was laughing ! "

" But I observe, my dear boy," said Versilov, and there was something nervous and sincere in his voice, that went to one's heart, as his words rarely did : " that you speak with too much heat on this subject. You said just now that you have taken to visiting ladies . . . of course, for me to question you . . . on that subject, as you expressed it. . . . But is not ' that woman ' perhaps on the list of your new acquaintances ? "

" That woman " . . . my voice suddenly quivered ; " listen, Andrey Petrovitch, listen. That woman is what you were talking of with Prince Sergay this morning, ' living life,' do you remember ? You said that living life is something so direct and simple, something that looks you so straight in the face, that its very directness and clearness make us unable to believe that it can be the very thing we're seeking so laboriously all our lives. . . . With ideas like that, you met the ideal woman and in perfection, in the ideal, you recognized ' all the vices ' ! That's what you did ! "

The reader can guess what a state of frenzy I was in.

" All the vices ! Oho ! I know that phrase," cried Versilov : " and if things have gone so far, that you are told of such a phrase, oughtn't I to congratulate you ? It suggests such a degree of intimacy, that perhaps you deserve credit for a modesty and reserve of which few young men are capable."

There was a note of sweet, friendly and affectionate laughter in his voice . . . there was something challenging and charming in his words, and in his bright face, as far as I could see it in the night. He was strangely excited. I beamed all over in spite of myself.

" Modesty, reserve ! Oh, no, no ! " I exclaimed blushing and at the same time squeezing his hand, which I had somehow seized and was unconsciously holding. " No, there's no reason ! . . . In fact there's nothing to congratulate me on, and nothing of the sort can ever, ever happen."

I was breathless and let myself go, I so longed to let myself go, it was so very agreeable to me.

" You know . . . Well, after all I will . . . just this once . . . ! You are my darling, splendid father ; you will allow me to call you father ; it's utterly out of the question for a son to speak to his father—for anyone, in fact, to speak to a third person—of his relations with a woman, even if they are of the purest ! In fact, the purer they are the greater the obligation of silence. It would be distasteful, it would be coarse ; in short, a confidant is out of the question ! But if there's nothing, absolutely nothing, then surely one may speak, mayn't one ? "

" As your heart tells you ! "

" An indiscreet, a very indiscreet question : I suppose in the course of your life you've known women, you've had intimacies ? . . . I only ask generally, generally, I don't mean anything particular ! " I blushed, and was almost choking with delight.

" We will assume there have been transgressions."

" Well then, I want to ask you this, and you tell me what you think of it, as a man of more experience : a woman suddenly says, as she is taking leave of you, casually, looking away, 'To-morrow at three o'clock I shall be at a certain place . . . at Tatyana Pavlovna's, for example,'" I burst out, taking the final plunge. My heart throbbed and stood still ; I even ceased speaking, I could not go on. He listened eagerly. " And so next day at three o'clock I went to Tatyana Pavlovna's, and this is what I thought : 'when the cook opens the door'—you know her cook—'I shall ask first thing whether Tatyana Pavlovna is at home ? And if the cook says Tatyana Pavlovna is not at home, but there's a visitor waiting for her,' what ought I to conclude, tell me if it were you . . . In short, if you . . ."

" Simply that an apointment had been made you. Then I suppose that did happen, and it happened to-day. Yes ? "

" Oh no, no, no, nothing, nothing of the sort ! It did happen, but it wasn't that ; it was an appointment, but not of that sort, and I hasten to say so or I should be a blackguard ; it did happen, but. . . ."

" My dear fellow, all this begins to be so interesting that I suggest . . ."

" I used to give away ten roubles and twenty-five roubles at a time to those who begged of me. For a drink ! just a few coppers, it's a lieutenant implores your aid, a former lieutenant begging of you ! "

Our road was suddenly barred by the figure of a tall beggar possibly, in fact, a retired lieutenant. What was most singular was that he was very well dressed for his profession, and yet he was begging.

3

I purposely do not omit this paltry incident of the wretched lieutenant, for my picture of Versilov is not complete without the petty details of his surroundings at that minute, which was so momentous for him—momentous it was, and I did not know it !

"If you don't leave off, sir, I shall call the police at once," Versilov said, suddenly raising his voice unnaturally, and standing still before the lieutenant. I could never imagine such anger from a man so philosophic, and for such a trivial cause. And, note, our conversation was interrupted at the point of most interest to him, as he had just said himself.

"What, you haven't a five-kopeck piece ? " the lieutenant cried rudely, waving his hand in the air. "And indeed what canaille have five kopecks nowadays ! the low rabble! the scoundrels ! He goes dressed in beaver, and makes all this to-do about a copper ! "

"Constable," cried Versilov.

But there was no need to shout, a policeman was standing close by, at the corner, and he had heard the lieutenant's abuse himself.

"I ask you to bear witness to this insult, I ask you to come to the police-station," said Versilov.

"O-ho, I don't care, there's nothing at all you can prove ! You won't show yourself so wonderfully clever ! "

"Keep hold of him, constable, and take us to the police-station," Versilov decided emphatically.

"Surely we are not going to the police-station ? Bother the fellow ! " I whispered to him.

"Certainly we are, dear boy. The disorderly behaviour in our streets begins to bore one beyond endurance, and if everyone did his duty it would make it better for us all. *C'est comique. mais c'est ce que nous ferons.*"

For a hundred paces the lieutenant kept up a bold and swaggering demeanour, and talked with heat ; he declared "that it was not the thing to do," that it was "all a matter of five kopecks," and so on, and so on. But at last he began whispering something to the policeman. The policeman, a sagacious man, with apparently a distaste for exhibitions of

" nerves " in the street, seemed to be on his side, though only to a certain degree. He muttered in an undertone, in reply, that " it was too late for that now," that " it had gone too far," and that " if you were to apologize, for instance, and the gentleman would consent to accept your apology, then perhaps . . . ."

"Come li-isten, honoured sir, where are we going ? I ask you what are we hurrying to and what's the joke of it ? " the lieutenant cried aloud : " if a man who is down on his luck is willing to make an apology . . . in fact, if you want to put him down . . . damn it all ! we are not in a drawing-room, we are in the street ! For the street, that's apology enough. . . ."

Versilov stopped, and suddenly burst out laughing ; I actually imagined that he had got the whole thing up for amusement, but it was not so.

" I entirely accept your apology, Monsieur l'officier, and I assure you that you are a man of ability. Behave like that in the drawing-room ; it will soon pass muster perfectly there, too, and meanwhile here are twenty kopecks for you ; eat and drink your fill with it ; pardon me, constable, for troubling you ; I would have thanked you more substantially for your pains, but you are so highly respectable nowadays. . . . My dear boy," he added turning to me, " there's an eating house close here, it's really a horrible sewer, but one could get tea there, and I invite you to a cup . . . this way, quite close, come along."

I repeat, I had never seen him so excited, though his face was full of brightness and gaiety ; yet I noticed that when he was taking the coin out of his purse to give it to the officer, his hands trembled, and his fingers refused to obey him, so that at last he asked me to take out the money, and give it to the man for him ; I cannot forget it.

He took me to a little restaurant on the canal side, in the basement. The customers were few. A loud barrel-organ was playing out of tune, there was a smell of dirty dinner napkins ; we sat down in a corner.

" Perhaps you don't know. I am sometimes so bored . . . so horribly bored in my soul . . . that I like coming to all sorts of stinking holes like this. These surroundings, the halting tune from ' Lucia,' the waiters in their unseemly Russian get-up, the fumes of cheap tobacco, the shouts from the billiard-room, it's all so vulgar and prosaic that it almost borders on the fantastic. . . . Well, my dear boy, that son of Mars interrupted us, I believe, at the most interesting moment. . . . Here's the tea ;

I like the tea here. . . . Imagine Pyotr Ippolitovitch suddenly
began to-day assuring the other lodger, the one marked with
small-pox, that during the last century a special committee of
lawyers was appointed in the English parliament to examine
the trial of Christ before the High Priest and Pilate, with the
sole object of finding how the case would have gone nowadays
by modern law, and that the inquiry was conducted with all
solemnity, with counsel for the prosecution and all the rest of
it. . . . And that the jury were obliged to uphold the original
verdict. . . . A wonderful story ! That fool of a lodger began
to argue about it, lost his temper, quarrelled and declared he
should leave next day. . . . The landlady dissolved in tears at
the thought of losing his rent . . . *Mais passons*. In these
restaurants they sometimes have nightingales. Do you know
the old Moscow anecdote à la Pyotr Ippolitovitch ? A nightingale
was singing in a Moscow restaurant, a merchant came in ; ' I
must have my fancy, whatever it costs, said he, ' what's the
price of the nightingale ? ' ' A hundred roubles.' ' Roast it
and serve it.' So they roasted it and served it up. ' Cut me
off two-pennorth.' I once told it to Pyotr Ippolitovitch, but he
did not believe it, and was quite indignant."

He said a great deal more. I quote these fragments as a
sample of his talk. He repeatedly interrupted me every time
I opened my mouth to begin my story. He began each time
talking of some peculiar and utterly irrelevant nonsense ; he
talked gaily, excitedly ; laughed, goodness knows what at, and
even chuckled in an undignified way, as I had never seen him do
before. He swallowed a glass of tea at one gulp, and poured
out another. Now I can understand it, he was like a man who
had received a precious, interesting, and long-expected letter,
and who lays it down before him and purposely refrains from
opening it, turning it over and over in his hands, examining the
envelope and the seal, going to see to things in another room, in
short deferring the interesting moment of perusal, knowing that
it cannot escape him. And all this he does to make his enjoyment more complete.

I told him all there was to tell, of course, everything from
the very beginning, and it took me perhaps an hour telling it.
And indeed how could I have helped telling him ? I had been
dying to talk of it that afternoon. I began with our very first
meeting at the old prince's on the day she arrived from Moscow ;
then I described how it had all come about by degrees. I left

nothing out, and indeed I could not have left anything out ; he led me on, he guessed what was coming and prompted me. At moments it seemed to me that something fantastic was happening, that he must have been sitting or standing behind the door, for those two months ; he knew beforehand every gesture I made, every feeling I had felt. I derived infinite enjoyment from this confession to him, for I found in him such intimate softness, such deep psychological subtlety, such a marvellous faculty for guessing what I meant from half a word. He listened as tenderly as a woman. And above all he knew how to save me from feeling ashamed ; at times he stopped me at some detail ; often when he stopped me he repeated nervously : " Don't forget details ; the great thing is, not to forget any details : the more minute a point is, the more important it may sometimes be." And he interrupted me several times with words to that effect. Oh, of course I began at first in a tone of superiority, superiority to her, but I quickly dropped into sincerity. I told him honestly that I was ready to kiss the spot on the floor where her foot had rested. The most beautiful and glorious thing was that he absolutely understood that she might " be suffering from terror over the letter " and yet remain the pure and irreproachable being she had revealed herself to be. He absolutely realized what was meant by the word " student." But when I was near the end of my story I noticed that behind his good-natured smile there were signs in his face from time to time of some impatience, some abruptness and preoccupation ; when I came to the letter, I thought to myself :

" Shall I tell him the exact truth or not ? " and I did not tell it, in spite of my enthusiasm. I note this here that I may remember it all my life. I explained to him, as I had done to her, that it had been destroyed by Kraft. His eyes began to glow ; a strange line, a line of deep gloom was visible on his forehead.

" You are sure you remember, my dear boy, that that letter was burned by Kraft in the candle ? You are not mistaken ? "

" I am not mistaken," I repeated.

" The point is that that scrap of paper is of such importance to her, and if you had only had it in your hands to-day, you might . . ." But what " I might " he did not say. " But you haven't it in your hands now ? "

I shuddered all over inwardly, but not outwardly. Outwardly I did not betray myself, I did not turn a hair; but I was still unwilling to believe in the question :

"Haven't it in my hands ! In my hands now ? How could I since Kraft burned it that day ? "

"Yes ? " A glowing intent look was fastened upon me, a look I shall never forget; he smiled, however, but all his good-nature, all the feminine softness that had been in his expression suddenly vanished. It was replaced by something vague and troubled; he become more and more preoccupied. If he had controlled himself at that moment, as he had till then, he would not have asked me that question about the letter; he had asked it, no doubt, because he was carried away himself. I say this, however, only now; at the time, I did not so quickly perceive the change that had come over him; I still went on plunging, and there was still the same music in my heart. But my story was over; I looked at him.

"It's strange," he said suddenly, when I had told him everything to the minutest detail : "it's a very strange thing, my dear boy: you say that you were there from three o'clock till four and that Tatyana Pavlovna was not at home ? "

"From three o'clock till half-past four exactly."

"Well, only fancy, I went to see Tatyana Pavlovna exactly at half-past four to the minute, and she met me in the kitchen : I nearly always go to see her by the back entrance."

"What, she met you in the kitchen ? " I cried, staggering back in amazement.

"And she told me she could not ask me in; I only stayed two minutes, I only looked in to ask her to come to dinner."

"Perhaps she had only just come home from somewhere ? "

"I don't know, of course not, though she was wearing a loose dressing-gown. That was at half-past four exactly."

"But . . . Tatyana Pavlovna didn't tell you I was there ? "

"No, she did not tell me you were there . . . otherwise I should have known it, and should not have asked you about it."

"Listen, that's awfully important. . . ."

"Yes . . . from a certain point of view; and you've turned quite white, my dear; but, after all, what is there important in it ? "

"They've been laughing at me as though I were a baby ! "

"It's simply ' that she was afraid of your impulsiveness,' as she expressed it herself—and so she felt safer with Tatyana Pavlovna there."

"But, good God, what a trick! Think, she let me say all that before a third person, before Tatyana Pavlovna; so she heard everything I said! It . . . it's horrible to conceive of!"

"*C'est selon, mon cher*, Besides, you spoke just now of ' breadth ' of view in regard to women and exclaimed ' Hurrah for breadth '!"

"If I were Othello and you Iago, you could not have done better. . . . I am laughing though! There can be no sort of Othello, because there have been no relations of the kind. And why laugh indeed? It doesn't matter! I believe she's infinitely above me all the same, and I have not lost my ideal! . . . If it was a joke on her part I forgive her. A joke with a wretched raw youth doesn't matter! Besides, I did not pose as anything, and the student—the student was there in her soul, and remained there in spite of everything; it was in her heart, it exists there, and will always exist there! Enough! Listen, what do you think: shall I go to her at once to find out the whole truth or not?"

I said "I am laughing," but there were tears in my eyes.

"Well, my dear boy, go if you want to."

"I feel as though I were defiled in soul, from having told you all this. Don't be angry, dear, but, I repeat, one can't tell things about a woman to a third person; no confidant will understand. Even an angel wouldn't understand. If you respect a woman, don't confide in anyone! If you respect yourself don't confide in anyone. Now I don't respect myself. Good-bye for the present; I can't forgive myself."

"Nonsense, my dear boy, you exaggerate. You say yourself that ' there was nothing in it.' "

We came out on the canal bank and said good-bye.

"Will you never give me a real warm kiss, as a child kisses its father?" he said, with a strange quiver in his voice. I kissed him fervently.

"Dear boy . . . may you be always as pure in heart as you are now."

I had never kissed him before in my life, I never could have conceived that he would like me to.

CHAPTER VI

1

" I'LL go, of course ! " I made up my mind as I hurried home, " I'll go at once. Very likely I shall find her at home alone ; whether she is alone or with some one else makes no difference : I can ask her to come out to me. She will receive me ; she'll be surprised, but she will receive me. And if she won't see me I'll insist on her seeing me, I'll send in word that it's most urgent. She will think it's something about that letter and will see me. And I'll find out all about Tatyana there . . . and what then ? If I am not right I will be her servant, if I am right and she is to blame it's the end of everything ! In any case it's the end of everything ! What am I going to lose ? I can lose nothing. I'll go ! I'll go ! "

I shall never forget and I recall with pride that I did *not* go ! It will never be known to anyone, it will die with me, but it's enough that I know of it and at such a moment I was capable of an honourable impulse.

" This is a temptation, and I will put it behind me," I made up my mind at last, on second thoughts. They had tried to terrify me with a fact, but I refused to believe it, and had not lost my faith in her purity ! And what had I to go for, what was there to find out about ? Why was she bound to believe in me as I did in her, to have faith in my " purity," not to be afraid of my " impulsiveness " and not to provide against all risks with Tatyana ? I had not yet, as far as she could see, deserved her confidence. No matter, no matter that she does not know that I am worthy of it, that I am not seduced by " temptations," that I do not believe in malicious calumnies against her ; I know it and I shall respect myself for it. I shall respect my own feeling. Oh, yes, she had allowed me to utter everything before Tatyana, she had allowed Tatyana to be there, she knew that Tatyana was sitting there listening (for she was incapable of not listening) ; she knew that she was laughing at me out there,—that was awful, awful ! But . . . but what if it were impossible to avoid it ? What could she have done in her position, and how could one blame her for it ? Why, I had told her a lie about Kraft, I had deceived her because that, too,

s

could not be helped, and I had lied innocently against my will. "My God!" I cried suddenly, flushing painfully, "what have I just done myself! Haven't I exposed her, too, before Tatyana, haven't I repeated it all to Versilov just now? Though, after all, there was a difference. It was only a question of the letter; I had in reality only told Versilov about the letter because there was nothing else to tell, and could be nothing else. Was not I the first to declare that "there could not be"? He was a man of insight. Hm! But what hatred there was in his heart for this woman even to this day! And what sort of drama must have taken place between them in the past, and about what? All due to vanity, of course! "*Versilov cannot be capable of any feeling but boundless vanity!*"

That last thought rose spontaneously in my mind and I did not even remark it. Such were the thoughts that floated through my mind one after another, and I was straightforward with myself: I did not cheat or deceive myself; and if there was anything I did not understand at that moment, it was not from sophistry with myself but only from lack of brains.

I returned home in great excitement, and—I don't know why —in a very cheerful, though confused state of mind. But I was afraid of analysing my feelings and did my utmost to distract my mind. I went in at once to see my landlady: it turned out that a terrible quarrel really had taken place between her husband and her. She was in advanced consumption, and though, perhaps, she was a good-natured woman, like all consumptives she was of uncertain temper. I began trying to reconcile them at once; I went to the lodger, who was a very vain little bank clerk, called, Tchervyak, a coarse pock-marked fool. I disliked him very much, but I got on with him quite well, for I often was so mean as to join him in turning Pyotr Ippolitovitch into ridicule. I at once persuaded him to keep on the lodgings, and indeed he would not in any case have really gone so far as to move. It ended in my reassuring the landlady completely, and even succeeding in very deftly putting a pillow under her head: "Pyotr Ippolitovitch would never have known how to do it," she commented malignantly. Then I busied myself in the kitchen preparing mustard plasters for her and succeeded in making two capital ones with my own hand. Poor Pyotr Ippolitovitch looked on envious, but I did not allow him to touch them, and was rewarded by liberal tears of gratitude from the lady. I remember I suddenly felt sick of it all, and suddenly realized that

I was not looking after the invalid from kindness at all, but from something else, some very different motive.

I waited for Matvey with nervous impatience : I had resolved that evening to try my luck at cards for the last time and . . . and, apart from my need to win, I had an intense longing to play ; but for that, my excitement would have been unbearable. If I had not gone anywhere I might have been unable to hold out and should have gone to her. It was almost time for Matvey to come, when the door was opened and an unexpected visitor, Darya Onisimovna, walked in. I frowned and was surprised. She knew my lodging, for she had been there once with some message from my mother. I made her sit down and looked at her inquiringly. She said nothing, and only looked straight into my face with a deferential smile.

" You've not come from Liza ? " it occurred to me to ask.

" No, it's nothing special."

I informed her that I was just going out ; she replied again that it was "nothing special," and that she was going herself in a minute. I suddenly for some reason felt sorry for her. I may observe that she had met with a great deal of sympathy from all of us, from my mother, and still more from Tatyana Pavlovna, but after installing her at Mme. Stolbyeev's all of us had rather begun to forget her, except perhaps Liza, who often visited her. I think she was herself the cause of this neglect, for she had a special faculty for effacing herself and holding herself aloof from people in spite of her obsequiousness and her ingratiating smiles. I personally disliked those smiles of hers, and her affected expression, and I even imagined on one occasion that she had not grieved very long for her Olya. But this time for some reason I felt very sorry for her.

And behold, without uttering a word, she suddenly bent forward with her eyes cast down, and all at once, throwing her arms round my waist, hid her face on my knees. She seized my hand, I thought she meant to kiss it, but she pressed it to her eyes, and hot tears trickled upon it. She was shaking all over with sobs, but she wept silently. It sent a pang to my heart, even though I felt at the same time somehow annoyed. But she was embracing me with perfect confidence and without the least fear that I might be vexed, though only just before she had smiled so timidly and cringingly.

I began begging her to calm herself.

" Kind, good friend, I don't know what to do with myself.

As soon as it gets dark, I can't bear it ; as soon as it gets dark I can't go on bearing it, and I feel drawn into the street, into the darkness. And I am drawn there by my imaginings. My mind is possessed by the fancy that as soon as ever I go out I shall meet her in the street. I walk and seem to see her. That is other girls are walking along the street and I walk behind them on purpose, and I think : ' Isn't it she, there she is,' I think, ' it really is my Olya ! ' I dream and dream. I turn giddy at last, and feel sick, and stumble and jostle against people ; I stumble as though I were drunk and some swear at me ; I hide by myself and don't go to see anyone, and wherever one goes, it makes one's heart more sick ; I passed by your lodging just now, and thought : ' I'll go in to him ; he is kinder than any of them, and he was there at the time.' Forgive a poor creature who's no use to anyone ; I'll go away directly ; I'm going. . . . ."

She suddenly got up and made haste to depart. Matvey arrived just then ; I made her get into the sledge with me, and left her at Mme. Stolbyeev's on my way.

2

I had of late begun to frequent Zerstchikov's gambling saloon. I had so far visited three gambling houses, always in company with Prince Sergay, who had introduced me to these places. At one of these houses the game was faro especially, and the stakes were high. But I did not care for going there : I saw that one could not get on there without a long purse and, also, that the place was crowded with insolent fellows and swaggering young snobs. This was what Prince Sergay liked ; he liked playing, too, but he particularly liked getting to know these young prodigals. I noticed that though he went in with me he kept away from me during the evening and did not introduce me to any of " his set " I stared about me like a wild man of the woods, so much so that I sometimes attracted attention. At the gambling table people spoke to one another freely ; but once I tried bowing next day to a young fop, with whom I had not only talked but laughed the previous evening, sitting beside him, and had even guessed two cards from him. Yet when I greeted him in the same room next day, he actually did not recognize me. Or what was worse, stared at me with simulated amazement, and passed by with a smile. So I quickly gave up the place and preferred to visit a " sewer "—I don't know what else to call it—it was a wretched sordid little place for roulette. managed by a kept woman, who, however, never showed herself in the saloon. It was all horribly free and easy there, and though officers and wealthy merchants sometimes frequented it, there was a squalid filthiness about the place, though that was an attraction to many. Moreover, I was often lucky there. But I gave that place up, too, after a disgusting scene, which occurred when the game was at its hottest and ended in a fight between two players. I began going instead to Zerstchikov's, to which Prince Sergay took me also. The man was a retired captain, and the tone at his rooms was very tolerable, military, curt, and businesslike, and there was a fastidiously scrupulous keeping up of the forms of punctilio. No boisterous practical jokers or very fast men frequented it. Moreover, the stakes played for were often considerable. Both faro and roulette were played. I had only been there twice before that evening, the 15th of November, but I believe Zerstchikov already knew me by sight ; I had made no acquaintances there, however. As luck would have it Prince Sergay did not turn up till about midnight, when he dropped in with Darzan after spending the evening at the gambling saloon of the young snobs which I had given up ; and so that evening I found myself alone and unknown in a crowd of strangers.

If I had a reader and he had read all I have written so far of my adventures, there would be certainly no need to inform him that I am not created for any sort of society. The trouble is I don't know how to behave in company. If I go anywhere among a great many people I always have a feeling as though I were being electrified by so many eyes looking at me. It positively makes me shrivel up, physically shrivel up, even in such places as a theatre, to say nothing of private houses. I did not know how to behave with dignity in these gambling saloons and assemblies ; I either sat still, inwardly upbraiding myself for my excessive mildness and politeness, or I suddenly got up and did something rude. And meanwhile all sorts of worthless fellows far inferior to me knew how to behave with wonderful aplomb—and that's what exasperated me above everything, so that I lost my self-possession more and more. I may say frankly, even at that time, if the truth is to be told, the society there, and even winning money at cards, had become revolting and a torture to me. Positively a torture. I did, of course,

derive acute enjoyment from it, but this enjoyment was at the
cost of torture : the whole thing, the people, the gambling, and,
most of all, myself in the midst of them, seemed horribly nasty.
" As soon as I win I'll chuck it all up ! " I said to myself every
time when I woke up in my lodgings in the morning after
gambling over night.　Then, again, how account for my desire to
win, since I certainly was not fond of money ?　Not that I am going
to repeat the hackneyed phrases usual in such explanations, that I
played for the sake of the game, for the pleasure of it, for the risk,
the excitement and so on, and not for gain.　I was horribly in
need of money, and though this was not my chosen path, not
my idea, yet somehow or other I had made up my mind to try it
by way of experiment.　I was continually possessed by one
overwhelming thought : " You maintained that one could
reckon with certainty on becoming a millionaire if only one had
sufficient strength of will ; you've tested your strength of will
already ; so show yourself as strong in this case : can more
strength of will be needed for roulette than for your idea ? "
that is what I kept repeating to myself.　And as I still retain
the conviction, that in games of chance, if one has perfect control
of one's will, so that the subtlety of one's intelligence and one's
power of calculation are preserved, one cannot fail to overcome
the brutality of blind chance and to win, I naturally could not
help growing more and more irritated when at every moment
I failed to preserve my strength of will and was carried away
by excitement, like a regular child.　" Though I was able to
endure hunger, I am not able to control myself in an absurd
thing like this ! " that was what provoked me.　Moreover, the
consciousness that however absurd and abject I might seem, I
had within me a rich store of strength which would one day make
them all change their opinion of me, that consciousness has been
from the days of my oppressed childhood the one spring of
life for me, my light, my dignity, my weapon and my consolation,
without which I might have committed suicide as a little child.
And so how could I help being irritated when I saw what a
pitiful creature I became at the gambling table ?　That is why
I could not give up playing !　I see it all clearly now.　This
was the chief reason, but apart from that my petty vanity was
wounded.　Losing had lowered me in the eyes of Prince Sergay,
of Versilov, though he did not deign to speak of it, of every one,
even of Tatyana Pavlovna ; that is what I thought, I felt.　Finally,
I will make another confession !　By that time I had begun

to be corrupted : it had become hard for me to give up a dinner
of seven dishes at the restaurant, to give up Matvey, and the
English shop, to lose the good opinion of my hairdresser, and all
that, in fact. I was conscious of it even at the time, but I refused
to admit the thought ; now I blush to write it.

3

Finding myself alone in a crowd of strangers, I established
myself at first at a corner of the table and began staking small
sums. I remained sitting there without stirring for two hours.
For those two hours the play was horribly flat—neither one
thing nor another. I let slip some wonderful chances and tried
not to lose my temper, but to preserve my coolness and confidence.
At the end of the two hours I had neither lost nor won. Out of
my three hundred roubles I had lost ten or fifteen roubles.
This trivial result exasperated me, and what's more an exceedingly unpleasant, disgusting incident occurred. I know that such
gambling saloons are frequented by thieves, who are not simply
pickpockets out of the street but well-known gamblers. I am
certain that the well-known gambler Aferdov is a thief ; he is
still to be seen about the town ; I met him not long ago driving
a pair of his own ponies, but he is a thief and he stole from me.
But this incident I will describe later ; what happened this
evening was simply a prelude.

I spent there two hours sitting at a corner of the table, and
beside me, on the left, there was all the time an abominable little
dandy, a Jew I believe ; he is on some paper though, and even
writes something and gets it published. At the very last moment
I suddenly won twenty roubles. Two red notes lay before me,
and suddenly I saw this wretched little Jew put out his hand
and remove one of my notes. I tried to stop him ; but with a
most impudent air he immediately informed me, without raising
his voice in the least, that it was what he had won, that he had
just put down a stake and won it ; he declined to continue the
conversation and turned away. As ill-luck would have it, I was in
a state of extreme stupidity at that moment : I was brooding over
a great idea, and with a curse I got up quickly and walked away ;
I did not want to dispute, so made him a present of the red note.
And indeed it would have been difficult to go into the matter
with an impudent thief, for I had let slip the right moment.

and the game was going on again. And that was my great
mistake, the effect of which was apparent later on : three or four
players near us saw how the matter ended, and noticing how
easily I had given way, took me for another of the same sort.

It was just twelve o'clock ; I walked into the other room, and
after a little reflection formed a new plan. Going back I changed
my notes at the bank for half imperials. I received over forty
of them. I divided them into ten lots, and resolved to stake
four half imperials ten times running on the zero. " If I win
it's my luck. If I lose, so much the better, I'll never play again."
I may mention that zero had not turned up once during those
two hours, so that at last no one was staking on zero.

I put down my stakes standing, silent, frowning and
clenching my teeth. At the third round, Zerstchikov called
aloud zero, which had not turned up all day. A hundred and
forty half imperials were counted out to me in gold. I had
seven chances left and I went on, though everything seemed
whirling round, and dancing before my eyes.

" Come here ! " I shouted right across the table to a player
beside whom I had been sitting before, a grey-headed man with
a moustache, and a purple face, wearing evening dress, who had
been for some hours staking small sums with ineffable patience
and losing stake after stake : " come this end ! There's luck
here ! "

" Are you speaking to me ? " the moustached gentleman
shouted from the other end of the table, with a note of menacing
surprise in his voice.

" Yes, you ! You'll go on losing for ever there ! "

" That's not your business, please not to interfere ! "

But I could not restrain myself. An elderly officer was sitting
facing me at the other side of the table. Looking at my stake
he muttered to his neighbour :

" That's queer, zero. No, I won't venture on zero."

" Do, colonel ! " I shouted laying down another stake.

" Kindly leave me alone, and don't force your advice upon
me," he rapped out sharply. " You are making too much
noise."

" I am giving you good advice ; would you like to bet on zero's
turning up directly : ten gold pieces, I'll bet that, will you take
it ? "

And I laid down ten half imperials.

" A bet of ten gold pieces ! That I can do," he brought out

drily and severely. "I'll bet against you that zero won't turn up."

"Ten louis d'or, colonel."

"What do you mean by ten louis d'or ? "

"Ten half imperials, colonel, and, in grand language, ten louis d'or."

"Well, then, say they are half imperials, and please don't joke with me."

I did not of course hope to win the bet ; there were thirty-six chances against one that zero would not turn up again ; but I proposed it out of swagger, and because I wanted to attract every one's attention. I quite saw that for some reasonnobody here liked me, and that they all would have taken particular pleasure in letting me know it. The roulette wheel was sent spinning,—and what was the general amazement when it stopped at zero again ! There was actually a general shout. The glory of my success dazed me completely. Again a hundred and forty half imperials were counted out to me. Zerstchikov asked me if I would not like to take part of them in notes, but I mumbled something inarticulate in reply, for I was literally incapable of expressing myself in a calm and definite way. My head was going round and my legs felt weak. I suddenly felt that I would take a fearful risk at once ; moreover, I had a longing to do something more, to make another bet, to carry off some thousands from some one. Mechanically I scooped up my notes and gold in the hollow of my hand, and could not collect myself to count them. At that moment I noticed Prince Sergay and Darzan behind me : they had only just come from their faro saloon, where as I heard afterwards they had lost their last farthing.

"Ah ! Darzan," I cried   "There's luck here ! Stake on zero ! "

" I've been losing, I've no money," he answered drily ; Prince Sergay actually appeared not to notice or recognize me.

" Here's money," I cried pointing to my heap of gold   " As much as you like."

" Hang it all ! " cried Darzan, flushing crimson ; "I didn't ask you for money, I believe."

" You are being called," said Zerstchikov pulling my arm.

The colonel who had lost ten half imperials to me had called to me several times almost abusingly.

" Kindly take this ! " he shouted, purple with rage. " It's

not for me to stand over you, but if I don't you'll be saying afterwards you haven't had the money. Count it."

" I trust you, I trust you, colonel, without counting ; only please don't shout at me like that and don't be angry," and I drew his heap of gold towards me.

" Sir, I beg you to keep your transports for some one else and not to force them on me," the colonel rasped out. " I've never fed pigs with you ! "

" It's queer to admit such people "—" Who is he ? "— " Only a lad," I heard exclamations in undertones.

But I did not listen, I was staking at random, not on zero this time. I staked a whole heap of hundred rouble notes on the first eighteen numbers.

" Let's go, Darzan," I heard Prince Sergay's voice behind me.

" Home ? " I asked, turning round to them. " Wait for me : we'll go together, I've had enough."

My stake won, I had gained a big sum. " Enough ! " I cried, and without counting the money I began with trembling hands, gathering up the gold and dropping it into my pockets, and clumsily crumpling the notes in my fingers, and trying to stuff them all at once into my side pocket. Suddenly Aferdov, who was sitting next to me on the right and had been playing for high stakes, laid a fat hand with a ring on the first finger over three of my hundred-rouble notes.

" Excuse me that's not yours," he brought out sternly and incisively, though he spoke rather softly.

This was the prelude, which was destined a few days afterwards to have such a serious sequel. Now I swear on my honour those three notes were mine, but to my misfortune, at the time, though I was convinced they were mine I still had the fraction of a doubt, and for an honest man, that is enough ; and I am an honest man. What made all the difference was that I did not know at the time that Aferdov was a thief : I did not even know his name then, so that at that moment I might very well imagine I had made a mistake, and that those three notes were really not in the heap that had just been paid me. I had not counted my gains at all, I had simply gathered up the heaps with my hands, and there had been money lying in front of Aferdov too, and quite close to mine, but in neat heaps and counted. Above all Aferdov was known here and looked upon as a wealthy man ; he was treated with respect : all this had an influence on me and again I did not protest. A terrible mistake ! The whole beastly incident was the result of my enthusiasm.

" I am awfully sorry, I don't remember for certain ; but I really think they are mine," I brought out with lips trembling with indignation. These words at once aroused a murmur.

" To say things like that, you ought to *remember* for certain, but you've graciously announced yourself that you *don't* remember for certain," Aferdov observed with insufferable superciliousness.

" Who is he ? "—" It can't be allowed ! " I heard several exclamations.

" That's not the first time he has done it ; there was the same little game over a ten-rouble note with Rechberg just now," a mean little voice said somewhere near.

" That's enough ! that's enough ! " I exclaimed, " I am not protesting, take it . . . where's Prince . . . where are Prince Sokolsky and Darzan ? Have they gone ? Gentlemen, did you see which way Prince Sokolsky and Darzan went ? " And gathering up all my money at last, I could not succeed in getting some of the half imperials into my pocket, and holding them in my hands I rushed to overtake Prince Sergay and Darzan. The reader will see, I think, that I don't spare myself, and am recording at this moment what I was then, and all my nastiness, so as to explain the possibility of what followed.

Prince Sergay and Darzan were going downstairs, without taking the slightest notice of my shouts, and calls to them. I had overtaken them, but I stopped for a moment before the hall-porter, and, goodness knows why, thrust three half imperials into his hand ; he gazed at me in amazement and did not even thank me. But that was nothing to me, and if Matvey had been there I should probably have pressed handfuls of gold upon him ; and so indeed I believe I meant to do, but as I ran out on the steps, I suddenly remembered that I had let him go home when I arrived. At that moment Prince Sergay's horse came up, and he got into his sledge.

" I am coming with you, prince, and to your flat ! " I cried. clutching the fur cover and throwing it open, to get into the empty seat ; but all at once Darzan skipped past me into the sledge, and the coachman snatched the fur cover out of my hands, and tucked it round them.

" Damn it all ! " I cried dumbfounded ; it looked as though I had unbuttoned the cover for Darzan's benefit, like a flunkey.

"Home !" shouted Prince Sergay.

"Stop !" I roared, clutching at the sledge, but the horse started, and I was sent rolling in the snow. I even fancied they were laughing. Jumping up I took the first sledge I came across, and dashed after Prince Sergay, urging on the wretched nag at every second.

4

As ill-luck would have it, the wretched beast crawled along with unnatural slowness, though I promised the driver a whole rouble. The driver did nothing but lash the beast to earn his rouble. My heart was sinking : I began trying to talk to the driver, but I could not even articulate my words, and I muttered something incoherent. This was my condition when I ran up to Prince Sergay's ! He had only just come back ; he had left Darzan on the way, and was alone. Pale and ill-humoured, he was pacing up and down his study. I repeat again he had lost heavily that evening. He looked at me with a sort of preoccupied wonder.

"You again !" he brought out frowning.

"To settle up with you for good, sir !" I said breathlessly. "How dared you treat me like that !"

He looked at me inquiringly.

"If you meant to drive with Darzan you might have answered that you were going with him, but you started your horse, and I. . . . ."

"Oh yes, you tumbled into the snow," he said and laughed into my face.

"An insult like that can be only answered with a challenge, so to begin with we'll settle accounts. . . . ."

And with a trembling hand I began pulling out my money and laying it on the sofa, on the marble table, and even on an open book, in heaps, in handfuls, and in rolls of notes ; several coins rolled on the carpet.

"Oh, yes, you've won, it seems ? . . . One can tell that from your tone."

He had never spoken to me so insolently before. I was very pale.

"Here . . . I don't know how much . . . it must be counted. I owe you three thousand . . . or how much ? . . . More or less ?"

' I am not pressing you to pay, I believe."

"No, it's I want to pay, and you ought to know why. I know that in that roll there's a thousand roubles, here ! " And I began with trembling fingers to count the money, but gave it up. "It doesn't matter, I know it's a thousand. Well, that thousand I will keep for myself, but all the rest, all these heaps, take for what I owe you, for part of what I owe you : I think there's as much as two thousand or may be more ! "

"But you are keeping a thousand for yourself then ? " said Prince Sergay with a grin.

"Do you want it ? In that case . . . I was meaning . . . I was thinking you didn't wish it . . . but if you want it here it is. . . ."

"No, you need not," he said turning away from me contemptuously, and beginning to pace up and down again.

"And what the devil's put it into your head to want to pay it back ? " he said, turning to me suddenly, with a horrible challenge in his face.

"I'm paying it back to be free to insist on your giving me satisfaction ! " I vociferated.

"Go to the devil with your everlasting words and gesticulations ! " he stamped at me suddenly, as though in a frenzy. "I have been wanting to get rid of you both for ages ; you and your Versilov."

"You've gone out of your mind ! " I shouted and indeed it did look like it.

"You've worried me to death with your high-sounding phrases, and never anything but phrases, phrases, phrases ! Of honour for instance ! Tfoo ! I've been wanting to have done with you for a long time. . . . I am glad, glad, that the minute has come. I considered myself bound, and blushed that I was forced to receive you . . . both ! But now I don't consider myself bound in any way, in any way, let me tell you ! Your Versilov induced me to attack Madame Ahmakov and to cast aspersions on her. . . . Don't dare to talk of honour to me after that. For you are dishonourable people . . . both of you, both of you ; I wonder you weren't ashamed to take my money ! "

There was a darkness before my eyes.

"I borrowed from you as a comrade," I began, speaking with a dreadful quietness. "You offered it me yourself, and I believed in your affection. . . ."

" I am not your comrade ! That's not why I have given you money, you know why it is."

" I borrowed on account of what you owed Versilov ; of course it was stupid, but I . . ."

" You could not borrow on Versilov's account without his permission . . . and I could not have given you his money without his permission. I gave you my own money, and you knew it ; knew it and took it ; and I allowed this hateful farce to go on in my house ! "

" What did I know ? What farce ! Why did you give it to me ? "

" *Pour vos beaux yeux, mon cousin !* " he said, laughing straight in my face.

" Go to hell ! " I cried. ": Take it all, here's the other thousand too ! Now we are quits, and to-morrow. . . ."

And I flung at him the roll of hundred rouble notes I had meant to keep to live upon. The notes hit him in the waistcoat and flopped on the floor.

With three rapid strides he stepped close up to me :

" Do you dare to tell me," he said savagely articulating his words as it were syllable by syllable : " that all this time you've been taking my money you did not know your sister was with child by me ? "

" What ! what ! " I screamed, and suddenly my legs gave way under me and I sank helplessly on the sofa. He told me himself afterwards that I literally turned as white as a hand-kerchief. I was stunned. I remember we still stared into each other's faces in silence. A look of dismay passed over his face ; he suddenly bent down, took me by the shoulder and began supporting me. I distinctly remember his set smile, in which there was incredulity and wonder. Yes, he had never dreamed of his words having such an effect, for he was absolutely convinced of my knowledge.

It ended in my fainting, but only for a moment : I came to myself ; I got on my feet, gazed at him and reflected—and suddenly the whole truth dawned upon my mind which had been so slow to awaken ! If some one had told me of it before and asked me what I should have done at such a moment, I should no doubt have answered that I should have torn him in pieces. But what happened was quite different and quite independent of my will : I suddenly covered my face with both hands and began sobbing bitterly. It happened of itself. All at once the child came out again in the young man. It seemed that fully half of my soul was still a child's. I fell on the sofa and sobbed out, "Liza! Liza! Poor unhappy girl!" Prince Sergay was completely convinced all at once.

"Good God, how unjust I've been to you!" he cried in deep distress. "How abominably I've misjudged you in my suspiciousness. . . . Forgive me, Arkady Makarovitch!"

I suddenly jumped up, tried to say something to him, stood facing him, but said nothing, and ran out of the room and out of the flat. I dragged myself home on foot, and don't know how I got there. I threw myself on the bed in the dark, buried my face in the pillow and thought and thought. At such moments orderly and consecutive thought is never possible; my brain and imagination seemed torn to shreds, and I remember I began dreaming about something utterly irrelevant, I don't know what. My grief and trouble came back to my mind suddenly with an ache of anguish, and I wrung my hands again and exclaimed: "Liza, Liza!" and began crying again. I don't remember how I fell asleep, but I slept sweetly and soundly.

CHAPTER VII

1

I WAKED up at eight o'clock in the morning, instantly locked my door, sat down by the window and began thinking. So I sat till ten o'clock. The servant knocked at my door twice, but I sent her away. At last at eleven o'clock there was a knock again. I was just going to shout to the servant again, but it was Liza. The servant came in with her, brought me in some coffee, and prepared to light the stove. It was impossible to get rid of the servant, and all the time Fekla was arranging the wood, and blowing up the fire, I strode up and down my little room, not beginning to talk to Liza, and even trying not to look at her. The servant, as though on purpose, was inexpressibly slow in her movements as servants always are when they notice they are preventing people from talking. Liza sat on the chair by the window and watched me.

"Your coffee will be cold," she said suddenly.

I looked at her: not a trace of embarrassment, perfect tranquillity, and even a smile on her lips.

" Such are women," I thought, and could not help shrugging my shoulders. At last the servant had finished lighting the stove and was about to tidy the room, but I turned her out angrily, and at last locked the door.

" Tell me, please, why have you locked the door again ? " Liza asked.

I stood before her.

" Liza, I never could have imagined you would deceive me like this ! " I exclaimed suddenly, though I had never thought of beginning like that, and instead of being moved to tears, an angry feeling which was quite unexpected stabbed me to the heart. Liza flushed; she did not turn away, however, but still looked straight in my face.

" Wait, Liza, wait, oh how stupid I've been ! But was I stupid ? I had no hint of it till everything came together yesterday, and from what could I have guessed it before ? From your going to Mme. Stolbyeev's and to that . . . Darya Onisimovna ? But I looked upon you as the sun, Liza, and how could I dream of such a thing ? Do you remember how I met you that day two months ago, at his flat, and how we walked together in the sunshine and rejoiced. . . . Had it happened then ? Had it ? "

She answered by nodding her head.

" So you were deceiving me even then ! It was not my stupidity, Liza, it was my egoism, more than stupidity, the egoism of my heart and . . . maybe my conviction of your holiness. Oh ! I have always been convinced that you were all infinitely above me and—now this ! I had not time yesterday in one day to realize in spite of all the hints. . . . And besides I was taken up with something very different yesterday ! "

At that point I suddenly thought of Katerina Nikolaevna, and something stabbed me to the heart like a pin, and I flushed crimson. It was natural that I could not be kind at that moment.

" But what are you justifying yourself for ? You seem to be in a hurry to defend yourself, Arkady, what for ? " Liza asked softly and gently, though her voice was firm and confident.

" What for ? What am I to do now ? if it were nothing but that question ! And you ask what for ? I don't know how to act ! I don't know how brothers do act in such cases. . . . I know they go with pistols in their hands and force them to marry. . . . I will behave as a man of honour ought ! Only I don't know how a man of honour ought to behave. . . . Why ?

Because we are not gentlefolk, and he's a prince and has to think of his career; he won't listen to honest people like us. We are not even brother and sister, but nondescript illegitimate children of a house-serf without a surname; and princes don't marry house-serfs. Oh, it's nauseating! And what's more, you sit now and wonder at me."

"I believe that you are very much distressed," said Liza flushing again, "but you are in too great a hurry, and are distressing yourself."

"Too great a hurry? Why, do you think I've not been slow enough! Is it for you, Liza, to say that to me?" I cried, completely carried away by indignation at last. "And what shame I've endured, and how that prince must despise me! It's all clear to me now, and I can see it all like a picture: he quite imagined that I had guessed long ago what his relation was to you, but that I held my tongue or even turned up my nose while I bragged of 'my honour'—that's what he may well have thought of me! And that I have been taking his money for my sister, for my sister's shame! It was that he loathed so, and I think he was quite right, too; to have every day to welcome a scoundrel because he was her brother, and then to talk of honour . . . it would turn any heart to stone, even his! And you allowed it all, you did not warn me! He despised me so utterly that he talked of me to Stebelkov, and told me yesterday that he longed to get rid of us both, Versilov and me. And Stebelkov too! 'Anna Andreyevna is as much your sister as Lizaveta Makarovna,' and then he shouted after me, 'My money's better than his.' And I, I insolently lolled on *his* sofa, and forced myself on his acquaintances as though I were an equal, damn them! And you allowed all that! Most likely Darzan knows by now, judging, at least, by his tone yesterday evening. . . . Everyone, everyone knew it except me!"

"No one knows anything, he has not told any one of his acquaintances, and he *could not*," Liza added. "And about Stebelkov, all I know is that Stebelkov is worrying him, and that it could only have been a guess on Stebelkov's part anyway. . . . I have talked to him about you several times, and he fully believed me that you know nothing, and I can't understand how this happened yesterday."

"Oh, I paid him all I owed him yesterday, anyway, and that's a load off my heart! Liza, does mother know? Of course she does; why, yesterday she stood up for you against me. . . .

T

Oh, Liza ! Is it possible that in your heart of hearts you think yourself absolutely right, that you really don't blame yourself in the least ? I don't know how these things are considered nowadays, and what are your ideas, I mean as regards me, your mother, your brother, your father. . . . Does Versilov know ? "

" Mother has told him nothing ; he does not ask questions, most likely he does not want to ask."

" He knows, but does not want to know, that's it, it's like him ! Well, you may laugh at a brother, a stupid brother, when he talks of pistols, but your mother ! Surely you must have thought, Liza, that it's a reproach to mother ? I have been tortured by that idea all night ; mother's first thought now will be : ' it's because I did wrong, and the daughter takes after the mother ! ' "

" Oh, what a cruel and spiteful thing to say ! " cried Liza, while the tears gushed from her eyes ; she got up and walked rapidly towards the door.

" Stay, stay ! " I caught her in my arms, made her sit down again, and sat down beside her, still keeping my arm round her.

" I thought it would be like this when I came here, and that you would insist on my blaming myself. Very well, I do blame myself. It was only through pride I was silent just now, and did not say so, I am much sorrier for you and mother than I am for myself. . . ."

She could not go on, and suddenly began crying bitterly.

" Don't, Liza, you mustn't, I don't want anything. I can't judge you. Liza, what does mother say ? Tell me, has she known long ? "

" I believe she has ; but I only told her a little while ago, when *this* happened," she said softly, dropping her eyes.

" What did she say ? "

" She said, ' bear it,' " Liza said still more softly.

" Ah, Liza, yes, ' bear it ! ' Don't do anything to yourself, God keep you ! "

" I am not going to," she answered firmly, and she raised her eyes and looked at me. " Don't be afraid," she added, " it's not at all like that."

" Liza, darling, all I can see is that I know nothing about it, but I've only found out now how much I love you. There's only one thing I can't understand, Liza ; it's all clear to me, but there's one thing I can't understand at all : what made you love him ? How could you love a man like that ? That's the question."

" And I suppose you've been worrying yourself all night about that too ? " said Liza, with a gentle smile.

" Stay, Liza, that's a stupid question, and you are laughing ; laugh away, but one can't help being surprised, you know ; you and *he*, you are such opposite extremes ! I have studied him : he's gloomy, suspicious ; perhaps he is very good-hearted, he may be, but on the other hand, he is above all extremely inclined to see evil in everything (though in that he is exactly like me). He has a passionate appreciation of what's noble, that I admit, but I fancy it's only in his ideal. Oh, he is apt to feel remorse, he has been all his life continually cursing himself, and repenting, but he will never reform ; that's like me, too, perhaps. Thousands of prejudices and false ideas and no real ideas at all. He is always striving after something heroic and spoiling it all over trifles. Forgive me, Liza, I'm a fool though ; I say this and wound you and I know it ; I understand it. . . ."

" It would be a true portrait," smiled Liza, " but you are too bitter against him on my account, and that's why nothing you say is true. From the very beginning he was distrustful with you, and you could not see him as he is, but with me, even at Luga. . . . He has had no eyes for anyone but me, ever since those days at Luga. Yes, he is suspicious and morbid, and but for me he would have gone out of his mind ; and if he gives me up, he will go out of his mind, or shoot himself. I believe he has realized that and knows it," Liza added dreamily as though to herself. " Yes, he is weak continually, but such weak people are capable at times of acting very strongly. . . . How strangely you talked about a pistol, Arkady ; nothing of that sort is wanted and I know what will happen. It's not my going after him, it's his coming after me. Mother cries and says that if I marry him I shall be unhappy, that he will cease to love me. I don't believe that ; unhappy, perhaps, I shall be, but he won't cease to love me. That's not why I have refused my consent all along, it's for another reason. For the last two months I've refused, but to-day I told him ' yes, I will marry you.' Arkasha, do you know yesterday " (her eyes shone and she threw her arms round my neck), " he went to Anna Andreyevna's and told her with absolute frankness that he could not love her . . . ? Yes, he had a complete explanation with her, and that idea's at an end ! He had nothing to do with the project. It was all Prince Nikolay Ivanovitch's notion, and it was pressed upon him by those tormentors, Stebelkov and some one else. . . . And to-day for that I've said ' *yes*.' Dear Arkady, he is very anxious to see you, and don't be offended because of what happened yesterday : he's not quite well this morning, and will be at home all day. He's really unwell, Arkady ; don't think it's an excuse. He has sent me on purpose, and told me to say that he ' needs ' you, that he has a great deal he must tell you, and that it would be awkward to say it here, in your lodging. Well, good-bye ! Oh, Arkady, I am ashamed to say it, as I was coming here I was awfully afraid that you would not love me any more. I kept crossing myself on the way, and you've been so good and kind ! I shall never forget it ! I am going to mother. And you try and like him a little, won't you ? "

I embraced her warmly, and told her :

" I believe, Liza, you're a strong character. And I believe that it's not you who are going after him, but he who is going after you, only . . ."

" Only, what made you love him ? ' that's the question ! ' " Liza put in with her old mischievous laugh, pronouncing the words exactly as I had done " that's the question ! " And as she said it she lifted her forefinger exactly as I do. We kissed at parting, but when she had gone my heart began to ache again.

2

I note merely for myself there were moments after Liza had gone when a perfect host of the most unexpected ideas rushed into my mind, and I was actually quite pleased with them.

" Well, why should I bother," I thought ; " what is it to me ? It's the same with every one or nearly so. What of it if it has happened to Liza ? Am I bound to save the honour of the family ? "

I mention all these details to show how far I was from a sound understanding of the difference between good and evil. It was only feeling saved me : I knew that Liza was unhappy, that mother was unhappy, and I knew this by my feeling when I thought of them, and so I felt that what had happened must be wrong.

Now I may mention beforehand that from that day, right up to the catastrophe of my illness, events followed one another with such rapidity that recalling them now I feel surprised myself that I was able to stand up against them, crushing as they were. They clouded my mind, and even my feelings, and if in the end I had been overwhelmed by them, and had committed a crime (I was within an ace of it), the jury might well have acquitted me. But I will try to describe it all in the exact order of events, though I forewarn the reader that there was little order in my thoughts at that time. Events came rushing on me like the wind, and my thoughts whirled before them like the dead leaves in autumn. Since I was entirely made up of other people's ideas, where could I find principles of my own when they were needed to form independent decisions? I had no guide at all.

I decided to go to see Prince Sergay that evening, that we might be perfectly free to talk things over, and he would be at home till evening. But when it was getting dark I received again a note by post, a note from Stebelkov; it consisted of three lines, containing an urgent and most persuasive request that I would call on him next morning at eleven o'clock on "most important business, and you will see for yourself that it is business." Thinking it over I resolved to be guided by circumstances, as there was plenty of time to decide before to-morrow.

It was already eight o'clock; I should have gone out much earlier, but I kept expecting Versilov; I was longing to express myself to him, and my heart was burning. But Versilov was not coming and did not come. It was out of the question for me to go to see my mother and Liza for a time, and besides I had a feeling that Versilov certainly would not be there all day. I went on foot, and it occurred to me on the way to look in at the restaurant on the canal side where we had been the day before. Sure enough, Versilov was sitting there in the same place.

"I thought you would come here," he said, smiling strangely and looking strangely at me. His smile was an unpleasant one, such as I had not seen on his face for a long time.

I sat down at the little table and told him in full detail about the prince and Liza, and my scene with Prince Sergay the evening before; I did not forget to mention how I had won at roulette. He listened very attentively, and questioned me as to Prince Sergay's intention to marry Liza.

"*Pauvre enfant*, she won't gain much by that perhaps. But very likely it won't come off . . . though he is capable of it. . . ."

" Tell me, as a friend : you knew it, I suppose, had an inkling of it ? "

" My dear boy, what could I do in the matter ? It's all a question of another person's conscience and of feeling, even though only on the part of that poor girl. I tell you again ; I meddled enough at one time with other people's consciences, a most unsuitable practice ! I don't refuse to help in misfortune so far as I'm able, and if I understand the position myself. And you, my dear boy, did you really suspect nothing all this time ? "

" But how could you," I cried, flaring up, " how could you, if you'd a spark of suspicion that I knew of Liza's position, and saw that I was taking money at the same time from Prince Sergay, how could you speak to me, sit with me, hold out your hand to me, when you must have looked on me as a scoundrel, for I bet anything you suspected I knew all about it and borrowed money from Prince Sergay knowingly ! "

" Again, it's a question of conscience," he said with a smile. " And how do you know," he added distinctly, with unaccountable emotion, " how do you know I wasn't afraid, as you were yesterday, that I might lose my ' ideal ' and find a worthless scamp instead of my impulsive, straightforward boy ? I dreaded the minute and put it off. Why not instead of indolence or duplicity imagine something more innocent in me, stupid, perhaps, but more honourable, *que diable !* I am only too often stupid, without being honourable. What good would you have been to me if you had had such propensities ? To persuade and try to reform in that case would be degrading ; you would have lost every sort of value in my eyes even if you were reformed. . . ."

" And Liza ? Are you sorry for her ? "

" I am very sorry for her, my dear. What makes you think I am so unfeeling. . . . On the contrary, I will try my very utmost. . . . And you. What of *your* affair ? "

" Never mind my affair ; I have no affairs of my own now. Tell me, why do you doubt that he'll marry her ? He was at Anna Andreyevena's yesterday and positively refused . . . that is disowned the foolish idea . . . that originated with Prince Nikolay Ivanitch . . . of making a match between them. He disowned it absolutely."

"Yes ? When was that ? And from whom did you hear it ? " he inquired with interest. I told him all I knew.

"H'm . . . ! " he pronounced as it were dreamily and ponder-

ing, "then it must have happened just about an hour . . .
before another explanation. H'm . . . ! oh, well, of course,
such an interview may have taken place between them . . .
although I know that nothing was said or done either on his
side or on hers . . . though, of course, a couple of words would
be enough for such an explanation. But I tell you what, it's
strange," he laughed suddenly ; " I shall certainly interest you
directly with an extraordinary piece of news ; if your prince did
make his offer yesterday to Anna Andreyevna (and, suspecting
about Liza, I should have done my utmost to oppose his suit,
entre nous soit dit), Anna Andreyevna would in any case have
refused him. I believe you are very fond of Anna Andreyevna,
you respect and esteem her. That's very nice on your part, and
so you will probably rejoice on her account ; she is engaged to
be married, my dear boy, and judging from her character I
believe she really will get married, while I—well, I give her my
blessing, of course."

"Going to be married ? To whom ? " I cried, greatly astonished.

"Ah, guess ! I won't torment you ; to Prince Nikolay
Ivanovitch, to your dear old man."

I gazed at him with open eyes.

"She must have been cherishing the idea for a long time ;
and no doubt worked it out artistically in all its aspects,"
he went on languidly, dropping out his words one by one.
"I imagine this was arranged just an hour after Prince
Sergay's visit. You see how inappropriate was his dashing in !
She simply went to Prince Nikolay Ivanovitch and made him
a proposal."

"What, 'made him a proposal' ? You mean he made her
a proposal ? "

"Oh, how could he ! She did, she herself, though to be sure
he is perfectly ecstatic. They say he is simply sitting now
wondering how it was the idea never occurred to him. I have
heard he has even taken to his bed . . . from sheer ecstasy, no
doubt."

"Listen, you are talking so ironically . . . I can hardly believe
it. And how could she propose to him ? What did she say ? "

"I assure you, my dear boy, that I am genuinely delighted,"
he answered, suddenly assuming a wonderfully serious air ; " he
is old, of course, but by every law and custom he can get married ;
as for her—again it's a matter of another person's conscience,

as I've told you already, my dear boy. However, she is quite competent to have her own views and make her own decision. But the precise details and the words in which she expressed herself I am not in a position to give you, my dear boy. But no doubt she was equal to doing it, in a way which neither you nor I would have imagined. The best of it all is that there's nothing scandalous in it, it's all *très comme il faut* in the eyes of the world. Of course, it's quite evident that she was eager for a good position in the world, but you know she deserves it. All this, my dear boy, is an entirely worldly matter. And no doubt she made her proposal in a magnificent and artistic style. It's an austere type, my dear boy, ' the girl-nun,' as you once described her ; ' the cool young lady' has been my name for her a long time past. She has almost been brought up by him, you know, and has seen more than one instance of his kindly feeling towards her. She assured me some time ago that she had ' such a respect for him and such a high opinion of him, such feeling for him and such sympathy with him,' and all the rest of it, so that I was to some extent prepared. I was informed of all this this morning in her name and at her request by my son, her brother Andrey Andreyevitch, whom I believe you don't know, and whom I see regularly twice a year. He respectfully approves of the step she has taken."

" Then it is public already ? Good heavens, I am amazed ! "

" No, it's certainly not public yet, not for some time. . . . I don't know . . . I am altogether out of it, in fact. But it's all true."

" But now Katerina Nikolaevna. . . . What do you think ? it won't suit Büring's tastes, will it ? "

" I don't know . . . actually that he will dislike it ; but you may be sure that on that side Anna Andreyevna is a highly respectable person. But what a girl she is ! Yesterday morning, immediately before this, she inquired of me ' whether I were in love with the widow Ahmakov ? ' Do you remember I told you of it yesterday with surprise ; it would have been impossible for her to marry the father if I had married the daughter ! Do you understand now ? "

" Oh, to be sure," I cried, " but could Anna Andreyevna really have imagined . . . that you could possibly want to marry Katerina Nikolaevna ? "

" Evidently she could, my dear boy, but, however . . . but, however, I believe it's time for you to go where you were going.

My head aches all the time, you know. I'll tell them to play Lucia. I love the solemnity of its dreariness, but I've told you that already . . . I repeat myself unpardonably. . . . Perhaps I'll go away from here though. I love you, my dear boy, but good-bye ; whenever I have a headache or toothache I thirst for solitude."

A line of suffering came into his face ; I believe now he really was suffering with his head, his head particularly. . . .

" Till to-morrow," I said.

" Why ' till to-morrow,' and what is to happen to-morrow ? " he said with a wry smile.

" I shall go to see you, or you come to see me."

" No, I shan't come to you, but you'll come running to me. . . ."

There was something quite malevolent in his face, but I had no thoughts to spare for him ; what an event !

3

Prince Sergay was really unwell, and was sitting alone with his head wrapped in a wet towel. He was very anxious to see me ; but he had not only a headache, he seemed to be aching morally all over. To anticipate events again ; all that latter time, right up to the catastrophe, it was somehow my fate to meet with people who were one after another so excited that they were all almost mad, so that I couldn't help being infected with the same malady myself. I came, I must confess, with evil feelings in my heart, and I was horribly ashamed, too, of having cried before him the previous night. And anyway Liza and he had so clearly succeeded in deceiving me that I could not help seeing myself as a fool. In short, my heart was vibrating on false notes as I went in. But all this affectation and false feeling vanished quickly. I must do him the justice to say that his suspiciousness had quickly disappeared, that he surrendered himself completely ; he betrayed almost childish affection, confidence and love. He kissed me with tears and at once began talking of the position. . . . Yes, he really did need me : his words and the sequence of his ideas betrayed great mental disorder.

He announced with great firmness his intention to marry Liza and as soon as possible. " The fact that she is not of noble birth does not trouble me in the least, believe me," he said to me ; " my grandfather married a serf-girl who sang in a neighbouring landowner's private theatre. My family, of course, have rested certain expectations upon me, but now they'll have to give way, and it will not lead to strife. I want to break with my present life for good, for good ! To have everything different, everything new ! I don't understand what made your sister love me ; but if it had not been for her I should not have been alive to this day. I swear from the depth of my soul that my meeting her at Luga was the finger of Providence. I believe she loved me because 'I had fallen so low'. . . can you understand that though, Arkady Makarovitch ? "

" Perfectly ! " I declared in a voice of full conviction. I sat at the table, and he walked about the room.

" I must tell you the whole story of our meeting, without reserve. It began with a secret I had guarded in my heart, of which she alone heard, because only to her could I bring myself to trust it. And to this day no one else knows it. I went to Luga then with despair in my heart, and stayed at Mme. Stolbyeev's, I don't know why, seeking solitude perhaps. I had only just resigned my commission in the regiment, which I had entered on my return from abroad, after my meeting with Andrey Petrovitch out there. I had some money at the time, and in the regiment I led a dissipated life, and spent freely ; well, the officers, my comrades, did not like me, though I tried not to offend anyone. And I will confess it to you, no one has ever liked me. There was a certain Cornet Stepanov, I must admit an extremely empty-headed worthless fellow not distinguished in any way. There was no doubt he was honest though. He was in the habit of coming to see me, and I did not stand on ceremony with him ; he used to sit in a corner, mute but dignified, for days together, and he did not get in my way at all. One day I told him a story that was going the round, with many foolish additions of my own, such as that the colonel's daughter was in love with me, and that the colonel had his eye upon me for her and so would do anything to please me. . . . In short, I will pass over the details, but it led to a very complicated and revolting scandal. It was not Stepanov who spread it but my orderly, who had overheard and remembered it all, for I had told an absurd story compromising the young lady. So, when there was an inquiry into the scandal, and this orderly was questioned by the officers, he threw the blame on Stepanov, that is, he said that it was to Stepanov I'd told the story. Stepanov was put in such a position that he could not deny having heard it ; it was a question of honour. And as two-thirds of the story had been lying on my part, the officers were indignant, and the commanding officer who had called us together was forced to clear the matter up. At this point the question was put to Stepanov in the presence of all : had he heard the story or not ? And at once he told the whole truth. Well, what did I do then, I, a prince whose line goes back a thousand years ? I denied it, and told Stepanov to his face that he was lying, in the most polite way, suggesting that he had ' misunderstood my words ' and so on. . . . I'll leave out the details again, but as Stepanov came to me so often I was able with some appearance of likelihood to put the matter in such a light that he might seem to be plotting with my orderly for motives of his own ; and this told in my favour. Stepanov merely looked at me in silence and shrugged his shoulders. I remember the way he looked at me and shall never forget it. Then he promptly resigned his commission ; but how do you suppose it ended ? Every officer without exception called on him and begged him not to resign. A fortnight later I, too, left the regiment ; no one turned me out, no one suggested my resigning, I alleged family reasons for my leaving the army. That was how the matter ended. At first I didn't mind, and even felt angry with them ; I stayed at Luga, made the acquaintance of Lizaveta Makarovna, but a month afterwards I began to look at my revolver and to think about death. I looked at everything gloomily, Arkady Makarovitch. I composed a letter to the commanding officer and my former comrades, with a full confession of my lie, and a vindication of Stepanov's honour. When I had written the letter I asked myself the question, should I send it and live, or should I send it and die ? I should never have decided that question. Chance, blind chance brought me near to Lizaveta Makarovna after a strange and rapid conversation with her. She had been at Mme. Stolbyeev's before that, we had met and parted with bows and had rarely spoken. I suddenly told her everything. It was then she held out a hand to me."

" How did she settle the question ? "

" I didn't send the letter. She decided that I should not send it. She argued that if I did send the letter I should, of course, have been doing an honourable action, sufficient to wash away all the filth of the past, and far more, but she doubted my having the strength to endure it. It was her idea that no one would have the strength to bear it, for then the future would be utterly ruined, and no new life would be possible. It is true Stepanov had suffered for it ; but he had been acquitted by public opinion, as it was. It was a paradox, of course ; but she restrained me, and I gave myself into her hands completely."

" Her reasoning was jesuitical but feminine," I cried ; " she had begun to love you already ! "

" It was my regeneration into a new life. I vowed to change, to begin a new life, to be worthy of myself and of her and —this is how it has ended ! It has ended in my going with you to roulette, in my playing faro ; I could not resist the fortune, I was delighted at being in the swim, delighted with all these people, with racehorses. . . . I tortured Liza, to my shame ! "

He rubbed his forehead with his hand and walked up and down the room.

" We are both, you and I, stricken by the same Russian curse, Arkady Makarovitch ; you don't know what to do, and I don't know what to do. If a Russian deviates ever so little from the rut of routine laid down for him by tradition, at once he is at a loss what to do. While he's in the rut everything's clear— income, rank, position in society, a carriage, visits, a wife—but ever so little off it—and what am I ? A leaf fluttering before the wind, I don't know what to do ! For the last two months I have striven to keep in the rut, I have liked the rut, I've been drawn to the rut. You don't know the depth of my downfall here ; I love Liza, but at the same time I've been thinking of Mme. Ahmakov ! "

" Is it possible ? " I cried in distress. " By the way, what did you say yesterday about Versilov's having instigated you to behave in a mean way to Katerina Nikolaevna ? "

" I may have exaggerated it, and perhaps I have been unfair to him in my suspiciousness as I have been to you. Let us drop the subject. Why, do you suppose that I have not been brooding over a lofty ideal of life all this time, ever since Luga, perhaps ? I swear that ideal has never left me, it has been with me continually, and has lost none of its beauty in my heart. I remembered the vow I made to Lizaveta Makarovna to reform. When Andrey Petrovitch talked about the aristocracy to me yesterday, he said nothing new, I can assure you. My ideal is firmly established : a few score acres (and only a few score, for I've scarcely anything left of the fortune), then absolutely complete abandonment of the world and a career ; a rural home, a family, and myself a tiller of the soil or something of the sort. Oh, in our family it's nothing new ; my uncle, my grandfather, too, tilled the soil with their own hands. We have been princes for a thousand years, as aristocratic and as ancient a name as the Rohans, but we are beggars. And this is how I will train my children : ' Remember always, all your life, that you are a nobleman, that the sacred blood of Russian princes flows in your veins, but never be ashamed that your father tilled the soil with his own hands—he did it like a prince.' I should not leave them property, nothing but that strip of land, but I would bring them up in the loftiest principles : that I should consider a duty. Oh, I should be helped by Liza, by work, by children ; oh, how we have dreamed of this together, dreamed of it here in this room. And would you believe it ? at the same time I was thinking of Mme. Ahmakov, and of the possibility of a worldly and wealthy marriage, though I don't care for the woman in the least ! And only after what Nastchokin said about Büring, I resolved to turn to Anna Andreyevna."

" But you went to decline the match ? That was an honourable action anyway, I suppose ! "

" You think so ? " he stopped short before me. " No, you don't know my nature, or else there is something I don't know myself, because it seems I have more than one nature. I love you sincerely, Arkady Makarovitch, and besides I am terribly to blame for the way I've treated you for the last two months, and so I want you as Liza's brother to know all this. I went to Anna Andreyevna to make her an offer of marriage, not to disown the idea."

" Is it possible ? But Liza told me . . ."

" I deceived Liza."

" Tell me, please, you made a formal offer and Anna Andreyevna refused it ? Was that it ? Was that it ? The facts are of great importance to me, prince."

" No, I did not make an offer at all, but that was only because I hadn't time ; she forestalled me, not in direct words, of course, though the meaning was clear and unmistakable—she ' delicately ' gave me to understand that the idea was henceforth out of the question."

" So it was the same as your not making her an offer, and your pride has not suffered ! "

" How can you reason like that ! My own conscience condemns me, and what of Liza, whom I have deceived . . . and meant to abandon ? And the vow I made to myself and my forefathers to reform and to atone for all my ignoble past ! I entreat you not to tell her that. Perhaps that is the one thing she would not be able to forgive me ! I have been ill since what happened yesterday. And now it seems that all is over, and the last of the Sokolskys will be sent to prison. Poor Liza ! I have been very anxious to see you all day, Arkady Makarovitch, to tell you as Liza's brother what she knows nothing of as yet. I am a criminal. I have taken part in forging railway shares ! "

" Something more ! What, you are going to prison ? " I cried jumping up and looking at him in horror. His face wore a look of the deepest gloom and utterly hopeless sorrow.

" Sit down," he said, and he sat down in the armchair opposite. " To begin with, you had better know the facts ; it was more than a year ago, that same summer that I was at Ems with Lidya, and Katerina Nikolaevna, and afterwards at Paris, just at the time when I was going to Paris for two months. In Paris, of course, I was short of money, and it was just then Stebelkov turned up, though I knew him before. He gave me some money and promised to give me more, but asked me in return to help him ; he wanted an artist, a draughtsman, engraver, lithographer, and so on, a chemist, an expert, and—for certain purposes. What those purposes were he hinted pretty plainly from the first. And would you believe it ? he understood my character—it only made me laugh. The point is that from my schooldays I had an acquaintance, at present a Russian exile, though he was not really a Russian, but a native of Hamburg. He had been mixed up in some cases of forging papers in Russia already. It was on this man that Stebelkov was reckoning, but he wanted an introduction to him and he applied to me. I wrote a couple of lines for him, and immediately forgot all about it. Afterwards he met me again and again, and I received altogether as much as three thousand from him. I had literally forgotten all about the business. Here I've been borrowing from him all the time with I O Us and securities, and he has been cringing before me like a slave, and suddenly yesterday I learned from him for the first time that I am a criminal."

" When, yesterday ? "

" Yesterday morning, when we were shouting in my study just before Nastchokin arrived. For the first time he had the effrontery to speak to me quite openly of Anna Andreyevna. I raised my hand to strike him, but he suddenly stood up and informed me that his interests were mine. and that I must remember that I was his accomplice and as much a swindler as he—though he did not use those words, that was the sense."

" What nonsense, why surely it's all imagination ? "

" No, it's not imagination. He has been here to-day and explained things more exactly. These forged documents have been in circulation a long time, and are still being passed about, but it seems they've already begun to be noticed. Of course, I've nothing to do with it, but ' you see though, you were pleased to give me that little letter,' that's what Stebelkov told me."

" So you didn't know, of course, what for, or did you know ? "

" I did know," Prince Sergay answered in a low voice, dropping his eyes ; " that's to say I knew and didn't know, you see. I was laughing, I was amused. I did it without thinking, for I had no need of forged documents at that time, and it wasn't I who meant to make them. But that three thousand he gave me then he did not put down in his account against me and I let it pass. But how do you know, perhaps I really am a forger. I could not help knowing, I am not a child ; I did know, but I felt in a merry humour and I helped scoundrels, felons . . . helped them for money ! So I, too, am a forger ! "

" Oh, you are exaggerating ; you've done wrong, but you're exaggerating ! "

" There's some one else in it, a young man called Zhibyelsky, some sort of attorney's clerk. He, too, had something to do with these forgeries, he came afterwards from that gentleman at Hamburg to see me about some nonsense ; of course, I didn't know what it was about myself—it was not about those forgeries I know that . . . but he has kept in his possession two documents in my handwriting, only brief notes—and, of course, they are evidence too ; I understood that to-day. Stebelkov makes out that this Zhibyelsky is spoiling everything ; he has stolen something, public money I believe, but means to steal something more and then to emigrate ; so he wants eight thousand, not a penny less, to help him on his way. My share of the fortune I had inherited would satisfy Stebelkov, but he said Zhibyelsky must be satisfied too. . . . In short I must give up my share of the fortune and ten thousand besides, that's their final offer. And then they will give me back my two letters. They're in collusion, that's clear."

" It's obviously absurd ! If they inform against you they

will betray themselves ! Nothing will induce them to give information."

"I understand that. They don't threaten to give information at all, they only say, ' We shall not inform, of course, but if it should be discovered, then . . .' that's what they say, and that's all, but I think it's enough ! But that's not the point; whatever happens, and even if I had those letters in my pocket now, yet to be associated with those swindlers, to be their accomplice for ever and ever ! To lie to Russia, to lie to my children, to lie to Liza, to lie to my conscience ! . . ."

"Does Liza know ? "

"No, she does not know everything. It would be too much for her in her condition. I wear the uniform of my regiment, and every time I meet a soldier of the regiment, at every second, I am inwardly conscious that I must not dare to wear the uniform."

"Listen," I cried suddenly ; " there's no need to waste time talking about it ; there's only one way of salvation for you ; go to Prince Nikolay Ivanitch, borrow ten thousand from him, ask him for it, without telling him what for, thén send for those two swindlers, settle up with them finally, buy back your letters . . . and the thing is over ! The whole thing will be ended, and you can go and till the land ! Away with vain imaginings and have faith in life ! "

"I have thought of that," he said resolutely. " I have been making up my mind all day and at last I have decided. I have only been waiting for you ; I will go. Do you know I have never in my life borrowed a farthing from Prince Nikolay Ivanitch. He is well disposed to our family and even . . . and has come to their assistance, but I, I personally, have never borrowed money from him. But now I am determined to. Our family, you may note, is an older branch of the Sokolskys than Prince Nikolay Ivanitch's ; they are a younger branch, collaterals, in fact, hardly recognized. . . . There was a feud between our ancestors. At the beginning of the reforms of Peter the Great, my great-grandfather, whose name was Peter too, remained an Old Believer, and was a wanderer in the forest of Kostroma. That Prince Peter married a second wife who was not of noble birth. . . . So it was then these other Sokolskys dropped out, but I. . . . What was I talking about ? . . ."

He was very much exhausted, and seemed talking almost unconsciously.

"Calm yourself," I said, standing up and taking my hat; "go to bed, that's the first thing. Prince Nikolay Ivanitch is sure not to refuse, especially now in the overflow of his joy. Have you heard the latest news from that quarter ? Haven't you, really ? I have heard a wild story that he is going to get married ; it's a secret, but not from you, of course."

And I told him all about it, standing, hat in hand. He knew nothing about it. He quickly asked questions, inquiring principally when and where the match had been arranged and how far the rumour was trustworthy. I did not, of course, conceal from him that it had been settled immediately after his visit to Anna Andreyevna. I cannot describe what a painful impression this news made upon him ; his face worked and was almost contorted, and his lips twitched convulsively in a wry smile. At the end he turned horribly pale and sank into a reverie, with his eyes on the floor. I suddenly saw quite clearly that his vanity had been deeply wounded by Anna Andreyevna's refusal of him the day before. Perhaps in his morbid state of mind he realized only too vividly at that minute the absurd and humiliating part he had played the day before in the eyes of the young lady of whose acceptance, as it now appeared, he had all the time been so calmly confident. And worst of all, perhaps, was the thought that he had behaved so shabbily to Liza, and to no purpose ! It would be interesting to know for what these foppish young snobs think well of one another, and on what grounds they can respect one another ; this prince might well have supposed that Anna Andreyevna knew of his connection with Liza—in reality her sister—or if she did not actually know, that she would be certain to hear of it sooner or later ; and yet he had " had no doubt of her acceptance ! "

" And could you possibly imagine," he said suddenly, with a proud and supercilious glance at me, " that now, after learning such a fact, I, I could be capable of going to Prince Nikolay Ivanitch and asking him for money ? Ask him, the accepted fiancé of the lady who has just refused me—like a beggar, like a flunkey ! No, now all is lost, and if that old man's help is my only hope, then let my last hope perish ! "

In my heart I shared his feeling, but it was necessary to take a broader view of the real position : was the poor old prince really to be looked upon as a successful rival ? I had several ideas fermenting in my brain. I had, apart from Prince Sergay's affairs, made up my mind to visit the old man next day.

U

For the moment I tried to soften the impression made by the news and to get the poor prince to bed ! " When you have slept, things will look brighter, you'll see ! " He pressed my hand warmly, but this time he did not kiss me. I promised to come and see him the following evening, and " we'll talk, we'll talk ; there's so much to talk of." He greeted these last words of mine with a fateful smile.

CHAPTER VIII

1

ALL that night I dreamed of roulette, of play, of gold, and reckonings. I seemed in my dreams to be calculating something at the gambling table, some stake, some chance, and it oppressed me all night like a nightmare. To tell the truth, the whole of the previous day, in spite of all the startling impressions I had received, I had been continually thinking of the money I had won at Zerstchikov's. I suppressed the thought, but I could not suppress the emotion it aroused, and I quivered all over at the mere recollection of it. That success had put me in a fever ; could it be that I was a gambler, or at least—to be more accurate—that I had the qualities of a gambler ? Even now, at the time of writing this, I still at moments like thinking about play ! It sometimes happens that I sit for hours together absorbed in silent calculations about gambling and in dreams of putting down my stake, of the number turning up, and of picking up my winnings. Yes, I have all sorts of " qualities," and my nature is not a tranquil one.

At ten o'clock I intended to go to Stebelkov's and I meant to walk. I sent Matvey home as soon as he appeared. While I was drinking my coffee I tried to think over the position. For some reason I felt pleased ; a moment's self-analysis made me realize that I was chiefly pleased because I was going that day to the old prince's. But that day was a momentous and startling one in my life, and it began at once with a surprise.

At ten o'clock my door was flung wide open, and Tatyana Pavlovna flew in. There was nothing I expected less than a visit from her, and I jumped up in alarm on seeing her. Her face was ferocious, her manner was incoherent, and I daresay if she had been asked she could not have said why she had hastened to me. I may as well say at once, that she had just received a piece of news that had completely overwhelmed her, and she had not recovered from the first shock of it. The news overwhelmed me, too. She stayed, however, only half a minute, or perhaps a minute, but not more. She simply pounced upon me.

" So this is what you've been up to ! " she said, standing facing me and bending forward. " Ah, you young puppy ! What have you done ! What, you don't even know ! Goes on drinking his coffee ! Oh, you babbler, you chatterbox, oh, you imitation lover . . . boys like you are whipped, whipped, whipped ! "

" Tatyana Pavlovna, what has happened ? What is the matter ? Is mother ? . . ."

" You will know ! " she shouted menacingly, ran out of the room—and was gone. I should certainly have run after her, but I was restrained by one thought, and that was not a thought but a vague misgiving : I had an inkling that of all her vituperation, " imitation lover " was the most significant phrase. Of course I could not guess what it meant, but I hastened out, that I might finish with Stebelkov and go as soon as possible to Nikolay Ivanitch.

" The key to it all is there ! " I thought instinctively.

I can't imagine how he learned it, but Stebelkov already knew all about Anna Andreyevna down to every detail ; I will not describe his conversation and his gestures, but he was in a state of enthusiasm, a perfect ecstasy of enthusiasm over this " master-stroke."

" She is a person ! Yes, she is a person ! " he exclaimed. " Yes, that's not our way ; here we sit still and do nothing, but as soon as she wants something of the best she takes it. She's an antique statue ! She is an antique statue of Minerva, only she is walking about and wearing modern dress ! "

I asked him to come to business ; this business was, as I had guessed, solely to ask me to persuade and induce Prince Sergay to appeal to Prince Nikolay Ivanitch for a loan. " Or it will be a very very bad look-out for him, though it's none of my doing ; that's so, isn't it ? "

He kept peeping into my face, but I fancy did not detect that I knew anything more than the day before. And indeed he could not have imagined it : I need hardly say that I did not by word or hint betray that I knew anything about the forged documents.

Our explanations did not take long, he began at once promising me money, " and a considerable sum, a considerable sum, if only you will manage that the prince should go. The matter is urgent, very urgent, and that's the chief point that the matter's so pressing ! "

I did not want to argue and wrangle with him, as I had done the day before, and I got up to go, though to be on the safe side I flung him in reply that " I would try " ; but he suddenly amazed me beyond all expression : I was on my way to the door when all at once he put his arm round my waist affectionately and began talking to me in the most incomprehensible way.

I will omit the details of the conversation that I may not be wearisome. The upshot of it was that he made me a proposition that I should introduce him to M. Dergatchev, " since you go there ! "

I instantly became quiet, doing my utmost not to betray myself by the slightest gesture. I answered at once, however, that I was quite a stranger there, and though I had been in the house, it was only on one occasion, by chance.

" But if you've been *admitted* once, you might go a second time ; isn't that so ? "

I asked him point-blank, and with great coolness, why he wanted it ? And to this day I can't understand such a degree of simplicity in a man who was apparently no fool, and who was a " business man," as Vassin had said of him ! He explained to me quite openly that he suspected " that something prohibited and sternly prohibited was going on at Dergatchev's, and so if I watch him I may very likely make something by it." And with a grin he winked at me with his left eye.

I made no definite answer, but pretended to be considering it and promised to " think about it," and with that I went hastily away. The position was growing more complicated : I flew to Vassin, and at once found him at home.

" What, you . . . too ! " he said enigmatically on seeing me.

Without inquiring the significance of this phrase, I went straight to the point and told him what had happened. He was evidently impressed, though he remained absolutely cool. He cross-examined me minutely.

" It may very well be that you misunderstood him."

" No, I quite understood him, his meaning was quite clear."

" In any case I am extremely grateful to you," he added with sincerity. " Yes, indeed, if that is so, he imagined that you could not resist a certain sum of money."

" And, besides, he knows my position : I've been playing all this time, and behaving badly, Vassin."

" I have heard about that."

" What puzzles me most of all is that he knows you go there constantly, too," I ventured to observe.

" He knows perfectly well," Vassin answered quite simply, " that I don't go there with any object. And indeed all those young people are simply chatterers, nothing more ; you have reason to remember that as well as anyone."

I fancied that he did not quite trust me.

" In any case I am very much obliged to you."

" I have heard that M. Stebelkov's affairs are in rather a bad way," I tried to question him once more. " I've heard, anyway, of certain shares . . ."

" What shares have you heard about ? "

I mentioned " the shares " on purpose, but of course not with the idea of telling him the secret Prince Sergay had told me the day before. I only wanted to drop a hint and see from his face, from his eyes, whether he knew anything about " shares." I attained my object : from a momentary indefinable change in his face, I guessed that he did perhaps know something in this matter, too. I did not answer his question " what shares," I was silent ; and it was worth noting that he did not pursue the subject either.

" How's Lizaveta Makarovna ? " he inquired with sympathetic interest.

" She's quite well. My sister has always thought very highly of you. . . ."

There was a gleam of pleasure in his eyes ; I had guessed long before that he was not indifferent to Liza.

" Prince Sergay Petrovitch was here the other day," he informed me suddenly.

" When ? " I cried.

" Just four days ago."

" Not yesterday ? "

" No, not yesterday." He looked at me inquiringly. " Later perhaps I may describe our meeting more fully, but for the moment I feel I must warn you," Vassin said mysteriously, " that he struck me as being in an abnormal condition of mind, and . . . of brain indeed. I had another visit, however," he added suddenly with a smile, " just before you came, and I was driven to the same conclusion about that visitor, too."

" Has Prince Sergay just been here ? "

" No, not Prince Sergay, I am not speaking of the prince just now. Andrey Petrovitch Versilov has just been here, and . . . you've heard nothing ? Hasn't something happened to him ? "

" Perhaps something has; but what passed between you exactly ? " I asked hurriedly.

" Of course, I ought to keep it secret . . . we are talking rather queerly, with too much reserve," he smiled again. "Andrey Petrovitch, however, did not tell me to keep it secret. But you are his son, and as I know your feelings for him, I believe I may be doing right to warn you. Only fancy, he came to me to ask the question : ' In case it should be necessary for him very shortly, in a day or two, to fight a duel, would I consent to be his second ? ' I refused absolutely, of course."

I was immensely astonished ; this piece of news was the most disturbing of all : something was wrong, something had turned up, something had happened of which I knew nothing as yet ! I suddenly recalled in a flash how Versilov had said to me the day before : " I shan't come to you, but you'll come running to me."

I rushed off to Prince Nikolay Ivanitch, feeling more than ever that the key to the mystery lay there. As he said good-bye, Vassin thanked me again.

2

The old prince was sitting before an open fire with a rug wrapped round his legs. He met me with an almost questioning air, as though he were surprised that I had come; yet almost every day he had sent messages inviting me. He greeted me affectionately, however. But his answers to my first questions sounded somewhat reluctant, and were fearfully vague. At times he seemed to deliberate, and looked intently at me, as though forgetting and trying to recall something which certainly. ought to be connected with me. I told him frankly that I had heard everything and was very glad. A cordial and good-natured smile came into his face at once and his spirits rose ; his mistrust and caution vanished at once as though he had forgotten them. And indeed he had, of course.

" My dear young friend, I knew you would be the first to come, and, and do you know, I thought about you yesterday : ' Who will be pleased ? he will ! ' Well, no one else will indeed ; but that doesn't matter. People are spiteful gossips, but that's no great matter. . . . *Cher enfant*, this is so exalted and so charming. . . . But, of course, you know her well. And Anna Andreyevna has the highest opinion of you. It's a grave and charming face out of an English keepsake. It's the most charming English engraving possible. . . . Two years ago I had a regular collection of such engravings. . . . I always had the intention, always ; I only wonder why it was I never thought of it."

"You always, if I remember rightly, distinguished Anna Andreyevna and were fond of her."

"My dear boy, we don't want to hurt anyone. Life with one's friends, with one's relations, with those dear to one's heart is paradise. All the poets. . . . In short, it has been well known from prehistoric times. In the summer you know we are going to Soden, and then to Bad-Gastein. But what a long time it is since you've been to see me, my dear boy ; what's been the matter with you ? I've been expecting you. And how much, how much has happened meanwhile, hasn't it ? I am only sorry that I am uneasy ; as soon as I am alone I feel uneasy. That is why I must not be left alone, must I ? That's as plain as twice two make four. I understood that at once from her first word. Oh, my dear boy, she only spoke two words, but . . . it was something like a glorious poem. But, of course, you are her brother, almost her brother, aren't you ? My dear boy, it's not for nothing I'm so fond of you ! I swear I had a presentiment of all this. I kissed her hand and wept."

He took out his handkerchief as though preparing to weep again. He was violently agitated, suffering, I fancy, from one of his "nervous attacks," and one of the worst I remember in the whole course of our acquaintance. As a rule, almost always in fact, he was ever so much better and more good-humoured.

"I would forgive everything, my dear boy," he babbled on. "I long to forgive every one, and it's a long time since I was angry with anyone. Art, *la poésie dans la vie*, philanthropy, and she, a biblical beauty, *quelle charmante* person, eh ? *Les chants de Salomon . . . non, c'est n'est pas Salomon, c'est David qui mettait une jeune belle dans son lit pour se chauffer dans sa vieillesse. Enfin* David, Salomon, all that keeps going round in my head—a regular jumble. Everything, *cher enfant* may be at the same time grand and ridiculous. *Cette jeune belle de la vieillesse de David—c'est tout un poème,* and Paul de Kock would have made of it a *scène de bassinoire,* and we should all have laughed. Paul de Kock has neither taste nor sense of proportion, though he is a writer of talent . . . Katerina Nikolaevna smiles . . . I said that we would not trouble anyone. We have begun our romance and only ask them to let us finish it. Maybe it is a dream, but don't let them rob me of this dream."

" How do you mean it's a dream, prince ? "

" A dream ? How a dream ? Well, let it be a dream, but let me die with that dream."

" Oh, why talk of dying, prince ? You have to live now, only to live ! "

" Why, what did I say ? That's just what I keep saying. I simply can't understand why life is so short. To avoid being tedious, no doubt, for life, too, is the Creator's work of art, in a perfect and irreproachable form like a poem of Pushkin's. Brevity is the first essential of true art. But if anyone is not bored, he ought to be allowed to live longer."

" Tell me, prince, is it public property yet ? "

" No, my dear boy, certainly not ! We have all agreed upon that. It's private, private, private. So far I've only disclosed it fully to Katerina Nikolaevna, because I felt I was being unfair to her. Oh, Katerina Nikolaevna is an angel, she is an angel ! "

" Yes, yes ! "

" Yes, and you say ' yes ' ? Why, I thought that you were her enemy, too. Ach, by the way, she asked me not to receive you any more. And only fancy, when you came in I quite forgot it."

" What are you saying ? " I cried, jumping up. " Why ? Where ? "

(My presentiment had not deceived me ; I had had a presentiment of something of this sort ever since Tatyana's visit.)

" Yesterday, my dear boy, yesterday. I don't understand, in fact, how you got in, for orders were given. How did you come in ? "

" I simply walked in."

" The surest way. If you had tried to creep in by stealth, no doubt they would have caught you, but as you simply walked in they let you pass. Simplicity, *cher enfant,* is in reality the deepest cunning."

" I don't understand : did you, too, decide not to receive me, then ! "

" No, my dear boy, I said I had nothing to do with it. . . . . That is I gave my full consent. And believe me, my dear boy, I am much too fond of you. But Katerina Nikolaevna insisted so very strongly. . . . So, there it is ! "

At that instant Katerina Nikolaevna appeared in the doorway. She was dressed to go out, and as usual came in to kiss her father.

Seeing me she stopped short in confusion, turned quickly, and went out.

" *Voilà !* " cried the old prince, impressed and much disturbed. " It's a misunderstanding ! " I cried. " One moment . . . I . . . I'll come back to you directly, prince ! "

And I ran after Katerina Nikolaevna.

All that followed upon this happened so quickly that I had no time to reflect, or even to consider in the least how to behave. If I had had time to consider, I should certainly have behaved differently ! But I lost my head like a small boy. I was rushing towards her room, but on the way a footman informed me that Katerina Nikolaevna had already gone downstairs and was getting into her carriage. I rushed headlong down the front staircase. Katerina Nikolaevna was descending the stairs, in her fur coat, and beside her—or rather arm-in-arm with her—walked a tall and severe-looking officer, wearing a uniform and a sword, and followed by a footman carrying his great-coat. This was the baron, who was a colonel of five-and-thirty, a typical smart officer, thin, with rather too long a face, ginger moustache and even eyelashes of the same colour. Though his face was quite ugly, it had a resolute and defiant expression. I describe him briefly, as I saw him at that moment. I had never seen him before. I ran down the stairs after them without a hat or coat. Katerina Nikolaevna was the first to notice me, and she hurriedly whispered something to her companion. He slightly turned his head and then made a sign to the footman and the hall-porter. The footman took a step towards me at the front door, but I pushed him away and rushed after them out on the steps. Büring was assisting Katerina Nikolaevna into the carriage.

" Katerina Nikolaevna ! Katerina Nikolaevna ! " I cried senselessly like a fool ! like a fool ! Oh, I remember it all ; I had no hat on !

Büring turned savagely to the footman again and shouted something to him loudly, one or two words, I did not take them in. I felt some one clutch me by the elbow. At that moment the carriage began to move ; I shouted again and was rushing after the carriage. I saw that Katerina Nikolaevna was peeping out of the carriage window, and she seemed much perturbed. But in my hasty movement I jostled against Büring unconsciously, and trod on his foot, hurting him a good deal, I fancy. He uttered a faint cry, clenched his teeth, with a powerful hand grasped me by the shoulder, and angrily pushed me away, so that I was sent flying a couple of yards. At that instant his great-coat was handed him, he put it on, got into his sledge, and once more shouted angrily to the footman and the porter, pointing to me as he did so. Thereupon they seized me and held me; one footman flung my great-coat on me, while a second handed me my hat and—I don't remember what they said; they said something, and I stood and listened, understanding nothing of it. All at once I left them and ran away.

3

Seeing nothing and jostling against people as I went, I ran till I reached Tatyana Pavlovna's flat: it did not even occur to me to take a cab. Büring had pushed me away before her eyes! I had, to be sure, stepped on his foot, and he had thrust me away instinctively as a man who had trodden on his corn—and perhaps I really had trodden on his corn! But she had seen it, and had seen me seized by the footman; it had all happened before her, before her! When I had reached Tatyana Pavlovna's, for the first minute I could say nothing and my lower jaw was trembling, as though I were in a fever. And indeed I was in a fever and what's more I was crying. . . . Oh, I had been so insulted!

"What! Have they kicked you out? Serve you right! serve you right!" said Tatyana Pavlovna. I sank on the sofa without a word and looked at her.

"What's the matter with him?" she said, looking at me intently. "Come, drink some water, drink a glass of water, drink it up! Tell me what you've been up to there now?"

I muttered that I had been turned out, and that Büring had given me a push in the open street.

"Can you understand anything, or are you still incapable? Come here, read and admire it." And taking a letter from the table she gave it to me, and stood before me expectantly. I at once recognized Versilov's writing, it consisted of a few lines: it was a letter to Katerina Nikolaevna. I shuddered and instantly comprehension came back to me in a rush. The contents of this horrible, atrocious, grotesque and blackguardly letter were as follows, word for word:

"DEAR MADAM
    KATERINA NIKOLAEVNA.

Depraved as you are in your nature and your arts, I should have yet expected you to restrain your passions and not to try your wiles on children. But you are not even ashamed to do that. I beg to inform you that the letter you know of was certainly not burnt in a candle and never was in Kraft's possession, so you won't score anything there. So don't seduce a boy for nothing. Spare him, he is hardly grown up, almost a child, undeveloped mentally and physically—what use can you have for him ? I am interested in his welfare, and so I have ventured to write to you, though with little hope of attaining my object. I have the honour to inform you that I have sent a copy of this letter to Baron Büring. "A. VERSILOV."

I turned white as I read, then suddenly I flushed crimson and my lips quivered with indignation.

"He writes that about me ! About what I told him the day before yesterday ! " I cried in a fury.

"So you did tell him ! " cried Tatyana Pavlovna, snatching the letter from me.

"But . . . I didn't say that, I did not say that at all ! Good God, what can she think of me now ! But it's madness, you know. He's mad . . . I saw him yesterday. When was the letter sent ? "

"It was sent yesterday, early in the day ; it reached her in the evening, and this morning she gave it me herself."

"But I saw him yesterday myself, he's mad ! Versilov was incapable of writing that, it was written by a madman. Who could write like that to a woman ? "

"That's just what such madmen do write in a fury when they are blind and deaf from jealousy and spite, and their blood is turned to venom. . . . You did not know what he is like ! Now they will pound him to a jelly. He has thrust his head under the axe himself ! He'd better have gone at night to the Nikolaevsky railway and have laid his head on the rail. They'd have cut it off for him, if he's weary of the weight of it ! What possessed you to tell him ! What induced you to tease him ! Did you want to boast ? "

"But what hatred ! What hatred ! " I cried, clapping my hand on my head. "And what for, what for ? Of a woman ! What has she done to him ? What can there have been between them that he can write a letter like that ? "

"Ha—atred ! " Tatyana Pavlovna mimicked me with furious sarcasm.

The blood rushed to my face again ; all at once I

seemed to grasp something new ; I gazed at her with searching inquiry.

" Get along with you ! " she shrieked, turning away from me quickly and waving me off. " I've had bother enough with you all ! I've had enough of it now ! You may all sink into the earth for all I care ! . . . Your mother is the only one I'm sorry for . . ."

I ran, of course, to Versilov. But what treachery ! What treachery !

4

Versilov was not alone. To explain the position beforehand : after sending that letter to Katerina Nikolaevna the day before and actually dispatching a copy of it to Baron Büring (God only knows why), naturally he was bound to expect certain "consequences " of his action in the course of to-day, and so had taken measures of a sort. He had in the morning moved my mother upstairs to my " coffin," together with Liza, who, as I learned afterwards, had been taken ill when she got home, and had gone to bed. The other rooms, especially the drawing-room, had been scrubbed and tidied up with extra care. And at two o'clock in the afternoon a certain Baron R. did in fact make his appearance. He was a colonel, a tall thin gentleman about forty, a little bald, of German origin, with ginger-coloured hair like Büring's, and a look of great physical strength. He was one of those Baron R.s of whom there are so many in the Russian army, all men of the highest baronial dignity, entirely without means, living on their pay, and all zealous and conscientious officers.

I did not come in time for the beginning of their interview ; both were very much excited, and they might well be. Versilov was sitting on the sofa facing the table, and the baron was in an armchair on one side. Versilov was pale, but he spoke with restraint, dropping out his words one by one ; the baron raised his voice and was evidently given to violent gesticulation. He restrained himself with an effort, but he looked stern, supercilious, and even contemptuous, though somewhat astonished. Seeing me he frowned, but Versilov seemed almost relieved at my coming.

" Good-morning, dear boy. Baron, this is the very young man mentioned in the letter, and I assure you he will not be in your way, and may indeed be of use." (The baron looked at me contemptuously.) " My dear boy," Versilov went on, " I am glad that you've come, indeed, so sit down in the corner please, till the baron and I have finished. Don't be uneasy, baron, he will simply sit in the corner."

I did not care, for I had made up my mind, and besides all this impressed me : I sat down in the corner without speaking, as far back as I could, and went on sitting there without stirring or blinking an eyelid till the interview was over. . . .

" I tell you again, baron," said Versilov, rapping out his words resolutely, " that I consider Katerina Nikolaevna Ahmakov, to whom I wrote that unworthy and insane letter, not only the soul of honour, but the acme of all perfection ! "

" Such a disavowal of your own words, as I have observed to you already, is equivalent to a repetition of the offence," growled the baron ; "your words are actually lacking in respect."

" And yet it would be nearest the truth if you take them in their exact sense. I suffer, do you see, from nervous attacks, and . . . nervous ailments, and am in fact being treated for them and therefore it has happened in one such moment . . ."

" These explanations cannot be admitted. I tell you for the third time that you are persistently mistaken, perhaps purposely wish to be mistaken. I have warned you from the very beginning that the whole question concerning that lady, that is concerning your letter to Mme. Ahmakov, must be entirely excluded from our explanation ; you keep going back to it. Baron Büring begged and particularly charged me to make it plain that this matter concerns him only ; that is, your insolence in sending him that ' copy ' and the postcript to it in which you write that ' you are ready to answer for it when and how he pleases.' "

" But that, I imagine, is quite clear without explanation."

" I understand, I hear. You do not even offer an apology, but persist in asserting that ' you are ready to answer for it when and how he pleases.' But that would be getting off too cheaply. And therefore I now, in view of the turn which you obstinately will give to your explanation, feel myself justified on my side in telling you the truth without ceremony, that is, I have come to the conclusion that it is ut-ter-ly impossible for Baron Büring to meet you . . . on an equal footing."

" Such a decision is no doubt advantageous for your friend, Baron Büring, and I must confess you have not surprised me in the least : I was expecting it."

I note in parenthesis : it was quite evident to me from the

first word and the first glance that Versilov was trying to lead
up to this outburst, that he was intentionally teasing and pro-
voking this irascible baron, and was trying to put him out of
patience. The baron bristled all over.

"I have heard that you are able to be witty, but being witty
is very different from being clever."

"An extremely profound observation, colonel."

"I did not ask for your approbation," cried the baron. "I did
not come to bandy words with you. Be so good as to listen.
Baron Büring was in doubt how to act when he received your
letter, because it was suggestive of a madhouse. And, of course,
means might be taken to . . . suppress you. However, owing
to certain special considerations, your case was treated with
indulgence and inquiries were made about you : it turns out that
though you have belonged to good society, and did at one time
serve in the Guards, you have been excluded from society and
your reputation is dubious. Yet in spite of that I've come here to
ascertain the facts personally, and now, to make things worse,
you don't scruple to play with words, and inform me yourself
that you are liable to nervous attacks. It's enough ! Baron
Büring's position and reputation are such that he cannot stoop
to be mixed up in such an affair. . . . in short, I am authorized,
sir, to inform you, that if a repetition or anything similar to your
recent action should follow hereafter, measures will promptly be
found to bring you to your senses, very quickly and very
thoroughly I can assure you. We are not living in the jungle,
but in a well ordered state ! "

"You are so certain of that, my good baron ? "

"Confound you," cried the baron, suddenly getting up ;
" you tempt me to show you at once that I am not ' your good
baron.' "

"Ach, I must warn you once again," said Versilov, and he too
stood up, "that my wife and daughter are not far off . . .
and so I must ask you not to speak so loud, for your shouts may
reach their ears."

"Your wife . . . the devil . . . I am sitting here talking
to you solely in order to get to the bottom of this disgusting
business," the baron continued as wrathfully as before, not dropping his voice in the least. "Enough ! " he roared furiously,
" you are not only excluded from the society of decent people,
but you're a maniac, a regular raving maniac, and such you've
been proved to be ! You do not deserve indulgence, and I can

tell you that this very day measures will be taken in regard to you . . . and you will be placed where they will know how to restore you to sanity . . . and will remove you from the town."

He marched with rapid strides out of the room. Versilov did not accompany him to the door. He stood gazing at me absent-mindedly, as though he did not see me ; all at once he smiled, tossed back his hair, and taking his hat, he too made for the door. I clutched at his hand.

"Ach, yes, you are here too. You . . . heard ? " he said, stopping short before me.

"How could you do it ? How could you distort . . . disgrace . . . with such treachery ! "

He looked at me intently, his smile broadened and broadened till it passed into actual laughter.

"Why, I've been disgraced . . . before her ! before her ! They laughed at me before her eyes, and he . . . and he pushed me away ! " I cried, beside myself.

"Really ? Ach, poor boy, I am sorry for you. . . . So they laughed at you, did they ? "

"You are laughing yourself, you are laughing at me ; it amuses you ! "

He quickly pulled his hand away, put on his hat and laughing, laughing aloud, went out of the flat. What was the use of running after him ? I understood and—I had lost everything in one instant ! All at once I saw my mother ; she had come down-stairs and was timidly looking about her.

"Has he gone away ? "

I put my arms around her without a word, and she held me tight in hers.

"Mother, my own, surely you can't stay ? Let us go at once, I will shelter you, I will work for you like a slave, for you and for Liza. Leave them all, all, and let us go away. Let us be alone. Mother, do you remember how you came to me at Touchard's and I would not recognize you ? "

"I remember, my own ; I have been bad to you all your life. You were my own child, and I was a stranger to you."

"That was his fault, mother, it was all his fault ; he has never loved us."

"Yes, yes, he did love us.'

"Let us go, mother."

"How could I go away from him, do you suppose he is happy?"

"Where's Liza ? "

"She's lying down; she felt ill when she came in; I'm frightened. Why are they so angry with him? What will they do to him now? Where's he gone? What was that officer threatening?"

"Nothing will happen to him, mother, nothing does happen to him, or ever can happen to him. He's that sort of man! Here's Tatyana Pavlovna, ask her, if you don't believe me, here she is." (Tatyana Pavlovna came quickly into the room.) "Good-bye, mother. I will come to you directly, and when I come, I shall ask you the same thing again. . . ."

I ran away. I could not bear to see anyone, let alone Tatyana Pavlovna. Even mother distressed me. I wanted to be alone, alone.

5

But before I had crossed the street, I felt that I could hardly walk, and I jostled aimlessly, heedlessly, against the passers-by, feeling listless and adrift; but what could I do with myself? What use am I to anyone, and—what use is anything to me now? Mechanically I trudged to Prince Sergay's, though I was not thinking of him at all. He was not at home. I told Pyotr (his man) that I would wait in his study (as I had done many times before). His study was a large one, a very high room, cumbered up with furniture. I crept into the darkest corner, sat down on the sofa and, putting my elbows on the table, rested my head in my hands. Yes, that was the question: "what was of any use to me now?" If I was able to formulate that question then, I was totally unable to answer it.

But I could not myself answer the question, or think about it rationally. I have mentioned already that towards the end of those days I was overwhelmed by the rush of events. I sat now, and everything was whirling round like chaos in my mind. "Yes, I had failed to see all that was in him, and did not understand him at all," was the thought that glimmered dimly in my mind at moments. "He laughed in my face just now: that was not at me, it was all Büring then, not me. The day before yesterday he knew everything and he was gloomy. He pounced on my stupid confession in the restaurant, and distorted it, regardless of the truth; but what did he care for the truth? He did not believe a syllable of what he wrote to her. All he wanted was to insult her, to insult her senselessly, without knowing what for;

he was looking out for a pretext and I gave him the pretext. . . . He behaved like a mad dog ! Does he want to kill Büring now ? What for ? His heart knows what for ! And I know nothing o. what's in his heart. . . . No, no, I don't know even now. Can it be that he loves her with such passion ? Or does he hate her to such a pitch of passion ? I don't know, but does he know himself ? Why did I tell mother that 'nothing could happen to him' ; what did I mean to say by that ? Have I lost him or haven't I ?

" . . . She saw how I was pushed away. . . . Did she laugh too, or not ? I should have laughed ! They were beating a spy, a spy. . . .

" What does it mean, " suddenly flashed on my mind, " what does it mean that in that loathsome letter he puts in that the document has not been burnt, but is in existence ? . . .

" He is not killing Büring but is sitting at this moment, no doubt, in the restaurant listening to ' Lucia ' ! And perhaps after Lucia he will go and kill Büring. Büring pushed me away, almost struck me ; did he strike me ? And Büring disdains to fight even Versilov, so would he be likely to fight with me ? Perhaps I ought to kill him to-morrow with a revolver, waiting for him in the street. . . ." I let that thought flit through my mind quite mechanically without being brought to a pause by it.

At moments I seemed to dream that the door would open all at once, that Katerina Nikolaevna would come in, would give me her hand, and we should both burst out laughing. . . . Oh, my student, my dear one ! I had a vision of this, or rather an intense longing for it, as soon as it got dark. It was not long ago I had been standing before her saying good-bye to her, and she had given me her hand, and laughed. How could it have happened that in such a short time we were so completely separated ! Simply to go to her and to explain everything this minute, simply, simply ! Good heavens ! how was it that an utterly new world had begun for me so suddenly ! Yes, a new world, utterly, utterly new. . . . And Liza, and Prince Sergay, that was all old. . . . Here I was now at Prince Sergay's. And mother—how could she go on living with him if it was like this ! I could, I can do anything, but she ? What will be now ? And the figures of Liza, Anna Andreyevna, Stebelkov, Prince Sergay, Aferdov, kept disconnectedly whirling round in my sick brain. But my thoughts became more and more formless and elusive ; I was glad when I succeeded in thinking of something and clutching at it.

x

"I have 'my idea'!" I thought suddenly; "but have I? Don't I repeat that from habit? My idea was the fruit of darkness and solitude, and is it possible to creep back into the old darkness? Oh, my God, I never burnt that 'letter'! I actually forgot to burn it the day before yesterday. I will go back and burn it in a candle, in a candle of course; only I don't know if I'm thinking properly. . . ."

It had long been dark and Pyotr brought candles. He stood over me and asked whether I had had supper. I simply motioned him away. An hour later, however, he brought me some tea, and I greedily drank a large cupful. Then I asked what time it was? It was half-past eight, and I felt no surprise to find I had been sitting there five hours.

"I have been in to you three times already," said Pyotr, "but I think you were asleep."

I did not remember his coming in. I don't know why, but I felt all at once horribly scared to think I had been asleep. I got up and walked about the room, that I might not go to sleep again. At last my head began to ache violently. At ten o'clock Prince Sergay came in and I was surprised that I had been waiting for him: I had completely forgotten him, completely.

"You are here, and I've been round to you to fetch you," he said to me. His face looked gloomy and severe, and there was not a trace of a smile. There was a fixed idea in his eyes.

"I have been doing my very utmost all day and straining every nerve," he said with concentrated intensity; "everything has failed, and nothing in the future, but horror. . . ." (N.B.—he had not been to Prince Nikolay Ivanitch's.) "I have seen Zhibyelsky, he is an impossible person. You see, to begin with we must get the money, then we shall see. And if we don't succeed with the money, then we shall see. . . . I have made up my mind not to think about that. If only we get hold of the money to-day, to-morrow we shall see everything. The three thousand you won is still untouched, every farthing of it. It's three thousand all except three roubles. After paying back what I lent you, there is three hundred and forty roubles change for you. Take it. Another seven hundred as well, to make up a thousand, and I will take the other two thousand. Then let us both go to Zerstchikov and try at opposite ends of the table to win ten thousand—perhaps we shall do something, if we don't win it— then. . . . This is the only way left, anyhow."

He looked at me with a fateful smile.

" Yes, yes ! " I cried suddenly, as though coming to life again ; " let us go. I was only waiting for you. . . ."

I may remark that I had never once thought of roulette during those hours.

" But the baseness ? The degradation of the action ? " Prince Sergay asked suddenly.

" Our going to roulette ! Why that's everything," I cried, " money's everything. Why, you and I are the only saints, while Büring has sold himself, Anna Andreyevna's sold herself, and Versilov—have you heard that Versilov's a maniac ? A maniac ! A maniac ! "

" Are you quite well, Arkady Makarovitch ? Your eyes are somehow strange."

" You say that because you want to go without me ! But I shall stick to you now. It's not for nothing I've been dreaming of play all night. Let us go, let us go ! " I kept exclaiming, as though I had found the solution to everything.

" Well, let us go, though you're in a fever, and there . . ."

He did not finish. His face looked heavy and terrible. We were just going out when he stopped in the doorway.

" Do you know," he said suddenly, " that there is another way out of my trouble, besides play ? "

" What way."

" A princely way."

" What's that ? What's that ? "

" You'll know what afterwards. Only let me tell you I'm not worthy of it, because I have delayed too long. Let us go, but you remember my words. We'll try the lackey's way. . . . And do you suppose I don't know that I am consciously, of my own free will, behaving like a lackey ? "

6

I flew to the roulette table as though in it were concentrated all hopes of my salvation, all means of escape, and yet as I have mentioned already, I had not once thought of it before Prince Sergay's arrival. Moreover, I was going to gamble, not for myself but for Prince Sergay, and with his money ; I can't explain what was the attraction, but it was an irresistible attraction. Oh, never had those people, those faces, those croupiers with their

monotonous shouts, all the details of the squalid gambling saloon
seemed so revolting to me, so depressing, so coarse, and so
melancholy as that evening !   I remember well the sadness and
misery that gripped my heart at times during those hours at the
gambling table.   But why didn't I go away ?   Why did I
endure and, as it were, accept this fate, this sacrifice, this
devotion ?   I will only say one thing : I can hardly say of myself
that I was then in my right senses.   Yet at the same time, I
had never played so prudently as that evening.   I was silent
and concentrated, attentive and extremely calculating ;   I was
patient and niggardly, and at the same time resolute at critical
moments.   I established myself again at the zero end of the table,
that is between Zerstchikov and Aferdov, who always sat on the
former's right hand ;   the place was distasteful to me, but I had
an overwhelming desire to stake on zero, and all the other places
at that end were taken.   We had been playing over an hour ;
at last, from my place, I saw Prince Sergay get up from his seat
and with a pale face move across to us and remain facing me the
other side of the table :   he had lost all he had and watched my
play in silence, though he probably did not follow it and had
ceased to think of play.   At that moment I just began winning,
and Zerstchikov was counting me out what I had won.   Suddenly,
without a word, Aferdov with the utmost effrontery took one of
my hundred-rouble notes before my very eyes and added it to the
pile of money lying before him.   I cried out, and caught hold of
his hand.   Then something quite unexpected happened to me :
it was as though I had broken some chain that restrained me,
as though all the affronts and insults of that day were concentrated in that moment in the loss of that hundred-rouble note.
It was as though everything that had been accumulating and
suppressed within me had only been waiting for that moment to
break out.

" He's a thief, he has just stolen my hundred roubles," I
exclaimed, looking round, beside myself.

I won't describe the hubbub that followed ; such a scandal was
a novelty there.   At Zerstchikov's, people behaved with propriety,
and his saloon was famous for it.   But I did not know what I was
doing.   Zerstchikov's voice was suddenly heard in the midst of
the clamour and din :

" But the money's not here, and it was lying here !   Four
hundred roubles ! "

Another scene followed at once ; the money in the bank had

disappeared under Zerstchikov's very nose, a roll of four hundred roubles. Zerstchikov pointed to the spot where the notes had only that minute been lying, and that spot turned out to be close to me, next to the spot where my money was lying, much closer to me than to Aferdov.

"The thief is here ! he has stolen it again, search him ! " I cried pointing to Aferdov.

"This is what comes of letting in all sorts of people," thundered an impressive voice in the midst of the general uproar. "Persons have been admitted without introduction ! Who brought him in ?   Who is he ? "

"A fellow called Dolgoruky."

"Prince Dolgoruky ? "

"Prince Sokolsky brought him," cried some one.

"Listen, prince," I yelled to him across the table in a frenzy ; "they think I'm a thief when I've just been robbed myself ! Tell them about me, tell them about me ! "

And then there followed something worse than all that had happened that day . . . worse than anything that had happened in my life : Prince Sergay disowned me. I saw him shrug his shoulders and heard him in answer to a stream of questions pronounce sharply and distinctly :

"I am not responsible for anyone. Please leave me alone."

Meanwhile Aferdov stood in the middle of the crowd loudly demanding that "he should be searched." He kept turning out his own pockets. But his demands were met by shouts of "No, no, we know the thief ! "

Two footmen were summoned and they seized me by my arms from behind.

"I won't let myself be searched, I won't allow it ! " I shouted, pulling myself away.

But they dragged me into the next room ; there, in the midst of the crowd, they searched me to the last fold of my garments. I screamed and struggled.

"He must have thrown it away, you must look on the floor," some one decided.

"Where can we look on the floor now ? "

"Under the table, he must have somehow managed to throw it away."

"Of course there's no trace . . ."

I was led out, but I succeeded in stopping in the doorway, and with senseless ferocity I shouted, to be heard by the whole saloon :

" Roulette is prohibited by the police. I shall inform against you all to-day ! "

I was led downstairs. My hat and coat were put on me, and . . . the door into the street was flung open before me.

CHAPTER IX

1

THE day had ended with a catastrophe, there remained the night, and this is what I remember of that night.

I believe it was one o'clock when I found myself in the street. It was a clear, still and frosty night, I was almost running and in horrible haste, but—not towards home.

" Why home ? Can there be a home now ? Home is where one lives, I shall wake up to-morrow to live—but is that possible now ? Life is over, it is utterly impossible to live now," I thought.

And as I wandered about the streets, not noticing where I was going, and indeed I don't know whether I meant to run anywhere in particular, I was very hot and I was continually flinging open my heavy raccoon-lined coat. " No sort of action can have any object for me now " was what I felt at that moment. And strange to say, it seemed to me that everything about me, even the air I breathed, was from another planet, as though I had suddenly found myself in the moon. Everything—the town, the passers-by, the pavement I was running on—all of these were *not mine*. " This is the Palace Square, and here is St. Isaak's," floated across my mind. " But now I have nothing to do with them." Everything had become suddenly remote, it had all suddenly become *not mine*. " I have mother and Liza —but what are mother and Liza to me now ? Everything is over, everything is over at one blow, except one thing : that I am a thief for ever."

" How can I prove that I'm not a thief ? Is it possible now ? Shall I go to America ? What should I prove by that ? Versilov will be the first to believe I stole it ! My ' idea ' ? What idea ? What is my ' idea ' now ? If I go on for fifty years, for a hundred years, some one will always turn up, to point at me and say : ' He's a thief, he began, " his idea " by stealing money at roulette.' "

Was there resentment in my heart ? I don't know, perhaps there was. Strange to say, I always had, perhaps from my earliest childhood, one characteristic : if I were ill-treated, absolutely wronged and insulted to the last degree, I always showed at once an irresistible desire to submit passively to the insult, and even to accept more than my assailant wanted to inflict upon me, as though I would say : " All right, you have humiliated me, so I will humiliate myself even more ; look, and enjoy it ! " Touchard beat me and tried to show I was a lackey, and not the son of a senator, and so I promptly took up the rôle of a lackey. I not only handed him his clothes, but of my own accord I snatched up the brush and began brushing off every speck of dust, without any request or order from him, and ran after him brush in hand, in a glow of menial devotion, to remove some particle of dirt from his dress-coat, so much so that he would sometimes check me himself and say, " That's enough, Arkady, that's enough." He would come and take off his overcoat, and I would brush it, fold it carefully, and cover it with a check silk handkerchief. I knew that my school-fellows used to laugh at me and despise me for it, I knew it perfectly well, but that was just what gratified me : " Since they want me to be a lackey, well, I am a lackey then ; if I'm to be a cad, well, I will be a cad." I could keep up a passive hatred and underground resentment in that way for years.

Well, at Zerstchikov's I had shouted to the whole room in an absolute frenzy :

" I will inform against you all—roulette is forbidden by the police ! " And I swear that in that case, too, there was something of the same sort : I was humiliated, searched, publicly proclaimed a thief, crushed. " Well then I can tell you, you have guessed right, I am worse than a thief, I am an informer." Recalling it now, that is how I explain it ; at the time I was incapable of analysis ; I shouted that at the time unintentionally, I did not know indeed a second before that I should say it : it shouted itself—the *characteristic* was there already in my heart.

There is no doubt that I had begun to be delirious while I was running in the streets, but I remember quite well that I knew what I was doing ; and yet I can confidently assert that a whole cycle of ideas and conclusions were impossible for me at that time ; I felt in myself even at those moments that " some thoughts I was able to think, but others I was incapable of." In the same way some of my decisions, though they were formed with perfect consciousness, were utterly devoid of logic. What is more, I remember very well that at some moments I could recognize fully the absurdity of some conclusion and at the same time with complete consciousness proceed to act upon it. Yes, crime was hovering about me that night, and only by chance was not committed.

I suddenly recalled Tatyana Pavlovna's saying about Versilov : "He'd better have gone at night to the Nikolaevsky Railway and have laid his head on the rails—they'd have cut it off for him."

For a moment that idea took possession of all my feelings, but I instantly drove it away with a pang at my heart : "If I lay my head on the rails and die, they'll say to-morrow he did it because he stole the money, he did it from shame—no, for nothing in the world ! " And at that instant I remember I experienced a sudden flash of fearful anger. "To clear my character is impossible," floated through my mind, "to begin a new life is impossible too, and so I must submit, become a lackey, a dog, an insect, an informer, a real informer, while I secretly prepare myself, and one day suddenly blow it all up into the air, annihilate everything and every one, guilty and innocent alike, so that they will all know that this was the man they had all called a thief . . . and then kill myself."

I don't remember how I ran into a lane somewhere near Konnogvardeysky Boulevard. For about a hundred paces on both sides of this lane there were high stone walls enclosing backyards. Behind the wall on the left I saw a huge stack of wood, a long stack such as one sees in timber-yards, and more than seven feet higher than the wall. I stopped and began pondering.

In my pocket I had wax matches in a little silver matchbox. I repeat, I realized quite distinctly at that time what I was thinking about and what I meant to do, and so I remember it even now, but why I meant to do it I don't know, I don't know at all. I only know that I suddenly felt a great longing to do it. "To climb over the wall is quite possible," I reflected ; at that moment I caught sight of a gate in the wall not two paces away, probably barred up for months together. "Standing on the projection below, and taking hold of the top of the gate I could easily climb on to the wall," I reflected, "and no one will notice me, there's no one about, everything's still ! And there I can sit on the wall and easily set fire to the woodstack. I can do it without getting down, for the wood almost touches the wall. The frost will make it burn all the better, I have only to take hold of a birch-log with my hand. . . . And indeed there's no need to reach a log at all : I can simply strip the bark off with my hand, while I sit on the wall, set light to it with a match and thrust it into the stack—and there will be a blaze. And I will jump down and walk away ; there will be no need to run, for it won't be noticed for a long while. . . ." That was how I reasoned at the time, and all at once I made up my mind.

I felt an extraordinary satisfaction and enjoyment, and I climbed up. I was very good at climbing : gymnastics had been my speciality at school, but I had my overboots on and it turned out to be a ·difficult task. I succeeded somehow in catching hold of one very slight projection above, and raised myself ; I lifted my other hand to clutch the top of the wall, but at that instant I slipped and went flying backwards.

I suppose I must have struck the ground with the back of my head, and must have lain for two or three minutes unconscious. When I came to myself I mechanically wrapped my fur coat about me, feeling all at once unbearably cold, and scarcely conscious of what I was doing, I crept into the corner of the gateway and sat crouching and huddled up in the recess between the gate and the wall. My ideas were in confusion, and most likely I soon fell into a doze. I remember now, as it were in a dream, that there suddenly sounded in my ears the deep heavy clang of a bell, and I began listening to it with pleasure.

2

The bell rang steadily and distinctly, once every two or three seconds ; it was not an alarm bell, however, but a pleasant and melodious chime, and I suddenly recognized that it was a familiar chime, that it was the bell of St. Nikolay's, the red church opposite Touchard's, the old-fashioned Moscow church which I remembered so well, built in the reign of Tsar Alexey Mihalovitch, full of tracery, and with many domes and columns, and that Easter was only just over, and the new-born little green leaves were trembling on the meagre birches in Touchard's front garden. The brilliant evening sun was pouring its slanting rays into our classroom, and in my little room on the left, where a year before Touchard had put me apart that I might not mix with " counts' and senators' children," there was sitting a visitor. Yes, I, who had no relations, had suddenly got a visitor for the first time since I had been at Touchard's. I recognized this visitor as soon as she came in : it was mother, though I had not seen her once since she had taken me to the village church and the dove had flown across the cupola. We were sitting alone together and I watched her strangely. Many years afterwards I learned that being left by Versilov, who had suddenly gone abroad, she had come on her own account to Moscow, paying for the journey out of her small means, and almost by stealth, without the knowledge of the people who had been commissioned to look after her, and she had done this solely to see me. It was strange, too, that when she came in and talked to Touchard, she did not say one word to me of being my mother. She sat beside me, and I remember I wondered at her talking so little. She had a parcel with her and she undid it : in it there turned out to be six oranges, several gingerbread cakes, and two ordinary loaves of French bread. I was offended at the sight of the bread, and with a constrained air I announced that our 'food' was excellent, and that they gave us a whole French loaf for our tea every day.

"Never mind, darling, in my foolishness I thought 'maybe they don't feed them properly at school,' don't be vexed, my own."

"And Antonina Vassilyevna (Touchard's wife) will be offended. My schoolfellows will laugh at me too. . . ."

"Won't you have them ; perhaps you'll eat them up ? "

"Please, don't. . . ."

And I did not even touch her presents ; the oranges and gingerbread cakes lay on the little table before me, while I sat with my eyes cast down, but with a great air of dignity. Who knows, perhaps I had a great desire to let her see that her visit made me feel ashamed to meet my schoolfellows, to let her have at least a glimpse that she might understand, as though to say, "See, you are disgracing me, and you don't understand what you are doing." Oh, by that time I was running after Touchard with a brush to flick off every speck of dust ! I was picturing to myself, too, what taunts I should have to endure as soon as she was gone, from my schoolfellows and perhaps from Touchard himself ; and there was not the least friendly feeling for her in my heart. I only looked sideways at her dark-coloured old dress, at her rather coarse, almost working-class hands, at her quite coarse shoes, and her terribly thin face ; there were already furrows on her forehead, though Antonina Vassilyevna did say that evening after she had gone : " Your mamma must have been very pretty."

So we sat, and suddenly Agafya came in with a cup of coffee on a tray. It was just after dinner, and at that time Touchard always drank a cup of coffee in his drawing-room. But mother thanked her and did not take the cup : as I learned afterwards she never drank coffee in those days, as it brought on palpitations of the heart. The fact was that Touchard inwardly considered her visit, and his permitting me to see her, an act of great condescension on his part, so that the cup of coffee sent her was, comparatively speaking, a signal proof of humanity which did the utmost credit to his civilization, feelings, and European ideas. And as though on purpose, mother refused it.

I was summoned to Touchard, and he told me to take all my lesson books and exercise books to show my mother : " That she may see what you have succeeded in attaining in my establishment." At that point Antonina Vassilyevna, pursing up her lips, minced out to me in a jeering and insulting way :

" Your mamma does not seem to like our coffee."

I collected my exercise books and carried them to my waiting mother, passing through the crowd of " counts' and senators' children " in the classroom who were staring at mother and me. And it actually pleased me to carry out Touchard's behests with literal exactitude. " Here are my lessons in French grammar, here are my dictation exercises, here are the conjugations of the auxiliary verbs *avoir* and *être*, here is the geography, descriptions of the principal towns of Europe, and all parts of the world," and so on. For half an hour or more I went on explaining in a monotonous little voice, keeping my eyes sedately cast down. I knew that my mother knew nothing of these learned subjects, could not perhaps even write, but in this too I was pleased with my part. But I did not succeed in wearying her : she listened all the time without interrupting me, with extraordinary and even reverent attention, so that at last I got tired of it myself and left off ; her expression was sad, however, and there was something pitiful in her face.

She got up to go at last ; Touchard suddenly walked in, and with an air of foolish importance asked her : " Whether she was satisfied with her son's progress ? " Mother began muttering incoherent thanks ; Antonina Vassilyevna came up too. Mother began begging them both "not to abandon the orphan, who was as good as an orphan now, but to treat him with kindness." . . . And with tears in her eyes she bowed to them both, each separately, and to each with a deep bow, exactly as "simple people" bow down when they ask a favour of the gentry. The Touchards had not expected this, and Antonina Vassilyevna was evidently softened, and revised her opinion about the cup of coffee. Touchard humanely responded with even greater dignity "that he made no distinction between the children, that here all were his children, and he was their father, that I was almost on an equal footing with the sons of senators and counts, and that she ought to appreciate that," and so on, and so on. Mother only bowed down, but was much embarrassed. At last she turned to me, and with tears shining in her eyes said : " Good-bye, darling."

She kissed me, that is I allowed myself to be kissed. She evidently wanted to go on kissing, embracing and hugging me, but either she herself felt ashamed before company, or felt hurt by something else, or guessed that I was ashamed of her, for she hurriedly went out, bowing once more to the Touchards. I stood still.

" *Mais suivez donc votre mère*," said Antonina Vassilyevna : " *il n'a pas de cœur, cet enfant !* "

Touchard responded by shrugging his shoulders, which meant, of course, " it's not without reason that I treat him as a lackey."

I obediently followed my mother ; we went out on to the steps. I knew that they were all looking at me out of the window. Mother turned towards the church and crossed herself three times ; her lips were trembling, the deep bell chimed musically and regularly from the belfry. She turned to me and could not restrain herself, she laid both hands on my head and began crying over it.

"Mother, stop . . . I'm ashamed . . . they can see from the window. . . ."

She broke out hurriedly :

"Well God . . . God be with you. . . . The heavenly angels keep you. Holy Mother, Saint Nikolay. . . . My God, my God ! " she repeated, speaking rapidly and making as many signs of the cross over me as she possibly could. "My darling, my darling ! Stay, my darling. . . ."

She hurriedly put her hand in her pocket and drew out a handkerchief, a blue checked handkerchief, with a tightly fastened knot at the corner, and began untying the knot . . . but it would not come untied. . . .

"Well never mind, take it with the handkerchief: it's clean, it may be of use perhaps. There are four fourpenny-bits in it, perhaps you'll need the money; forgive me, darling, I have not got any more just now . . . forgive me, darling."

I took the handkerchief. I wanted to observe that we were allowed very liberal diet by M. Touchard and Antonina Vassily-evna, and were not in need of anything, but I restrained myself and took the handkerchief.

Once more she made the sign of the cross over me, once more she whispered a prayer, and suddenly—suddenly bowed to me exactly as she had done to the Touchards upstairs—a prolonged low bow—I shall never forget it! Then I shuddered, I don't know why. What had she meant by that bow? "Was she confessing the wrong she had done me?" as I fancied once long afterwards—I don't know. But at the time it made me more ashamed than ever that they "were looking out of window and that Lambert would, most likely, begin beating me."

At last she went away. The apples and oranges had been devoured by the sons of counts and senators, and the four fourpenny-bits were promptly taken from me by Lambert and spent at the confectioner's on tarts and chocolates, of which I was not offered a taste.

Fully six months had passed and it was a wet and windy October. I had quite forgotten about mother. Oh, by then hate, a blind hatred of everything had crept into my heart, and was its sustenance, though I still brushed Touchard as before; but I hated him with all my might, and every day hated him more and more. It was then that in the melancholy dusk of one evening I began rummaging for something in my little box, and suddenly in the corner I saw her blue cotton handkerchief; it had been lying there ever since I had thrust it away. I took it out and even looked at it with some interest. The corner of the handkerchief still retained the creases made by the knot, and even the round impress of the money was distinctly visible; I put the handkerchief in again, however, and pushed the box back. It was the eve of a holiday, and the bells were ringing for the all-night service. The pupils had all gone to their homes after dinner, but this time Lambert had stayed for Sunday. I don't know why he hadn't been fetched. Though he used still to beat me, as before, he used to talk to me a great deal, and often needed me. We talked the whole evening about Lepage's pistols, which neither of us had seen, and Circassian swords and how they cut, how splendid it would be to establish a band of brigands, and finally Lambert passed to the familiar obscene subjects which were his favourite topics, and though I wondered at myself, I remember I liked listening. Suddenly I felt it unbearable, and I told him I had a headache. At ten o'clock we went to bed; I turned away with my head under the quilt and took the blue handkerchief from under my pillow: I had for some reason fetched it from the box an hour before, and as soon as our beds were made I put it under the pillow. I put it to my face and suddenly began kissing it: "Mother, mother," I whispered, and my whole chest contracted as though in a vice. I closed my eyes, and saw her face with the quivering lips when she crossed herself facing the church, and afterwards made the sign of the cross over me, and I said to her, "I'm ashamed, they are looking at us." "Mother darling, mother, were you really with me once? . . . Mother darling, where are you now, my far-away visitor? Do you remember your poor boy, whom you came to see? . . . Show yourself to me just this once, come to me if only in a dream, just that I may tell you how I love you, may hug you and kiss your blue eyes, and tell you that I'm not ashamed of you now, and tell you that I loved you even then, and that my heart was aching then, though I simply sat like a lackey. You will never know, mother, how I loved you then! Mother, where are you now? Do you hear me? Mother, mother, do you remember the dove in the country? . . ."

"Confound him. . . . What's the matter with him!" Lambert grumbled from his bed. "Stop it, I'll give it you! You won't let me sleep. . . ." He jumped out of bed at last, ran to me, and began pulling off the bedclothes, but I kept tight hold of the quilt, which I had wrapped round my head.

"You are blubbering; what are you blubbering about, you fool? I'll give it you!" and he thumped me, he thumped me hard on my back, on my side, hurting me more and more and . . . and I suddenly opened my eyes. . . .

It was bright daylight, and the snow on the wall was glistening with hoarfrost. . . . I was sitting huddled up, almost frozen, and almost numb in my fur coat, and some one was standing over me, waking me up, abusing me loudly, and kicking me in the ribs with his right foot. I raised myself and looked: I saw a man wearing a splendid bear-lined coat, and a sable cap. He had black eyes, foppish pitch-black whiskers, a hook nose, white teeth grinning at me, a face white and red like a mask. . . . He bent down over me very close, and a frosty vapour came from his lips at each breath.

"Frozen, the drunken fool! You'll freeze like a dog; get up! Get up!"

"Lambert," I cried.

"Whoever are you?"

"Dolgoruky."

"Who the devil's Dolgoruky?"

"*Simply* Dolgoruky! . . . Touchard. . . . The one you stuck a fork into, in the restaurant! . . ."

"Ha-a-a!" he cried, with a slow smile of recollection (could he possibly have forgotten me?), "ha! So it's you, it's you!"

He lifted me up and put me on my legs; I could hardly stand, could hardly walk; he led me, supporting me with his arm. He looked into my eyes as though considering and recalling, and listening to me intently, and I babbled on continuously without pause, and I was delighted, so delighted to be talking, and so delighted too that it was Lambert. Whether for some reason I looked on him as my "salvation," or whether I pounced on him at that moment because I took him for some one of another world, I don't know—I did not consider it then—but I pounced on him without considering. What I said then, I don't remember at all, and I doubt whether any of it was coherent, I doubt whether I even pronounced a word clearly; but he listened very attentively. He took the first sledge we came upon, and within a few minutes I was sitting in his room in the warmth.

3

Every man, whoever he may be, must certainly preserve a recollection of something which has happened to him, upon which he looks, or is inclined to look, as something fantastic, exceptional, outside the common order of things, almost miraculous, whether it be a dream, a meeting, a divination, a presentiment or anything of that kind. I am to this day inclined to look upon this meeting with Lambert as something almost supernatural . . . judging, that is, from the circumstances and consequences of that meeting. It all happened from one point of view, however, perfectly naturally; he was simply returning from one of his nocturnal pursuits (the nature of it will be explained later on) half-drunk, and stopping at the gate for a moment, caught sight of me. He had only been in Petersburg a few days.

The room in which I found myself was small and furnished in an unsophisticated style, a typical example of the ordinary Petersburg furnished lodgings of the middling sort. Lambert himself, however, was very well and expensively dressed. On the floor there lay two trunks, only half unpacked. A corner of the room was shut off by a screen which concealed the bed.

" Alphonsine ! " cried Lambert.

" *Présente !* " responded from behind the screen a cracked female voice with a Parisian accent, and two minutes later Mlle. Alphonsine emerged, just out of bed, hurriedly dressed in a loose wrapper, a queer creature, tall and as lean as a rake, a brunette with a long waist and a long face, with dancing eyes and sunken cheeks, who looked terribly the worse for wear.

" Make haste " (he spoke to her in French, I translate), " they must have got a samovar ; hot water quick, red wine and sugar, a glass here, look sharp, he's frozen, it's a friend of mine . . . he's been sleeping the night in the snow. . . ."

" *Malheureux !* " she exclaimed with a theatrical air, clasping her hands.

" Now then ! " he shouted, holding up his finger and speaking exactly as though to a dog ; she at once desisted and ran to carry out his orders.

He examined me and felt me over ; tried my pulse, touched my forehead and my temple. " It's strange," he muttered, " that you did not freeze. . . . However, you were entirely covered with your fur coat, head and all, so that you were sitting in a sort of nest of fur. . . ."

A glass of something hot arrived, I sipped it greedily and it revived me at once ; I began babbling again ; I was half lying on the sofa in a corner and was talking all the time, I talked even as I sipped—but what I said, again I scarcely remember ; moments and even whole intervals of time I've completely forgotten. I repeat : whether he understood anything of what I said, I don't know ; but one thing I distinctly gathered afterwards, and that was that he succeeded in understanding me sufficiently to deduce that he must not take his meeting with me lightly. . . . I will explain later in its proper place how he came to make this calculation.

I was not only extremely lively, but at moments, I believe, cheerful. I remember the sun suddenly flooding the room with light when the blinds were drawn up, and the crackling stove which some one was lighting, who and how I forget. I remember, too, the tiny black lap-dog which Mlle. Alphonsine held in her arms, coquettishly pressing it to her heart. This lap-dog attracted me so much that I left off talking and twice stretched out towards it, but Lambert waved his hand, and Alphonsine with her lap-dog instantly vanished behind the screen.

He was very silent himself, he sat facing me and bending close down to me, listened without moving ; at times he smiled, a broad slow smile, showing his teeth, and screwing up his eyes as though reflecting intensely and trying to guess something. I have a clear recollection only of the fact that when I told him about the " document," I could not express myself intelligibly and tell the story consecutively, and from his face I quite saw that he could not understand me, but that he would very much have liked to understand, so much so that he even ventured to stop me with a question, which was risky, as at the slightest interruption I broke off and forgot what I was talking of. How long we sat and talked like this I don't know and cannot even imagine. He suddenly got up and called to Alphonsine.

" He needs rest ; he may have to have the doctor. Do everything he asks, that is . . . *vous comprenez, ma fille ? Vous avez l'argent*, no ? here ! " and he drew out a ten-rouble note. He began whispering with her : " *Vous comprenez ? vous comprenez ?* " he repeated to her, holding up his finger menacingly to her, and frowning sternly. I saw that she was dreadfully afraid of him.

" I'll come back, and you had better go to sleep," he said, smiling to me, and took his cap. " *Mais vous n'avez pas dormi de tout, Maurice !* " Alphonsine began pathetically. " *Taisez-vous je dormirai après*," and he went out.

" *Sauvée*," she murmured, pathetically pointing after him.

" *Monsieur, Monsieur*," she began declaiming at once, taking up an attitude in the middle of the room, " *jamais homme ne fut si cruel, si Bismarck que cet être, qui regarde une femme, comme une saleté de hazard. Une femme, qu'est-ce que ça dans notre époque ? Tue-la !' voilà le dernier mot de l'Académie française !* "

Y

I stared at her open-eyed ; I saw everything double, I had a vision of two Alphonsines. . . . I suddenly noticed that she was crying, I started and realized that she had been talking to me for a long time, and that I must have been asleep or unconscious.

" . . . *Hélas ! de quoi m'aurait servi de le découvrir plutôt,*" she exclaimed, " *et n'aurais-je pas autant gagné à tenir ma honte cachée toute ma vie ? Peut-être n'est-il pas honnête à une demoiselle de s'expliquer si librement devant monsieur, mais enfin je vous avoue que s'il m'était permis de vouloir quelque chose, oh, ce serait de lui plonger au cœur mon couteau, mais en détournant les yeux, de peur que son regard exécrable ne fit trembler mon bras et ne glaçât mon courage ! Il a assassiné ce pape russe, monsieur, il lui arracha sa barbe rousse pour la vendre à un artiste en cheveux au pont de Maréchaux, tout près de la maison de Monsieur Andrieux—hautes nouveautés, articles de Paris, linge, chemises, vous savez, n'est-ce pas ? . . . Oh, monsieur, quand l'amitié rassemble à table épouse, enfants, sœurs, amis, quand une vive allégresse enflamme mon cœur, je vous le demande, monsieur : est-il bonheur préférable à celui dont tout jouit ? Mais il rit, monsieur, ce monstre exécrable et inconcévable, et si ce n'était pas par l'entremise de Monsieur Andrieux, jamais, oh, jamais je ne serais . . . Mais quoi, monsieur, qu'avez vous, monsieur ?* "

She rushed up to me. I believe I had an attack of shivering, perhaps a fainting fit. I cannot express what a painful and miserable impression this half-crazy creature made upon me. She imagined perhaps that she had been commanded to entertain me : at any rate she did not leave my side for one instant. She had perhaps at one time or another been on the stage ; she declaimed in a terrible way, pirouetted, talked incessantly, while I had long been silent. All I could understand from her story was that she had been closely connected with " *la maison de M. Andrieux—hautes nouveautés, articles de Paris, etc.,*" and perhaps was one of the family of la Maison de M. Andrieux ; but she had somehow been torn for ever from M. Andrieux, *par ce monstre furieux et inconcévable,* and that was the point of the tragedy. . . . She sobbed, but I fancied that this was all part of the performance, and that she was not really crying at all ; sometimes I fancied that she would suddenly drop to pieces, like a skeleton ; she articulated her words in a jangling, broken voice ; the word *préferable,* for instance, she pronounced *préfér-a-able,* and on the syllable *a* positively baa-ed like a sheep. Coming to myself on one occasion I found her executing a pirouette in the middle of the room, but she was not actually dancing, the pirouette had some connection with her story, and she was simply impersonating some figure in it. Suddenly she rushed and opened a little, old, out-of-tune piano that was in the room, and began strumming on it and singing. I believe that for ten minutes or more I lost consciousness completely, I fell asleep, but the lap-dog yelped and I waked up again ; for a moment consciousness returned completely and suddenly flooded my mind with light ; I jumped up in horror :

"Lambert, I am at Lambert's ! " I thought, and snatching up my hat, I rushed to my fur coat.

"*Où allez-vous, monsieur ?* " cried the vigilant Alphonsine.

"I want to get out, I want to go away ! Let me out, don't keep me. . . ."

"*Oui, monsieur !* " Alphonsine assented vigorously, and she rushed to open the door into the corridor herself. "*Mais ce n'est pas loin, monsieur, c'est pas loin du tout, ça ne vaut pas la peine de mettre votre chouba, c'est ici près, monsieur !* " she shouted for the benefit of the whole corridor. Running out of the room I turned to the right.

"*Par ici, monsieur, c'est par ici !* " she shouted at the top of her voice, clutching at my coat with her long bony fingers, and with the other hand pointing to the left of the corridor, where I did not at all want to go. I broke away and ran to the outer door opening on to the stairs.

"*Il s'en va, il s'en va !* " Alphonsine ran after me shouting in her cracked voice ; "*mais il me tuera, monsieur, il me tuera !* " But I was already on the stairs and, though she ran after me down stairs, I succeeded in opening the front door, dashing out into the street, and jumping into the first sledge I met. I gave the driver my mother's address. . . .

4

But the clear consciousness that had flickered up for one moment was soon dimmed. I still have a faint recollection of the drive and being taken up to my mother's, but there I sank almost at once into complete unconsciousness. Next day, as they told me afterwards, and indeed I remember it myself, I had a moment of lucidity again. I found myself in Versilov's room and on his sofa. I remember around me the faces of Versilov, my mother, Liza; I remember particularly Versilov's speaking to me about Zerstchikov, and about Prince Sergay, and showing me some letter to soothe me. They told me afterwards that I kept asking with horror about someone called Lambert, and kept hearing the barking of some lap-dog. But the faint light of consciousness was soon quenched again : by the evening of the second day I was completely prostrate with brain-fever. But I will anticipate events, and explain what had happened.

When I had run out in the street from Zerstchikov's that evening, and when calm had been restored there, Zerstchikov, who had returned to the table, proclaimed aloud that a regrettable mistake had been made : the missing money, four hundred roubles, had been found in a pile of other money, and the bank account turned out to be quite correct. Then Prince Sergay, who had remained in the room, went up to Zerstchikov and insisted that he should make a public declaration of my innocence and should, moreover, send me an apology in the form of a letter. Zerstchikov on his side accepted this suggestion as a very proper one, and promised, in the presence of all, to send me next day a letter of explanation and apology. Prince Sergay gave him Versilov's address. And Versilov did in fact receive next day a letter addressed to me in Zerstchikov's hand, and more than thirteen hundred roubles belonging to me, which I had left on the roulette table. And so the affair with Zerstchikov ended : this joyful news did much to hasten my recovery, when I regained consciousness.

When Prince Sergay returned from the gambling saloon that night he wrote two letters—one to me, and the other to his old regiment, in which he had behaved so scandalously to Cornet Stepanov. He dispatched both letters next morning. After that, he wrote a report for the authorities, and with that report in his hand he went early in the morning to the officer in command of his regiment and announced to him that he, " a common criminal, who had taken part in the forging of the X—— railway shares, surrendered to justice and asked to be tried." Therewith he handed him the report in which all this was set out in writing. He was arrested.

Here is the letter he wrote to me that night, word for word :

" Precious Arkady Makarovitch,

" Having tried the lackey's way of escape, I have lost the right to comfort my soul a little with the thought that I was able in the end to dare to do what was just and fine. I have sinned against my fatherland and against my family, and for this I, the last of my family, am punishing myself. I don't know how I could have caught at the bare idea of self-preservation, and for a time have dreamed of buying them off with money! I should have still remained to all eternity a criminal in my conscience! Even if those people had given back the notes that compromised me, they would never have been induced to let me alone as long as I lived! What remained? To live with them, to be on a level with them all my life—that was the fate awaiting me! I could not accept it, and have at last found in myself strength enough, or perhaps only despair enough, to act as I am acting now.

" I have written a letter to my old regiment, to my fellow officers, clearing Stepanov's character. This is not and cannot be an atonement: it is only the last will and testament of a man who will be dead to-morrow. That is how one must look at it.

" Forgive me for turning away from you in the gambling saloon; it was because at the moment I was not sure of you. Now that I am a dead man I can make this confession . . . from the other world.

" Poor Liza! she knows nothing of this decision; let her not curse me, but judge of it herself. I cannot defend myself and cannot even find the words to explain anything to her. I must tell you, too, Arkady Makarovitch, that when she came to me yesterday morning for the last time, I confessed that I had deceived her, and owned that I had been to Anna Andreyevna with the intention of making her an offer. I could not, seeing her love, keep this upon my conscience in face of my last determination, and I told her. She forgave me, she forgave everything, but I could not believe her; it is not forgiveness; in her place I could not forgive.

" Remember me a little.

" Your unhappy friend,
" The Last Prince Sokolsky."

I lay unconscious for exactly nine days.

PART III

CHAPTER I

1

Now for something quite different.

I keep declaring : " something different, something different," yet I keep on scribbling of nothing but myself. Yet I have announced a thousand times already that I don't want to describe myself at all, and I firmly meant not to do so when I began my story : I quite understand that I'm not of the slightest interest to the reader. I am describing and want to describe other people, not myself, and if I keep coming in it's only a lamentable mistake, because I can't avoid it, however much I should like to. What I regret most is that I describe my own adventures with such heat ; by doing so I give ground for supposing that I am still the same as I was. The reader will remember, however, that I have exclaimed more than once, " Oh, if one could only change the past and begin all over again ! " I could not have uttered that exclamation if I were not radically changed and had not become an entirely different man now ; that is quite evident. And no one can imagine how sick I am of these apologies and prefaces, which I am continually forced to squeeze into the very middle of my narrative !

To return.

After nine days' unconsciousness I came to myself, regenerated but not reformed ; my regeneration was a stupid one, however, of course, if the word is taken in the wide sense, and perhaps if it had happened now it would have been different. The idea, or rather the feeling, that possessed me was, as it had been a thousand times before, the desire to get away altogether, but this time I meant to go away, not as in the past, when I had so often considered the project and been incapable of carrying it out. I didn't want to revenge myself on anyone, and I give

my word of honour that I did not, though I had been insulted
by all of them. I meant to go away without loathing, without
cursing, and never to return, but I wanted to do this by my
own effort, and by real effort unassisted by any one of them,
or by anyone in the whole world; yet I was almost on the
point of being reconciled with every one! I record this absorbing
dream not as a thought, but as an overwhelming sensation. I
did not care to formulate it as long as I was in bed. Sick and
helpless I lay in Versilov's room, which they had given up to
me; I recognized, with a pang, how abjectly helpless I was.

What was tossing on the bed was not a man but a feeble straw,
and this impotence was not only through illness—and how
degrading I felt it! And so from the very depth of my being,
from all the forces in me, a protest began to rise, and I was
choking with a feeling of infinitely exaggerated pride and defiance.
Indeed, I can't remember any time in my whole life when I was
so full of arrogant feeling as I was during the early days of
my convalescence, that is, while I was tossing like a weak straw
on my bed.

But for the time I held my peace, and even made up my mind
not to think of anything! I kept peeping at their faces, trying
to guess from them all I wanted to know. It was evident that
they too did not want to ask questions or be inquisitive, but
talked of something irrelevant. This pleased me and at the
same time mortified me; I won't attempt to explain the contra-
diction. I did not see Liza so often as my mother, though she
came in to see me every day, and indeed twice a day. From
fragments of their talk and from their whole air I gathered that
Liza had a great deal on her hands and that she was indeed often
absent from home on business of her own: the very fact that
she could have " business of her own " was something like a
grievance to me; but all these were morbid, purely physical,
sensations, which are not worth describing. Tatyana Pavlovna
came, too, almost daily to see me, and though she was by no
means tender with me, she did not abuse me as usual, which
annoyed me extremely—so much so that I said to her openly:
" You know, Tatyana Pavlovna, when you're not scolding you
are very tedious." " Well, then, I won't come and see you,"
she blurted out, and went away. And I was pleased that I had
got rid of one of them, at least.

Most of all I worried my mother; I was irritable with her.
I developed a terrific appetite and grumbled very much that

the meals were late (and they never were late). Mother did not know how to satisfy me. Once she brought some soup, and began, as usual, feeding me with it herself, and I kept grumbling as I ate it. And suddenly I felt vexed that I was grumbling : " She is perhaps the only one I love, and I am tormenting her." But I was none the less ill-humoured, and I suddenly began to cry from ill-humour ; and she, poor darling, thought I was crying from tenderness, stooped down and began kissing me. I restrained myself and endured it, but at that instant I positively hated her. But I always loved my mother, and at that very time I loved her and did not hate her at all, but it happened as it always does—that the one you love best you treat worst.

The only person I hated in those days was the doctor. He was a young man with a conceited air, who talked abruptly and even rudely, as though all these scientific people had only yesterday discovered something special, when in reality nothing special had happened ; but the " mediocrity," the man in the street, is always like that. I restrained myself for a long time, but at last I suddenly broke out and informed him before every one that he was hanging about unnecessarily, that I should get better just as well without him ; that, though he looked like a scientific man, he was filled with nothing but conventional ideas and did not even understand that medicine had never cured anyone ; that, in fact, he was in all probability grossly ill-educated, " like all the specialists who had become so high and mighty among us of late years." The doctor was very much offended (showing by that very fact that he was that sort of person) ; however, he still came as before. I told Versilov at last that if the doctor did not give up coming, that I should say something to him ten times as disagreeable. Versilov only observed that it was impossible to say anything even twice as disagreeable as I had said, let alone ten times. I was pleased at his saying that.

He was a man, though ! I am speaking of Versilov. He, he was the sole cause of it all, and, strange to say, he was the only one towards whom I did not feel resentful. It was not only his manner to me that won me over. I imagine that we felt at that time that we owed each other many explanations . . . and for that very reason it would be our best course never to explain. It's extremely pleasant in such situations to have to do with a man of intelligence : I have mentioned already, in the second part of my story, that he told me briefly and clearly of Prince

Sergay's letter to me about Zerstchikov, about what he, Prince Sergay, had said to the latter, and so on. As I had made up my mind to keep quiet, I only asked him two or three brief questions ; he answered them clearly and exactly but entirely without superfluous words and, what was best of all, without feeling. I was afraid of superfluous feeling at that time.

I said nothing about Lambert, but the reader will readily understand that I thought a great deal about him. In my delirium I spoke more than once about Lambert ; but, recovering from my delirium and looking about me, I quickly reflected that everything about Lambert remained a secret, and that every one, even Versilov, knew nothing about him. Then I was relieved and my fears passed away ; but I was mistaken, as I found out later to my astonishment. He had come to the house during my illness, but Versilov said nothing to me about it, and I concluded that Lambert had lost all trace of me for ever. Nevertheless, I often thought of him ; what is more, I thought of him not only without repulsion, not only with curiosity, but even with sympathy, as though foreseeing from him something new, some means of escape in harmony with my new feelings and plans. In short, I made up my mind to think over Lambert as soon as I should be ready to think over anything. I will note one strange fact : I had entirely forgotten where he lived and in what street it had all happened. The room, Alphonsine, the lap-dog, the corridor, all I remembered, so that I could have sketched them at once ; but where it had all happened—that is, in what street and in what house—I had utterly forgotten. And, what is strangest of all, I only realized this three or four days after I had regained complete consciousness, when I had been occupied with the thought of Lambert for a long time.

These, then, were my first sensations on my resurrection. I have noted only what was most on the surface, and most probably I was not able to detect what was most important. In reality, perhaps, what was really most important was even then taking shape and becoming defined in my heart ; I was not, of course, always vexed and resentful simply at my broth's not being brought me. Oh, I remember how sad I was then and how depressed, especially at moments when I had remained a long while alone. As ill-luck would have it, they soon saw that I was dreary with them and that their sympathy irritated me, and they began more and more often to leave me alone— superfluous delicacy of perception on their part.

2

On the fourth day of consciousness I was lying in my bed at three o'clock in the afternoon, and there was no one with me. It was a bright day, and I knew that at four o'clock, when the sun would set, its slanting red rays would fall on the corner of my wall, and throw a patch of glaring light upon it. I knew that from the days before, and that that would certainly happen in an hour's time, and above all, that I knew of this beforehand, as certainly as twice two make four, exasperated me to fury. I turned round impulsively and suddenly, in the midst of the profound stillness, I clearly distinguished the words : " Lord Jesus Christ, have mercy upon us." The words were pronounced in a half-whisper, and were followed by a deep-drawn sigh, and then everything was still again. I raised my head quickly.

I had before, that is the previous day, and even the day before that, noticed something special in our three rooms downstairs. In the little room beyond the dining-room where mother and Liza were accustomed to sleep, there was evidently now some one else. I had more than once heard sounds, both by day and by night, but only for brief moments, and complete stillness followed immediately and lasted for several hours, so that I took no notice of the sounds. The thought had occurred to me the evening before that Versilov was in there, especially as he soon afterwards came in to me, though I knew for a fact from their conversation that during my illness Versilov had been sleeping out in another lodging. I had known for some time past that mother and Liza had moved into my former " coffin " upstairs (to make it quieter for me, I imagined) and I had even once wondered how the two of them could have possibly fitted themselves into it. And now it suddenly appeared that there was some person living in their old room, and that that person was not Versilov. With an ease which I had not the least expected (for I had till then imagined I was quite helpless) I dropped my feet over the bed, slipped them into slippers, threw on a grey astrachan dressing-gown which lay close at hand (Versilov had sacrificed it for my benefit), and made my way through the parlour to what had been mother's bedroom. What I saw there completely astounded me ; I had never expected anything of the kind, and I stood still in the doorway pertified. There was sitting there a very grey-headed old man, with a big and very white beard, and it was clear that he had been sitting there for a long time. He was not sitting on the bed but on mother's little bench, resting his back against the bed. He held himself so upright, however, that he hardly seemed to need a support for his back, though he was evidently ill. He had over his shirt a short jacket lined with fur. His knees were covered with mother's plaid, and on his feet were slippers. He was, it could be discerned, tall, broad-shouldered, and of a hale appearance, in spite of his invalid state, though he was somewhat thin and looked ill. He had rather a long face and thick but not very long hair; he looked about seventy. On a little table, within reach, lay three or four books and a pair of silver-rimmed spectacles. Though I had not the slightest idea of meeting him, I guessed instantly who he was, though I was still unable to imagine how he could have been sitting all those days, almost beside me, so quietly that till that time I had heard nothing of him.

He did not stir on seeing me, he looked intently at me in silence, just as I did at him, the only difference being that I stared at him with the greatest astonishment, and he looked at me without the slightest. Scrutinizing me, on the contrary, from head to foot during those five or ten seconds of silence, he suddenly smiled and even laughed a gentle noiseless laugh, and though the laugh was soon over, traces of its serene gaiety remained upon his face and above all in his eyes, which were very blue, luminous and large, though they were surrounded by innumerable wrinkles, and the eyelids were swollen and drooping. This laugh of his was what had most effect on me.

I consider that in the majority of cases people are revolting to look at when they are laughing. As a rule something vulgar, something as it were degrading, comes to the surface when a man laughs, though he is almost unconscious of the impression he is making in his mirth, as little in fact as anyone knows what he looks like when he is asleep. One person's face will look intelligent asleep, while another man, intelligent in waking life, will look stupid and ridiculous when he is sleeping. I don't know what this is due to : I only mean to say that people laughing, like people asleep, have no idea what they look like. The vast majority of people don't know how to laugh at all. It is not a matter of knowing how, though : it's a gift and it cannot be cultivated. One can only cultivate it, perhaps, by training oneself to be different, by developing and improving and by struggling against the evil instincts of one's character : then a man's laugh might very likely change for the better. A man will sometimes give himself away completely by his laugh, and you suddenly know him through and through. Even an unmistakably intelligent laugh will sometimes be repulsive. What is most essential in laughter is sincerity, and where is one to find sincerity ? A good laugh must be free from malice, and people are constantly laughing maliciously. A sincere laugh free from malice is gaiety, and where does one find gaiety nowadays ? People don't know how to be gay (Versilov made this observation about gaiety and I remember it). A man's gaiety is what most betrays the whole man from head to foot. Sometimes one will be for a long time unable to read a character, but if the man begins to laugh his whole character will suddenly lie open before you. It is only the loftiest and happiest natures whose gaiety is infectious, that is, good-hearted and irresistible. I am not talking of intellectual development, but of character, of the whole man. And so if you want to see into a man and to understand his soul, don't concentrate your attention on the way he talks or is silent, on his tears, or the emotion he displays over exalted ideas ; you will see through him better when he laughs. If a man has a good laugh, it means that he is a good man. Take note of every shade ; a man's laugh must never, for instance, strike you as stupid, however gay and good-humoured he may be. If you notice the slightest trace of stupidity in his laughter, you may be sure that that man is of limited intelligence, though he is continually dropping ideas wherever he goes. Even if his laugh is not stupid, but the man himself strikes you as being ever so little ridiculous when he laughs, you may be sure that the man is deficient in personal dignity, to some extent anyway. Or if the laughter though infectious, strikes you for some reason as vulgar, you may be sure that that man's nature is vulgar, and all the generous and lofty qualities you have observed in him before are either intentionally assumed or unconsciously borrowed and that the man is certain to deteriorate, to go in for the profitable, and to cast off his noble ideas without regret as the errors and enthusiasm of youth.

I am intentionally introducing here this long tirade on the subject of laughter and am sacrificing the continuity of my story for the sake of it, for I consider it one of the most valuable deductions I have drawn from life, and I particularly recommend it to the attention of girls who are ready to accept the man of their choice, but are still hesitating and watching him mistrustfully, unable to make their final decision ; and don't let them jeer at a wretched raw youth for obtruding his moral reflections on marriage, a subject which he knows nothing about. But I only understand that laughter is the surest test of the heart. Look at a baby—some children know how to laugh to perfection ; a crying baby is disgusting to me, but a laughing, merry one is a sunbeam from paradise, it is a revelation from the future, when man will become at last as pure and simple-hearted as a child. And, indeed, there was something childlike and incredibly attractive in the momentary laughter of this old man. I went up to him at once.

3

" Sit down, sit down a bit, you can scarcely stand on your legs, I dare say," he urged me, motioning me to a seat beside him, and still gazing into my face with the same luminous gaze. I sat down beside him and said :

" I know you, you are Makar Ivanovitch."

" Yes, darling. It's very good that you are up. You are young, it is good for you. The old monk looks towards the grave, but the young must live."

" But are you ill ? "

" Yes, dear, chiefly in my legs ; my feet brought me as far as the door, and here I've sat down and they are swollen. I've had it since last Friday when there were degrees " (*i.e.* when there was a frost) "I used to rub them with ointment you see ; the year before last the doctor, Edmond Karlovitch, prescribed it me in Moscow, and the ointment did good, aye, it did good ; but now it's no use. And my chest, too, is choked up. And since yesterday my spine has been bad, as though dogs were gnawing it. . . . I don't sleep at nights."

" How is it I haven't heard you here at all ? " I broke in. He looked at me as though considering something.

" Only don't wake your mother," he added as though suddenly remembering something. " She has been busy close at hand all night, and as quiet as a mouse ; and now I know she is lying down. Ach, it's bad for a sick monk," he sighed ; " the soul hangs by a thread it seems, yet it still holds on, and still is glad of the light ; and it seems, if all life were to begin over again, the soul would not shrink even from that ; though maybe such a thought is sinful."

" Why sinful ? "

" Such a thought is a dream, and the old monk should take leave with blissful resignation. Again, if one goes to meet death with murmur or repining that is a great sin, but if from the gladness of the spirit one has grown to love life, I fancy God will forgive, even a monk. It's hard for a man to tell of every sin what is sinful and what is not ; therein is mystery passing the mind of man. A monk must be content at all times, and ought to die in the full light of his understanding, in holy peace and blessedness, filled full with days, yearning for his last hour, and rejoicing when he is gathered as the ear of wheat to the sheaf, and has fulfilled his mystery."

" You keep talking of ' mystery ' ; what does it mean ' having fulfilled his mystery ' ? " I asked, and looked round towards the door. I was glad that we were alone, and that all around the stillness was unbroken. The setting sun cast a dazzling light on the window. His talk was rather highflown and rambling, but very sincere ; there was a sort of intense exaltation in it, as though he really were delighted at my coming. But I noticed unmistakable signs that he was feverish, extremely so in fact. I, too, was ill ; I, too, had been in a fever, from the moment I went in to him.

" What is the mystery ? Everything is a mystery, dear ; in all is God's mystery. In every tree, in every blade of grass that same mystery lies hid. Whether the tiny bird of the air is singing, or the stars in all their multitudes shine at night in heaven, the mystery is one, ever the same. And the greatest mystery of all is what awaiteth the soul of man in the world beyond. So it is, dear ! "

" I don't know in what sense you . . . I am not speaking, of course, to tease you, and I assure you I believe in God ; but all these mysteries have long been discovered by human intelligence, or if they have not yet been discovered they will be, for certain, and probably in a very short time. The botanist knows perfectly well how the tree grows. The psychologist and the anatomist know why the bird sings, or soon will know, and as for the stars, they are not only all counted, but all their motions have been calculated with the greatest exactitude, so that they can predict even a thousand years beforehand the very minute of the appearance of some comet . . . and now even the composition of the most remote star is known. You take a microscope, that is a sort of magnifying glass that magnifies a thousand times, and look through it at a drop of water, and you will see in it a whole new world, a whole world of living creatures, yet this, too, was once a mystery, but it has been revealed by science."

"I've heard about that, darling, I have heard folk tell of it more than once. To be sure, it's a great and glorious thing ; all has been vouchsafed to man by God's will ; not for naught did the Lord breathe into him the breath of life ; 'live and learn.' "

"That's a commonplace. You're not antagonistic to science though, not a clerical ? though I don't know whether you'll understand ? "

"No, darling, I did not study science in my youth, and though I am not learned I do not repine at that ; if it's not for me it will be for another. Maybe better so, for every man has his allotted part, for science, dear, is not of use for all. All men are unbridled, each wants to astonish all the world, and I should have perhaps more than all if I had been learned. But now being very un-learned, how can I be puffed up when I know nothing ? You, now, are young and clever, you must study—such is the lot ordained you. Understand all things, that when you meet an infidel or an evil-doer you may be able to answer him, and he may not lead you astray with his frantic words, or confound your unripe thoughts. That glass I saw not so long ago."

He took breath and heaved a sigh. There was no doubt that my coming in was a source of great satisfaction to him. His desire to be communicative was almost morbid. What is more, I am certainly not mistaken in declaring that at moments he looked at me with extraordinary affection ; he laid his hand on mine caressingly, stroked me on the shoulder . . . though there were minutes when I must confess he seemed to forget all about me, as though he had been sitting alone, and though he went on talking warmly, it seemed at times as though he were talking to the air.

"In the Gennadiev desert, dear, there lives a man of great understanding. He is of noble birth, and by rank a major, and he has great possessions. When he lived in the world he would not be bound by marriage ; he has been withdrawn from the world for nearly ten years, loving still and silent resting-places, and keeping his heart free from worldly vanities. He follows all the monastic rules, but will not become a monk.

and he has so many books, dear, as I have never seen in any other
man's possession ; he told me himself that his books were worth
eight thousand roubles. His name is Pyotr Valerianitch. He
has taught me a great deal at different times, and I loved listening to him exceedingly. I said to him once : ' How is it, sir,
that with your great understanding, after living here ten years
in monastic obedience, and in complete renunciation of your will,
how is it you don't take honourable vows, so as to be still more
perfect,' and he said to me thereupon, " You talk of my understanding, old man, but perhaps my understanding has held me in bondage
and I have not kept it in submission. And you speak of my
obedience ; maybe I've long since lost the right measure for myself. And you talk of the renunciation of my will ; I am ready to
be deprived of my money on the spot and to give up my rank and to
lay all my medals and ribbons on the table, but my pipe of tobacco,
though I've been struggling for ten years, I can't do without.
What sort of a monk should I be, and how could you glorify the
renunciation of my will ? ' And I marvelled then at this humility.
Well, last year, about St. Peter's day, I went again to that desert
—the Lord led me there—and I saw standing in his cell that very
thing, a microscope ; he had ordered it for a great sum of money
from abroad. ' Stay,' said he, ' old man, I'll show you a marvellous thing you have never hitherto looked upon ; you see a drop
of water as pure as a tear ; well, look what is in it and you will
see that the mechanicians will soon seek out all the mysteries
of God and not leave one for either you or me ! ' That is what
he said, I remember. But I had looked through such a microscope thirty-five years before that, at Alexandr Vladimirovitch
Malgasov's, who was our old master, Andrey Petrovitch's maternal
uncle. It was from him the property came on his death to Andrey
Petrovitch. He was a grand gentleman, a great general, and he
used to keep a pack of hounds, and I lived many years with
him as huntsman ; so he, too, set up this microscope ; he
brought it with him, and he told all the servants to come up
one after another, male and female, and look through ; he showed
them a flea and a louse and the end of a needle, and a hair and a
drop of water. And it was diverting, they were afraid to go up
and afraid of the master—he was hasty. Some did not know how
to look properly, and the elder saw nothing ; others were frightened
and cried out ; the elder Savin Makarov covered his eyes with
both hands and cried, ' Do what you will with me, I won't go
near ! ' There was much foolish laughter. I didn't confess to

z

Pyotr Valerianitch, though, that I had seen this marvel before more than thirty-five years ago, because I saw it was a great pleasure to him showing it ; I began, on the contrary, admiring it and marvelling. He waited a bit and asked, 'Well, old man, what do you say now ? ' And I lifted myself up and said to him, ' The Lord said, Let there be light and there was light,' and thereupon he said to me all at once, 'And was there not darkness ? ' And he said that so strangely, he did not even laugh. I wondered at him then, and he seemed to be angered and said no more."

" The fact of the matter is your Pyotr Valerianitch is eating rice and raisins in the monastery, and bowing to the ground, while he does not believe in God, and you hit on the wrong moment, that's all," I said. " And what's more, he is rather an absurd person : I suppose he must have seen that microscope a dozen times before, why should he go off his head when he saw it for the thirteenth ? What nervous susceptibility . . . he must have got that from living in a monastery."

" He was a man of pure life and lofty mind," the old man pronounced impressively, " and he was not an infidel. There was a cloud over his mind and his heart was not at peace. Very many such men have come nowadays from the ranks of the gentry and learned. And something more I will tell you, a man punishes himself. But you watch them and do not worry them, and before you lie down to sleep at night remember them in your prayers, for such are seeking God. Do you pray at night ? "

" No, I regard it as an empty ceremony. I must own, though, that I like your Pyotr Valerianitch. He's not a man of straw, anyway, but a real person, rather like a man very near and well-known to us both."

The old man only paid attention to the first part of my answer.

" You're wrong, my dear, not to pray ; it is a good thing, it cheers the heart before sleep, and rising up from sleep and awakening in the night. Let me tell you this. In the summer in July we were hastening to the monastery of Our Lady for the holy festival. The nearer we got to the place the greater the crowd of people, and at last there were almost two hundred of us gathered together, all hastening to kiss the holy and miraculous relics of the two great saints, Aniky and Grigory. We spent the night, brother, in the open country, and I waked up early in the morning when all was still sleeping and the dear sun had not yet peeped out from behind the forest. I lifted up my head, dear,

I gazed about me and sighed. Everywhere beauty passing all utterance ! All was still, the air was light ; the grass grows— Grow, grass of God, the bird sings—Sing, bird of God, the babe cries in the woman's arms—God be with you, little man ; grow and be happy, little babe ! And it seemed that only then for the first time in my life I took it all in. . . . I lay down again, I slept so sweetly. Life is sweet, dear ! If I were better, I should like to go out again in the spring. And that it's a mystery makes it only the better ; it fills the heart with awe and wonder ; and that awe maketh glad the heart : ' All is in Thee my Lord, and I, too, am in Thee ; have me in Thy keeping.' Do not repine, young man ; it is even more beautiful because it is a mystery," he added fervently.

"It's the more beautiful for being a mystery. . . . I will remember those words. You express yourself very inaccurately, but I understand you. . . . It strikes me that you understand and know a great deal more than you can express ; only you seem to be in delirium." . . . I added abruptly, looking at his feverish eyes and pale face. But he did not seem to hear my words.

"Do you know, dear young man," he began again, as though going on with what he had been saying before : " Do you know there is a limit to the memory of a man on this earth ? The memory of a man is limited to a hundred years. For a hundred years after his death his children or his grandchildren who have seen his face can still remember him, but after that though his memory may still remain, it is only by hearsay, in thought, for all who have seen his living face have gone before. And his grave in the churchyard is overgrown with grass, the stones upon it crumble away, and all men, and even his children's children, forget him ; afterwards they forget even his name, for only a few are kept in the memory of men—and so be it ! You may forget me, dear ones, but I love you from the tomb. I hear, my children, your gay voices ; I hear your steps on the graves of your kin : live for a while in the sunshine, rejoice and I will pray to God for you, I will come to you in your dreams . . . it is all the same—even in death is love ! . . . ."

I was myself in the same feverish state as he was ; instead of going away or persuading him to be quiet, or perhaps putting him to bed, for he seemed quite delirious, I suddenly seized his arm and bending down to him and squeezing his hand, I said in an excited whisper, with inward tears :

"I am glad of you. I have been waiting a long time for you, perhaps. I don't like any of them ; there is no ' seemliness ' in them . . . I won't follow them, I don't know where I'm going, I'll go with you." . . . But luckily mother suddenly came in, or I don't know how it would have ended. She came in only just awake and looking agitated ; in her hand she had a table-spoon and a glass ; seeing us she exclaimed :

"I knew it would be so ! I am late with his quinine and he's all in a fever ! I overslept myself, Makar Ivanovitch, darling ! "

I got up and went out. She gave him his quinine and put him to bed. I, too, lay down on mine in a state of great excite-ment. I tossed about pondering on this meeting with intense interest and curiosity. What I expected from it I don't know. Of course, my reasoning was disconnected, and not thoughts but fragments of thoughts flitted through my brain. I lay with my face to the wall, and suddenly I saw in the corner the patch of glowing light which I had been looking forward to with such curses, and now I remember my whole soul seemed to be leaping for joy, and a new light seemed penetrating to my heart. I remember that sweet moment and I do not want to forget it. It was only an instant of new hope and new strength. . . . I was convalescent then, and therefore such transports may have been the inevitable result of the state of my nerves ; but I have faith even now in that bright hope—that is what I wanted to record and to recall. Of course, even then I knew quite well that I should not go on a pilgrimage with Makar Ivanovitch, and that I did not know the nature of the new impulse that had taken hold of me, but I had pronounced one word, though in delirium, "There is no seemliness in their lives ! "   "Of course," I thought in a frenzy, "from this minute I am seeking ' seemliness,' and they have none of it, and that is why I am leaving them."

There was a rustle behind me, I turned round : mother stood there bending down to me and looking with timid inquiry into my face. I took her hand.

"Why did you tell me nothing about our dear guest, mother ? " I asked suddenly, not knowing I was going to say it. All the uneasiness vanished from her face at once, and there was a flush as it were of joy, but she made me no reply except the words :

"Liza, don't forget Liza, either ; you've forgotten Liza."

She said this in a hurried murmur, flushing crimson, and would have made haste to get away, for above all things she hated displaying her feelings, and in that she was like me, that is reverent and delicate ; of course, too, she would not care to begin on the subject of Makar Ivanovitch with me ; what we could say to each other with our eyes was quite enough. But though I hated demonstrativeness, I still kept her by her hand ; I looked tenderly into her eyes, and laughed softly and tenderly, and with my other hand stroked her dear face, her hollow cheeks. She bent down and pressed her forehead to mine.

" Well, Christ be with you," she said suddenly, standing up, beaming all over : " get well, I shall count on your doing so. He is ill, very ill. Life is in God's hands. . . . Ach, what have I said, oh that could not be ! . . ."

She went away. All her life, in fear and trembling and reverence, she had honoured her legal husband, the monk, Makar Ivanovitch, who with large-hearted generosity had forgiven her once and for ever.

CHAPTER II

1

I HAD not ' forgotten ' Liza ; mother was mistaken. The keensighted mother saw that there was something like coolness between brother and sister, but it was rather jealousy than lack of love. In view of what followed, I will explain in a couple of words. Ever since Prince Sergay's arrest, poor Liza had shown a sort of conceited pride, an unapproachable haughtiness, almost unendurable ; but every one in the house knew the truth and understood how she was suffering, and if at first I scowled and was sulky at her manner with us, it was simply owing to my petty irritability, increased tenfold by illness—that is how I explain it now. I had not ceased to love Liza ; on the contrary, I loved her more than ever, only I did not want to be the first to make advances, though I understood that nothing would have induced her either to make the first advances.

As soon as all the facts came out about Prince Sergay, that is, immediately after his arrest, Liza made haste at once to take up an attitude to us, and to every one else, that would not admit of the possibility of sympathy or any sort of consolation and excuses for Prince Sergay. On the contrary, she seemed continually priding herself on her luckless lover's action as though it were the loftiest heroism, though she tried to avoid all discussion of the subject. She seemed every moment to be telling us all (though I repeat that she did not utter a word), ' None of you would do the same—you would not give yourself up at the dictates of honour and duty, none of you have such a pure and delicate conscience ! And as for his misdeeds, who has not evil actions upon his conscience ? Only every one conceals them, and this man preferred facing ruin to remaining ignoble in his own eyes.' This seemed to be expressed by every gesture Liza made. I don't know, but I think in her place I should have behaved almost in the same way. I don't know either whether those were the thoughts in her heart, in fact I privately suspect that they were not. With the other, clear part of her reason, she must have seen through the insignificance of her ' hero,' for who will not agree now that that unhappy man, noble-hearted in his own way as he was, was at the same time an absolutely insignificant person ? This very haughtiness and as it were antagonism towards us all, this constant suspiciousness that we were thinking differently of him, made one surmise that in the secret recesses of her heart a very different judgment of her unhappy friend had perhaps been formed. But I hasten to add, however, that in my eyes she was at least half right ; it was more pardonable for her than for any of us to hesitate in drawing the final conclusion. I will admit with my whole heart that even now, when all is over, I don't know at all how to judge the unhappy man who was such a problem to us all.

Home was beginning to be almost a little hell on account of her. Liza whose love was so intense was bound to suffer terribly. It was characteristic of her to prefer to suffer in silence. Her character was like mine, proud and domineering, and I thought then, and I think now that it was that that made her love Prince Sergay, just because he had no will at all, and that from the first word, from the first hour, he was utterly in subjection to her. This comes about of itself, in the heart, without any preliminary calculation ; but such a love, the love of the strong woman for the weak man, is sometimes incomparably more intense and more agonizing than the love of equal characters, because the stronger unconsciously undertakes responsibility for the weaker. That is what I think at any rate.

All the family from the first surrounded her with the tenderest care, especially mother ; but Liza was not softened, she did not respond to sympathy, and seemed to repulse every sort of help. At first she did talk to mother, but every day she became more

reluctant to speak, more abrupt and even more harsh. She
asked Versilov's advice at first, but soon afterwards she chose
Vassin for her counsellor and helper, as I learned afterwards
with surprise. . . .

She went to see Vassin every day ; she went to the law courts,
too, by Prince Sergay's instructions ; she went to the lawyers, to
the crown prosecutor ; she came in the end to being absent from
home for whole days together. Twice a day, of course, she
visited Prince Sergay, who was in prison, in the division for
noblemen, but these interviews, as I was fully convinced later,
were very distressing to Liza. Of course no third person can
judge of the relations of two lovers. But I know that Prince
Sergay was always wounding her deeply, and by what do you
suppose ? Strange to say, by his continual jealousy. Of that,
however, I will speak later ; but I will add one thought on the
subject : it would be hard to decide which of them tormented
the other more. Though with us she prided herself on her hero,
Liza perhaps behaved quite differently alone with him ; I
suspect so indeed from various facts, of which, however, I will
also speak later.

And so, as regards my feeling and my attitude towards Liza,
any external change there was was only simulated, a jealous
deception on both sides, but we had never loved each other
more than at that time. I must add, too, that though Liza
showed surprise and interest when Makar Ivanovitch first
arrived, she had since for some reason begun to treat him almost
disdainfully, even contemptuously. She seemed intentionally
to take not the slightest notice of him.

Having inwardly vowed " to be silent," as I explained in the
previous chapter, I expected, of course theoretically, that is in
my dreams, to keep my word. Oh, with Versilov, for instance, I
would have sooner begun talking of zoology or of the Roman
Emperors, than of *her* for example, or of that most important
line in his letter to her, in which he informed her that ' the document was not burnt but in existence '—a line on which I began
pondering to myself again as soon as I had begun to recover
and come to my senses after my fever. But alas ! from the
first steps towards practice, and almost before the first steps,
I realized how difficult and impossible it was to stick to
such resolutions : the day after my first acquaintance with
Makar Ivanovitch, I was fearfully excited by an unexpected
circumstance.

2

I was excited by an unexpected visit from Darya Onisimovna, the mother of the dead girl, Olya. From my mother I had heard that she had come once or twice during my illness, and that she was very much concerned about my condition. Whether "that good woman," as my mother always called her when she spoke of her, had come entirely on my account, or whether she had come to visit my mother in accordance with an established custom, I did not ask. Mother usually told me all the news of the household to entertain me when she came with my soup to feed me (before I could feed myself) : I always tried to appear uninterested in these domestic details, and so I did not ask about Darya Onisimovna; in fact, I said nothing about her at all.

It was about eleven o'clock; I was just meaning to get out of bed and install myself in the armchair by the table, when she came in. I purposely remained in bed. Mother was very busy upstairs and did not come down, so that we were left alone. She sat down on a chair by the wall facing me, smiled and said not a word. I foresaw this pause, and her entrance altogether made an irritating impression on me. Without even nodding to her, I looked her straight in the face, but she too looked straight at me.

" Are you dull in your flat now the prince has gone ? " I asked, suddenly losing patience.

" No, I am not in that flat now. Through Anna Andreyevna I am looking after his honour's baby now."

" Whose baby ? "

" Andrey Petrovitch's," she brought out in a confidential whisper, glancing round towards the door.

" Why, but there's Tatyana Pavlovna. . . ."

" Yes, Tatyana Pavlovna, and Anna Andreyevna, both of them, and Lizaveta Makarovna also, and your mamma . . . all of them. They all take an interest; Tatyana Pavlovna and Anna Andreyevna are great friends now."

A piece of news ! She grew much livelier as she talked. I looked at her with hatred.

" You are much livelier than when you came to see me last."

" Oh, yes."

" I think, you've grown stouter ? "

She looked strangely at me :

" I have grown very fond of her, very."

" Fond of whom ? "

" Why, Anna Andreyevna. Very fond. Such a noble young lady, and with such judgment. . . ."

" You don't say so ! What about her, how are things now ? "

" She is very quiet, very."

" She was always quiet."

" Always."

" If you've come here with scandal," I cried suddenly, unable to restrain myself, " let me tell you that I won't have anything to do with it, I have decided to drop . . . everything, every one. . . . I don't care—I am going away ! . . ."

I ceased suddenly, for I realized what I was doing. I felt it degrading to explain my new projects to her. She heard me without surprise and without emotion. But again a pause followed, again she got up, went to the door and peeped into the next room. Having assured herself that there was no one there, and we were alone, she returned with great composure and sat down in the same place as before.

" You did that prettily ! " I laughed suddenly.

" You are keeping on your lodging at the clerk's ? " she asked suddenly, bending a little towards me, and dropping her voice as though this question were the chief object for which she had come.

" Lodging ? I don't know. Perhaps I shall give it up. . . How do I know ? "

" They are anxiously expecting you : the man's very impatient to see you, and his wife too. Andrey Petrovitch assured them you'd come back for certain."

" But what is it to you ? "

" Anna Andreyevna wanted to know, too ; she was very glad to learn that you were staying."

" How does she know so positively that I shall certainly stay on at that lodging ? "

I wanted to add, " And what is it to her," but I refrained from asking through pride.

" And M. Lambert said the same thing, too."

" Wha-at ? "

" M. Lambert, he declared most positively to Andrey Petrovitch that you would remain, and he assured Anna Andreyevna of it, too."

I felt shaken all over. What marvels! Then Lambert already knew Versilov, Lambert had found his way to Versilov—Lambert and Anna Andreyevna—he had found his way to her too! I felt overcome with fever, but I kept silent. My soul was flooded with a terrible rush of pride, pride or I don't know what. But I suddenly said to myself at that moment, "If I ask for one word in explanation, I shall be involved in that world again, and I shall never have done with it." There was a glow of hate in my heart. I resolutely made up my mind to be mute, and to lie without moving; she was silent too, for a full minute.

"What of Prince Nikolay Ivanovitch?" I asked suddenly, as though I had taken leave of my senses. The fact is, I asked simply to change the subject, and again I chanced to ask the leading question; like a madman I plunged back again into that world from which I had just before, with such a shudder, resolved to flee.

"His honour is at Tsarskoe Syelo. He is rather poorly; and as the hot days have begun in town, they all advised him to move to their house at Tsarskoe for the sake of the air."

I made no answer.

"Madame and Anna Andreyevna visit him there twice a week, they go together."

Anna Andreyevna and Madame (that is *she*) were friends then! They go together! I did not speak.

"They have become so friendly, and Anna Andreyevna speaks so highly of Katerina Nikolaevna. . . ."

I still remained silent.

"And Katerina Nikolaevna is in a whirl of society again; it's one fête after another; she is making quite a stir; they say all the gentlemen at court are in love with her . . . and everything's over with M. Büring, and there's to be no wedding; so everybody declares . . . it's been off ever since *then*."

That is since Versilov's letter. I trembled all over, but I did not utter a word.

"Anna Andreyevna is so sorry about Prince Sergay, and Katerina Nikolaevna too, and they all say that he will be acquitted and that Stebelkov will be condemned. . . ."

I looked at her with hatred. She got up and suddenly bent down to me.

"Anna Andreyevna particularly told me to find out how you are," she said quite in a whisper; "and she particularly begged you to go and see her as soon as you begin to go out ; good-bye. Make haste and get well and I'll tell her. . . ."

She went away. I sat on the edge of the bed, a cold sweat came out on my forehead, but I did not feel terror : the incredible and grotesque news about Lambert and his machinations did not, for instance, fill me with horror in the least, as might have been expected from the dread, perhaps unaccountable, with which during my illness and the early days of my convalescence I recalled my meeting with him on that night. On the contrary, in that first moment of confusion, as I sat on the bed after Darya Onisimovna had gone, my mind did not dwell on Lambert, but . . . more than all I thought about the news of *her*, of her rupture with Büring, and of her success in society, of her fêtes, of her triumphs, of the "stir" she was making. "She's making quite a stir," Darya Onisimovna's phrase, was ringing in my ears. And I suddenly felt that I had not the strength to struggle out of that whirlpool ; I had known how to control myself, to hold my tongue and not to question Darya Onisimovna after her tales of marvels ! An overwhelming thirst for that life, for *their* life, took possession of my whole spirit and . . . and another blissful thirst which I felt as a keen joy and an intense pain. My thoughts were in a whirl ; but I let them whirl. . . . "Why be reasonable," I felt. "Even mother kept Lambert's coming a secret," I thought, in incoherent snatches. "Versilov must have told her not to speak of it. . . . I would rather die than ask Versilov about Lambert ! "

"Versilov," the thought flashed upon me again. "Versilov and Lambert. Oh, what a lot that's new among them ! Bravo, Versilov ! He frightened the German Büring with that letter ; he libelled her, *la calomnie . . . il en reste tonjours quelque chose*, and the German courtier was afraid of the scandal. Ha ! ha ! it's a lesson for her."

"Lambert . . . surely Lambert hasn't found his way to her ? To be sure he has ! Why shouldn't she have an intrigue with him ? "

At this point I suddenly gave up pondering on this senseless tangle, and sank back in despair with my head on my pillow. "But it shall not be," I exclaimed with sudden determination. I jumped out of bed, put on my slippers and dressing-gown, and went straight to Makar Ivanovitch's room, as though there were in it a talisman to repel all enticements, a means of salvation, and an anchor to which I could cling.

It may really have been that I was feeling this at the time with my whole soul; else why should I have leaped up with such a sudden and irresistible impulse and rushed in to Makar Ivanovitch in such a state of mind ?

3

But to my surprise I found other people—my mother and the doctor—with Makar Ivanovitch. As I had for some reason imagined I should find the old man alone, as he had been yesterday, I stopped short in the doorway in blank amazement. Before I had time to frown, Versilov came in followed by Liza. . . . So they had all met for some reason in Makar Ivanovitch's room " just when they were not wanted ! "

" I have come to ask how you are," I said, going straight up to Makar Ivanovitch .

"Thank you, my dear, I was expecting you ; I knew you would come ; I was thinking of you in the night."

He looked into my face caressingly, and I saw that perhaps he liked me best of them all, but I could not help seeing instantly that, though his face was cheerful, his illness had made progress in the night. The doctor had only just been examining him very seriously. I learned afterwards that the doctor (the same young man with whom I had quarrelled had been treating Makar Ivanovitch ever since he arrived) had been very attentive to the patient and had diagnosed a complication of various diseases in him—but I don't know their medical terms. Makar Ivanovitch, as I observed from the first glance, was on the warmest, friendliest terms with him ; I disliked that at that instant ; but I was of course in a very bad mood at the moment.

" Yes, Alexandr Semyonovitch, how is our dear invalid today," inquired Versilov. If I had not been so agitated, it would have been most interesting to me to watch Versilov's attitude to this old man ; I had wondered about it the day before. What struck me most of all now was the extremely soft and pleasant expression in Versilov's face, there was something perfectly sincere in it. I have noted already, I believe, that Versilov's face became wonderfully beautiful as soon as it became ever so little kindly.

" Why, we keep quarrelling," answered the doctor.

" With Makar Ivanovitch ? I don't believe it ; it's impossible to quarrel with him."

" But he won't obey ; he doesn't sleep at night. . . ."

" Come give over, Alexandr Semyonovitch, that's enough scolding," said Makar Ivanovitch laughing. " Well, Andrey Petrovitch, how have they treated our good lady ? Here she's been sighing and moaning all the morning, she's worrying," he added, indicating mother.

" Ach, Andrey Petrovitch," cried my mother, who was really very uneasy ; "do make haste and tell us, don't keep us in suspense ; how has it been settled for her, poor thing ? "

" They have found her guilty and sentenced her ! "

" Ach ! " cried my mother.

" But not to Siberia, don't distress yourself—to a fine of fifteen roubles, that's all ; it was a farce ! "

He sat down, the doctor sat down too ; they were talking of Tatyana Pavlovna ; I knew nothing yet of what had happened. I sat down on Makar Ivanovitch's left, and Liza sat opposite me on the right ; she evidently had some special sorrow of her own to-day, with which she had come to my mother ; there was a look of uneasiness and irritation in her face. At that moment we exchanged glances, and I thought to myself, " we are both disgraced, and I must make the first advances." My heart was suddenly softened to her. Versilov meanwhile had begun describing what had happened that morning.

It seemed that Tatyana Pavlovna had had to appear before the justice of the peace that morning, on a charge brought against her by her cook. The whole affair was utterly absurd ; I have mentioned already that the ill-tempered cook would sometimes, when she was sulky, refuse to speak, and would not say a word to her mistress for a whole week at a time. I mentioned, too, Tatyana's weakness in regard to her, how she put up with anything from her and absolutely refused to get rid of her. All these whimsical caprices of old maiden ladies are, in my eyes, utterly beneath contempt and so undeserving of attention. And I only mention this story here because this cook is destined to play a leading and momentous part in the sequel of my story.

So Tatyana Pavlovna, driven out of all patience by the obstinate Finnish woman, who had refused to answer a word for several days, had suddenly at last struck her, a thing she had never done before. Even then the cook did not utter the slightest sound, but the same day she communicated the fact to a discharged midshipman called Osyetrov, who earned a precarious existence by undertaking cases of various sorts and of course, by getting up such cases as this for the courts. It had ended in Tatyana Pavlovna's being summoned before the justice of the peace, and when the case was tried Versilov had for some reason appeared as a witness.

Versilov described all this with extraordinary gaiety and humour, so that even mother laughed; he even mimicked Tatyana Pavlovna and the midshipman and the cook. The cook had from the very beginning [announced to the court that she wanted a money fine, "For if they put my mistress in prison, whom am I going to cook for?" In answer to the judge, Tatyana Pavlovna answered with immense condescension, not even deigning to defend herself; on the contrary, she had concluded with the words, "I did beat her and I shall do it again," whereupon she was promptly fined three roubles for her impudent answer. The midshipman, a lean lanky young man, would have begun with a long speech in defence of his client, but broke down disgracefully to the amusement of the whole court.

The hearing was soon over, and Tatyana Pavlovna was condemned to pay fifteen roubles to the injured Marya.

Tatyana Pavlovna promptly drew out her purse, and proceeded on the spot to pay the money, whereupon the midshipman at once approached her, and was putting out his hand to take it, but Tatyana Pavlovna thrust aside his hand, almost with a blow, and turned to Marya. "Don't you trouble, madam, you needn't put yourself out, put it down in our accounts, I'll settle with this fellow." "See, Marya, what a lanky fellow you've picked out for yourself," said Tatyana Pavlovna, pointing to the midshipman, hugely delighted that Marya had spoken to her at last.

"He is a lanky one to be sure," Marya answered slily. "Did you order cutlets with peas? I did not hear this morning, I was in a hurry to get here." "Oh no, with cabbage, Marya, and please don't burn it to a cinder, as you did yesterday." "No, I'll do my best to-day, madam, let me have your hand," and she kissed her mistress's hand in token of reconciliation; she entertained the whole court in fact.

"Ah, what a woman!" said mother, shaking her head, very much pleased with the news and Andrey Petrovitch's account of it, though she looked uneasily on the sly at Liza.

" She has been a self-willed lady from her childhood," smiled Makar Ivanovitch.

" Spleen and idleness," opined the doctor.

" Is it I am self-willed ? Is it I am spleen and idleness ? " asked Tatyana Pavlovna, coming in upon us suddenly, evidently very well pleased with' herself. " It's not for you to talk nonsense, Alexandr Semyonovitch ; when you were ten years old, you knew whether I was idle, and you've been treating yourself for spleen for the last year and have not been able to cure yourself, so you ought to be ashamed ; well, you've picked me to pieces enough ; thanks for troubling to come to the court, Andrey Petrovitch. Well, how are you, Makarushka ; it's only you I've come to see, not this fellow," she pointed to me, but at once gave me a friendly pat on the shoulder ; I had never before seen her in such a good humour. " Well, how is he ? " turning suddenly to the doctor and frowning anxiously.

" Why, he won't lie in bed, and he only tires himself out sitting up like this."

" Why, I only sit up like this a little, with company," Makar Ivanovitch murmured with a face of entreaty, like a child's.

" Yes, we like this, we like this ; we like a little gossip when our friends gather round us ; I know Makarushka," said Tatyana Pavlovna.

" Yes you're a quick one, you are ! And there's no getting over you ; wait a bit, let me speak : I'll lie down, darling, I'll obey, but you know, to my thinking, ' If you take to your bed, you may never get up,' that's what I've got at the back of my head, friend."

" To be sure I knew that was it, peasant superstitions : ' If I take to my bed,' they say, ' ten to one I shan't get up,' that's what the peasants very often fear, and they would rather keep on their legs when they're ill than go to a hospital. As for you, Makar Ivanovitch, you're simply home-sick for freedom, and the open road—that's all that's the matter with you, you've got out of the habit of staying long in one place. Why, you're what's called a pilgrim, aren't you ? And tramping is almost a passion in our peasantry. I've noticed it more than once in them, our peasants are tramps before everything."

" Then Makar is a tramp according to you ? " Tatyana Pavlovna caught him up.

" Oh, I did not mean that, I used the word in a general sense. Well yes, a religious tramp, though he is a holy man, yet he is a tramp. In a good respectful sense, but a tramp . . . . I speak from the medical point of view. . . ."

"I assure you," I addressed the doctor suddenly : "that you and I and all the rest here are more like tramps than this old man from whom you and I ought to learn, too, because he has a firm footing in life, while we all of us have no firm standpoint at all. . . . But how should you understand that, though ! "

I spoke very cuttingly, it seemed, but I had come in feeling upset. I don't know why I went on sitting there, and felt as though I were beside myself.

"What are you saying ? " said Tatyana Pavlovna, looking at me suspiciously. "How did you find him, Makar Ivanovitch ? " she asked, pointing her finger at me.

"God bless him, he's a sharp one," said the old man, with a serious air, but at the words "sharp one " almost every one laughed. I controlled myself somehow ; the doctor laughed more than anyone. It was rather unlucky that I did not know at the time of a previous compact between them. Versilov, the doctor, and Tatyana Pavlovna had agreed three days before to do all they could to distract mother from brooding and apprehension on account of Makar Ivanovitch, whose illness was far more dangerous and hopeless than I had any suspicion of then. That's why they were all making jokes, and trying to laugh. Only the doctor was stupid, and did not know how to make jokes naturally : that was the cause of all that followed. If I had known of their agreement at that time, I should not have done what I did. Liza knew nothing either.

I sat listening with half my mind ; they talked and laughed and all the time my head was full of Darya Onisimovna, and her news, and I could not shake off the thought of her ; I kept picturing how she had sat and looked, and had cautiously got up, and peeped into the next room. At last they all suddenly laughed. Tatyana Pavlovna, I don't in the least know why, called the doctor an infidel : "Why, all you doctors are infidels ! "

"Makar Ivanovitch ! " said the doctor, very stupidly pretending to be offended and to be appealing to him as an umpire, " am I an infidel ? "

"You an infidel ? No you are not an infidel," the old man answered sedately, looking at him instantly. "No, thank God ! " he said, shaking his head : "you are a merry-hearted man."

"And if a man's merry-hearted, he's not an infidel ? " the doctor observed ironically.

"That's in its own way an idea," observed Versilov ; he was not laughing, however.

"It's a great idea," I could not help exclaiming, struck by the thought.

The doctor looked round inquiringly.

"These learned people, these same professors " (probably they had been talking about professors just before), began Makar Ivanovitch, looking down : " at the beginning, ough, I was frightened of them. I was in terror in their presence, for I dreaded an infidel more than anything. I have only one soul, I used to think ; what if I lose it, I shan't be able to find another ; but, afterwards, I plucked up heart. ' After all,' I thought, ' they are not gods but just the same as we are, men of like passions with ourselves.' And my curiosity was great. ' I shall find out,' I thought, ' what this infidelity is like.' But afterwards even that curiosity passed over."

He paused, though he meant to go on, still with the same gentle sedate smile. There are simple souls who put complete trust in every one, and have no suspicion of mockery. Such people are always of limited intelligence, for they are always ready to display all that is precious in their hearts to every newcomer. But in Makar Ivanovitch I fancied there was something else, and the impulse that led him to speak was different, and not only the innocence of simplicity : one caught glimpses as it were of the missionary in him. I even caught, with pleasure, some sly glances he bent upon the doctor, and even perhaps on Versilov. The conversation was evidently a continuation of a previous discussion between them the week before, but unluckily the fatal phrase which had so electrified me the day before cropped up in it again, and led me to an outburst which I regret to this day.

"I am afraid of the unbeliever, even now perhaps," the old man went on with concentrated intensity ; "only, friend Alexandr Semyonovitch, I tell you what, I've never met an infidel, but I have met worldly men ; that's what one must call them. They are of all sorts, big and little, ignorant and learned, and even some of the humblest class, but it's all vanity. They read and argue all their lives, filling themselves with the sweetness of books, while they remain in perplexity and can come to no conclusion. Some quite let themselves go, and give up

2 A

taking notice of themselves. Some grow harder than a stone and their hearts are full of wandering dreams ; others become heartless and frivolous, and all they can do is to mock and jeer. Another will, out of books, gather some flowers, and those according to his own fancy ; but he still is full of vanity, and there is no decision in him. And then again : there is a great deal of dreariness. The small man is in want, he has no bread and naught to keep his babes alive with, he sleeps on rough straw, and all the time his heart is light and merry ; he is coarse and sinful, yet his heart is light. But the great man drinks too much, and eats too much, and sits on a pile of gold, yet there is nothing in his heart but gloom. Some have been through all the sciences, and are still depressed, and I fancy that the more intellect a man has, the greater his dreariness. And then again : they have been teaching ever since the world began, and to what good purpose have they taught, that the world might be fairer and merrier, and the abode of every sort of joy ? And another thing I must tell you : they have no seemliness, they don't even want it at all ; all are ruined, but they boast of their own destruction ; but to return to the one Truth, they never think ; and to live without God is naught but torment. And it seems that we curse that whereby we are enlightened and know it not ourselves : and what's the sense of it ? It's impossible to be a man and not bow down to something ; such a man could not bear the burden of himself, nor could there be such a man. If he rejects God, then he bows down to an idol—fashioned of wood, or of gold, or of thought. They are all idolaters and not infidels, that is how we ought to describe them—though we can't say there are no infidels. There are men who are down-right infidels, only they are far more terrible than those others, for they come with God's name on their lips. I have heard of them more than once, but I have not met them at all. There are such, friend, and I fancy, too, that there are bound to be."

"There are, Makar Ivanovitch," Versilov agreed suddenly : " there are such, ' and there are bound to be.' "

"There certainly are, and 'there are certainly bound to be,' " I burst out hotly, and impulsively, I don't know why ; but I was carried away by Versilov's tone, and fascinated by a sort of idea in the words " there are bound to be." The conversation was an absolute surprise to me. But at that minute something happened also quite unexpected.

4

It was a very bright day; by the doctor's orders Makar Ivanovitch's blind was as a rule not drawn up all day; but there was a curtain over the window now, instead of the blind, so that the upper part of the window was not covered; this was because the old man was miserable at not seeing the sun at all when he had the blind, and as we were sitting there the sun's rays fell suddenly full upon Makar Ivanovitch's face. At first, absorbed in conversation, he took no notice of it, but mechanically as he talked he several times turned his head on one side, because the bright sunlight hurt and irritated his bad eyes. Mother, standing beside him, glanced several times uneasily towards the window; all that was wanted was to screen the window completely with something, but to avoid interrupting the conversation she thought it better to try and move the bench on which Makar Ivanovitch was sitting a little to the right. It did not need to be moved more than six or at the most eight inches. She had bent down several times and taken hold of the bench, but could not move it; the bench with Makar Ivanovitch sitting on it would not move. Feeling her efforts unconsciously, in the heat of conversation, Makar Ivanovitch several times tried to get up, but his legs would not obey him. But mother went on straining all her strength to move it, and at last all this exasperated Liza horribly. I noticed several angry irritated looks from her, but for the first moment I did not know to what to ascribe them, besides I was carried away by the conversation. And I suddenly heard her almost shout sharply to Makar Ivanovitch :

" Do get up, if it's ever so little : you see how hard it is for mother."

The old man looked at her quickly, instantly grasped her meaning, and hurriedly tried to stand up, but without success ; he raised himself a couple of inches and fell back on the bench.

" I can't, my dearie," he answered plaintively, looking, as it were, meekly at Liza.

" You can talk by the hour together, but you haven't the strength to stir an inch ! "

" Liza ! " cried Tatyana Pavlovna. Makar Ivanovitch made another great effort.

"Take your crutches, they are lying beside you; you can get up with your crutches!" Liza snapped out again.

"To be sure," said the old man, and he made haste to pick up his crutches.

"He must be lifted!" said Versilov, standing up; the doctor, too, moved, and Tatyana Pavlovna ran up, but before they had time to reach him Makar Ivanovitch, leaning on the crutches, with a tremendous effort, suddenly raised himself and stood up, looking round with a triumphant air.

"There, I have got up!" he said almost with pride, laughing gleefully; "thank you, my dear, you have taught me a lesson, and I thought that my poor legs would not obey me at all. . . ."

But he did not remain standing long; he had hardly finished speaking, when his crutch, on which he was leaning with the whole weight of his body, somehow slipped on the rug, and as his "poor legs" were scarcely any support at all, he fell heavily full length on the floor. I remember it was almost horrible to see. All cried out, and rushed to lift him up, but, thank God, he had broken no bones; he had only knocked his knees with a heavy thud against the floor, but he had succeeded in putting out his right hand and breaking his fall with it. He was picked up and seated on the bed. He was very pale, not from fright, but from the shock. (The doctor had told them that he was suffering more from disease of the heart than anything.) Mother was beside herself with fright, and still pale, trembling all over and still a little bewildered, Makar Ivanovitch turned suddenly to Liza, and almost tenderly, in a soft voice, said to her:

"No, my dearie, my legs really won't hold me!"

I cannot express what an impression this made on me, at the time. There was not the faintest note of complaint or reproach in the poor old man's words; on the contrary, it was perfectly evident that he had not noticed anything spiteful in Liza's words, and had accepted her shout as something quite befitting, that is, that it was quite right to pitch into him for his remissness. All this had a very great effect on Liza too. At the moment when he fell she had rushed forward, like all the rest of us, and stood numb with horror, and miserable, of course, at having caused it all; hearing his words, she almost instantly flushed crimson with shame and remorse.

"That's enough!" Tatyana Pavlovna commanded suddenly:

" this comes of talking too much ! It's time we were off ; it's a bad look-out when the doctor himself begins to chatter ! "

" Quite so," assented Alexandr Semyonovitch who was occupied with the invalid. " I'm to blame, Tatyana Pavlovna ; he needs rest."

But Tatyana Paklovna did not hear him : she had been for half a minute watching Liza intently.

" Come here, Liza, and kiss me, that is if you care to kiss an old fool like me," she said unexpectedly.

And she kissed the girl, I don't know why, but it seemed exactly the right thing to do ; so that I almost rushed to kiss Tatyana Pavlovna myself. What was fitting was not to overwhelm Liza with reproach, but to welcome with joy and congratulation the new feeling that must certainly have sprung up in her. But instead of all those feelings, I suddenly stood up and rapped out resolutely :

" Makar Ivanovitch, you used again the word ' seemliness,' and I have been worrying about that word yesterday, and all these days . . . in fact, all my life I have been worrying about it, only I didn't know what it was. This coincidence I look upon as momentous, almost miraculous. . . . I say this in your presence . . ."

But I was instantly checked. I repeat I did not know their compact about mother and Makar Ivanovitch ; they considered me, of course judging from my doings in the past, capable of making a scene of any sort.

" Stop him, stop him ! cried Tatyana Pavlovna, utterly infuriated. Mother began trembling. Makar Ivanovitch, seeing the general alarm, was alarmed too.

" Arkady, hush ! " Versilov cried sternly.

" For me, my friends," I said raising my voice : " to see you all beside this babe (I indicated Makar) is unseemly ; there is only one saint here—and that is mothér, and even she . . ."

" You are alarming him," the doctor said emphatically.

" I know I am the enemy to every one in the world " (or something of the sort), I began faltering, but looking round once more, I glared defiantly at Versilov.

" Arkady," he cried again, " just such a scene has happened once here already between us. I entreat you, restrain yourself now ! "

I cannot describe the intense feeling with which he said this. A deep sadness, sincere and complete, was manifest in his face.

What was most surprising was that he looked as though he were guilty ; as though I were the judge, and he were the criminal. This was the last straw for me.

" Yes," I shouted to him in reply : " just such a scene we had before, when I buried Versilov, and tore him out of my heart . . . but then there followed a resurrection from the dead . . . but now . . . now there will be no rising again ! But . . . but all of you here shall see what I am capable of : you have no idea what I can show you ! "

Saying this, I rushed into my room. Versilov ran after me.

5

I had a relapse ; I had a violent attack of fever, and by nightfall was delirious. But I was not all the time in delirium ; I had innumerable dreams, shapeless and following one another, in endless succession. One such dream or fragment of a dream I shall remember as long as I live. I will describe it without attempting to explain it ; it was prophetic and I cannot leave it out.

I suddenly found myself with my heart full of a grand and proud design, in a large lofty room ; I remember the room very well, it was not at Tatyana Pavlovna's, I may observe, anticipating events. But although I was alone, I felt continually with uneasiness and discomfort that I was not alone at all, that I was awaited, and that something was being expected of me. Somewhere outside the door people were sitting and waiting for what I was going to do. The sensation was unendurable . " Oh, if I could only be alone ! " And suddenly *she* walked in. She looked at me timidly, she was very much afraid, she looked into my eyes. *In my hand I had the letter*. She smiled to fascinate me, she fawned upon me ; I was sorry, but I began to feel repulsion. Suddenly she hid her face in her hands. I flung the letter on the table with unutterable disdain, as much as to say, ' You needn't beg, take it, I want nothing of you ! I revenge myself for all your insults by contempt." I went out of the room, choking with immense pride. But at the door Lambert clutched me in the darkness ! " Fool, fool ! " he whispered, holding me by the arm with all his might, " she will have to open a high-class boarding-house for wenches in Vassilyevsky Island." (N.B.—to get her living, if her father, hearing of the

letter from me, were to deprive her of her inheritance, and
drive her out of the house.   I quote what Lambert said, word
for word, as I dreamed it.)

   " Arkady Makarovitch is in quest of ' seemliness,' " I heard
the low voice of Anna Andreyevna, somewhere close by on the
stairs ; but there was a note, not of approval, but of insufferable
mockery in her words.   I returned to the room with Lambert.
But, seeing Lambert, *she* began to laugh.   My first impression
was one of horrible dismay, such dismay that I stopped short
and would not go up to her.   I stared at her, and could not
believe my eyes, as though she had just thrown off a mask : the
features were the same, but each feature seemed distorted by an
insolence that was beyond all bounds.   " The ransom, the
ransom, madam ! " cried Lambert, and both laughed louder than
ever, while my heart went cold.   " Oh, can that shameless creature
be the woman one glance from whom set my heart glowing with
virtue ! "

   " You see what these proud creatures in their good society
are ready to do for money ! " cried Lambert.   But the shameless
creature was not even abashed by that ; she laughed at my
being so horrified.   Oh, she was ready to pay the ransom, that
I saw, and . . . and what came over me ?   I no longer felt
pity or disgust ; I was thrilled as I had never been before. . . .
I was overwhelmed by a new and indescribable feeling, such as
I had never known before, and strong as life itself. . . . I could
not have gone away now for anything on earth !   Oh, how it
pleased me that it was so shameful !   I clutched her hands ; the
touch of her hands sent an agonizing thrill through me, and I
put my lips to her insolent crimson lips, that invited me, quivering with laughter.

   Oh, away with that vile memory ?   Accursed dream !   I
swear that until that loathsome dream nothing like that shameful
idea had ever been in my mind.   There had never been even an
unconscious dream of the sort (though I had kept the " letter "
sewn up in my pocket, and I sometimes gripped my pocket with
a strange smile).   How was it all this came to me so complete ?
It was because I had the soul of a spider !   It shows that all
this had long ago been hatching in my corrupt heart, and lay
latent in my desires, but my waking heart was still ashamed, and
my mind dared not consciously picture anything of the sort.
But in sleep the soul presented and laid bare all that was hidden
in the heart, with the utmost accuracy, in a complete picture and

in prophetic form. And was *that* what I had threatened to *show* them, when I had run out of Makar Ivanovitch's room that morning ? But enough : for the time no more of this ! That dream is one of the strangest things that has happened in my life.

CHAPTER III

1

THREE days later I got up from my bed, and as soon as I was on my legs I felt that I should not go back to it again. I felt all over that convalescence was at hand. All these little details perhaps would not be worth writing, but then several days' followed which were not remarkable for anything special that happened, and yet have remained in my memory as something soothing and consolatory, and that is rare in my reminiscences. I will not for the time attempt to define my spiritual condition ; if I were to give an account of it the reader would scarcely believe in it. It will be better for it to be made clear by facts themselves. And so I will only say one thing : let the reader remember the *soul of the spider ;* and that in the man who longed to get away from them all, and from the whole world for the sake of " seemliness ! " The longing for " seemliness " was still there, of course, and very intense, but how it could be linked with other longings of a very different sort is a mystery to me. It always has been a mystery, and I have marvelled a thousand times at that faculty in man (and in the Russian, I believe, more especially) of cherishing in his soul his loftiest ideal side by side with the most abject baseness, and all quite sincerely. Whether this is breadth in the Russian which takes him so far or simply baseness—that is the question !

But enough of that. However that may be, a time of calm followed. All I knew was that I must get well at all costs and as quickly as possible that I might as soon as possible begin to act, and so I resolved to live hygienically and to obey the doctor (whoever he might be), disturbing projects I put off with great good sense (the fruit of this same breadth) to the day of my escape, that is, to the day of my complete recovery. How all the peaceful impressions and sensations in that time of stillness were consistent with the painfully sweet and agitated throbbings of my heart when I dreamed of violent decisions I do not know,

but again I put it all down to " breadth." But there was no
trace now of the restlessness I had suffered from of late. I put
it all off for the time, and did not tremble at the thought of the
future as I had so recently, but looked forward to it, like a wealthy
man relying on his power and his resources. I felt more and
more proud and defiant of the fate awaiting me, and this was
partly due, I imagine, to my actual return to health, and the
rapid recovery of my vital forces. Those few days of final and
complete recovery I recall even now with great pleasure.

Oh, they forgave me everything, that is my outburst, and
these were the people whom I had called " unseemly " to their
faces ! That I love in people ; that is what I call intelligence
of the heart ; anyway, this attracted me at once, to a certain
degree, of course. Versilov and I, for instance, talked together
like the best of friends, but only to a certain point : if at times
we became ever so little too expansive (and we were over-
expansive at times) we pulled ourselves up at once as though a
trifle ashamed of something. There are cases when the victor
cannot help feeling abashed before the vanquished, and just
because he has gained the upper hand over him. I was evidently
the victor ; and I was ashamed.

That morning, that is the one on which I got up again after
my relapse, he came in to see me, and then I learned from him
for the first time of their compact in regard to mother and
Makar Ivanovitch. He added that though the old man was
better, the doctor would not answer for the future. I promised
him with my whole heart that I would be more careful of my
behaviour in the future. While Versilov was telling me all this
I detected for the first time that he was most genuinely concerned about the old man, far more, indeed, than I could have
expected from a man like him : and that he looked upon him
as a being for some reason particularly precious to himself, not
simply for mother's sake. This at once interested me and
almost surprised me, and I must confess if it had not been for
Versilov I should have overlooked and failed to appreciate a
great deal in this old man, who has left one of the most lasting
and original impressions on my mind.

Versilov seemed to be afraid of my attitude to Makar Ivanovitch, that is he distrusted my intelligence and my tact, and he
was therefore particularly pleased afterwards when he discerned
that I knew how to behave with a man of quite different ideas
and conceptions, could, in fact, be broad-minded and make

allowances. I must confess, too (and I don't think it's humiliating to do so), that in this man of the people I found something absolutely new to me in regard to certain feelings and conceptions, something I had known nothing of, something far more serene and consolatory than my own previous ideas on those subjects. It was none the less impossible sometimes to keep from being impatient at some positive superstitions in which he believed with the most revolting placidity and steadfastness. But this, of course, was only due to his lack of education ; his soul was rather happily constructed, so much so that I have never met a man superior in that respect.

2

What attracted one first of all, as I have observed already, was his extraordinary pure-heartedness and his freedom from *amour-propre ;* one felt instinctively that he had an almost sinless heart. He had " gaiety " of heart, and therefore " seemliness." The word " gaiety " he was very fond of and often used. He sometimes showed an almost abnormal exaltation, an almost abnormal fervour, partly, I imagine, because the fever never really left him ; but that did not mar his beautiful serenity. There were contrasts in him, too : side by side with his marvellous simplicity (at times, to my vexation, he completely failed to detect irony) there was a sort of sly subtlety, most frequently apparent in controversy. And he was fond of controversy, though at times only through caprice. It was evident that he had been on foot over a great part of Russia, had heard a great deal ; but I repeat, what he liked best of all was religious emotion, and therefore everything that led up to it, and he was fond of telling incidents that moved one to tenderness and reverence.

He was fond of telling stories in general. I listened to many tales from him of his own wanderings and various legends of the lives of the " ascetics " of ancient times. I'm not familiar with these stories, but I believe that he told them all wrong, adapting them for the most part from the traditions current among the peasantry. It was simply impossible to accept some of his versions. But together with evident distortions or even inventions there were continual flashes of something wonderfully complete, full of peasant feeling, and always touching. . . . I recall, for instance, one long story out of the life of " Marya of Egypt." Of this " life " and of all such " lives " I had had no idea at all till then. I frankly confess that it was almost impossible to hear the story without tears, not from tender feeling, but from a sort of strange ecstasy. One felt something strange and burning like the parched sandy desert upon which the holy woman wandered among lions. I don't want to talk of this though, and, indeed, I am not competent to do so.

Apart from the tender feeling of his stories I particularly liked certain extremely original views on disputed questions of modern life. He told me once, for instance, of something that had happened recently with a retired soldier ; he had almost witnessed the incident. A soldier had come home to his village from serving in the army and did not like going back to live with peasants, the peasants did not like him either. The man went wrong, took to drinking, and robbed some one. There was no strong evidence against him, but he was taken up and tried. The lawyer was defending him successfully—there was no proof against him, but suddenly, after listening a long time, the prisoner suddenly stood up and interrupted him. " No, you stop," said he, and then he told the whole story " to the tiniest grain of dust " ; he confessed his full guilt with tears and penitence. The jury went out, were shut up to confer, and suddenly they all came back. " No, not guilty ! " Every one shouted, and rejoiced, and the soldier stood rooted to the spot; he seemed turned into a post, and couldn't make head or tail of it ; he didn't understand a word of the judge's exhortation to him when he dismissed him. The soldier came out to freedom and still couldn't believe it. He began to fret, sank into brooding, gave up eating and drinking, spoke to no one, and on the fifth day he took and hanged himself. " That's what it is to live with sin on the soul," said Makar Ivanovitch in conclusion. Of course that's a foolish story, and there are masses of such stories nowadays in all the newspapers, but I liked his tone, and most of all some phrases of quite a new significance. Describing, for instance, how the soldier was disliked by the peasants when he went back to the village, Makar Ivanovitch used the expression, " And we know what a soldier is : a soldier's a peasant spoilt." Speaking afterwards of the lawyer who had almost won the case, he said : " We know what a lawyer is : a lawyer's a conscience for hire." Both these expressions he brought out without effort and almost without noticing them, and yet those

two utterances revealed a complete and special attitude of
mind on those subjects, not borrowed but peculiar to Makar
Ivanovitch if not to the whole peasantry. These judgments
among the peasants in regard to certain subjects are sometimes
really marvellous in their originality.

"And how do you look upon the sin of suicide, Makar Ivanovitch ? " I asked him, apropos of the same story.

" Suicide is the greatest human sin," he answered with a sigh,
" but God alone is judge of it, for He alone knows all, every
limit, every measure. We must pray without ceasing for such
sinners. Whenever you hear of such a sin pray fervently at
bedtime for the sinner ; if only you breathe a sigh for him to
God, even though you don't know his name—the more acceptable
will be your prayer for him."

" But will my prayer be any help to him if he is condemned
already ? "

" How can you tell ? There are many, ah, many without
faith who thereby confound those of little knowledge. Heed
them not, for they know not what foolishness they are speaking.
The prayer of the living for the condemned may still, in truth,
benefit him. So what a plight for him who has no one to pray
for him. Therefore, at your evening prayer say also at the
end : ' Lord Jesus, have mercy on all those also who have none
to pray for them.' Very acceptable and pleasant will be this
prayer. Also for all living sinners—' Lord, who holdest all
destinies in Thy hand, save all sinners that repent not ! '—
that, too, is a good prayer."

I promised him I would pray, feeling that I was giving him
immense pleasure by this promise. And his face did, in fact,
beam with joy ; but I hasten to add that in such cases he did
not take up a superior attitude to me, as a monk speaking to
a raw youth ; on the contrary, he very often liked listening to
me. He was never weary in fact of hearing me talk on various
subjects, realizing that though a " youth " I was immeasurably
superior to him in education. He was very fond, for instance,
of talking of the life of hermits in the desert, and thought of
the " desert " as something far above " pilgrimage." I hotly
opposed him, laying stress on the egoism of these people, who
had abandoned the world and all the services they might have
rendered mankind, simply with the egoistic idea of their own
salvation. At first he didn't quite understand ; I suspect,
indeed, he didn't understand at all, but he zealously defended

the "desert." "At first, of course, one grieves (that is when first one goes to dwell in the desert), but then each day one is more glad at heart, and at last one looks upon the face of God."

Then I drew a picture to him of the useful activity in the world of the man of science, the doctor, or any friend of humanity, and roused him to real enthusiasm, for I spoke with warmth; he kept eagerly assenting to my words, "That's so, dear, that's so! God bless you, your thoughts are true."

But when I had finished he did not seem to agree entirely.

"To be sure, to be sure," he sighed deeply, "but are there many who hold fast and are not led astray? Though money be not their God, yet it is a demi-god—a great temptation, and then there's the female sex, and then doubt and envy. And so they will forget their great work, and will be absorbed in little things. But in the desert a man strengthens himself for every great deed. My dear, what is there in the world?" he exclaimed with intense feeling. "But is it only a dream? Take a grain of sand and sow it on a stone; when that yellow grain of sand of yours on the stone springs up, then your dream will come true in the world. That's a saying of ours. Very different from Christ's ' Go and give all that thou hast to the poor and become the servant of all.' Then thou wilt be a thousandfold richer than ever before; for not by bread alone, not by rich garments, not by pride, not by envy, wilt thou be happy, but by love multiplied immeasurably. Not a little riches, not a hundred-thousand, not a million, but the whole world wilt thou gain! Now we gather and have not enough and squander senselessly, but then there will be no orphans nor beggars, for all will be my people, all will be akin. I have gained all, I have bought all, every one! Now it is no uncommon thing for the rich and powerful to care nothing for the length of their days, and to be at a loss to invent a pastime; then thy days and thy hours will be multiplied a thousandfold, for thou wilt grudge the loss of a single minute, and wilt rejoice in every minute in gaiety of heart. Then thou wilt attain wisdom, not from books alone, but wilt be face to face with God Himself; and the earth will shine more brightly than the sun, and there shall be no more sorrow nor sighing, nothing but one priceless Paradise. . . ."

It was these enthusiastic outbursts that I believe Versilov liked particularly. He was in the room on this occasion.

"Makar Ivanovitch," I interrupted suddenly, feeling immensely stirred myself (I remember that evening), "why, it's communism, absolute communism, you're preaching!"

And as he knew absolutely nothing of the doctrine of communism, and heard the word indeed for the first time, I began at once expounding to him all I knew on the subject. I must confess my knowledge was scanty and confused, even now, in fact, it is not very ample. But in spite of that I discoursed with great heat on what I did know. To this day I recall with pleasure the extraordinary impression I made on the old man. It was more than an impression. It was really an overwhelming effect. He was passionately interested, too, in the historical details, asking, "Where? How? Who arranged it? Who said so?" I have noticed, by the way, that that is characteristic of the Russian peasant. If he is much interested he is not content with general ideas, but insists on having the most solid and exact facts. It was just for such details that I was at a loss, and as Versilov was present I felt ashamed of my incompetence, and that made me hotter than ever. In the end Makar Ivanovitch could do nothing but repeat with emotion, "Yes: yes!" though he had evidently lost the thread and did not understand. I felt vexed, but Versilov interrupted the conversation and said it was bedtime. We were all in the room and it was late. But when he peeped into my room a few minutes later I asked him at once what he thought of Makar Ivanovitch, and what was his opinion of him? Versilov laughed gaily (but not at my mistakes about communism—he did not mention them in fact). I repeat again, he seemed absolutely devoted to Makar Ivanovitch, and I often caught a very attractive smile on his face when he was listening to the old man. At the same time this smile did not prevent his criticising him.

"Makar Ivanovitch is above all not a peasant but a house-serf," he pronounced with great readiness, "who has been a servant, born a servant, and of servants. The house-serfs and servants used to share a very great deal in the interests of their masters' private, spiritual, and intellectual life in the past. Note that to this day Makar Ivanovitch is most interested in the life of the gentry and upper class. You don't know yet how much interest he takes in recent events in Russia. Do you know that he is a great politician? Don't feed him on honey, but tell him where anyone is fighting and whether we are going to fight. In old days I used to delight him by such accounts.

He has the greatest respect for science, and of all sciences is fondest of astronomy. At the same time he has worked out for himself something so independent that nothing you could do would shake it. He has convictions, firm, fairly clear . . . and genuine. Though he's so absolutely uneducated he is often able to astound one by his surprising knowledge of certain ideas which one would never have expected to find in him. He extols the ' desert ' with enthusiasm, but nothing would induce him to retire to the desert or enter a monastery, because he is above all things a ' tramp,' as he was so charmingly called by Alexandr Semyonovitch (and by the way there's no need for you to be angry with him). Well, and what more ? He's some-thing of an artist, many of his sayings are his own, though some are not. He's somewhat halting in his logic, and at times too abstract ; he has moods of sentimentality, but of a thoroughly peasant kind, or rather moods of that tenderness universally found among peasants, which the people introduce so freely into their religious feelings. As for his purity of heart and freedom from malice, I won't discuss them ; it's not for you and me to begin upon that. . . ."

3

To complete my picture of Makar Ivanovitch I'll repeat some of his stories, choosing those taken from private life. These stories were of a strange character. It was impossible to extract any sort of moral or general tendency from them, except perhaps that they were all more or less touching. There were some, however, which were not touching, some, in fact, were quite gay, others even made fun of certain foolish monks, so that he actually discredited his own convictions by telling them. I pointed this out to him, but he did not understand what I meant. Sometimes it was difficult to imagine what induced him to tell the story, so that at times I wondered at his talkativeness and put it down to the loquacity of old age and his feverish condition.

" He is not what he used to be," Versilov whispered to me once, " he was not quite like this in the old days. He will soon die, much sooner than we expect, and we must be prepared."

I have forgotten to say that we had begun to have something like " evenings." Besides my mother, who never left him, Versilov was in his little room every evening ; I came too—and indeed I had nowhere else to go. Of late Liza, too, had always been present, though she came a little later than the rest of us, and always sat in silence. Tatyana Pavlovna came too, and, though more rarely, the doctor. Somehow I suddenly began to get on with the doctor, and though we were never very friendly there were no further scenes between us. I liked a sort of simple-mindedness which I detected in him, and the attachment he showed to our family, so that I made up my mind at last to forgive him his professional superciliousness, and, moreover, I taught him to wash his hands and clean his nails, even if he couldn't put on clean linen. I explained to him bluntly that this was not a sign of foppishness or of elegant artificiality, but that cleanliness is a natural element of the trade of a doctor, and I proved it to him. Finally, Lukerya often came out of the kitchen and stood at the door listening to Makar Ivanovitch's stories. Versilov once called her in from the door, and asked her to sit down with us. I liked his doing this, but from that time she gave up coming to the door. Her sense of the fitting !

I quote one of his stories, selecting it simply because I remember it more completely. It is a story about a merchant, and I imagine that such incidents occur by thousands in our cities and country towns, if only one knew how to look for them. The reader may prefer to skip the story, especially as I quote it in the old man's words.

4

I'll tell you now of a wonderful thing that happened in our town, Afimyevsk. There was a merchant living there, his name was Skotoboynikov, Maxim Ivanovitch, and there was no one richer than he in all the countryside. He built a cotton factory, and he kept some hundreds of hands, and he exalted himself exceedingly. And everything, one may say, was at his beck and call, and even those in authority hindered him in nothing, and the archimandrite thanked him for his zeal : he gave freely of his substance to the monastery, and when the fit came upon him he sighed and groaned over his soul and was troubled not a little over the life to come. A widower he was and childless ; of his wife there were tales that he had beaten her from the first year of their marriage, and that from his youth up he had been apt to be too free with his hands. Only all that had happened long ago ; he had no desire to enter into the bonds of another marriage. He had a weakness for strong drink, too, and when the time came he would run drunk about the town, naked and shouting; the town was of little account and was full of iniquity. And when the time was ended he was moved to anger, and all that he thought fit was good, and all he bade them do was right. He paid his people according to his pleasure, he brings out his reckoning beads, puts on his spectacles : " How much for you, Foma ? " " I've had nothing since Christmas, Maxim Ivanovitch ; thirty-nine roubles is my due." " Ough ! what a sum of money ! That's too much for you ! It's more than you're worth altogether ; it would not be fitting for you ; ten roubles off the beads and you take twenty-nine." And the man says nothing ; no one dares open his lips ; all are dumb before him.

" I know how much I ought to gi˙e him," he says. " It's the only way to deal with the folk here. The folk here are corrupt. But for me they would have perished of hunger, all that are here. The folk here are thieves again. They covet all that they behold, there is no courage in them. They are drunkards too ; if you pay a man his money he'll take it to the tavern and will sit in the tavern till he's naked—not a thread on him, he will come out as bare as your hand. They are mean wretches. A man will sit on a stone facing the tavern and begin wailing : ' Oh mother, my dear mother, why did you bring me into the world a hopeless drunkard ? Better you had strangled me at birth, a hopeless drunkard like me ! ' Can you call that a man ? That's a beast, not a man. One must first teach him better, and then give him money. I know when to give it him."

That's how Maxim Ivanovitch used to talk of the folk of Afimyevsk. Though he spoke evil of them, yet it was the truth. The folk were froward and unstable.

There lived in the same town another merchant, and he died. He was a young man and light-minded. He came to ruin and lost all his fortune. For the last year he struggled like a fish on the sand, and his life drew near its end. He was on bad terms with Maxim Ivanovitch all the time, and was heavily in debt to him. And he left behind a widow, still young, and five children. And for a young widow to be left alone without a husband, like a swallow without a refuge, is a great ordeal, to say nothing of five little children, and nothing to give them to eat. Their last possession, a wooden house, Maxim Ivanovitch had taken for a debt. She set them all in a row at the church porch,

2 B

the eldest a boy of seven, and the others all girls, one smaller than another, the biggest of them four, and the youngest babe at the breast. When Mass was over Maxim Ivanovitch came out of church, and all the little ones, all in a row, knelt down before him—she had told them to do this beforehand—and they clasped their little hands before them, and she behind them, with the fifth child in her arms, bowed down to the earth before him in the sight of all the congregation : " Maxim Ivanovitch, have mercy on the orphans ! Do not take away their last crust ! Do not drive them out of their home ! " And all who were present were moved to tears, so well had she taught them. She thought that he would be proud before the people and would forgive the debt, and give back the house to the orphans. But it did not fall out so. Maxim Ivanovitch stood still. " You're a young widow," said he, " you want a husband, you are not weeping over your orphans. Your husband cursed me on his deathbed." And he passed by and did not give up the house. " Why follow their foolishness (that is, connive at it) ? If I show her benevolence they'll abuse me more than ever. All that nonsense will be revived and the slander will only be confirmed."

For there was a story that ten years before he had sent to that widow before she was married, and had offered her a great sum of money (she was very beautiful), forgetting that that sin is no less than defiling the temple of God. But he did not succeed then in his evil design. Of such abominations he had committed not a few, both in the town and all over the province,.and indeed had gone beyond all bounds in such doings.

The mother wailed with her nurslings. He turned the orphans out of the house, and not from spite only, for, indeed, a man sometimes does not know himself what drives him to carry out his will. Well, people helped her at first and then she went out to work for hire. But there was little to be earned, save at the factory ; she scrubs floors, weeds in the garden, heats the bath-house, and she carries the babe in her arms, and the other four run about the streets in their little shirts. When she made them kneel down at the church porch they still had little shoes, and little jackets of a sort, for they were merchant's children : but now they began to run barefoot. A child soon gets through its little clothes we know. Well, the children didn't care : so long as there was sunshine they rejoiced, like birds, did not feel their ruin, and their voices were like little bells. The widow thought " the winter will come and what shall I do with you

then ? If God would only take you to Him before then ! "
But she had not to wait for the winter. About our parts the
children have a cough, the whooping-cough, which goes from
one to the other. First of all the baby died, and after her the
others fell ill, and all four little girls she buried that autumn
one after the other ; one of them, it's true, was trampled by the
horses in the street. And what do you think ? She buried
them and she wailed. Though she had cursed them, yet when
God took them she was sorry. A mother's heart !

All she had left was the eldest, the boy, and she hung over
him trembling. He was weak and tender, with a pretty little
face like a girl's, and she took him to the factory to the foreman
who was his godfather, and she herself took a place as nurse.

But one day the boy was running in the yard, and Maxim
Ivanovitch suddenly drove up with a pair of horses, and he had
just been drinking ; and the boy came rushing down the steps
straight at him, and slipped and stumbled right against him as
he was getting out of the droshky, and hit him with both hands
in the stomach. He seized the boy by the hair and yelled,
" Whose boy is it ? A birch ! Thrash him before me, this
minute." The boy was half-dead with fright. They began
thrashing him ; he screamed. " So you scream, too, do you ?
Thrash him till he leaves off screaming." Whether they thrashed
him hard or not, he didn't give up screaming till he fainted
altogether. Then they left off thrashing him, they were
frightened. The boy lay senseless, hardly breathing. They did
say afterwards they had not beaten him much, but the boy
was terrified. Maxim Ivanovitch was frightened ! " Whose
boy is he ? " he asked. When they told him, " Upon my word
Take him to his mother. Why is he hanging about the factory
here ? " For two days afterwards he said nothing. Then he
asked again : " How's the boy ? " And it had gone hard with
the boy. He had fallen ill, and lay in the corner at his mother's,
and she had given up her job to look after him, and inflammation
of the lungs had set in.

" Upon my word ! " said Maxim Ivanovitch, " and for so little !
It's not as though he were badly beaten. They only gave him
a bit of a fright. I've given all the others just as sound a
thrashing and never had this nonsense." He expected the
mother to come and complain, and in his pride he said nothing.
As though that were likely ! The mother didn't dare to complain. And then he sent her fifteen roubles from himself, and

a doctor ; and not because he was afraid, but because he thought better of it. And then soon his time came and he drank for three weeks.

Winter passed, and at the Holy Ascension of Our Lord, Maxim Ivanovitch asks again : " And how's that same boy ? " And all the winter he'd been silent and not asked. And they told him, " He's better and living with his mother, and she goes out by the day." And Maxim Ivanovitch went that day to the widow. He didn't go into the house, but called her out to the gate while he sat in his droshky. " See now, honest widow," says he. " I want to be a real benefactor to your son, and to show him the utmost favour. I will take him from here into my house. And if the boy pleases me I'll settle a decent fortune on him ; and if I'm completely satisfied with him I may at my death make him the heir of my whole property as though he were my own son, on condition, however, that you do not come to the house except on great holidays. If this suits you, bring the boy to-morrow morning, he can't always be playing knuckle-bones." And saying this, he drove away, leaving the mother dazed. People had overheard and said to her, " When the boy grows up he'll reproach you himself for having deprived him of such good fortune." In the night she cried over him, but in the morning she took the child. And the lad was more dead than alive.

Maxim Ivanovitch dressed him like a little gentleman, and hired a teacher for him, and sat him at his book from that hour forward ; and it came to his never leaving him out of his sight, always keeping him with him. The boy could scarcely begin to yawn before he'd shout at him, " Mind your book ! Study ! I want to make a man of you." And the boy was frail ; ever since the time of that beating he'd had a cough. " As though we didn't live well in my house ! " said Maxim Ivanovitch, wondering ; " at his mother's he used to run barefoot and gnaw crusts ; why is he more puny than before ? " And the teacher said, " Every boy," says he, " needs to play about, not to be studying all the time ; he needs exercise," and he explained it all to him reasonably. Maxim Ivanovitch reflected. " That's true," he said. And that teacher's name was Pyotr Stepano-vitch ; the Kingdom of Heaven be his ! He was almost like a crazy saint, he drank much, too much indeed, and that was the reason he had been turned out of so many places, and he lived n the town on alms one may say, but he was of great intelligence and strong in science. " This is not the place for me," he thought to himself, "I ought to be a professor in the university ; here I'm buried in the mud, my very garments loathe me." Maxim Ivanovitch sits and shouts to the child, "Play ! " and he scarcely dares to breathe before him. And it came to such a pass that the boy could not hear the sound of his voice without trembling all over. And Maxim Ivanovitch wondered more and more. "He's neither one thing nor the other ; I picked him out of the mud, I dressed him in *drap de dames* with little boots of good material, he has embroidered shirts like a general's son, why has he not grown attached to me ? Why is he as dumb as a little wolf ? " And though people had long given up being surprised at Maxim Ivanovitch, they began to be surprised at him again—the man was beside himself : he pestered the little child and would never let him alone. "As sure as I'm alive I'll root up his character. His father cursed me on his deathbed after he'd taken the last sacrament. It's his father's character." And yet he didn't once use the birch to him (after that time he was afraid to). He frightened him, that's what he did. He frightened him without a birch.

And something happened. One day, as soon as he'd gone out, the boy left his book and jumped on to a chair. He had thrown his ball on to the top of the sideboard, and now he wanted to get it, and his sleeve caught in a china lamp on the sideboard, the lamp fell to the floor and was smashed to pieces, and the crash was heard all over the house, and it was an expensive thing, made of Saxony china. And Maxim Ivanovitch heard at once, though he was two rooms away, and he yelled. The boy rushed away in terror. He ran out on the verandah, across the garden, and through the back gate on to the river-bank. And there was a boulevard running along the river-bank, there were old willows there, it was a pleasant place. He ran down to the water, people saw, and clasped his hands at the very place where the ferry-boat comes in, but seemed frightened of the water, and stood as though turned to stone. And it's a broad open space, the river is swift there, and boats pass by ; on the other side there are shops, a square, a temple of God, shining with golden domes. And just then Mme. Ferzing, the colonel's wife, came hurrying down to the ferry with her little daughter. The daughter, who was also a child of eight, was wearing a little white frock ; she looked at the boy and laughed, and she was carrying a little country basket, and in it a hedgehog. "Look, mother," said she, "how the boy is looking at my hedgehog ! " "No," said the lady, " he's frightened of something. What are you afraid of, pretty boy ? " (All this was told afterwards.) " And what a pretty boy," she said ; " and how nicely he's dressed. Whose boy are you ? " she asked. And he'd never seen a hedgehog before, he went up and looked, and forgot everything at once— such is childhood ! " What is it you have got there ? " he asked. " It's a hedgehog," said the little lady, " we've just bought it from a peasant, he found it in the woods." " What's that," he asked, " what is a hedgehog ? " and he began laughing and poking it with his finger, and the hedgehog put up its bristles, and the little girl was delighted with the boy. " We'll take it home with us and tame it," she said. " Ach," said he, " do give me your hedgehog ! " And he asked her this so pleadingly, and he'd hardly uttered the words, when Maxim Ivanovitch came running down upon him. " Ah, there you are ! Hold him ! " (He was in such a rage, that he'd run out of the house after him, without a hat.) Then the boy remembered everything, he screamed, and ran to the water, pressed his little fists against his breast, looked up at the sky (they saw it, they saw it !) and leapt into the water. Well, people cried out, and jumped from the ferry, tried to get him out, but the current carried him away. The river was rapid, and when they got him out, the little thing was dead. His chest was weak, he couldn't stand being in the water, his hold on life was weak. And such a thing had never been known in those parts, a little child like that to take its life ! What a sin ! And what could such a little soul say to our Lord God in the world beyond ?

And Maxim Ivanovitch brooded over it ever after. The man became so changed one would hardly have known him. He sorrowed grievously. He tried drinking, and drank heavily, but gave it up—it was no help. He gave up going to the factory too, he would listen to no one. If anyone spoke to him, he would be silent, or wave his hand. So he spent two months, and then he began talking to himself. He would walk about talking to himself. Vaskovo, the little village down the hill, caught fire, and nine houses were burnt; Maxim Ivanovitch drove up to look. The peasants whose cottages were burnt came round him wailing ; he promised to help them and gave orders, and then he called his steward again and took it back. " There's no need," said he, " don't give them anything," and he never said why. " God has sent me to be a scorn unto all men," said he, " like some monster, and therefore so be it.

Like the wind," said he, "has my fame gone abroad." The archimandrite himself came to him. He was a stern man, the head of the community of the monastery. "What are you doing?" he asked sternly.

"I will tell you." And Maxim Ivanovitch opened the Bible and pointed to the passage:

"Whoso shall offend one of these little ones, which believe in me, it were better for him that a millstone were hanged about his neck and that he were drowned in the depth of the sea." (Math. xviii, 6.)

"Yes," said the archimandrite, "though it was not said directly of this, yet it fits it well. It is sad when a man loses his measure—the man is lost. And thou hast exalted thyself."

And Maxim Ivanovitch sits as though a stupor had come upon him. The archimandrite gazed upon him.

"Listen," said he, "and remember. It is said: 'the word of a desperate man flies on the wind.' And remember, also, that even the angels of God are not perfect. But perfect and sinless is one only, our Lord Jesus Christ, and Him the angels serve. Moreover, thou didst not will the death of that child, but wast only without wisdom. But this," said he, "is marvellous in my eyes. Thou hast committed many even worse iniquities. Many men thou hast ruined, many thou hast corrupted, many thou hast destroyed, no less than, if thou hadst slain them. And did not his sisters, all the four babes, die almost before thine eyes? Why has this one only confounded thee? For all these in the past thou hast not grieved, I dare say, but hast even forgotten to think of them. Why art thou so horror-stricken for this child for whom thou wast not greatly to blame?"

"I dream at night," Maxim Ivanovitch said.

"And what?"

But he told nothing more. He sat mute. The archimandrite marvelled, but with that he went away. There was no doing anything with him.

And Maxim Ivanovitch sent for the teacher, for Pyotr Stepanovitch; they had not met since that day.

"You remember him?" says he.

"Yes."

"You painted a picture with oil colours, here in the tavern," said he, "and took a copy of the chief priest's portrait. Could you paint me a picture?"

"I can do anything, I have every talent. I can do everything."

" Paint me a very big picture, to cover the whole wall, and paint in it first of all the river, and the slope, and the ferry, and all the people who were there, the colonel's wife, and her daughter and the hedgehog. And paint me the other bank too, so that one can see the church and the square and the shops, and where the cabs stand—paint it all just as it is. And the boy by the ferry, just above the river, at that very place, and paint him with his two little fists pressed to his little breast. Be sure to do that. And open the heavens above the church on the further side, and let all the angels of heaven be flying to meet him. Can you do it or not ? "

" I can do anything."

" I needn't ask a dauber like you. I might send for the finest painter in Moscow, or even from London itself, but you remember his face. If it's not like, or little like, I'll only give you fifty roubles. But if it's just like, I'll give you two hundred. You remember his eyes were blue. . . . And it must be made a very, very big picture."

It was prepared. Pyotr Stepanovitch began painting and then he suddenly went and said :

" No, it can't be painted like that."

" Why so ? "

" Because that sin, suicide, is the greatest of all sins. And would the angels come to meet him after such a sin ? "

" But he was a babe, he was not responsible."

" No, he was not a babe, he was a youth. He was eight years old when it happened. He was bound to render some account."

Maxim Ivanovitch was more terror-stricken than ever.

" But I tell you what, I've thought something," said Pyotr Stepanovitch, " we won't open the heaven, and there's no need to paint the angels, but I'll let a beam of light, one bright ray of light, come down from heaven as though to meet him. It's all the same as long as there's something."

So he painted the ray. I saw that picture myself afterwards, and that very ray of light, and the river. It stretched right across the wall, all blue, and the sweet boy was there, both little hands pressed to his breast, and the little lady, and the hedgehog, he put it all in. Only Maxim Ivanovitch showed no one the picture at the time, but locked it up in his room, away from all eyes ; and when the people trooped from all over the town to see it, he bade them drive every one away. There was a great talk about it. Pyotr Stepanovitch seemed as though he were beside himself. " I can do anything now," said he. " I've only to set up in St. Petersburg at the court." He was a very polite man, but he liked boasting beyond all measure. And his fate overtook him ; when he received the full two hundred roubles, he began drinking at once, and showed his money to every one, bragging of it, and he was murdered at night, when he was drunk, and his money stolen by a workman with whom he was drinking, and it all became known in the morning.

And it all ended so that even now they remember it everywhere there. Maxim Ivanovitch suddenly drives up to the same widow. She lodged at the edge of the town in a working-woman's hut ; he stood before her and bowed down to the ground. And she had been ill ever since that time and could scarcely move.

" Good mother," he wailed, " honest widow, marry me, monster as I am. Let me live again ! "

She looks at him more dead than alive.

" I want us to have another boy," said he. " And if he is born, it will mean that that boy has forgiven us both, both you and me. For so the boy has bidden me."

She saw the man was out of his mind, and in a frenzy, but she could not refrain.

" That's all nonsense," she answered him, " and only cowardice. Through the same cowardice I have lost all my children. I cannot bear the sight of you before me, let alone accepting such an everlasting torture."

Maxim Ivanovitch drove off, but he did not give in. The whole town was agog at such a marvel. Maxim Ivanovitch sent match-makers to her. He sent for two of his aunts, working women in the chief town of the province. Aunts they were not, but kinsfolk of some sort, decent people. They began trying to turn her, they kept persuading her and would not leave the cottage. He sent her merchants' wives of the town too, and the wife of the head priest of the cathedral, and the wives of officials ; she was besieged by the whole town, and she got really sick of it.

" If my orphans had been living," she said, " but why should I now ? Am I to be guilty of such a sin against my children ? "

The archmandrite, too, tried to persuade her. He breathed into her ear :

" You will make a new man of him."

She was horrified, and people wondered at her.

" How can you refuse such a piece of luck ? "

And this was how he overcame her in the end.

" Anyway he was a suicide," he said, " and not a babe, but a youth, and owing to his years he could not have been admitted to the Holy Communion, and so he must have been bound to give at least some account. If you enter into matrimony with me, I'll make you a solemn promise, I'll build a church of God to the eternal memory of his soul."

She could not stand out against that, and consented. So they were married.

And all were in amazement. They lived from the very first day in great and unfeigned harmony, jealously guarding their marriage vow, and like one soul in two bodies. She conceived that winter, and they began visiting the churches, and fearing the wrath of God. They stayed in three monasteries, and consulted prophecy. He built the promised church, and also a hospital, and almshouses in the town. He founded an endowment for widows and orphans. And he remembered all whom he had injured, and desired to make them restitution ; he began to give away money without stint, so that his wife and the archimandrite even had to restrain him ; " for that is enough," they said. Maxim Ivanovitch listened to them. " I cheated Foma of his wages that time," said he. So they paid that back to Foma. And Foma was moved even to tears. " As it is I'm content . . ." says he, " you've given me so much without that." It touched every one's heart in fact, and it shows it's true what they say that a living man will be a good example. And the people are good-hearted there.

His wife began to manage the factory herself, and so well that she's remembered to this day. He did not give up drinking, but she looked after him at those times, and began to nurse him. His language became more decorous, and even his voice changed. He became merciful beyond all wont, even to animals. If he saw from the window a peasant shamelessly beating his horse on the head, he would send out at once, and buy the horse at double its value. And he received the gift of tears. If any one talked to him he melted into tears. When her time had come, God answered their prayers at last, and sent them a son, and for the first time Maxim Ivanovitch became glad ; he gave alms freely, and forgave many debts, and invited the whole town to the christening. And next day he was black as night. His wife saw that something was wrong with him, and held up to him the new-born babe.

" The boy has forgiven us," she said ; " he has accepted our prayers and our tears for him."

And it must be said they had neither of them said one word on that subject for the whole year, they had kept it from each other in their hearts. And Maxim Ivanovitch looked at her, black as night. " Wait a bit," said he, " consider, for a whole year he has not come to me, but last night he came in my dream."

" I was struck to the heart with terror when I heard those strange words," she said afterwards.

The boy had not come to him in his dream for nothing. Scarcely had Maxim Ivanovitch said this, when something happened to the new-born babe, it suddenly fell ill. And the child was ill for eight days; they prayed unceasingly and sent for doctors, and sent for the very best doctor in Moscow by train. The doctor came, and he flew into a rage.

" I'm the foremost doctor," said he, " all Moscow is awaiting me."

He prescribed a drop, and hurried away again. He took eight hundred roubles. And the baby died in the evening.

And what after that ? Maxim Ivanovitch settled all his property on his beloved wife, gave up all his money and all his papers to her, doing it all in due form according to law, then he stood before her and bowed down to the earth.

" Let me go, my priceless spouse, save my soul while it is still possible. If I spend the time without profit to my soul, I shall not return. I have been hard and cruel, and laid heavy burdens upon men, but I believe that for the woes and wanderings that lie before me, God will not leave me without requital, seeing that to leave all this is no little cross and no little woe."

And his wife heard him with many tears.

" You are all I have now upon the earth, and to whom am I left ? " said she, " I have laid up affection in my heart for you this year."

And every one in the town counselled him against it and besought him ; and thought to hold him back by force. But he would not listen to them, and he went away in secret by night, and was not seen again. And the tale is that he perseveres in pilgrimage and in patience to this day, and visits his dear wife once a year.

CHAPTER IV

1

I AM now approaching the culminating catastrophe to which
my whole story is leading up. But before I can continue I
must give a preliminary explanation of things of which I knew
nothing at the time when I was taking part in them, but which
I only understood and fully realized long afterwards, that is
when everything was over. I don't know how else to be clear,
as otherwise I should have to write the whole story in riddles.
And so I will give a simple and direct explanation, sacrificing so-
called artistic effect, and presenting it without any personal
feelings, as though I were not writing it myself, something after
the style of an *entrefilet* in the newspaper.

The fact is that my old schoolfellow, Lambert, might well,
and indeed with certainty, be said to belong to one of those disreputable gangs of petty scoundrels who form associations for
the sake of what is now called *chantage*, an offence nowadays
defined and punished by our legal code. The gang to which
Lambert belonged had been formed in Moscow and had already
succeeded in a good many enterprises there (it was to some extent exposed later on). I heard afterwards that they had in
Moscow an extremely experienced and clever leader, a man no
longer young. They embarked upon enterprises, sometimes
acting individually and sometimes in concert.   While they
were responsible for some filthy and indecent scandals (accounts
of which have, however, already been published in the newspapers) they also carried out some subtle and elaborate intrigues
under the leadership of their chief. I found out about some of
them later on, but I will not repeat the details. I will only
mention that it was their characteristic method to discover
some secret, often in the life of people of the greatest respecta-
bility and good position.   Then they would go to these persons
and threaten to make public documentary evidence (which they
often did not possess) and would demand a sum of money as
the price of silence.   There are things neither sinful nor criminal
which even honourable and strong-minded people would dread
to have exposed. They worked chiefly upon family secrets.
To show how adroit their chief sometimes was in his proceedings,

I will describe in three lines and without any details one of their exploits. A really wicked and sinful action was committed in a certain honourable family; the wife of a well-known and highly respected man entered into a secret love-affair with a young and wealthy officer. They scented this out, and what they did was to give the young man plainly to understand that they would inform the husband. They hadn't the slightest proof, and the young man knew that quite well, and indeed they did not conceal it from him. But the whole ingenuity and the whole cunning of their calculations lay in the reflection that on receiving information, even without proofs, the husband would take exactly the same steps as though he had positive proofs. They relied upon their knowledge of the man's character, and of the circumstances of the family. The fact was that one member of the gang was a young man belonging to a very good set, and he had been able to collect information beforehand. They extracted a considerable sum from the lover, and without any risk to themselves, because their victim was himself eager for secrecy.

Though Lambert took part in this affair, he was not actually one of the Moscow gang; acquiring a taste for the work he began by degrees and experimentally acting on his own account. I may mention beforehand that he was not altogether well fitted for it. He was very sharp and calculating, but hasty, and what's more, simple, or rather naïve, that is he had very little knowledge of men or of good society. I fancy, for instance, that he did not realize the capacity of the Moscow chief, and imagined that the organization and conduct of such projects were very easy. And he imagined that almost every one was as great a scoundrel as he was himself, and if once he had conceived that a certain person was afraid, or must be afraid for this reason or for that, he would be as certain that the man was afraid as though it were an axiomatic truth. I don't know how to express this; I'll explain the fact more clearly later, but in my opinion he had rather a coarse-grained intelligence, and not only had he no faith in certain good and generous feelings, but perhaps he had actually no conception of them.

He had come to Petersburg because he had long conceived of Petersburg as offering a wider scope for his energies, and because in Moscow he had got into a scrape, and because some one was looking for him there with extremely evil intentions. On arriving in Petersburg he at once got into touch with an old comrade, but he found the outlook unpromising and nothing to be done on a large scale. His acquaintance had increased, but nothing had come of it. " They're a wretched lot here, no better than boys," he said to me himself afterwards. And behold, one fine morning at sunrise he found me half-frozen under a wall, and at once dropped upon the scent of what he regarded as a " very rich job."

It all rested on my ravings as I thawed! in his lodgings. I was practically delirious then ! But from my words it was manifest that of all the affronts I had suffered on that momentous day, the thing which most rankled in my heart, and was most vivid in my memory, was the insult I had received from Büring and from her; I should not otherwise have talked of nothing else in my delirium at Lambert's, but should have raved of Zerstchikov for example, but it was only of the former I had talked, as I learned afterwards from Lambert himself. And besides, I was in a sort of ecstasy, and looked upon both Lambert and Alphonsine on that awful morning as, so-to-say, champions and deliverers. Afterwards, as I got better and lay in bed, wondering what Lambert could have learned from my ravings, and to what extent I had babbled, it never occurred to me even to suspect that he could have found out so much. Oh, of course, from the gnawing at my conscience I suspected even then that I had said a great deal I should not have said, but, I repeat, I never imagined that it had gone so far. I hoped, too, that I was not able to articulate my words clearly, and indeed I reckoned upon this, as I distinctly remembered it. And yet it turned out in fact that my articulation had been much more distinct than I afterwards supposed and hoped. But the worst of it was that all this only came to light afterwards, and long afterwards, and that was a misfortune for me.

From my deliriums, my ravings, my mutterings, my transports, and so on, he learned, to begin with, almost all the surnames correctly, and even some addresses. And, secondly, he was able to get a fairly correct idea of the consequence of the persons concerned (the old prince, *her*, Büring, Anna Andreyevna, and even Versilov); thirdly, he learned that I had been insulted and was threatening revenge; and lastly, and chiefly, that there was in existence a mysterious, hidden document, a letter, such, that if it were shown to a half-crazy old prince he would learn that his own daughter thought him a lunatic and was already consulting lawyers to get him locked up—and would either go quite mad,

or would turn her out of the house, and leave her out of his
will, or would marry a certain Mlle. Versilov whom he already
wanted to marry, and was being prevented from marrying. In
short, Lambert understood a great deal; no doubt a great deal
still remained obscure, but the expert blackmailer had anyway
dropped on a trustworthy scent. When I ran away afterwards from Alphonsine he promptly found out my address (in the
simplest possible way, by going to the address bureau); and
then immediately made the necessary inquiries, from which
he discovered that all these persons about whom I had babbled
to him did actually exist. Then he promptly took the first
step.

The most important fact was the existence of the *document*,
and that I was in possession of it, and that that document was
of the highest value—of that Lambert had no doubt. Here I
omit one circumstance, which will come in better later, in its
proper place, and will only mention here that that circumstance
was what principally confirmed Lambert in the conviction of
the real existence and, still more, of the value of the document.
It was, I may say beforehand, a momentous circumstance, of
which I could have no conception either at the time or afterwards,
until the final catastrophe, when everything was discovered and
became evident of itself. And so, convinced of the main facts,
his first step was to go to Anna Andreyevna.

Yet one thing perplexes me to this day: how he, Lambert,
succeeded in gaining admittance to, and fastening himself upon,
such an unapproachable and superior personage as Anna Andreyevna. It is true that he gathered information about her, but
what of that? It is true that he was extremely well dressed,
spoke French with a Parisian accent, and had a French surname,
but surely Anna Andreyevna must have discerned that he was a
scoundrel at once? Or is one to suppose that a scoundrel was
just what she wanted at that time? But surely that cannot be
so?

I never could find out the details of their interview, but I
have often pictured the scene to myself in my imagination.
What is most likely is that from the first word Lambert posed as
a friend of my childhood, anxious over a dear and cherished
comrade. But no doubt at that first interview he succeeded in
hinting quite clearly that I had a document, and letting her know
that it was a secret, and that only he, Lambert, was in possession
of it, and that I was intending to revenge myself on Mme.

Ahmakov by means of it, and so on, and so on. Above all he could explain to her as precisely as possible the importance and value of this document. As for Anna Andreyevna she was in such a position that she must have caught at any information of this kind, must have listened with the closest attention, and . . . must have risen to the bait through " the struggle for existence." Just at that time they had abstracted her fiancé from her, and had carried him off under guardianship to Tsarskoe ; and they had even put her under supervision, too. And then a find like this ! This was not a case of some old woman whispering in her ear, of tearful lamentations, of scheming and backbiting, there was a letter, an actual piece of writing, that is a positive proof of the treacherous design of his daughter, and of all those who had snatched him from her, and that, therefore, he must be saved even by flight, to her, to Anna Andreyevna, and must be married to her in twenty-four hours, otherwise he would be at once spirited away into a lunatic asylum.

And perhaps the fact that Lambert attempted no subterfuges with the young lady even for a moment, but practically blurted straight out from the first word :

" Mademoiselle, either remain an old maid or become a princess and a millionaire. There is a document and I will steal it from the lad and give it to you . . . for a note of hand from you for thirty thousand."

I positively imagine that that's just how it was. Oh, he thought they were all as scoundrelly as himself ; I repeat he had that sort of simplicity, that sort of innocence of the scoundrel . . . However it happened, it may very well be that even when she was demeaning herself like this, Anna Andreyevna was not embarrassed for a minute, but could perfectly well control herself and listen to the blackmailer talking in his own style—and all from " the breadth of her nature." Oh, no doubt she flushed a little at first, and then she mastered herself and listened. And when I imagine that proud, unapproachable, genuinely dignified girl, with her brains, too, hand in hand with Lambert, well . . . what a mind ! A Russian mind, so large, with such a desire for breadth, a woman's too, and in such circumstances !

Now I'll make a résumé. By the time I went out after my illness, Lambert had two plans (I know that for a fact now). The first was to get an IOU for not less than thirty thousand from Anna Andreyevna for the letter, and then to help her to frighten the prince, to abduct him and to get her married to him at once—something of that sort anyway. The plan for this was complete. They were only waiting for my help, that is for the document.

The second plan was to desert Anna Andreyevna, throw her over, and sell the letter to Mme. Ahmakov, if that would pay him better. In this he was reckoning on Büring. But Lambert had not yet applied to Mme. Ahmakov, and was only on her track. He was waiting for me too.

Oh, he needed me, that is, not me but the letter ! He had formed two plans in regard to me also. The first was, if necessary, to act in concert with me, and to go halves with me, first taking possession of me morally and physically. But the second plan attracted him much more. It was to deceive me as a silly boy, and to steal the letter from me, or even simply to take it from me by force. This was his favourite plan, and the one he cherished in his dreams. I repeat, there was a circumstance which made him reckon with certainty on the success of his second plan, but, as I have said already, I will explain that later. In any case he awaited me with nervous impatience. Everything depended upon me, every step and every decision.

And I must do him the justice to say that he knew how to restrain himself till the time came, in spite of his hasty temper. He did not come to see me all the while I was ill, he only came once to the house and saw Versilov ; he did not worry or frighten me, he kept up an attitude of complete independence as regards me till the day and hour of my going out. As for the possibility of my giving up the letter, telling about it, or destroying it, he had no anxiety on that score. From my words he had been able to gather how much importance I attached to secrecy, and how afraid I was that some one might find out about the letter. And that I should go straight to him and to no one else, on the first day I was well enough, he did not doubt in the least either. Darya Onisimovna came to see me partly by his orders, and he knew that my curiosity and apprehension were already aroused, and that I should not hold out. . . . And, indeed, he had taken all precautions, he was in a position to know what day I was going out, so that I could hardly have eluded him if I had wanted to.

But however eagerly Lambert may have been expecting me, Anna Andreyevna perhaps was awaiting me even more eagerly. I must say frankly that Lambert was to some extent right in his reckoning when he contemplated throwing her over, and it was her own fault. In spite of the agreement that no doubt existed between them (in what form I don't know, but I have no doubt about it), Anna Andreyevna up to the very last moment was not fully open with him. She did not lay all her cards on the table. She hinted at complete agreement on her part and at all sorts of promises—but she confined herself to hints. She listened perhaps to his whole plan in detail ; but she only approved in silence. I have good evidence for this conclusion, and the reason of it all was *that she was waiting for me.* She would rather have had to do with me than with the rascally Lambert—that's a fact I have no doubt of. That I understand ; but her mistake was in letting Lambert at last understand it. And it would not have suited him at all, if passing him by she had enticed the letter out of me and entered into a compact with me. Moreover, at that time he had complete confidence in the " soundness of the job " ; another man in his place would have had fears and still have been uncertain ; but Lambert was young, insolent, and filled with impatient greed for gain ; he knew little of human nature, and confidently assumed that all were scoundrels. Such a man could have no doubts, especially as he had already observed all sorts of traits in Anna Andreyevna which supported his belief.

One last point, and the most important : did Versilov know anything by that time, and had he even then taken part with Lambert in any plan, however remote ? No, no, no, at that time he had not. Though, perhaps, even then a fatal word had been dropped. But enough, enough, I am hastening too far ahead.

Well, and what of me ? Did I know anything, and what did I know on the day I went out ? When I began this *entrefilet* I declared that I knew nothing on that day, but found out about everything much later, and only when it was all over. That's the truth, but is it the full truth ? No, it is not ; I certainly knew something already, I knew a great deal, indeed. But how ? Let the reader remember my *dream !* If I could have had such a dream, if it could have surged up from my heart and taken that shape, I must have had, not a knowledge but a presentiment of a very great deal of what I have just explained, though in actual fact I only discovered it when everything was over. I had no knowledge of it, but my heart was throbbing with forebodings, and evil spirits had possession of my dreams. And it was to that man that I rushed, fully knowing what sort of man he was and foreseeing everything even in detail. And why did

I rush to him ? Imagine ; it seems to me now at the very minute when I am writing that I knew exactly at the time why I was rushing to him, though, again, I knew nothing then. Perhaps the reader will understand this. Now to get on with my story, fact by fact.

2

It begins two days before my outburst, when Liza came home in the evening in a state of agitation. She felt terribly humiliated and indeed something insufferable had happened to her.

I have already mentioned the terms she was on with Vassin. She went to see him not simply to show us that she did not need us, but because she really had a high opinion of him. Their acquaintance had begun at Luga, and I always fancied that Vassin was not indifferent to her. In the misfortunes that had over- whelmed her she might naturally have wished for the advice of a calm, resolute, always lofty mind such as she supposed Vassin's to be. Besides, women are not very clever in appre- ciating a man's mind at its true value when they like a man ; and they will gladly accept paradoxes as the closest reasoning, if they fall in with their own desires. What Liza liked in Vassin was his sympathy for her in her position and, as she had fancied at first, his sympathy with Prince Sergay. When, later on, she suspected his feeling for her, she could not help appreciating the sympathy he showed for his rival. When she told Prince Sergay that she sometimes went to consult Vassin, he had from the first shown the greatest uneasiness ; he began to be jealous. Liza was offended at this, and purposely maintained her friendly relations with Vassin. Prince Sergay said nothing, but was gloomy. Liza confessed to me (long afterwards) that Vassin had very soon ceased to attract her ; he was composed, and just this everlasting unruffled composure, which had so attracted her at first, afterwards seemed to her distasteful. One would have thought he was practical, and he did, in fact, give her some apparently good advice, but all his advice, as ill-luck would have it, appeared later on impossible to carry out. He gave his opinions sometimes too conceitedly, and showed no trace of diffidence with her, becoming more and more free in his manner as time went on, which she ascribed to his unconsciously feeling less and less respect for her position. Once she thanked him for his invariable goodwill to me, and for talking to me as an intellectual equal though he was so superior to me (she was repeating my words). He answered :

" That's not so, and not for that reason. It's because I see no difference between him and other people. I don't consider him more foolish than the clever, or more evil than the good. I treat every one alike because every one's alike in my eyes."

" Why, do you mean to say you see no differences ? "

" Oh, of course, people are all different in one way or another, but differences don't exist for me because the differences between people don't concern me ; to me they are all the same and everything's the same ; and so I'm equally kind to all."

" And don't you find it dull ? "

" No, I'm always satisfied with myself."

" And there's nothing you desire ? "

" Of course there is. But nothing I desire very much. There's scarcely anything I want, not another rouble. Whether I wear cloth of gold or remain as I am is all the same to me. Cloth of gold would add nothing to me. Tit-bits don't tempt me. Could places or honours be worth the place that I am worth ? "

Liza declared on her honour that these were literally his words. But it's not fair to criticize them like this without knowing the circumstances under which they were uttered.

Little by little Liza came also to the conclusion that his indulgent attitude to Prince Sergay was not due to sympathy for her, but was perhaps only because " all were alike to him, and differences did not exist for him." But in the end he did apparently begin to lose his indifference, and to take up an attitude not only of disapproval, but even of contemptuous irony towards Prince Sergay. This incensed Liza, but Vassin remained unaffected. Above all, he always expressed himself gently, and showed no indignation even in his disapproval, but confined himself to logical exposition of her hero's worthlessness ; but there was irony in this very logic. Finally he demonstrated almost directly the " irrationality," the perverse violence of her love. " Your feelings have been mistaken, and a mistake once recognized ought invariably to be corrected."

This had happened on that very day ; Liza indignantly got up from her place to go, but it will hardly be believed what this rational man did next, and how he concluded. With the air of a man of honour, and even with feeling, he offered her his hand. Liza bluntly called him a fool to his face and walked out.

To suggest deserting a man in misfortune because that man was

" unworthy of her," and above all to suggest it to a woman who was with child by that very man—there you have the mind of these people ! I call this being dreadfully theoretical and knowing nothing whatever of life, and put it down to a prodigious conceit. And what's more, Liza saw quite clearly that he was actually proud of his action, because he knew of her condition. With tears of indignation she hurried off to Prince Sergay, and he positively surpassed Vassin. One would have thought that after what she told him he might have been convinced that he had no cause for jealousy ; but he became perfectly frantic. But jealous people are always like that ! He made a fearful scene and insulted her so outrageously that she almost resolved to break off all relations with him.

She came home, however, still controlling herself, but she could not help telling mother. Oh, that evening the ice was completely broken, and they were on their old affectionate terms again ; both, of course, shed tears as usual in each other's arms, and Liza apparently regained her composure, though she was very gloomy. She sat through the evening in Makar Ivanovitch's room, without uttering a word, but without leaving the room. She listened very attentively to what he said. Ever since the incident with the bench she had become extremely and, as it were, timidly respectful to him, though she still remained taciturn.

But this time Makar Ivanovitch suddenly gave an unexpected and wonderful turn to the conversation. I may mention that Versilov and the doctor had talked of his health with very gloomy faces that morning. I may mention, too, that we had for some days been talking a great deal about mother's birthday, and making preparations to celebrate it in five days' time. Apropos of her birthday Makar Ivanovitch suddenly launched into reminiscences of mother's childhood, and the time when she " couldn't stand up on her little feet." " She was never out of my arms," the old man recalled. " I used to teach her to walk too sometimes. I set her up in a corner three steps away and called her, and she used to totter across to me, and she wasn't frightened, but would run to me laughing, she'd rush at me and throw her arms round my neck. I used to tell you fairy-tales later on, Sofia Andreyevna ; you were very fond of fairy-tales, you'd sit on my knee listening for two hours at a stretch. They used to wonder in the cottage, ' just see how she's taken to Makar.' Or I'd carry you off into the woods, I'd seek out a raspberry-bush, I would sit you down by it, and cut you a whistle-pipe out of wood. When we'd had a nice walk, I'd carry you home in my arms—and the little thing would fall asleep. Once she was afraid of a wolf ; she flew to me all of a tremble, and there wasn't a wolf there at all."

" I remember that," said mother.

" Can you really remember it ? "

" I remember a great deal. Ever since I remember anything in life I have felt your love and tender care over me," she said in a voice full of feeling, and she suddenly flushed crimson.

Makar Ivanovitch paused for a little.

" Forgive me, children, I am leaving you. The term of my life is close at hand. In my old age I have found consolation for all afflictions. Thank you, my dear ones."

" That's enough, Makar Ivanovitch darling," exclaimed Versilov in some agitation. " The doctor told me just now that you were a great deal better. . . ."

Mother listened in alarm.

" Why, what does he know, your Alexandr Semyonovitch—he's a dear man and nothing more. Give over, friends, do you think that I'm afraid to die ? After my morning prayer to-day I had the feeling in my heart that I should never go out again from here ; it was told me. Well, what of it, blessed be the name of the Lord. Yet I have a longing to be looking upon all of you still. Job, after all his sufferings, was comforted looking upon his new children, and forgot the children that were gone—it is impossible ! Only with the years the sorrow is mingled with the joy and turned to sighs of gladness. So it is in the world. Every soul is tried and is comforted. I thought, children, to say one little word to you," he went on with a gentle, exquisite smile which I shall never forget, and he turned to me, " be zealous for the Holy Church, my dear, and if the time calls for it—die for her ; but wait a bit, don't be frightened, it won't be at once," he added, laughing. " Now perhaps you don't think of it, afterwards you will think of it. And something more. Any good thing you bethink yourself to do, do it for the sake of God and not for envy. Stand firmly to your cause, and do not give way through any sort of cowardice ; act steadily, neither rushing nor turning about ; well, that is all I want to tell you. Only accustom yourself to pray daily and unceasingly. I say this now, maybe you'll remember it. I should like to say something to you, too, Andrey Petrovitch, sir, but God will find your heart without my words.

And for long years we have ceased to speak of that, ever since that arrow pierced my heart. Now that I am departing I would only remind you of what you promised then. . . ."

He almost whispered the last words, with his eyes cast down.

"Makar Ivanovitch!" Versilov said in confusion, and he got up from his chair.

"There, there, don't be troubled, sir, I only recalled it . . . and in the sight of God I am more to blame than any of you, seeing that though you were my master I ought not to have allowed this weakness, and therefore, Sofia, fret not your soul too much, for all your sin is mine, and you scarcely had full judgment in those days, so I fancy; nor maybe you either, sir," he smiled with lips that quivered from some sort of pain, "and though I might then have taught you, my wife, even with the rod and indeed ought to have, yet I pitied you when you fell in tears before me, and hid nothing, and kissed my feet. Not to reproach you have I recalled this, beloved, but only to remind Andrey Petrovitch . . . for you remember, sir, yourself your promise, as a nobleman, and all will be covered with the wedding crown. I speak before the children, master . . ."

He was extremely agitated and looked at Versilov as though expecting from him some word of confirmation. I repeat it was all so sudden, so unexpected, that I sat motionless. Versilov was no less agitated: he went up to mother in silence and warmly embraced her; then mother, also in silence, went up to Makar Ivanovitch and bowed down to his feet.

In short the scene was overwhelming; on this occasion we were by ourselves. Even Tatyana Pavlovna was not present. Liza drew herself up in her chair and listened in silence; suddenly she stood up and said firmly to Makar Ivanovitch:

"Bless me, too, Makar Ivanovitch for my great anguish. To morrow will decide my whole fate, and you will pray for me to-day."

And she went out of the room. I knew that Makar Ivanovitch knew all about her already from mother. But it was the first time I had seen mother and Versilov side by side: till then I had only seen her as his slave near him. There was still so much I did not understand and had not detected in that man whom I had condemned, and so I went back to my room in confusion. And it must be said that it was just at this time that my perplexity about him was greatest. He had never seemed to me so mysterious and unfathomable as just at that time; but it's just about that that I'm writing this whole account ; all in its good time.

" It turns out though," I thought to myself as I got into bed, " that he gave his word ' as a nobleman ' to marry mother if she were left a widow. He said nothing of that when he told me about Makar Ivanovitch before."

Liza was out the whole of the following day, and when she came back, rather late, she went straight to Makar Ivanovitch. I thought I would not go in that I might not be in their way, but soon, noticing that mother and Versilov were already there, I went in. Liza was sitting by the old man crying on his shoulder, and he with a sorrowful face was stroking her head.

Versilov told me in my room afterwards that Prince Sergay insisted on having his way, and proposed marrying Liza at the first opportunity before his trial was over. It was hard for Liza to make up her mind to it, though she scarcely had the right to refuse. And indeed Makar Ivanovitch " commanded " her to be married. Of course all this would have come about of itself, and she would certainly have been married of her own accord and without hesitation, but at the moment she had been so insulted by the man she loved, and she was so humiliated by this love even in her own eyes that it was difficult for her to decide. But apart from her mortification there was another circumstance deterring her of which I could have no suspicion.

" Did you hear that all those young people on the Petersburg Side were arrested ? " Versilov added suddenly.

" What ? Dergatchev ? " I cried.

" Yes, and Vassin, too."

I was amazed, especially to hear about Vassin.

" Why, was he mixed up in anything ? Good heavens, what will happen to them now ! And just when Liza was being so severe upon him ! . . . What do you think ? What may happen to them ? It's Stebelkov, I swear it's Stebelkov's doing."

" We won't go into it," said Versilov, looking at me strangely (as people look at a man who has no knowledge or suspicion of something). " Who can tell what is going on among them, and who can tell what may happen to them ? I didn't come to speak of that. I hear you meant to go out to-morrow. Won't you be going to see Prince Sergay ? "

" The first thing ; though I must own it's very distasteful to me. Why, have you some message to send him ? "

" No, nothing. I shall see him myself. I'm sorry for Liza.

And what advice can Makar Ivanovitch give her ? He knows nothing about life or about people himself. Another thing, my dear boy " (it was a long time since he had called me " my dear boy "), " there are here too . . . certain young men . . . among whom is your old schoolfellow, Lambert . . . I fancy they are all great rascals. . . . I speak simply to warn you. . . . But, of course, it's your business, and I have no right . . ."

" Andrey Petrovitch ! " I clutched his hand, speaking without a moment's thought and almost by inspiration as I sometimes do (the room was almost in darkness). " Andrey Petrovitch, I have said nothing ; you have seen that of course, I have been silent till now, do you know why ? To avoid knowing your secrets. I've simply resolved not to know them, ever. I'm a coward. I'm afraid your secrets may tear you out of my heart altogether, and I don't want that to happen. Since it's so, why should you know my secrets ? It doesn't matter to you where I go. Does it ? "

" You are right ; but not a word more, I beseech you ! " he said, and went away. So, by accident, we had the merest scrap of an explanation. But he only added to my excitement on the eve of my new step in life next day, and I kept waking up all night in consequence. But I felt quite happy.

3

Next day I went out of the house at ten o'clock in the morning, doing my utmost to steal out quietly without taking leave or saying anything. I, so to speak, slipped out. Why I did so I don't know ; but if even mother had seen that I was going out and spoken to me I should have answered with something spiteful. When I found myself in the street and breathed the cold outdoor air I shuddered from an intense feeling—almost animal—which I might call " carnivorous." What was I going for, where was I going ? The feeling was utterly undefined and at the same time I felt frightened and delighted, both at once.

" Shall I disgrace myself to-day or not ? " I thought to myself with a swagger, though I knew that the step once taken that day would be decisive, and could not be retrieved all my life. But it's no use talking in riddles.

I went straight to the prison to Prince Sergay. I had received a letter for the superintendent from Tatyana Pavlovna two days before, and I met with an excellent reception. I don't know whether he was a good man, and it's beside the point; but he permitted my interview with the prince and arranged that it should take place in his room, courteously giving it up for our use. The room was the typical room of a government official of a certain standing, living in a government building—I think to describe it is unnecessary.

So it turned out that Prince Sergay and I were left alone.

He came in dressed in some sort of half-military attire, but wearing very clean linen and a dandified tie ; he was washed and combed, at the same time he looked terribly thin and very yellow. I noticed the same yellowness even in his eyes. In fact he was so changed in appearance that I stood still in amazement.

" How you have changed ! " I cried.

" That's nothing. Sit down, dear boy," half-fatuously he motioned me to the armchair and sat down opposite, facing me. " Let's get to the point. You see, my dear Alexey Makarovitch . . ."

" Arkady," I corrected him.

" What ? Oh yes ! No matter ! Oh yes ! " He suddenly collected himself. " Excuse me, my dear fellow, we'll return to the point."

He was, in fact, in a fearful hurry to turn to something. He was entirely from head to foot absorbed by something ; some vital idea which he wanted to formulate and expound to me. He talked a great deal and fearfully fast, gesticulating and explaining with strained and painful effort, but for the first minute I really could make nothing of it.

" To put it briefly " (he had used this expression " To put it briefly " ten times already), " to put it briefly," he concluded, " I troubled you yesterday, Arkady Makarovitch, and so urgently through Liza begged you to come to me, as though the place were on fire, but seeing that the essential part of the decision is bound to be momentous and conclusive for me . . ."

" Excuse me, prince," I interrupted, " did you send me a message yesterday ? Liza said nothing to me about it."

" What ? " he cried, suddenly stopping short in extreme astonishment, almost in alarm.

" She gave me no message at all. She came home last night so upset that she couldn't say a word to me."

Prince Sergay leapt up from his seat

"Are you telling me the truth, Arkady Makarovitch ? If so this . . . this . . ."

"Why, what is there so serious about it ? Why are you so uneasy ? She simply forgot or something."

He sat down and seemed overcome by a kind of stupor. It seemed as though the news that Liza had given me no message had simply crushed him. He suddenly began talking rapidly and waving his hands, and again it was fearfully difficult to follow him.

"Stay ! " he exclaimed suddenly, pausing and holding up his finger. "Stay, this . . . this . . . if I'm not mistaken this is a trick ! . . ." he muttered with the grin of a maniac, " and it means that . . ."

"It means absolutely nothing," I interposed, " and I can't understand how such a trivial circumstance can worry you so much. . . . Ach, prince, since that time—since that night, do you remember . . ."

"Since what night, and what of it ? " he cried pettishly, evidently annoyed at my interrupting him.

" At Zerstchikov's, where we saw each other last. Why, before your letter. . . . Don't you remember you were terribly excited then, but the difference between then and now is so great that I am positively horrified when I look at you."

" Oh yes," he pronounced in the tone of a man of polite society, seeming suddenly to remember. " Oh yes ; that evening . . . I heard. . . . Well, and are you better ? How are you after all that, Arkady Makarovitch ? . . . But let us return to the point. I am pursuing three aims precisely, you see ; there are three problems before me, and I . . ."

He began rapidly talking again of his " chief point." I realized at last that I was listening to a man who ought at once to have at least a vinegar compress applied to his head, if not perhaps to be bled. All his incoherent talk turned, of course, around his trial, and the possible issue of it, and the fact that the colonel of his regiment had visited him and given him a lengthy piece of advice about something which he had not taken, and the notes he had just lately sent to some one, and the prosecutor, and the certainty that they would deprive him of his rights as a nobleman and send him to the Northern Region of Russia, and the possibility of settling as a colonist and regaining his position, in Tashkent, and his plans for training his son (which Liza would bear him) and handing something down to him " in the wilds of Archangel, in the

Holmogory." " I wanted your opinion, Arkady Makarovitch, believe me I so feel and value . . . If only you knew, if only you knew, Arkady Makarovitch, my dear fellow, my brother, what Liza means to me, what she has meant to me here, now, all this time ! " he shouted, suddenly clutching at his head with both hands.

" Sergay Petrovitch, surely you won't sacrifice her by taking her away with you ! To the Holmogory ! " I could not refrain from exclaiming. Liza's fate, bound to this maniac for life, suddenly, and as it were for the first time, rose clearly before my imagination. He looked at me, got up again, took one step, turned and sat down again, still holding his head in his hands.

" I'm always dreaming of spiders ! " he said suddenly.

" You are terribly agitated. I should advise you to go to bed, prince, and to ask for a doctor at once."

" No, excuse me—of that afterwards. I asked you to come and see me chiefly to discuss our marriage. The marriage, as you know, is to take place here, at the church. I've said so already. Permission has been given for all this, and, in fact, they encourage it. . . . As for Liza . . ."

" Prince, have pity on Liza, my dear fellow ! " I cried. " Don't torture her, now, at least, don't be jealous ! "

" What ! " he cried, staring at me intently with eyes almost starting out of his head, and his whole face distorted into a sort of broad grin of senseless inquiry. It was evident that the words " don't be jealous " had for some reason made a fearful impression on him.

" Forgive me, prince, I spoke without thinking. Oh prince, I have lately come to know an old man, my nominal father. . . . Oh, if you could see him you would be calmer. . . . Liza thinks so much of him, too."

" Ah, yes, Liza . . . ah, yes, is that your father ? Or . . . pardon, mon cher, something of the sort . . . I remember . . . she told me . . . an old man. . . . I'm sure of it, I'm sure of it. I knew an old man, too . . . mais passons. . . . The chief point is to make clear what's essential at the moment, we must . . ."

I got up to go away. It was painful to me to look at him.

" I don't understand ! " he pronounced sternly and with dignity, seeing that I had got up to go.

" It hurts me to look at you," I said.

" Arkady Makarovitch, one word, one word more ! " He clutched me by the shoulder with quite a different expression and gesture, and sat me down in the armchair. " You've heard about those . . . you understand ? " he bent down to me.

" Oh yes, Dergatchev. No doubt it's Stebelkov's doing ! " I cried impulsively.

" Yes, Stebelkov. And . . . you don't know ? "

He broke off and again he stared at me with the same wide eyes and the same spasmodic, senselessly questioning grin, which grew broader and broader. His face gradually grew paler. I felt a sudden shudder. I remembered Versilov's expression when he had told me of Vassin's arrest the day before.

" Oh, is it possible ? " I cried, panic-stricken.

" You see, Arkady Makarovitch, that's why I sent to you to explain . . . I wanted . . ." he began whispering rapidly.

" It was you who informed against Vassin ! " I cried.

" No ; you see, there was a manuscript. Vassin gave it only a few days ago to Liza . . . to take care of. And she left it here for me to look at, and then it happened that they quarrelled next day . . ."

" You gave the manuscript to the authorities ! "

" Arkady Makarovitch, Arkady Makarovitch ! "

" And so you," I screamed, leaping up, emphasizing every word, " without any other motive, without any other object, simply because poor Vassin was *your rival*, simply out of jealousy, you gave up the *manuscript entrusted to Liza* . . . gave it up to whom ? To whom ? To the Public Prosecutor ? "

But he did not answer, and he hardly could have answered, for he stood before me like a statue, still with the same sickly smile and the same fixed look. But suddenly the door opened and Liza came in. She almost swooned when she saw us together.

" You're here ? So you're here ? " she cried, her face suddenly distorted, seizing my hand. " So you . . . *know* ? "

But she could read in my face already that I " knew." With a swift irresistible impulse I threw my arms round her and held her close ! And at that minute for the first time I grasped in all its intensity the hopeless, endless misery which shrouded in unbroken darkness the whole life of this . . . wilful seeker after suffering.

" Is it possible to talk to him now," she said, tearing herself away from me. " Is it possible to be with him ? Why are you here ? Look at him look at him ! And can one, can one judge him ? "

Her face was full of infinite suffering and infinite compassion as exclaiming this she motioned towards the unhappy wretch.

He was sitting in the armchair with his face hidden in his hands. And she was right. He was a man in a raging fever and not responsible. They put him in the hospital that morning, and by the evening he had brain fever.

4

Leaving Prince Sergay with Liza I went off about one o'clock to my old lodging. I forgot to say that it was a dull, damp day, with a thaw beginning, and a warm wind that would upset the nerves of an elephant. The master of the house met me with a great display of delight, and a great deal of fuss and bustle, which I particularly dislike, especially at such moments. I received this drily, and went straight to my room, but he followed me, and though he did not venture to question me, yet his face was beaming with curiosity, and at the same time he looked as though he had a right to be curious. I had to behave politely for my own sake ; but though it was so essential to me to find out something (and I knew I should learn it), I yet felt it revolting to begin cross-examining him. I inquired after the health of his wife, and we went in to see her. The latter met me deferentially indeed, but with a businesslike and taciturn manner ; this to some extent softened my heart. To be brief, I learned on this occasion some very wonderful things.

Well, of course, Lambert had been and he came twice afterwards, and " he looked at all the rooms, saying that perhaps he would take them." Darya Onisimovna had come several times, goodness knows why. " She was very inquisitive," added my landlord.

But I did not gratify him by asking what she was inquisitive about. I did not ask questions at all, in fact. He did all the talking, while I kept up a pretence of rummaging in my trunk (though there was scarcely anything left in it). But what was most vexatious, he too thought fit to play at being mysterious, and noticing that I refrained from asking questions, felt it incumbent upon him to be more fragmentary and even enigmatic in his communications.

" The young lady has been here, too," he added, looking at me strangely.

" What young lady ? "

" Anna Andreyevna ; she's been here twice ; she made the acquaintance of my wife. A very charming person, very pleasant. Such an acquaintance is quite a privilege, Arkady Makarovitch."

And as he pronounced these words he positively took a step towards me. He seemed very anxious that I should understand something.

" Did she really come twice ? " I said with surprise.

" The second time she came with her brother."

" That was with Lambert," I thought involuntarily.

" No, not with Mr. Lambert," he said, seeming to guess at once, as though piercing into my soul with his eyes. " But with her real brother, young Mr. Versilov. A *kammer-junker*, I believe."

I was very much confused. He looked at me, smiling very caressingly.

" Oh, and some one else came and was asking after you, that ma'amselle, a French lady, Mamselle Alphonsine de Verden. Oh, how well she sings and recites poetry. She'd slipped off to see Prince Nikolay Ivanovitch at Tskarskoe, to sell him a dog, she told me, a rare kind, black, and no bigger than your fist . . ."

I asked him to leave me alone on the pretext of a headache. He immediately fell in with my request, even breaking off in the middle of a sentence, and not only without the slightest sign of huffiness, but almost with pleasure, waving his hand mysteriously, as though to say, " I understand, I understand," and though he did not actually say this he could not resist the satisfaction of walking out of the room on tiptoe.

There are very vexatious people in the world.

I sat for an hour and a half alone, deliberating ; rather, not really deliberating but dreaming. Though I was perplexed I was not in the least surprised. I even expected to hear something more, other marvels. " Perhaps they have already hatched them," I thought. I had for a long time been firmly persuaded that the machinery of their plot was wound up and was in full swing. " They're only waiting for me," I thought again with a sort of irritable and pleasant self-satisfaction. That they were eagerly awaiting me, and were scheming to carry out some plan at my lodging was clear as day. " The old prince's wedding, can it be ? He's surrounded by a regular network of intrigue. But am I going to permit it, my friends ? That's the question," I said in conclusion with haughty satisfaction.

" Once I begin I shall be carried away by the whirlpool like a chip. Am I free now, this minute, or am I not ? When I go back to mother this evening can I still say to myself as I have done all these days ' I am my own master ' ? "

That was the gist of my questions, or rather of the throbbing at my heart in the hour and a half I spent sitting on the bed in the corner, with my elbows on my knees and my head propped in my hands. But I knew, I knew even then that all these questions were utter nonsense, and that I was drawn only by *her* —by her, by her alone ! At last I have said this straight out and have written it with pen on paper, though even now as I write this a year later I don't know what name to give to the feeling I had then !

Oh, I was sorry for Liza, and my heart was full of a most unfeigned grief. Nothing but the feeling of pain on her account could have calmed or effaced in me for a time that "carnivorousness " (I recall that word). But I was immensely spurred on by curiosity and a sort of dread and another feeling—I don't know what ; but I know and I knew then that it was an evil feeling. Perhaps my impulse was to fall at *her* feet, or perhaps I wanted to put her to every torture, and " quickly, quickly " to show her something. No grief, no compassion for Liza, could stop me. Could I have got up and gone home . . . to Makar Ivanovitch ?

" And is it quite impossible to go to them, to find out everything from them, and to go away from them for ever, passing unscathed among marvels and monsters ? "

At three o'clock, pulling myself together and reflecting that I might be late, I went out hastily, took a cab, and flew to Anna Andreyevna.

CHAPTER V

1

As soon as I was announced, Anna Andreyevna threw down her sewing and rushed to meet me in the outermost of her rooms, a thing which had never happened before. She held out both hands to me and flushed quickly. She led me into her room in silence, sat down to her needlework again, made me sit down beside her. She did not go on with her sewing, but still scrutinized me with the same fervent sympathy, without uttering a word.

" You sent Darya Onisimovna to me," I began bluntly, rather overwhelmed by this exaggerated display of sympathy, though I found it agreeable.

She suddenly began talking without answering my question.

" I have heard all about it, I know all about it. That terrible night. . . . Oh, what you must have gone through ! Can it be true ! Can it be true that you were found unconscious in the frost ? "

" You heard that . . . from Lambert. . . ." I muttered, reddening.

" I heard it all from him at the time ; but I've been eager to see you. Oh, he came to me in alarm ! At your lodging . . . where you have been lying ill, they would not let him in to see you . . . and they met him strangely . . . I really don't know how it was, but he kept telling me about that night ; he told me that when you had scarcely come to yourself, you spoke of me, and . . . and of your devotion to me. I was touched to tears, Arkady Makarovitch, and I don't know how I have deserved such warm sympathy on your part, especially considering the condition in which you were yourself ! Tell me, M. Lambert was the friend of your childhood, was he not ? "

" Yes, but what happened ? . . . I confess I was indiscreet, and perhaps I told him then a great deal I shouldn't have."

" Oh, I should have heard of that wicked horrible intrigue apart from him ! I always had a presentiment that they would drive you to that, always. Tell me, is it true that Büring dared to lift his hand against you ? "

She spoke as though it were entirely owing to Büring and *her* that I had been found under the wall. And she is right too, I thought, but I flared up :

" If he had lifted his hand against me, he would not have gone away unpunished. And I should not be sitting before you now without having avenged myself," I answered hotly. It struck me that she wanted for some reason to irritate me, to set me against somebody (I knew of course against whom) ; yet I fell in with it.

" You say that you had a presentiment that I should be driven *to this,* but on Katerina Nikolaevna's side it was of course only a misunderstanding . . . though it is true that she was too hasty in allowing her kindly feeling for me to be influenced by that misunderstanding. . . ."

" I should think she was too hasty indeed ! " Anna Andreyevna assented quickly, with a sort of ecstasy of sympathy. "Oh, if only you knew the intrigue that is being hatched there now ! Of course, Arkady Makarovitch, of course it is difficult for you to realize now all the delicacy of my position," she brought out, blushing and casting down her eyes. "Since I saw you last . . . that very morning I took a step which not every one would be able to understand and interpret rightly ; so it is hardly likely that it would be understood by anyone with your still uncorrupted mind, and your fresh, loving, unsophisticated heart. Believe me, my dear friend, I appreciate your devotion to me, and I shall repay it with my everlasting gratitude. In the world, of course, they will throw stones at me, they have thrown them already. But even if they were right, from their odious point of view, which of them could, which of them dare judge me ? I have been abandoned by my father from childhood up ; we Versilovs are an ancient noble Russian family, yet we are adventurers, and I am eating the bread of charity. Was it not natural I should turn to one who has taken the place of a father to me, at whose hands I have received nothing but kindness during all these years ? My feelings for him are known only to God, and he alone can judge them, and I refuse to accept the judgment of the world upon the step I have taken. When there is, moreover, at the bottom of this the most cunning, the most evil intrigue, and the plot to ruin a trusting, noble-hearted father is the work of his own daughter, is it to be endured ? No, I will save him if I have to ruin my reputation. I am ready to be with him simply as a nurse, to take care of him, and to look after him, but I will not let hateful, cold, mercenary worldliness triumph ! "

She spoke with unwonted fire, very possibly half assumed, though at the same time sincere, because it was evident how deeply involved she was in the matter. Oh, I felt that she was lying (though sincerely, for one can lie sincerely). And that she was now evil ; but it is wonderful how it often is, in dealing with women : this assumption of perfect refinement, these lofty manners, these inaccessible heights of well-bred grandeur and proud chastity—all this quite threw me out of my reckoning, and I began agreeing with her on every point, so long as I was with her ; that is, I could not bring myself to contradict her, anyway. Oh, a man is in absolute moral slavery to a woman, especially if he is a generous man ! Such a woman can convince a generous man of anything she likes. "She and Lambert, my goodness ! " I thought, looking at her in perplexity. To tell the whole truth, however, I don't know what to think of her to this day ; truly her feelings were known only to God, and, besides, human beings are such complicated machines, that one cannot analyse them in some cases, and above all if the human being in question is a woman.

"Anna Andreyevna, what is it you exactly want me to do ? " I asked, with a good deal of decision however.

"How ? What do you mean by your question, Arkady Makarovitch ? "

"I fancy, from everything . . . and from certain other considerations . . ." I explained stammering, "that you sent to me because you expected something from me ; so what is it exactly ? "

Without answering my question, she immediately began talking again, as rapidly and as earnestly as before :

"But I cannot, I am too proud to enter into explanations and negotiations with unknown persons, like M. Lambert. I have been waiting for you, I don't want M. Lambert. My position is awful, desperate, Arkady Makarovitch ! I am forced to duplicity, hemmed in by the machinations of that woman—and that is more than I can endure. I am driven almost to the humiliation of intriguing, and I have been waiting for you as my saviour. You must not blame me for looking greedily about me to find one friend at least, and so I cannot help being glad to see a friend : he, who could think of me and even utter my name, half frozen on that night, must be devoted to me. That's what I've been thinking all this time and that is why I rely on you."

She looked into my face with impatient inquiry. And again I had not the heart to disillusion her, and to tell her plainly that Lambert had deceived her, and that I had by no means told him that I was so devoted to her, and that her name was not the only one I mentioned. And so by my silence I confirmed, as it were, Lambert's lie. Oh, she knew very well, I am convinced, that Lambert had been exaggerating and simply lying to her, solely in order to have a plausible excuse to call upon her, and to get into touch with her ; though she looked into my face as though she were convinced of my truth and devotion, she must have known that I did not bring myself to contradict her from delicacy of feeling, and the awkwardness of youth. But whether I was right in this surmise, I don't know. Perhaps I am horribly evil-minded.

"My brother is taking my part," she said with sudden heat, seeing that I was not disposed to speak.

"I'm told you have been at my lodgings," I muttered in confusion.

"Yes . . . you know poor Prince Nikolay Ivanitch has no place now where he can take refuge from this intrigue, or rather from his own daughter, unless in your lodgings, that is the lodgings of a friend ; you know he looks upon you at least as a friend ! . . . And if you will only do something for his benefit, then do this—if only you can, if only you have the generosity and courage . . . and, and finally if it is really true, that there is *something you can do*. Oh, it is not for my sake, it's not for my sake, but for the sake of the poor old man, the only person who genuinely loved you, and who has become as attached to you as though you were his own son, and is still missing you ! For myself I expect nothing, even from you— since even my own father has played me such a treacherous, such a spiteful trick."

"I believe, Andrey Petrovitch . . ." I began.

"Andrey Petrovitch," she repeated with bitter mockery ; "Andrey Petrovitch, in answer to a direct question from me, told me on his word of honour that he had never had any intentions in regard to Katerina Nikolaevna and I completely believed it when I took that step ; and yet it seemed that his composure only lasted till he heard of Baron Büring."

"That's wrong, " I cried, "there was a moment when I too believed in his love for that woman, but it's a mistake . . . and even if it were so, he might, I should think, be perfectly composed about it now . . . since the retirement of that gentleman."

"What gentleman ? "

"Büring."

"Who has told you of his retirement ? Perhaps the gentle man in question never had any such views," she jeered malignantly ; I fancied too, that she looked at me jeeringly.

"Darya Onisimovna told me," I muttered in confusion, which I was not able to conceal, and which she saw only too clearly.

"Darya Onisimovna is a very nice person, and, of course, I cannot forbid her loving me, but she has no means of knowing what does not concern her."

My heart began to ache ; and, as she had been reckoning on

rousing my indignation, I did in fact begin to feel indignant, but not with "that woman," but for the time being with Anna Andreyevna herself. I got up.

"As an honourable man, I ought to warn you, Anna Andreyevna, that your expectations . . . in regard to me . . . may turn out to be utterly unfounded. . . ."

"I expect you to be my champion," she said, looking at me resolutely : "abandoned as I am by every one . . . your sister, if you care to have it so, Arkady Makarovitch."

Another instant, and she would have burst into tears.

"Well, you had better not expect anything, for, 'perhaps' nothing will come of it," I muttered with an indescribable feeling of disgust.

"How am I to understand your words ? " she said, showing her consternation too plainly.

"Why, that I am going away from you all, and—that's the end of it ! " I suddenly exclaimed almost furiously, "and the *letter*—I shall tear up. Good-bye."

I bowed to her, and went out without speaking, though at the same time I scarcely dared to look at her, but had hardly gone downstairs when Darya Onisimovna ran after me, with a half sheet of paper folded in two. Where Darya Onisimovna had sprung from, and where she had been sitting while I was talking with Anna Andreyevna, I cannot conceive. She did not utter a word, but merely gave me the paper, and ran away. I unfolded it : on the paper, clearly and distinctly written, was Lambert's address, and it had apparently been got ready several days before. I suddenly recalled that when Darya Onisimovna had been with me that day, I had told her that I did not know where Lambert lived, meaning, "I don't know and don't want to know." But by this time I had learned Lambert's address from Liza, whom I had specially asked to get it for me from the address bureau. Anna Andreyevna's action seemed to me too definite, even cynical : although I had declined to assist her, she was simply sending me straight to Lambert, as though she had not the slightest faith in my refusal. It was quite clear to me that she knew everything about the letter, and from whom could she have learnt it if not from Lambert, to whom she was sending me that I might co-operate with him.

There was no doubt that they all, every one of them, looked upon me as a feeble boy without character or will, with whom they could do anything, I thought with indignation.

2

Nevertheless, I did go to Lambert's. Where else could I have satisfied my curiosity ? Lambert, as it appeared, lived a long way off, in Cross Alley, close to the Summer Gardens, still in the same lodgings ; but when I ran away from him that night I had so completely failed to notice the way and the distance, that when I got his address from Liza, four days earlier, I was surprised and could scarcely believe that he lived there. As I was going upstairs I noticed at the door of the flat, on the third storey, two young men, and thought they had rung the bell before I came and were waiting for the door to be opened. While I was mounting the stairs they both, turning their backs on the door, scrutinized me very attentively. " The flat is all let out in rooms, and they must be going to see another lodger," I thought, frowning, as I went up to them. It would have been very disagreeable to me to find anyone else at Lambert's. Trying not to look at them, I put out my hand to the bell.

" *Attendez !* " one of them cried to me.

" Please, please don't ring again yet," said the other young man in a soft musical voice, slightly drawling the words. " Here we'll finish this, and then we'll all ring altogether. Shall we ? "

I waited. They were both very young men, about twenty or twenty-two ; they were doing something rather strange at the door, and I began to watch them with surprise. The one who had cried " *attendez* " was a very tall fellow, over six feet, thin and lean, but very muscular, with a very small head in proportion to his height, and with a strange, as it were comic expression of gloom on his rather pock-marked though agreeable and by no means stupid face. There was a look as it were of exaggerated intentness and of unnecessary and excessive determination in his eyes. He was very badly dressed : in an old wadded overcoat, with a little fur collar of mangy-looking raccoon ; it was too short for him and obviously second-hand. He had on shabby high boots almost like a peasant's, and on his head was a horribly crushed, dirty-looking top-hat. His whole appearance was marked by slovenliness ; his ungloved hands were dirty and his long nails were black. His companion, on the other hand, was smartly dressed, judging from his light skunk fur coat, his elegant hat, and the light new gloves on his slender fingers ;

he was about my height, and he had an extremely charming expression on his fresh and youthful face.

The tall fellow was taking off his tie—an utterly threadbare greasy ribbon, hardly better than a piece of tape—and the pretty-looking youth, taking out of his pocket another newly purchased black tie, was putting it round the neck of the tall fellow, who, with a perfectly serious face, submissively stretched out his very long neck, throwing his overcoat back from his shoulders.

"No ; it won't do if the shirt is so dirty," said the younger one, "the effect won't be good, it will only make it look dirtier. I told you to put on a collar. I don't know how . . . do you know how to do it," he said, turning suddenly to me.

"What ? " I asked.

"Why, fasten his tie. You see it ought to go like this, to hide his dirty shirt, or else the whole effect is spoilt whatever we do. I have just bought the tie for a rouble at Filip's, the hairdresser's, on purpose for him."

"Was it—that rouble ? " muttered the tall one.

"Yes, I haven't a farthing now. Then you can't do it ? In that case we must ask Alphonsine."

"To see Lambert ? " the tall fellow asked me abruptly.

"Yes," I answered with no less determination, looking him in the face.

"Dolgorowky ? " he went on with the same air and the same voice.

"No, not Korovkin," I answered as abruptly, mistaking what he said.

"Dolgorowky ? " the tall fellow almost shouted again, and he took a step towards me almost menacingly. His companion burst out laughing.

"He says 'Dolgorowky' and not Korovkin," he explained to me. "You know in the *Journal des Débats* the French constantly distort Russian names. . . ."

"In the *Indépendance*," growled the tall fellow.

". . . Well, it's just the same in the *Indépendance*. Dolgoruky, for instance, they write Dolgorowky—I have seen it myself, and Valonyev is always written comte Wallonieff."

"Doboyny ! " cried the tall fellow.

"Yes, there's Doboyny, too, I've seen it myself ; and we both laughed ; some Russian Madame Doboyny abroad . . . but there's no need to mention them all, you know," he said, turning suddenly to the tall fellow.

" Excuse me, are you M. Dolgoruky ? "

" Yes, my name is Dolgoruky ; how do you know it ? "

The tall one suddenly whispered something to the pretty-looking lad ; the latter frowned and shook his head, but the tall fellow immediately addressed me ;

" *Monsieur le prince, vous n'avez pas de rouble d'argent pour nous, pas deux, mais un seul, voulez-vous ?* "

" Oh, how horrid you are," cried the boy.

" *Nous vous rendons,*" concluded the tall one, mispronouncing the French words coarsely and clumsily.

" He's a cynic, you know," the boy laughed to me ; " and do you suppose he can't speak French ? He speaks like a Parisian, but he is mimicking those Russians who are awfully fond of talking aloud in French together before other people, though they can't speak it themselves. . . ."

" *Dans les wagons,*" the tall fellow explained.

" To be sure, in railway carriages ; oh, what a bore you are ! There's no need to explain. Why will you always pretend to be a fool ? "

Meanwhile I took out a rouble and offered it to the tall fellow.

" *Nous vous rendons,*" said the latter, pocketing the rouble ; and turning to the door with a perfectly unmoved and serious face, he proceeded to kick it with his huge coarse boot and without the faintest sign of ill-humour. . . .

" Ah, you will be fighting with Lambert again ! " the boy observed uneasily. " You had much better ring the bell ! "

I rang the bell, but the tall fellow continued kicking the door nevertheless.

" *Ah, sacré* . . ." we heard Lambert's voice the other side of the door, and he quickly opened it.

" *Dites donc, voulez-vous que je vous casse la tête, mon ami !* " he shouted to the tall man.

" *Mon ami, voilà Dolgorowky, l'autre mon ami,*" the tall fellow replied with dignified gravity, staring at Lambert, who was red with anger. As soon as the latter saw me, he seemed suddenly transformed.

" It's you, Arkady ! At last ! Then you are better, better are you at last ? "

He seized my hands, pressing them warmly ; he was in fact so genuinely delighted that I felt pleased at once, and even began to like him.

" I've come to you first of all ! "

" Alphonsine ! " cried Lambert.

She instantly skipped out from behind the screen.

" *Le voilà !* "

" *C'est lui !* " cried Alphonsine, clasping and unclasping her hands ; she would have rushed to embrace me, but Lambert protected me.

" There, there, there, down, down ! " he shouted to her as though she were a dog. " It's like this, Arkady : some fellows have agreed to dine together to-day at the Tatars'. I shan't let you go, you must come with us. We'll have dinner ; I'll get rid of these fellows at once, and then we can have a chat. Come in, come in ! We'll set off at once, only wait a minute . . ."

I went in and stood in the middle of that room, looking about me, and remembering it. Lambert behind the screen hurriedly dressed. The tall fellow and his companion followed us in, in spite of Lambert's words. We all remained standing.

" *Mlle. Alphonsine, voulez-vous me baiser ?* " growled the tall man.

" *Mlle. Alphonsine,*" the younger one was beginning, showing her the tie, but she flew savagely at both of them.

" *Ah, le petit vilain !* " she shouted to the younger one ; " *ne m'approchez pas, ne me salissez pas, et vous, le grand dadais, je vous planque à la porte tous les deux, savez vous cela !* "

Though she warned him off with contempt and disgust, as though she were really afraid of being soiled by contact with him (which I could not at all understand because he was such a pretty fellow, and turned out to be just as well dressed when he took off his overcoat), the younger of the two men kept asking her to tie his tall friend's cravat for him, and to put him on one of Lambert's clean collars first. She was on the point of beating them in her indignation at such a suggestion, but Lambert overhearing, shouted to her behind the screen not to hinder them, but to do as they asked ; " they won't leave off if you don't," he added, and Alphonsine instantly produced a collar and began to fasten the tall man's cravat without the slightest sign of disinclination. The man stretched out his neck just as he had done on the stairs, while she tied his cravat.

" *Mlle. Alphonsine, avez vous vendu votre bologne ?* " he asked.

" *Qu'est-ce que ca, ma bologne ?* "

The younger man explained that "ma bologne" meant a lapdog.

"*Tiens, quel est ce baragouin ?*"

"*Je parle comme une dame russe sur les eaux minérales,*" observed *le grand dadais*, still with his neck outstretched.

"*Qu'est-ce que ça qu'une dame russe sur les eaux minérales et . . . où est donc votre jolie montre, que Lambert vous a donnée,*" she said suddenly to the younger one.

"What, no watch again," Lambert chimed in irritably behind the screen.

"We've eaten it up ! " growled *le grand dadais*.

"I sold it for eight roubles : it was only silver gilt, and you said it was gold ; so now at the shop it's only sixteen roubles," the younger answered Lambert, defending himself reluctantly.

"We must put an end to this ! " Lambert said even more irritably. "I don't buy you clothes, my young friend, and give you good things, for you to spend them on your tall friend. . . . What was that tie too that you bought him ? "

"That was only a rouble ; that was not with your money. He had no cravat at all, and he ought to buy a hat too."

"Nonsense ! " Lambert was really angry. "I gave him enough for a hat too, and he goes off and wastes it on oysters and champagne. He positively reeks ; he's dirty and untidy ; you can't take him anywhere. How can I take him out to dinner ? "

"I'm a cad," growled the *dadais*. "*Nous avons un rouble d'argent que nous avons prêté chez notre nouvel ami.*"

"Don't you give him anything, Arkady," Lambert cried again.

"Excuse me, Lambert ; I ask you plainly for ten roubles," cried the boy, growing suddenly angry and flushing, which made him look twice as handsome as before ; "and don't ever dare to say such stupid things as you did just now to Dolgoruky. I must have ten roubles to pay Dolgoruky back that rouble at once, and with the rest I'll buy Andreyev a hat, so you see."

Lambert came out from behind the screen :

"Here are three yellow notes, and three roubles, and there's nothing more till Tuesday, and don't dare . . . or else. . . ."

Le grand dadais fairly snatched the money from him.

"*Dolgorowky,* here is the rouble *nous vous rendons avec beaucoup de grâce.* Petya, come along ! " he called to his companion. Then holding up the two notes and waving them in the air, while he stared fixedly at Lambert, he yelled at the top of his voice :

"*Ohé Lambert !   Où est Lambert, as-tu vu Lambert ?* "

"How dare you, how dare you," Lambert yelled too, in terrible wrath : I saw that underlying all this was something in the past of which I knew nothing, and I looked on in astonishment. But the tall fellow was not in the least alarmed by Lambert's wrath ; on the contrary, he yelled louder than ever : "Ohé Lambert ! " and so on. And so shouting, they went out on the stairs. Lambert was running after them, but he turned back.

"I'll throw them out by the scr-r-ruff of their necks ! They cost more than they are worth. . . . Come along, Arkady ! I'm late. I am expected there by another . . . fellow I need . . . a beast too. . . . They're all beasts ! A low lot, a low lot ! " he shouted again, almost gnashing his teeth ; but all at once he recovered himself completely.

"I am glad that you have come at last. Alphonsine, not a step out of the house ! Let us go."

At the steps a smart turn-out was waiting for him. We got in ; but all the way he could not quite regain his composure and get over a sort of rage against the two young men. I was surprised at his taking it so seriously ; and what's more, at their being so disrespectful to Lambert, and his seeming almost frightened of them.

From the old impression that had been stamped on me from childhood, it still seemed to me that every one must be afraid of Lambert, as in spite of all my independence, I certainly stood in awe of him myself at that moment.

"I tell you now they are all a low lot," Lambert persisted. "Would you believe it that tall ruffian pestered me, the day before yesterday, in decent company. He stood in front of me and shouted : ' Ohé Lambert ! ' in decent company ! Every one laughed, and do you know, it was for me to give him money —would you believe it. I gave it him. Oh, that—r-r-ruffian ! Would you believe it ? He was an ensign in a regiment, but he was kicked out, and, you wouldn't imagine it, but he is a man of education : he was brought up in a good family, you would hardly believe it ! He has ideas, he might . . . and damn it all ! And he is a perfect Hercules. He is of use, though of not much use. And you can see he does not wash his hands. I

interested a lady in his case, an old lady of very good position,
telling her that he was penitent, and on the point of committing
suicide from remorse, and he went to see her, sat down and
began whistling. And the other, the pretty fellow, is a general's
son ; his family is ashamed of him. I got him off when he was
arrested, I saved him, and you see how he repays me. There
are no people worth their salt here ! I'll pay them out, I'll pay
them out ! "

"They know my name ; did you talk to them about me ? "

" Yes, it was stupid of me. Please stay on a little after dinner,
control your feelings. . . . There's an awful *canaille* coming.
Yes, he's an awful *canaille*, and awfully cunning ; they are all
rascals here, there's not an honest man about ! Well, we'll
finish—then. . . . What's your favourite dish ? But it doesn't
matter, the fare is always good. I'll pay, don't you worry. It's
a good thing you are well dressed. I can give you money.
You must come often. Only fancy, I've stood them meat and
drink here, it's fish pie every day of the week ; that watch he
sold—it's the second time. That little fellow, Trishatov, you
saw him ; Alphonsine is sick at the very sight of him, and won't
let him come near her ; and here in the presence of officers he
calls out : ' I must have woodcock.' I stood him woodcock !
But I'll pay them out."

" Do you remember, Lambert, how we went to a restaurant
together in Moscow, and you stuck a fork into me, and how you
had fifty roubles then ! "

" Yes, I remember ! Damn it, I remember ! I like you . . .
you may believe it. Nobody likes you ; but I like you ; I'm
the only one that does, you remember that. . . . The pock-
marked fellow that is coming here is a cunning *canaille* ; don't
you answer any of his questions ; if he begins talking, it's all right ;
but if he begins questioning, make some nonsensical answer, or
hold your tongue."

At any rate, in his excitement he did not question me much
on the way. I even felt insulted at his having such confidence
in me, and not even suspecting that I mistrusted him ; I fancied
that I detected in him the absurd idea that he could still order
me about. " And what's more, he's awfully ignorant and ill-
bred," I thought, as I went into the restaurant.

3

I had been into that restaurant, in the Morskaya, before, during my disgraceful period of degradation and depravity, and so the impression of those rooms, of those lackeys looking at me, and recognizing me as a familiar visitor, and finally the impression made on me by the mysterious company of Lambert's friends, amongst whom I found myself so suddenly, and to whom I seemed already to belong, and above all an obscure feeling that of my own freewill I was going into something abominable, and that I should certainly end up by doing something horrid— all this seemed to go through me in a flash. There was a moment when I very nearly went away ; but the moment passed and I remained.

The " pock-marked man," of whom for some reason Lambert was so much afraid, was already waiting for us. He was one of those men of stupidly practical appearance, whom I have always from my childhood detested ; he was about forty-five, of middle height, with hair just turning grey. He was disgustingly close-shaven, except for two little neatly trimmed grey whiskers, like sausages, one on each side of his extremely flat and spiteful-looking face. He was of course dull, solemn, and taciturn, and even conceited, as such nonentities always are. He looked at me very attentively, but he did not say a word. Lambert was so stupid that though he sat us down at the same table together, he did not think it necessary to introduce us, and so he may well have taken me for one of the blackmailers associated with Lambert. To the two young men (who arrived almost simultaneously with us) he did not address a single word during the whole of dinner, but it was evident that he knew them well. He talked only to Lambert, and then almost in a whisper, and indeed Lambert did most of the talking, and the pock-marked man confined himself to fragmentary and wrathful ejaculations, which sounded like an ultimatum. He behaved superciliously, was ill-humoured and sarcastic, while Lambert on the other hand was extremely excited and was evidently trying to persuade him all the time, probably urging him on to some undertaking. On one occasion I put out my hand to take a bottle of red wine ; the pock-marked man immediately took a bottle of sherry and handed it to me, though he had not said a word to me till then.

" Try this," he said, offering me the bottle. I guessed, on the spot, that he too, knew everything in the world about me—my story, and my name, and perhaps the fact that Lambert was counting upon me. The idea that he was taking me for a satellite maddened me again, and Lambert's face betrayed an intense and very stupid uneasiness when the pock-marked man addressed me ; the latter noticed it and laughed. "There's no doubt that Lambert depends on all of them," I thought, hating him at that instant with my whole soul. In this way, though we were sitting at the same table, throughout the whole dinner we were divided into two groups ; the pock-marked man with Lambert, facing each other close to the window, while I was beside the grubby Andreyev, and Trishatov sat facing me. Lambert hurried on the dinner, continually urging the waiters to make haste with the dishes. When the champagne was brought he held out his glass to me :

" To your health, let's clink glasses ! " he said, breaking off his conversation with the pock-marked man.

" And will you let me clink with you too ? " said the pretty youth, holding out his glass across the table. Till the champagne arrived he had been very silent, and seemed pensive. The *dadais* said nothing at all, but sat silent and ate a great deal.

" With pleasure," I answered Trishatov. We clinked glasses and drank.

" But I'm not going to drink your health," observed the *dadais* turning to me ; " not because I desire your death, but so that you may not drink any more here to-day." He spoke gloomily and ponderously. "Three glasses is enough for you. I see you are looking at my unwashed fist ! " he went on, putting his fist on the table. " I don't wash it, but as it is I put it at Lambert's service for smashing other people's heads when he's in a tight place." And saying this he brought down his fist on the table with such force that he set all the plates and glasses rattling. Besides us there were people dining at four other tables, all of them officers or gentlemen of dignified appearance. It was a fashionable restaurant ; all broke off their conversation for a moment and looked round to our corner ; and indeed I fancied we had attracted curiosity for some time past. Lambert flushed crimson.

" Ah, he's at it again ! I thought I had asked you to behave yourself, Nikolay Semyonovitch," he said to Andreyev in a furious whisper. The latter gave him a prolonged stare.

"I don't want my new friend Dolgorowky to drink a great deal here to-day."

Lambert flushed more hotly than ever.

The pock-marked man listened in silence but with evident pleasure. Andreyev's behaviour seemed to please him, for some reason. I was the only one who did not understand why I was not to drink much wine.

"He says that because he's only just had some money! You shall have another seven roubles directly after dinner—only do let us have dinner, don't disgrace us," Lambert hissed at him.

"Aha!" the *dadais* growled triumphantly. At this the pock-marked man was absolutely delighted, and he sniggered spitefully.

"Listen, you really . . ." began Trishatov to his friend with uneasiness and almost distress in his voice, evidently anxious to restrain him. Andreyev subsided, but not for long; that was not his intention. Just across the table, five paces from us, two gentleman were dining, engaged in lively conversation. Both were middle-aged gentleman, who looked extremely conscious of their own dignity; one was tall and very stout, the other was also very stout but short, they were discussing in Polish the events of the day in Paris. For some time past the *dadais* had been watching them inquisitively and listening to their talk. The short Pole evidently struck him as a comic figure, and he promptly conceived an aversion for him after the manner of envious and splenetic people, who often take such sudden dislikes for no reason whatever. Suddenly the short Pole pronounced the name of the deputy, Madier de Montjeau, but, as so many Poles do, he pronounced it with an accent on the syllable before the last, instead of on the last syllable; this was enough for the *dadais*, he turned to the Poles, and drawing up himself with dignity, he suddenly articulated loudly and distinctly as though addressing a question to them:

"Madier de Montjeáu?"

The Poles turned to him savagely.

"What do you want?" the tall stout Pole shouted threateningly to him in Russian.

The *dadais* paused. "Madier de Montjeáu," he repeated suddenly again, to be heard by the whole room, giving no sort of explanation, just as he had stupidly set upon me at the door with the reiterated question "Dolgorowky." The Poles jumped up from their seats, Lambert leapt up from the table and rushed to Andreyev, but leaving him, darted up to the Poles and began making cringing apologies to them.

"They are buffoons, Pani, they are buffoons," the little Pole repeated contemptuously, as red as a carrot with indignation. "Soon it will be impossible to come!" There was a stir all over the room too, and a murmur of disapproval, though laughter was predominant.

"Come out . . . please . . . come along!" Lambert muttered completely disconcerted, doing his utmost to get Andreyev out of the room. The latter looking searchingly at Lambert, and judging that he would now give the money, agreed to follow him. Probably he had already extorted money from Lambert by the same kind of disgraceful behaviour. Trishatov seemed about to run after them too, but he looked at me and checked himself.

"Ach, how horrid," he said hiding his eyes with his slender fingers.

"Very horrid," whispered the pock-marked man, looking really angry at last.

Meanwhile Lambert came back looking quite pale, and gesticulating eagerly, began whispering something to the pock-marked man. The latter listened disdainfully, and meanwhile ordered the waiter to make haste with the coffee; he was evidently in a hurry to get off. And yet the whole affair had only been a schoolboyish prank. Trishatov got up with his cup of coffee, and came and sat down beside me.

"I am very fond of him," he said to me with a face as open as though he had been talking to me like this all his life. "You can't imagine how unhappy Andreyev is. He has wasted all his sister's dowry on eating and drinking, and in fact all they had he spent on eating and drinking during the year he was in the service, and I see now he worries. And as for his not washing, it's just through despair. And he has awfully strange ideas: he'll tell you all of a sudden that he's both a scoundrel and an honest man—that it's all the same and no difference: and that there's no need to do anything, either good or bad, they are just the same, one may do good or bad, but that the best of all is to be still, not taking off one's clothes for a month at a time, to eat, and drink, and sleep—and nothing else. But believe me, he only says that. And do you know, I really believe he played the fool like this just now to break off with

Lambert once for all. He spoke of it yesterday. Would you believe it, sometimes at night or when he has been sitting long alone, he begins to cry, and, do you know, when he cries, it's different from anyone else ; he howls, he howls in an awful way, and you know it's even more pitiful . . . and he's such a big strong fellow, and then all of a sudden—to see him howling. It is sad, poor fellow, isn't it ? I want to save him, though I am a wretched hopeless scamp myself, you wouldn't believe. Will you let me in, Dolgoruky, if I ever come and see you ? "

" Oh, do come, I really like you."

" What for ? Well, thank you. Listen, will you drink another glass ? But after all you'd better not. He was right when he said you had better not drink any more," he suddenly gave me a significant wink, " but I'll drink it all the same. I have nothing now, but would you believe it, I can't hold myself back in anything ; if you were to tell me I must not dine at a restaurant again, I should be ready to do anything, simply to dine there. Oh, we genuinely want to be honest, I assure you, but we keep putting it off,

" *And the years pass by and the best of our years !*

" I am awfully afraid that he will hang himself. He'll go and do it without telling anyone. He's like that. They are all hanging themselves nowadays ; why, I don't know—perhaps there are a great many people like us. I, for instance, can't exist without money to spend. Luxuries matter a great deal more to me than necessities.

" I say, are you fond of music ? I'm awfully fond of it. I'll play you something when I come and see you. I play very well on the piano and I studied music a very long time. I've studied seriously. If I were to compose an opera, do you know I should take the subject from Faust. I am very fond of that subject. I am always making up a scene in the cathedral, just imagining it in my head, I mean. The Gothic cathedral, the interior, the choirs, the hymns ; Gretchen enters, and mediæval singing, you know, so that you can hear the fifteenth century in it. Gretchen overwhelmed with grief ; to begin with a recitative, subdued but terrible, full of anguish ; the choirs hunder on, gloomily, sternly, callously,

" *Dies irae, dies illa !*

" And all of a sudden—the voice of the devil, the song of the

2 E

devil. He is unseen, there is only his song, side by side with the hymns, mingling with the hymns, almost melting into them, but at the same time quite different from them—that must be managed somehow. The song is prolonged, persistent, it must be a tenor, it must be a tenor. It begins softly, tenderly : ' Do you remember, Gretchen, when you were innocent, when you were a child, you came with your mother to this cathedral and lisped your prayers from an old prayer-book ? ' But the song gets louder and louder, more intense ; on higher notes : there's a sound of tears in them, misery unceasing, and hopeless, and finally despair. ' There's no forgiveness, Gretchen, there's no forgiveness for you here ! ' Gretchen tries to pray, but only cries of misery rise up from her soul—you know when the breast is convulsed with tears—but Satan's song never ceases, and pierces deeper and deeper into the soul like a spear ; it gets higher and higher, and suddenly breaks off almost in a shriek : ' The end to all, accursed one ! ' Gretchen falls on her knees, clasps her hands before her—and then comes her prayer, something very short, semi-recitative, but naive, entirely without ornament, something mediæval in the extreme, four lines, only four lines altogether—Stradella has some such notes—and at the last note she swoons ! General confusion. She is picked up, carried out, and then the choir thunders forth. It is, as it were, a storm of voices, a hymn of inspiration, of victory, overwhelming, something in the style of our

' Borne on high by angels '

—so that everything is shaken to its foundations, and it all passes into the triumphant cry of exaltation ' Hosanna ! '—as though it were the cry of the whole universe and it rises and rises, and then the curtain falls ! Yes, you know if only I could, I should have done something ; only I can never do anything now, I do nothing but dream. I am always dreaming ; my whole life has turned into a dream. I dream at night too. Ah, Dolgoruky, have you read Dickens' ' Old Curiosity Shop ' ? "

" Yes, why ? "

" Do you remember—wait, I will have another glass—do you remember, there's one passage at the end, when they— that mad old man and that charming girl of thirteen, his grand-child, take refuge after their fantastic flight and wandering in some remote place in England, near a Gothic mediæval church, and the little girl has received some post there, and shows the church to visitors . . . then the sun is setting, and the child in the church porch, bathed in the last rays of light, stands and gazes at the sunset, with gentle pensive contemplation in her child soul, a soul full of wonder as though before some mystery, for both alike are mysteries, the sun, the thought of God, and the church, the thought of man, aren't they ?   Oh, I don't know how to express it, only God loves such first thoughts in children. . . . While near her, on the step, the crazy old grandfather gazes at her with a fixed look . . . you know there's nothing special in it, in that picture of Dickens, there's absolutely nothing in it, but yet one will remember it all one's life, and it has survived for all Europe—why ?   It's splendid !   It's the innocence in it !   And I don't know what there is in it, but it's fine.   I used always to be reading novels when I was at school. Do you know I had a sister in the country only a year older than me. . . . Oh, now it's all sold, and we have no country-place ! I was sitting with her on the terrace under our old lime trees, we were reading that novel, and the sun was setting too, and suddenly we left off reading, and said to one another that we would be kind too, that we would be good—I was then preparing for the university and . . . Ach, Dolgoruky, you know, every man has his memories ! . . ."

And he suddenly let his pretty little head fall on my shoulder and burst out crying.   I felt very very sorry for him.   It is true that he had drunk a great deal of wine, but he had talked to me so sincerely, so like a brother, with such feeling. . . . Suddenly, at that instant, we heard a shout from the street, and there was a violent tapping at the window (there was a large plate-glass window on the ground floor, so that anyone could tap on the window with his fingers from the street).   This was the ejected Andreyev.

"*Ohé Lambert !   Où est Lambert ?   As-tu vu Lambert ?* " we heard his wild shout in the street.

"Ah ! yes, here he is !   So he's not gone away ? " cried the boy, jumping up from his place.

"Our account ! " Lambert cried through his clenched teeth to the waiter.   His hands shook with anger as he paid the bill, but the pock-marked man did not allow Lambert to pay for him.

"Why not ?   Why, I invited you, you accepted my invitation."

"No, excuse me," the pock-marked man pulled out his purse, and reckoning out his share he paid separately.

"You'll offend me, Semyon Sidorovitch."

"That's what I wish," Semyon Sidorovitch snapped out,

taking his hat, and without saying good-bye to anybody, he walked alone out of the room. Lambert tossed the money to the waiter and hurriedly ran after him, even forgetting my existence in his confusion. Trishatov and I walked out last of all. Andreyev was standing like a post at the door, waiting for Trishatov.

"You scoundrel!" cried Lambert, unable to restrain himself.

"There, there!" Andreyev grunted at him, and with one swing of his arm he knocked off his round hat, which went spinning along the pavement. Lambert flew abjectly to pick it up.

"*Ving-cinq roubles!*" Andreyev showed Trishatov the note, which he had just got from Lambert.

'That's enough," Trishatov shouted to him. "Why must you always make an uproar? . . . And why have you wrung twenty-five roubles out of him? You only ought to have had seven."

"Why did I wring it out of him? He promised us a private dinner with Athenian women, and instead of women he regaled us with the pock-marked man, and what's more, I did not finish my dinner and I've been freezing here in the cold, it's certainly worth eighteen roubles. He owed me seven, so that makes twenty-five."

"Go to the devil both of you!" yelled Lambert. "I'll send you both packing, I'll pay you out . . ."

"Lambert, I'll send you packing. I'll pay you out!" cried Andreyev. "*Adieu, mon prince,* don't drink any more wine! *Petya, marche! Ohé Lambert! Où est Lambert? As-tu vu Lambert?*" he roared for the last time as he strode away.

"So I shall come and see you, may I?" Trishatov murmured hurriedly, and hastened after his friend.

I was left alone with Lambert.

"Well . . . come along!" he brought out, seeming stupefied and breathing with difficulty.

"Where shall I come along? I'm not coming anywhere with you!" I made haste to reply defiantly.

"You're not coming," he said, startled and apprehensive. "Why, I have only been waiting for us to be alone!"

"But where to go?" I must confess I, too, had a slight ringing in my head, from the three glasses of champagne and the two wine-glasses of sherry I had drunk.

"This way, this way. Do you see?"

"But this is an oyster bar; you see it is written up. It smells so horrid . . ."

" That's only because you have just had dinner. We won't have oysters, but I'll give you some champagne. . . ."

" I don't want any ! You want to make me drunk."

" That's what they told you ; they've been laughing at you. You believe blackguards like that ! "

" No, Trishatov's not a blackguard. But I know how to take care of myself—that's all ! "

" So you've a will of your own, have you ? "

" Yes, I have a character; more than you have, for you're servile to everybody you meet. You disgraced us, you begged pardon of the Poles like a lackey. I suppose you've often been beaten in restaurants ? "

" But we must have a talk, you fool ! " he cried with the same contemptuous impatience, which almost implied, what are you driving at ? " Why, you are afraid, aren't you ? Are you my friend or not ? "

" I am not your friend and you are a swindler. We'll go along simply to show you I'm not afraid of you. Oh, what a horrid smell, it smells of cheese ! How disgusting ! "

CHAPTER VI

1

I must beg the reader to remember again that I had a slight giddiness in my head ; if it had not been for that I should have acted and spoken differently. In the shop, in a back room, one could indeed have eaten oysters, and we sat down to a table covered with a filthy cloth. Lambert ordered champagne ; a glass of cold wine of a golden colour was set before me and seemed looking at me invitingly ; but I felt annoyed.

" You see, Lambert, what annoys me most is that you think you can order me about now as you used to do at Touchard's, while you are cringing upon everybody here."

" You fool ! Aië, let's clink glasses."

" You don't even deign to keep up appearances with me : you might at least disguise the fact that you want to make me drunk."

" You are talking rot and you're drunk. You must drink some more and you'll be more cheerful. Take your glass, take it ! "

" Why do you keep on ' take it ' ? I am going and that's the end of it."

And I really did get up. He was awfully vexed :

" It was Trishatov whispered that to you : I saw you whispering. You are a fool for that. Alphonsine is really disgusted if he goes near her. . . . He's a dirty beast, I'll tell you what he's like."

" You've told me already. You can talk of nothing but your Alphonsine, you're frightfully limited."

" Limited ? " he did not understand. "They've gone over now to that pock-marked fellow. That's what it is ! That's why I sent them about their business. They're dishonest. That fellow's a blackguard and he's corrupting them. I insisted that they should always behave decently."

I sat still and as it were mechanically took my glass and drank a draught.

" I'm ever so far ahead of you in education," I said. But he was only too delighted that I went on sitting there, and at once filled up my glass.

" And you know you're afraid of them ! " I went on taunting him, and no doubt I was even nastier than he was at that moment. " Andreyev knocked your hat off, and you gave him twenty-five roubles for it."

" I did give it him, but he'll pay me back. They are rebellious, but I'll be quits with them."

" You are awfully upset by that pock-marked man. And do you know it strikes me that I'm the only one left you. All your hopes now are resting on me—aren't they ? "

" Yes, Arkasha, that is so : you are the only friend left me ; you are right in saying that ! " he slapped me on the shoulder.

What could be done with a man so crude ; he was utterly obtuse, and took irony for serious praise.

" You could save me from bad things if you would be a good comrade, Arkady," he went on, looking at me caressingly.

" In what way could I save you ? "

" You know yourself what it is. Without me, like a fool, you will certainly be stupid ; but I'd get you thirty thousand and we would go halves and you know how. Why, think who you are ; you're nothing—no name, no position, and here you'd win first prize straight off : and having such a fortune, you'll know how to make a career ! "

I was simply astounded at this attack. I had taken for granted that he would dissemble, but he had begun upon it with such bluntness, such schoolboyish bluntness. I resolved to listen to him from a desire to be open-minded and . . . from intense curiosity.

"Look here, Lambert, you won't understand this, but I'm consenting to listen to you because I'm open-minded," I declared firmly, and again I took a gulp at my glass. Lambert at once filled it up.

"I'll tell you what, Arkady: if a fellow like Büring had dared to abuse me and strike me in the presence of a lady I adored, I don't know what I should have done ! But you put up with it, I'm ashamed of you : you're a poor creature ! "

"How dare you say that Büring struck me ! " I shouted, turning crimson. "It was more I struck him than he me."

"No, it was he struck you, not you struck him."

"You're lying, I trod on his foot too ! "

"But he shoved you back, and told the footman to drag you away . . . and she sat and looked on from her carriage and laughed at you ; she knows that you have no father and that you can be insulted."

"I don't understand this schoolboyish conversation, Lambert, and I'm ashamed of it. You are saying this to irritate me, and as crudely and as openly as though I were a boy of sixteen. You've been plotting with Anna Andreyevna ! " I cried, trembling with anger, and still mechanically sipping my wine.

"Anna Andreyevna's a sly jade ! She's humbugging you and me and all the world ! I have been waiting for you, because you can best finish off with that woman."

"With what woman ? "

"With Madame Ahmakov. I know all about it. You told me yourself that she is afraid of that letter you've got . . ."

"What letter . . . you're talking nonsense. . . . Have you seen her ? " I muttered in confusion.

"Yes, I saw her. She's beautiful. *Très belle ;* and you've taste."

"I know you've seen her but you did not dare speak to her, and I wish you did not dare to speak of her either."

"You're a boy, and she laughs at you—so there ! We had a virtuous lady like that in Moscow. Ough, didn't she turn up her nose ! but she began to tremble when we threatened that we would tell all we knew and she knuckled under directly ; and we got all we wanted both ways, money, and—you understand ? Now she's virtue unapproachable again in society—foo ! my word, isn't she high and mighty, and hasn't she got a turn-out. Ah, you should have seen that little back room it happened in ! You've not lived ; if only you knew the little back rooms they don't shrink from . . ."

" I've thought that," I could not help muttering.

"They're corrupt to their very finger-tips ; you don't know what they're capable of ! Alphonsine lived in a house like that, and she was disgusted."

" I have thought of that," I chimed in again.

" But they beat you, and you complain . . ."

"Lambert, you're a blackguard, you're a damned beast ! " I cried, suddenly pulling myself together and beginning to tremble. " I have dreamed all this, you were in it and Anna Andreyevna . . . Oh, you damned brute ! Did you really think I was such a scoundrel ? I dreamed it because I knew that you would say this. And besides, all this can't be so simple that you can talk to me about it so simply and directly."

" He is in a rage, tut, tut, tut ! " Lambert drawled, laughing and triumphant. " Well, Arkasha, my boy, now I've found out all I wanted to know. That's why I was so eager to see you. Listen, you love her I see, and want to revenge yourself on Büring. That's what I wanted to find out. I've been suspecting it all this time while I've been waiting to see you. *Ceci posé, celà change la question.* And so much the better, for she loves you too. So you must marry her without a moment's delay, that's the best thing ; you can't do anything else, that's your safest position. And then remember, Arkady, that you have a friend in me of whom you can make any use you like. And that friend will help you, and will marry you : I'll move heaven and earth, Arkasha ! And you can give your old friend thirty thousand for his trouble afterwards, eh ? And I'll help you, don't doubt that. I know all the ins and outs of the business, and they shall give you the whole dowry, and you'll be a wealthy man with a career before you ! "

Though my head was in a whirl I looked at Lambert with wonder. He was in earnest, and not merely in earnest in what he said, but in believing in the possibility of my marrying ; I could see that he thoroughly believed in it himself, and, in fact, caught at the idea with enthusiasm. I saw, of course, too, that he was entrapping me like a schoolboy (I certainly must have seen it even then) ; but the thought of marrying her so thrilled me that though I wondered how Lambert could believe in such a fantastic notion, yet, at the same time I tried violently to believe in it myself, though I did not for an instant lose consciousness of the fact that it could not possibly come to pass. All this was mingled together at the same time.

" But is it possible ? " I faltered.

" Why not ? you will show her the letter, she'll be frightened and marry you to keep her money."

I made up my mind not to stop Lambert in his vile suggestions, for he disclosed them to me with such simplicity and did not suspect that I might be revolted by them ; I did mutter, however, that I should not like to marry her simply by force.

" I don't want to use force for anything ; how can you be so base as to think me capable of it ! "

" Hoity-toity ! Why, she'll marry you of her own accord : it won't be your doing, she'll be frightened and marry you herself, and she'll marry you because she loves you, too," Lambert put in hastily.

" That's a lie ; you're laughing at me. How do you know she loves me ? "

" Of course she does. I know it. And Anna Andreyevna assumes it. It's the truth in earnest. I'm telling you that Anna Andreyevna assumes it. And I'll tell you something else when you come to me, and you'll see that she does love you. Alphonsine has been at Tsarskoe ; she found out there . . ."

" What could she find out there ? "

" You come back with me ; she'll tell you herself, and it will please you. Why, aren't you as good as anybody, you are handsome, you are well educated."

" Yes, I am well educated," I answered, hardly able to breathe ; my heart was thumping and, of course, not only from the wine.

" You are handsome, you are well dressed."

" Yes, I'm well dressed."

" And you are good-natured. . . ."

" Yes, I'm good-natured."

" Why shouldn't she consent ? Büring won't take her without money anyway, and you can deprive her of her money—so she'll be in a fright : you'll marry her and punish Büring. Why, you told me yourself that night after you were frozen that she was in love with you."

" Can I have told you that ? I'm sure I did not tell you that."

" Yes, you did."

" I was delirious when I said that. I suppose I told you of the letter too ? "

" Yes, you told me you had such a letter ; I thought at the time : how can he let slip his luck if he has such a letter ? "

" It's all a mad idea, and I'm not so stupid as to believe it," I muttered ; " to begin with there's a difference in our ages, and besides I've no surname."

" But she'll marry you though ; she can't help marrying you when it's a question of so much money—I'll arrange that. And, what's more, she loves you. You know that old prince is very well disposed to you ; through his protection, you know, you can form connections ; and what does it matter if you have no name, nowadays nothing of that's necessary : once you pocket the money you'll get on and get on, and in ten years' time you will be such a millionaire that all Russia will resound with your fame, so you won't need a name then. Why, you can buy a title in Austria. And when you get married, keep her well in hand. They want a firm hand. If a woman's in love, she likes to feel a man's got a tight grip on her. Women like will in a man. When you frighten her with the letter, from that hour you will show her you have strength of will. ' Ah,' she'll say ' he's so young, and yet he has will.' "

I sat, as it were, spell-bound. I should never with anyone else have sunk to such an idiotic conversation. But in this case a sort of voluptuous craving drew me on to continue it. Besides, Lambert was so stupid and so low that no one could feel ashamed of anything before him.

" No, do you know, Lambert," I said suddenly : " you may say what you like, but a great deal of this is absurd ; I have been talking to you because we were schoolfellows, and we need not be ashamed of saying anything to one another ; but I would not have demeaned myself to it with anyone else for any consideration. And, first of all, tell me why you keep repeating so positively that she's in love with me ? That was quite good what you said just now about having capital ; but you see, Lambert, you don't know anything of good society : all this is still with them on the most patriarchal, family system, so to say, and, therefore, as so far she does not know my abilities and what a position I may achieve in the world, she'll be ashamed of me. But I won't conceal from you, Lambert, that there really is one point that might give one hope. You see : she might marry me from gratitude, because I might save her from a man she hates. And she is afraid of that man."

" Ah, you mean your father ? Why, is he so much in love

with her ? " Lambert said, pricking up his ears with peculiar curiosity.

" Oh no ! " I cried : " and how horrid you are, and at the same time how stupid, Lambert ! Why, if he were in love with her, how could I want to marry her ? After all we are father and son, that would be shameful. He loves my mother, my mother, and I saw how he held her in his arms. I did think at one time he loved Katerina Nikolaevna, but now I know for certain that though he may once have loved her, he has hated her for a long time now . . . and wants to revenge himself on her, and she's afraid of him, for I tell you, Lambert, he is very terrible when he begins to revenge himself. He becomes almost insane. When he's in a rage with her, he doesn't stick at anything. This is a feud in the old style on account of the loftiest principles. In our time we don't care a hang for any general principles ; nowadays there are no general principles but only special cases. Ah, Lambert, you don't understand, you are as stupid as a post ; I am talking to you about these principles, but I am sure you don't understand. You are awfully uneducated. Do you remember you used to beat me ! Now I'm stronger than you are— do you know that ? "

" Arkasha, come home with me ! We'll spend the evening and drink another bottle, and Alphonsine will sing to the guitar."

" No, I'm not coming. Listen, Lambert, I've got an ' idea.' If I don't succeed and don't marry, I shall fall back on the ' idea ' ; but you haven't an idea."

" All right, all right, you shall tell me about it, come along."

" I am not coming," I said, getting up. " I don't want to, and I'm not coming. I shall come and see you, but you are a black-guard. I'll give you thirty thousand, but I am cleaner and better than you. . . . I see, you want to deceive me all round. But I forbid you even to think of her : she's above every one, and your plan is so low that I really wonder at you, Lambert. I want to be married, that's a different matter ; but I don't want money, I despise money. I wouldn't take it if she begged me to on her knees . . . but marriage, marriage, that's a different matter. But you know that was quite right what you said, that one ought to keep a tight hand on her. It's a good thing to love, to love passionately, with all the generosity of which a man is capable, and which can never be found in a woman ; but to be despotic is a good thing too. For, do you know, Lambert, a woman loves despotism. You understand woman, Lambert.

But you are wonderfully stupid in everything else. And do you know, Lambert, you are not at all such a blackguard as you seem, you're simple. I like you. Ah, Lambert, why are you such a rogue ? What a jolly time we might have if you weren't ! You know Trishatov's a dear."

These last incoherent phrases I muttered in the street. Oh, I set all this down in every trivial detail, that the reader may see that with all my enthusiasm and my vows and promises to reform, and to strive for "seemliness," I was capable then of falling so easily and into such filth. And I swear that if I were not fully convinced that I am no longer the same, but have gained strength of character by practical life, I should not have confessed all this to the reader.

We went out of the shop, and Lambert supported me slightly, putting his arm round me. Suddenly I looked at him, and saw in his fixed, terribly intent and perfectly sober eyes the very same expression as I had seen that morning when I was frozen and when he had led me to the cab with his arm round me in the same way, and listened, all eyes and ears, to my incoherent babble. Men who are drunk but not quite hopelessly drunk, sometimes have moments of absolute soberness.

" I'm not going home with you for anything," I declared firmly and coherently, looking at him sarcastically and putting aside his arm.

" Come, nonsense. I'll tell Alphonsine to make tea for us, come ! "

He was horribly confident that I should not get away ; he put his arm round me and held me with a sort of relish, as his prey, and the prey was what he needed of course, that evening and in that condition ! It will be clear later why.

" I'm not coming ! " I repeated. " Cab ! "

At that instant a sledge drove up and I jumped into it.

" Where are you off to ? What are you about ! " yelled Lambert, clutching at my fur coat in extreme dismay.

" And don't dare to follow me ! " I cried, " don't drive after me." At that very instant the sledge started, and my coat was torn out of Lambert's hands.

" You'll come all the same ! " he shouted after me in an angry voice.

" I shall come if I want to. I can do as I like ! " I retorted, turning round in the sledge.

2

He did not follow me, of course, because there did not happen to be another sledge at hand, and I succeeded in getting out of his sight. I drove on as far as the Haymarket, and there I stopped and dismissed the sledge. I had a great desire to walk. I was not conscious of being tired or of being much intoxicated, I felt full of vigour ; I was aware of a fresh flow of energy, of an exceptional readiness for any sort of enterprise, and of innumerable pleasant ideas in my brain.

My heart was thudding violently and loudly, I could hear every beat. And everything seemed so charming, so easy. When I passed the sentry at the Haymarket I felt inclined to go up and kiss him. There was a thaw, the market-place was dingy and evil-smelling, but I was delighted even with the market-place.

" I am in the Obuhovsky Prospect," I thought, " and afterwards I shall turn to the left and come out in the Semyonovsky Polk. I shall take a short cut, that's delightful, it's all delightful. My coat is unbuttoned, how is it no one snatches it off, where are the thieves ? They say there are thieves in the Haymarket ; let them come, I might give them my fur coat. What do I want with a fur coat ? A fur coat is property. *La propriété c'est le vol*. But what nonsense, and how nice everything is ! It's nice that the snow is melting. Why frost ? There's no need of a frost at all. It's nice to talk nonsense too. What was it I said to Lambert about principles ? I said there were no general principles, but only special cases ; that was stuff, utter stuff ! And I said it on purpose, out of swagger. I am a little ashamed, but after all it doesn't matter, I'll make up for it. Don't be ashamed, don't distress yourself, Arkady Makarovitch. Arkady Makarovitch, I like you. I like you very much, in fact, my young friend. It's a pity you're a little rascal . . . and . . . and . . . ah, yes . . . ah ! "

I suddenly stood still, and my heart began to ache with ecstasy again.

" Good God ! what was it he said ? He said that she loves me. Oh, he is a scoundrel, he told a lot of lies, that was to make me stay the night with him. But perhaps not. He said Anna Andreyevna thinks so too. . . . Ba ! But Darya Onisimovna might have found out something about it for him ; she pokes her nose into everything. And why didn't I go to him ? I should have found out everything ! H'm ! He has a plan, and I had a presentiment of it all, every bit of it. The dream. A bold scheme, M. Lambert, only let me tell you it won't be so. Perhaps it will though, perhaps it will ! And can he bring off my marriage ? Perhaps he can. He is naïve and he believes it. He is stupid and impudent like all practical people. Stupidity and impudence combined are a great force. But confess, you were really afraid of Lambert, Arkady Makarovitch ! And what does he want with honest people ? He says so seriously : 'There isn't an honest man here !' Why, what are you yourself ? And what am I ! Don't scoundrels need honest men ? In swindling honest men are more needed than anywhere. Ha ! ha ! You did not know that till now, Arkady Makarovitch, you were so innocent. Good God ! What if he really were to bring about my marriage ! ''

I stood still again. Here I must confess something stupid (as it is all so long ago) : I must confess that I had long before been wishing to be married—at least not wishing, and it would never have happened (and I can guarantee it never will in the future), but more than once—a great many times in fact— I had dreamed how splendid it would be to be married, especially as I was falling asleep at night. I began to dream of it when I was about sixteen. I had a schoolfellow of my own age at the high school, called Lavrovsky, such a quiet, sweet, pretty boy, not particularly distinguished in any other way, however. I hardly ever talked to him. One day we happened to be sitting side by side, and he was very dreamy, and suddenly he said to me : ' Ah, Dolgoruky, what do you think, we ought to be married now ; yes, really when should we be married if not now ; now would be the very best time, and yet it's impossible.' And he said that so frankly. And I agreed with it at once entirely, for I already had visions of something of the sort. For several days afterwards we met and talked, as it were, in secret, only of that however. But afterwards, I don't know how it happened, but we left off talking to each other and drifted apart. And from that time I began to dream of marriage. This, of course, would not have been worth mentioning, only I wanted to show how far back this feeling sometimes goes. . . .

" There is only one serious objection," I mused, as I went on again. " Oh, of course, the trivial difference in our ages is no real obstacle, but she is such an aristocrat and I am simply

Dolgoruky! It's awfully horrid! H'm! Couldn't Versilov marry mother and petition the government for me to be legitimatized as a reward for his services, so to say. . . . He's been in the service, so must have rendered services; he was a mediator at the emancipation. . . . Oh, damn it all, how loathsome."

I suddenly uttered this exclamation and stood still for the third time, but this time I felt as though I had been crushed to the earth. The agonizing feeling of humiliation from the consciousness that I could desire anything so shameful as the change of my surname by being legitimized, this treachery to my whole childhood, all this in one flash shattered my previous mood, and all my joyfulness was dissipated like smoke. "No, I'll never tell that to anyone," I thought, turning crimson : " I've sunk so low because I'm in love and stupid. . . . No, if Lambert is right in anything, it is that nowadays, in our age, the man is what matters, and afterwards his money. Or rather not his money, but rather his property. With a capital like that I would throw myself into the 'idea,' and all Russia would ring with my fame in ten years, and I would revenge myself on them all. And there's no need to stand on ceremony with her. Lambert's right there. She'll be frightened and simply marry me. She'll consent in the simplest and most abject way, and marry me." " You don't know, you don't know in what little back room that happened ! " I remembered Lambert's words. "That's true," I went on musing : " Lambert's right in everything, a thousand times more right than Versilov and I and all the idealists ! He is a realist. She shall see that I have strength of will, and she will say : ' He has will ! ' Lambert's a scoundrel, and all he wants is to get thirty thousand out of me, and yet he is the only friend I have. There is no other sort of friendship and there can be no other, that's all been invented by unpractical people. And I shan't be even degrading her ; shall I be degrading her ? Not in the least : all women are like that ! Are there any women who are not abject ? That's why she must have a man over her ; that's why she's created a subordinate creature. Woman is vice and temptation, and man is honour and generosity. So it will be to the end of time. And what if I do mean to use that ' document ' ? That does not matter. That does not prevent honour or generosity. Pure, unadulterated Schillers don't exist, they are invented. It does not matter if one has to pass through filth to get there, as long as the goal is magnificent. It will all be washed off, it will all be smoothed away afterwards. And now it's only

' breadth,' it's only life, it's only vital truth—that's what it is called nowadays."

Oh, I repeat again : I must be forgiven for recording all my drunken ravings at the time. Of course this is only the essence of what I thought then, but I fancy I used those very words. I was bound to record them because I have sat down to write in order to condemn myself. And what is to be condemned, if not that ? Can there be anything graver in my life ? Wine is no justification. *In vino veritas.*

Entirely absorbed in such dreams I did not notice that I had reached home, that is, mother's lodgings. I did not even notice going in, but as soon as I slipped into our tiny entrance, I realized at once that something unusual was happening.

There were loud voices and outcries in the room, and I could hear that mother was crying. In the doorway I almost fell over Lukerya, who was running from Makar Ivanovitch's room to the kitchen. I flung down my fur coat and went in to Makar Ivanovitch, for they were all gathered together in his room.

There I found mother and Versilov. Mother was supported in his arms, and he was pressing her to his heart. Makar Ivanovitch was sitting as usual on his little bench, but he seemed overcome with weakness, and Liza had her arms round his shoulders and with an effort was holding him up ; and it was evident that he was on the point of falling. I took a rapid step towards him and realized with a shudder that the old man was dead.

He had only just died, one minute before I arrived. Only ten minutes before he had felt just as usual. No one was with him then but Liza ; she had been sitting with him, telling her grief, and he had been stroking her head just as he had done the day before. Suddenly he began to tremble (Liza told us), tried to stand up, tried to cry out, and began falling on his left side, and was silent. "Rupture of the heart !" said Versilov. Liza uttered a scream that could be heard all over the house, and they had all run in at once, and all that only the minute before I came in.

"Arkady," Versilov cried, "run instantly to Tatyana Pavlovna. She's sure to be at home. Ask her to come at once. Take a sledge. Make haste, I entreat you ! "

His eyes were shining. I remember that clearly. I did not notice in his face anything like simple pity, anything like tears. The others, mother, Liza, and Lukerya, were crying. I was struck, on the contrary—and I remember this very well—by a look of unusual excitement almost of elation in his face. I ran for Tatyana Pavlovna.

It was not far to go, as the reader knows already. I did not take a sledge, but ran all the way without stopping. My mind was in confusion, and yet there was something almost like elation in my heart, too. I realized something momentous was happening. Every trace of drunkenness had disappeared completely, and with it every ignoble thought, by the time I was ringing at Tatyana Pavlovna's door.

The Finnish cook opened the door : " Not at home ! " she said and would have shut it at once.

" Not at home ? " I cried, and rushed headlong into the passage. " Impossible ! Makar Ivanovitch is dead ! "

" Wha—at ! " I heard Tatyana Pavlovna cry out in her drawing-room, through the closed door.

" He is dead ! Makar Ivanovitch is dead ! Andrey Petrovitch begs you to go this minute ! "

" What nonsense you're talking."

The bolt clicked, but the door only opened an inch. " What has happened, tell me ! . . ."

" I don't know, he was dead when I arrived. Andrey Petrovitch says it's rupture of the heart ! "

" I'll come at once, this minute. Run and tell them I'm coming, run along ! run along ! run along ! What are you stopping for ? "

But through the half-opened door I had distinctly seen some one come suddenly out from behind the curtain that screened Tatyana Pavlovna's bed, and that some one was standing at the back of the room behind Tatyana Pavlovna. Mechanically and instinctively I clutched at the lock and would not let the door be shut.

" Arkady Makarovitch, is it really true that he's dead ? " I heard a soft, smooth, ringing voice, a well-known voice that thrilled everything in my heart at once. In the question was a note of some emotion that deeply stirred *her* heart.

" Oh, if that's how it is," cried Tatyana Pavlovna, abandoning the door, " if that's how it is—you may settle it to please yourself. It's your own doing ! "

She ran full speed out of the flat, flinging on her kerchief and her fur coat as she went downstairs. We were left alone. I threw off my fur coat, took a step forward, and shut the door.

She stood before me as she had done that time before, with a bright face, and just as she had done then, she held out both hands to me. As though I had been struck down I literally fell at her feet.

3

I was beginning to cry, I don't know why; I don't remember how she made me sit down beside her, I only remember, as one of my most precious memories, that we sat side by side, hand in hand, and talked eagerly : she was questioning me about the old man and his death, and I was telling her about him—so that it might have been supposed that I had been crying over Makar Ivanovitch, though that would have been the acme of absurdity ; and I know that she could not possibly have suspected me of such childish banality. All at once I pulled myself together and felt ashamed. I imagine now that I cried simply from joy, and I believe she knew that perfectly well, so that my heart is quite at rest when I remember it.

It suddenly struck me as very strange that she should go on questioning me about Makar Ivanovitch.

"Why, did you know him ? " I asked in surprise.

"Yes. I have never seen him, but he has played a part in my life, too. I was told a great deal about him at one time, by that man whom I fear. You know what man I mean."

"All I know is that 'that man' has been in the past much nearer to your heart than you told me before," I said. I don't know what I meant to express by this, but I spoke as it were reproachfully and with a frown.

"You say he was kissing your mother just now ? Holding her in his arms ? You saw that yourself ? " she did not hear what I said, but went on cross-examining me.

"Yes, I saw it ; and, believe me," I hastened to assure her, seeing her joy, " it was with true and generous feeling."

"God grant it," she said, crossing herself. "Now he is set free. That admirable old man simply held his life in bondage. His death will mean for him a renewal of duty . . . and dignity, as they were renewed once before. Oh, he is before all things generous, he will give peace of heart to your mother, whom he loves more than anything on earth, and will at last be at peace himself, and thank God—it's high time."

"He is dear to you ? "

" Yes, very dear, though not in the way he would have liked to be and you mean by your question."

" And is it for yourself or for him that you are afraid now ? " I asked suddenly.

" Oh, these are deep questions, let us leave them."

" Let us leave them, of course ; but I knew nothing of this, nor of too much else perhaps ; but may you be right, now everything will begin anew, and if anyone is to be renewed, it's I first of all. I have been base in my thoughts in regard to you, Katerina Nikolaevna, and not more than an hour ago, perhaps, I was guilty of a low action in regard to you, but do you know I am sitting beside you and feel no pang of conscience. For everything now is over, and everything is beginning anew, and the man who was plotting vileness against you an hour ago I don't know, and don't want to know ! "

" Come, calm yourself," she smiled ; " one would think you were a little delirious."

" And how can one condemn oneself beside you, whether one is good or vile—you are as far beyond one as the sun. . . . Tell me, how could you come out to me after all that's happened ? Oh, if only you knew what happened only an hour ago ! And what a dream has come true."

" I expect I know all that," she smiled softly : " you have just been wanting to punish me in some way, you swore to ruin me, and would certainly have killed, or at least have beaten, anyone who had dared to say one word against me."

Oh, she smiled and jested : but this was only from her excessive kindness, for her heart at that moment, as I realized later, was full of such an immense anxiety of her own, such a violent overmastering emotion, that she can only have talked to me and have answered my foolish irritating questions, she can only have done that as one sometimes answers the persistent prattle of a little child, simply to get rid of it. I understood that dully and felt ashamed, but I could not help persisting.

" No," I cried, unable to control myself. " No, I did not kill the man who spoke ill of you, I encouraged him instead ! "

" Oh, for goodness' sake, please don't ; there's no need to tell me anything," she said, suddenly putting out her hand to stop me, with a look of compassion in her face; but I leapt up from my seat and was standing before her, to tell her everything, and if I had told her, nothing of what happened afterwards would have happened, for it would certainly have ended in my confessing everything and returning the document to her. But she suddenly laughed.

"There's no need, there's no need of anything, no facts at all! I know all your misdoings; I'm ready to bet that you meant to marry me or something of that sort, and you have only just been plotting about it with some one, with some accomplice, some old school friend. . . . Why I believe I've guessed right!" she cried, looking gravely at my face.

"What . . . how could you guess!" I faltered like a fool, tremendously impressed.

"Well, what next! But that's enough, that's enough! I forgive you, but no more about it," she waved her hand again, with unmistakable impatience. "I am given to dreaming myself, and if you only knew what shifts I have recourse to in my dreams when I let myself go! That's enough, you make me forget what I was going to say. I am very glad that Tatyana Pavlovna has gone away; I have been very anxious to see you, and we could not have talked as we are doing before her. I believe I was to blame for what happened. I was! Of course I was!"

"You to blame? But I had betrayed you to *him*, and—what can you have thought of me! I have been thinking of that all this time, all these days, I've been thinking and feeling about it every minute." (It was not a lie.)

"There was no need for you to distress yourself so much, I quite understood at the time how it had all happened; you simply spoke too freely in your joy, and told him that you were in love with me and that I . . . well, that I listened to you. Just what you would do at twenty. You love him more than anyone in the world, don't you, and look to him to be your friend, your ideal? I quite understood that, but it was too late. Oh yes, I was to blame: I ought to have sent for you at the time, and have set your mind at rest, but I felt annoyed; and I told them not to admit you; that's what led to the scene at the entrance, and then that night. And do you know, like you, I've been dreaming all this time of meeting you secretly, only I did not know how to arrange it? And what do you suppose I dreaded more than anything? That you would believe what he said against me."

"Never!" I cried.

"The memory of our meetings in the past is dear to me; the boy in you is very dear to me, and perhaps, too, that very sincerity . . . you know, I'm a very serious person, I am one of the most serious and gloomy characters among modern women, let me tell you . . . ha—ha—ha ! We'll have another talk some time, but now I'm not quite myself, I am upset and . . . I believe I'm a little hysterical. But, at last, at last, *he* will let me, too, live in peace."

This exclamation broke from her unconsciously ; I understood it at once, and did not want to catch it up, but I trembled all over.

" He knows I've forgiven him ! " she exclaimed suddenly again, as though to herself.

" Could you really forgive him that letter ? And how could he tell that you forgave him ? " I could not help exclaiming.

" How could he tell ? Oh, he knows," she went on answering me, yet she looked as though she had forgotten my existence and were talking to herself. " He has come to his senses now. And how could he not know that I forgave him, when he knows every secret of my soul by heart ? Why, he knows that I am a little after his kind myself."

" You ? "

" Why, yes, he knows that. Oh, I'm not passionate, I'm calm : but like him I should like all men to be fine. . . . Of course there was something made him love me."

" How could he say that you had all the vices."

" He only said that ; he has another secret in his heart. And didn't he write an awfully funny letter ? "

" Funny ? " (I was listening to her with strained attention. I imagined that she really was hysterical, and . . . was speaking, perhaps, not for my benefit ; but I could not resist the question.)

" Oh yes, funny, and how I should have laughed, if . . . if I hadn't been frightened. Though I'm not such a coward, don't think it ; but I didn't sleep all night after that letter, it seemed written in blood and frenzy . . . and after such a letter what was left to come. I love life, I'm horribly afraid for my life, I'm horribly cowardly in that. . . . Ah, listen," she cried, suddenly darting at me, " go to him, he's alone now, he can't be there still, most likely he's gone off somewhere alone ; make haste and find him, you must make haste, run to him, show him that you are his son and love him, prove that you are the dear kind boy, my student whom I . . . Oh, God give you happiness, I love nobody, and it is better so, but I want every one to be happy, every one, and him above all, and let him know that . . . at once . . . I should be very glad."

She got up and suddenly disappeared behind the curtain. At that instant tears were shining on her face (hysterical after her laughter). I remained alone, agitated and confused. I was completely at a loss to what to ascribe such emotion in her, an emotion which I never should have suspected. Something seemed to be clutching at my heart.

I waited five minutes, ten ; the profound silence suddenly struck me, and I ventured to peep out of the door, and to call. In answer to my call Marya appeared and informed me in the most stolid tone, that the lady had put on her things long, long ago and gone out by the back way.

CHAPTER VII

1

THIS was enough for me. I snatched up my fur coat and, throwing it on as I went, rushed off with the thought : " She bade me go to him, but where shall I find him ? "

But together with everything else I was struck by the question, " Why does she suppose that something has happened, and that now *he* will leave her in peace ? Of course, because he will marry mother, but what is she feeling ? Is she glad that he will marry mother, or is she unhappy about it ? And was that why she was hysterical ? Why is it I can't get to the bottom of it ? "

I note this second thought that flashed upon me, literally in order to record it : it is important. That evening was a momentous one. And really one is forced to believe in pre-destination : I had not gone a hundred steps in the direction of mother's lodging when I came across the man I was looking for. He clutched me by the shoulder and stopped me.

" It's you ! " he cried joyfully, and at the same time with the greatest astonishment. " Only fancy, I've been at your lodgings," he began quickly. " I have been looking for you, I've been asking for you, you are the one person I want in the whole universe ! Your landlord told me some extraordinary tale ; but you weren't there, and I came away and even forgot to tell him to ask you to run round to me at once, and, would you believe it, I set off, nevertheless, with the positive conviction that fate could not fail to send you to me now when most I need you, and here you are the first person to meet me ! Come home with me : you've never been to my rooms."

In fact we had been looking for each other, and something of the same sort had happened to each of us. We walked very rapidly.

On the way he uttered only a few brief phrases, telling me he had left mother with Tatyana Pavlovna and so on. He walked holding my arm. His lodging was not far off and we soon arrived. I had, in fact, never been in these rooms of his. It was a small flat of three rooms, which he had taken or rather Tatyana Pavlovna had taken simply for that "tiny baby." The flat had always been under Tatyana Pavlovna's supervision, and in it had been installed a nurse with the baby (and now Darya Onisimovna, too), but there had always been a room there for Versilov, the outermost of the three, a fairly good and spacious room, snugly furnished, like a study for literary pursuits. On the table, on the shelves, and on a whatnot there were numbers of books (while at mother's there were none at all) ; there were manuscripts and bundles of letters—in fact, it all looked snug and as though it had been long inhabited, and I know that in the past Versilov had sometimes, though not very often, moved into this flat altogether, and had stayed there even for weeks at a time. The first thing that caught my attention was a portrait of mother that hung over the writing table ; a photograph in a magnificent carved frame of rare wood, obviously taken abroad and judging from its size a very expensive one. I had never heard of this portrait and knew nothing of it before, and what struck me most of all was the likeness which was remarkable in a photograph, the spiritual truth of it, so to say ; in fact it looked more like a real portrait by the hand of an artist than a mere mechanical print. When I went in I could not help stopping before it at once.

" Isn't it, isn't it ? " Versilov repeated behind me, meaning, " Isn't it like ? " I glanced at him and was struck by the expression of his face. He was rather pale, but there was a glowing and intense look in his eyes which seemed shining with happiness and strength. I had never seen such an expression on his face.

" I did not know that you loved mother so much ! " I blurted out, suddenly delighted.

He smiled blissfully, though in his smile there was a suggestion of something like a martyr's anguish, or rather something humane and lofty . . . I don't know how to express it ; but highly developed people, I fancy, can never have triumphantly and complacently happy faces. He did not answer, but taking the portrait from the rings with both hands brought it close to him, kissed it, and gently hung it back on the wall.

" Observe," he said ; " photographs very rarely turn out good likenesses, and that one can easily understand : the originals, that is all of us, are very rarely like ourselves. Only on rare occasions does a man's face express his leading quality, his most characteristic thought. The artist studies the face and divines its characteristic meaning, though at the actual moment when he's painting, it may not be in the face at all. Photography takes a man as he is, and it is extremely possible that at moments Napoleon would have turned out stupid, and Bismarck tender. Here, in this portrait, by good luck the sun caught Sonia in her characteristic moment of modest gentle love and rather wild shrinking chastity. And how happy she was when at last she was convinced that I was so eager to have her portrait. Though that photograph was taken not so long ago, still she was younger then and handsomer ; yet even then she had those hollow cheeks, those lines on her forehead, that shrinking timidity in her eyes, which seems to gain upon her with the years, and increase as time goes on. Would you believe it, dear boy ? I can scarcely picture her now with a different face, and yet you know she was once young and charming. Russian women go off quickly, their beauty is only a passing gleam, and this is not only due to racial peculiarity, but is because they are capable of unlimited love. The Russian woman gives everything at once when she loves— the moment and her whole destiny and the present and the future : she does not know how to be thrifty, she keeps nothing hidden in reserve ; and their beauty is quickly consumed upon him whom they love. Those hollow cheeks, they too were once a beauty that has been consumed on me, on my brief amusement. You are glad that I love your mother, and perhaps you didn't believe that I did love her ? Yes, my dear, I did love her very much, but I've done her nothing but harm. . . . Here is another portrait—look at that, too."

He took it from the table and handed it me. It, too, was a photograph, a great deal smaller, in a thin oval wooden frame— it was the face of a young girl, thin and consumptive, and at the same time very good-looking ; dreamy and yet strangely lacking in thought. The features were regular, of the type suggesting the pampering of generations, but it left a painful impression :

it looked as though some fixed idea had taken possession of this creature and was torturing her, just because it was too much for her strength.

" That . . . that is the girl you meant to marry and who died of consumption . . . *her* step-daughter ? " I said rather timidly.

" Yes, I meant to marry her, she died of consumption, *her* step-daughter. I knew that you knew . . . all that gossip. Though you could have known nothing about it but the gossip. Put the portrait down, my boy, that was a poor, mad girl and nothing more."

" Really mad ? "

" Or imbecile ; I think she was mad though. She had a child by Prince Sergay. It came about through madness not through love ; it was one of Prince Sergay's most scoundrelly actions. The child is here now in the next room, and I've long wanted to show it to you. Prince Sergay has never dared come here to look at the child ; that was the compact I made with him abroad. I took the child to bring up with your mother's permission. With your mother's permission I meant at the time to marry that unhappy creature . . ."

" Could such permission have been possible ? " I protested warmly.

" Oh yes, she allowed it : jealousy could only have been felt of a woman, and that was not a woman."

" Not a woman to anyone but mother ! I shall never in my life believe that mother was not jealous ! " I cried.

" And you're right. I guessed it was so when everything was over, that is when she had given her permission. But enough of that. It all came to nothing through Lidya's death, and perhaps it wouldn't have come off if she had lived, and even now I don't let mother come to see the child. It was only an episode. My dear boy, I've been looking forward to having you here for ever so long. I've been dreaming of how we should get to know each other here. Do you know how long ?—for the last two years."

He looked at me sincerely and truthfully, and with a warmth of heart in which there was no reserve. I gripped his hand :

" Why have you put it off, why did you not invite me long ago ? If only you knew all that has been . . . which would not have been if only you had sent for me earlier ! . . ."

At that instant the samovar was brought in, and Darya Onisimovna suddenly brought in the baby asleep.

" Look at it," said Versilov ; " I am fond of it, and I told them to bring it in now that you might look at it. Well, take it away again, Darya Onisimovna. Sit down to the samovar. I shall imagine that we have always lived together like this, and that we've been meeting every evening with no parting before us. Let me look at you : there, sit like this, that I can see your face. How I love your face. How I used to imagine your face when I was expecting you from Moscow. You ask why I did not send for you long ago ? Wait a little, perhaps you will understand that now."

" Can it be that it's only that old man's death that has set your tongue free ? That's strange . . ."

But though I said that, I looked at him with love. We talked like two friends in the highest and fullest sense of the word. He had asked me to come here to make something clear to me, to tell me something, to justify himself ; and yet everything was explained and justified before a word was said. Whatever I might hear from him now, the result was already attained, and we both knew that and were happy, and looked at each other knowing it.

" It's not the death of that old man," he answered : " it's not his death alone, there is something else too, which has happened at the same time. . . . God bless this moment and our future for a long time to come ! Let us talk, my dear boy. I keep wandering from the point and letting myself be drawn off. I want to speak about one thing, but I launch into a thousand side issues. It's always like that when the heart is full. . . . But let us talk ; the time has come and I've been in love with you, boy, for ever so long . . ."

He sank back in the armchair and looked at me once more.

" How strange it is to hear that, how strange it is," I repeated in an ecstasy of delight. And then I remember there suddenly came into his face that habitual line, as it were, of sadness and mockery together, which I knew so well. He controlled himself and with a certain stiffness began.

2

" You see, Arkady, if I had asked you to come earlier what should I have said to you ? That question is my whole answer."

" You mean that now you are mother's husband, and my

father, while then . . . You did not know what to say to me
before about the social position ? Is that it ? "

"Not only about that, dear boy. I should not have known
what to say to you : there was so much I should have had to be
silent about. Much that was absurd, indeed, and humiliating,
because it was like a mountebank performance—yes, a regular
show at a fair. Come, how could we have understood each other
before, when I've only understood myself to-day at five o'clock
this afternoon, just two hours before Makar Ivanovitch's death ?
You look at me with unpleasant perplexity. Don't be uneasy :
I will explain the facts, but what I have just said is absolutely
true ; my whole life has been lost in mazes and perplexity, and
suddenly they are all solved on such a day, at five o'clock this
afternoon ! It's quite mortifying, isn't it ? A little while ago I
should really have felt mortified."

I was listening indeed with painful wonder ; that old expression of
Versilov's, which I should have liked not to meet that evening after
what had been said, was strongly marked. Suddenly I exclaimed :

"My God ! You've received something from her . . . at five
o'clock this afternoon ? "

He looked at me intently, and was evidently struck at my
exclamation : and, perhaps, at my expression : "from her."

"You shall know all about it," he said, with a dreamy smile,
"and, of course, I shall not conceal from you anything you ought
to know ; for that's what I brought you here for ; but let us put
that off for a time. You see, my dear boy, I knew long ago that
there are children who brood from their earliest years over their
family through being humiliated by the unseemliness of their
surroundings and of their parents' lives. I noticed these brooding
natures while I was still at school, and I concluded then that it all
came from their being prematurely envious. Though I was myself
a brooding child, yet . . . excuse me, my dear, I'm wonderfully
absent-minded. I only meant to say that almost all this time
I have been continually uneasy about you. I always imagined
you one of those little creatures doomed to solitude, though
conscious of being gifted. Like you, I was never fond of my
schoolfellows. It is sad for those natures who are flung back
on their own resources and dreams, especially when they have a
passionate, premature and almost vindictive longing for 'seemliness'—yes, 'vindictive.' But enough, dear boy, I'm wandering from the point. Before I had begun to love you, I was
picturing you and your solitary wild dreams. . . . But enough ;

I've actually forgotten what I had begun to speak about. But all this had to be said, however. But what could I have said to you before ? Now I see your eyes looking at me, and I feel it's my *son* looking at me. Why, even yesterday I could not have believed that I should ever be sitting and talking to my boy as I am to-day."

He certainly did seem unable to concentrate his mind, and at the same time he seemed, as it were, softened.

" I have no need to dream and brood now ; it's enough for me, now, that I have you ! I will follow you ! " I said, dedicating myself to him with my whole heart.

" Follow me ? But my wanderings are just over, they have ended to-day : you are too late, my dear boy. To-day is the end of the last act, and the curtain has gone down. This last act has dragged on long. It began very long ago—the last time I rushed off abroad. I threw up everything then, and you must know, my dear, I broke off all relations for good with your mother, and told her I was doing so myself. That you ought to know. I told her then I was going away for ever ; that she would never see me again. What was worst of all, I even forgot to leave her any money. I did not think of you either, not for one minute. I went away meaning to remain in Europe and never to return home, my dear. I emigrated."

" To Herzen ? To take part in the revolutionary propaganda abroad ? Probably all your life you have been taking part in political conspiracies ? " I cried, unable to restrain myself.

" No, my dear, I've never taken part in any conspiracy. But how your eyes sparkle ; I like your exclamations, my dear. No, I simply went away then from a sudden attack of melancholy. It was the typical melancholy of the Russian nobleman, I really don't know how to describe it better. The melancholy of our upper class, and nothing else."

" Of the serf-owner . . . the emancipation of the serfs," I was beginning to mutter, breathless.

" Serf-owner ? You think I was grieving for the loss of it ? That I could not endure the emancipation of the serfs. Oh no, my boy ; why, we were all for the emancipation. I emigrated with no resentful feeling. I had only just been a mediator, and exerted myself to the utmost, I exerted myself disinterestedly, and I did not even go away because I got very little for my liberalism. We none of us got anything in those days, that is to say again, not those that were like me. I went away more in pride than in penitence, and, believe me, I was far from imagining that the time had come for me to end my life as a modest shoemaker. *Je suis gentilhomme avant tout et je mourrai gentilhomme!* Yet all the same I was sad. There are, perhaps, a thousand of my sort in Russia, no more perhaps really, but you know that is quite enough to keep the idea alive. We are the bearers of the idea, my dear boy! . . . I am talking, my darling, in the strange hope that you may understand this rigmarole. I've brought you here acting on a caprice of the heart: I've long been dreaming of how I might tell you something . . . you, and no one else. However . . . however . . ."

" No, tell me," I cried : " I see the look of sincerity in your face again. . . . Tell me, did Europe bring you back to life again ? And what do you mean by the ' melancholy of the nobleman ! ' Forgive me, darling, I don't understand yet."

" Europe bring me back to life ? Why, I went to bury Europe ! "

" To bury ? " I repeated in surprise.

He smiled.

" Arkady dear, my soul was weary then, and I was troubled in spirit. I shall never forget my first moments in Europe that time. I had stayed in Europe before, but this was a special time, and I had never gone there before with such desperate sadness, and . . . with such love, as on that occasion. I will tell you about one of my first impressions, one of the dreams I had in those days, a real dream. It was when I was in Germany, I had only just left Dresden, and in absence of mind I passed the station at which I ought to have got out, and went off on to another line. I had to get out at once to change, it was between two and three in the afternoon, a fine day. It was a little German town : I was directed to an hotel. I had to wait ; the next train was at eleven o'clock at night. I was quite glad of the adventure, for I was in no particular haste to get anywhere, and was simply wandering from place to place, my dear. The hotel turned out to be small and poor, but all surrounded by green trees and flower-beds, as is always the case in Germany. They gave me a tiny room, and as I had been travelling all night I fell asleep, after dinner, at four o'clock in the afternoon.

" I dreamed a dream that was a complete surprise to me, for I had never had any dreams of the sort before. In the gallery at Dresden there is a picture by Claude Lorraine, called in the catalogue ' Acis and Galatea,' but I used to call it ' The Golden

Age,' I don't know why. I had seen it before, but I had noticed it again in passing three days earlier. I dreamed of this picture, but not as a picture, but, as it were, a reality. I don't know exactly what I did dream though : it was just as in the picture, a corner of the Grecian Archipelago, and time seemed to have gone back three thousand years ; blue smiling waves, isles and rocks, a flowery shore, a view like fairyland in the distance, a setting sun that seemed calling to me—there's no putting it into words. It seemed a memory of the cradle of Europe, and that thought seemed to fill my soul, too, with a love as of kinship. Here was the earthly paradise of man : the gods came down from the skies, and were of one kin with men. . . . Oh, here lived a splendid race ! they rose up and lay down to sleep happy and innocent ; the woods and meadows were filled with their songs and merry voices. Their wealth of untouched strength was spent on simple-hearted joy and love. The sun bathed them in warmth and light, rejoicing in her splendid children . . . Marvellous dream, lofty error of mankind ! The Golden Age is the most unlikely of all the dreams that have been, but for it men have given up their life and all their strength, for the sake of it prophets have died and been slain, without it the peoples will not live and cannot die, and the feeling of all this I lived through, as it were, in that dream ; rocks and sea, and the slanting rays of the setting sun—all this I seemed still to see when I woke up and opened my eyes, literally wet with tears. I remembered that I was glad, a sensation of happiness I had never known before thrilled my heart till it ached ; it was the love of all humanity. It was by then quite evening ; through the green of the flowers that stood in the windows of my little room, broke slanting rays that flooded me with light. And then, my dear—that setting sun of the first day of European civilization which I had seen in my dream was transformed for me at once on waking, into the setting sun of the last day of civilization ! One seemed to hear the death-knell ringing over Europe in those days. I am not speaking of the war and the Tuileries ; apart from that, I knew that all would pass away, the whole face of the old world of Europe—sooner or later, but I, as a Russian European, could not accept it. Yes, they had only just burnt the Tuileries. . . .

"Oh, rest assured, I know it was logical ; I quite understand the irresistible force of the idea, but as the bearer of the idea of the highest Russian culture, I could not accept it, for the highest Russian thought is the reconciliation of ideas, and who in the whole world could understand such a thought at that time; I was a solitary wanderer. I am not speaking of myself personally—it's the Russian idea I'm speaking of. There all was strife and logic; there the Frenchman was nothing but a Frenchman, the German was nothing but a German, and this more intensely so than at any time in their whole history; consequently never had the Frenchman done so much harm to France, or the German to Germany, as just at that time! In those days in all Europe there was not one European: I alone among all the vitriol-throwers could have told them to their face that their Tuileries was a mistake. And I alone among the avenging reactionists could have told them that the Tuileries, although a crime, was none the less logical. And that, my boy, was because I, as a Russian, was the *only European* in Russia. I am not talking of myself, I am talking of the whole Russian idea. I have been a wanderer, my boy. I was a wanderer, and I knew well that I must wander and be silent. But yet I was sad. I cannot help respecting my position as a Russian nobleman. My boy, I believe you are laughing?"

"No, I'm not laughing," I said in a voice full of feeling, "I'm not laughing at all; you thrilled my heart by your vision of 'The Golden Age,' and, I assure you, I'm beginning to understand you. But, above all, I'm glad that you have such a respect for yourself. I hasten to tell you so. I never expected that of you!"

"I've told you already that I love your exclamations, dear boy," he smiled again at my naïve exclamation, and getting up from his chair, began unconsciously walking up and down the room. I, too, got up. He went on talking in his strange language which was yet so deeply pregnant with thought.

3

"Yes, boy, I tell you again, I cannot help respecting my position as a Russian nobleman. Among us has been created by the ages, a type of the highest culture never seen before, and existing nowhere else in the world—the type of world-wide compassion for all. It is a Russian type, but since it is taken from the most highly cultured stratum of the Russian people, I have the honour of being a representative of it. That type is the custodian of the future of Russia. There are, perhaps, only a thousand of us in Russia, possibly more, possibly less—but all

Russia has existed, so far, only to produce that thousand. I shall be told with indignation that the result is poor, if so many ages and so many millions of people have been spent to produce only this thousand. I don't think it little."

I listened with strained attention. A conviction, the guiding principle of a whole life, was emerging. That "thousand men" made his personality stand out in such strong relief!

I felt that his expansiveness with me was due to some external shock. He talked so warmly to me because he loved me ; but the reason he had suddenly begun to talk, and the reason he so wanted to talk to me especially, I could not guess.

"I emigrated," he went on ; "and I regretted nothing I had left behind. I had served Russia to the utmost of my abilities as long as I was there ; when I went away I went on serving her, too, but in a wider sense. But serving her in that way I served her far more than if I had remained only a Russian, just as the Frenchman at that time was a Frenchman, and a German only a German. In Europe they don't understand that yet. Europe has created a noble type of Frenchman, of Englishman, and of German, but of the man of the future she scarcely knows at present. And, I fancy, so far she does not want to know. And that one can well imagine ; they are not free and we are free. I, with my Russian melancholy, was the only one free in Europe. . . .

"Take note, my dear, of a strange fact : every Frenchman can serve not only his France, but humanity, only on condition that he remains French to the utmost possible degree, and it's the same for the Englishman and the German. Only to the Russian, even in our day, has been vouchsafed the capacity to become most of all Russian only when he is most European, and this is true even in our day, that is, long before the millennium has been reached. That is the most essential difference between us Russians and all the rest, and in that respect the position in Russia is as nowhere else. I am in France a Frenchman, with a German I am a German, with the ancient Greeks I am a Greek, and by that very fact I am most typically a Russian. By that very fact I am a true Russian, and am most truly serving Russia, for I am bringing out her leading idea. I am a pioneer of that idea. I was an emigrant then, but had I forsaken Russia ? No, I was still serving her. What though I did nothing in Europe, what if I only went there as a wanderer (indeed, I know that was so) it was enough that I went there with my thought and my consciousness. I carried thither my Russian melancholy. Oh, it was not only the bloodshed in those days that appalled me, and it was not the Tuileries, but all that was bound to follow it. They are doomed to strife for a long time yet, because they are still too German and too French, and have not yet finished struggling in those national characters. And I regret the destruction that must come before they have finished. To the Russian, Europe is as precious as Russia : every stone in her is cherished and dear. Europe is as much our fatherland as Russia. Oh, even more so. No one could love Russia more than I do, but I never reproached myself that Venice, Rome, Paris, the treasures of their arts and sciences, their whole history, are dearer to me than Russia. Oh, those old stones of foreign lands, those wonders of God's ancient world, those fragments of holy marvels are dear to the Russian, and are even dearer to us than to the inhabitants of those lands themselves ! They now have other thoughts and other feelings, and they have ceased to treasure the old stones. . . . There the conservative struggles only for existence ; and the vitriol-thrower is only fighting for a crust of bread. Only Russia lives not for herself, but for an idea, and, you must admit, my dear, the remarkable fact that for almost the last hundred years Russia has lived absolutely not for herself, but only for the other States of Europe ! And, what of them ! Oh, they are doomed to pass though fearful agonies before they attain the Kingdom of God."

I must confess I listened in great perplexity ; the very tone of his talk alarmed me, though I could not help being impressed by his ideas. I was morbidly afraid of falsity. I suddenly observed in a stern voice :

" You spoke just now of the ' Kingdom of God.' I've heard that you used to preach, used to wear chains ? "

" Let my chains alone," he said with a smile : " that's quite a different matter. I did not preach anything in those days, but that I grieved for their God, that is true. Atheism was proclaimed . . . only by one group of them, but that made no difference ; it was only the hot-heads, but it was the first active step—that's what mattered. In that, too, you have their logic ; but there's always melancholy in logic. I was the outcome of a different culture, and my heart could not accept it. The ingratitude with which they parted from the idea, the hisses and pelting with mud were intolerable to me. The brutality of the process shocked me. Reality always has a smack of the brutal about it, even when there's an unmistakable striving towards the ideal, and, of course, I ought to have known that ; but yet I was

2 G

a man of another type ; I was free to choose, and they were not, and I wept, I wept for them, I wept for the old idea. And I wept, perhaps, with real tears, with no figure of speech."

" Did you believe so much in God ? " I asked incredulously.

" My dear boy, that question, perhaps, is unnecessary. Supposing I did not believe very much, yet I could not help grieving for the idea. I could not help wondering, at times, how man could live without God, and whether that will ever be possible. My heart always decided that it was impossible ; but at a certain period perhaps it is possible . . . I have no doubt that it is coming ; but I always imagined a different picture. . . ."

" What picture ? "

It was true that he had told me before that he was happy ; there was, of course, a great deal of enthusiasm in his words ; that is how I take a great deal that he said. Respecting him as I do, I can't bring myself to record here, on paper, all our conversation ; but some points in the strange picture I succeeded in getting out of him I will quote. What had always worried me most was the thought of those " chains," and I wanted to clear up the matter now, and so I persisted. Some fantastic and extremely strange ideas, to which he gave utterance then, have remained in my heart for ever.

" I picture to myself, my boy," he said with a dreamy smile, " that war is at an end and strife has ceased. After curses, pelting with mud, and hisses, has come a lull, and men are left alone, according to their desire : the great idea of old has left them ; the great source of strength that till then had nourished and fostered them was vanishing like the majestic sun setting in Claude Lorraine's picture, but it was somehow the last day of humanity, and men suddenly understood that they were left quite alone, and at once felt terribly forlorn. I have never, my dear boy, been able to picture men ungrateful and grown stupid. Men left forlorn would begin to draw together more closely and more lovingly ; they would clutch one another's hands, realizing that they were all that was left for one another ! The great idea of immortality would have vanished, and they would have to fill its place ; and all the wealth of love lavished of old upon Him, who was immortal, would be turned upon the whole of nature, on the world, on men, on every blade of grass. They would inevitably grow to love the earth and life as they gradually became aware of their own transitory and finite nature, and with a special love, not as of old, they would begin to observe and would discover in nature phenomena and secrets which they had not suspected before, for they would look on nature with new eyes, as a lover looking on his beloved. On awakening they would hasten to kiss one another, eager to love, knowing that the days are short, and that is all that is left them. They would work for one another, and each would give up all that he had to all, and by that only would be happy. Every child would know and feel that every one on earth was for him like a father or mother. 'To-morrow may be my last day,' each one would think, looking at the setting sun ; ' but no matter, I shall die, but all they will remain and after them their children,' and that thought that they will remain, always as loving and as anxious over each other, would replace the thought of meeting beyond the tomb. Oh, they would be in haste to love, to stifle the great sorrow in their hearts. They would be proud and brave for themselves, but would grow timid for one another ; every one would tremble for the life and happiness of each ; they would grow tender to one another, and would not be ashamed of it as now, and would be caressing as children. Meeting, they would look at one another with deep and thoughtful eyes, and in their eyes would be love and sorrow. . . .

"My dear boy," he broke off with a smile, "this is a fantasy and a most improbable one ; but I have pictured it to myself so often, for all my life I could not have lived without it, and the thought of it. I am not speaking of my belief : my faith is great, I am a deist, a philosophic deist, like all the thousand of us I imagine, but . . . but it's noteworthy that I always complete my picture with Heine's vision of ' Christ on the Baltic Sea.' I could not get on without Him, I could not help imagining Him, in fact, in the midst of His bereaved people. He comes to them, holds out His hands, and asks them, ' How could they forget Him ? ' And then, as it were, the scales would fall from their eyes and there would break forth the great rapturous hymn of the new and the last resurrection . . .

"Enough of that, my dear ; but my ' chains ' are all nonsense ; don't trouble your mind about them. And another thing : you know that I am modest and sober of speech ; if I'm talking too freely now, it's . . . due to various feelings, and it's with you ; to no one else shall I ever speak like this. I add this to set your mind at rest."

But I was really touched ; there was none of the falsity I had dreaded, and I was particularly delighted to see clearly that he really had been melancholy and suffering, and that he really, undoubtedly, had loved much, and that was more precious to me than anything. I told him this with impulsive eagerness.

" But do you know," I added suddenly, " it seems to me that in spite of all your melancholy in those days you must have been very happy ? "

He laughed gaily.

" You are particularly apt in your remarks to-day," he said. " Well, yes, I was happy. How could I be unhappy with a melancholy like that ? No one is freer and happier than a Russian wanderer in Europe, one of our thousand. I am not laughing when I say that, and there's a great deal that's serious in it. And I would not have given up my melancholy for any happiness. In that sense I've always been happy, my dear, all my life. And through being happy I began then, for the first time in my life, really to love your mother."

" How do you mean for the first time in your life ? "

" It was just that. Wandering and melancholy, I suddenly began to love her as I had never loved her before, and I sent for her at once."

" Oh, tell me about that, too, tell me about mother."

" Yes, that's why I asked you here," he smiled gaily. " And do you know I was afraid that you'd forgiven the way I treated your mother for the sake of Herzen, or some little conspiracy...."

CHAPTER VIII

1

As we talked the whole evening and stayed together till midnight, I am not recording the whole conversation, but am only selecting what cleared up for me one enigmatic point in his life.

I will begin by saying that I have no doubt that he loved my mother, and though he did abandon her and " break off all relations with her " when he went away, it was of course, only because he was bored or something of that kind, which is apt to happen indeed to every one on earth, but which is always difficult to explain. Abroad, after some length of time, however, he suddenly began to love mother again, at a distance, that is in thought, and sent for her. I shall be told perhaps that it was a " caprice," but I think differently : to my mind it was a question of all that can be serious in human life, in spite of the apparent sloppiness which I am ready, if you like, to some extent to admit. But I swear that I put his grieving for Europe unmistakably on a level with, and in fact incomparably higher than, any modern practical activity in the construction of railways. His love for humanity I recognize as a most sincere and deep feeling, free from any sort of pose, and his love for mother as something quite beyond dispute, though perhaps a little fantastic. Abroad, in melancholy and happiness, and I may add in the strictest monastic solitude (this fact I learned afterwards through Tatyana Pavlovna), he suddenly thought of mother—to be exact, thought of her " hollow cheeks," and at once sent for her.

" My dear," he blurted out among other things, " I suddenly reflected that my serving the idea did not release me, as a morally rational creature, from the duty of making, in the course of my life, at least one fellow-creature happy, in a practical way."

" Can such a bookish thought have really been the reason of it ? " I asked him with surprise.

" It's not a bookish thought. Though—perhaps it is. It was everything together ; you know I loved your mother really, sincerely, not bookishly. If I hadn't loved her, I shouldn't have sent for her, but should have made happy some casual German, man or woman, if I had formulated that thought. To make in one's lifetime at least one fellow-creature happy, in a practical way, that is really happy, I would make a binding duty for every educated man ; just as I would make it a law or an obligation for every peasant to plant at least one tree in his life to counteract the deforestation of Russia ; though indeed one tree in one's lifetime isn't much, one might order him to plant one every year. The man of higher education and culture, pursuing higher ideas, sometimes loses sight of reality altogether becomes ridiculous, capricious and cold, and indeed I may say stupid, not only in practical life but in theory. The duty not to neglect practice and to make at least one real person happy would correct everything and would give fresh life even to the philanthropist himself.

" As a theory this is very absurd ; but if it were adopted in practice and became a habit, it would not be stupid at all. I have experienced it myself : so soon as I began to develop this idea of a new creed, and at first of course in jest, I suddenly began to realize the depth of the love for your mother that lay hidden in my heart. Until then I had not understood that I loved her. While I lived with her I was only charmed with her while she was pretty, then I began to be moody and changeable. It was only in Germany that I understood that I loved her. It began with her hollow cheeks, of which I could never think, and sometimes not even see, without a pain in my heart, real physical pain. There are memories that hurt, my dear, that cause actual pain. Almost everyone has some such memories, only people forget them, but it does happen that they suddenly recall them, or perhaps only some feature of them, and then they cannot shake them off. I began to recall a thousand details of my life with Sonia. In the end they recalled themselves, and came crowding on my mind, and almost tortured me while I was waiting for her coming. What distressed me most of all was the memory of her everlasting submissiveness to me, and the way she continually thought herself inferior to me, in every respect, even—imagine it—physically; she was ashamed and flushed crimson when I looked at her hands and fingers, which were by no means aristocratic, and not her fingers only—she was ashamed of everything in herself, in spite of my loving her beauty. She was always shrinkingly modest with me, but what was wrong was that in it there was always a sort of fear, in short she thought herself something insignificant beside me, something almost unseemly in fact. I used really sometimes to think at first that she still looked upon me as her master, and was afraid of me, but it was not that at all. Yet, I assure you, no one was more capable of understanding my failings, and I have never in my life met a woman with so much insight and delicacy of heart. Oh, how unhappy she was if I insisted at first, when she was so pretty, on her dressing smartly; it was a question of vanity, and some other feeling, that was wounded. She realized that it would never be in her line to be a lady, and that in any dress but her own she would simply be ridiculous. As a woman she did not want to be ridiculous in her dress, and knew that every woman has *her own* style of dress, which thousands and hundreds of thousands of women will never understand—so long as they are dressed in the fashion. She feared my ironical looks—that was what she feared!

"But it was particularly sad for me to recall the look of deep amazement which I often caught fixed upon me, during the time we were together : in her eyes there was the fullest comprehension of her lot and of the future awaiting her, so that I too felt weighed down, by that look in them, though I must admit, in those days, I did not discuss things with her, and treated all this somewhat disdainfully. And, you know, she wasn't always such a timorous, shy creature as she is now ; even now it happens that she will all at once grow gay, and look as pretty as a girl of twenty ; and in those days in her youth she was very fond of chattering and laughing, only with people she was at home with, with girls and women belonging to the household ; and how she started if I came on her unawares, if she were laughing, how she blushed, and how timorously she looked at me ! Once, not long before I went abroad, almost on the eve of my breaking off all relations with her, in fact, I went into her room and found her alone, at a little table, without any work in her hands, but deep in thought, resting her elbow on the table. It had hardly ever happened to her before to sit without work. At that time I had quite given up showing her affection. I succeeded in stealing in very quietly, on tiptoe, and suddenly embracing and kissing her. . . . She leapt up—and I shall never forget the rapture, the bliss in her eyes, and suddenly it was succeeded by a swift rush of colour, and her eyes flashed. Do you know what I read in those flashing eyes ? ' You are kissing me as a charity—that's what it is ! ' She began sobbing hysterically, making the excuse that I had startled her, but even at the time it made me think. And, in fact, all such reminiscences are very dreary things, dear boy. It's like those *painful* scenes which you sometimes find in the works of great artists, which one remembers ever afterwards with pain ; for instance, Othello's last monologue in Shakespeare, Yevgeny, at the feet of Tatyana, or the meeting of the runaway convict with the little girl on the cold night at the well, in ' Les Miserables ' of Victor Hugo ; it stabs the heart once for all, and leaves a wound for ever. Oh, how eager I was for Sonia to come and how I longed to hold her in my arms ! I dreamed with feverish impatience of a complete new programme of existence ; I dreamed that gradually, by systematic efforts, I would break down that constant fear of me in her soul, would make her appreciate her own value, and all in which she was actually superior to me. Oh, I knew quite well, even then, that I always began to love your mother as soon as we were parted, and always grew cold to her at once as soon as we were together again ; but that time, it was different, then it was different."

I was astonished : " And *she ?* " the idea flashed across me.

" Well, and how did mother and you meet then ? " I asked cautiously.

" Then ?   Oh, we didn't meet then at all.   She only got as far as Königsberg, and stopped there, and I was on the Rhine. I didn't go to her, and I told her to stay there and wait.   We only saw each other again long after, oh, long after, when I went to her to ask her to consent to my marriage. . . ."

2

Now I'm coming to the core of it all, that is, as far as I was able to grasp it myself ; for, indeed, his own account began to be somewhat disconnected.   His talk became ten times as incoherent and rambling as soon as he reached this part of the story.

He met Katerina Nikolaevna suddenly, just when he was expecting mother, at the moment of most impatient expectation. They were all, at the time, on the Rhine, at some spa, all drinking the waters.   Katerina Nikolaevna's husband was by then almost dying, he had, at any rate, been given up by the doctors.   She made an impression on him at the first meeting, as it were cast a sort of spell upon him.   It was a case of fate.   It's remarkable that recalling it and writing it down now, I don't remember that he once used the word " love " in connection with her, or spoke of " being in love."   The word " fate " I remember.

And, of course, it was fate.   He did *not choose* it, " he did not want to love her."   I don't know whether I can give a clear account of it, but his whole soul was in revolt at the fact that this could have happened to him.   Everything in him that was free was annihilated by this meeting.   And the man was fettered for life to a woman who had really nothing to do with him.   He did not desire this slavery of passion.   To state the fact plainly, Katerina Nikolaevna is a type rare amongst society women—a type perhaps unique in that circle.   That is, she is an extremely good-natured and straightforward woman.   I've heard, indeed I know for a fact that this was what made her irresistible in the fashionable world whenever she made her appearance in it.   (She used at times to withdraw into complete seclusion.)

Versilov did not believe, of course, when he first met her, that she was like that ; in fact, he believed she was the exact opposite, that she was a hypocrite and a Jesuit.   At this point I will anticipate by quoting her own criticism of him : she declared that he could not help thinking what he did of her " because an idealist always runs his head against reality and is more inclined than other people to assume anything horrid."

I don't know if this is true of idealists in general, but it was entirely true of him, no doubt. I may perhaps add here my own judgment, which flashed across my mind while I was listening to him then : I thought that he loved mother, more so to say with the humane love one feels for all mankind, than with the simple love with which women are loved as a rule, and that as soon as he met a woman whom he began to love with that simple love, he at once turned against that love—most probably because the feeling was new to him. Perhaps, though, this idea is incorrect ; I did not of course utter it to him. It would have been indelicate, and he really was in such a condition that it was almost necessary to spare him : he was agitated ; at some points in his story he simply broke off, and was silent for some moments, walking about the room with a vindictive face.

She soon divined his secret. Oh, perhaps she flirted with him on purpose ; even the most candid women are base in these cases, and it is their overwhelming instinct. It ended in a rupture full of rankling bitterness, and I believe he tried to kill her ; he frightened her, and would have killed her, perhaps, " but it was all turned to hatred." Then there came a strange period : he was suddenly possessed by the strange idea of torturing himself by a discipline, " the same as that used by the monks. Gradually, by systematic practice, you overcome your will, beginning with the most absurd and trivial things, and end by conquering your will completely, and become free." He added that this practice of the monks is a serious thing ; in the course of a thousand years it has been brought by them to a science. But what is most remarkable is that he gave himself up to this idea of discipline, not in order to get rid of the image of Katerina Nikolaevna, but in the full conviction that he had not only ceased to love her, but hated her. He so thoroughly believed in his hatred for her as to conceive the idea of loving and marrying her step-daughter, who had been seduced by Prince Sergay, to persuade himself absolutely of this new love, and to win the poor imbecile's heart completely, by his devotion making her perfectly happy. Why, instead of devoting himself to her, he did not think of mother, who was all this time waiting for him at Königsberg, remained for me inexplicable. . . . He quite forgot mother, indeed, and even neglected to send money for her maintenance, so that Tatyana Pavlovna had to come to her rescue ; yet finally he did go to mother " to ask her permission " to marry the young lady, pleading that " such a bride was not a woman." Oh, perhaps all this is only a portrait of a theoretical man, as Katerina Nikolaevna said of him later. But why is it, though, that these theoretical people (if they really are theoretical people) are capable of such very real suffering, and end in such very real tragedy ? On that evening, however, I looked at it differently, and I was disturbed by the thought :

" All your development, your whole soul, has been won by the suffering and the struggle of your whole life, while her perfection has cost her nothing. That's unjust. . . . Woman is revolting in that way." I said this without the least intention of flattering him, speaking with warmth and indignation.

" Perfection ? Her perfection ? But she has no sort of perfection ! " he said suddenly, seeming almost surprised at my words. " She is the most ordinary woman, she is really a contemptible woman. . . . But she is bound to have every perfection ! "

" Why is she bound to ? "

" Because she has such power, she is bound to have every sort of perfection ! " he cried vindictively.

" The saddest thing is that you are so harassed even now," I could not help blurting out suddenly.

" How harassed ! " he repeated my words again, standing still before me as though in some perplexity. And suddenly a slow, gentle, dreamy smile lighted up his whole face, and he held up his finger as though considering. Then as though waking up, he took from the table an open letter, and flung it down in front of me.

" Read it ! You must know everything . . . and why have you made me rake up all this bygone foolishness ? . . . It has only roused up nasty and spiteful feelings in my heart. . . ."

I cannot describe my astonishment. The letter was from her to him, received by him that afternoon at five o'clock. I read it, almost shaking with emotion. It was not long, and was written so simply and straightforwardly, that as I read it I seemed to see her before me and hear her words. With the most simple truthfulness (and so almost touchingly) she confessed her terror, and then simply besought him to " leave her in peace." In conclusion, she told him that she definitely was to marry Büring. Till then she had never written a word to him.

And this is what I could make out of his explanation:

As soon as he had read the letter that day, he was aware of a new sensation : for the first time in those fatal two years he felt not the slightest hatred for her, or the slightest shock of emotion, such as had "driven him out of his mind" at a mere rumour of Büring. "On the contrary, I sent her my blessing, with perfect sincerity," he told me, with deep feeling. I heard these words with ecstasy. Then all the passion and agony that had possessed him had vanished all at once of itself, like a dream, like an obsession that had lasted two years. Hardly yet able to believe in himself he hastened to mother's and—arrived at the very moment when she was set free by the death of the old man who had bequeathed her to him. The coincidence of these two events had deeply stirred his soul. Not long afterwards he rushed to find me—and that immediate thought of me I shall never forget.

I shall never forget the end of that evening either. The whole man was suddenly transformed again. We did not separate till late at night. The effect that all he told me had upon me I will describe later, in its proper place, and will confine myself now to a few words, in conclusion, about him. Reflecting upon it now, I realize that what captivated me so much at the time was his humility, so to speak, with me, his frank sincerity with a boy like me ! "It was infatuation, but my blessings on it ! " he exclaimed. "But for that blind obsession I might perhaps have never discovered in my heart my sole queen, my suffering darling—your mother." These passionate words, wrung from him by over-mastering feeling, I note particularly, in view of what followed. But at the time he gained complete possession of my heart and conquered it.

I remember in the end we became very cheerful. He asked for some champagne, and we drank to mother, and to the "future." Oh, he was so full of life, and so eager to live ! But we suddenly became extremely merry, not from the wine : we only drank two glasses. I don't know why, but in the end we laughed almost helplessly. We began talking of quite extraneous matters ; he began telling me an anecdote and I told him one. And our laughter and our anecdotes, were by no means malicious or amusing, but we were merry. He was unwilling to let me go : "Stay, stay a little longer," he repeated, and I stayed. He even came out to see me home ; it was an exquisite evening, with a slight frost. " Tell me, have you sent her an answer yet ? " I asked, quite casually, as I pressed his hand for the last time at the cross road.

" No, not yet, but that's no matter. Come to-morrow, come early. . . . Oh, and another thing : drop Lambert altogether and tear up that ' document,' and make haste about it. Goodbye ! "

Saying this he went away quickly ; I remained standing still, and so much taken aback that I could not bring myself to call after him. The expression, the " document," startled me particularly : how could he have known of it, and that particular word too, if not from Lambert ? I went home in great confusion. And how can it have happened, the question flashed upon me suddenly, that such an obsession for two years can have vanished like a dream, like a vapour, like a phantom.

CHAPTER IX

1

But I waked up next morning feeling fresher and in better heart. I unconsciously reproached myself, indeed, with perfect sincerity, for a certain levity, and, as it were, superciliousness, with which it seemed to me, recalling it, I had listened to some parts of his " confession " the evening before. Supposing it had been to some extent muddled, and some revelations had been, as it were, a little delirious and incoherent, he had not, of course, prepared to deliver a speech when he invited me the day before. He had simply done me a great honour in turning to me, as his one friend at such a moment, and I shall never forget his doing it. On the contrary, his confession was " touching," though people may laugh at me for saying so, and if there were glimpses from time to time of something cynical, or even something that seemed ridiculous, I was not so narrow as to be unable to understand and accept realism, which did not, however, detract from the ideal. The great point was now that I understood the man, and I even felt, and was almost vexed at feeling, that it had all turned out to be so simple : I had always in my heart set that man on a supreme pinnacle, in the clouds, and had insisted on shrouding his life in mystery, so that I had naturally wished not to fit the key to it so easily.

In his meeting *with her*, however, and in the sufferings he had endured for two years, there was much that was complex. " He did not want to live under the yoke of fate ; he wanted to be free, and not a slave to fate ; through his bondage to fate he had been forced to hurt mother, who was still waiting for him at Königsberg. . . ." Besides, I looked upon him in any case as a preacher : he cherished in his heart the golden age, and knew all about the future of atheism ; and then the meeting with *her* had shattered everything, distorted everything ! Oh, I was not a traitor to her, but still I was on his side, Mother, for instance, I reflected, would have been no hindrance, nor would marriage with her be so indeed. That I understood ; that was something utterly different from his meeting with *that woman*. Mother, it is true, would not have given him peace either, but that was all the better : one cannot judge of such men as of others, and their life must always be different ; and that's not unseemly at all ; on the contrary, it would be unseemly if they settled down and became altogether like other ordinary people. His praises of the nobility, and his words : " *Je mourrai gentilhomme,*" did not disconcert me in the least ; I understood what sort of *gentilhomme* he was ; he was a man ready to abandon everything, and to become the champion of political rights for all, and the leading Russian thought of a universal harmony of ideas. And even though all this might be nonsense, that is " the universal harmony of ideas " (which is of course inconceivable), yet the very fact that he had all his life bowed down to an idea, and not to the stupid golden calf, was good. My God ! why, conceiving " my idea," had I, I myself—could I— have been bowing down to the golden calf, could I have been aiming only at money, then ? I swear that all I wanted was the idea ! I swear I would not have had one chair, one sofa upholstered in velvet, and I would have eaten the same plate of soup as now, if I had had millions. I dressed and hurried off impatiently to see him. I may add that in regard to his outburst yesterday about the " document," I was ever so much more at ease in my mind than I had been the day before. To begin with, I hoped to have it out with him, and besides, what was there in Lambert's having wormed his way in to him, and having talked to him of something ? But what rejoiced me most was an extraordinary sensation : it came from the thought that " he no longer loved *her* " ; I put absolute faith in it, and felt as if some one had lifted a fearful weight off my heart. I recall a conjecture that flashed upon me at the time : that the unseemliness and senselessness of his last violent outbreak, on hearing about Büring, and the sending of that insulting letter, that that final crisis might be taken as a sign and augury of a change in his feeling, and an approaching return to sanity ; it must be as it is in illness, I thought, and, in fact, he is bound to reach the opposite extreme, it is a pathological episode, and nothing more.

This thought made me happy.

" And let her arrange her life as she pleases, let her marry her Büring as much as she likes, so long as he, my father, my friend, loves her no longer," I exclaimed.

I had, however, certain secret feelings of my own, on which I do not care to enlarge in my notes here.

That's enough. And now, without further reflections, I will give an account of the awful event that followed, and how the facts worked together to bring it about.

2

At ten o'clock, just as I was getting ready to go out, to see him of course, Darya Onisimovna appeared. I asked her joyfully : " whether she came from him ? " and heard with vexation that she did not come from him, but from Anna Andrey-evna, and that she, Darya Onisimovna, " had left the lodging as soon as it was light."

" What lodging ? "

" Why, the same where you were yesterday. You know, the lodging where you were yesterday, where the baby is ; it is taken in my name now, and Tatyana Pavlovna pays the rent. . . ."

" Oh, well, that's nothing to me ! " I interrupted with annoy-ance. " Is he at home, anyway ? Shall I find him ? "

And to my surprise I heard from her that he had gone out even before she had ; so she had gone out as soon as it was light, and he had gone out even earlier.

" Then has he come back yet ? "

" No, he's certainly not back yet, and perhaps he won't come back at all," she declared, turning upon me the same sharp and furtive eye, and keeping it fixed on me, as she had done on the occasion I have described, when she visited me as I lay ill in bed. What infuriated me most was that their mysteries and imbecilities should be forced on me again, and that these people could not get on without secrets and intrigues.

"Why do you say : 'he will certainly not come back'? What do you mean by that? He has gone to see mother, that's all!"

"I d—don't know."

"And what have you come for?"

She told me that she had just come from Anna Andreyevna, who had sent her for me, and urgently expected me at once, or else it would be "too late." These last enigmatic words finally exasperated me :

"Why too late? I don't want to come and I'm not coming! I won't let them take possession of me again! I don't care a damn for Lambert, you can tell her so, and if she sends Lambert to me, I'll kick him out, you can tell her so!"

Darya Onisimovna was awfully alarmed.

"Oh no," she said, taking a step towards me, clasping her hands as though she were beseeching me. "Don't be so hasty. There's something very important the matter, very important to yourself, to them, too, to Andrey Petrovitch, to your mamma, to every one. . . . Go and see Anna Andreyevna at once, she can't wait any longer . . . I assure you, on my honour . . . and afterwards you can make your decision."

I looked at her with surprise and repulsion.

"Nonsense, it will be nothing, I'm not coming!" I shouted obstinately and vindictively: "Now everything's different! Though how could you understand that? Good-bye, Darya Onisimovna, I won't go on purpose, I won't question you on purpose. You simply bother me. I don't want to know anything about your mysteries."

As she did not go away, however, but still stood waiting, I snatched up my fur coat and cap, and went out myself, leaving her in the middle of the room. There were no letters or papers in my room, and I never used to lock my door when I went out. But before I had reached the front door my landlord ran after me downstairs, without his hat, and not in full uniform.

"Arkady Makarovitch! Arkady Makarovitch!"

"What now?"

"Have you no instructions to leave?"

"No, nothing."

He looked at me with eyes like gimlets, in evident uneasiness :

" About your room, for instance ? "

" What about my room ?   Why, I sent you the rent when it was due ? "

" Oh no, sir, I was not thinking of the money," he said with a broad smile, his eyes still piercing into me like pins.

" Why, what on earth's the matter with you all ? " I shouted at last, growing almost savage.   " What do you want too ? "

He waited for a few seconds longer, still seeming to expect something from me.

" Well, then, you will give instructions later . . . if you are not in the humour now," he muttered, grinning more broadly than ever ; " you go on and I'll see to it."

He ran back upstairs. Of course all this might well make one reflect. I purposely avoid omitting a single detail in all that petty tomfoolery, for every little detail helped to make up the final situation and had its place in it, a fact of which the reader will be convinced. But that they really did bother me was true. If I was upset and irritated, it was at hearing again in their words that tone of intrigue and mystery of which I was so sick, and which so brought back the past. But to continue.

It turned out that Versilov was not at home, and it appeared that he really had gone out as soon as it was light.   " To mother's, of course " : I stuck obstinately to my idea. I did not question the nurse, rather a stupid peasant woman, and there was no one else in the lodging. I ran to mother's and I must admit I was so anxious that I took a sledge half-way. *He had not been at mother's since the evening before.* There was no one with mother except Tatyana Pavlovna and Liza. Liza began getting ready to go out as soon as I went in.

They were all sitting upstairs, in my " coffin." In the drawing room Makar Ivanovitch was laid out on the table, and an old man was reading the psalter over him in an even, monotonous voice. For the future I am not going to describe anything more that does not relate to the matter in hand. I will only say that the coffin, which they had already made, was standing in the middle of the room, and was not a plain one, though it was black ; it was upholstered in velvet, and the pall was of an expensive sumptuousness that was not in keeping with the character of a monk, or with the convictions of the dead man ; but such was the special desire of my mother and Tatyana Pavlovna, who arranged the matter together.

I had not of course expected to find them cheerful ; but the peculiar overwhelming distress mixed with uneasiness and anxiety, which I read in their eyes, struck me at once, and I instantly concluded that " sorrow for the dead was certainly not the only cause." All this, I repeat, I remember perfectly.

In spite of everything I embraced mother tenderly and at once asked about *him*. A gleam of tremulous curiosity came into mother's eyes at once. I made haste to mention that we had spent the whole evening together, till late at night, but that to-day he had been away from home since early morning, though at parting last night he had asked me to come as early as I could this morning. Mother made no answer, and Tatyana Pavlovna, seizing a favourable moment, shook her finger at me meaningly.

" Good-bye, brother," Liza blurted out, going quickly out of the room. I ran after her, of course, but she stopped short at the outer door.

" I thought you would guess you must come with me," she said in a rapid whisper.

" Liza, what's the matter ? "

" I don't know what, but a great deal, no doubt the last chapter of ' the same old story.' He has not come, but they have heard something about him. They won't tell you, you needn't trouble yourself, and you won't ask, if you are sensible ; but mother's shattered. I've not asked about anything either. Good-bye."

She opened the door.

" And, Liza, about you, yourself, have you nothing to tell me ? " I dashed after her into the entry. Her terribly exhausted and despairing face pierced my heart. She looked at me, not simply with anger, but with a sort of exasperated fury, laughed bitterly, and waved me off.

" If only he were dead I should thank God ! " she flung up at me from the stairs, and was gone. She said this of Prince Sergay, and he, at that very time, was lying delirious and unconscious.

I went upstairs, sad but excited. " The same old story ! What same old story ? " I thought defiantly, and I had suddenly an irresistible impulse to tell them at least a part of the impression left upon me by his last night's confession, and the confession too. " They're thinking some evil of him now, so let them know all about it ! " floated through my mind.

I remember that I succeeded very cleverly in beginning to

tell them my story. Instantly their faces betrayed an intense curiosity. This time Tatyana Pavlovna positively fixed me with her eyes ; but mother showed more reserve ; she was very grave, but the glimmer of a faint, beautiful, though utterly hopeless smile came into her face, and scarcely left it all the time I was talking. I told the story well, of course, though I knew that it would be almost beyond their comprehension. To my surprise Tatyana Pavlovna did not attack me, did not insist on minute details, or try to pick holes as she usually did as soon as I began telling anything. She only pinched up her lips and screwed up her eyes, as though making an effort to get to the bottom of it. At times I positively fancied that they understood it all, though that could hardly have been so. . . . I spoke for instance of his convictions, but principally of his enthusiasm last night, his enthusiastic feeling for mother, his love for mother and how he had kissed her portrait. . . . Hearing this they exchanged a rapid silent glance with each other, and mother flushed all over, though both continued silent. Then . . . then I could not of course *before mother* touch on the principal point, that is his meeting with *her* and all the rest of it, above all *her* letter to him the day before, and his moral resurrection after getting that letter ; and that indeed was the chief point, so that all his feeling, with which I had hoped to please mother so much, naturally remained inexplicable, though of course that was not my fault ; I had told all that could be told extremely well. I ended in complete confusion ; their silence was still unbroken and I began to feel very uncomfortable with them.

" Most likely he's come back now, and may be at my lodgings waiting for me," I said, and got up to go.

" Go and see ! go and see ! " Tatyana Pavlovna urged me resolutely.

" Have you been downstairs ? " mother asked me, in a sort of half whisper, as she said good-bye.

" Yes, I have been, and I bowed down and prayed for him. What a peaceful, serene face he has, mother ! Thank you, mother, for not sparing expense over his coffin. At first I thought it strange, but I thought, at once, that I should have done the same."

" Will you come to the church to-morrow ? " she asked, and her lips trembled.

" What do you mean, mother ? " I asked in surprise. " I shall come to the requiem service to-day, and I shall come again ;

and . . . besides, to-morrow is your birthday, mother darling !
To think that he died only three days before ! "

I went away painfully surprised : how could she ask such
questions, whether I were coming to the funeral service in the
church ? "If that's what they think of me, what must they think
of *him* ? "

I knew that Tatyana Pavlovna would run after me and I
purposely waited at the outer door of the flat ; but she
pushed me out on to the stairs and closed the door behind
her.

"Tatyana Pavlovna, don't you expect Andrey Petrovitch to-
day or to-morrow, then ? I am alarmed. . . ."

"Hold your tongue. Much it matters your being alarmed.
Tell me, tell me what you kept back when you were telling us
about that rigmarole last night ! "

I didn't think it necessary to conceal it, and feeling almost
irritated with Versilov I told her all about Katerina Nikolaevna's
letter to him the day before and of the effect of the letter, that
is of his resurrection into a new life. To my amazement the
fact of the letter did not surprise her in the least, and I guessed
that she knew of it already.

" But you are lying."

" No, I'm not."

" I dare say," she smiled malignantly, as though meditating :
" risen again, has he, so that's the latest, is it ? But is it true
that he kissed her portrait ? "

" Yes, Tatyana Pavlovna."

" Did he kiss it with feeling, he wasn't putting it on ? "

" Putting it on, as though he ever did ! For shame, Tatyana
Pavlovna ; you've a coarse soul, a woman's soul."

I said this with heat ; but she did not seem to hear me ; she
seemed to be pondering something again, in spite of the terrible
chilliness of the stairs. I had on my fur coat, but she was in
her indoor dress.

" I might have asked you to do something, the only pity is
you're so stupid," she said with contempt and apparent vexation.
"Listen, go to Anna Andreyevna's, and see what's going on there.
. . . But no, don't go ; a booby's always a booby ! Go along,
quick march, why do you stand like a post ? "

" And I'm not going to Anna Andreyevna's. Anna Andreyevna
sent to ask me herself."

" She did ? Darya Onisimovna ? " she turned to me quickly ;

she had been on the point of going away, and had already opened the door, but she shut it again with a slam.

"Nothing will induce me to go to Anna Andreyevna's," I repeated with spiteful enjoyment; "I won't go because I've just been called a booby, though I've never been so sharp-sighted as to-day. I see all you're doing, it's as clear as day, but I'm not going to Anna Andreyevna all the same!"

"I know it," she exclaimed, but again pursuing her own thoughts, and taking no notice of my words at all. "They will devour her now completely, and draw her into a deadly noose."

"Anna Andreyevna?"

"Fool!"

"Then whom do you mean? Surely not Katerina Nikolaevna? What sort of deadly noose?"

I was terribly frightened, a vague but terrible idea set my whole heart quivering. Tatyana Pavlovna looked at me searchingly.

"What are you up to there?" she asked suddenly. "What are you meddling in there? I've heard something about you too, you'd better look out!"

"Listen, Tatyana Pavlovna, I'll tell you a terrible secret, only not just now, there's not time now, but to-morrow, when we're alone; but in return you tell me the whole truth, how and what you mean by a deadly noose, for I am all in a tremble. . . ."

"Much I care for your trembling," she exclaimed. "What's this other secret you want to tell to-morrow? Why, you know nothing whatever!" she transfixed me with a questioning look. "Why, you swore then that Kraft had burnt the letter, didn't you?"

"Tatyana Pavlovna, I tell you again, don't torment me," I persisted in my turn, not answering her question, for I was beside myself. "Take care, Tatyana Pavlovna, that your hiding this from me may not lead to something worse . . . why, yesterday he was absolutely turning over a new leaf!"

"Go along, you idiot! you are like a love-sick sparrow yourself, I'll be bound; father and son in love with the same idol! Foo, horrid creatures!"

She vanished, slamming the door indignantly. Furious at the impudent, shameless cynicism of these last words, a cynicism of which only a woman would have been capable, I ran away, deeply insulted. But I won't describe my vague sensations as

I have vowed to keep to facts which will explain everything now ; on my way of course, I called in at his lodging, and heard from the nurse that he had not been home at all.

" And isn't he coming at all ? "

" Goodness knows."

3

Facts, facts ! . . . But will the reader understand ? I remember how these facts overwhelmed me and prevented me from thinking clearly, so that by the end of the day my head was in a perfect whirl. And so I think I must say two or three words by way of introduction.

The question that tormented me was this : if he really had gone through a spiritual change and had ceased to love her, in that case where should he have been now ? The answer was : first of all with me whom he had embraced the evening before, and next with mother, whose portrait he had kissed. And yet, in spite of these natural alternatives, he had suddenly, " as soon as it was light," left home and gone off somewhere, and Darya Onisimovna had for some reason babbled of his not being likely to return. What's more, Liza had hinted at the " last chapter " of some " same old story," and of mother's having some news of him, and the latest news, too ; moreover, they undoubtedly knew of Katerina Nikolaevna's letter, too (I noticed that), and yet they did not believe in " his resurrection into a new life " though they had listened to me attentively. Mother was crushed, and Tatyana Pavlovna had been diabolically sarcastic at the word " resurrection." But if all this was so, it must mean that some revulsion of feeling had come over him again in the night, another crisis, and this—after yesterday's enthusiasm, emotion, pathos ! So all his " resurrection " had burst like a soap-bubble, and he, perhaps, was rushing about somewhere again now, in the same frenzy as he had been after hearing the news of Büring ! There was the question, too, what would become of mother, of me, of all of us, and . . . and, finally, what would become of *her ?* What was the deadly noose Tatyana had babbled of when she was sending me to Anna Andreyevna ? So that " deadly noose " was there, at Anna Andreyevna's ! Why at Anna Andreyevna's ? Of course I should run to Anna Andreyevna's ; I had said that I wouldn't go on purpose, only in annoyance ; I would run there at once, but what was it Tatyana had said about the "document"? And hadn't he himself said to me the evening before: "Burn the document"?

These were my thoughts, this was what strangled me, too, in a deadly noose; but what I wanted most of all was *him*. With him I could have decided everything—I felt that; we should have understood each other in two words! I should have gripped his hands, pressed them; I should have found burning words in my heart—this was the dream that haunted me. Oh, I would have calmed his frenzy. . . . But where was he? Where was he?

And, as though this were not enough, Lambert must needs turn up at such a moment, when I was so excited! When I was only a few steps from my door I met him; he uttered a yell of delight on seeing me, and seized me by the arm.

"I've been to see you thr-r-ree times already. . . . *Enfin!* come and have lunch."

"Stay, have you been to my rooms; was Andrey Petrovitch there?"

"No, there was no one there. Dr-r-rop them all! You're a fool, you were cross yesterday; you were drunk, and I've something important to tell you; I heard a splendid piece of news this morning, about what we were discussing yesterday. . . ."

"Lambert," I interrupted hurriedly, breathing hard and unconsciously declaiming a little. "I am only stopping with you now to finish with you for good. I told you yesterday, but you still won't understand. Lambert, you're a baby and as stupid as a Frenchman. You persist in thinking that it's the same as it was at Touchard's, and that I'm as stupid as at Touchard's. . . . But I'm not so silly as I was at Touchard's. . . . I was drunk yesterday, but not from wine, but because I was excited; and if I seemed to agree with the stuff you talked, it was because I pretended, so as to find out what you were driving at. I deceived you, and you were delighted and believed it and went on talking nonsense. Let me tell you that marrying her is such nonsense that it wouldn't take in a schoolboy in the first form. How could you imagine I should believe it? Did you believe it? You believed it because you have never been in aristocratic society, and don't know how things are done among decent people. Things aren't done so simply in aristocratic society, and it's not possible for her so simply to go and get married. . . . Now I will tell you plainly what it is you want: you mean to entice me, so as to make me drunk, and to get me to give up the document, and to join you in some scoundrelly plot against Katerina Nikolaevna ! So I tell you it's nonsense ! I'll never come to you. And you may as well know that to-morrow or the day after that letter will be in her own hands, for it belongs to her, for it was written by her, and I'll give it to her myself, and if you care to know where, I can tell you that through Tatyana Pavlovna, her friend, I shall give it at Tatyana Pavlovna's, and in Tatyana Pavlovna's presence, and I'll take nothing from her for giving it her. And now be off and keep away from me for ever, or else . . . or else, I shan't treat you so civilly next time, Lambert. . . ."

As I finished I was in a slight shudder all over. A very serious thing and the nastiest habit in life, which vitiates everything in all one does, is . . . is showing off. Some evil spirit prompted me to work myself up with Lambert, till rapping out the words with relish, and raising my voice higher and higher, in my heat I ended up by dragging in the quite unnecessary detail, that I should return the document through Tatyana Pavlovna, and in her lodging ! But I had such a longing to crush him ! When I burst out so directly about the letter, and suddenly saw his stupid alarm, I immediately felt a desire to overwhelm him by giving him precise details. And this womanish, boastful babbling was afterwards the cause of terrible misfortunes, for that detail about Tatyana Pavlovna and her lodging was naturally caught up and retained by a scoundrel who had a practical mind for little things ; in more exalted and important matters he was useless and unintelligent, but for such trifles he had a keen sense, nevertheless. If I had held my tongue about Tatyana Pavlovna, great disasters would not have occurred. Yet when he heard what I said, for the first minute he was terribly upset.

" Listen," he muttered. " Alphonsine . . . Alphonsine will sing. . . . Alphonsine has been to see *her ;* listen. I have a letter, almost a letter, in which Mme. Ahmakov writes of you ; the pock-marked fellow got it for me, do you remember him— and you will see, you will see, come along ! "

" You are lying ; show me the letter ! "

" It's at home, Alphonsine has got it ; come along ! "

He was lying and talking wildly, of course, trembling for fear I should run away from him ; but I suddenly abandoned him in the middle of the street, and when he seemed disposed to follow me I stood still and shook my fist at him. But he already stood hesitating, and let me get away ; perhaps a new plan had dawned upon him. But the meetings and surprises in store for me were not yet over. . . . And when I remember the whole of that disastrous day, it always seems as though all those surprises and unforeseen accidents were somehow conspiring together and were showered on my head from some accursed horn of plenty. I had scarcely opened the door of my lodging when in the entry I jostled against a tall young man, of dignified and elegant exterior with a long pale face, wearing a magnificent fur coat. He had a pince-nez on his nose ; but as soon as he saw me he took it off (evidently as a mark of politeness), and courteously lifting his top-hat, but without stopping, however, said to me with an elegant smile : " Hullo, *bonsoir*," and passing me went downstairs. We recognized each other at once, though I had only once seen him for a moment in Moscow. It was Anna Andreyevna's brother, the young *kammer-junker*, Versilov's son, and consequently almost my brother. He was accompanied by my landlady. (The landlord was not yet back from his office.) As soon as he had gone, I simply pounced on her :

" What has he been doing here ? Has he been in my room ? "

" He's not been in your room at all. He came to see me . . ." she snapped out briefly and dryly, and returned to her room.

" No, you can't put me off like that," I cried. " Kindly answer me ; why did he come ? "

" My goodness ! Am I always to tell you why people come to see me ? We may have our own interests to consider, mayn't we ? The young man may have wanted to borrow money ; he found out an address from me. Perhaps I promised it him last time. . . ."

" Last time ? When ? "

" Oh my goodness, why it's not the first time he's been ! "

She went away. The chief thing I gathered was the change of tone. They had begun to be rude to me. It was clear that this was another secret ; secrets were accumulating with every step, with every hour. For the first time young Versilov had come with his sister, with Anna Andreyevna, when I was ill ; I remember that perfectly, as well as Anna Andreyevna's amazing words the day before, that, perhaps, the old prince would stay at my rooms. . . . But all this was so mixed up and so monstrous that I could scarcely gather anything from it. Clapping my hands to my forehead, and not even sitting down to rest, I ran to Anna Andreyevna's ; it appeared that she was not at home, and I received from the porter the information that " she had gone to Tsarskoe ; and might, perhaps, not be back till about this time to-morrow."

She was at Tsarskoe, and no doubt with the old prince, and her brother was examining my lodgings ! " No, that shall not be," I cried, gnashing my teeth ; " and if there really is some ' deadly noose ' I will defend ' the poor woman ' ! "

From Anna Andreyevna's I did not return home, for there suddenly flashed upon my feverish brain the thought of the restaurant on the canal side, where Andrey Petrovitch had the habit of going in his gloomy hours. Delighted at this conjecture, I instantly ran thither ; it was by now four o'clock and was already beginning to get dark. In the restaurant I was told that he had been there, stayed a little while and had gone away, but, perhaps, he would come back. I suddenly determined to wait for him, and ordered dinner ; there was a hope any how.

I ate my dinner, ate, indeed, more than I wanted, so as to have a right to stay as long as possible, and I stayed, I believe, four hours. I won't describe my disappointment and feverish impatience, everything within me seemed shaking and quivering. That organ, those diners—oh, all the dreariness of it is stamped upon my soul, perhaps for the rest of my life ! I won't describe the ideas that whirled in my head like a crowd of dry leaves in autumn after a hurricane ; it really was something like that, and I confess that I felt at times that my reason was beginning to desert me.

But what worried me till it was a positive pain (in a side-current, of course, besides my chief torment) was a persistent poisonous impression, persistent as a venomous autumn fly, which one does not think about but which whirls about one, pesters one, and suddenly bites one painfully ; it was only a reminiscence, an incident of which I had never spoken to anyone in the world before. This was what it was, since it seems I must tell this, too.

4

When it was settled that I was to leave Moscow and come to Petersburg, I received instructions through Nikolay Semyonovitch to wait for money to be sent me for the journey. From whom the money was coming I did not ask ; I knew it was from Versilov, and as I dreamed day and night of my meeting with him, making exalted plans about it while my heart almost swooned within me, I had quite given up speaking about him aloud even to Marie Ivanovna. I remember that I had money of my own, but I proceeded to wait expectantly for the money to come by post.

Suddenly, however, Nikolay Semyonovitch, returing home, informed me (as usual briefly and without going off into explanations) that I was to go next day to Myasnitsky, at eleven o'clock in the morning, to Prince V.'s flat, and that there Andrey Petrovitch's son, the *kammer-junker*, Versilov, who had just arrived from Petersburg and was staying with his schoolfellow, Prince V., would hand over to me a sum of money for my journey. On the face of it the arrangement was simple enough : Andrey Petrovitch might well send the money by his son rather than by post ; but the news crushed me and filled me with alarm. I had no doubt that Versilov wished to bring his son, my brother, and me together ; this threw a light upon the intentions and feelings of the man of whom I dreamed ; but a question of the utmost magnitude presented itself to me : how should I, and how must I behave at this utterly unexpected interview, and how could I best keep up my dignity ?

Next day, exactly at eleven o'clock, I turned up at Prince V.'s flat, which, as I was able to judge, was splendidly furnished, though it was a bachelor's establishment. I was kept waiting in the hall where there were several lackeys in livery. And from the next room came sounds of loud talk and laughter : Prince V. had other visitors besides the *kammer-junker*. I told the footman to announce me, and, I fancy, in rather haughty terms. Anyway, he looked at me strangely, and, as I fancied, not so respectfully as he should have done. To my amazement he was a very long time in announcing me, five minutes, and all the while the same laughter, and the same sounds of conversation reached me.

I waited standing, knowing that it would be impossible and unseemly for me, " just as much a gentleman," to sit down in a hall where there were footmen. My pride would have prevented me under any circumstances from entering the drawing-room without a special invitation ; over-fastidious pride perhaps it was, but that was only fitting. To my amazement the two lackeys who were left in the hall had the impertinence to sit down. I turned away to avoid noticing it, and yet I could not help quivering all over, and suddenly turning and stepping up to one of the footmen, I *ordered* him to go " at once " and take in my name again. In spite of my stern expression and extreme excitement, the lackey looked at me lazily, without getting up, and the other one answered for him :

" It's been taken in, don't disturb yourself."

I made up my mind to wait only another minute or possibly even less, and then *to go*. I was very well-dressed : my suit and overcoat were new anyway, and my linen was perfectly fresh, Marie Ivanovna had seen to that with a special view to the occasion. But I learned for a fact, much later, when I was in Petersburg, that these lackeys had heard the evening before from young Versilov's valet that " the young gentleman's bastard brother, a student, was coming." I know this now for a fact.

The minute passed. It's a strange sensation when one decides and cannot decide. " Shall I go or not, shall I go or not ? " I repeated to myself every second, almost in a fever, and suddenly the lackey who had taken my name returned. Between his fingers he held fluttering four red notes—forty roubles !

" Here, sir, will you please take forty roubles ! "

I boiled over. This was such an insult ! All the night before I had been dreaming of the meeting Versilov had arranged between us two brothers ; I had spent the whole night in feverish visions of the demeanour I ought to adopt, that I might not discredit—not discredit the whole cycle of ideas which I had worked out in my solitude, and which might have made me feel proud in any circle. I dreamed of how proud, gentlemanly, and sad, perhaps, I would be even in Prince V.'s society, and how in that way I should be admitted into that circle—oh, I'm not sparing myself, and so be it, for it's just such details that I ought to record ! And then—to be given forty roubles by a lackey in the hall, and after being kept ten minutes waiting, and not even in an envelope, not even on a salver, but straight from the lackey's fingers !

I shouted so violently at the lackey that he started and stepped back ; I told him he must go back at once and " his master must bring the money himself "—in fact, my request was, of course, incoherent and incomprehensible to the man. But I shouted so that he went. To make things worse my shouting was heard in the room, and the talk and laughter suddenly subsided.

Almost at the same time I heard footsteps, dignified, quiet, unhurried, and a tall figure of a handsome and haughty-looking young man (he seemed to me then even thinner and paler than when I met him to-day) appeared in the doorway a yard from the door leading into the passage. He was wearing a magnificent red silk dressing-gown and slippers, and had a pince-nez on his nose. Without uttering a word he fixed me with his pince-nez and proceeded to stare at me. I took one step towards him like a wild beast, and began glaring at him defiantly. But he only scrutinized me for a moment, ten seconds at the utmost ; suddenly I detected on his lips a scarcely perceptible, but most malignant smile—what made it so malignant was that it was scarcely perceptible : he turned round without a word and went back into the room, just as deliberately, just as quietly and smoothly as he had come. Oh, these insolent fellows are trained by their mothers from childhood to be insolent ! I lost my head of course. . . . Oh, why did I lose my head !

Almost at that moment the same lackey reappeared with the same notes in his hand.

" Be so good as to take this, it is sent you from Petersburg, but his honour can't see you : ' perhaps another time, when he's more at leisure.' " I felt that these last words were his own addition. But I was still overwhelmed with confusion. I took the money and walked to the door, I took it simply because I was confused, I ought not to have taken it ; but the lackey, no doubt wanting to mortify me further, ventured upon a regular flunkey's impertinence ; he flung the door extra wide open before me, and pronounced with exaggerated emphasis and dignity, as I went out :

" This way, if you please ! "

" You blackguard," I roared at him, and I raised my hand, but I did not bring it down ; " and your master's a blackguard, too ! Tell him so directly," I added, and went down the stairs.

" Don't you dare ! If I were to report that to my master, you would be taken, that very minute, with a note to the police station. And don't you dare threaten me ! "

I went down the stairs. It was a grand open staircase, and above I could be watched as I went down the red carpeted stairs. All three lackeys came out and stood looking over the banisters. I made up my mind to keep quiet, of course : to brawl with lackeys was impossible. I walked the whole length of the stairs without increasing my pace ; I believe I even moved more slowly.

Oh, there may be philosophers (and shame upon them !) who

will say that all this is nonsense, the irritability of a milksop; let them say so, but for me it was a wound—a wound which has not healed to this day, even to the present moment, when I am writing this, when all is over and even avenged. Oh, I swear I am not given to harbouring malice and I am not revengeful. No doubt I always, even before my illness, wanted to revenge myself when I was insulted, but I swear it was only to revenge myself by magnanimity. Let me revenge myself magnanimously, but so that he felt it and understood, and I should have been avenged ! And, by the way, I must add : that though I am not revengeful I have a good memory for injuries, in spite of being magnanimous ; I wonder whether others are the same ? Then, oh, then I went with generous feelings, perhaps absurd, but no matter : better they were absurd and generous, than not absurd but mean, vulgar and mediocre ! I never told anyone of that meeting with " my brother," even Marie Ivanovna, even Liza : that interview was exactly like an insulting slap in the face. And now I came across this gentleman when I least expected to meet him ; he smiles to me, takes off his hat and says *bonsoir* in quite a friendly way. That gave one something to think about of course. . . . But the wound was reopened.

5

After sitting for more than four hours in the restaurant I suddenly rushed away as though I were in a fit, again to Versilov's of course, and again, of course, I did not find him at home ; he had not been to the house at all ; the nurse was bored, and she asked me to send Darya Onisimovna ; as though I had thoughts for that ! I ran to mother's, but did not go in. Calling Lukerya into the passage I learnt from her that he had not been there either, and that Liza, too, was not at home. I saw that Lukerya, too, would have liked to ask me something, and also, perhaps, to give me some commission ; but I had no thoughts for that ! There was one last hope left—that he had gone to my lodging ; but I had no faith in this.

I have already stated that I was almost out of my mind. And lo, and behold ! in my room I found Alphonsine and my landlord. They were coming out, it is true, and in Pyotr Ippolitovitch's hand was a candle.

" What's this ? " I yelled at the landlord, almost senselessly. " How dare you take that hussy into my room ? "

" *Tien*," cried Alphonsine : " *et les amis ?* "

" Get out," I roared.

" *Mais c'est un ours !* " she whisked out into the passage, pretending to be alarmed, and instantly disappeared into the landlady's room. Pyotr Ippolitovitch, still holding the candle in his hand, came up to me with a severe face.

" Allow me to observe, Arkady Makarovitch, that you are too hasty ; with all respect to you, Mademoiselle Alphonsine is not a hussy, but quite the contrary, indeed, is here, not as your visitor, but as my wife's, with whom she has been for some time past acquainted."

" And how dared you take her into my room ? " I repeated, clutching at my head, which almost suddenly began to ache violently.

" By chance. I went in to shut the window, which I had opened to air the room ; and as Alphonsine Karlovna and I were continuing our conversation, she came into your room simply following me."

" That's a lie. Alphonsine's a spy, Lambert's a spy ! Perhaps you're a spy, too ! And Alphonsine came into my room to steal something."

" That's as you please. You'll say one thing to-day, but to-morrow you'll speak differently. And I've let our rooms for some time, and have moved with my wife into the little room so that Alphonsine Karlovna is almost as much a lodger here as you are."

" You've let your rooms to Lambert ? " I cried in dismay.

" No, not to Lambert," he answered with the same broad grin, in which, however, the hesitation I had seen in the morning was replaced by determination. " I imagine that you know to whom and only affect not to know for the sake of appearances, and that's why you're angry. Good-night, sir ! "

" Yes, yes, leave me, leave me alone ! " I waved my hand, almost crying, so that he looked at me in surprise ; he went away, however. I fastened the door with the hook and threw myself on my bed with my face in the pillow. And that is how I passed that awful day, the first of those three momentous days with which my story concludes.

CHAPTER X

1

BUT, again anticipating the course of events, I find it is necessary to explain to the reader something of what is coming, for the logical sequence of the story is obscured by such numerous incidents, that otherwise it would be impossible to understand it.

That something is the " deadly noose " to which Tatyana Pavlovna let slip an allusion. It appeared that Anna Andreyevna had ventured at last on the most audacious step that could be imagined in her position ; she certainly had a will of her own ! On the pretext of his health the old prince had been in the nick of time carried off to Tsarskoe Syelo so that the news of his approaching marriage with Anna Andreyevna might not be spread abroad, but might for the time be stifled, so to say, in embryo, yet the feeble old man, with whom one could do anything else, would not on any consideration have consented to give up his idea and jilt Anna Andreyevna, who had made him an offer. On this subject he was a paragon of chivalry, so that he might sooner or later bestir himself and suddenly proceed to carry out his intentions with that irresistible force which is so very frequently met with in weak characters, for they often have a line beyond which they cannot be driven. Moreover, he fully recognised the delicacy of the position of Anna Andreyevna, for whom he had an unbounded respect ; he was quite alive to the possibility of rumours, of gibes, of injurious gossip. The only thing that checked him and kept him quiet for the time was that Katerina Nikolaevna had never once allowed herself to drop the faintest hint reflecting on Anna Andreyevna in his presence, or to raise the faintest objection to his intention of marrying her ; on the contrary, she showed the greatest cordiality and every attention to her father's fiancée. In this way Anna Andreyevna was placed in an extremely awkward position, perceiving with her subtle feminine instinct that she would wound all the old prince's tenderest feelings, and would arouse his distrust and even, perhaps, his indignation by the slightest criticism of Katerina Nikolaevna, whom he worshipped, too, and now more than ever just because she had so graciously and dutifully consented to his marriage. And so for the present the conflict was waged on that plane : the two rivals vied with one another in delicacy and patience, and as time went on the prince did not know which of them to admire the most, and like all weak but tender-hearted people, he ended by being miserable and blaming himself for everything. His depression of spirits reached a morbid point, I was told : his nerves were thoroughly upset, and instead of regaining health in Tsarskoe, he was, so I was assured, on the point of taking to his bed.

Here I may note in parenthesis what I only learnt long after-wards that Büring had bluntly proposed to Katerina Niko-laevna that they should take the old gentleman abroad, inducing him to go by some sort of strategy, letting people know privately meanwhile that he had gone out of his mind, and obtaining a doctor's certificate to that effect abroad. But Katerina Niko-laevna would not consent to that on any account ; so at least it was declared afterwards. She seems to have rejected the project with indignation. All this is only a rather roundabout rumour, but I believe it.

And just when things had reached this apparently hopeless position, Anna Andreyevna suddenly learnt through Lambert that there was in existence a letter, in which the daughter had consulted a lawyer about declaring her father insane. Her proud and revengeful mind was roused to the utmost. Recalling previous conversations with me and putting together many trifling circumstances, she could not doubt the truth of it. Then, inevitably, the plan of a bold stroke matured in her resolute, inflexible, feminine heart. . . . That plan was to tell the prince all about it, suddenly, with no preliminaries or negotiations, to frighten him, to give him a shock, to prove to him that what inevitably awaited him was the lunatic asylum, and if he were perverse, if he refused to believe and expressed indignation, to show him his daughter's letter, as though to say, " Since there was once an intention of declaring him insane, it might well be tried again in order to prevent his marriage." Then to take the frightened and shattered old man to Petersburg—*straight to my lodging*.

It was a terrible risk, but she had complete confidence in her powers. Here I will digress for a moment to observe that the later course of events proved that she had not been mistaken as to the effect of this blow ; what is more, the effect of it exceeded her expectations. The news of the existence of this letter produced, perhaps, a far stronger effect on the old prince than she or any of us had anticipated. I had no idea until then that the old prince had heard of this letter before ; but like all weak and timid people he did not believe the rumour, and did his utmost to dismiss it from his mind in order to preserve his serenity; what is more, he reproached himself for his baseness in being ready to believe it. I may add that the fact, that is the existence of the letter, had a far greater effect on Katerina Nikolaevna than I had expected. . . . In fact, this scrap of paper turned out to be of far greater consequence than I, carrying it in my pocket, had imagined. But I am running too far ahead.

But why, I shall be asked to my lodgings ? Why convey the old prince to my pitiful little den, and alarm him, perhaps, by the sordidness of his surroundings ? If not to his own home (where all her plans might be thwarted at once), why not to some " sumptuous " private apartments, as Lambert urged ? But it was just on this that Anna Andreyevna reckoned in her desperate step.

Her chief object was to confront the prince with the document ; but nothing would have induced me to give it up. And as there was no time to lose, Anna Andreyevna, relying on her power to carry off the position, resolved to begin without the document, bringing the old prince straight to me—for what purpose ? To catch me by that same step ; so to say, to kill two birds with one stone. She reckoned on working upon me by the sudden blow, the shock, the unexpectedness of it. She anticipated that when I found the old man in my room, when I saw his helplessness and his alarm, and heard them all imploring me, I should give in and show the document ! I must confess her calculation was crafty and clever, and showed psychological insight; what is more, she was very nearly successful. . . . As for the old man, Anna Andreyevna had succeeded in bringing him away, and had forced him to believe her simply by telling him that she was bringing him *to me*. All this I learned later ; the mere statement that the letter was in my hands extinguished in his timid heart the last doubts of the fact—so great were his love and respect for me !

I may remark, too, that Anna Andreyevna herself never for a moment doubted that I still had the letter and had not let it go out of my hands ; her great mistake was that she had a wrong conception of my character and was cynically reckoning on my innocence, my good-nature, and even my sentimentality ;

2 I

and, on the other hand, she imagined that even if I had made up my mind to give up the letter, to Katerina Nikolaevna for instance, I should only do so under special conditions, and she made haste to anticipate those conditions by the suddenness, the unexpectedness of her master-stroke.

And, finally, Lambert confirmed her in all this. I have mentioned already that Lambert's position at this time was most critical ; the traitor would have liked above everything to lure me from Anna Andreyevna so that with him I might sell the letter to Mme. Ahmakov, which he, for some reason, considered a more profitable course ; but since nothing would induce me to give up the document till the last moment, he decided, at any rate, to act with Anna Andreyevna also, that he might not risk losing everything, and therefore he did his utmost to force his services on her till the very last hour, and I know that he even offered to procure a priest, if necessary . . . but Anna Andreyevna had asked him, with a contemptuous smile, not to suggest this. Lambert struck her as horribly coarse, and aroused her utmost aversion ; but to be on the safe side she still accepted his services, as a spy for instance. By the way, I do not know for certain to this day whether they bought over Pyotr Ippolitovitch, my landlord, and whether he got anything at all from them for his services, or whether he simply worked for them for the joy of intrigue ; but that he acted as a spy upon me, and that his wife did also, I know for a fact.

The reader will understand now that though I was to some extent forewarned, yet I could not have guessed that the next day, or the day after, I should find the old prince in my lodgings and in such circumstances. Indeed, I never could have conceived of such audacity from Anna Andreyevna. One may talk freely and hint at anything one likes, but to decide, to act, and to carry things out—well, that really is character !

2

To continue.

I waked up late in the morning. I slept an exceptionally sound and dreamless sleep, as I remember with wonder, so that I waked up next morning feeling unusually confident again, as though nothing had happened the day before. I intended not going first to mother's but straight to the church of the cemetery, with the idea of returning to mother's after the ceremony and remaining the rest of the day. I was firmly convinced that in any case I should meet him sooner or later at mother's.

Neither Alphonsine nor the landlord had been at the flat for a long time. I would not on any account question the landlady, and, indeed, I made up my mind to cut off all relations with them for the future, and even to give up my lodgings as soon as I could ; and so, as soon as my coffee had been brought, I put the hook on the door again. But suddenly there was a knock at the door, and to my surprise it turned out to be Trishatov.

I opened the door at once and, delighted to see him, asked him to come in, but he refused.

" I will only say two words from the door . . . or, perhaps, I will come in, for I fancy one must talk in a whisper here ; only I won't sit down. You are looking at my horrid coat : Lambert took my great-coat."

He was, in fact, wearing a wretched old great-coat, which did not fit him. He stood before me without taking off his hat, a gloomy, dejected figure, with his hands in his pockets.

" I won't sit down, I won't sit down. Listen, Dolgoruky, I know nothing in detail, but I know that Lambert is preparing some treachery against you at once, and you won't escape it— and that's certain. And so be careful ; I was told by that pock-marked fellow, do you remember him ? But he did not tell me anything more about it, so I can't tell you. I've only come to warn you—good-bye."

" But sit down, dear Trishatov ; though I'm in a hurry I'm so glad to see you. . . ." I cried.

" I won't sit down, I won't sit down ; but I shall remember you were glad to see me. Oh, Dolgoruky, why deceive others ? I've consciously of my own free will consented to every sort of abomination, to things so vile, that I can't speak of them before you. Now we are at the pock-marked fellow's. Good-bye. I am not worthy to sit down with you."

" Nonsense, Trishatov, dear. . . ."

" No, you see, Dolgoruky, I keep a bold face before every one, and I'm going to have a rollicking time. I shall soon have a better fur coat than my old one, and shall be driving a fast trotter. But I shall know in my own mind that I did not sit down in your room, because I judge myself unworthy, because I'm low compared with you. It will always be nice for me to remember that when I'm in the midst of disgraceful debauchery. Good-bye, good-bye. And I won't give you my hand; why, Alphonsine won't take my hand. And please don't follow me or come to see me, that's a compact between us."

The strange boy turned and went out. I had no time then, but I made up my mind to seek him out as soon as I had settled our affairs.

I won't describe the rest of that morning, though there is a great deal that might be recalled. Versilov was not at the funeral service in the church, and I fancy from their faces I could have gathered that they did not expect him there. Mother prayed devoutly and seemed entirely absorbed in the service; there were only Liza and Tatyana Pavlovna by the coffin. But I will describe nothing, nothing. After the burial we all returned and sat down to a meal, and again I gathered by their faces that he was not expected to it. When we rose from the table, I went up to mother, embraced her and congratulated her on her birthday; Liza did the same after me.

" Listen, brother," Liza whispered to me on the sly; "they are expecting him."

" I guessed so, Liza. I see it."

" He's certainly coming."

" So they must have heard something positive," I thought, but I didn't ask any question. Though I'm not going to describe my feelings, all this mystery began to weigh like a stone upon my heart again in spite of my confident mood. We all settled down in the drawing-room, near mother, at the round table. Oh, how I liked being with her then, and looking at her! Mother suddenly asked me to read something out of the Gospel. I read a chapter from St. Luke. She did not weep, and was not even very sorrowful, but her face had never seemed to me so full of spiritual meaning. There was the light of thought in her gentle eyes, but I could not trace in them any sign that she expected something with apprehension. The conversation never flagged; we recalled many reminiscences of Makar Ivanovitch; Tatyana Pavlovna, too, told us many things about him of which I had no idea before. And, in fact, it would make an interesting chapter if it were all written down. Even Tatyana Pavlovna wore quite a different air from usual: she was very gentle, very affectionate, and, what is more, also very quiet, though she talked a good deal to distract mother's mind. But one detail I remember well: mother was sitting on the sofa, and on a special round table on her left there lay, apparently put there for some purpose, a plain antique ikon, with halos on the heads of the saints, of which there were two. This ikon had belonged to Makar Ivanovitch—I knew that, and knew also that the old man had never parted from it, and looked upon it with superstitious reverence. Tatyana Pavlovna glanced at it several times.

" Listen, Sofia," she said, suddenly changing the conversation ; "instead of the ikon's lying down, would it not be better to stand it up on the table against the wall, and to light the lamp before it ? "

" No, better as it is," said mother.

" I dare say you're right ; it might seem making too much fuss. . . ."

I did not understand at the time, but this ikon had long ago been verbally bequeathed by Makar Ivanovitch to Andrey Petrovitch, and mother was preparing to give it to him now.

It was five o'clock in the afternoon ; we were still talking when I noticed a sudden quiver in mother's face ; she drew herself up quickly and began listening, while Tatyana Pavlovna, who was speaking at the time, went on talking without noticing anything. I at once turned to the door, and an instant later saw Andrey Petrovitch in the doorway. He had come in by the back stairs, through the kitchen and the passage, and mother was the only one of us who had heard his footsteps. Now I will describe the whole of the insane scene that followed, word by word, and gesture by gesture ; it was brief.

To begin with, I did not, at the first glance anyway, observe the slightest change in his face. He was dressed as always, that is almost foppishly ; in his hand was a small but expensive nosegay of fresh flowers. He went up and handed it to mother with a smile ; she was looking at him with frightened perplexity, but she took the nosegay, and a faint flush at once glowed on her pale cheeks, and there was a gleam of pleasure in her eyes.

" I knew you would take it like that, Sonia," he said. As we all got up when he came in, he took Liza's easy-chair, which was on the left of mother, and sat down in it without noticing he was taking her seat. And so he was quite close to the little table on which the ikon was lying.

" Good evening to you all ; I felt I must bring you this nosegay on your birthday, Sonia, and so I did not go to the funeral, as I could not come to the grave with a nosegay ; and you didn't expect me at the funeral, I know. The old man certainly won't be angry at these flowers, for he bequeathed us joy himself, didn't he ? I believe he's here somewhere in the room."

Mother looked at him strangely ; Tatyana Pavlovna seemed to wince.

" Who's here in the room ? " she asked.

" Makar Ivanovitch. Never mind. You know that the man who is not entirely a believer in these marvels is always more prone to superstition. . . . But I had better tell you about the nosegay : how I succeeded in bringing it I don't know. Three times on the way I had a longing to throw it in the snow and trample on it."

Mother shuddered.

" A terrible longing. You must have pity on me and my poor head, Sonia. I longed to, because they are too beautiful. Is there any object in the world more beautiful than a flower ? I carried it, with snow and frost all round. Our frost and flowers —such an incongruity ! I wasn't thinking of that though, I simply longed to crush it because it was so lovely. Sonia, though I'm disappearing again now, I shall soon come back, for I believe I shall be afraid. If I am afraid, who will heal me of my terrors, where can I find an angel like Sonia ? . . . What is this ikon you've got here ? Ah, Makar Ivanovitch's, I remember. It belonged to his family, his ancestors ; he would never part from it ; I know, I remember he left it to me ; I quite remember . . . and I fancy it's an unorthodox one. Let me have a look at it."

He took up the ikon, carried it to the light and looked at it intently, but, after holding it a few seconds only, laid it on the table before him. I was astonished, but all his strange speech was uttered so quickly that I had not time to reflect upon it. All I remember is that a sick feeling of dread began to clutch at my heart. Mother's alarm had passed into perplexity and compassion ; she looked on him as some one, above all, to be pitied ; it had sometimes happened in the past that he had talked almost as strangely as now. Liza, for some reason, became suddenly very pale, and strangely made a sign to me with a motion of her head towards him. But most frightened of all was Tatyana Pavlovna.

" What's the matter with you, Andrey Petrovitch darling ? " she inquired cautiously.

" I really don't know, Tatyana Pavlovna dear, what's the

matter with me. Don't be uneasy, I still remember that you are Tatyana Pavlovna, and that you are dear. But I've only come for a minute though ; I should like to say something nice to Sonia, and I keep trying to find the right word, though my heart is full of words, which I don't know how to utter ; yes, really, all such strange words somehow. Do you know I feel as though I were split in two "—he looked round at us all with a terribly serious face and with perfectly genuine candour. " Yes, I am really split in two mentally, and I'm horribly afraid of it. It's just as though one's second self were standing beside one ; one is sensible and rational oneself, but the other self is impelled to do something perfectly senseless, and sometimes very funny ; and suddenly you notice that you are longing to do that amusing thing, goodness knows why ; that is you want to, as it were, against your will; though you fight against it with all your might, you want to. I once knew a doctor who suddenly began whistling in church, at his father's funeral. I really was afraid to come to the funeral to-day, because, for some reason, I was possessed by a firm conviction that I should begin to whistle or laugh in church, like that unfortunate doctor, who came to rather a bad end. . . . And I really don't know why, but I've been haunted by the thought of that doctor all day ; I am so haunted by him that I can't shake him off. Do you know, Sonia, here I've taken up the ikon again " (he had picked it up and was turning it about in his hand), " and do you know, I have a dreadful longing now, this very second, to smash it against the stove, against this corner I am sure it would break into two halves—neither more nor less."

What was most striking was that he said this without the slightest trace of affectation or whimsical caprice ; he spoke quite simply, but that made it all the more terrible ; and he seemed really frightened of something ; I noticed suddenly that his hands were trembling a little.

" Andrey Petrovitch ! " cried mother, clasping her hands.

" Let the ikon alone, let it alone, Andrey Petrovitch, let it alone, put it down ! " cried Tatyana Pavlovna, jumping up. " Undress and go to bed. Arkady, run for the doctor ! "

" But . . . but what a fuss you're making," he said gently, scrutinising us all intently. Then he suddenly put both elbows on the table and leaned his head in his hands.

" I'm scaring you, but I tell you what, my friends, try to

comfort me a little, sit down again, and all be calm, if only for a minute ! Sonia, I did not come to talk of this at all ; I came to tell you something, but it was quite different. Good-bye, Sonia, I'm going off on my wanderings again, as I have left you several times before . . . but, no doubt, I shall come back to you again one day—in that sense you are inevitable. To whom should I come back, when all is over ? Believe, Sonia, that I've come to you now as to an angel, and not as to an enemy ; how could you be an enemy to me, how could you be an enemy ! Don't imagine that I came to break this ikon, for do you know, Sonia, I am still longing to break it all the same. . . ."

When Tatyana Pavlovna had cried out " Let the ikon alone," she had snatched it out of his hands and was holding it in hers. Suddenly, at his last word, he jumped up impulsively, snatched the ikon in a flash from Tatyana's hands, and with a ferocious swing smashed it with all his might against the corner of the tiled stove. The ikon was broken into two pieces. . . . He turned to us and his pale face suddenly flushed red, almost purple, and every feature in his face quivered and worked.

" Don't take it for a symbol, Sonia ; it's not as Makar's legacy I have broken it, but only to break something . . . and, anyway, I shall come back to you, my last angel ! You may take it as a symbol, though ; of course it must have been so ! . . ."

And with sudden haste he went out of the room, going again through the kitchen (where he had left his fur coat and cap). I won't attempt to describe what happened to mother : in mortal terror she stood clasping her hands above her, and she suddenly screamed after him :

" Andrey Petrovitch, come back, if only to say good-bye, dear ! "

" He'll come, Sofia, he'll come ! Don't worry yourself ! " Tatyana shrieked, trembling all over in a terrible rage, a really brutal rage. " Why, you heard he promised to come back himself ! Let him go and amuse himself for the last time, the fool. He's getting old—and who'll nurse him when he's bedridden except you, his old nurse ? Why, he tells you so himself, he's not ashamed. . . ."

As for us, Liza was in a swoon ; I would have run after him, but I rushed to mother. I threw my arms round her and held her tight. Lukerya ran in with a glass of water for Liza, but mother soon came to herself, she sank on the sofa, hid her face in her hands, and began crying.

" But . . . but you'd better run after him," Tatyana Pavlovna shouted suddenly with all her might, as though she had suddenly waked up. " Go along . . . go along . . . overtake him, don't leave him for a minute, go along, go along ! " She pulled me forcibly away from mother. " Oh, I shall run myself."

" Arkasha, oh, run after him, make haste ! " mother cried suddenly, too.

I ran off, full speed, through the kitchen and through the yard, but there was no sign of him anywhere. In the distance I saw black shadows in the darkness ; I ran after them and examined each passer-by carefully as I overtook them. So I ran on to the cross-roads.

" People are not angry with the insane," suddenly flashed through my mind, " but Tatyana was wild with rage at him, so he's not mad at all. . . ." Oh, it seemed to me all the time that it was symbolic, and that he was bent on putting an end to everything as he did to the ikon, and showing that to us, to mother, and all. But that second self was unmistakably beside him, too ; of that there could be no doubt. . . .

3

He was nowhere to be found, however, and I could not run to him. It was difficult to believe that he would have simply gone home. Suddenly an idea flashed upon me and I rushed off to Anna Andreyevna.

Anna Andreyevna had just returned, and I was shown up at once. I went in, controlling myself as far as I could. Without sitting down, I at once described to her the scene which had just taken place, that is the "second self." I shall never forget the greedy but pitilessly composed and self-complacent curiosity with which she listened, also standing, and I shall never forgive her for it.

" Where is he ? Perhaps you know ? " I ended, insistently. " Tatyana Pavlovna sent me to you yesterday. . . ."

" I sent for you, too, yesterday. Yesterday he was at Tsarskoe Syelo ; he came to see me, too. And now " (she looked at her watch), " now it is seven o'clock. . . . So he's pretty sure to be at home."

"I see that you know all about it—so tell me, tell me," I cried.

"I know a good deal; but I don't know everything. Of course, there's no reason to conceal it from you. . . ." She scanned me with a strange glance, smiling and as though deliberating. "Yesterday morning, in answer to her letter, he made Katerina Nikolaevna a formal offer of marriage."

"That's false," I said, opening my eyes wide.

"The letter went through my hands; I took it to her myself, unopened. This time he behaved 'chivalrously' and concealed nothing from me."

"Anna Andreyevna, I can't understand it!"

"Of course, it's hard to understand it, but it's like a gambler who stakes his last crown, while he has a loaded pistol ready in his pocket—that's what his offer amounts to. It's ten to one she won't accept his offer; but still he's reckoning on that tenth chance, and I confess that's very curious; I imagine, though, that it may be a case of frenzy, that 'second self,' as you said so well just now."

"And you laugh? And am I really to believe that the letter was given through you? Why, you are the fiancée of her father? Spare me, Anna Andreyevna!"

"He asked me to sacrifice my future to his happiness, though he didn't really ask; it was all done rather silently. I simply read it all in his eyes. Oh, my goodness, what will he do next! Why, he went to Königsberg to ask your mother's leave to marry Katerina Nikolaevna's step-daughter. That's very like his pitching on me for his go-between and confidante yesterday."

She was rather pale. But her calmness was only exaggerated sarcasm. Oh, I forgave her much then, as I began to grasp the position. For a minute I pondered; she waited in silence.

"Do you know," I laughed suddenly, "you delivered the letter because there was not the slightest risk for you, because there's no chance of a marriage, but what of him? Of her, too? Of course she will reject his offer and then . . . what may not happen then? Where is he now, Anna Andreyevna?" I cried. "Every minute is precious now, any minute there may be trouble!"

"He's at home. I have told you so. In the letter to Katerina Nikolaevna, which I delivered, he asked her in *any case* to grant him an interview in his lodgings to-day at seven o'clock this evening. She promised."

" She's going to his lodging ? How can that be ? "

" Why not, the lodging is Darya Onisimovna's ; they might very well meet there as her guests. . . ."

" But she's afraid of him. . . . He may kill her."

Anna Andreyevna only smiled.

" In spite of the terror which I detected in her myself, Katerina Nikolaevna has always from the first cherished a certain reverence and admiration for the nobility of Andrey Petrovitch's principles and the loftiness of his mind. She is trusting herself to him this once, so as to have done with him for ever. In his letter he gave her the most solemn and chivalrous promise that she should have nothing to fear. . . . In short, I don't remember the words of the letter, but she trusted herself . . . so to speak, for the last time . . . and so to speak, responding with the same heroic feelings. There may have been a sort of chivalrous rivalry on both sides."

" But the second self, the second self ! " I exclaimed ; " besides, he's out of his mind ! "

" Yesterday, when she gave her promise to grant him an interview, Katerina Nikolaevna probably did not conceive of the possibility of that."

I suddenly turned and was rushing out . . . to him, to them, of course ! But from the next room I ran back for a second.

" But, perhaps, that is just what would suit you, that he should kill her ! " I cried, and ran out of the house.

I was shaking all over, as though in a fit, but I went into the lodging quietly, through the kitchen, and asked in a whisper to see Darya Onisimovna ; she came out at once and fastened a gaze of intense curiosity upon me.

" His honour . . . he's not at home."

But in a rapid whisper I explained, bluntly and exactly, that I knew all about it from Anna Andreyevna, and that I had just come from her.

"Darya Onisimovna, where are they ? "

" They are in the room where you sat the day before yesterday, at the table."

" Darya Onisimovna, let me go in ! "

" That's impossible ! "

" Not in there, but in the next room. Darya Onisimovna, Anna Andreyevna wishes it, perhaps ; if she didn't wish it, she wouldn't have told me herself. They won't hear me . . . she wishes it herself. . . ."

" And if she doesn't wish it ? " said Darya Onisimovna, her eyes still riveted upon me.

" Darya Onisimovna, I remember your Olya ; let me in."

Her lips and chin suddenly began to quiver.

" Dear friend . . . for Olya's sake . . . for the sake of your feeling . . . don't desert Anna Andreyevna. My dear ! you won't desert her, will you ? You won't desert her ? "

" No, I won't ! "

" Give me your solemn promise, you won't rush out upon them, and won't call out if I hide you in there ? "

" I swear on my honour, Darya Onisimovna."

She took me by my coat, led me into a dark room—next to the one where they were sitting—guided me, almost noiselessly, over the soft carpet to the doorway, stationed me at the curtain that hung over it, and lifting the curtain a fraction of an inch showed me them both.

I remained ; she went away. Of course, I remained. I knew that I was eavesdropping, spying on other people's secrets, but I remained. How could I help remaining with the thought of the 'second self' in my mind ! Why, he had smashed the ikon before my eyes !

4

They were sitting facing one another at the table at which we had yesterday drunk to his " resurrection." I got a good view of their faces. She was wearing a simple black dress, and was as beautiful and apparently calm as always. He was speaking ; she was listening with intense and sympathetic attention. Perhaps there was some trace of timidity in her, too. He was terribly excited. I had come in the middle of their conversation, and so for some time I could make nothing of it. I remember she suddenly asked :

" And I was the cause ? "

" No, I was the cause," he answered ; " and you were only innocently guilty. You know that there are the innocently guilty. Those are generally the most unpardonable crimes, and they almost always bring their punishment," he added, laughing strangely. " And I actually thought for a moment that I had forgotten you and could laugh at my stupid passion . . . but you know that. What is he to me, though, that man you're going to marry ? Yesterday I made you an offer, forgive me for it ; it was absurd and yet I had no alternative but that. . . . What could I have done but that absurd thing ? I don't know. . . ."

As he said this, he laughed hopelessly, suddenly lifting his eyes to her ; till then he had looked away as he talked. If I had been in her place, I should have been frightened at that laugh, I felt that. He suddenly got up from his chair.

" Tell me, how could you consent to come here ? " he asked suddenly, as though remembering the real point. " My invitation and my whole letter was absurd. . . . Stay, I can quite imagine how it came to pass that you consented to come, but— why did you come ? that's the question. Can you have come simply from fear ? "

" I came to see you," she said, looking at him with timid caution. Both were silent for half a minute. Versilov sank back in his chair, and in a voice soft but almost trembling and full of intense feeling began :

" It's so terribly long since I've seen you, Katerina Nikolaevna, so long that I scarcely thought it possible I should ever be sitting beside you again as I now am, looking into your face and listening to your voice. . . . For two years we've not seen each other, for two years we've not talked. I never thought to speak to you again. But so be it, what is past is past, and what is will vanish like smoke to-morrow—so be it ! I assent because there is no alternative again, but don't let your coming be in vain," he added suddenly, almost imploringly ; " since you have shown me this charity and have come, don't let it be in vain ; answer me one question ! "

" What question ? "

" You know we shall never see each other again, and what is it to you ? Tell me the truth for once, and answer me one question which sensible people never ask. Did you ever love me, or was I . . . mistaken ? "

She flushed crimson.

" I did love you," she brought out.

I expected she would say that. Oh, always truthful, always sincere, always honest !

" And now ? " he went on.

" I don't love you now."

" And you are laughing ? "

" No, I laughed just now by accident, because I knew you would ask, ' And now.' And I smiled at that, because when one guesses right one always does smile. . . ."

It seemed quite strange to me ; I had never seen her so much on her guard, almost timid, indeed, and embarrassed.

His eyes devoured her.

" I know that you don't love me . . . and—you don't love me at all ? "

" Perhaps not at all. I don't love you," she added firmly, without smiling or flushing. " Yes, I did love you, but not for long. I very soon got over it."

" I know, I know, you saw that it was not what you wanted, but . . . what do you want ? Explain that once more. . . ."

" Have I ever explained that to you ? What do I want ? Why, I'm the most ordinary woman ; I'm a peaceful person. I like . . . I like cheerful people."

" Cheerful ? "

" You see, I don't know even how to talk to you. I believe that if you could have loved me less, I should have loved you then," she smiled timidly again. The most absolute sincerity was transparent in her answer ; and was it possible she did not realise that her answer was the most final summing up of their relations, explaining everything. Oh, how well he must have understood that ! But he looked at her and smiled strangely.

" Is Büring a cheerful person ? " he went on, questioning her.

" He ought not to trouble you at all," she answered with some haste. " I'm marrying him simply because with him I shall be most at peace. My whole heart remains in my own keeping."

" They say that you have grown fond of society, of the fashionable world again ? "

" Not fond of it. I know that there is just the same disorderliness in good society as everywhere else ; but the outer forms are still attractive, so that if one lives only to pass the time, one can do it better there than anywhere."

" I've often heard the word ' disorderliness ' of late ; you used to be afraid of my disorderliness, too—chains, ideas, and imbecilities ! "

" No, it was not quite that. . . ."

" What then, for God's sake tell me all, frankly."

" Well, I'll tell you frankly, for I look on you as a man of great intellect. . . . I always felt there was something ridiculous about you." When she had said this she suddenly flushed crimson, as though she feared she had said something fearfully indiscreet.

"For what you have just said I can forgive you a great deal," he commented strangely.

"I hadn't finished," she said hurriedly, still flushing. "It's I who am ridiculous to talk to you like a fool."

"No, you are not ridiculous, you are only a depraved, worldly woman," he said, turning horribly white. "I did not finish either, when I asked you why you had come. Would you like me to finish? There is a document, a letter in existence, and you're awfully afraid of it, because if that letter comes into your father's hands, he may curse you, and cut you out of his will. You're afraid of that letter, and you've come for that letter," he brought out. He was shaking all over, and his teeth were almost chattering. She listened to him with a despondent and pained expression of face.

"I know that you can do all sorts of things to harm me," she said, as if warding off his words, "but I have come not so much to persuade you not to persecute me, as to see you yourself. I've been wanting to meet you very much for a long time. But I find you just the same as ever," she added suddenly, as though carried away by a special and striking thought, and even by some strange sudden emotion.

"Did you hope to see me different, after my letter about your depravity? Tell me, did you come here without any fear?"

"I came because I once loved you; but do you know, I beg you not to threaten me, please, with anything. While we are now together, don't remind me of my evil thoughts and feelings. If you could talk to me of something else I should be very glad. Let threats come afterwards; but it should be different now. . . . I came really to see you for a minute and to hear you. Oh, well, if you can't help it, kill me straight off, only don't threaten me and don't torture yourself before me," she concluded, looking at him in strange expectation, as though she really thought he might kill her. He got up from his seat again, and looking at her with glowing eyes, said resolutely:

"While you are here you will suffer not the slightest annoyance."

"Oh yes, your word of honour," she said, smiling.

"No, not only because I gave my word of honour in my letter, but because I want to think of you all night. . . ."

"To torture yourself?"

"I picture you in my mind whenever I'm alone. I do nothing

but talk to you. I go into some squalid, dirty hole, and as a contrast you appear to me at once. But you always laugh at me as you do now. . . ." He said this as though he were beside himself. . . .

"I have never laughed at you, never!" she exclaimed in a voice full of feeling, and with a look of the greatest compassion in her face. "In coming here I tried my utmost to do it so that you should have no reason to be mortified," she added suddenly. "I came here to tell you that I almost love you. . . . Forgive me, perhaps I used the wrong words," she went on hurriedly.

He laughed.

"How is it you cannot dissemble? Why is it you are such a simple creature? Why is it you're not like all the rest? . . . Why, how can you tell a man you are turning away that you 'almost love him'?"

"It's only that I could not express myself," she put in hurriedly. "I used the wrong words; it's because I've always felt abashed and unable to talk to you from the first time I met you, and if I used the wrong words, saying that I almost love you, in my thought it was almost so—so that's why I said so, though I love you with that . . . well, with that *general* love with which one loves every one and which one is never ashamed to own. . . ."

He listened in silence, fixing his glowing eyes upon her.

"I am offending you, of course," he went on, as though beside himself. "This must really be what they call passion. . . . All I know is that in your presence I am done for, in your absence, too. It's just the same whether you are there or not, wherever you may be you are always before me. I know, too, that I can hate you intensely, more than I can love you. But I've long given up thinking about anything now—it's all the same to me. I am only sorry I should love a woman like you."

His voice broke; he went on, as it were, gasping for breath.

"What is it to you? You think it wild of me to talk like that!" He smiled a pale smile. "I believe, if only that would charm you, I would be ready to stand for thirty years like a post on one leg. . . . I see you are sorry for me; your face says 'I would love you if I could but I can't. . . .' Yes? Never mind, I've no pride. I'm ready to take any charity from you like a beggar—do you hear, any . . . a beggar has no pride."

She got up and went to him. "Dear friend," she said, with

inexpressible feeling in her face, touching his shoulder with her hand, " I can't hear you talk like that ! I shall think of you all my life as some one most precious, great-hearted, as something most sacred of all that I respect and love. Andrey Petrovitch, understand what I say. Why, it's not for nothing I've come here now, dear friend . . . dear to me then and now : I shall never forget how deeply you stirred my mind when first we met. Let us part as friends, and you will be for me the most earnest and dearest thought in my whole life."

" Let us part and then I will love you ; I will love you—only let us part. Listen," he brought out, perfectly white, " grant me one charity more : don't love me, don't live with me, let us never meet ; I will be your slave if you summon me, and I will vanish at once if you don't want to see me, or hear me, only . . . *only don't marry anyone !* "

It sent a pang to my heart to hear those words. That naïvely humiliating entreaty was the more pitiful, the more heartrending for being so flagrant and impossible. Yes, indeed, he was asking charity ! Could he imagine she would consent ? · Yet he had humbled himself to put it to the test ; he had tried entreating her ! This depth of spiritual degradation was insufferable to watch. Every feature in her face seemed suddenly distorted with pain, but before she had time to utter a word, he suddenly realised what he had done.

" I will *strangle* you," he said suddenly, in a strange distorted voice unlike his own.

But she answered him strangely, too, and she, too, spoke in a different voice, unlike her own.

" If I granted you charity," she said with sudden firmness, " you would punish me for it afterwards worse than you threaten me now, for you would never forget that you stood before me as a beggar. . . . I can't listen to threats from you ! " she added, looking at him with indignation, almost defiance.

" ' Threats from you,' you mean—from such a beggar. I was joking," he said softly, smiling. " I won't touch you, don't be afraid, go away . . . and I'll do my utmost to send you that letter—only go ; go ! I wrote you a stupid letter, and you answered my stupid letter in kind by coming ; we are quits. This is your way." He pointed towards the door. (She was moving towards the room in which I was standing behind the curtain.)

" Forgive me if you can," she said, stopping in the doorway.

" What if we meet some day quite friends and recall this

2 K

scene with laughter ? " he said suddenly, but his face was quivering all over like the face of a man in convulsions.

"Oh, od grant we may ! " she cried, clasping her hands, though she watched his face timidly, as though trying to guess what he meant.

"Go along. Much sense we have, the pair of us, but you . . . Oh, you are one of my own kind ! I wrote you a mad letter, and you agreed to come to tell me that ' you almost love me.' Yes, we are possessed by the same madness ! Be always as mad, don't change, and we shall meet as friends— that I predict, that I swear ! "

"And then I shall certainly love you, for I feel that even now ! " The woman in her could not resist flinging those last words to him from the doorway.

She went out. With noiseless haste I went into the kitchen, and scarcely glancing at Darya Onisimovna, who was waiting for me, I went down the back staircase and across the yard into the street, but I had only time to see her get into the sledge that was waiting for her at the steps. I ran down the street.

CHAPTER XI

1

I RAN to Lambert. Oh, how I should have liked to give a show of logic to my behaviour, and to find some trace of common sense in my actions that evening and all that night ; but even now, when I can reflect on it all, I am utterly unable to present my conduct in any clear and logical connection. It was a case of feeling, or rather a perfect chaos of feelings, in the midst of which I was naturally bound to go astray. It is true there was one dominant feeling, which mastered me completely and over- whelmed all the others, but . . . need I confess to it ? Especi- ally as I am not certain. . . .

I ran to Lambert, beside myself of course. I positively scared Alphonsine and him for the first minute. I have always noticed that even the most profligate, most degraded Frenchmen are in their domestic life extremely given to a sort of bourgeois routine, a sort of very prosaic daily ceremonial of life established once and for ever. Lambert quickly realised, however, that something had happened, and was delighted that I had come to

him at last, and that I was *in his clutches.* He had been thinking of nothing else day and night ! Oh, how badly he needed
me ! And behold now, when he had lost all hope, I had suddenly
appeared of my own accord, and in such a frantic state—just
in the state which suited him.

"Lambert, wine !" I cried : " let's drink, let's have a jolly
time. Alphonsine, where's your guitar ? "

I won't describe the scene, it's unnecessary. We drank, and
I told him all about it, everything. He listened greedily. I
openly of my own accord suggested a plot, a general flare-up.
To begin with, we were by letter to ask Katerina Nikolaevna to
come to us. . . .

"That's possible," Lambert assented, gloating over every
word I said.

Secondly, we must send a copy of the "document" in full,
that she might see at once that she was not being deceived.

"That's right, that's what we must do !" Lambert agreed,
continually exchanging glances with Alphonsine.

Thirdly, Lambert must ask her to come, writing as though he
were an unknown person and had just arrived from Moscow,
and I must bring Versilov.

"And we might have Versilov, too," Lambert assented.

"Not might, but must !" I cried. "It's essential ! It's for
his sake it's all being done !" I explained, taking one sip after
another from my glass. (We were all three drinking, while I
believe I really drank the whole bottle of champagne, while they
only made a show of drinking.) "Versilov and I will sit in the
next room"—(Lambert would have to take the next room !)—
"and suddenly when she had agreed to everything—to paying the
cash, and to his *other* demands too, for all women were abject
creatures, then Versilov and I would come in and convict her
of being abject, and Versilov, seeing what a horrid woman
she was, would at once be cured, and reject her with scorn.
Only we ought to have Büring too, that he might see her
put to shame."

" No, we don't want Büring," Lambert observed.

" We do, we do," I yelled again : " you don't know anything
about it, Lambert, for you are a fool ! On the contrary, let it
make a scandal in fashionable society, it will be our revenge
on fashionable society, and upon her, and let her be punished !
Lambert, she will give you an IOU. . . . I don't want money,
I don't care a damn for money, but you can stoop to pick it up

and stuff it in your pocket, and my curse with it, but I shall crush her ! "

" Yes, yes," Lambert kept approving, "you are right there." He kept exchanging glances with Alphonsine.

"Lambert, she has an awful reverence for Versilov : I saw that for certain just now," I babbled to him.

" It's a good thing you did peep and see it all. I should never have thought that you would have made such a good spy and that you had so much sense ! " He said this to flatter me.

"That's a lie, Frenchman ; I'm not a spy, but I have plenty of sense ! And do you know, Lambert, she loves him, really ! " I went on making desperate efforts to express myself. " But she won't marry him because Büring's an officer in the guards, and Versilov is only a noble-hearted man, and a friend of humanity : to their thinking a comic person and nothing else ! Oh, she understands his passion and gloats over it, flirts, is carried away by it, but won't marry him ! She's a woman, she's a serpent ! Every woman is a serpent, and every serpent is a woman ! He must be cured ; we must tear the scales off his eyes ; let him see what she is and be cured. I will bring him to you, Lambert ! "

" Just so," Lambert kept repeating, filling up my glass every minute.

He was in a perfect tremble of anxiety to avoid contradicting or offending me and to make me go on drinking. It was so coarse and obvious that even at the time I could not help noticing it. But nothing could have made me go away ; I kept drinking and talking, and was desperately anxious to give full expression to what I was feeling. When Lambert brought in another bottle, Alphonsine was playing some Spanish air on the guitar ; I was almost in tears.

"Lambert, do you know everything ? " I exclaimed with intense feeling. "That man must be saved, for he's spell-bound . . . by sorcery. If she were to marry him, he would spurn her from him the day after the wedding . . . for that does happen sometimes. For such a wild outrageous love is like a fit, like a deadly noose, like an illness, and—as soon as it is gratified— the scales fall from the eyes at once and the opposite feeling comes—loathing and hatred, the desire to strangle, to crush. Do you know the story of Avisage, Lambert ? Have you read it ? "

"No, I don't remember : a novel ? " muttered Lambert.

"Oh, you know nothing, Lambert, you're fearfully, fearfully

ignorant . . . but I don't care a damn for that. It's no matter. Oh, he loves mother, he kissed her portrait; he'll spurn that woman next morning and come back to mother of himself; but then it will be too late, so we must save him now. . . ."

In the end I began crying bitterly, but I still went on talking and drank a fearful quantity of champagne. It was most characteristic of Lambert that all that evening he did not once ask about the " document " : where it was, that I should show it, should put it on the table. What would have been more natural than to inquire about it, since we were planning to take action ? Another point : we kept saying that we must do " this," that we certainly would do " this," but of the place, the time and manner —we did not say a word ! He only assented to all I said and kept looking at Alphonsine, that was all ! Of course, I was incapable of reflecting on that at the time, but I remember it.

I ended by falling asleep on his sofa without undressing. I slept a long time and waked up very late. I remember that after waking I lay for a long time on the sofa, as it were petrified, trying to reflect and remember, and pretending that I was still asleep. But it appeared that Lambert was not in the room, he had gone out. It was past nine o'clock, the stove had been heated and was crackling exactly as it had done when I found myself the first time at Lambert's after that night. But Alphonsine was behind the screen keeping guard on me; I noticed it at once, for she had twice peeped out and glanced at me, but each time I shut my eyes and pretended to be asleep. I did this because I was overwhelmed and wanted to think over my position. I felt with horror all the ineptitude and loathsomeness of my confession to Lambert, my plotting with him, the blunder I had made in running to him ! But, thank God, the letter was still in my keeping; it was still sewn up in my side pocket; I felt with my hand—it was there ! So all I had to do was to get up and run away, I need not care what Lambert thought of me afterwards. Lambert was not worth it.

But I was ashamed of myself ! I was my own judge, and— my God, what was there in my heart ! But there's no need to describe that hellish, insufferable feeling, and that consciousness of filth and vileness. But yet I must confess it, for I feel the time has come. It must be recorded in my story. So let it be known that I meant to shame her, and planned to be almost a witness of her yielding to Lambert's demands—oh, the baseness !—not for the sake of saving Versilov in his madness and bringing him back to mother, but because . . . perhaps because I was myself in love and jealous ! Jealous of whom : of Büring, of Versilov ? Of anyone she might look at, or talk to at a ball, while I should be standing in a corner ashamed of myself. . . . Oh, the hideousness of it !

In short, I don't know of whom I was jealous on her account ; but all I felt and knew the evening before was that as certainly as twice two make four, she was lost to me, that that woman would spurn me and laugh at me for falseness and absurdity ! She was truthful and honest, while I—I was a spy, using letters to threaten her !

All this I have kept hidden in my heart ever since, but now the day has come and I make up my account, but, again, for the last time. Perhaps fully half, or perhaps even seventy-five per cent. of what I am saying is a libel upon myself ! That night I hated her in a kind of delirium, and afterwards like a drunken rowdy. I have said already that it was a chaos of feelings and sensations in which I could distinguish nothing clearly myself. But still I have had to confess it, for though only a part of what I felt, it was certainly present.

With an overpowering sense of disgust, and a firm determination to cancel all that had happened, I suddenly jumped up from the sofa ; but as I jumped up, Alphonsine instantly popped out. I seized my overcoat and cap and told her to tell Lambert that I had been raving the evening before, that I had slandered a woman, that I had been joking, and that Lambert must not dare come near me again. . . . All this I expressed in a blundering fashion, talking hurriedly in French, and, of course, anything but clearly, but, to my surprise, Alphonsine understood everything perfectly ; and what was most surprising of all, she seemed positively relieved at something.

"*Oui, oui,*" she said approvingly, "*c'est une honte ! Une dame. . . . Oh, vous être génereux, vous ! Soyez tranquille, je ferai voir raison à Lambert. . . .*"

So that I was even at that moment puzzled to explain the sudden change in her attitude, and consequently I suppose in Lambert's. I went away, however, saying nothing ; all was in confusion within me, and I was hardly capable of reasoning. Oh, afterwards I could explain it all, but then it was too late ! Oh, what a hellish plot it was ! I will pause here and explain it beforehand, as otherwise it will be impossible for the reader to understand it,

The fact was that at my very first interview with Lambert, when I was thawing in his lodging, I had muttered to him like a fool that the letter was sewn up in my pocket; then I had suddenly fallen asleep for a time on the sofa in the corner, and Lambert had promptly felt my pocket and was convinced that there was a piece of paper sewn up in it. Several times afterwards he made sure that the paper was still there ; when we were dining, for instance, at the "Tatar's," I remember that he several times put his arms round my waist on purpose. Grasping the importance of the letter he made a separate plan of his own of which I had no suspicion at all. I, like a fool, imagined all the time that he urged me to come home so persistently to get me to join his gang and to act only in concert with him, but, alas ! he invited me with quite a different object ! He wanted to make me dead drunk, and when I was stretched snoring and unconscious, to rip open my pocket and take possession of the letter. This was precisely what he and Alphonsine had done that night ; Alphonsine had unpicked the pocket, taking out the letter, *her letter*, the document I had brought from Moscow, they had taken a piece of plain notepaper the same size, put it in the pocket and sewn it up again, as if nothing had happened, so that I might notice no difference. Alphonsine had sewn it up. And I, up to the very end, for another day and a half—still went on believing that I was in possession of the secret, and that Katerina Nikolaevena's fate was still in my hands.

A last word : that theft of the letter was the cause of everything and of all the other disasters that followed.

2

The last twenty-four hours of my story have come and I am at the end !

It was, I believe, about half-past ten, when excited, and, as far as I remember, strangely absent-minded, but with a firm determination in my heart, I dragged myself to my lodgings. I was not in a hurry, I knew how I was going to act. And scarcely had I stepped into the passage when I realised at once that a new calamity had occurred, and an extraordinary complication had arisen : the old prince had just been brought from Tsarskoe-Syelo and was in the flat ; with him was Anna Andreyevna !

He had been put not in my room but in the two rooms next to

mine that had been occupied by my landlord and his wife. The day before, as it appeared, some changes and improvements had been made in the room, but only of the most superficial kind. The landlord and his wife had moved into the little room of the whimsical lodger marked with small-pox whom I have mentioned already, and that individual had been temporarily banished, I don't know where.

I was met by the landlord, who at once whisked into my room. He looked less sure of his ground than he had done the evening before, but was in an unusual state of excitement, so to say, at the climax of the affair. I said nothing to him, but, moving aside into a corner and clutching my head in my hands, I stood so for a moment. He thought for the first moment that I was "putting it on," but at last his fortitude gave way, and he could not help being scared.

"Can anything be wrong ? " he muttered. " I've been waiting for you to ask," he added, seeing I did not answer, "whether you preferred that door to be opened so that you may have direct access to the prince's rooms . . . instead of going by the passage ? " He pointed to the door at the side always locked, which led to the landlord's rooms, now the old prince's apartments.

"Look here, Pyotr Ippolitovitch," I turned to him with a stern air, " I humbly beg you to go to Anna Andreyevna and ask her to come here at once to discuss the situation. Have they been here long ? "

" Going on for an hour."

" Go and fetch her then."

He went and brought the strange reply " that Anna Andreyevna and Prince Nikolay Ivanitch were impatiently expecting me in the next room "; so Anna Andreyevna would not come. I smoothed out my coat, which was creased from sleeping in it that night, brushed it, washed, combed my hair ; I did all this deliberately, realising how necessary it was to be careful, and I went in to the old prince.

The prince was sitting on the sofa at a round table, and Anna Andreyevna in another corner, at another table covered with a cloth, on which the landlady's samovar, polished as it had never been before, was boiling for tea. I walked in with the same stern look on my face, and the old man instantly noticed this and winced, and the smile on his face was instantly replaced by a look of terror ; but I could not keep it up, I instantly laughed and held out my hands to him ; the poor old fellow simply flung himself into my arms.

I realised unmistakably at once the condition of the man I had to deal with. To begin with, it was as clear as twice two make four that in the interval since I had seen him last they had turned the old man, till lately almost hale, and to some extent rational, and not altogether without will-power, into a sort of mummy, a scared and mistrustful child. I may add, he quite knew why they had brought him here, and everything had been done as I have explained already. He was suddenly shocked, crushed, and overwhelmed by being told of his daughter's treachery and of a possible madhouse. He had allowed himself to be carried off, so scared that he hardly knew what he was doing ; he was told that I was in possession of the secret and that I had the proof that would establish the fact conclusively. I may mention at once : it was just that proof that would establish the fact which he dreaded more than anything in the world. He was expecting me to go in to him with a sort of death sentence in my face and a document in my hand, and was immensely delighted that I was ready meanwhile to laugh and chatter of other things. While we were embracing he shed tears. I must confess I shed a tear also ; I felt suddenly very sorry for him. Alphonsine's little lap-dog broke into a bark as shrill as a bell, and made dashes at me from the sofa. He had not parted from this tiny dog since he had had it and even slept with it.

" *Oh je disais, qu'il a du cœur!* " he exclaimed, indicating me to Anna Andreyevna.

" But how much stronger you look, prince, how well and fresh and strong you look ! " I observed. Alas ! It was just the opposite : he looked like a mummy and I only said it to cheer him up !

" *N'est-ce pas, n'est-ce pas ?* " he repeated joyfully. " Oh, I've regained my health wonderfully."

" But drink your tea, and if you'll give me a cup I'll drink some with you."

" That's delightful ! ' Let us drink the cup that cheers ' . . . or how does it go, that's in some poem. Anna Andreyevna, give him some tea ; *il prend toujours par les sentiments*. . . . Give us some tea, my dear."

Anna Andreyevna poured out the tea, but suddenly turning to me began with extreme solemnity :

" Arkady Makarovitch, we both, my benefactor, Prince

Nikolay Ivanitch and I, have taken refuge with you. I consider that we have come to you, to you alone, and we both beg of you to shelter us. Remember that the whole fate of this saintly, this noble and injured man, is in your hands . . . we await the decision, and count upon the justice of your heart ! "

But she could not go on ; the old prince was reduced to terror and almost trembling with alarm.

" *Après, après, n'est-ce pas, chère amie,*" he kept repeating, holding out his hands to her.

I cannot express how disagreeably her outburst impressed me. I made no response but a chilly and dignified bow ; then I sat down to the table, and with undisguised intention began talking of other things, of various trifles, laughing and making jokes. . . . The old man was evidently grateful to me and was enthusiastically delighted ; but enthusiastic as his gaiety was, it was evidently insincere and might any moment have been followed by absolute dejection : that was clear from the first glance.

" *Cher enfant,* I hear you've been ill. . . . *Ah, pardon,* I hear you've been busy with spiritualism all this time."

" I never thought of such a thing," I said smiling.

" No ? who was it told me about spiritualism ? "

" It was your landlord here, Pyotr Ippolitovitch," Anna Andreyevna explained, " he's a very amusing man and knows a great many anecdotes ; shall I ask him in ? "

" *Oui, oui, il est charmant* . . . he knows anecdotes, but better send for him later. We'll send for him and he'll tell us stories, *mais après.* Only fancy, they were laying the table just now and he said : ' Don't be uneasy, it won't fly about, we are not spiritualists.' Is it possible that the tables fly about among the spiritualists ? "

" I really don't know, they say so, they say they jump right off the ground."

" *Mais c'est terrible ce que tu dis,*" he looked at me in alarm.

" Oh, don't be uneasy, of course that's nonsense."

" That's what I say too. Nastasya Stepanovna Salomeyev . . . you know her, of course . . . oh no, you don't know her . . would you believe it she believes in spiritualism, too ; and only fancy, *chère enfant,*" he turned to Anna Andreyevna, " I said to her, there are tables in the Ministry of Finance and eight pairs of clerks' hands are lying on them, writing all the while, so why is it the tables don't dance there ? Fancy if they suddenly all began dancing ! The revolt of the tables in the

Ministry of Finance or popular education—that's the last straw."

"What charming things you say, prince, just as you always did," I exclaimed, trying to laugh as genuinely as possible.

"*N'est-ce pas ? Je ne parle pas trop, mais je dis bien.*"

"I will bring Pyotr Ippolitovitch," Anna Andreyevna said, getting up. There was a gleam of pleasure in her face : she was relieved at seeing how affectionate I was with the old prince. But she had hardly gone out when the old man's face changed instantly. He looked hurriedly at the door, glanced about him, and stooping towards me from the sofa, whispered to me in a frightened voice :

"*Cher ami !* Oh, if I could see them both here together ! *Oh, cher enfant !*"

"Prince, don't distress yourself. . . ."

"Yes, yes, but . . . we'll reconcile them, *n'est-ce pas ?* It's a foolish petty quarrel between two most estimable women, *n'est-ce pas ?* You are my only hope. . . . We'll set everything straight here ; and what a queer place this is," he looked about him almost fearfully ; "and that landlord, you know . . . he's got such a face. . . . Tell me ! He's not dangerous ? "

"The landlord ? Oh no, how could he be dangerous ? "

"*C'est ça.* So much the better. *Il semble qu'il est bête, ce gentilhomme.* Cher enfant, for Christ's sake don't tell Anna Andreyevna that I'm afraid of everything here ; I praised everything from the first moment, I praised the landlord too. Listen, do you know the story of what happened to Von Sohn—do you remember ? "

"Well, what of it ? "

"*Rien, rien de tout.* . . . *Mais je suis libre ici, n'est-ce pas ?* What do you think, nothing could happen to me here . . . of the same sort ? "

"But I assure you, dear prince . . . upon my word ! "

"*Mon ami, mon enfant !*" he exclaimed suddenly, clasping his hands before him, not seeking to disguise his alarm : "if you really have something . . . some document . . . in fact— if you have something to say to me, don't say it ; for God's sake don't say anything at all . . . put it off as long as you can. . . ."

He was on the point of throwing himself in my arms ; tears were flowing down his face ; I cannot describe how it made my heart ache ; the poor old man was like a pitiful frightened child stolen from his home by gypsies and carried away to live with strangers, but we were not allowed to embrace. The door opened and Anna Andreyevna walked in, not with the landlord, but with her brother, the *kammer-junker*. This new surprise petrified me. I got up and was making for the door.

"Arkady Makarovitch, allow me to introduce you," Anna Andreyevna said aloud, so that I was compelled to stop.

"I know your brother *too* well already," I rapped out, laying special emphasis on the word "too."

"Ah, that was a terrible blunder! And I'm so sor-r-ry, dear, and . . . Andrey Makarovitch," the young man began lisping, coming up to me with an extraordinarily free-and-easy air and seizing my hand, which I was incapable of withdrawing, "it was all the fault of my Stepan; he announced you so stupidly that I mistook you for some one else: that was in Moscow," he explained to his sister: "afterwards, I did everything I could to look you up and explain, but I was ill, ask her. *Cher prince, nous devons être amis même par droit de naissance. . . .*"

And the impudent young man had the effrontery to put his arm round my shoulder, which was the height of familiarity. I drew back, but overcome by embarrassment preferred to beat a hasty retreat, without saying a word. Going back to my room I sat down on my bed in uncertainty and agitation. I felt suffocated by the atmosphere of intrigue, but I could not deal Anna Andreyevna such a direct and crushing blow. I suddenly felt that she, too, was dear to me, and that her position was an awful one.

3

As I had expected, she came into my room herself, leaving the prince with her brother, who immediately began telling him some society scandal, as fresh as hot cakes, which at once distracted the impressionable old man's attention and cheered him up. I got up from the bed in silence, with a look of inquiry.

"I have told you everything, Arkady Makarovitch," she began directly, "our fate is in your hands."

"But I told you beforehand that I cannot . . . the most sacred duties prevent me doing what you desire. . . ."

"Yes? Is that your answer? Well, let me perish, but what of the old prince? What do you expect? Why, he'll be out of his mind by the evening!"

"No, he'll go out of his mind if I show him the letter in which his daughter writes to a lawyer about certifying him insane!" I cried with heat. "That's what would be too much for him. Do you know he won't believe that letter, he's told me so already!"

I lied, saying he had said this of the letter; but it was effective.

"He has said so already? I thought so! In that case I'm lost. He's been crying already and asking to go home."

"Tell me, what's your plan exactly?" I asked insistently. She flushed from exasperated haughtiness, so to speak, but she controlled herself:

"With that letter of his daughter's in our hands, we are justified in the eyes of the world. I should send it at once to Prince V. and to Boris Mihalovitch Pelistchev, the friends of his childhood; both persons highly respected and influential in society, and I know that some years ago they were indignant with the conduct of his greedy and merciless daughter. They will of course reconcile him with his daughter at my request. I shall insist on it myself; but the position of affairs will be completely changed. And my relations, too, the Fanariotovs, will, I judge, make up their minds to support my rights; but what weighs most with me is his happiness: I want him to understand and appreciate who is really devoted to him. Of course I've always reckoned most on your influence with him, Arkady Makarovitch; you are so fond of him. . . . And who does care for him except you and me? He has done nothing but talk about you these last few days; he was pining for you 'his young friend. . . .' I need not say that for the rest of my life my gratitude will be unmeasured. . . ."

She was actually promising me a reward—money perhaps.

I interrupted her sharply.

"Whatever you say I cannot," I brought out with an air of immovable determination. "I can only repay you with equal frankness and explain my final decision: I shall, at the earliest possible moment, put this fatal letter into Katerina Nikolaevna's hands, but only on condition that all that has happened shall not be made a scandal, and that she gives me her word beforehand that she will not interfere with your happiness; that's all that I can do."

"That's impossible!" she said, flushing all over. The mere idea that Katerina Nikolaevna would *spare* her roused her to indignation.

" I shall not change, Anna Andreyevna."

" Perhaps you will change."

" You had better apply to Lambert ! "

" Arkady Makarovitch, you don't know what misery may come from your obstinacy," she said with grim exasperation.

" Misery will follow, that's true . . . my head is going round. I've had enough of you : I've made up my mind—and that's the end of it. Only I beg you for God's sake don't bring your brother in to me."

" But he is very anxious to make up for . . ."

" There is nothing to make up for ! I don't want it, I don't wish for it, I don't wish for it ! " I exclaimed, clutching my head. (Oh, perhaps I treated her too disdainfully then.) " Tell me, though, where will the prince sleep to-night ? Surely not here ? "

" He will stay the night here in your flat, and with you."

" I am moving into another lodging this evening."

And uttering these ruthless words I seized my cap and began putting on my great-coat. Anna Andreyevna watched me in sullen silence. I felt sorry for her—oh, I felt sorry for that proud girl ! But I rushed out of the flat, without leaving her one word of hope.

4

I will try to be brief. My decision was taken beyond recall, and I went straight to Tatyana Pavlovna. Alas ! A great calamity might have been averted if I had only found her at home ; but as though of design, I was pursued by ill-luck all that day. I went of course to my mother's, in the first place to see her, and secondly, because I reckoned certainly on meeting Tatyana Pavlovna there. But she was not there either ; she had only just gone away, while mother was lying down ill, and Liza was left alone with her. Liza begged me not to go in, and not to wake mother : " She has not slept all night, she's so worried ; thank God she has fallen asleep at last." I embraced Liza and said two or three words to her, telling her I had made an immense and momentous resolution, and should carry it out at once. She listened without particular surprise, as though to the usual thing. Oh, they had all grown used by then to my constantly repeated ' final resolutions,' and the feeble cancelling of them afterwards. But this time, this time it would be a different matter. I went to the eating-house on the canal side and sat down there to wait awhile in the certainty of finding Tatyana Pavlovna afterwards. I must explain, though, why I found it so necessary to see that lady. The fact is that I wanted to send her at once to Katerina Nikolaevna, to ask her to come back with her, meaning in Tatyana Pavlovna's presence to return the letter, explaining everything once for all. In short, I wanted nothing but what was fitting; I wanted to put myself right once and for all. At the same time I was quite determined to put in a few words on behalf of Anna Andreyevna and, if possible, to take Katerina Nikolaevna, together with Tatyana Pavlovna (by way of a witness), back with me to see the prince, there to reconcile the hostile ladies, to bring the old prince back to life and . . . and . . . in fact, in that little group anyway, to make every one happy on the spot, that very day, so that there would be none left unhappy but Versilov and mother. I could have no doubt of my success. From gratitude for my restoration of the letter from which I should ask nothing of her in return, Katerina Nikolaevna would not have refused me such a request. Alas! I still imagined I was in possession of the document. Oh, what a stupid and ignominious position I was in, though without suspecting it!

It was getting quite dark, about four o'clock, when I called at Tatyana Pavlovna's again. Marya answered gruffly that she had not come in. I remember very well now the strange look Marya gave me from under her brows; but of course it did not strike me at the time. I was suddenly stung by another idea. As I went down the stairs, from Tatyana Pavlovna's, vexed and somewhat dejected, I thought of the poor old prince, who had held out his hands to me that morning, and I suddenly reproached myself bitterly for having deserted him, perhaps indeed from feeling personally aggrieved.

I began uneasily imagining that something really very bad might have happened in my absence, and hurriedly went home. At home, however, all that had been happening was this.

When Anna Andreyevna had gone out of my room in a rage, that morning, she had not yet lost heart; I must mention that she had already, that morning, sent to Lambert, then she sent to him again, and as Lambert appeared to be still absent from home, she finally dispatched her brother to look for him. In face of my opposition the poor girl was resting her last hopes on Lambert and his influence on me; she expected him with impatience, and only wondered that after hovering round her and never leaving her side till that day, he should now have suddenly deserted her and vanished. Alas! she could not possibly have imagined that Lambert, being now in possession of the document, had made entirely different plans, and so, of course, was keeping out of the way and hiding from her on purpose.

And so in her anxiety and growing uneasiness Anna Andreyevna was scarcely capable of entertaining the old man : his uneasiness was growing to threatening proportions, he kept asking strange and timorous questions, he began looking suspiciously at her, and several times fell to weeping. Young Versilov did not stay long. After he had gone Anna Andreyevna was reduced to bringing in Pyotr Ippolitovitch, on whom she was relying, but he did not please the old prince at all, and even aroused his aversion. In fact the old prince, for some reason, regarded Pyotr Ippolitovitch with increasing distrust and suspicion. As ill-luck would have it, the landlord launched again into a disquisition on spiritualism, and described all sorts of tricks which he said he had seen himself at séances. He declared that one medium had, before the whole audience, cut off people's heads, so that blood flowed, and every one saw it, and afterwards'put them back on their necks, and that they grew on again, also in the sight of the whole audience, and all this happened in the year eighteen hundred and fifty-nine. The old prince was so frightened, and at the same time for some reason was so indignant, that Anna Andreyevna was obliged to get rid of the story-teller promptly ; fortunately, dinner arrived, ordered expressly the evening before from somewhere near (through Lambert and Alphonsine) from a remarkable French cook who was out. of a place, and wanted to find a situation in a nobleman's family or a club. The dinner and the champagne that accompanied it greatly cheered the old prince ; he ate a great deal and was very jocose. After dinner he felt heavy and drowsy, of course, and as he always took a nap after dinner, Anna Andreyevna made up a bed for him. He kept kissing her hand as he fell asleep and declaring that she was his paradise, his hope, his houri, "his golden flower"—in fact he dropped into the most Oriental expressions. At last he fell asleep, and it was just then I came back.

Anna Andreyevna came in to me hurriedly, clasped her hands before me, and said. that not for her own sake, but for the prince's she besought me not to go away, but to go in to him as soon as he waked up. "He will be lost without you, he will have a nervous attack; I'm afraid he may break down before night. . . ." She added that she herself would be compelled to be away "possibly for a couple of hours, and so she would be leaving the prince in my sole charge." I promised her warmly that I would remain till the evening, and that when the prince waked up I would do my very best to entertain him.

"And I will do my duty!" she declared with energy.

She went out. I may add, anticipating events, that she went out to look for Lambert herself; this was her last hope; she also went to her brother's, and to her relations, the Fanariotovs'; it may well be understood what her state of mind must have been when she returned.

The old prince waked up about an hour after her departure. I heard him groan through the wall, and at once ran in to him; I found him sitting on the bed in his dressing-gown, but so terrified by his isolation, the light of the solitary lamp, and the strange room, that when I went in he started, jumped up and screamed. I flew up to him, and when he recognised me, he began embracing me with tears of joy.

"I was told that you had moved into another lodging, that you had taken fright, and run away."

"Who can have told you that?"

"Who could? You see I may have imagined it myself, or some one may have told me. Only fancy, I've just had a dream: an old man with a beard came in carrying an ikon, an ikon broken in two, and all at once he said, ' So shall your life be broken in two!' "

"Good heavens! You must have heard from some one that Versilov broke an ikon in two yesterday?"

"*N'est-ce pas?* I heard so, I heard so! I heard from Darya Onisimovna yesterday morning. She brought my trunk here and the dog."

"And so you dreamed of it."

"Yes, I suppose so, and that old man kept shaking his finger at me. Where is Anna Andreyevna?"

"She'll be back directly."

"Where from? Has she gone away, too?" he exclaimed piteously.

"No, no, she'll be here directly, and she asked me to stay with you."

2 L

"*Oui.* And so our Andrey Petrovitch has gone off his head, 'so rapidly and unexpectedly!' I always predicted that that's how he'd end. Stay, my dear. . . ."

He suddenly clutched me by my coat, and drew me towards him.

"The landlord," he whispered : " brought in some photographs just now, horrid photographs of women, naked women in various oriental poses, and began showing them me in a glass. . . . I admired them of course, though I did not like them, but you know that's just as they brought horrid women to that poor fellow, so as to make him drunk more easily. . . ."

"Why, you are talking of Von Sohn, but that's enough, prince ! The landlord's a fool and nothing more ! "

"A fool and nothing more ! *C'est mon opinion !* My dear, rescue me from here if you can ! " He suddenly clasped his hands before me.

"Prince, I will do everything I can ! I am entirely at your service. . . . Dear prince, wait a little and perhaps I will put everything right ! "

"*N'est-ce pas ?* We'll cut and run and we'll leave my trunk here to look as though we are coming back."

"Where should we run to ! And what of Anna Andreyevna?"

"No, no, we'll go with Anna Andreyevna. . . . Oh, *mon cher*, there's a regular muddle in my head. . . . Stay : there in my bag on the right, is Katya's portrait. I slipped it in on the sly so that Anna Andreyevna, and still more, that Darya Onisimovna should not notice it ; take it out, for goodness' sake make haste, be careful, mind we are not caught. . . . Couldn't you fasten the door with the hook ? "

I did in fact, find in the bag a photograph of Katerina Nikolaevna in an oval frame. He took it in his hands, carried it to the light, and tears suddenly flowed down his thin yellow cheeks.

"*C'est un ange, c'est un ange du ciel !* " he exclaimed : " I never have been as good to her as I ought . . . and see what's happened now ! *Cher enfant,* I don't believe a word of it, not a word of it ! My dear, tell me : can you imagine, they are wanting to put me in a madhouse ? *Je dis des choses charmantes et tout le monde rit* . . . and all of a sudden they take a man like that to a madhouse ! "

"That's never happened ! " I cried, " that's a mistake. I know her feelings."

" You know her feelings, too ? That's splendid ! My dear, you've given me new life. How could they say things against you ! My dear, fetch Katya here, and let them kiss each other before me, and I will take them home, and we'll get rid of the landlord ! "

He stood up, clasped his hands, and fell on his knees before me.

" *Cher*," he whispered, shaking like a leaf in a sort of insane terror : " My dear, tell me the whole truth : where will they put me now ? "

" My God ! " I cried, raising him up, and making him sit on the bed : " why you don't believe in me at last ; do you think that I'm in the plot too ? I won't let anyone lay a finger on you ! "

" *C'est-ça*, don't let them," he faltered, clutching me tightly by the elbow with both hands, and still trembling. " Don't let anyone touch me ! And don't tell me lies yourself about anything . . . for will they take me away from here ? Listen, that landlord, Ippolit or whatever his name is . . . isn't a doctor ? "

" A doctor ? "

" This . . . this isn't a madhouse, here, in this room ? "

But at that instant the door opened, and Anna Andreyevna came in. She must have been listening at the door, and, could not resist opening the door too suddenly—and the prince, who started at every creak, shrieked, and flung himself on his face on the pillow. Finally he had something like a fit, which ended in sobs.

" See ? This is your doing," I said to her, pointing to the old man.

" No, it's your doing ! " she raised her voice harshly, " I appeal to you for the last time, Arkady Makarovitch, will you unmask the diabolical intrigue against this defenceless old man, and sacrifice ' your mad and childish dreams of love,' to save your *own* sister ? "

" I will save you all, but only in the way I told you this morning ! I am running off again, and perhaps in an hour Katerina Nikolaevna will be here herself ! I will reconcile you all, and you will all be happy ! " I exclaimed almost with inspiration.

" Fetch her, fetch her here," cried the prince in a flutter. " Take me to her ! I want to see Katya and to bless her," he exclaimed, lifting up his hands and springing off the bed.

" You see," I said to Anna Andreyevna, motioning towards him : " you hear what he says : now at all events no ' document ' will be any help to you."

" I see, but it might help to justify my conduct in the opinion of the world, as it is, I'm disgraced ! Enough, my conscience is clear. I am abandoned by everyone, even by my own brother, who has taken fright at my failure. . . . But I will do my duty and will remain by this unhappy man, to take care of him and be his nurse ! "

But there was no time to be lost. I ran out of the room : " I shall come back in an hour, and shall not come back alone," I cried from the doorway.

CHAPTER XII

1

At last I found Tatyana Pavlovna at home ! I at once explained everything to her—all about the " document," and every detail of what was going on at my lodgings. Though she quite understood the position, and might have fully grasped what was happening in two words, yet the explanation took us, I believe, some ten minutes. I did the talking, I put aside all shame and told her the whole truth. She sat in her chair silent and immovable, drawing herself up straight as a knitting needle, with her lips compressed, and her eyes fixed upon me, listening greedily. But when I finished she promptly jumped up from her chair, and with such impetuosity that I jumped up too.

" Ach, you puppy ! So you really had that letter sewn up in your pocket and it was sewn up there by that fool Marya Ivanovna ! Oh, you shameless villains ! So you came here to conquer hearts and take the fashionable world by storm. You wanted to revenge yourself on the devil knows who, because you're an illegitimate son, eh ? "

"Tatyana Pavlovna, don't dare to abuse me ! " I cried. " Perhaps you in your abuse have been the cause from the very beginning of my vindictiveness here. Yes, I am an illegitimate son, and perhaps I worked to revenge myself for being an illegitimate son, and perhaps I did want to revenge myself on the devil knows who, the devil himself could scarcely find who is guilty ; but remember, I've cut off all connection with these villains, and have conquered my passions. I will lay the document before her in silence and will go away without even waiting for a word from her; you'll be the witness of it!"

"Give me the letter, give me the letter, lay it on the table at once; but you are lying, perhaps."

"It's sewn up in my pocket. Marya Ivanovna sewed it up herself; and when I had a new coat made here I took it out of the old one and sewed it up in the new coat; here it is, feel it, I'm not lying!"

"Give it me, take it out," Tatyana Pavlovna stormed.

"Not on any account, I tell you again; I will lay it before her in your presence and will go away without waiting for a single word; but she must know and see with her eyes that it is my doing, that I'm giving it up to her of my own accord, without compulsion and without recompense."

"Showing off again? You're in love, puppy, eh?"

"You may say horrid things to me as much as you like. I've deserved them, but I'm not offended. Oh, I may seem to her a paltry boy who has been keeping watch on her and plotting against her; but let her recognise that I have conquered myself and put her happiness above everything on earth! Never mind, Tatyana Pavlovna, never mind! I keep crying to myself: courage and hope! What if this is my first step in life, anyway it is ending well, it is ending honourably! And what if I do love her," I went on fervently with flashing eyes; "I am not ashamed of it: mother is a heavenly angel, but she is an earthly queen! Versilov will go back to mother, and I've no cause to be ashamed to face her; you know I once heard what Versilov and she were saying, I stood behind the curtain. . . . Oh, we are all three possessed by the same madness. Oh, do you know whose phrase that is 'possessed by the same madness'? They are his words, Andrey Petrovitch's! But do you know, perhaps there are more than three of us possessed by the same madness? Yes, I don't mind betting, you're a fourth —possessed by the same madness! Shall I say it—I will bet that you've been in love with Andrey Petrovitch all your life and perhaps you are so still . . ."

I repeat I was carried away by excitement and a sort of happiness, but I could not finish; she suddenly, with super-human quickness, seized me by the hair and twice shook me backwards and forwards with all her might. . . . Then she suddenly abandoned me and retreated into the corner, and hid her face in her handkerchief.

" You young puppy ! Never dare say that to me again ! " she brought out, crying.

All this was so unexpected, that I was naturally thunderstruck. I stood gazing at her, not knowing what to do.

" Foo, you stupid ! Come here and give me a kiss, though I am an old fool ! " she said suddenly, laughing and crying : " and don't you dare, don't you ever dare to say that to me again . . . but I love you and have always loved you . . . you stupid."

I kissed her. I may mention in parenthesis that Tatyana Pavlovna and I were friends from that time forward.

" But oh ! what am I doing ? " she said suddenly, slapping herself on the forehead ; " but what were you saying : the old prince is at your lodging ? But is it true ? "

" I assure you he is."

" Oh, my goodness ! Ach, it makes me sick ! " she hurried to and fro about the room. " And they are doing what they like with him there ! Ech, is there nothing will frighten the fools ! And ever since the morning ! Oh, oh, Anna Andreyevna. Oh, oh, the nun ! And she of course, Militrissa, knows nothing about it."

" What Militrissa ? "

" Why, your earthly queen, your ideal ! Ach, but what's to be done now ? "

" Tatyana Pavlovna," I cried, coming to myself, " we've been talking nonsense and have forgotten what matters ; I ran out to fetch Katerina Nikolaevna, and they're all waiting for me there."

And I explained that I should give up the letter only on condition that she promised to be reconciled to Anna Andreyevna at once, and even agree to the marriage . . .

" Quite right, too," Tatyana Pavlovna interposed," and I've said the same thing to her a hundred times. Why, he'll die before the wedding—he won't be married anyhow, and if he leaves money to Anna in his will, why their names are in it as it is, and will remain there."

" Surely it's not only the money that Katerina Nikolaevna cares about ? "

" No, she has been afraid all along that the letter was in Anna's hands, and I was afraid of it, too ! We were keeping watch on her. The daughter did not want to give the old father a shock, and the German, Büring, certainly did feel anxious about the money."

" And after that she can marry Büring ? "

" Why, what's one to do with a little fool ? It's a true saying, a fool's a fool and will be a fool for ever. He gives her a certain calm you see ; ' Since I must marry some one,' she said, ' I'll marry him, he will suit me better than anyone ' ; she says ; but we shall see afterwards how he suits her. One may tear one's hair afterwards, but then it's too late."

" Then why do you allow it ? You are fond of her, aren't you ? Why, you told her to her face you were in love with her ! "

" Yes, I am in love with her, and I love her more than all the rest of you put together, but she's a senseless little fool all the same."

" Well, run and fetch her now, and we will settle it all, and take her to her father ourselves."

" But we can't, we can't, you little stupid ! That's just it ! Ach, what are we to do ! Ach, it makes me sick ! " She fell to rushing to and fro again, though she snatched up her shawl " Ech, if only you had come to me four hours earlier, but now it's eight o'clock, and she went off just now to the Pelistchevs' to dinner, and afterwards she was going with them to the opera."

" Good heavens ! can't we run to the opera then . . . oh, no, we can't. What will become of the old man now ? He may die in the night ! "

" Listen, don't go there, but go to your mother's for the night, and early to-morrow . . ."

" No, I won't desert the old man, whatever happens."

"Well, don't desert him ; you are right there. But do you know I'll run round to her and leave a note . . . I write in our own words (she'll understand), that the document's here and that she must be here at ten o'clock to-morrow morning— punctually ! Don't worry yourself, she'll come, she'll obey me ; and then we'll put everything right. And you run home, and use all your little arts to please the old prince, put him to bed, and perhaps he'll hold out till the morning ! Don't frighten Anna either, I am fond of her too ; you are unjust to her, because you can't understand : she feels injured, she has been injured from a child ; ach, you've all been a burden on me ! Oh, don't forget, tell her from me, that I'll see to this business myself, and with a good will, and tell her not to worry, and her pride shall not suffer. . . . You see of late we've done nothing but quarrel—we've been spitting and scolding at one another ! Come, run along. . . . But stay, show me your pocket again . . . is it true, is it true ? Oh, is it true ? Give me that letter if only for the night, what is it to you ? Leave it, I won't eat it. You may let it slip out of your hands in the night you know. . . . You'll change your mind ? "

" Not for anything ! " I shouted. " Here, feel it, look at it, but I won't leave it for anything ! "

" I see it's paper," she said, feeling it with her fingers. " Oh, very well, go along, and I'll go round to her, maybe I'll look in at the theatre, too, that was a good idea of yours ! But run along, run along ! "

" Tatyana Pavlovna, wait a minute. How is mother ? "

" She's alive."

" And Andrey Petrovitch ? "

She waved her hand.

" He will come to himself ! "

I ran off, feeling cheered, and more hopeful, although I had not been successful, as I had reckoned to be, but alas ! destiny had decided otherwise, and there were other things in store for me— there certainly is a fate in things.

2

From the stairs I heard a noise in my lodging, and the door of the flat turned out to be open. At the door stood a servant in livery whom I did not know. Pyotr Ippolitovitch and his wife were both in the passage, too, looking scared and expectant. The door into the prince's room was open, and I could hear within a voice of thunder, which I could recognise at once—the voice of Büring. I had hardly taken two steps forward when I saw the old prince trembling and in tears, led out into the passage by Büring and Baron R., the gentleman who had called on Versilov about the duel. The prince was sobbing loudly, embracing and kissing Büring. Büring was shouting at Anna Andreyevna, who had followed the old prince into the passage. Büring was threatening her, and I believe stamped at her—in fact the coarse German soldier came to the surface in spite of his aristocratic breeding. It afterwards came out that he had somehow got hold of the notion that Anna Andreyevna was guilty of something positively criminal, and certainly would have to answer for her conduct before a court of law. In his ignorance he exaggerated it as the ignorant commonly do, and so considered he had the right to be unceremonious in the extreme. He had not yet got to the bottom of the business : he had been informed of it by an anonymous letter (which I shall have to refer to later) and he had rushed round in that state of fury in which even the most sharp-witted people of his nationality are sometimes prepared to fight like brigands. Anna Andreyevna had met all this outburst with the utmost dignity, but I missed that. All I saw was that, after bringing the old man into the passage, Büring left him in the hands of Baron R., and rushing impetuously back to her, shouted, probably in reply to some remark of hers :

" You're an intriguing adventuress, you're after his money ! You've disgraced yourself in society and will answer for it in a court of law ! . . ."

" You're taking advantage of an unfortunate invalid and driving him to madness. . . . and you're shouting at me because I'm a woman, and there's no one to defend me . . ."

" Oh, yes, you are his betrothed, a fine betrothed," Büring chuckled, with spiteful violence.

" Baron, Baron . . . *chère enfant, je nous aime,*" wailed the prince, stretching out his hands towards Anna Andreyevna.

" Go along, prince, go along, there's been a plot against you, and maybe your life was threatened," shouted Büring.

" *Qui, oui, je comprends, j'ai compris au commencement* . . ."

" Prince," Anna Andreyevna raised her voice. " You are insulting me, and letting me be insulted ! "

" Get along with you," Büring shouted at her suddenly.

That I could not endure.

" Blackguard ! " I yelled at him : " Anna Andreyevna, I'm here to defend you ! "

What happened then I cannot describe exactly, and will not attempt to. The scene that followed was horrible and degrading. I seemed suddenly to lose my reason. I believe I dashed up and struck him, or at least gave him a violent push. He struck me with all his might on my head so that I fell on the floor. When I came to, I rushed after them down stairs. I remember that my nose was bleeding. At the entrance a carriage was waiting for them, and while they were getting the prince in, I ran up, and in spite of the lackey, who pushed me back I rushed at Büring again. At this point the police turned up, I don't know how.

Büring seized me by the collar and in a threatening voice ordered the police to take me into custody. I shouted that he ought to come with me, that we might make our affirmation together, and that they dare not take me almost from my own lodging. But as it had all happened in the street and not in the flat, and as I shouted and fought like a drunken man, and as Büring was wearing his uniform, the policeman took me. But flying into a perfect frenzy, I believe at that point I struck the policeman too. Then I remember two of them suddenly appeared and carried me off. I faintly remember they took me to a room full of tobacco smoke, with all sorts of people standing and sitting about in it waiting and writing ; here too I went on shouting, and insisting on making a statement. But things had gone beyond that, and were complicated by violence and resisting the police, besides I looked absolutely disreputable. Some one shouted at me angrily. Meanwhile the policeman charging me with fighting was describing the colonel . . .

"What's your name ? " some one shouted to me.

"Dolgoruky," I yelled.

"Prince Dolgoruky ? "

Beside myself, I answered by a very coarse word of abuse, and then . . . then I remember they dragged me to a very dark little room, set apart for drunkards. Oh, I'm not complaining. Readers will have seen of late in the newspapers a complaint made by a gentleman who was kept all night under arrest, tied up, and in a room set apart for drunkards, but I believe he was quite innocent while I had done something. I threw myself on the common bed which I shared with two unconscious sleepers. My head ached, my temples throbbed, and so did my heart. I must have been unconscious, and I believe I was delirious. I only remember waking up in the middle of the night, and sitting on the bed. I remembered everything at once and understood it in all its bearings, and, with my elbow propped on my knees and my head in my hands, I sank into profound meditation.

Oh, I am not going to describe my feelings, and there is no time to do it, but I will note one thing only : perhaps I never spent moments more consolatory to my soul than those moments of reflection in the middle of the night on that prison bed. This will perhaps strike the reader as strange, and he may be inclined to set it down to brag and the desire to be original—and yet it was just as I have said. It was one of those minutes which come perhaps to every one, but only come once in a lifetime. At such moments men decide their fate, define their point of view, and say to themselves once and for all : " That's where the truth lies, and that is the path to take to attain it." Yes, those moments were the light of my soul. Insulted by haughty Büring and expecting to be insulted next day by that aristocratic lady, I knew that I could revenge myself on them, but I decided not to revenge myself. I decided, in spite of every temptation, that I would not produce the letter, and publish it to the whole world (the idea had been floating in my mind) ; I repeated to myself that next day I would put that letter before her, and, if need be, instead of gratitude, would bear her ironical smile, but in any case I would not say a word but would go away from her for ever. . . . There is no need to enlarge on this, however. What would happen next day here, how I should be brought before the authorities, and what they would do with me —I almost forgot to think about. I crossed myself with love in my heart, lay down on the bed, and fell into a sound childlike sleep.

I waked up late, when it was daylight. I found myself alone in the room. I sat down to wait in silence and waited about an hour ; it must have been about nine o'clock when I was suddenly summoned. I might go into greater detail but it is not worth while, for all this is now irrelevant ; I need only record what matters. I must note, however, that to my great astonishment I was treated with unexpected courtesy ; I was questioned, I answered, and I was at once allowed to depart. I went out in silence, and to my satisfaction saw in their faces some surprise at a man who was able to keep up his dignity even in such circumstances. If I had not noticed that, I should not have recorded it. Tatyana Pavlovna was waiting for me at the entrance. I will explain in a couple of words why I was let off so easily.

Early in the morning, by eight o'clock perhaps, Tatyana Pavlovna had flown round to my lodging, that is to Pyotr Ippolitovitch's, expecting to find the old prince still there, and she heard at once of all the horrors of the previous day, above all that I had been arrested. She instantly rushed off to Katerina Nikolaevna (who on returning from the theatre the evening before had had an interview with the father who had been restored to her). Tatyana Pavlovna waked her up, alarmed her and insisted that I should be at once released.

With a note from her she flew at once to Büring's and demanded from him forthwith another note, to the proper authorities, with an urgent request from Büring himself that I should be released, as I had been arrested through a misunderstanding. With this note she presented herself to the prison and her request was respectfully granted.

3

Now I will go on with my story.

Tatyana Pavlovna pounced on me, put me in a sledge, and took me home with her, she immediately ordered the samovar, and washed and brushed me herself in the kitchen. In the kitchen she told me in a loud voice that at half-past eleven Katerina Nikolaevna would come herself—as they had agreed that morning—to meet me. Marya overheard this. A few minutes later she brought in the samovar, and two minutes later, when Tatyana Pavlovna called her, she did not answer ; it appeared that she had gone out for something. I beg the reader to make special note of this ; it was about a quarter to ten I believe. Though Tatyana Pavlovna was angry at her disappearance without asking leave, she only thought she had gone out to the shop, and immediately forgot about it. And, indeed, we had no thoughts to spare for it, we talked away without ceasing, for we had plenty to talk about, so that I, at least, scarcely noticed Marya's disappearance ; I beg the reader to make a note of that.

As for me, I was in a sort of delirium, I poured out my feelings, and above all we were expecting Katerina Nikolaevna, and the thought that in an hour I should meet her at last, and at such a turning-point in my life, made me tremble and quiver. At last, when I had drunk two cups of tea, Tatyana Pavlovna suddenly stood up, took a pair of scissors from the table, and said :

" Let me have your pocket, I must take out the letter, we can't unpick it when she's here."

" Yes," I exclaimed and unbuttoned my coat.

" What a muddle it's in ! who sewed it up ? "

" I did, I did, Tatyana Pavlovna."

" Well, I can see you did. Come, here it is. . . ."

We took it out . . . the old envelope was the same, but inside was a blank sheet of paper.

" What's this ? " cried Tatyana Pavlovna, turning it round and round . . . " what's the matter with you ? "

But I was standing pale and speechless . . . and I suddenly sank helplessly into a chair. I really almost fainted.

" What does it mean ? " wailed Tatyana Pavlovna. " Where is your letter ? "

" Lambert ! " I jumped up suddenly, slapping myself on the forehead as I guessed.

With breathless haste I explained to her—the night at Lambert's and our plot ; I had, however, confessed that to her the night before.

" They've stolen it, they've stolen it ! " I cried, stamping on the floor and clutching at my hair.

" That's terrible ! " cried Tatyana Pavlovna, grasping what had happened.

" What time is it ? "

It was about eleven.

" Ech, there's no Marya ! . . . Marya, Marya ! "

" What is it, mistress ? " Marya responded from the kitchen.

" Are you here ? What are we to do now ! I will fly to her. . . . Ah, slow coach, slow coach ! "

" And I to Lambert," I yelled, " and I will strangle him if need be."

" Mistress," Marya piped suddenly from the kitchen, " here's a person asking for you very particularly."

But before she had time to finish, the person burst in from the kitchen, making a great outcry and lamentation. It was Alphonsine. I will not describe the scene in detail ; the scene was a fraud and a deception, but I must say Alphonsine acted it splendidly. With tears of repentance and with violent gesticulations she babbled (in French, of course), that she had unpicked the letter herself, that it was now in Lambert's hands, and that Lambert, together with that " brigand," *cet homme noir,* meant to entice *Mme. la générale* to shoot her, immediately within an hour . . . that she knew all this from them, and that she had suddenly taken fright because she saw they had a pistol, *le pistolet,* and now she had rushed off to us, that we might go, might save, might warn. . . . That *cet homme noir. . . .*"

In fact, it all sounded very probable, the very stupidity of some of Alphonsine's expressions only increased its apparent truthfulness.

" What *homme noir* ? " cried Tatyana Pavlovna.

" *Tien, j'ai oublié son nom. . . Un homme affreux. . . Tiens, Versilov.*"

"Versilov, it cannot be," I cried !

"Oh, yes, it can ! " wailed Tatyana Pavlovna : "come, tell us my good woman without dancing about, don't wave your arms about ; what do they want ? Explain, my good woman ; I don't believe they mean to shoot her."

"My good woman " did explain as follows (N.B.—it was all a lie, I must remind the reader again) : Versilov was to sit at the door and when she went in Lambert was to show her *cette lettre*, then Versilov was to rush in and they would. . . . . Oh ! *ils feront leur vengeance !* that she, Alphonsine, was afraid there would be trouble, because she had had a share in the business herself, *cette dame, la générale* would certainly come at once, at once, because they had sent her a copy of the letter, and she would see at once that they really had the letter, and would go to interview them, but only Lambert had written the letter, so she knew nothing about Versilov ; and Lambert had introduced himself as a stranger who had come from a lady in Moscow, *une dame de Moscou* (N.B.—Marie Ivanovna !)

"Ach, I feel sick ! Ach, I feel sick ! " exclaimed Tatyana Pavlovna.

"*Sauvez la, sauvez la !* " cried Alphonsine.

Oh, of course there was something inconsistent, even at first sight, in this mad story, but there was no time to think it over, for in essentials it sounded very probable. Of course, one might still suppose, and with the greatest likelihood, that Katerina Nikolaevna, on receiving Lambert's summons, would come first to Tatyana Pavlovna's to discuss the matter with us ; and on the other hand, this might not happen, and she might go straight to him, and then—she was lost ! It was difficult to believe that she would rush off to a stranger like Lambert at the first summons ; yet, again, this might somehow happen, after seeing the copy and satisfying herself that they really had her letter, and then there would be disaster anyway ! Above all, we had no time even to reflect.

"Versilov will murder her ! if he has stooped to make use of Lambert he'll murder her ! It's the second self," I cried.

"Ah that 'second self ' ! " cried Tatyana Pavlovna, wringing her hands. "Well, this is no use," she said decidedly, "take your cap and coat and quick march together. Lead us straight to them, my good woman. Ach, it's a long way. Marya, Marya, if Katerina Nikolaevna comes, tell her I shall be back directly and make her sit and wait for me, and if she does not want to wait, lock the door and keep her by force. Tell her I told her to. A hundred roubles for you, Marya, if you deserve it."

We ran down stairs. No doubt nothing better could have been suggested, for, in any case, the chief scene of danger was in Lambert's lodging, and if Katerina Nikolaevna did really come first to Tatyana Pavlovna's lodgings, Marya could always detain her. Yet after she had called a sledge, Tatyana Pavlovna changed her mind.

" You go with her," she bade me, leaving me with Alphonsine " and if need be, die there, do you understand ? I'll follow you directly, but first I'll whisk round to her, maybe I shall find her, for say what you like, I feel suspicious ! "

And she flew off to Katerina Nikolaevna.

Alphonsine and I went our way towards Lambert's. I urged on the driver and continued to question Alphonsine, but she confined herself to exclamations, and finally took refuge in tears. But God saved and preserved us all when everything was hanging on a thread. We had not driven a quarter of the way when I suddenly heard a shout behind me ; some one was calling me by my name. I looked round—Trishatov was driving after us in another sledge.

" Where are you going," he shouted in alarm, " and with her, with Alphonsine ? "

" Trishatov," I cried, " you told the truth, there is trouble ! I am going to that scoundrel, Lambert's ! Let's go together, the more the better ! "

" Turn back, turn back at once," shoulted Trishatov, " Lambert's deceiving you, and Alphonsine's deceiving you. The pock-marked fellow sent me ; they are not at home, I met Versilov and Lambert just now ; they were driving to Tatyana Pavlovna's . . they're there now. . . ."

I stopped the driver and jumped out to join Trishatov. To this day I don't know how I could make up my mind so quickly, but I believed him at once, and made up my mind. Alphonsine raised a terrible outcry, but we did not trouble ourselves about her, and I don't know whether she followed us or went home, anyway, I did not see her again.

In the sledge, Trishatov told me breathlessly that there was some sort of plot on foot, that Lambert had been plotting with the pock-marked man, but that the latter had betrayed him at the last moment, and had sent Trishatov to Tatyana Pavlovna's to warn her not to believe Lambert and Alphonsine. Trishatov added that he knew nothing more, and that the pock-marked gentleman had told him nothing more, for he had been in a hurry himself, and it had all been settled in haste. "I saw you driving," Trishatov went on, "and drove after you."

It was clear, of course, that this pock-marked individual also knew the whole story, since he had sent Trishatov straight to Tatyana Pavlovna's, but that was another mystery. But to avoid a muddle I will, before describing the catastrophe, explain the actual fact, and for the last time anticipate the order of events.

4

AFTER stealing the letter Lambert at once got into communication with Versilov. How Versilov could have brought himself to join Lambert—I won't discuss for the time ; that will come later ; what was chiefly responsible was the "second self !" After joining Versilov, Lambert still had to entice Katerina Nikolaevna as cunningly as he could. Versilov assured him at once that she would not come. But ever since the day before yesterday, when I met him in the street in the evening, broke off all relations with him, and told him that I should give back the letter at Tatyana Pavlovna's lodgings and in her presence— Lambert had arranged to keep a watch on Tatyana Pavlovna's lodgings ; Marya was bought over as a spy. Marya was given twenty roubles, and after the theft of the letter, Lambert visited Marya a second time, settling with her finally, and promising to pay her two hundred roubles for her services.

That was why Marya had rushed from the flat and galloped off in a sledge to Lambert's, with the news, as soon as she heard that Katerina Nikolaevna was to be at Tatyana Pavlovna's at half-past eleven, and that I, too, should be present. This was just the information she was to bring Lambert ; that was precisely the duty assigned her. Versilov happened to be with Lambert at that very moment. In one moment Versilov had devised the diabolical plan. They say that madmen are at times extraordinarily cunning.

The plot was to lure both of us, Tatyana and me, out of the flat at all costs, if only for a quarter of an hour, but before Katerina Nikolaevna arrived. Then they meant to wait in the street, and as soon as Tatyana Pavlovna and

I had come out, to run into the flat, which Marya was to open to them, and there to await Katerina Nikolaevna. Alphonsine, meantime, was to do her utmost to detain us where and how she pleased. Katerina Nikolaevna would be sure to come, as she promised, at half-past eleven, so that she would certainly be there long before we could be back. (Of course, Katerina Nikolaevna had received no summons from Lambert. Alphonsine had told us a lie and Versilov had invented the story in all its details, and Alphonsine had simply played the part of the frightened traitor.) Of course, it was a risk, but they probably reasoned that if it answered all would be well, if it failed nothing would have been lost, for the document would still be in their possession. But it did answer and could not possibly have failed to do so, for we could not but follow Alphonsine on the barest supposition that what she said might be true. I repeat again : there was no time to reflect.

5

We ran with Trishatov into the kitchen and found Marya in a fright. She was horrified to notice that when she let Versilov and Lambert in, that the latter had a revolver in his hand. Though she had taken money, the revolver had not entered into her calculations. She was bewildered and rushed at me as soon as she saw me.

" The lady has come and they've got a pistol ! "

" Trishatov, stay here in the kitchen," I said, "and as soon as I shout, run as quickly as you can to help me."

Marya opened the door in the passage and I slipped into Tatyana Pavlovna's bedroom—into the tiny cupboard of a room in which there was only space for Tatyana Pavlovna's bed, and in which once I had already accidentally played the eavesdropper. I sat down on the bed and at once found a peephole for myself in the curtain.

There was already a noise in the room and they were talking loudly ; I may mention that Katerina Nikolaevna arrived at the flat just a minute after them. I heard the noise and talk from the kitchen : Lambert was shouting. She was sitting on the sofa, and he was standing before her shouting like a fool. Now I know why he lost his head so stupidly : he was in a hurry and afraid they would be discovered. I will explain later who it was he feared. The letter was in his hand. But Versilov was not in the room. I was ready to rush in at the first sign of danger. I record only the gist of the conversation, perhaps a good deal I don't remember correctly, but I was too much excited to remember with perfect accuracy.

" This letter's worth thirty thousand roubles, and you are surprised ! It's worth a hundred thousand, and I only ask thirty ! " Lambert said in a loud voice, terribly excited.

Though Katerina Nikolaevna was evidently frightened, she looked at him with a sort of contemptuous wonder.

" I see that a trap has been laid for me, and I don't understand it," she said : " but if only that letter is really in your hands." . . . .

" But here it is, see for yourself ! Isn't that it ? An IOU for thirty thousand and not a farthing less ! " Lambert interrupted her.

" I've no money."

" Write an IOU—here's paper. Then go and get the money, and I will wait a week—no more. . . . Give me the money and then I will give you back the IOU and give you the letter."

" You take such a strange tone. You are making a mistake. That letter will be taken from you, if I go to-day and lodge a complaint."

" To whom ? Ha-ha-ha ? What of the scandal, and we shall show the letter to the prince ! Where are they going to find it ? I don't keep the document at my lodging. I shall show it to your father through a third person. Don't be obstinate, madam, be thankful that I'm not asking much, any other man would ask for something else besides . . . you know what . . . which many a pretty woman would not refuse in such trying circumstances, that's what I mean . . . ha-ha-ha ! *Vous êtes belle, vous !* "

Katerina Nikolaevna rose impetuously, turned crimson—and spat in his face. Then she turned quickly towards the door. It was at this point that the fool, Lambert, pulled out the revolver.

Like an unimaginative fool he had put blind faith in the effect of the document ; his chief error lay in not distinguishing what sort of woman he had to deal with, because, as I have said already, he thought every one was as mean in their feelings as he was. He angered her from the first word by his rudeness, though perhaps otherwise she might not have declined to consider the question of payment.

"Don't stir !" he yelled, furious at her spitting at him, clutching her by the shoulder, and showing her the revolver—simply, of course, to frighten her. She uttered a shriek and sank on the sofa. I burst into the room ; but, at the same instant, Versilov ran in at the other door. (He had been standing outside the door waiting.) In a flash he had snatched the revolver from Lambert, and with all his might hit him on the head with it. Lambert staggered and fell senseless ; the blood streamed from his head upon the carpet.

She saw Versilov, turned suddenly as white as a sheet, gazed at him for some moments immovable with indescribable horror, and fell into a swoon. He rushed to her. It all flashes before my eyes as I write. I remember with what terror I saw his flushed almost purple face and his bloodshot eyes. I believe that though he saw me in the room he did not recognise me. He caught her as she fell unconscious, and with amazing ease lifted her up in his arms, as though she were a feather, and began aimlessly carrying her about the room like a baby. It was a tiny room, but he paced to and fro from corner to corner, evidently with no idea why he was doing so. In one instant he had lost his reason. He kept gazing at her, at her face. I ran after him ; what I was most afraid of was the revolver, which he seemed to have forgotten in his right hand, and was holding close to her head. But he pushed me away, once with his elbow, and the second time with his foot. I wanted to shout to Trishatov, but I was afraid of irritating the madman. At last I drew back the curtain and began entreating him to put her on the bed. He went up and laid her down on it, stood over her, and gazed at her face ; and, suddenly bending down, kissed her twice on her pale lips. Oh, I realised at last that this was a man utterly beside himself. He suddenly waved the revolver over her, but, as though realising, turned the revolver and aimed it at her face. I instantly seized his arm and shouted to Trishatov. I remember we both struggled with him, but he succeeded in pulling away his arm and firing at himself. He would have shot her and then himself, but since we would not let him get at her, he pressed the revolver against his heart ; I succeeded, however, in pushing his arm upwards, and the bullet struck him in the shoulder. At that instant Tatyana Pavlovna burst into the room shrieking ; but he was already lying senseless on the carpet beside Lambert.

CHAPTER XIII

CONCLUSION

1

ALMOST six months have passed since that scene, much has happened, much has completely changed, and a new life has begun for me since then. . . . But I must settle what I have left doubtful in my story.

To me at least, the first question at the time, and long afterwards was : how Versilov could have brought himself to act in concert with a man like Lambert, and what were his objects in doing so ? Little by little, I have arrived at an explanation of a sort ; to my thinking, at those moments, that is, all that last day and the day before, Versilov can have had no definite aim, and I believe, indeed, he did not reflect on the matter at all, but acted under the influence of a whirlwind of conflicting emotions. But the theory of actual madness I cannot accept, especially as he is not in the least mad now. But the "second self" I do accept unquestionably. What is a second self exactly ? The second self, according to a medical book, written by an expert, which I purposely read afterwards, is nothing else than the first stage of serious mental derangement, which may lead to something very bad. And in that scene at my mother's, Versilov himself had with strange frankness described the "duality" of his will and feelings. But I repeat again : though that scene at mother's and that broken ikon were undoubtedly partly due to the influence of a real "second self," yet I have ever since been haunted by the fancy that there was in it an element of a sort of vindictive symbolism, a sort of resentment against the expectations of those women, a sort of angry revolt against their rights and their criticism. And so hand in hand with the "second self" he broke the ikon, as though to say "that's how your expectations will be shattered ! " In fact, even though the "second self" did come in, it was partly simply a whim. . . . But all this is only my theory ; it would be hard to decide for certain.

It is true that in spite of his adoration for Katerina Nikolaevna, he had a deep-rooted and perfectly genuine disbelief in her moral qualities. I really believe that he waited outside the door then, to see her humiliated before Lambert. But did he desire it, if even he waited for it ? Again I repeat : I firmly believe that he had no desire, no intention even. He simply wanted to be there, to rush in afterwards, to say something, perhaps to insult, perhaps even to kill her. . . . Anything might happen then ; but when he came with Lambert he had no idea what would happen. I may add that the revolver was Lambert's and that he himself came unarmed. Seeing her proud dignity, and above all, exasperated by Lambert's blackguardliness in threatening her, he dashed in—and only then went mad. Did he mean to shoot her at that instant ? In my opinion he did not know what he was doing, but he certainly would have shot her if we had not thrust aside his hand.

His wound proved to be not a fatal one, and it healed, but he was ill in bed rather a long time, at mother's, of course.

Now as I am writing these lines it is the middle of May, an exquisite spring day, and our windows are open. Mother is sitting beside him : he strokes her cheeks and hair and gazes into her face with tender emotion. Oh, this is only the half of the old Versilov, he never leaves mother's side now, and will never leave her again. He has even gained the "gift of tears," as Makar Ivanovitch, of precious memory, said in his story about the merchant. I fancy, however, that Versilov has a long life before him. With us he is perfectly good-natured and candid as a child, though he never loses his sense of proportion and self-control, and does not talk too freely. All his intellect and his moral nature have remained unchanged, though all his ideal side has become more marked. I may say frankly that I have never loved him so much as now, and I regret that I have neither time nor space to say more about him.

I will, however, tell one recent anecdote about him (and there are many). He had quite recovered by Lent, and in the sixth week declared that he would fast and take the sacrament. He had not taken the sacrament for thirty years or more I believe. Mother was delighted ; they began preparing Lenten dishes, rather expensive, dainty ones, however. In the next room I heard him on Monday and Tuesday chanting to himself "The Bridegroom cometh," and he was delighted with the verses and the chant. He spoke beautifully of religion several times during those days ; but on Wednesday the fast suddenly came to an end. Something suddenly irritated him, some " amusing contrast," as he expressed it, laughing; he disliked something in the exterior of the priest, in the surroundings; whatever it was, he returned and said with a gentle smile: "My friends, I love God, but I am not fitted for that." The same day roast beef was served at dinner.

But I know that even now mother often sits beside him, and in a low voice, with a gentle smile, begins to talk to him of the most abstract subjects: now she has somehow grown *daring* with him, but how this has come to pass I don't know. She sits beside him and speaks to him usually in a whisper. He listens with a smile, strokes her hair, kisses her hand, and there is the light of perfect happiness in his face. He sometimes has attacks that are almost like hysterics. Then he takes her photograph, the one he kissed that evening, gazes at it with tears, kisses it, recalls the past, gathers us all round him, but at such moments he says little. . . .

Katerina Nikolaevna he seems to have completely forgotten and has never once mentioned. Nothing has been said of marriage with my mother so far, either. They did think of taking him abroad for the summer; but Tatyana Pavlovna strongly opposed it, and he did not desire it himself. They will spend the summer at a villa, in some country place in the neighbourhood of Petersburg. By the way we are all still living at the expense of Tatyana Pavlovna. One thing I will add: I am dreadfully sorry that I have several times in this narrative allowed myself to take up a disrespectful and superior attitude in regard to Versilov. But as I wrote I imagined myself precisely at each of the moments I was describing. As I finish my narrative and write the last lines, I suddenly feel by the very process of recalling and recording, I have re-educated myself. I regret a great deal I have written, especially the tone of certain sentences and pages, but I will not cross them out or correct a single word.

I have stated that he never says one word of Katerina Nikolaevna; but I really believe that he is quite cured of his passion. Of her I never speak except sometimes to Tatyana Pavlovna, and then in secret. Katerina Nikolaevna is now abroad; I saw her before she went away, and visited her several times. Since she has been abroad I have received two letters from her, and have answered them. But of what was in her letter and what we discussed I will say nothing; that is another story, a quite *new* story, and perhaps it is still in the future; indeed there are some things of which I say nothing even to Tatyana

Pavlovna, but enough of that. I will only add that she is not married, and that she is travelling with the Pelistchevs. Her father is dead and she is the richest of widows. At this moment she is in Paris.

Her rupture with Büring took place very quickly, and as it were of itself, that is, extremely naturally. I will describe it, however.

On the morning of that terrible scene, the pock-marked man to whom Trishatov and his tall friend had gone over, succeeded in letting Büring know of the proposed crime. This was how it happened. Lambert still tried to pursuade him to work with him, and, when he gained possession of the letter, he told him all the details of the undertaking, up to the very last moment, that is, when Versilov suggested the trick to get rid of Tatyana Pavlovna. But at the last moment the pock-marked man, who had more sense than the rest, and foresaw the possibility of a serious crime being committed, preferred to betray Lambert. He reckoned upon Büring's gratitude as something more secure than the fantastic plan made by Lambert, who was clumsy and hotheaded, and by Versilov, who was almost mad with passion. All this I learned afterwards from Trishatov. I know nothing, by the way, of Lambert's relations with the pock-marked man, and I cannot understand why Lambert could not have acted without him. A question of far more interest for me is why Lambert needed Versilov when, having the letter in his possession, he might perfectly well have dispensed with the latter's assistance. The answer is clear to me now. Versilov was of use to Lambert from his knowledge of all the circumstances; moreover, if their plans miscarried, or some accident happened, Lambert reckoned on throwing all responsibility on Versilov. And since the latter did not want money, Lambert thought his help very opportune.

But Büring did not arrive in time. When he reached the scene of action an hour later, Tatyana Pavlovna's flat wore a very different aspect. Five minutes after Versilov had fallen on the carpet, covered with blood, Lambert, whom we all believed to be dead, raised his head and got up. He looked about him with amazement, quickly grasped the position, went into the kitchen without saying a word, put on his coat, and disappeared for ever. The document he left on the table. I have heard that he was not seriously ill but only slightly indisposed afterwards ; the blow from the revolver had stunned him and drawn blood. but had done no further harm.

Meanwhile Trishatov had run for the doctor ; but before the doctor arrived, Versilov, too, returned to consciousness, though before that Tatyana Pavlovna succeeded in bringing Katerina Nikolaevna to herself and taking her home. And so when Büring ran in upon us he found in Tatyana Pavlovna's flat only me, the doctor, Versilov, and my mother, who had been fetched by Trishatov, and though still ill, had come in haste, beside herself with anxiety. Büring stared at us with amazement, and as soon as he learned that Katerina Nikolaevna had gone home he went off to see her without saying another word to us.

He was perturbed ; he saw clearly that now scandal and gossip were almost inevitable. The affair did not make any great scandal, however. The pistol-shot could not be concealed, it is true ; but the chief facts remained almost unknown. All that was discovered by the investigation that was made was that a certain V., a man passionately in love, though almost fifty and with a family, had declared his feelings to the young lady, a person worthy of the highest respect, who did not share his sentiments, and in a sudden access of madness had shot himself. Nothing more than this came out, and in that form the story even got into the papers, no names being mentioned but only initials. I know that Lambert was not troubled in any way.

Nevertheless Büring was alarmed. To make matters worse he chanced to learn of the interview between Katerina Nikolaevna and Versilov two days before the catastrophe. This enraged him, and he rather incautiously ventured to observe to Katerina Nikolaevna that after that he was not surprised that such extraordinary adventures could happen to her. Katerina Nikolaevna refused him on the spot, without anger, but without hesitation. All her preconceived ideas of the judiciousness of marrying such a man vanished like smoke. Possibly she had seen through him long before, and perhaps the shock she had been exposed to had changed some of her views and feelings. But of that again I will say nothing. I will only add that Lambert made his escape to Moscow, and that I have heard he got into trouble over something there. Trishatov I have lost sight of since that day, though I am still trying to track him ; he vanished after the death of his friend " *le grand dadais*," who shot himself.

2

I have mentioned the death of the old prince Nikolay Ivanovitch. The good-natured, kindly old man died not long after his adventure. His death took place, however, quite a month later in his bed at night, from a stroke. I never saw him again after the day he was in my flat. I was told that during that month he became far more rational, more tender in his manner even, he ceased to be apprehensive, shed no more tears, and did not once utter a word about Anna Andreyevna. All his affection was centred on his daughter. On one occasion, a week before his death, Katerina Nikolaevna suggested inviting me to entertain him, but he actually frowned : I simply state this fact without trying to explain it. His estate turned out to be in good order at his death, and he left a very considerable fortune as well. A third of this fortune was by his will divided between his innumerable goddaughters ; but it struck every one as strange, that there was no mention of Anna Andreyevna in his will at all ; her name was omitted. But I know for a fact that a few days before his death, the old man summoned his daughter and his friends, Pelistchev and Prince V., and instructed Katerina Nikolaevna, in view of the possibility of his speedy decease, to set aside out of his fortune sixty thousand roubles for Anna Andreyevna. He expressed his wishes briefly, clearly and precisely, not indulging in a single exclamation or explanation. After his death, and when his affairs were put in order, Katerina Nikolaevna, through her lawyer, informed Anna Andreyevna that the sixty thousand roubles were at her disposal ; but drily, with no unnecessary words, Anna Andreyevna declined the money : she refused to accept it in spite of every assurance that this had been the old prince's desire. The money still lies waiting for her, and Katerina Nikolaevna still hopes to induce her to change her mind ; but this will never happen, of that I am positive, for I am now one of Anna Andreyevna's closest and most intimate friends. Her refusal made rather a stir, and people talked about it. Her aunt, Madame Fanariotov, who had been anoyed at first by her scandalous affair with the old prince, suddenly took a different view of it, and, after she refused the money, made her a solemn assurance of her respect. Her brother, on the other hand, quarrelled with her finally on account of it. But though I often go to see Anna Andreyevna, I cannot say that we ever discuss anything very intimate ; we never refer to the past ; she is very glad to see me, but talks to me chiefly of abstract subjects. Among other things, she has told me that she is firmly resolved to go into a convent ; that was not long ago ; but I don't believe this, and look upon it simply as an expression of bitterness.

But what is really tragic is what I have to tell of my sister Liza's fate. That is real unhappiness. What are all my failures beside her bitter lot ? It began with Prince Sergay Petrovitch's dying in the hospital before his trial. He died before Prince Nikolay Ivanovitch. Liza was left to face the world with her unborn child. She did not shed tears and was outwardly calm, she became gentle and resigned ; but all her old fire seemed to have vanished for ever. She helped mother meekly, nursed Andrey Petrovitch through his illness, but became very silent and never seemed to notice anyone or anything, as though nothing mattered to her, as though she were simply passing by. When Versilov was better, she began to sleep a great deal. I used to take her books, but she did not read ; she became terribly thin. I did not dare to try to comfort her, though I often went in to her intending to ; but in her presence I could not approach her, and I found no words to speak to her. It went on like this till something terrible happened : she fell down our stairs ; she did not fall far, only three steps, but it brought on a miscarriage, and she was ill all the rest of the winter. Now she is on her feet again, but her health has been shaken and it will be a long time before she is strong. She is still dreamy and silent with us, but she has begun to talk with mother a little. These last few days we have had bright, clear spring sunshine, and I am all the while inwardly recalling that sunny morning last autumn, when she and I walked along the street, both full of joy and hope and love for one another. Alas, what has happened since then ? I don't complain, for me a new life has begun, but for her ? Her future is a problem, and I cannot look at her even now without pain.

Three weeks ago I did succeed, however, in interesting her with news of Vassin. He was released at last and is now at liberty. That judicious person gave, so I am told, the most precise explanation and the most interesting information which completely cleared his character in the eyes of those on whom his fate depended. Moreover his celebrated manuscript turned out to be no more than a translation from the French, upon which he had intended to write an article for a magazine. He is now in the X. province, and his stepfather, Stebelkov, is still in prison on the same charge, which I hear grows more extensive and complicated as it goes on. Liza heard the news of Vassin with a strange smile, and even observed that that was just what was sure to have happened to him. But she was evidently pleased, no doubt that Prince Sergay's action had not brought worse harm to Vassin. Of Dergatchev and his friends I have nothing to say here.

I have finished. Perhaps some reader may care to know : what has become of my " idea," and what is the new life that is beginning for me now, to which I refer so mysteriously ? But that new life, that new way which is opening before me is my " idea," the same as before, though in such a different form, that it could hardly be recognised. But I cannot enter into that in this story, that is something quite different. My old life has passed away completely, and the new is just beginning. But I will add one essential matter : Tatyana Pavlovna, a true and dear friend to me, pesters me almost every day with exhortations to enter the university : " When you've taken your degree," she says, " then you can consider the position, but now you must finish your studies." I must confess I am considering her suggestion, but I don't know how I shall decide. Among other objections I have urged that I have not the right to continue my studies, as it is my duty now to work to maintain mother and Liza ; but she offers to undertake this, and she says her means are sufficient to do so all the time I am at the university. I have determined at last to ask the advice of some one. Looking about me, I have chosen that some one carefully and critically. I have fixed on Nikolay Semyonovitch, my former tutor in Moscow, the husband of Marie Ivanovna. Not so much that I need advice about anything, but I feel an irresistible longing to hear the opinion of this outsider, who is a rather coldly egoistic, but undoubtedly clever man. I have sent him my whole manuscript, asking him to keep it secret from every one, especially Tatyana Pavlovna, because I have not shown it to any one so far. The manuscript came back to me a fortnight later, and with it a rather long letter. From this letter I make a few extracts, as I find in them a certain general view and something that may be explanatory. Here are the extracts.

3

" . . . You could never have employed your leisure time more profitably, my ever precious Arkady Makarovitch, than in writing this autobiography ! You have given yourself, so to say, an unflinching account of your first stormy, perilous steps on the path of life. I quite believe that you may by this exposition have to a great extent ' re-educated yourself,' to use your own expression. I shall not, of course, venture upon the smallest criticism : though every page makes one reflect . . . for instance, the circumstance, that you so long and so obstinately retained possession of the ' document '—is highly characteristic. . . . But that is only one remark out of hundreds, which I permitted myself. I greatly appreciate also, the fact of your deciding to confide to me, and apparently to me alone, ' the secret of your idea,' to use your own expression. But your request that I should give you my opinion on that ' idea ' I must resolutely refuse : to begin with, it would be out of place in a letter, and secondly, I am not prepared to give an answer off-hand ; I must ruminate upon it further. I will only observe that your ' idea ' is distinguished by originality, whereas young men of the present generation, for the most part, throw themselves into ready-made ideas, of which there is always an ample provision, and which are a source of danger. Your idea, for instance, did at any rate save you for the time from the ideas of Messrs. Dergatchev and Co., certainly less original than yours. Finally I am absolutely in agreement with that honoured lady, Tatyana Pavlovna, whom I had till now failed to esteem as she deserves, though I know her personally. Her plan that you should enter the university will be of the greatest possible benefit for you. Study and life will undoubtedly in three or four years widen the horizon of your ideas and aspirations, and if after the university you still desire to return to your ' idea,' there will be nothing to prevent it.

" Now allow me, though you have not requested it, to give you frankly some thoughts and impressions that have occurred to my mind while perusing your extremely candid ' autobiography.' Yes, I agree with Andrey Petrovitch, that one might well feel anxiety about you and your *solitary youth*. And there are more than a few lads like you, and there really is always a danger of their talents leading them astray, either into secret sensuality, or a latent desire for lawlessness. But this thirst for lawlessness proceeds most frequently, perhaps, from a latent craving for discipline and 'seemliness'—(I am using your own words). Youth is pure, just because it is youth. Perhaps in these precocious impulses of madness, there lie concealed a craving for discipline and a search for truth, and whose fault is it that some young people of to-day see that truth and that discipline in such stupid and ridiculous things, that one cannot imagine how they can believe in them! I may mention, by the way, that in the recent past, a generation ago at most, such interesting lads were not so much to be pitied, for in those days they almost always ended by successfully attaching themselves to our most highly cultivated class and merging into it and even if they did at the onset recognise their own lack of order and consistency, the lack of nobility even in their family surroundings, the lack of an ancestral tradition, and of fine finished forms of social life, it was a gain for them, for they consciously strove towards all this and thereby learned to prize it. Nowadays the position is somewhat different, for there is scarcely anything the young can attach themselves to.

"I will explain by comparison, or, so to say, by analogy. If I had been a Russian novelist and had talent I should certainly have chosen my heroes from the old nobility, because only in that type of cultivated Russian is it possible to find at least that outward semblance of fine order and æsthetic beauty so necessary in a novel to produce an artistic effect on the reader. I am not joking when I say this, although I am not a nobleman myself, as you are indeed aware. Pushkin selected the subject for his future novels from the 'Traditions of the Russian Family,' and believe me that everything beautiful we have had so far is to be found therein. Everything that has been brought to some sort of perfection, anyway. I don't say this because I am accepting unconditionally the truth and justness of that beauty; but at least there were completely worked out forms of honour and duty which have never existed anywhere in Russia except in the nobility, even in the most rudimentary shape. I speak as a calm man seeking calm.

"Whether that honour was a good thing, and whether that duty was a true one—is a secondary question. What to my mind is of most consequence is the finality of the forms and the existence of some sort of order, not prescribed from above, but developed from within. Good heavens, what matters most of all for us is to have any sort of order of our own ! All hopes for the future and, so to say, restfulness of outlook lie in our having something at last built up, instead of this everlasting destruction, instead of chips flying in all directions, rubbish and disorder which has led to nothing for two hundred years.

"Don't accuse me of Slavophilism ; I only say this from misanthropy, for my heart is heavy ! Something is happening to us to-day and in the recent past, the very opposite of what I have imagined above. It is not that the worthless attach themselves to the highest stratum of society, but, on the contrary, with light-hearted haste, fragments are torn from what is fine and noble and thrown into one mass with the lawless and the envious. And there have been many instances of fathers and heads of what have been cultured families, laughing at what their children perhaps would have liked to believe in. What is more, they eagerly display to their children their spiteful pleasure at the sudden licence to be dishonest, which they have all at once deduced, wholesale, from something. I am not speaking of the true progressives, dear Arkady Makarovitch, but only of that rabble, so numerous it seems, of whom it has been said '*grattez le Russe et vous verrez le Tatare*,' and believe me there are by no means so many true liberals, true and noble friends of humanity among us, as we have imagined.

"But all this is theorising ; let us come back to our supposed novelist. The position of our novelist in this case would be perfectly definite ; he could not write in any other form but the historical, for there is no fine type in our day, and if there were remnants of it left they would not, according to the prevalent ideas of the day, have retained their beauty. Oh ! and in historical form it is possible to depict a multitude of extremely attractive and consolatory details ! It is possible so to fascinate the reader indeed that he will take the historical picture for the possible and the actual. Such a work, if executed with great talent, would belong not so much to Russian literature as to Russian history.

"It would be a picture artistically worked out of the Russian ideal, having a real existence so long as it was not guessed that it was an ideal. The grandson of those heroes who have been depicted in a picture of a Russian family of the upper middle cultivated class during three generations, side by side with and in connection with Russian history—that descendant of his forefathers would not be depicted in his modern type except in a somewhat misanthropic solitary and distinctly melancholy aspect. He is even bound to appear a somewhat strange figure, so that the reader might from the first glance recognise him as one retreating from the field of action, and might be convinced there was no field of action left for him. A little further and even that misanthrope, that grandson of heroes, will disappear entirely; new characters will appear, unknown to us as yet, and a new ideal; but what sort of characters? If they are without beauty, then the Russian novel is impossible in the future. But alas! will the novel be the only thing impossible?

"I will not pursue this further, but will hasten back to your manuscript. Consider, for instance, both the families of M. Versilov (for this once I will venture to be quite open). I won't enlarge on Andrey Petrovitch himself; but he is anyway of a good old family. He is a nobleman of ancient lineage, and at the same time a Parisian communard. He is a true poet and loves Russia, yet denies her absolutely. He is without any sort of religion, but yet almost ready to die for something indefinite, to which he cannot give a name, but in which he fervently believes, like a number of Russian adherents of European civilisation of the Petersburg period of Russian history. But enough of him. As for his legitimate family, I won't discuss his son, and indeed, he is not worthy of the honour. All who have eyes know what upstarts like that come to in Russia, and what they bring others to as well. Then his daughter, Anna Andreyevna—she is surely a girl of strong character? A figure on the scale of the Mother Abbess Mitrofania, not that I mean to predict anything criminal —which would be unjust on my part.

"If you can assure me, Arkady Makarovitch, that that family is an exceptional phenomenon it will rejoice my heart. But would it not be on the contrary a truer conclusion, that a multitude of unquestionably aristocratic Russian families are with irresistible force passing in masses into exceptional families and mingling with them in the general lawlessness and chaos. A typical example of such an exceptional family is sketched by you in your manuscript. Yes, Arkady Makarovitch, you are *a member of an exceptional family*, in contrary distinction to the aristocratic types who have had such a very different childhood and adolescence from yours.

"I must say I should not like to be a novelist whose hero comes of an exceptional family!

"To describe him is an ungrateful task and can have no

beauty of form. Moreover these types are in any case transitory, and so a novel about them cannot have artistic finish. One may make serious mistakes, exaggerations, misjudgments. In any case, one would have to guess too much. But what is the writer to do who doesn't want to confine himself to the historical form, and is possessed by a longing for the present ? To guess . . . and make mistakes.

" But such an autobiography as yours might serve as material for a future work of art, for a future picture of a lawless epoch already passed. Oh, when the angry strife of the day has passed, and the future has come, then a future artist will discover beautiful forms for depicting past lawlessness and chaos. Then such autobiographies as yours—so long as they are sincere—will be of use and provide material in spite of their chaotic and fortuitous character . . . they will preserve at any rate some faithful traits by which one may guess what may have lain hidden in the heart of some raw youth of that troubled time—a knowledge not altogether valueless since from raw youths are made up the generations."